COZY IN KANSAS

THREE ROMANCE MYSTERIES

NANCY MEHL

BARBOUR
PUBLISHING

Cover thumbnails:
Design by Kirk DouPonce, DogEared Design
Illustration by Jody Williams

Published by Barbour Publishing, Inc., P.O. Box 719, Uhrichsville, OH 44683, www.barbourbooks.com

Our mission is to publish and distribute inspirational products offering exceptional value and biblical encouragement to the masses.

 Member of the
Evangelical Christian
Publishers Association

Printed in the United States of America.

THE DEAD OF WINTER

Dedication:

To Pastor David Brace, who was the very first person to tell me I could fly. Your belief in me changed my life. To Pastor Rob Rotola, who encouraged me to spread my wings and fly even higher. To my heavenly Father, who gave me wings in the first place. It's all for You.

Acknowledgements:

Creating a fictional town presents an author with many challenges. My thanks to the following people for helping me to translate Winter Break, Kansas, out of my imagination and onto the printed page. Deputy Sheriff Robert P. (Pat) Taylor. Your help has been invaluable. Bob Slotta, a super guy who deserves the title of "The Twainiac." Henry Sweets, curator of the Mark Twain Boyhood Home and Museum. Darrin W. Figgins, funeral director for Garnand Funeral Home in Hugoton, Kansas. Jinwen Liu. For the lessons in Mandarin. To my family. You are my greatest blessing.

1

I gripped the steering wheel in a desperate attempt to keep my car from sliding on the ice-covered road. My decision to leave the main highway had been a huge mistake. I should have realized that the weather would worsen the closer I got to Winter Break. The fury of the storm outside matched the tempest that raged inside me. I was going back to a place I'd abandoned years ago. A mixture of memories tumbled around wildly inside my head. Some brought back feelings of safety and love. Others reminded me of the person I used to be, the person I'd tried hard to leave behind. I finally eased the car slowly to the shoulder. Should I see the storm as an ominous sign? A warning that I was venturing into dangerous territory?

I held my trembling hands in front of the car's heater, grateful my parents had given me their late-model sedan before taking off for China. The car was much nicer than anything I could afford as a lowly college student. I wasn't worried about it quitting on me, but I was definitely concerned about the worsening weather conditions. I'd narrowly missed two deer that had bounded across the road in front of my car. They'd probably felt safe, shielded by a thick blanket of white. Unfortunately, suddenly finding themselves caught in the glare of my headlights had destroyed their sense of security and frightened them only a little less than it had me. I wasn't sure if they'd heard me scream, but the sound still rang in my ears.

I hit the tuning button on the radio, but the numbers ran wildly up the dial. I was a long way out of Wichita. There was nothing for the tuner to lock onto. How much farther was Winter Break? Because of the blizzard, I couldn't find any familiar landmarks.

Winter Break. Named by wagon trains on their way west, the town was founded as a place of refuge when the strong storms of winter erupted. The location didn't actually provide any special protection; it was simply one of the last stops on the trail before hitting the rocky terrain that would eventually become Colorado Territory. Weary travelers knew that steep mountain trails could easily become final resting places for those caught inside Mother Nature's frozen fury. As they waited in Winter Break for the promise of spring, many turned back, deciding that the promise of gold wasn't worth the struggles they faced from weather, disease, Indians, or fellow pioneers who made their way west by stealing what they could from other nomads. As the years went on, Winter Break became nothing more than an odd spot on the Kansas map. Winter came early and left late there. It seemed comfortable in the small town, choosing to settle in until it was finally defeated by the inevitable encroachment of summer.

I put the car into gear and eased back onto the road. With my high beams on and my speed as close to a crawl as possible, I had only a few feet of visibility. However, there wasn't any other traffic on the road. No one else was foolish enough to be out here.

The slow pace gave me plenty of time to think about Aunt Bitty. My late great-aunt Bitty, that is. It would take me awhile before I could think of her in the past tense. When I was a little girl, I'd called her "Grape Aunt Bitty." To make it easier, she simply became Aunt Bitty.

Bitty was the most alive person I'd ever known. She and I had forged a special bond when I was younger. I'd loved her old secondhand bookstore in Winter Break. I'd spent many summers and winter vacations there, sitting on the hardwood floors, sipping either homemade lemonade or cups of thick hot chocolate topped with melting marshmallows while I read through her collection of gently used classics. *Huckleberry Finn*, *The Adventures of Tom Sawyer*, *The Chronicles of Narnia*, *The Bobbsey Twins*, *Nancy Drew*. An eclectic assortment to be sure, but the hot summer days and cold winter nights had drifted by on wings of magic, and Bitty's store had been my enchanted castle.

Visits to Winter Break had led to my decision to choose English as my major, over the heartfelt protests of my parents. As I got closer to graduation, uncertainty began to haunt me. What could I possibly do with a degree in English? Become an editor? A teacher? Both noble professions, but for some reason, something else wiggled around inside me. A desire for something I'd never been able to put a name to. Of course, it's very difficult to follow a path laid out in the dark. My only option had been to put my future in God's hands. And I had more than once. Phantom whispers of my mother's voice echoed through the quiet inside the car. "Ivy, every time you worry, you take your situation right out of God's hands. Quit worrying and start trusting!"

Easy for her to say. She and my father had always known exactly what they were meant to do. Running a mission in China had been their goal even before they were married. Although they'd never said it, I was pretty sure the only thing that hadn't gone according to their master plan was me. Mother was thirty when she'd gotten pregnant. All my life, I'd sensed that, although my parents loved me, my existence had derailed their ambitions. Once I was in college, it didn't take them long to sell our home, along with almost all of their possessions, and head to China. I was happy for them, but I couldn't help feeling a little abandoned. It was probably selfish, but it felt odd not having any family nearby. Except, of course, Aunt Bitty.

Something flashed across the windshield, breaking my reverie. Surely it wasn't another deer. I started to press lightly on the brake when a light flickered through the veil of white that surrounded the car. Was it another vehicle? I peered through the snow that blew straight at my windshield while the wipers fought furiously to keep my field of vision clear. There it was again. The light wasn't moving. Could I have finally made it to Winter Break?

As if providing an answer to my question, a sign announcing the city limits appeared on the right side of the road. I could barely make it out, but I didn't really need to. From here, I knew the way.

Three years had passed since I'd been to see my aunt, but I had the strangest feeling I'd left only yesterday. Through the snow, I could make out the sheriff's office right next to the only grocery store in Winter Break. The faded sign reading LABAN'S FOOD-A-RAMA swung violently in the wind-driven snow. The lights were on, signaling that Old Man Tater was still up. Dewey Tater, now in his seventies, had run the Food-a-Rama ever since he was twenty-two, after his father, Laban, died of a heart attack. Dewey stayed in Winter Break to take care of his mother until her death ten years ago. Now he lived here alone. Since he'd never married, the Food-a-Rama would probably close for good after Dewey passed away. His life sounded rather sad, but Dewey was well liked, had a lot of friends, and seemed to be perfectly happy. His sense of humor and even temper had been particularly helpful to us kids when we'd call up the store to ask if "Mr. Tater had any taters for sale," or when Amos Parker stole two bottles of strawberry pop and got caught.

Dewey was known for extending credit to almost everyone in town at one time or another. Most of the folks in Winter Break were farmers. There were lean years and times of bounty. Dewey helped people balance out the ups and downs of their lives, and they loved and trusted him. That's why they had eventually elected him mayor of Winter Break. Not that the mayor had much to do in a town of a little over six hundred people, but it was the thought that counted.

I rounded the first corner of Main Street and found myself in front of Miss Bitty's Bygone Bookstore. True to his word, Amos had turned on the lights. I parked right in front of the entrance. Well, maybe *parked* isn't the right word. *Slid to a stop* is more accurate.

I struggled to open the car door as the wind fought to keep it shut. After finally winning the brief battle, I pushed the trunk button on my key fob. Nothing happened. I hit it again, leaning against the car while my face was pelted with small crystals of ice. The trunk lid was frozen shut, and my suitcases were inside. I pushed on the trunk several times with my gloved hands. After yelling at the resistant lid a couple of times, I finally popped it open. I grabbed my two suitcases and skated toward the bookstore entrance. Amos had promised to unlock the door and turn on the heat. I said a brief prayer of thanks for his efforts. I wasn't in the mood to face another frozen lock.

I twisted the large brass knob and practically fell inside. As the door closed behind me, I heard the familiar sound of Bitty's bell. The tinkling of the little silver bell over the door and the smell of old books and lemon oil threw me headlong into the past. For a moment, I was a ten-year-old girl again, searching the ceiling-to-floor shelves for new worlds and wonderful stories to take me away from the awkwardness of puberty, braces, zits, boys, and the uncertainness of life in general. I leaned against the timeworn door, waiting for Bitty to come around the corner. "Ah, it's my beautiful Ivy," she'd sing out whenever I came to stay. And somehow she always made me feel beautiful, even though I wasn't.

This place had been a sanctuary. My sanctuary. I closed my eyes and breathed it in. I'd almost forgotten how wonderful it was. Bitty had turned this old house into a charming bookstore. Her precious books lined the walls in what used to be the living room. The room beyond that, at one time a combination dining room and kitchen, had been turned into a sitting room for patrons who wanted to cuddle up with a book in one of the mismatched, overstuffed chairs or couches scattered around the room. Bitty's rocking chair sat near the carved stone fireplace in the corner. Tears stung my eyelids. Bitty was really gone, yet something of her remained. The bookstore was still here. And I was here.

I picked up my suitcases and set them down at the bottom of the stairs just to the right of the entryway. Bitty's apartment was nestled above the bookstore on the second floor. I'd stay there until I could finalize the funeral arrangements and settle the estate. Christmas break was a little over a month long. Things would have to be resolved before my next semester began. According to Dewey, Bitty had taken care of almost everything—except what to do with the store. Dewey had informed me when he called to tell me about Bitty's accident that she'd left all her worldly goods to me. I was contemplating what I could possibly do with an old, used-book store, when I heard the door creak open in back of me. The bell tinkled again, and the icy wind swooped in. I turned around to see Amos Parker standing in the doorway.

It had been a long time since we'd seen each other, but I would have known him in a second. He still had the same turned-up nose, ruffled blond hair, and mischievous grin. The only differences were that he was a little older, and he was wearing a deputy sheriff's uniform. Yep, the boy who stole strawberry pop from the Food-a-Rama now kept the law in Stevens County. Of course, in Winter Break itself, there weren't a lot of dangerous criminals. Mostly loose dogs, cats stuck in trees, and an occasional runaway cow. Oh, and old Odie Rimrucker. Used to be he would get locked up every Friday night for drunk and disorderly. But he was always sober and in church by Sunday morning, remorseful and repentant for his sins. Deputy Sheriff Morley Watson waited every Friday night for Odie to come and turn himself in. When Deputy Watson died of a stroke several years ago, Bitty told me it broke Odie's heart. He swore never to touch another drop of alcohol again. I wondered if his promise had held.

"My goodness, Ivy," Amos said, a smile picking at the corners of his mouth, "you turned out to be very pretty."

"Why, thank you, Amos, but I'm wondering why you sound so surprised."

He laughed. "I'll take the fifth. I doubt there's anything I could say that wouldn't get me in trouble."

"Smart move. And by the way, I don't go by Ivy anymore. I use my middle name, Samantha. Everyone calls me Sam."

His eyebrows arched in surprise. "Sam? I don't know. . . . You've always been Ivy to me. Might be hard to change that now."

Amos peeled off his jacket and gloves and hung them on the ancient wooden coatrack near the door. Then he followed me through the bookstore and into the sitting room. I motioned to a large plush chair near the fireplace while I slid into Aunt Bitty's rocking chair across from him. We sat in front of a crackling fire he had obviously set in anticipation of my arrival.

I shook my head. "Sorry, no choice. I didn't want to live with the name Ivy Towers in the real world. Not many people have my mother's sense of humor. Sam suits me fine. Besides, Ivy was a little girl. I've grown up."

Amos leaned back into the thick cushions of the chair and stared into the dancing flames in the fireplace. "That's too bad. I liked Ivy Towers. She was my friend." He turned his head and gazed into my eyes. "I don't know Sam Towers. I hope she's as caring and compassionate as Ivy."

I smiled. "Oh, she's okay. Maybe a little more practical, but all in all, no one to fear. I don't think you have anything to worry about."

"Good. I'm relieved."

I thought I saw a shadow of something flicker through his expression. For some reason, it made me feel a little flustered. Amos looked like the same person I'd spent hours with, sharing my deepest secrets, but now there was something harder in his face, a look in his eyes I'd never seen before. Truth was, we'd both changed, and I didn't really know him anymore.

"How long has it been, Ivy. . .I mean Sam?" he asked.

"Well, let me see," I responded, trying to work out the answer in my head. "I haven't been back since before I started college. That's three years. But you left when? A couple of years before that?"

"Yeah, I think so. That makes it somewhere around five years since we've seen each other."

I found that rocking gently back and forth in Bitty's chair in front of the warm, comforting fire made me sleepy. I couldn't stifle a yawn. "Sorry," I said sheepishly.

Amos waved away my apology.

"Didn't you go to live with your dad in Oklahoma?" I asked.

His smile didn't reach his eyes. "Yes, but it didn't work out. I imagined my father to be the answer to all my problems. I was bored living in Winter Break. I thought I would 'find myself' in the big city." He laughed, but it was tinged with a note of bitterness.

"And now you're back here?" I asked, stating the obvious.

This time his smile was genuine. For just a moment, I saw my old friend and confidant. "I finally realized that I couldn't *find* myself in a place I didn't belong. Everything I wanted was here." He looked down, his face flushed. "Well, almost everything."

I wanted to ask him what he meant, but I was exhausted and needed some shut-eye. "Amos, what happened to Bitty? I didn't quite understand from Dewey's phone call."

Amos shook his head, his forehead knit in a frown. "I don't know, S–Sam. Isaac called me at the office. He said he'd found your aunt on the floor—that she'd fallen from her ladder."

"So Isaac still works for her," I said mostly to myself. Isaac Holsapple had been her part-time assistant for as long as I could remember. He was a strange little man who kept to himself but seemed totally committed to Bitty and her bookstore.

From my vantage point I could see Bitty's old wooden library ladder. I'd watched her roll back and forth in front of the tallest bookshelves, almost as if it were a part of her. How could she have lost her footing?

"How did she fall? Did the ladder come off the track?" I asked.

"No, it was still connected. I found her lying on the floor next to the ladder. When she fell, she hit her head hard." He looked down at his boots and took a deep breath. "She was already gone when I got here, Ivy."

I didn't bother to correct him again. All I could think of was Bitty lying alone on the floor. "Did she die right away?" I meant to ask this question out loud, but it came out in a whisper.

Amos scooted forward in his chair and reached out to me, closing his hand over mine. "There wasn't any indication that she moved again after she fell, Ivy," he said softly. "She probably died instantly. Actually, she looked quite peaceful. Except for the blood. . ."

"Blood? Why would she bleed if she hit her head on the floor? That doesn't make sense."

Amos frowned and let go of my hand. "I don't think anyone ever said she hit her head on the floor. Maybe you just assumed. . ."

I was confused. "Then what happened?"

"She struck her head on the bottom of the ladder. On the metal fixture that covers the rollers."

Of course. Why was I surprised? The iron hardware that covered the casters jutted out on both sides. "I'm sorry, Amos. That makes sense." I tried to smile but couldn't. I was tired, sad, and disgusted. I didn't want to think about the spot where Bitty's body had been, but my eyes were drawn to it, even though my mind fought the urge. Amos noticed.

"I cleaned it up, Ivy," he said quietly. "You can't tell anything happened there."

A sense of relief and gratitude washed through me. I wasn't sure I could have faced bloodstains. I had other questions, but I was too tired to ask them now. "Thank you, Amos. I really appreciate it. Would you mind if we talked more tomorrow? I'm so exhausted, my brain is fuzzy."

"Of course. I'm sorry." As he stood up, he reached over and patted my shoulder. It felt strange to be so close to him again. "I'll see you tomorrow. You rest. If you need any help making the final arrangements, please let me know. I'm sure you want to wrap things up here and get back to your life."

"I don't know. I'm on break from school. Maybe I'll hang around for a while. Catch up with old friends."

I don't know what I expected, but the look Amos shot me didn't convey his excitement at my intention to spend some time in Winter Break.

"There's not really anything here for you, Sam," he said. "It's been a long time. Town's changed. People change, too. Might be best if you get things squared away and get back to Wichita."

"You. . .you're probably right. We'll see. I'll think about it tomorrow after I get unpacked."

He stood there for a few moments and stared at me. I started to feel a little uncomfortable, but I wasn't sure why.

Finally, he looked away. "I'll call you tomorrow afternoon if I don't hear from you first. Again, if there's anything you need. . ."

"Thank you," I said. "I really appreciate all your help."

He nodded. "You're welcome. Dewey has your keys and some papers he needs to go over with you. And he brought some supplies over. We stocked Bitty's kitchen so you'd have enough food to get you by for a few days."

I smiled my thanks, but without warning, tears filled my eyes. Being back in Winter Break was stirring up my emotions in a way I hadn't expected.

"Everything will be okay," he said, his voice softening a little. "I'll be here for you."

Once again, I saw the face of my old, trusted friend. At first I thought

Amos was going to put his arms around me, but then he pulled back, grabbed his coat and hat, and headed for the front door. He glanced back once before leaving. "I'll see you tomorrow, Ivy."

I stood in the bookstore for a few minutes before heading upstairs to Bitty's apartment. I couldn't take my eyes off the library ladder. Two questions swirled around in my head. *How in the world could she have fallen off? And why did Amos Parker want me out of Winter Break?*

I awoke Saturday morning to the sound of ice bouncing off the roof. Great. Ice on top of snow. Perfect weather to organize a funeral.

I turned over on my back and stared up at the ceiling. What had I gotten myself into? My mother had offered to fly back from China to take care of her aunt's final arrangements, but I'd told her to stay put, volunteering myself since I was so much closer. It had seemed the right thing to do at the time, even though I hated the idea of returning to this town without Aunt Bitty's being here. Now that I was actually in Winter Break, I felt overwhelmed with the responsibility. Dewey Tater had reassured me over the phone that everything was in good shape and that Bitty had made detailed preparations, but I was still worried. Taking care of her final wishes was important to me. I wanted to give her the kind of send-off she deserved.

I pulled myself up in bed and looked around. The spare bedroom was exactly as it had been the last time I stayed here. In fact, some of my things still adorned the room; my set of Nancy Drew books sat on top of the oak dresser, and my gold-colored jewelry box with its gaudy, fake ruby rhinestones was next to them. The old iron bed gave a familiar squeak as I sat up, and the same brightly colored rag rug lay on the floor next to the bed, waiting to keep my bare feet warm on a cold winter's morning.

I slid my feet into my slippers and padded out into the hallway. After a stop at the bathroom, I entered Bitty's cozy little kitchen. It was waiting for her, ready to begin breakfast and get the day started. I was the intruder, the interloper trying to take her place. But no one else could ever replace Bitty Flanagan—especially me.

Ever since I'd first stepped into the old bookstore, I'd had the strangest feeling of being watched. I felt it strongly at that moment. In my mind, I could see Bitty sitting at her kitchen table, greeting me with a smile as I emerged from my bedroom. "Good morning, Sleeping Beauty," she'd always call out. Last night, I'd kept expecting to see her standing on her library ladder with a book in her hand, saying, "Now, Ivy. I think this book is just the right one for a day like today." Her presence wouldn't be easily exorcised from this place. It was a part of the building...part of each of the books lining the walls downstairs...part of me.

I stood there in the silence of the morning, wishing she really would appear and tell me this was all just a bad joke, but the only sound I heard was the dinging of frozen drizzle ricocheting off the roof.

As I opened the refrigerator door in search of caffeine, I almost stumbled over a small bowl of water sitting next to another empty bowl. I'd forgotten all about Bitty's cat. Miss Skiffins was named after a character in *Great Expectations*. Where was she? I hadn't heard from her since my arrival the night before. As if on cue, I heard a soft *meow* from behind me.

"Well, hello, Miss Skiffins," I said to the small calico cat that approached me cautiously. "I'm sure you'd rather see your mistress here this morning, but you'll have to put up with me." I rummaged around in the cabinets until I found several cans of cat food. I pulled the top off a can of tuna-flavored rations and dumped the contents into the empty bowl. I was rewarded with a rub against my shins before the hungry animal attacked the smelly offering. The sound of purring filled the small room. It felt good to take care of Bitty's cat. They had been very close friends. It dawned on me that I would have to find Miss Skiffins a home before I left. My brief euphoria skipped away, replaced by a cautionary sense of gloom. This was a small town. What if no one wanted a tiny calico cat?

Just as I located the coffee can, someone knocked on the street-side door downstairs. I looked down at my black sweatpants and pink Shakespeare T-shirt that proclaimed ALL THE WORLD'S A STAGE. Oh well. At least I was covered up. I reached for my hair and ran my hands through it a couple of times. One thing about supercurly hair—you get pretty much the same effect when you hand comb it as you do after several minutes in front of the mirror with a brush and hair gel. Bitty and I had shared more than a love of books. We both had inherited curly dark red hair and bright green eyes.

I patted Miss Skiffins and ran downstairs. I half expected to see Amos standing outside the large oak entry door embedded with thick, etched glass, but instead, it was Old Man Tater. For some reason, seeing him there caused a lump in my throat. Dewey Tater was a big part of Winter Break—and a huge part of my childhood. I unlocked the door and held it open. Dewey stepped inside, his boots tracking in snow and ice. He looked down at the rapidly melting mush on the carpet in front of the door.

"Sorry, Ivy," he said in a voice that sounded like old, dried paper rustling in an invisible breeze.

"Don't worry about it, Dewey." Although I tried to keep my tone steady, the old man peered at me from under his parka hood with a look that told me I hadn't fooled him one little bit. He opened up his arms, and I tumbled unceremoniously into a much-needed bear hug.

"Everything will be okay," he said, his words muffled slightly by the side of my head.

I pulled out of his embrace and smiled up at him. "Sorry. I didn't realize how much I missed Winter Break until I saw you."

He nodded. "Coming home can do that."

I opened my mouth to protest. This wasn't home. Home was. . . To be honest, I wasn't sure where home was. Even though I lived in Wichita, my dorm room was only a temporary place to roost. I certainly hadn't nested.

Dewey hung up his coat. "Thought we'd go over some of Bitty's arrangements if it's okay." His vivid blue eyes still twinkled with personality and intelligence. Although his hair was grayer, his face more lined, he still had something—a spark of some kind that hadn't diminished one bit.

"Sure. How 'bout some coffee?" I asked. "I was just getting ready to make some."

"Sounds great, Ivy. I brought some paperwork. I'll get everything ready while you get the coffeemaker going."

For the first time, I noticed the aged and battered briefcase he'd brought in with him. Bitty's last requests. A chill ran through me. The idea of hot coffee suddenly sounded even better than it had before.

Dewey ambled toward the sitting room. He put the case on the polished oak table that sat off to one side of the room then grabbed a couple of dark green padded leather chairs that had been pushed up against the far wall. The table had been a meeting spot for many, many book clubs and town meetings over the last forty years. Now the fate of all of Bitty's worldly goods would be decided there.

"I'll get the fire going while you work on that coffee," Dewey said.

I nodded at him and headed for the stairs. I was grateful to have a few minutes to myself. My emotions jumped around frantically inside me like inept circus acrobats. This was supposed to be a quick trip. Check the arrangements for Bitty's funeral. Tie up any loose ends. Go home. But I hadn't thought the situation out very well before leaving Wichita. It wasn't going to be that easy. There was something I hadn't counted on—the attachment I felt to this place. It was much stronger than I'd realized. In fact, my link to Bitty was almost overwhelming. I'd put her, and Winter Break, out of my mind for the past several years. I'd relegated the whole experience to my childhood. After all, I was growing up, putting away childish things. But I was quickly discovering that my link to the past wasn't so easily broken. It was still alive inside me. I just wasn't sure what that meant to me now.

I started the coffee then grabbed a pair of jeans and a sweatshirt from my suitcase. After changing and actually brushing my hair, I felt more like myself. Maybe Ivy would go back into the past where she belonged. Sam needed to be the person in charge now. I hoped she was strong enough to stand against the ghosts of my former life.

I filled two mugs with coffee, grabbed some sugar and creamer, and joined Dewey at the table next to the rapidly growing fire.

After a couple of sips, he pushed some papers toward me. "It's all pretty straightforward," he said. "Bitty left everything to you. All her bank accounts are in your name. Do you remember signing forms about that?"

I nodded. At the time, I'd put my John Henry on everything Mother told me to. She and Daddy knew they wouldn't be nearby if Bitty should pass away suddenly. She was almost seventy at the time, and my parents planned to be in China for a long time. Someone from the family had to be available. Maybe I should have asked a few more questions, but nineteen-year-olds have a lot of things on their minds. It just hadn't seemed important. What a difference a few years could make.

I looked over the bank statements. "There's over twenty thousand dollars in this business account," I said. "How in the world did Bitty make any money in this tiny town?"

Dewey chuckled. "You didn't think she only sold books to people in Winter Break, did you? Your aunt has customers all over the country. In fact, she's sold quite a few books to buyers overseas. She has an excellent reputation for finding valuable, collectible books."

"I don't know what I thought, to be honest," I said. "I guess I figured Bitty sold old books to people who couldn't afford new ones. I knew she had a few special volumes, but I thought they were hers—something she collected for herself."

Dewey's comments reminded me of something. "I found a couple of boxes of books by her desk. They've both been opened, but it doesn't look as if they've been gone through. Must be a shipment she got in but didn't have time to unpack."

"I'm sure that's exactly what it is." Dewey cleared his throat and frowned at me. "Miss Bitty's Bygone Bookstore was much more than discarded books, Ivy. Your aunt was an expert on rare books. She could find 'em and sell 'em. A lot of people benefited from her expertise. You should be proud of her."

Yes, I should have been. I also should have shown more interest in what Bitty did, but my time in the bookstore had been spent on myself and my own enjoyment. I felt ashamed. I hadn't given Bitty the respect or attention she'd deserved. Now I'd never have the chance.

Dewey shoved several new papers toward me. "You own the bookstore outright since your name is on the title. Also, all the contents are yours." He frowned. "Somewhere there's a list of individual items she wanted her friends to have, but I'm not sure where it is. It's not a legal document, just something she kept around here. I'd look through her desk for it. Even though everything belongs to you, you'll want to honor her wishes. When you find that list, let me know. I'll help you match the people to the things. Might be some folks mentioned that you don't know."

"Okay. I'll look for it a little later."

"Bitty didn't write down anything in particular for your mother. She knew you would make certain she got whatever she wanted." He shrugged. "Bitty tried to give her some of your great-grandmother's things several years ago, but your mother turned them down. Since your grandmother, Bitty's only sister, had already passed, she felt your mother should have some of the family heirlooms."

"That doesn't surprise me," I said. "My mother's only goal in life was to go to China. Before she left, she got rid of almost all of her own possessions. She doesn't seem to value family history much." I could hear the resentment in my voice. I wondered if Dewey noticed it. If he did, he didn't give any indication.

"She may change her mind someday, Ivy. You protect a few of Bitty's things for her, okay?"

"I'll try." I was wondering where in the world I was going to store "Bitty's things." I didn't even have enough storage for "my things," sparse as they were.

Dewey picked up his coffee mug and took a sip. "Many a morning I sat here with your aunt, drinking her coffee and talking about our lives. I'm going to miss that." His eyes grew misty, and he swiped at them with the back of his hand.

"You and Bitty were friends for a long time, weren't you, Dewey?"

His gaze became dreamy. "Yes, a long, long time," he said. "She was my best friend."

I waited a few moments before saying anything else. I didn't want to interrupt his private thoughts. When he reached for his cup again, I asked, "What am I supposed to do with the bookstore, Dewey? Is there anyone in Winter Break who might want to buy it?"

He smiled and shook his head. "I doubt it. Most people here already have their niches carved out. I don't think many Winter Break people understand this place." His forehead wrinkled in thought. "Well, except for Lila Hatcher."

"Lila Hatcher? I don't know the name."

He leaned back in his chair. "Lila and your aunt were pretty close. Maybe she spoke of her to you? She was teaching Lila all about old books."

"Oh yes. Now that you mention it, I do remember something about that." What I remembered was the feeling of guilt I'd had when Bitty talked about her new friend who shared her interest in literature. I used to be the person Bitty talked to about her latest TBR pile. *TBR* stood for *to be read*. At one time, my aunt and I kept each other updated on our lists, sometimes changing them because of suggestions from each other. Obviously, Lila had taken my place.

"Lila moved here a couple of years ago. Lives in the big Biddle house on Oak," Dewey said.

"The Biddle house? What happened to Cecil and Marion?"

Dewey grinned. "Don't look so worried. They moved to Florida. Cecil's arthritis needed a warmer climate."

"I'm glad they're okay. They were such a nice couple. Marion always made candy apples for us kids on the Fourth of July."

Dewey's eyes crinkled with amusement. It was obvious his face was used to wrinkling that way. The deep lines around his eyes spoke of his easygoing, happy nature. "I remember those apples. Wasn't just you kids who were crazy about 'em."

"Why do you think this Lila woman might be interested in the bookstore?"

Before answering, Dewey cleared his throat and took another sip of coffee. "I didn't say I thought she'd be interested. I said she was someone who might understand it. Lila spent quite a bit of time here. She and Bitty were good friends. Of course, Bitty was friends with everyone. She took her Bible seriously. She didn't believe in gossip, and she always tried to think the best of every person. I can't tell you how many times she quoted the verses in First Corinthians about love. If someone had set Miss Skiffins on fire and roasted marshmallows over her, your aunt wouldn't have had an unkind word to say."

It was my turn to laugh. "That might be pushing it a little, even for Aunt Bitty."

Dewey grinned. "Okay. But you get my drift."

"I never realized that you and Bitty were so close," I said. "I'm glad."

A hint of sadness shone in his eyes. "I'll miss her a lot, Ivy. But I know where she is, and I know I'll join her there soon. I keep my mind focused on that. It's how I make it from day to day. 'The goodness of God gives me strength.'"

"I remember Pastor Taylor saying that same thing many times." I'd always enjoyed attending Faith Community Church in Winter Break. It was smaller than our big church in Wichita, but I loved the family feeling there. For many people in Winter Break, church was the center of almost everything they did. "That reminds me. I need to talk to him about the service. It's Saturday already. We don't want to have the funeral on Sunday. I guess Monday would be best."

"Sounds okay. You don't have to rush it, though, Ivy. You set it at a time that will work for you."

I'd intended to ask Dewey to call me Sam when we first sat down at the table, but for some reason, I couldn't do it now. I was Ivy to him, and for the first time in a long time, it felt okay. "I doubt that Mr. Buskin would want me to wait too long," I said. "I mean, don't we need to get Bitty buried as soon as possible?"

Dewey looked startled. "You knew she was cremated, didn't you?"

It was my turn to look surprised. "What? No. I had no idea."

Dewey stood up and walked over to the fireplace. He grabbed a poker and jabbed at the logs. The flames flared up again, sending a rush of warmth my way. "She decided on cremation after she found out how much less it would cost than regular burial. Your aunt didn't like spending money on herself. She decided this would give her more to pass on to you—and be less of a bother." He put the tool back in its holder and turned around. "And maybe," he said mildly, "she wasn't sure how fast someone could get here if something happened to her. She knew your mother would be out of the country, and she didn't know if you would be available."

His words stung me. Bitty hadn't trusted her family to come if something happened to her. Tears filled my eyes.

"Now don't you go feeling bad, Ivy. Bitty knew you loved her. She thought the world of you. And she was so proud, especially with you studying English in college. She always suspected she might have had something to do with your interest in English and literature."

"She was right," I said, dabbing at my eyes with the side of my hand. "She definitely passed along her love of the written word."

Dewey sat down again. "That's good to hear. That's mighty good to hear."

"Bitty certainly seems to have everything arranged, Dewey," I said, glancing through the paperwork. "I know her well enough to understand that she felt the need to have all her ducks in a row, but from what you told me on the phone, she finalized several things in the past couple of months. Do you find that a little odd?"

He shrugged. "You know your aunt prided herself on having everything planned out as much as possible. She started making her final arrangements when she was still in her sixties. She wanted everything to go off without a hitch when she met her Maker." He looked off into space for a moment. "It did seem a little strange to me that she got so focused on all kinds of little details just lately. It was almost as if she knew she wasn't going to be around much longer." He smiled and shook his head. "Course, that was Bitty. She spent her life trying to be prepared for everything that might happen. That was one of her few weaknesses. And those lists she made. I swear, she would have submitted a list to the Lord for every day of her life, if He'd been interested. I told her that He might have a few ideas of His own, and she should let Him have a say so every once in a while. She tried, she really did, but it was a struggle." He grinned at me. "Never saw anyone so organized. I'll bet she's got the heavenly host on a pretty tight schedule already."

Aunt Bitty and I were obviously more alike than I'd realized. I was a list person, too, although I wasn't as obsessed as my aunt was. I felt better when everything was mapped out ahead of time. I wasn't about to confess my

Achilles' heel to Dewey Tater, so I just nodded as though I agreed with him.

Dewey straightened up. "So that's about it," he said. "There's a small insurance policy in here made out to you. You'll have to contact them yourself. You can proceed with the rest of this as if it's yours, 'cause it is. Again, I'd look in her desk for that list of things set aside for some of her friends. This stuff she kept in a box with instructions that I was to open it and give it to you if something happened. I've done that. She probably wouldn't have cared if I'd gone through her desk, but since she didn't tell me to, I felt…I don't know." He shrugged his shoulders. "I didn't want to breach her privacy. Or yours."

"Thanks, Dewey. But I think you're right. She wouldn't have minded."

"Oh, before I forget." He reached into the pocket of his jeans. "Here are all of her keys." He held up a key ring. "This is to the front door," he said, pointing to a square, gold-colored key. He pushed it out of the way and held up another one. "This is to the back door." He let that drop. "This is the key to Isaac's apartment next door, and this is to the valuables box these papers and checkbooks came out of. I put that box back in her closet where she kept it. There are a few other keys I don't recognize—you'll have to find out where they fit. And this one," he said gently, "is to your aunt's desk." His gaze moved to the antique cherrywood desk in the corner of the main room. I could still see my aunt sitting there, holding court as the queen of Miss Bitty's Bygone Bookstore. I knew Dewey could envision her, too.

We were silent for a few seconds, each lost in our own thoughts. Dewey reached out and touched my arm. "You let me know if you need anything, okay? Why don't I walk you over to Buskin's Funeral Home?"

I nodded. "That would be nice. I think I'd like to unpack, maybe take a shower before we go."

Dewey nodded. "I understand. Should I come back and get you around eleven? We can have a quick lunch at the Redbird before we see Elmer."

Ruby's Redbird Café. With everything else happening, I'd forgotten all about it. My mouth started to water just at the mention of Winter Break's only restaurant. Run by Ruby Bird for over thirty years, it was the town's most important attraction, even drawing visitors from neighboring cities. In fact, once in a while, old customers came back to see Ruby after moving across the county. If their travels brought them within two hundred miles of the Redbird Café, it meant a quick trip to Winter Break.

Ruby made breakfast plates that could feed three people: eggs fried just right with crispy edges and soft middles; homemade sausage with just a touch of spice; buttery hash browns; fried apples; creamy grits; and hot, fresh cinnamon bread that seemed to melt in your mouth. Her homemade soups were legend, and her pies had been known to save marriages, heal broken hearts, and bring families back together.

Almost everyone in town knew the story of Dolly and Pete Palavich, who had once owned a farm just outside town. Dolly had packed her bags, determined to find a man who appreciated her, when Pete showed up with one of Ruby's shoofly pies. Although it was hard for Pete to tell Dolly how much he loved her, the pie did the job for him. Dolly decided to stay. They were married for fifty-one years before Pete passed away.

But the thing Ruby was really famous for was her one-pound cheeseburgers. Ruby's Redbird Burger was something you'd never taste anywhere on this earth except at the Redbird Café. Although she wouldn't tell anyone her secret recipe, most of the townsfolk knew she added minced onions and jalapeños to the beef, along with some extra-sharp New York cheddar cheese stuck in the middle somehow. Then she grilled them and covered them with more cheddar cheese, lettuce, tomato, grilled onions, and mustard. No one ever, ever asked Ruby to add ketchup to her burgers. To Ruby, adding ketchup to a hamburger was a sin, pure and simple.

A lot of people had tried to recreate the Redbird Burger, but without success. Ruby had a secret ingredient. Something she kept to herself. All anyone could hope for was that before Ruby passed away, she'd reveal the mystery to someone she trusted. The thought that the Redbird Burger could be lost forever was too much for love-struck burger connoisseurs to comprehend. It was a major concern for the citizens of Winter Break, even prompting town meetings designed to wrestle the top-secret information from the obstinate restaurateur. So far, all strategies had failed miserably.

Ruby found the whole "Redbird Burger controversy," as it was called, quite humorous. She loved to tease her customers by claiming loudly to anyone who would listen that she planned to "go to my grave with the very last Redbird Burger clutched in my cold, dead hand."

Needless to say, Redbird Burger aficionados didn't find it the least bit funny.

After happily agreeing to Dewey's proposal, I saw him to the door and was on my way back upstairs when my gaze fell on Bitty's desk. Curiosity got the best of me, and I decided to see what was inside.

First I moved the two boxes of newly arrived books into the corner near the bookshelves. I'd go through them later. It took me a few moments to actually sit down on Bitty's antique swivel desk chair. In my whole life, I'd never seen anyone but my aunt sit in this chair. If she had been a queen, her desk chair would have been her throne. Unfortunately, Bitty had moved to another kingdom, and I had temporarily taken her place. As I slid the key Dewey had given me into the locked desk drawer, it hit me for the first time that this wasn't actually Bitty's desk anymore. It was mine. Frankly, the whole idea hit me like a slap in the face. I gazed around the bookstore. It was all mine.

I'd never really owned anything before. Even the house I grew up in had belonged to someone else. Now I lived in a dorm room as a temporary occupant. A strange feeling came over me. For just a moment, I felt an odd sense of belonging to something. But as quickly as the thought came, I pushed it away. This was Bitty's world. My world was back in Wichita, studying English. I forced myself to put my focus back on the task at hand.

I unlocked the deep top drawer of the desk and pulled it open. There were quite a few papers inside, as well as several large bound books with the word *Accounts* on the outside. I pulled the top one out and leafed through it. It was just as Dewey had said. Rows and rows of names and transactions filled the pages. Bitty had customers all over the planet. Although most of the addresses were in the States, several entries referenced overseas addresses.

I put the book on top of the desk, intending to spend more time going over it later. Then I pulled out a folder that housed a stack of papers. Most of the information seemed to be work related, until I came upon a large envelope with the words *Last Will and Testament* written on it. Inside were several handwritten sheets. Glancing over the first several pages, I saw that Bitty had written down exactly what Dewey had already told me. She wanted everything she owned turned over to me. A letter-sized envelope slid out from the middle of the papers and fell to the floor. I leaned over to pick it up and saw that my name was written on it. A letter left for me from Bitty. My throat constricted with emotion. I put the envelope on top of the desk next to the account book. I would read it later when I had time to give it the proper attention it deserved.

At the bottom of the various pages, I found what I'd been looking for: a list of items with a person's name written next to each one. There were eight names on the list. Isaac Holsapple, Dewey Tater, Ruby Bird, Alma Pettibone, Pastor Taylor, Amos Parker, Dr. Lucy Barber, and Lila Hatcher. I didn't know Dr. Barber, but I'd heard about the young doctor who'd moved into the area a couple of years earlier. If I remembered correctly, she lived in nearby Hugoton. I could tell that Bitty had actually started the list quite some time ago. A couple of the names were crossed off and added again at the bottom. She must have changed her mind about what she wanted to leave them.

Each corresponding item willed to the mentioned individuals appeared to be a book or a set of books. That made sense. Books were Bitty's most treasured possessions. I put all the other pages back into the large envelope and laid the list on top of Bitty's book of accounts that was on top of the desk next to the envelope with my name on it. The rest of the papers went back into the drawer, which I locked. At some point I would go through everything more carefully, but right now there wasn't much time left to shower and get ready to meet Dewey. Maybe I would get a chance later tonight. Besides, I could clearly hear a Redbird Burger calling my name.

I stared at the envelope with my name on it for a few moments before I went upstairs. I had to assume that Bitty had made all her final arrangements because at her age, she wanted to be prepared, but being this organized still seemed rather unusual. Could she really have sensed that her time on earth was drawing to a close? But how could that be? I felt a sudden chill that had nothing to do with the temperature outside.

A hot shower tends to make everything seem better somehow. After showering and changing clothes, I was ready to take on a Redbird Burger with gusto. I checked my watch on the way downstairs—twenty minutes to eleven. I had time to read Bitty's letter while I waited for Dewey to arrive.

The accounts book was where I'd left it, along with the list of books and recipients. The letter from my aunt was still there, but it had been moved. It now sat on the edge of the desk, with a message scribbled on it next to my name. I picked it up and read: *Please don't leave town. Bitty was murdered. Don't let her killer go free!*

3

A little after eleven, Dewey and I were safely tucked into a booth at the Redbird Café. I thought Ruby was going to lose her ever-present white blond wig at the sight of me coming through her front door. "Why, Ivy Towers," she screeched. "Where in blue blazes have you been keeping yourself? It's about time you came home!"

Ruby was well into her seventies. For as long as I could remember, she had sported a platinum hairpiece in the style of Marilyn Monroe. I had to believe that after all these years, it wasn't the very same wig. She must be down to the great-great-granddaughter of the original by now. It looked absolutely atrocious—but it was Ruby. I couldn't imagine her without it. Ruby was larger than life. Her choice of headgear matched her eccentric personality.

Longtime Winter Break residents knew that Ruby's boisterous behavior hid a secret heartache. Ruby had first come to town in her twenties, a young bride with a new baby. Her husband, Elbert, brought his family to western Kansas to help run his uncle Leonard's farm. Leonard had suffered a stroke that eventually proved fatal. After his death, Elbert, Ruby, and baby Bert stayed on, turning the place into one of the most successful dairy farms in this part of the country. But in the sixties, disaster struck. Elbert was hit by lightning while rounding up cows. He died instantly. Ruby and fifteen-year-old Bert tried to run the farm alone, but it proved to be too much for the diminutive widow and her young son. Several of their neighbors pitched in and offered their help, but with their own farms to run, they weren't able to give the Birds enough assistance to keep going.

Then one day when Bert was only sixteen, he disappeared. Most people in town believed he'd run away, tired and discouraged from trying to fill his daddy's shoes. Ruby was heartbroken. Eventually, she sold the farm and used the money to open the Redbird Café.

The story of the missing Bert Bird remained one of Winter Break's longest-running legends. I'd heard most of the speculation, which ran from the possible to the ridiculous: Bert ran away and became a hippie, showing up in a movie about Woodstock; Bert ran away and joined the circus; Bert became a famous movie producer in Hollywood; Bert was murdered and his ghost still haunts the peach tree groves down by Winter Break Lake; and my favorite—Bert went searching for the much-ballyhooed Lost Gambler's Gold, supposedly buried by a wealthy gambler on his way back from California. Legend had it that he was attacked and killed by Indians not long after hiding the booty he'd won from unlucky gold miners. His treasure was supposedly buried somewhere in Winter Break. The treasure carried a curse, and the hapless Bert had fallen prey to the spirit of the long-dead adventurer. Kids in Winter Break still told stories about the ill-fated gambler reaching out from beneath the ground and calling, "Where's my gold? Do you have it?" then grabbing them around the ankles. The tale had caused many a sleepless night for the town's young people.

After ordering two Redbird Burgers and jawing with Ruby for a while, Dewey and I made small talk while we waited for our gastronomic Redbird adventure to arrive. I wanted to tell him about the odd message written on Bitty's envelope, but to be honest, I wasn't certain if I should. Normally, Dewey would be my first choice as a confidant, but I needed some time to think. The note wasn't geared to frighten me. It appeared to be written by someone who really believed Bitty was murdered. I wanted time to think the situation through. Then I would formulate a plan and decide who I should tell—and who I shouldn't.

Dewey was saying something about Alma Pettibone at the post office. I shook off thoughts about Ruby and Bert and forced myself to concentrate on Dewey.

"Then she placed cherry bombs in every single postal box. When they blew up, it was quite a sight. The whole town watched the old post office take off straight into space. I hear it's still circling the earth."

My confused expression caused Dewey to chuckle. "Oh, you're back. I've been talking nonsense for quite a while. Where have you been?"

I shook my head, mortified by my lack of attention. "I'm sorry, Dewey. I have a lot on my mind, what with Bitty and the bookstore...."

He reached over and touched my hand. "I know that, Ivy. I understand. Sorry I teased you."

His compassionate response made me feel ashamed that I had harbored any mistrust toward him. I started to tell him about the note, but before I could get the words out, Ruby showed up with our hamburgers. The things were so big they were frightening. The aroma took me back to my childhood. In Winter Break, eating an entire Redbird Burger was the dividing line between childhood and the mysterious world of adults. Once you finished one of Ruby's famous Redbird Burgers, life changed. Other kids looked at you with new respect. Even now, as Ruby delivered her culinary masterpiece, a hush fell over the diner. I wasn't sure, but I thought I saw a man in the corner remove his cap.

"You eat up, honey," Ruby hollered as she set the monstrosity in front of me. "You need some meat on those bones!"

I had no plans to go anywhere near a scale for at least a week after this meal. It would take that long for my "bones" to recover from the shock they were about to receive.

Dewey bent his head and said a short prayer, which made me feel a little better. At least now I had some heavenly protection. It took awhile to figure out how to pick the thing up, but when I did, I chomped down, waiting for what I knew was coming. And it did. I'm not sure what the Lord plans to serve at the Marriage Supper of the Lamb, but I won't be surprised if the table is laid out with Ruby's Redbird Burgers.

After a few minutes of chewing and swallowing, I finally remembered where I was—and that I still had a problem. Dewey seemed to come back to himself, too. The glassy-eyed look that is normal during the enjoyment of a Redbird Burger cleared a little from Dewey's expression, and he smiled at me.

"Does it taste the way you remembered?" he asked, a little grease dribbling down his chin.

I shook my head. "I think it's even better. This has to be why some people never leave Winter Break. They're addicted to Ruby and her cooking."

Dewey grinned. "You're probably right."

I was about to the halfway point, so I put the burger down to rest a little before approaching the second stretch. Maybe my mind was clouded with hamburger grease, but I found myself saying, "Dewey, do you think there's anything strange about the way Aunt Bitty died? I mean, she was almost one with that ladder, she was so used to it. Don't you find it odd that she could fall off like that?"

Dewey, who was also resting for the final sprint in the Ruby race, frowned at me. "I guess I was surprised a little, Ivy. But obviously something went wrong and she fell. There's no other explanation." He stared at me for a moment. "Sometimes it's best to accept things and go on, even if it's hard."

For some reason his comment struck me as being somewhat callous, but Dewey Tater wasn't an insensitive person. In fact, just the opposite. Without thinking it through, I blurted out, "So it never occurred to you that something else might be behind her accident?"

Dewey's face turned so white it scared me. "Ivy Towers, why in the world would you say something like that?" He lowered his voice so no one in the restaurant could hear him. "There's not a soul in this town that would hurt Bitty. For goodness' sake. I hope you don't repeat that to anyone else."

I'd upset Dewey. The realization made my stomach a little queasy. Or maybe it was the Redbird Burger, but whatever it was, I felt bad. Dewey was someone I respected. It was obvious I wouldn't be able to share my suspicions with him, and I certainly couldn't tell him about the message left on the envelope. I flashed him an apologetic smile. "You're right, Dewey. Sorry. I guess living in the big city puts ideas in your head. I shouldn't have brought it up. Let's forget it."

He nodded, but his face still held a shadow of suspicion—or something else. I would have given the second half of my burger to know what he was thinking. Well, maybe not. But there was definitely more to Bitty and Dewey than met the eye. All of a sudden, something Dewey said earlier today about having coffee in the mornings with Bitty, along with a few of his other comments, clicked on a light in my brain.

"Dewey. You and my aunt—were you. . ." I couldn't quite find the words.

Dewey hung his head for a moment. When he looked up, there were tears in his eyes. "I loved your aunt with all my heart, Ivy. And she loved me, too. We even talked about getting married."

"I had no idea, Dewey. That's wonderful." I reached over and touched his arm. "I'm so happy she had you in her life. I wish she'd lived long enough to marry you."

He pulled a handkerchief out of the pocket of his shirt and blew his nose. "I do, too, Ivy. But wedding or not, we loved each other. That's the most important thing."

"Dewey, please don't take this wrong, but I'm surprised you and Bitty were so close. I knew you were friends, but you haven't seemed all that upset about her death."

"You mean because I'm not constantly bawling my eyes out in front of you?" He shook his head. "I miss her every second. It hurts. A lot." His eyes locked on mine. "But I truly believe that Bitty is alive and waiting for me. And I don't think we'll be apart much longer. I have my gaze set on heaven." He stared somewhere past me—looking at something only he could see. "'Where your treasure is, there will your heart be also.'" He smiled at me. "I guess I'm looking to my treasure, Ivy. That's all."

I was moved by his words and desperately wanted to ask more questions. Like how long had he and my aunt been in love? Why didn't they marry years ago? Unfortunately, this wasn't the time to get that personal. Besides, there'd been enough revelations for one morning. I stared at the rest of my hamburger and stirred up all the courage I had to continue my burger battle. Before I could begin round two, a voice cut through my beef-dazed stupor.

"Excuse me. Are you Ivy Towers?"

I looked up into eyes the color of deep blue evening skies and a smile so warm and brilliant I felt momentarily blinded. Okay, maybe I'm being a little overly dramatic, but this was one good-looking guy.

I responded brilliantly. "Huh?"

His smile grew wider. "I'm looking for Ivy Towers."

"I–I'm Ivy Towers." I looked at Dewey, who nodded to confirm the fact that I was who I said I was. "Can I help you?"

"May I sit down a minute?"

I bobbed my head up and down, which he obviously took as a yes.

"I'm sorry to interrupt your lunch."

Lunch? What lunch? Even though I wouldn't have believed it, Ruby's Redbird Burger had just taken second place in my heart. This guy was something. Tall, his dark hair just long enough to be romantic without being scruffy, black leather coat and gloves, and the kind of features you usually see only on the front of trashy romance novels. Not that I would know anything about that, of course.

"That's okay," I managed to squeak out. "What can I do for you?" I had a list of possibilities forming in my mind, but I was pretty sure his suggestion wasn't going to be among them.

He handed me a business card that I took without removing my eyes from his face. "I'm Noel Spivey. I did business with your aunt from time to time. I heard she passed away. I'm terribly sorry."

"Why, thank you," I said, grateful to have finally remembered the English language. "That's kind of you to say. Are you from around here, Mr. Spivey?"

And yes. I already saw the problem. Ivy Spivey. But I could overcome it. I'd been calling myself Sam for many years now. The name change would force me to bury Ivy for good.

And no, I wasn't jumping too far ahead. It's good to get things lined up as soon as possible. Saves headaches later.

"Actually, I live in Denver."

"You drove quite a ways in some pretty bad weather to get here," Dewey interjected. "What's so important?"

I glanced over at Dewey in surprise. His tone was a little rude, and that wasn't like him.

"Well, I'd like a chance to talk to Ms. Towers about that," Noel said. "I deal in rare books. I thought she might be interested in selling her aunt's inventory." He flashed another charming smile. "I hope it doesn't seem inappropriate—my coming here so soon after Miss Flanagan's death. I could have called sometime next week, but I really wanted to attend her funeral if possible. I had a lot of respect for her."

"No," I said after sending a warning look to Dewey. "I think it's very thoughtful. I appreciate it."

Dewey scowled but kept his mouth shut.

"Thank you, Ms. Towers. Now I need to find a place to stay. Are there any motels in Winter Break?"

I started to tell him that the closest motel would be in Hugoton, but Dewey interrupted me before I could get the words out.

"No motel here," he said grudgingly, "but I heard that Sarah Johnson has a room for rent. She has a clean home and she's a good cook. You'd be quite comfortable there."

Noel looked relieved. "Thanks for the information. I would really rather not get out on those roads again. It's pretty icy. If you could just point me in the right direction. . ."

Dewey told him how to get to Sarah's house while I tried to look him over without being too obvious. I really wished I'd taken the time to put some makeup on before I left the bookstore. It pays to remember that what your mother told you about clean underwear works with makeup, too. I'd certainly learned my lesson.

As Noel got ready to leave, he held out his hand. "Thank you for your time, Ms. Towers."

"Please. Call me Sam," I said.

He looked confused. "I thought your name was Ivy."

I shook my head and gave him my best smile. I hoped that mutilated shreds of Redbird Burger weren't stuck between my teeth. "I was known as Ivy when I was a child. My name is actually Ivy Samantha. I go by Sam."

"Then Sam it is." He held my hand a little longer than necessary. I didn't fight it. "Do you have a time set for your aunt's service yet?"

I explained that I was on my way to make those arrangements and offered to call him with the information later in the afternoon. He left with the telephone number of the bookstore and my promise to meet with him about my aunt's books after the funeral.

I watched him walk out of Ruby's, as did every other female in the place. I put his card in my coat pocket then turned my attention back to Dewey and the rest of my hamburger. For some reason, the added pounds that were waiting to jump onto my hips seemed more important than they had just a few minutes earlier. As I pushed my plate away, I could swear I heard a sigh of disappointment sweep through the room. I noticed that Dewey was still sullen.

"What's the matter? You seem upset," I said.

He shook his head. "I don't know. Something about that guy." Dewey leaned back and crossed his arms over his chest. "How'd he know about Bitty dying? Only place it's been reported is in the Hugoton newspaper. Seems unlikely that a guy who lives in Denver would be reading the *Hugoton Gazette*."

It was a good question. I added it to the growing list of questions I had about my aunt's death. As I watched Dewey finish his Redbird Burger, I realized that my list was getting pretty long. I was becoming more and more suspicious about Aunt Bitty's accident.

Suddenly, Winter Break, Kansas, didn't feel quite so friendly.

4

Dewey and I waddled over to Buskin's Funeral Home after turning down Ruby's offer of hot apple pie to top off our Redbird Burgers. I couldn't find the words to explain to her how impossible it was to put one more ounce of food into my already-suffering stomach, so I just shook my head and headed for the door. Ruby's partial deafness kept her from hearing Dewey mumble something about not having hollow legs.

As we walked out, she screeched, "I'm fryin' up a mess of fresh catfish tonight. Mashed potatoes whipped with cream and butter. Homemade biscuits and—"Thankfully, Dewey closed the door behind us, cutting off the rest of Ruby's cholesterol-laden proclamation. At that moment, I wasn't certain I would ever be able to eat again.

It was so cold outside, I felt that I'd walked smack into an open freezer. The ice and snow had finally stopped falling, but the clouds that drifted overhead looked as though they still had some business to attend to.

Dewey and I didn't talk on our way to Buskin's. It was only a couple of blocks away, and we weren't tempted to open our mouths since any conversation might slow us down. Survival instinct had kicked in. Continual movement was our only defense against becoming permanent popsicles.

When we reached Buskin's, Dewey, ever the gentleman, held the door open for me. Frankly, I wouldn't have blamed him if he'd run inside and left me to fend for myself. Self-preservation is a powerful instinct. Once we stepped into the main lobby, I had to stand still a few seconds just to soak in the surrounding warmth and get my muscles moving again.

"Why, there you are, Miss Ivy."

I elevated my frozen eyeballs a little to see Elmer Buskin peering at me from beneath his bushy gray eyebrows. His ever-present smirk was properly glued in place. For a man whose life was spent dealing with the dead, he always seemed suspiciously happy about it.

"He–hello, Mr. B–B–Buskin. It–it's b–been a long t–time." I was pretty sure my teeth would stop chattering at some point. If not, future conversations with me were going to require a lot of patience.

"Yes. Yes, it has, Miss Ivy. And now we meet again under these dark circumstances." His bloodshot eyes didn't match his black funeral director suit, but they did go very well with his bright red bow tie. Most people in town suspected that Elmer Buskin kept a little nip in his office and indulged from time to time. As kids, Amos and I used to tell anyone who would listen that he drank embalming fluid. When Aunt Bitty heard it, she gave us both a good talking to, expounding on the evils of gossip and "bearing false witness." It hadn't stopped us from saying it, but at least we felt guilty about it every time we did. That surely counted for something.

"Please. Let's go to my office where we can talk," Elmer said. Everything about Elmer Buskin was odd, from the way he looked to the way he acted. But one of his strangest features was his voice. Although he tried to sound appropriately funereal, his high-pitched voice and pronounced speech impediment caused him to sound like a cross between Darth Vader and Tweety Pie. Dewey and I followed him through the overly ostentatious lobby. Faded red brocade wallpaper accented the darkened oriental rugs. The crystal chandelier, which still swung slightly from the wind that had swept inside when we opened the front doors, was decorated with dust and cobwebs. Buskin's Funeral Home was a secondhand Rose dressed up in high-society castoffs. Unfortunately, her garments were threadbare and worn. Dewey had told me that Elmer could barely keep his head above water. Most Winter Break people picked one of the two funeral homes in Hugoton when they faced a death in the family. The facilities were much nicer and more modern. Besides, some folks were a little afraid of Elmer Buskin. Whether it was the man himself, the rumors spread by imaginative kids conjuring up ghost stories on dark, stormy nights, or simply Elmer's occupation, most people kept their distance. Except, of course, my aunt Bitty. She would have viewed giving her mortal remains to a funeral home outside of Winter Break as extreme disloyalty, bordering on rudeness. And Aunt Bitty was never, ever rude.

Elmer's office was just as shabby as the lobby. Dewey and I sat down on two burgundy Queen Anne–styled chairs positioned in front of Elmer's desk. They looked old enough to have actually held the derriere of the long-dead regent herself. The finish was worn off the arms, and the legs of my chair wobbled badly. I had to grab the edge of the plywood desk to steady myself. Dewey looked a little concerned about the noises coming from underneath him. He was a big man, and the creaks and moans emanating from the ancient chair were dire warnings of impending collapse. Finally, he stood up, professing to be tired of sitting and having the need to stretch his legs.

Elmer proceeded as if he hadn't noticed anything wrong. "I want to tell you how sorry I am about your aunt," he said to me. "She was a wonderful person. So kind. And such a pretty woman." Except it came out more like "tuch a pitty woman."

"Thank you, Mr. Buskin," I said. "I appreciate everything you've done for

Aunt Bitty. Is there anything we need to do besides make arrangements for the memorial service?"

"No. Everything else was taken care of by your aunt. She prepaid for all the services we have provided."

"And I understand that she chose cremation?"

He nodded. "Yes, she did. I still remember what she said to me about it. 'Just return me to dust, Elmer. I'm not worried about it. God will know where I am. That's all that counts.'"

It sounded exactly like something Aunt Bitty would say. In my mind, I could see her standing in this very room, pointing her finger at Elmer for emphasis, her voice strong with conviction, her emerald eyes flashing.

"And you've already taken care of that?" I asked.

"Yes, although we don't do it here. We take our clients to Dodge City. After the cremation, we bring them back to Winter Break." Elmer stood up and walked over to a door behind him. He disappeared for a few seconds then reentered carrying a small wooden box, which he placed on the desktop in front of me.

With a sick feeling in the pit of my stomach, I realized I was looking at Aunt Bitty's mortal remains. "Th–that's Aunt Bitty?"

His usually insipid smile slipped. "No, Miss Ivy," he said, his voice trembling slightly. "That most certainly is not Bitty Flanagan. You could never reduce a woman like that to a little pile of ash."

As I stared up at him, a tear escaped from the side of his right eye and splashed down on the simple box.

"You got that right, Elmer," Dewey said, his voice husky.

I felt my own eyes get wet. Strange little Elmer Buskin had cared deeply for Bitty. In that moment, he went from being a parody to a person in my eyes. And I felt true remorse for ever having made fun of him. Aunt Bitty was reaching beyond the grave to teach me one more time that true love includes kindness—and that judging a book by its cover is always a mistake.

"I don't really know much about cremation," I said. "But can't we put Bitty—I mean her remains—into something a little nicer?"

Elmer removed a handkerchief from his pocket. After loudly blowing his nose into it, he sat down again. "This is the container your aunt chose. 'No fuss, Elmer,' she said. 'Don't you let anyone turn my death into more than what it really is. A home-going.'" He shook his head. "Even though it was my intention to respect her wishes, I anticipated your desire to give her a nicer resting place." He pulled open his desk drawer and withdrew a folder. "Here are a few choices for urns. Of course, if you don't see anything here you like, I can order something else." He handed me the pictures, along with his magnifying glass. I could see the pictures just fine without it, but I took it anyway, not wanting to hurt his feelings.

I held the glass over the colorful sheet. There were metal containers as well as some made of stone and wood. There were even some glass urns that looked like something you'd set around the house for decoration. As I was looking over the choices, none of which made me think of Bitty, Elmer reached over and pulled another sheet from underneath the page I was contemplating. He laid it on top of the other glossy advertisements. The flyer displayed a picture of a dark green brass urn in the shape of a book. And on its side was a gold cross. It was just right. It was Bitty. I heard Dewey express his approval.

"Mr. Buskin, this urn is perfect. How long will it take to get it here if I order it immediately?"

Elmer reached down somewhere below his chair. He grunted as he pulled up a cardboard box. After placing it on the table, he opened it and took out the very urn we'd been looking at.

"Now, Elmer," Dewey said. "You already bought it? Must have put you out a pretty penny. What if we hadn't picked it?"

Elmer's eyes twinkled happily. "I just knew this was the one. I felt it in my bones. After awhile, you get some intuition in this business. I picked it up the same day I drove your aunt to Dodge City."

"Thank you, Mr. Buskin," I said gratefully. "You did the right thing. I'll write you a check from Aunt Bitty's account as soon as I get things set up with the bank on Monday morning. How much do I owe you?"

Elmer waved his hand dismissively. "You owe me nothing, Miss Ivy. Your aunt paid good money for everything except this. This is on me. My gift to her."

I started to protest, but Dewey put his hand on my arm and shook his head. In my heart, I understood. Elmer wanted to give something to a woman he respected. I had to let him do it whether he could afford it or not.

"Then I thank you, Mr. Buskin," I said. "And I know that somehow Bitty knows about your kindness, and she appreciates it. If there's anything I can do—"

"Miss Ivy, there *is* something you could do for me," he interrupted. "You could start calling me Elmer instead of Mr. Buskin. It was okay when you were a child, but now you're all grown up. I think friends should be able to call each other by their first names, don't you?"

"I agree. Then you should drop the *Miss* and just call me Ivy." The words slipped out before I realized I hadn't told him to call me Sam. Great. If I didn't start setting people straight, I was always going to be Ivy Towers to the folks of Winter Break.

We went over the arrangements for a memorial service on Monday afternoon at the church. Elmer told me I could choose to have the urn present during the service or not. It was up to me.

"I don't know," I said carefully. "Why don't you let me think about that. If I decide to display it, what happens after the service?" I was hoping against hope that Bitty hadn't left instructions for her ashes to be scattered somewhere. I saw a sitcom episode once where an intrepid soul, trying to dispose of a relative's remains, hadn't made allowance for wind direction. The ashes were blown back all over him. That scenario gave me the shivers. I didn't want to find myself in a situation that left me trying to wash Aunt Bitty out of my hair.

Elmer cleared his throat. "Well, you can certainly bury the urn in Winter Break Cemetery if you wish, but Bitty didn't intend for that to happen. Your aunt wanted her ashes to stay in the bookstore."

"But how could she possibly request something like that?" I asked. "I have no idea what will happen to the store. What if it doesn't stay a bookstore? What if the new owners don't want to be bothered? What if—"

Dewey stopped me with a touch of his hand, his forehead wrinkled in exasperation. "Ivy Towers. For a smart young woman, sometimes you are rather dense. Haven't you figured it out yet?"

I guess my answer should have been no, because I hadn't a clue what he was talking about. "Figured out what?"

Dewey clucked his tongue and shook his head. "Your aunt left you the bookstore because she hoped you would run it, girl. And she wanted her ashes to stay in the store because as much as she desired to be in the presence of God, she was human. She hoped to leave a little bit of herself in the place she loved the most—with the person she loved the most. You."

I was so taken aback, I could barely speak. "Dewey," I finally sputtered, "I'm in school. I have plans. Why would Bitty think I would give up my life to live in Winter Break?"

Dewey Tater just smiled at me. You know, one of those "you poor little dumb cluck" smiles. Very unchristian thoughts filled my mind. I pushed them away and decided to ignore him.

"Mr.—I mean Elmer, if you would please transfer Bitty to the new urn, I would appreciate it. Let's display it at her funeral. I'll get back to you as to what to do with her. . .uh, remains after the service. Is that okay?"

Elmer nodded while looking back and forth between Dewey and me. I felt like one of two feuding parents trying to decide how to handle custody of their child.

I stood up, shook hands with Elmer, told Dewey I'd see him later, and skedaddled out of the funeral home as fast as I could. My last look at Dewey came as I was going out the front door. He and Elmer Buskin stood in the hallway outside Elmer's office with their arms folded, staring at me as if I were wild game that had just escaped their trap.

I kept my head tugged against my chest to protect my face from freezing while I walked back to the bookstore. I was embarrassed to have acted so strongly to Dewey's declaration of Aunt Bitty's wishes. Why did I feel so defensive? It should be easy for me to tell anyone that life in Winter Break was not my destiny. I had other plans. But it wasn't easy—and I couldn't figure out why.

By the time I got to the bookstore, I was so stiff I had a hard time getting the key in the front door lock. When it finally clicked, I was close to tears. It wasn't just the outrageous cold; it was everything. My trip to Winter Break had turned into something I hadn't planned on. I was dealing with sadness over Aunt Bitty's death, confusion over my feelings about this small town, and the suspicion that my dear aunt might have actually been murdered.

I slowly peeled off my frozen coat, muffler, and gloves, then danced around a little to get my blood flowing. Good thing I was alone. I'm sure I looked a little loony.

I was almost to the sitting room when I remembered to call Noel Spivey. Those incredible blue eyes floated in front of me. I found myself smiling in spite of myself. I went back to the coatrack and fished his card out of my pocket. I carried it over to Aunt Bitty's desk and sat down. His card read *Noel Spivey—dealer in rare books, specializing in literary first editions, fine printing and binding, artist's books, illustrated books in limited editions, and children's books. Member of ABAA—Antiquarian Booksellers Association of America.* His contact information was at the bottom of the card. It listed a Denver address and phone number. Denver. It seemed so far away from Winter Break, although it wasn't really. Still, I was certain Noel was finding out how different the two places actually were.

I looked up Sarah's number in Bitty's phone book. When she answered, I asked for Noel. He must have been nearby, because it took only a couple of seconds for him to get to the phone. When he said hello, I told him about the service on Monday.

"Thank you, Sam," he said. "I hope you won't think I'm intruding on a difficult time, and I will completely understand if you say no, but I was wondering if we could have dinner together tonight. I promise not to bring up anything about your aunt's books if you'd rather not. It's just that I don't know anyone here, and I'm feeling a little out of my element."

Rather than shouting "Yes, please!" through the receiver and frightening him, I kept my cool and pretended to consider it. However, the idea of heading back to Ruby's made me feel a little dizzy. I quickly formulated a plan and asked him to come to dinner at the bookstore. That way we could eat, and he would get a chance to look around. He happily agreed, and we set a date for seven o'clock. That would give me time to conjure up something a little lighter than Ruby's fare. Besides, I was curious to see what he would offer for Bitty's books. I needed to know all my options.

I put down the phone and found myself staring at the envelope with my name on it, the message begging me to find Bitty's murderer still there, of course. I don't know if a small part of my brain hoped I'd imagined it, but I hadn't. I was still staring at the message and contemplating opening the envelope when the entry bell tinkled and the front door blew open.

Amos stomped inside, trying to knock the ice and snow off his boots and onto the entry rug. I was going to have to get used to the idea that this was actually a public place, and people were going to be walking in whenever they wanted to. Locking the door might help, but during the day, it seemed wrong somehow. Bitty had always welcomed the residents of Winter Break into her cozy bookstore, not only during regular business hours but also at off-hours for group meetings or social get-togethers.

"Hey—Ivy—I mean Sam," he called out.

I was beginning to feel that my name was *Ivy-I-Mean-Sam.* Maybe it would be best to give up and let everyone in Winter Break call me Ivy. I could go back to being Sam when I returned to my other life. Trying to be someone else in Winter Break was close to impossible. It was wearing me out and confusing some of the good people around me.

"Hi, Amos. What's up?" As he hung up his coat, I remembered the envelope in my hand. The drawers of the desk were locked and the keys were in my purse. I carefully slid it under the desk pad while I wondered if I'd ever get a chance to read Bitty's letter.

"I just wanted to know how things were going. Did you get everything squared away with Elmer?"

I started to answer, but Amos didn't wait for a response. He headed straight for the sitting room. Obviously Aunt Bitty hadn't had many conversations in the main store area. The sitting room was like some kind of magnet. People were automatically drawn to it.

I stood up and followed him, hoping he wasn't planning to stay long. I needed to go through Bitty's kitchen to see if I had something to fix for dinner. If not, I'd have to make a trip to Dewey's store. I glanced at the old grandfather clock that sat between two of the floor-to-ceiling bookshelves. I was startled to see it wasn't working. Amos noticed me staring at it and strolled back over to where I stood.

"You actually have to wind it, Ivy—I mean Sam," he said. He took a key off the top of the clock, opened the face, and pulled the weights back up. After setting the correct time, he closed and locked the cabinet and placed the key back where he'd found it.

"I know that, Amos. I used to wind it for Bitty. I just forgot." The steady *ticktock* coming from the clock was a comforting sound. I was surprised I hadn't noticed that it had wound down before now. Its steady tone was an important part of the ambiance of Miss Bitty's Bygone Bookstore. "Amos," I said, "would you do me a favor?"

"Sure, what do you need?" he asked.

"Two things. Would you start a fire in the fireplace? I haven't had time."

"No problem," he said, heading toward the massive stone fireplace. "And the other thing?"

"Stop calling me Sam. It isn't working. I shouldn't have expected people here to see me as anyone but Ivy."

He turned and smiled at me. "It isn't that we can't learn to call you something else; it's just hard to understand the reason behind it. We all know you as Ivy. None of us knows *Sam*, and frankly, I doubt that many people in Winter Break want you to be someone else. We all like Ivy."

I stopped in my tracks and watched him grab some wood from the wood box. "But what if I am more Sam than Ivy now? Would that disappoint you?"

He positioned the wood in the grate before answering me. When he finished, he turned around once more to stare at me, but this time, he wasn't smiling. "Ivy, I'm sure you've changed some—we all have. I think you see *Sam* as someone more mature and worldly than *Ivy*. But even though we grow up, we still need to accept ourselves as the people God created us to be. I'm not sure you've done that. You can call yourself *Flibber Jibber* for all I care, but maybe it isn't your name you should be thinking about. Maybe you need to find out who the real Ivy Towers is."

I kept my mouth shut, but I could feel the rush of indignation inside me. Amos would never understand the insecurity I'd felt as a teenager. The only place I'd ever felt comfortable with myself was in Winter Break. Out in the real world, I was the kid standing in line, waiting for an invitation to life, trying to find something that would make me feel a part of the world. As Ivy, it had never happened. As Sam, I finally felt I'd made some headway. I wasn't where I wanted to be, but I certainly wasn't where I used to be. I had no intention of going back.

Amos watched me for a few moments, probably waiting for me to acknowledge his advice, but I couldn't think of anything to say that wouldn't start an argument, so I said nothing. Eventually, he went back to building the fire. Out of the corner of my eye, I could see him shaking his head.

Miss Skiffins had come downstairs to see what was going on. She rubbed up against my leg, so I picked her up and brought her into the sitting room. We were getting to be pretty good friends, even though I knew it probably wasn't a good idea. I still didn't have any idea what would happen to her when I left, but I certainly needed to start formulating some kind of plan.

Amos had the fire going but was muttering under his breath.

"Is something wrong, Amos?"

"If you want me to start fires for you, you need to get a set of tongs," he said. "It makes it easier to turn the logs so they'll burn evenly."

He sounded rather cross, and I took exception to it. "Excuse me, but I haven't had much time to go shopping. Perhaps you could look everything over and make me a list of the things I'm lacking. I wouldn't want you to be inconvenienced in any way."

He mumbled something under his breath that I'm sure wasn't meant to compliment my social skills.

"I don't know why you're getting upset with me, Amos. They're Bitty's tools. Did you lecture her, too?"

He used a poker to flip the logs over. After positioning them the way he wanted them and replacing the fire screen, he sat down in the overstuffed chair next to the hearth. "Bitty Flanagan wouldn't let anyone build a fire in her fireplace, Ivy. She was very independent and liked things a certain way. To tell you the truth, it feels odd to be here without her, using her things."

"I know how to start a fire, you know," I said, still a little annoyed.

"I know you do. Don't get me wrong—I like doing things for people. It makes me feel good. Bitty was a wonderful woman who loved to give to others, but it was hard for her to receive much in return. To tell you the truth, it was a little frustrating."

"I guess it's because she had to spend so much of her life taking care of herself," I said.

"I'm sure that's true," Amos replied. "Sorry I got upset. I guess this whole thing with Bitty has me kinda jumpy."

I smiled at him to let him know he was forgiven. Then I pulled Bitty's rocking chair closer, and Miss Skiffins and I cuddled up in front of the quickly growing fire. As I rocked back and forth, I felt myself begin to relax. I was so comfortable, I could almost forget that the temperature outside was in the single digits. In fact, for a few minutes, I actually forgot that Noel was coming over for dinner and I still hadn't checked out the kitchen for menu possibilities. Remembering the plans I'd made jump-started me out of complacency.

"Amos, I really don't want to rush you, but I have plans tonight, and I still have a lot to do. Did you come over for a reason, or did you just stop by for a visit?"

He was silent for a moment. Finally, he said, "I suppose you're seeing that Spivey guy tonight?"

"How do you know about Noel Spivey?"

"This is Winter Break, Ivy. It doesn't take long for gossip to spread."

I felt my face turn hot. When I was a kid, I'd endured a lot of teasing because my face became a deep crimson when I was angry. It wasn't a good look for me, especially with my dark red hair. I could only hope Amos wouldn't notice. "First of all, it isn't anyone's business who I invite over here," I said. "And second, even though I don't owe you an explanation, Noel is coming over to look at Bitty's books. He's made an offer to buy me out. You should be quite happy about that since you've been trying to get rid of me ever since I got here."

Amos frowned. "Believe me, it isn't that I want you to leave. That's not it at all."

"Amos Parker, there's something you're not telling me. What is it? If it has anything to do with me or Bitty, you need to tell me. I'm not leaving Winter Break until you do."

He sighed and shook his head. "Ivy Towers, you are the most exasperating person I've ever known. The only person more bullheaded than you is. . .me, I guess."

He became quiet and seemed to be turning something over in his mind. His silence amplified the sounds around me: the soft purring that came from the cat that had fallen asleep in my lap, the snapping of the logs in the fireplace, and the steady ticking of the clock behind us.

Finally, he leaned forward in his chair. His fingers were clasped so tightly together, his knuckles were white. The look on his face made my stomach do a flip-flop.

"Ivy," he said slowly, "it is not my intention to frighten you. Believe me, all I want to do is to protect you. But I can see now that the more I push you to leave, the more you're going to dig your heels in."

"You've got that right," I said. "You might as well go on and say what's on your mind."

His hazel eyes locked on mine. "Ivy, it's my belief that Bitty didn't fall off that ladder by accident. I think someone helped her along. And I'm worried that whatever they were after is still here. I want you out of town because I'm afraid your life may be in danger."

5

A mos's pronouncement didn't really surprise me. I was already suspicious about Bitty's death. But hearing someone else say it out loud sent chills running down my spine. And I had to admit that it hadn't occurred to me that I might be at risk. Maybe it was because Bitty's bookstore had always been a safe haven for me, or maybe I hadn't taken the time to think that far ahead. But I was certainly thinking about it now.

I admitted to Amos that I was also suspicious about Bitty's *accident*. "For one thing," I said, "she rode that ladder like it was soldered to her. Then there's the mysterious message I received this morning."

"Message? What message?"

I stood up slowly, trying not to wake Miss Skiffins. I handed her to Amos. "Here, take her. I'll show you."

He took the cat, who opened one sleepy eye to see what was going on then fell right back into contented oblivion.

I went to Bitty's desk and pulled the envelope out from underneath the desk pad where I'd hidden it when Amos arrived. I brought it to him, and as he took it from my hand, I couldn't stop my fingers from trembling. I could only hope he hadn't noticed.

Miss Skiffins was happily cuddled up on the arm of Amos's chair. I decided to leave her where she was. Amos didn't seem to mind having her nearby. Maybe finding Miss Skiffins a good home would be easier than I'd anticipated. I sat down again, waiting for Amos's reaction to the odd note.

"You haven't opened this yet?" he said.

I shook my head. "I will. I. . .I want a few minutes when there aren't any distractions."

"Okay, but don't put it off too long, Ivy. It was important to Bitty that you read it or she wouldn't have left it for you."

"I'm aware of that, Amos." I could feel my temper rising. I pushed it back down. He was only trying to help.

"Do you have any idea who wrote this?" he asked after rereading the message carefully.

"None. The envelope was on the desk where I left it before I took a shower. Someone wrote that while I was upstairs."

"Was the front door locked?"

I shrugged. "I've gone over and over it in my mind, Amos. The last person here before I went upstairs was Dewey Tater. I walked him to the door, but I can't remember whether or not I locked it. I thought I did. Dewey had just given me Bitty's keys. It would have made sense for me to use them. I had it in my mind to lock the door because I didn't want anyone wandering in while I was in the shower. The problem is, I don't actually remember turning the lock." I shook my head. "I'm sorry. I just can't say for certain."

"It's okay," Amos said. "Who else has keys to this place, Ivy?"

"As far as I know, I'm the only one. It's possible Dewey might have another set. Maybe Isaac, but I'm not certain about that."

"Isaac Holsapple? When was the last time you saw him?"

"I haven't seen him at all. He hasn't been around."

"I suppose that's not unusual," Amos said. "He only worked for Bitty the first half of the week. Isaac came in on Mondays to start cataloging the new books. Tuesdays, he put the cataloged books on the shelves, and Wednesdays, he went to the post office to bring over any new shipments. Sometimes your aunt would let him open the new boxes, but that was it. She did everything else."

"What about the rest of the week?"

"On Thursdays, Bitty sorted through all the new books that had come in and prepared any books that were supposed to be mailed out. She took those books to the post office on Friday. She wouldn't let anyone else mail out books. She'd hand them personally to Alma because she wanted to make certain they were processed immediately."

This was understandable. Everyone knew that Alma Pettibone had a tendency to get caught up in her daytime soaps, and sometimes letters and packages didn't get prepared in time for the regular pickup. If you had something important to mail, it was best to stand at the counter and watch while Alma stamped it and put it in the pickup bin.

I was surprised. "You certainly know a lot about the goings-on in the bookstore."

He shrugged. "Bitty and I were friends, Ivy. I tried to stop by every day. You didn't have to spend much time with Bitty to figure out her schedule. She was as regular as. . .well, that old grandfather clock—once you wind it, that is."

I ignored the dig at my failure to attend to Bitty's clock. "You said Isaac found her Wednesday morning?"

"Yes. He went to the post office around ten. After he brought the mail back, Bitty sent him to Dewey's for some packaging tape, and then to Ruby's to pick up a couple of egg salad sandwiches. I guess they always ate egg salad together on Wednesdays. It was their habit."

"What time did he find Bitty?"

"He picked up the sandwiches a little after eleven. He called me about eleven thirty."

"Are you the only one he called?"

"No," Amos said. "Before he called me, he called Lucy. I mean Dr. Barber."

Amos looked a little uncomfortable when he mentioned the new doctor. I wondered why. "I thought Dr. Barber's office was in Hugoton."

"You're right; it is. But she was in town that morning, checking on Huey Martin's lumbago. Isaac saw her when he was at Ruby's. He called her over there."

I thought about the timeline. "So Isaac leaves Ruby's a little after eleven. It only takes a few minutes to walk here from Ruby's, yet it takes him over twenty minutes to call you? Does that seem reasonable?"

Amos absently ran his hands through his hair, a familiar sign of frustration. "I don't know, Ivy. I asked Lucy what time he called her. She couldn't quite remember. After she got here and realized that Bitty was beyond help, she told Isaac to call me." He stared past me, his forehead wrinkled in thought. "There wasn't much time for him to do anything except what he says he did. Besides," he said, "Isaac worshipped your aunt. I don't believe for one minute he would ever do anything to hurt her."

I wasn't as confident as Amos. I'd always thought Isaac was a little strange. Although he mostly kept to himself, he used to make me feel distinctly uncomfortable. I asked Bitty about him once. She'd looked at me sternly and said, "Now, Ivy, God made everyone different. Just because someone isn't just like you, it doesn't mean that He hasn't stuffed that person full of beautiful gifts."

Maybe so, but I'd never been able to find anything remotely beautiful about Isaac Holsapple. He was small and hunched over with a big nose and squinty eyes. His long salt-and-pepper hair was always messy, even though his clothes were always perfectly ironed and in place. He'd moved to Winter Break and started working for Bitty many years ago, not long after she opened the bookstore. Her fiancé, Robert, had been killed in an accident. Mother told me that Bitty had thrown herself into the bookstore so she could "forget." When I was a young girl, the story made me sad. But I'd never seen my great-aunt spend one moment sorrowing over what might have been. She was too busy enjoying life, the people around her, and the bookstore she loved.

"You haven't told me why you're suspicious about Bitty's death," I said.

Amos leaned back in his chair. "There are several things that bother me, Ivy. As you said, Bitty was an expert on that ladder. She was in good shape for her age. In fact, she was in better shape than most people half her age." He stared at the crackling flames in the fireplace. "Then there's the position of her body. It just didn't look quite right to me."

I didn't like the images that came into my mind as I imagined Bitty falling from her trusty library ladder, so I decided to push on. "Anything else, Amos?"

He nodded. "You may think this is silly, but there is something else that worries me."

"At this point, everything is important. Tell me."

He rubbed his hands together as though he were cold even though we sat in front of a roaring fire. I understood how he felt. The idea of anyone harming Aunt Bitty made me feel that I'd been dropped outside in a snowbank. It not only didn't make sense; it was unfathomable.

"Your aunt was the most organized person I ever knew," Amos said. "Her life ran like a well-oiled machine. She had a plan for everything, and she worked that plan as if it were cut in stone and delivered by the Lord God Himself.

"Every morning she and Dewey Tater had breakfast at 7:00 a.m. I know this because I used to stop by and eat with them whenever I could. At eight thirty, Dewey left to open his store, and Bitty cleaned up the breakfast dishes. She put those dishes in the dishwasher, turned it on, and started getting ready to open the bookstore at precisely nine o'clock. I watched her follow this same pattern every morning I was here. It never changed unless it was a day when she had to go to Hugoton for a doctor's or dentist's appointment, or if she drove out of town for an auction or estate sale."

"I know Aunt Bitty was organized to the max, but what does that have to do with anything?"

"I'm getting there," he said, looking a little perturbed by my interruption. "Sometimes during the day, she might fix herself a cup of herbal tea, but that was usually only in the afternoon."

I interrupted him. "Amos, I still don't see why this is important."

He lowered his voice as if someone else could hear us, but unless Miss Skiffins planned to sell our secrets for catnip, we were pretty safe. "I told you this might sound like an odd thing to be concerned about, but the morning Bitty died, there were two cups with saucers sitting on the kitchen cabinet."

"Oh, Amos. That doesn't sound like an important clue. Maybe she was making tea for her and Isaac."

"No way. Isaac doesn't drink anything with caffeine in it. Says it makes him too nervous. I've known him a long time. He's almost religious about it."

"Okay. What if Bitty didn't have time to run the dishwasher?" I offered.

He shook his head again. "The dishwasher had been turned on that morning. I checked it. The dishes inside it were warm. Besides a few other dishes, probably from the previous night's dinner, there were two cups and two small plates from breakfast. And anyway, these weren't empty cups, Ivy. There were

45

tea bags still sitting inside them and a pan of water heating on the stove. By the time I found it, the water was almost all boiled away."

"So you think someone was here Wednesday morning."

"Yes. Bitty was making tea because she was expecting company. The problem is, I've asked everyone I can think of, and no one admits to stopping by."

I thought for a moment. "Could it have been a book buyer from out of town?"

"No. No one saw any cars out front Wednesday morning. As nosy as everyone is in this town, someone would have noticed a strange car."

"So you believe that between the time Isaac left and the time he came back, someone came into the bookstore without being seen by anyone else in town and killed Aunt Bitty."

Amos held up his hands in mock surrender. "I know it sounds unlikely, but I just can't shake the feeling that something besides a simple accident happened here. And now with this. . ." He held up the envelope with the scrawled note.

"Amos, if you thought Bitty's death looked suspicious, why didn't you call someone? Start an investigation? And why let Elmer take her body before an expert had a chance to look at her injuries?"

He sighed. "Because this is Winter Break, Ivy. No one gets murdered here. Dr. Barber called it an accident. I figured she'd know. And to be honest, I was so upset about losing Bitty, I didn't start putting all of this together until after she had already been sent to Dodge City. By that time, it was too late. And before you ask, I can't call anyone from the outside in now to investigate. I don't have a shred of evidence except a couple of teacups. Believe me, I get the Andy Taylor treatment enough without having to go out of my way to stir it up."

The grandfather clock in the bookstore bonged a warning that my time was running out. "Look," I said, standing up, "you've got to get out of here so I can get ready for my meeting with Noel Spivey. We'll talk more about this tomorrow after church, okay?"

Amos reached over and patted Miss Skiffins once more before pulling himself up from his chair. "Okay. But hide that envelope. Lock it up. If the person who killed Bitty is still in town, the last thing we want to do is to tip anyone off that we're suspicious."

I'd already started toward the front door, when Amos grabbed my arm and spun me around. "Listen, Ivy. I still think you should leave town. The only reason anyone would have to murder your aunt was because she had something someone wanted. We don't know if it's still here or not. If it is. . ."

As I gazed into his eyes, I felt a stirring of something I thought was buried long ago. The last thing I wanted was to have feelings for Amos Parker. After all, those emotions belonged to Ivy, not to me. I pulled away from him.

"First of all, Amos, if there was something in here that someone wanted badly enough to kill for it, it's long gone by now. I mean, think about it. This place has been basically unprotected since Bitty died. I don't believe you need to worry about that any longer."

He shrugged. "You could be right. But if the killer finds out you're snooping around, trying to find out what really happened, you could be putting yourself in danger."

"You listen to me, Amos Parker. If someone really did kill my aunt Bitty, there's no way I'm leaving Winter Break until we catch him. You and I have to put our heads together and solve this. Bitty deserves no less."

Amos walked over to the door and pulled his coat from the rack. "You're right. But I want you to be careful. You have to start locking this door. Don't open it unless you're sure it's safe. And don't tell anyone about our suspicions." He zipped up his coat and pointed his finger at me. "And I mean *anyone*. Not even Dewey. Okay?"

"Too late," I said sheepishly. "I already mentioned something to Dewey."

Amos's forehead wrinkled with concern. "What did he say?"

"He got really upset, Amos. He wouldn't even discuss it."

"Can't say I'm surprised. He's been through a lot. Dewey loved your aunt very much. He was really hurt when she postponed their wedding."

His words took me by surprise. "What? I. . .I didn't know that. Do you know why?"

Amos shrugged. "I have no idea. Whatever it was, it didn't seem to change their relationship much. They still spent every day together." He pulled on his hat. "You remember what I said. Be careful, okay?"

"I will. I promise."

As he turned to walk out the door, I called out to him. "Andy Taylor was a better lawman than any of those big-city detectives who looked down on him, you know. And he was always right."

Amos's slow smile told me that he understood. I watched him leave and was surprised to find myself missing him.

6

By the time Amos left, I had only a couple of hours to get ready for Noel Spivey's visit. A quick trip upstairs told me that Dewey had given me enough supplies to put together a dinner for two. It wouldn't be fancy, but it would be food.

I got dressed, tried to do something with my hair, and applied a little makeup. Then I threw together a tuna casserole and popped it in the oven. Thankfully, Dewey had put a package of rolls in the bread box. A can of corn rounded out the meal. I poured the corn into a pan and turned the burner on low. After adding a little butter and salt, I cast a critical eye at Bitty's kitchen. Although it was certainly cozy, it was really too small for company. I decided to serve dinner on the big table in the sitting room.

After carrying our place settings and silverware downstairs, I remembered that I'd promised my mother a phone call. "Shoot," I said out loud. Miss Skiffins looked up from the chair where Amos had left her. She gazed at me wide-eyed, as if disturbing her sleep was a punishable offense in her world. "Sorry," I said softly. She made a little trilling noise, signaling absolution, I guess. Then she closed her eyes once again.

I ran upstairs, trying to remember the time difference between the United States and China. Mother had told me more than once. What was it? Were they thirteen or fourteen hours ahead of us or behind us? Either my parents were still in bed or they'd been up only a short time. I decided to call them after dinner. I was pretty sure they'd be happier to hear from me when they were fully awake. What was that proverb about greeting someone early in the morning? I couldn't quite remember it word for word, but I was pretty sure the writer wasn't encouraging the practice. Besides, it was never a good idea to talk to my mother before she had her first cup of coffee. Mother had very few vices, but coffee was something she enjoyed with a vengeance. I had to hope she could get some in China; otherwise some of her conversions were going to be taken by force.

After setting the table, I brought the tuna casserole down last. I didn't like the way Miss Skiffins was eyeing it, so I made one last trek upstairs to lock her up. She would have to go in Bitty's bedroom since my room didn't have a door. Funny how I'd been here almost twenty-four hours and still hadn't ventured into my aunt's room.

I slowly turned the door handle. Miss Skiffins looked up into my face as if asking if she was finally going to see her beloved mistress. I'm sure she was wondering why she'd been stuck with me instead of her rightful owner. As I opened the door, the aroma of my aunt's perfume was like a gentle caress. *Jean Nate.* It was the only fragrance she wore. I sucked in a deep breath, trying to ignore the lump in my throat.

While I fumbled for the light switch, Miss Skiffins wriggled out of my arms. She ran straight for the bed and jumped up on the colorful quilted comforter. I entered the room, closing the door behind me so she couldn't escape. After sniffing around a little, probably looking for Bitty, she conceded defeat and curled up next to the pillows.

I didn't have much time, but I spent the next few moments breathing in Bitty's presence. It was almost as if she were still here. Her lilac housecoat with its pale ivory ribbons lay on an old Victorian-styled chair in the corner that had belonged to her mother. Various framed pictures adorned the walls and dresser. A closer look revealed that the childish drawings were mine, and most of the photographs were of me. It had been years since I'd visited this room. Even when I'd stayed here, I'd kept to my own room, not thinking that an old woman's bedroom would hold anything of interest to me.

It was evident that Bitty had seen me almost as her own child. And perhaps in some ways it was true. In many aspects she had been more of a mother to me than my own had. I felt a deep stab of grief. Not for Bitty; I knew where she was, and I knew she was happy. It was the idea that there would be no more Bitty Flanagan in the world. I felt that we had all lost something important. Something that couldn't be replaced. I was certain I would never again find anyone quite like her.

Miss Skiffins was already fast asleep, probably dreaming of Bitty. I quietly closed the door and went downstairs to wait for Noel.

He knocked on the door at precisely seven o'clock. As he stepped inside, I was struck once again by how gorgeous he was. I didn't want to be too impressed; I knew that what was inside a person was more important than the outside, but I could certainly appreciate the excellent job God had done on the exterior of this man. It would be downright disrespectful to ignore His fine handiwork.

He took off his coat and hung it on the coatrack, taking special care to make sure it was secure. He wore designer jeans and a cerulean blue cable-knit sweater that complemented his azure eyes and dark hair.

"Thank you for asking me over, Sam," he said, smiling. "I know this is a difficult time for you."

"It's okay. I have been a little worried about what to do with the bookstore. You might be an answer to prayer. But let's eat first. Then we'll talk business, okay?"

He nodded his agreement, flashing me another one of his million-dollar smiles.

I'd felt pretty good about how I looked until that moment. Being honest with myself, I had to accept the unfortunate truth that I wasn't the prettiest person in the room anymore.

As I showed him to the sitting room, he stopped near a display case that held some special books Bitty kept under lock and key. Even in the low light of the store, I saw his face pale. "Oh my goodness," he said softly. "Do you know what these are?"

I circled back to where he stood, gazing into the glass-covered case. "Yes. My aunt told me those were all first editions of C. S. Lewis's Chronicles of Narnia series. Some of them are signed by the illustrator, Pauline. . .something."

"Baynes. Pauline Baynes. Are you certain? Do you know which ones are signed?"

I shook my head. "Although I don't know much about any of the other books here, Aunt Bitty spoke to me about this set more than once. She was quite proud of it. As you can see, she had collected only four of the set. There are seven, I believe. If I remember right, two of these books are signed and two are not."

I swear, if he hadn't been a rather refined person, I think he would have drooled on the glass.

"Are they worth much?" I asked.

The look he gave me made me realize that I didn't have enough knowledge about Bitty's books to sell them. I was going to have to sharpen my rare book smarts.

"Sam, I would have to inspect them to give you an accurate estimate, but you're looking at somewhere around ten to twelve thousand dollars here. And if *The Silver Chair* is one of the books signed by Baynes. . .well, a book like that just sold for nine thousand dollars."

Now it was my turn to feel the blood drain from my face. "Goodness gracious," I said. "I. . .I had no idea."

He frowned. "Making you an offer on your stock is going to be difficult if you don't know the value of it."

I felt really stupid. Why in the world did Bitty leave me this bookstore? She had to know I was ignorant about it. Then I remembered what Dewey told me at the funeral home. Bitty expected me to stay here and run things. I guess she thought I'd learn as I went. Now I was in a pickle.

"Look, let's eat. Then we'll talk about the store. To be honest, I haven't decided whether I'm going to sell it or keep it."

Noel seemed to take my declaration calmly and proceeded over to the table for dinner. I, on the other hand, couldn't believe what I'd just said. I had no intention of keeping the bookstore. Where in the world had those words come from?

Noel was busy looking at our dinner fare, so I risked a look up at the ceiling while I reminded my aunt that I had a life and she needed to quit interfering in it.

"Everything looks good," Noel said, breaking me out of my one-way discussion with Aunt Bitty.

I wondered if he was being kind. It occurred to me that he was probably used to high-class fare. A simple tuna casserole might be too pedestrian for his tastes. I stood there in my simple denim smock and twenty-dollar department store faux-suede Mary Janes, feeling out of place and ignorant. I was fourteen again—a goofy, gawky nerd. I had to remind myself that the insecure little girl was gone. I was Sam: smart, savvy, and mature. Why had I suddenly dropped back into the role of the teenager who never felt she belonged?

"It. . .it might not be what you're used to," I said, hoping I didn't sound as unsure as I felt.

I was rewarded with another utterly disarming smile. "I'm on the road so much, I'm used to greasy fast-food hamburgers and cold, stringy chicken. This is a banquet." He pulled out a chair for me. "I'm so hungry, I'm liable to forget my manners and dig in before you have a chance to get to the table. For your own good, I think you'd better sit down."

I obeyed, and within a few seconds we were eating. The casserole was good. I'd made it the way Aunt Bitty had taught me. In fact, most of my cooking expertise came from Bitty. Mother wasn't a very good cook. Preparing meals had always been a chore for her. Aunt Bitty had loved to cook, and she had always taken the time to teach me her recipes. She even allowed me to make dinner from time to time. Pretty heady stuff to a teenager.

Noel really did seem to be enjoying his meal, and I found myself relaxing a little. "So you deal in rare books," I said between bites. "Do you have a store?"

He shook his head. "No, almost all my work is done on the Internet and through private bidders."

I smiled. "Aunt Bitty never took to the Internet. She said she liked to deal with human beings face-to-face, not through a computer screen."

Noel laughed. "That sounds like Bitty. I talked to her more than once about setting up an Internet store, but she wasn't interested. Your aunt was very independent."

"You're right about that, but I think she did pretty well for herself. I'm amazed by what I've found since I got here. I never realized my aunt was so knowledgeable."

Noel reached for another roll. "She knew a lot about books, Sam, but she

51

didn't know much about business. She could have made five times the money if she'd put her business on the Net. She built up customers slowly and carefully over time, but the Internet brings in thousands of customers who are looking for exactly what you have. The idea of a bookstore in a small town like this. . . Well, it just isn't practical."

I watched him slather butter on his roll. For some reason I felt defensive, and I couldn't understand why. What he said made sense. Why did I want to jump up and demand that he take it back? After swallowing the bitter bile of resentment that filled my throat, I said timidly, "But I love this bookstore." He looked at me with pity. Not quite what I was going for.

"I know. I'm sorry. This store means something to you because it belonged to your aunt. I was talking strictly from a business viewpoint. I should have been more understanding."

My temporary flash of temper melted away. After all, he was so cute. . . .

"Let's talk about you for a while, Sam," he said. "Tell me about your life. What do you do when you're not in Winter Break?"

I told him about school, tried to explain my parents, which wasn't easy, and talked about graduation and my general lack of direction. By the time I quit jabbering, he was finished eating. My plate was still full, but I really wasn't hungry anyway. It was nice to have someone ask about my life as if he were really interested.

I wolfed down a few bites, just enough to make it look as if I'd given it the old college try. When I pushed my plate away, Noel poured us both some coffee from the carafe I'd filled and placed on the table so I wouldn't have to go back upstairs. He was quiet as he filled our cups, and his face was knit in a frown. Finally, he said, "Sam, I think you're a very smart, capable woman. I'm going to make you a very nice offer for the inventory in this bookstore. I'm also going to suggest something to you. You don't have to answer now, but I would like you to think about it." He sipped his coffee and stared at me for a moment before continuing. "I think you should take the money I give you and come to Denver. You'll have enough money for a nice apartment and a sufficient income to live on for a while. I have a friend who runs a large publishing house just outside the city. He's just expanded and is looking for additional staff. You'd be a cinch for the job of acquisitions editor. It pays great and you'd be able to work with books and authors. You'd love it."

"It sounds wonderful, Noel, but I haven't graduated yet. I won't get my degree until the spring."

He leaned across the table and took my hand. "Don't worry about that. If I recommend you, you'll get the job. Finish your degree later if you want to."

The confusion over what to do with my life lifted. Here was a chance to use my knowledge about literature in a way that would be fun and exciting.

My mouth was ready to shout "Yes!" but for some reason, "Let me think about it" came out instead.

He squeezed my hand. "Of course. I completely understand. You don't know me very well, and this is all very sudden." He gazed into my eyes while my heart did flip-flops like a frantic little fish out of water. "I'd really like us to get to know each other, Sam. I think you're a very special person. I intend to hang around for a few days after the funeral, if it's okay."

"It's definitely okay," I said impulsively.

He pressed my hand again and grinned. "Great."

I stared dumbly at him until I realized it was my turn to talk. "Let me get these dishes," I said. "Would you like some ice cream? All I have is butter pecan." Amos had obviously had a hand in that selection. He knew butter pecan was my very favorite ice cream. When looking for dinner possibilities, I'd found a half gallon of it in the freezer.

"Sounds great," Noel said. "Can I help with the dishes?"

Under normal circumstances, I might have accepted his offer, but I needed some time to myself, so I declined. I wanted to check my hair and makeup and try to lower my heart rate a little. Passing out in front of Noel Spivey wasn't something I wanted to do. Having "the vapors" was passé, and it was way too early in our relationship for mouth-to-mouth resuscitation—although the idea was definitely interesting.

I gathered our dishes together and headed upstairs. I could feel his eyes on me, and it made me nervous. The plates rattled slightly in my trembling hands. I hoped he didn't realize how much he affected me. I didn't want to come off as some naive country bumpkin. Instead, I wanted to appear to be the kind of woman who could be an acquisitions editor, although I wasn't sure what one looked like. To be honest, I wasn't even certain what an acquisitions editor did. But at the moment, I didn't really care. Noel would be in Denver. I would be in Denver. That was really all that mattered.

I made it to the kitchen and put the plates on the counter. Then I searched for a couple of bowls. I'd just pulled the ice cream out of the freezer when I remembered seeing some caramel syrup when I was going through the cabinets. Sure enough, I found a jar sitting next to the sugar. I loved it slopped all over my ice cream and wondered if Noel might like some, too. I could have just taken it downstairs and let Noel decide if he wanted some, but I was afraid to carry too much at one time. Falling on my fanny in front of the man I might marry someday wouldn't get us started out on the right foot.

I started back down the stairs but stopped before I had a chance to call out to Noel. He was squatting next to Bitty's desk, going through the boxes of books that had come in before she died. He seemed frantic and upset. At one point, I heard him use a word that had probably never been uttered before in

Miss Bitty's Bygone Bookstore.

I watched him for several seconds, unsure of what to do. Finally, I crept backward up the stairs so he wouldn't see or hear me. Then I went back to the kitchen, spooned out the ice cream, and returned to the stairs. I clomped down each step like some kind of loopy elephant, wanting to make certain he heard me. Fortunately, he was no longer near the boxes as I ventured downstairs. As I turned the corner at the bottom, I saw that he was back at the table in the sitting room, looking as if he'd been there the whole time.

I was confused. What was he looking for? If he wanted to know what was in those boxes, why hadn't he just asked me? I tried to reassure myself that he was probably looking out after his own interests. If he was going to buy my books, he wanted to know what he was getting. But I still couldn't understand why he hadn't waited. I gladly would have shown him everything.

"Here you go," I said, setting a bowl in front of him. "Sorry I took so long."

He gave me that Cary Grant smile of his. Or Hugh Grant, for people who don't love old movies the way I do. "No problem. I enjoy sitting here. It's a lovely room."

"Thank you. When Aunt Bitty bought this house, she transformed it into what it is now. I think she did a wonderful job of keeping its Victorian charm. Almost everything is original except for the paint, wallpaper, and of course, the bookshelves."

"Really. How interesting." He picked up his spoon and started in on his ice cream.

We talked very little while we ate. I liked Noel very much. He was handsome, successful, handsome, charming, handsome... Okay, I clearly needed to reset my priorities, but goodness gracious, he was so hand—never mind.

I'd planned to let him look through the books after dinner, but now I wasn't comfortable with it. Aunt Bitty used to tell me that if something felt wrong, God was probably giving you a warning. It was best to pay attention. I decided to go with her advice.

I took one last bite and pushed the bowl away. "Noel," I said, "I'm terribly sorry, but I'd like to wait until after the service on Monday to go through the inventory. I hope you don't mind, but I'm awfully tired. Are you upset?"

"Of course not," he said with sincerity. "I already told you that we didn't need to do this now. Let's leave it alone until Tuesday, shall we?"

"Thank you. I appreciate your understanding." I gave him my best smile, the one Aunt Bitty used to call my "try guessing what I'm up to" smirk. I hoped Noel wouldn't interpret it the same way.

He stood up. "Thank you for the wonderful dinner. It was such a nice break from restaurant food." He shook his head. "I had lunch at the restaurant down the street today. The food was quite good, but the owner was a little. . .I don't know. Worrisome, I guess."

Even though I had other things on my mind, I had to laugh. "Yes, Ruby is certainly different, but she's okay."

His expression told me he wasn't convinced. I was so used to the eccentricities of the citizens of Winter Break that I'd forgotten how they must appear to normal people.

As I walked him to the door, I noticed that his gaze swung toward the boxes in the corner. I'd already decided to go through those boxes after he left. I wanted to know exactly what was in them.

After putting on his coat, Noel turned to me. "Thank you, Sam, for allowing me to spend time with you. I truly enjoyed myself. I wish we'd met under different circumstances."

Before I had a chance to brace myself, he bent down and kissed me on the cheek. His lips were soft, and he smelled like expensive aftershave lotion and leather. It wasn't an unpleasant combination.

After he left, I went to the desk and got the key. I was careful to lock the door. Peeping through a window shade that covered one of the front windows, I watched him get in his car and drive away.

A line from *Alice in Wonderland* and *Through the Looking Glass* by Lewis Carroll flashed through my mind.

"Curiouser and curiouser," I said softly to myself.

7

I washed the dishes and cleaned up the table in the sitting room. The whole time my mind kept turning over the suspicions Amos had about Bitty's death. His comments had only created more questions. Why would anyone want to kill Bitty? Who was she expecting the morning she died? And who wrote that message on the envelope?

I was also bothered by the fact that my aunt broke off her engagement with Dewey. Why? Did she find out something about him that concerned her? Could he have hurt her because of it? I had to admit that Dewey Tater was the last person I would suspect of murder, but at this point, I couldn't afford to rule anyone out.

And what about Isaac Holsapple? He'd always seemed absolutely devoted to Bitty. Yet it was odd that he still hadn't shown his face, especially since he lived in the apartment next door. During her original renovations, Bitty had sectioned off part of the house and turned it into small, separate living quarters. I had no idea why; perhaps she knew she'd need an assistant someday and wanted to be ready. Isaac moved in a few months after the bookstore opened.

According to Amos, Isaac was the one who found Bitty's body. Maybe he'd killed her then covered it up by calling the doctor and Amos. But why? Could there be something in the bookstore he wanted? Something valuable? That possibility seemed unlikely. If Isaac had his eye on something, why didn't he just take it and leave town? In all these years, there must have been a number of valuable books. Why kill her now?

I had to set some time aside to carefully inspect Bitty's accounting books. If there was anything unusual, chances were I would find it there. Tonight I'd look through her new shipment. I wished I could ask Noel for help. As an expert, he could certainly tell me if there was anything valuable among the old books. But how could I trust him? After catching him going through those boxes, I had to wonder if he had some kind of ulterior motive. Besides, if he wanted to make an offer on the inventory, what would prevent him from lying about the value of Bitty's stock? It was hard to distrust him. I really liked him, and my gut told me he was a good person. But my gut had also told me that wrapping up Bitty's affairs in Winter Break wouldn't take much effort. That's why it's not a good idea to always go with your gut, no matter what the detective novels say. Not that I would know anything about that, of course.

I had to find a way to learn a lot about rare and collectible books, and I needed to do it yesterday. The Internet would be a great source of information, but Aunt Bitty didn't have a computer. I didn't want to mess with setting up service in the bookstore since I didn't plan to be in Winter Break very long. I remembered seeing a computer on Elmer's desk. I wondered if he'd either let me use it or allow me to connect my laptop up there. I decided to ask him tomorrow at church.

In the meantime, Amos and I would have to poke around to see if we could catch a murderer. There was always the possibility that Bitty's killer was someone I didn't know. If that was the case, uncovering the truth was going to be very difficult.

I finished the dishes, released Miss Skiffins from her temporary prison, and went downstairs to look through the books Noel had found so interesting. I also intended to read Bitty's letter. For some reason I dreaded it. Not because I didn't love her to pieces, but because I felt guilty about not visiting her for so long. I was afraid her letter would make me feel even worse than I did now, if that was possible.

I checked the time. It was a little after nine. Mother and Dad would definitely be up and around by now. I'd written their number down on a piece of paper and put it in my pocket. I pulled it out and sat down at Bitty's desk. I dialed all the numbers, but I kept getting a message telling me that the circuits were busy. Finally, I dialed 00 for the international operator. About a minute later, the phone was ringing at the mission. I heard someone pick up the receiver.

"*Wei. Ni hao?*"

Per my mother's instructions, I responded with "*Qing jiao* Mr. and Mrs. Towers?"

"Ivy, is that you?" my father said.

"Dad?"

"Yes, dear. Who else did you think it would be?"

"I didn't recognize your voice. You sound like a native."

"Of course it's me. However, your mother did meet a very handsome Chinese gentleman last night who seemed quite taken with her. If you call again and another man answers the phone, you'll know I've been summarily dismissed."

"Now, Dad. You know Mother couldn't do without you."

"Let's hope so. She's been giving me the fish eye all morning. I may be on my way out."

In the background, I heard my mother say, "Oh, Mickey. Sometimes you are so ridiculous! Give me that phone."

"I have to go, sweetie. Here's Mother."

I barely had time to say good-bye before my mother's voice came through the receiver. "Ivy. How are you? Are you in Winter Break?"

I proceeded to tell her where I was and what was going on. Well, not everything. I had no intention of sharing my suspicions about Bitty's death. Mother wasn't the type to believe in conspiracies or evil agendas. If I told her the truth, she would have considered me completely batty and insisted that I go home. In my mother's eyes, I was still twelve years old, slightly fumble brained, and wandering through life in some kind of hopeless fog.

"Now, Ivy, you will have everything wrapped up before school starts, won't you?" she asked after my recitation.

"That's my plan, Mother."

"School is the most important thing. Even with only an English degree, you'll be ahead of some job seekers who have no degree at all."

The little jab about my degree made it all the way through the electronic signals that connected Winter Break to Beijing. Funny how being thousands of miles away from my parents still didn't offer any protection from my mother's disapproval.

I'd like to think that what I said next was completely unplanned. In a way it was, and in another way, it wasn't. Suffice it to say that as soon as the words were out of my mouth, I wanted to push them back down my throat. But there it was.... "Mother, the funniest thing. Dewey Tater says that Aunt Bitty wanted me to stay in Winter Break and run the bookstore. What do you think of that?"

The number of miles separating us made absolutely no difference. My mother's reaction covered the distance in record time. I was surprised there wasn't a sonic boom.

"Ivy Samantha Towers! That's the most ridiculous thing I ever heard," she sputtered. "How could you possibly consider an idea like that? It's bad enough that Aunt Bitty threw her life away to live in that one-horse town, but to think that my own daughter would ever consider doing the same thing? Why, it's... it's...it's ludicrous. That's what it is. Ludicrous!"

Putting her out of her misery was the only kind thing to do. "Relax, Mother. I didn't say I seriously considered it. I know I have to go back and finish my last semester. Don't worry."

Mother gave an audible sigh of relief. "Well, thank goodness for small favors. I'm glad you're being sensible about this." She was silent for a moment. "Look, Ivy. I know you loved your aunt. I did, too. She was my mother's sister. But we have to remind ourselves that God has a plan for our lives. In my opinion, Bitty's independent spirit led her on the wrong path. She never found her purpose. I don't want the same for you. Remember that Daddy and I would love to have you come here after graduation. You're smart when it comes to language. You could pick up Mandarin in no time at all, and you could be so much help to us. You keep that in mind, okay?"

"Yes, Mother. I will."

I said good-bye to both of them, promising to call again in a few days. When I put the phone down, my emotions were all jumbled up. I really did want to find God's will for my life. Anyway, I thought I did. Maybe I was waiting for a bush to burn. It would probably take something just as dramatic, because so far, I wasn't picking up anything that remotely resembled a road map for my future. I tried to push my mother's voice out of my head. It was getting late, and I still had things to do.

I sat down on the floor next to the two new boxes of books. I went through the first box. Seventeen books. All old. All in pretty good shape. Most were first editions. At least I knew enough to look for that. There were some books by Mark Twain, as well as some from Zane Grey. There were several books by authors I'd never heard of, a couple of books of poetry, and a first edition of *The Pilgrim's Progress and Other Allegorical Works* by John Bunyan. Of course, I had no idea of their value. It would be fun to research them, though.

I finally finished the first box. I left the books stacked up on the floor, next to their respective box. I wanted to make a list of titles and authors for my investigation. Then I moved to the second box. Inside were books containing art by Norman Rockwell, several children's books, a set of Dickenses without a printing date, and once again, several other books by authors I didn't recognize.

At the bottom of the second box, I found a note that would have been impossible to see unless the books were removed.

Dear Miss Flanagan,
    As I packed up these boxes, I discovered a few additional books. They may not have any value. If they do, you can just send me whatever you think is fair. This is a very difficult time. Thank you for being so under-standing and compassionate. Your honesty and concern have made things easier.

The note was signed *Olivia.*

I had no idea who Olivia was. Neither did I know what Noel was looking for in these boxes. I decided to put his unusual behavior in my mental file titled "Things That Seem Suspicious." That file was getting remarkably full.

I pushed myself up from the floor and unlocked the desk drawer. Then I removed the envelope with Bitty's letter and sat down to read it. A blast of cold air from the front windows made me decide that I would rather sit in front of the fire. Although the bookstore itself was fairly warm, the icy temperatures outside made the area near the front of the store much colder than anywhere else in the old building.

I pulled up one of the shades to see big, fat flakes of snow falling lazily from the sky. The streetlight outside highlighted their leisurely dance. I watched for a few minutes, taking in their incredible beauty. Funny how Wichita hardly ever saw snow anymore, while Winter Break seemed to draw it like a magnet. I'd really missed it.

I'd started to think a lot about Christmas. My original plan had been to go back to school and stay in one of the dorm rooms rented to students who had nowhere else to go during the break. However, the way things were going, it was beginning to look as if I might need to stay in town awhile longer. Of course, that would mean Christmas in Winter Break.

Bitty and I had enjoyed quite a few holidays together, but Christmas was my favorite. She had made everything so special. Evenings spent by the fire, reading various Christmas stories and drinking hot chocolate; decorating the bookstore together; sitting next to her while she read the story of the birth of Christ from the Bible; standing outside and gazing up at the stars on Christmas Eve, thanking the Lord for His amazing love. All these memories came pouring back into my mind. I'd forgotten about them, relegating them to that invisible closet into which I'd shoved almost all of my Winter Break memories.

A little *meow* and the feel of soft cat hair on my leg reminded me that I also had to look after Miss Skiffins until I could find her a new home. I'd meant to talk to Amos about her, but I'd forgotten. In the meantime, the tiny cat settled it for me. I was staying here for Christmas.

I carried Aunt Bitty's letter, along with her furry friend, into the sitting room. The fire had burned down somewhat. I picked up another log and threw it on top of the embers. Then I settled down in Bitty's rocking chair to read. Miss Skiffins chose the overstuffed chair across from me.

I slowly opened the envelope, noticing for the first time the lingering scent of Jean Nate. I began to read slowly, still afraid of the emotions I might experience through my aunt's last communication.

My dearest Ivy:

If you're reading this letter it is because I am gone. I would tell you not to cry, but I know you will. You must remember, though, that I am with my Father, and my joy is overflowing. If you are sad, it is because we will have to miss each other for a while. As I write this, that seems almost too difficult to bear. But I know that once I am in His presence, sorrow will vanish. I am counting on that.

By now you've discovered that I've left you my bookstore. You're probably wondering why. It is because no one could possibly love it more than you do. It is important that you know, however, that I do not require you to run it. You are free to do whatever you want to do. You may sell it or you may stay. That is entirely up to you.

Many years ago I came to Winter Break with a broken heart. I was at a loss to find my place in the world. Although I originally came to visit my best friend, Emily Steiff, I fell in love with the town. With money my father sent me, I decided to buy the building that now houses the bookstore. Back then it was just an old house that needed a lot of fixing up. Working on it became therapy for me. I still wonder how it turned into a bookstore. It was as if the house always knew what it was supposed to be. One day it was a house, and the next day, it was a bookstore.

Everyone thought I was crazy to stay in Winter Break, including my parents, your grandparents, and your mother. But for the first time, I felt I had found the place I belonged. I was home. And so I stayed.

Now you're in Winter Break, perhaps at your own crossroads. You are not alone. Dewey and Amos will do everything they can to help you. Also remember what Pastor Taylor says: "The goodness of God gives me strength."

God has never let me down, Ivy. Never. I have failed Him many times, but His love for me is constant and unchanging.

So, my beautiful Ivy, I want you to know this: I count it a privilege to have been your "Grape Aunt Bitty." The truth is, you have always been more like a daughter to me. I believe you understand me more than anyone ever has. I always felt that someday you would come back to Winter Break, but perhaps that was just the silly wish of an old woman.

God has a plan for you, my darling. You will find it. I have no doubt of that.

Love God, love people, live life, and always forgive. Even yourself. These are the guideposts of my life and they've never led me the wrong way. They will also light your path.

I have faith in you.

All my love,
Bitty (Mark 12:30–31)

PS: Remember, some people spend their whole lives searching for something that is standing right in front of them.

Bitty was right about the crying. In fact, I had a really good boo-hoo fest. Even Miss Skiffins opened one of her eyes to see what the ballyhoo was all about.

COZY IN KANSAS

Bitty was telling me that she loved me and that she wasn't blaming me for not visiting her before she died. Her concern was that I forgive myself. For her, I would try. But right now, it felt impossible. How did my priorities get so upside down that I forgot what was most important? My fear of being Ivy shouldn't have been more important than my love for my aunt.

I sat and rocked for quite a while, thinking. What was it about Bitty that had allowed her to see her path so clearly? Why hadn't I found mine? I asked God to open up His plan for me. "My aunt Bitty seems to think You have a place for me, Father," I whispered. "Help me to find my way. Please."

Finally, I got up to go to bed. I was looking forward to going to church in the morning. Many of my old friends would be there. And I'd get to see Pastor Taylor again. He was very special to me. I'd never connected to any pastor the way I had to him.

I carried Bitty's letter over to the desk and opened the drawer to place it inside. Because it was dark and I couldn't clearly see the lock, I turned on the old desk lamp. Although I'd seen Bitty's notepad sitting near her phone more than once, the way the light shone on it made it look like there was writing on it. I put my envelope inside the drawer, locked it again, and picked up the notepad. Although they hadn't been obvious in the light of day, I was now able to see indentions on the top sheet of paper. I grabbed a pencil from the holder on the desk and began to lightly scribble across the top of the page, using the side of the pencil lead. You know, like something someone might see on one of those CSI shows on TV. Not that I would know anything about that, of course.

Slowly, the words began to take shape. It was one of Bitty's lists. When I finished, I put the pencil down and held the piece of paper directly under the desk light.

Wednesday
   1. *I—PO*
   2. *Pack t.c.*
   3. *D—coming here?*
   4. *BM for I—Don't forget!*
   5. *DRL—chk*
   6. *W clk*
   7. *Put c in o*
   8. *O—extra? Call*
   9. *Ivy. Call?*
   10. *PT—Ap W?*

I'd forgotten my aunt's way of making lists. They were written in her own brand of shorthand. No one but Bitty could decipher her notes. I think she liked it that way. But this list was written on Wednesday, the day she died. Could there be something here that could lead us to the truth?

I carefully tore off the top sheet of paper, opened the desk drawer again, put the list inside, and relocked the drawer. Maybe this would help us to find the person who killed Bitty. I'd tell Amos about it tomorrow.

As I stood up and reached over to turn off the lamp, I thought I saw something move at the window. It spooked me so much, a small shriek escaped through my lips before I could stop myself. Was someone out there? Watching me?

I walked slowly toward the window and looked out. All I could see was the falling snow and the empty street, highlighted by the glow of the street-lamp. Had I imagined it?

I lowered the shade and began climbing the stairs toward Bitty's apartment. The shadow at the window only added to my growing apprehension. The same feeling of being watched that I'd experienced that morning had returned—in spades. Either my imagination was out of control, or someone was worried about me. Or what I might find out.

I called Miss Skiffins, and she came running up the stairs. We climbed into bed, and she cuddled next to me until I fell asleep. I dreamed that Aunt Bitty was alive and hiding somewhere in Winter Break.

But no one would tell me where she was.

8

I woke up Sunday morning feeling decidedly cranky. Lying in bed, reminding myself, "This is the day the Lord has made. I will rejoice and be glad in it," helped. My mother started every day repeating that verse over and over. I think it gave her the strength to make it to her first cup of coffee. Actually, I really admired her for her commitment to enjoying the life God had given her. "Ivy," she'd say when I was in a bad mood, "God made this day just for you. He's placed blessings in your pathway. If you don't look for them, you might miss them."

Even though I was frustrated by a lack of sleep and concerns over finding out the truth about Bitty, I was looking forward to church. It had been a long time since I'd been able to attend a service at Winter Break's Faith Community Church. When I was younger, it seemed as if Pastor Ephraim Taylor was able to see straight into my soul. His sermons applied to my life, and I always left church feeling that God had spoken something personally to me. Aunt Bitty told me that Pastor Taylor had the ability to speak "a word in due season." For a while, I thought it had something to do with the time of the year, but eventually I figured out that it meant he was so surrendered to God, the Holy Spirit could lead him to preach exactly what people needed to hear.

I repeated the rejoicing scripture one more time and rolled out of bed. I almost knocked a surprised Miss Skiffins right off the covers and onto the floor. After calming her and finding my slippers, we made our way to the kitchen. I fed her, put on some coffee, then got dressed for church.

Church had always been an integral part of Winter Break. A little over half the town attended Faith Community. Another ninety or so were members of the First Mennonite Church down by the river. Actually, the original name of the church was Gutenberg First Mennonite Church, but no one in Winter Break used the *Gutenberg* part anymore. Most of the church members were part of the Baumgartner family that migrated from Gutenberg, Germany. The original Baumgartners were German immigrants who took up farming after settling in Winter Break several generations ago. Heirs of the great-grandchildren and the great-great-grandchildren still lived in Winter Break and continued to farm the family land. Once in a while, a brave Baumgartner escaped Winter Break, but for the most part, these deserters were dismissed as lost lambs who had unfortunately succumbed to the call of the world. After the shock of their betrayal wore off, their names were never mentioned again. Eventually, it was as if they'd never existed—unless of course they came back. Then all was forgiven and the duly chastened Baumgartner took his or her rightful place back in the bosom of the family.

Although some churches might feel somewhat competitive with each other, especially in a small town, this was not the case in Winter Break. Everyone at Faith Community understood that First Mennonite was a family church with a long-standing tradition, and the members of First Mennonite understood that most people who weren't related to them might feel more comfortable at Faith Community. For the most part, the churches worked together as one body as the scriptures taught. However, everyone realized that while some members were arms, legs, or feet, about ninety of them were Baumgartners.

In a town of a little over six hundred citizens, that left quite a few people who had no church home. They were, of course, considered to be fields ready for harvest, and both groups did everything they could to bring in the sheaves, regardless of what church they ended up in. Unfortunately, some of these "sheaves" weren't interested in coming in and were quite vocal about it. But Christians in Winter Break had no intention of giving up. The fields would be plucked before Judgment Day, and that's all there was to it. I suspected, although no one would ever admit it, that somewhere there was an unofficial tabulation being kept and that many of the town's faithful believed that sitting near the Great White Throne was a tall trophy made of pure gold, waiting to be awarded to the Winter Break church that won the Salvation Super Bowl. I kind of doubted that God saw it that way. The important thing was that Winter Break Christians were committed to preaching the Word, whether their targets thought they needed to hear it or not.

I checked my makeup, grabbed my purse, and was on my way down the stairs when someone knocked on the front door. At first I couldn't tell who it was because his back was turned, but when I opened the door, I found Amos standing on the steps, dressed in a dark blue suit and a black trench coat. It was the first time I'd seen him in anything besides his uniform since I'd arrived in Winter Break. I'd forgotten how attractive he could be.

"Thought I'd drive you to church, Ivy," he said. "If that's okay."

For some reason, I suddenly felt shy, but I mumbled something about appreciating his thoughtfulness. Within a few minutes, I was safely ensconced in his patrol car, and we were on our way to church.

Since Winter Break is a pretty small town, I had only a few minutes to tell him about Aunt Bitty's list and the note from Olivia. I also told him a little bit about my dinner with Noel, but at the last minute, I decided not to tell him about finding Noel going through the boxes of books. It wasn't that I wanted to keep it a secret, but I didn't think he would be objective about Noel, and I hadn't made up my mind about him yet. I didn't want someone else doing my thinking for me. Amos and I agreed to go back to Bitty's after lunch and look at the list together.

As we pulled into the church parking lot, I noticed that several men from the church were waiting to help anyone who needed a little support across the snow-covered parking lot. It was obvious that an attempt had been made to clear it, but last night's snow had added another slippery layer.

"Wait a minute. I'll come around and get you," Amos said as he parked the car. I wasn't used to being treated like a helpless woman, so I ignored his comment and opened my door. I no sooner stepped out of the car than I felt my feet slip out from underneath me. Thankfully, Amos was able to grab me before I landed smack on my derriere. He held me while I got my balance. Being so close felt funny—but nice. Then I looked up into his face and saw something familiar. It was the same look he'd had the day he left to go to live with his father. I'd almost forgotten about it. "I guess there's really nothing for me here, Ivy," he'd said before he got on the bus for Oklahoma. "Mama's married again. She and her new husband are moving to California. I don't want to live with them, and no one in this town cares anything about me."

The pressure of Amos's arms around me brought me back to the present. "I swear, Ivy Towers," he said softly, "you must not know that scripture about a haughty spirit going before a fall. Why are you so contrary?"

I struggled out of his embrace. "I'm not contrary, Amos Parker. I'm just stubborn." I had to smile. "Sorry. Guess I'm just not used to such gentlemanly conduct. I'll do better next time."

He chuckled and shook his head. "Like there's ever going to be a next time."

I reached over and took his arm. "Now, now. Let's not get an attitude." I pulled out my best Scarlet O'Hara voice. "Why, kind sir, if you would be so considerate as to escort me into the church, I would be eternally grateful."

He rolled his eyes. "Now you're overdoing it."

I batted my eyelashes at him. "So sorry."

He grunted but couldn't conceal a smile. We trudged through the snow and finally made it to the church entrance. A man swung the door open for us.

"O–Odie?" I stuttered. "Odie Rimrucker?"

It was Odie all right, but instead of greasy hair flying every which way and soiled, mismatched clothing, this Odie was neat and clean with slicked-back hair, a nice suit, and a sparkle in his eye.

"Why, Ivy Towers," he said with a big grin, "I heard you was back. It's been a long time, girl. My goodness gracious, you look jes' the same as you did when you was little. Pretty red hair and all." He reached out and locked me in a big bear hug. I was too surprised to react. Was this really Odorous Odie?

After he let me go and I caught my breath, I greeted him with a smile and a "Nice to see you, too." After we'd walked a few feet past him, I asked Amos about him.

"I'll tell you about it after church," he whispered. "It's quite a story."

As we entered the sanctuary, I saw several familiar faces. Emily Baumgartner, one of the friends I'd made during my excursions to Winter Break, waved and started toward me. But before she could reach me and I could ask her what a Baumgartner was doing away from the family church, a thin, bejeweled hand grabbed my arm. I turned to see a middle-aged woman with a hat almost bigger than she was, smiling at me sweetly.

"You must be little Ivy," she said in a soft, high-pitched voice. "Your dear, dear aunt talked about you all the time."

I felt Amos's hand on my shoulder. "Ivy, this is Lila Hatcher, your aunt's best friend."

Tears filled the woman's large, hazy blue eyes. "That's the truth, dear. She was my trusted friend and confidante. I don't know what I'm going to do without her. I hope you'll stay here and carry on her legacy. I'm sure we can become friends, too."

She held out her hand, and I took it. Her skin was like soft leather, and I could feel the remnants of hand cream clinging to it. "Thank you," I said. "Unfortunately, I'm just here to make her final arrangements and close the bookstore. I'll be going back to school in January."

Her eyes widened. "Oh, my dear," she said. "I hope you'll change your mind. I can't imagine Winter Break without our bookstore."

"I'm sorry." I didn't want to be rude, but Emily was waiting to greet me, and the service was about to start. "Maybe we can visit some other time when we're not so rushed."

"Please, dear," Lila said, "I would like to host an open house after the funeral tomorrow. Say about two thirty? Would that be all right with you? That will allow all of Bitty's friends to gather together and extend their condolences."

The idea of a social gathering hadn't occurred to me, but it was a good idea. "Thank you, Ms. Hatcher. I think that would be very nice."

"It's Lila, honey," she said, patting my arm. "I'm so glad. It gives me a chance to do something for Bitty. We'll talk more when there's time." Her eyes flushed with tears once more as she turned and walked away.

I felt a tap on the back and turned to see Emily smiling at me. "Oh, Ivy," she said. "I'm so glad to see you, but I'm so sorry it had to be like this."

She wrapped her arms around me and hugged me tightly. I'd forgotten what good friends we'd been. I was beginning to see that I'd forgotten a lot of things about Winter Break.

I gently pulled myself out of her arms. "Okay," I said. "You have to tell me how in the world a Baumgartner wound up at Faith Community. Did you defect, or were you kicked out?"

She laughed in a light, lilting way that brought back warm summer days spent sitting on the dock at Lake Winter Break, talking about boys and life in general.

"Neither one, smarty-pants. The only way a Baumgartner escapes the fold is to quit being a Baumgartner." She held up her left hand and wiggled her fingers, one of which sported a wedding ring.

"Emily! Who. . ."

Before I had a chance to finish my question, Buddy Taylor, Pastor Taylor's son, stepped up behind Emily and put his hands on her shoulders. "Was brave enough to take on the Baumgartner clan?" he finished. "You get one guess."

Buddy planted a kiss on the top of Emily's head, which wasn't difficult since Buddy was over six feet tall and Emily was exactly five feet and one-half inch. I knew this because she had lamented the fact constantly. She'd always wanted to leave Winter Break and become a model. Unfortunately, not many agencies were looking for models of Emily's stature.

I laughed. "Congratulations, you two." I slapped Buddy lightly on the arm. "If I remember right, you teased poor Emily every chance you could get. What was that all about?"

He wrapped his arms around his beaming wife. "When you're a kid, it's hard to tell a girl you're crazy about her. I guess the only way I could get her attention was by being a big pain in the—"

"Buddy!" Emily whispered. "Don't you say that word in church."

"Neck? What's wrong with saying 'neck' in church?" Buddy asked innocently.

Emily shook her head while Amos and I tried not to laugh. People were starting to stare.

"Okay, okay, I give," Buddy said. "But Amos knows what I mean, don't you, Amos?"

I looked at Amos just in time to see him flush the color of an overripe tomato. He pushed me lightly from behind. "We'll see you two later," he said gruffly. "There's Pastor Taylor. The service is getting ready to start."

We found a couple of seats a few pews from the front. Pastor Taylor seated himself on a chair next to the back wall on the small stage. Faith Community always had a rather long praise and worship service before the sermon. Pastor Taylor said he liked to step into the pulpit after praise had saturated the sanctuary. It made preaching much easier.

A young woman about my age stepped up and took the microphone. I didn't know her. Then three more people took the tiny platform. A young man of about seventeen or eighteen sat at the drums, and Bev Taylor, Pastor Taylor's wife, took her place at the piano. The woman at the podium encouraged us all to stand up.

As the strains of "Awesome God" began, I felt myself drawn immediately into worship. I felt as if God had stepped into the sanctuary with us. The worship leader took us through several wonderful songs, including some of my favorite old hymns, and then wrapped up her portion of the service with a song I'd never heard before. The words so touched my heart that when we were finished, I was surprised to find tears on my face. The words echoed in my heart. *I'm desperate for You. . .lost without You.* How long had it been since I'd felt desperate for God? School seemed to take all my time and concentration. Had I substituted it for God's presence?

Amos handed me a tissue, and I wiped my face as we sat down. I really liked my church in Wichita. I had friends there, but school kept me from attending regularly. I had to admit to myself that even when I *was* in church, I never experienced this kind of worship.

Pastor Taylor made a few announcements; then he stopped and looked at me. "We are all aware that Bitty Flanagan went home to be with her Lord this week," he said. "Although we will definitely miss her wonderful spirit, we rejoice to know that she is safely in the arms of God. We're happy to have her niece, Ivy, home again. I hope you will all get a chance to tell her how much Bitty meant to us." His voice trembled as he finished the last part of his sentence.

I heard sniffs and muffled sobs throughout the room. My goodness, Bitty had certainly touched the lives of the people in Winter Break. It was amazing.

"Bitty's memorial service will be here tomorrow at one o'clock. Following the service, Lila Hatcher will host an open house at her home. She encourages everyone who knew Bitty to come by for some food and good memories. It will give all of us a chance to let Ivy know how special Bitty was to us and how glad we are to have her home.

"One other thing. Bitty and I talked once about her funeral. She told me she didn't want a bunch of flowers sitting around dying on her account. It was her wish that people give a memorial gift to the church instead of sending flowers. I think we should do what she said, but I, for one, intend to do both." His voice broke. "My family is giving a check to the missionary fund in her name, and we already called the Flower Market in Hugoton and ordered the most beautiful display we could afford." He took a handkerchief from his pocket and blew his nose. "I think Bitty Flanagan should go out in style. You all do whatever you feel led to do, but I hope you go out of your way to honor her in the best way you can."

A chorus of amens and hallelujahs rang out in the church. I felt as if the entire town of Winter Break had wrapped its arms around me in a big hug. Their love for Bitty had translated right over to me. I was so moved, it took me a few minutes to refocus myself on Pastor Taylor's sermon. I picked up his words just in time to hear him say:

"Jeremiah chapter 29, verse 11, says: "'For I know the plans I have for you," declares the Lord, . . . "plans to give you hope and a future.' " He closed his Bible and stepped in front of the pulpit.

"God, the creator of heaven and earth, is thinking about *you*," he said. "In fact, He planned for you even before you were born. You are not some generality bouncing around in life without purpose. The future He has planned for you isn't anything to be afraid of. It is full of His blessings. It will fulfill all the desires of your heart. How can you trust this? Because God made you. Only He knows what will truly bring you joy. But it requires something from you. A sacrifice."

He walked back to his pulpit and picked up his Bible. "Matthew 10:39 tells us what that sacrifice is along with what it will cost and what you will receive in return. 'Whoever finds his life will lose it, and whoever loses his life for my sake will find it.' "

Pastor Taylor paused and gazed at the crowd seated in the sanctuary. "The only way we will ever find the life God has prepared for us is to lay our lives on the altar. What is keeping you from giving all of your life to God?"

As he continued his sermon, his words kept running around in my head. Was I really living for God? Why couldn't I find the path God had for me? My parents wanted me to come to China and minister with them. Maybe that really was my calling. There wasn't any other opportunity in my life that presented me with a chance to do so much good for other people.

Then there was the job offer in Denver. It would be a chance to make something successful out of my life. I could be *Sam* there. I could leave Ivy behind forever. I'd wanted that for a long, long time.

I didn't get much more out of Pastor Taylor's sermon because I wasn't listening. I spent the rest of the time trying to figure out what God wanted from me. Could He have sent Noel Spivey to Winter Break?

As I mentally bounced back and forth between Denver and China, I felt confusion. If God was trying to tell me something, I sure wasn't getting it.

A nudge from Amos's elbow reminded me that I needed to be listening instead of daydreaming. Pastor Taylor gave the closing prayer and dismissed us. As I turned to go, I found myself surrounded by Faith Community Church members. I knew most of them, but there were a few new faces in the crowd. Dewey talked to Amos while I focused on the other people around me. After they had all offered their condolences and exited the sanctuary, I finally saw

Isaac Holsapple. He was standing off to the side of the sanctuary, watching me. His thin face, long nose, and dark, darting eyes had always reminded me of a weasel. His thinning hair was just as unkempt as always, but there wasn't as much of it left. Isaac was growing older. Odd that I'd never thought of him as either young or old. He never seemed to change. He was just Isaac.

We stared at each other for a few seconds. I made a move toward him, and he scampered out the door without speaking.

"Amos," I said quietly, glancing around the room to make sure no one remained. "Why is Isaac hiding from me? If he's innocent, why won't he talk to me?"

Amos shook his head. "I can't answer that, Ivy. I've known Isaac all my life. He's an odd duck, but I've never seen him harm anyone. I think he's just really shy around people."

I picked up my coat and Bible from the pew. "Did Bitty ever say anything about him to you?" I asked.

Amos took my coat and held it up so that I could slip my arms in the sleeves. "No," he said thoughtfully. "Now that you mention it, she didn't talk much about him at all. I always thought it was a little odd. Not that your aunt gossiped about people; she didn't. But with Isaac, she seemed especially secretive."

When we reached the front lobby, we found Pastor Taylor and his wife standing near the front door.

"Ivy!" Pastor Taylor said loudly. "I'm so glad to see you. It's been a few years now, hasn't it?"

"About three," I said.

Bev reached out to hug me. "Oh, Ivy. When I look at you, I see Bitty. You two are so alike."

Pastor Taylor shook hands with Amos. "I hope you're taking good care of our girl here," he said.

Amos chuckled. "As much as I can, Pastor. Our Ivy has become quite independent."

"Honey, is there anything we can do for you?" Bev asked. "Anything at all?"

"No," I said. Then something occurred to me. "Well, maybe there is."

Encouraged by the looks on their faces, I took a deep breath and dove in. "Bitty was cremated, you know. And. . .I. . .I'm not sure what to do with her ashes. Elmer said something about keeping them in the store, but unless someone buys the whole store and keeps it open, that isn't going to work. Could. . .could you take them after the service tomorrow? I know you'll do the right thing. I don't want to take Bitty's remains with me. I think she needs to stay here in Winter Break."

I saw them exchange glances. "Sure, Ivy," Pastor Taylor said with a frown.

"If that's what you want us to do."

I nodded, feeling relieved. "Yes, please. I can't leave without knowing this has been settled."

Amos grabbed my elbow. "I'm starving," he said. "We need to get to Ruby's before all the fried chicken is gone."

I said my good-byes to the Taylors while Amos steered me out the door. When we got to Ruby's, the place was packed. We had to wait about ten minutes for a table. The way Amos acted, you'd think he hadn't eaten for a year.

The only thing Ruby served on Sundays was her pan-fried chicken along with mashed potatoes and chicken gravy, green beans with bacon, rolls, and peach cobbler with ice cream for dessert. For one price, you got all you could eat. Sunday protocol consisted of stuffing yourself at Ruby's then heading home for a long Sunday afternoon nap. That was about all you could do when you were full of Ruby's chicken. Sleeping through a major part of the digestion process was your only protection.

The wives in Winter Break loved their Sunday routine. It meant that their husbands would ask for something "light" for dinner, if they asked for anything at all.

I knew we had work to do that afternoon, so with great effort I kept myself to two pieces of chicken and one helping of everything else. It wasn't easy. Ruby's flaky, butter-crusted entrée left the Colonel's chicken lying like roadkill in its path.

Between bites I asked Amos about Odie Rimrucker.

Amos wiped his mouth with his napkin, took a sip of coffee, and gazed forlornly at the food still sitting on his plate. Taking a break was a costly sacrifice, but he took it like a man. "You remember the mess Odie used to be?"

I nodded. Odie was as low class as you could be in Winter Break. No matter what your problem was, you could always comfort yourself with the knowledge that you were better off than Odie.

"You also remember that after Morley Watson died, Odie claimed he'd never drink again?"

I nodded again. "That happened a little over three years ago. Did he keep his promise?"

Amos picked up his fork in readiness for the end of the story. I guess it paid to be prepared. "He stopped for a while, but then one Friday night, he wandered over to Hiram Ledbetter's and came back with a jar of 'medicine.'"

Winter Break had no bars, and Dewey refused to sell alcohol in his store. This forced those who imbibed to either purchase their supplies in Hugoton or buy a jar of Ledbetter's Life-Preserving Liniment. I never understood the name since no one ever suggested that you rub the stuff on your skin. In fact, there may have been a warning about contact with human flesh. But few people in town called it what it really was—moonshine, plain and simple. Deputy Watson warned Hiram more than once about his illegal still, but Hiram moved the thing around so much, it was tough to find. After awhile, Deputy Watson gave up. Most people in town acted as if they had no idea that Ledbetter's Liniment was hundred proof. Perhaps it was easier than admitting that Hiram Ledbetter was craftier than the law in Winter Break.

"Did he drink it?" I asked.

"Yep. In fact, he drank so much, he passed out for two whole days. Old Doc Evans came over from Hugoton and checked him out. He said that all we could do was let Odie sleep. Doc said he'd either live or die. It was in God's hands."

"My goodness," I said. "Did anyone keep an eye on him?"

Amos actually released the death grip on his fork a little. "This is the interesting part, the part you don't know. Someone watched over him all right. It was Bitty. She took him in. Let him sleep it off. When he finally started to stir, she nursed him back to consciousness. No one knows what happened after that, Ivy, but after four days with Bitty, Odie Rimrucker walked out of her place a different man. He got cleaned up, went back to church, and has been on the wagon ever since."

It was my turn to forget about Ruby's chicken. "Bitty never told me anything about that."

Amos smiled and shook his head. "She wouldn't. Bitty didn't believe in blabbing about her good deeds. You know that."

Yes, I knew that all right. She'd done many wonderful things for me. Good deeds that even my parents didn't know about. I'd always been able to tell her everything, without fear of condemnation.

"You have no idea what she said to Odie that made him quit drinking?"

Amos shook his head. "No. Even Pastor Taylor asked him about it, but Odie wouldn't say anything. He said it was something private between him and Bitty."

I stuck a bite of mashed potatoes in my mouth, but I was really chewing over Amos's story. Bitty had never been a drinker. What did she do that no one else had been able to do? Odie had been preached to, scolded, locked up, loved on, forgiven, and prayed over for more than twenty years. Now that Bitty was gone, I'd probably never know.

Amos took my silence and my forkful of Ruby's creamy whipped potatoes as a sign that he was free to pick up where he'd left off. He chomped into another chicken breast with a gusto that was usually reserved for cheering on his favorite basketball team, the Wichita State Shockers. Amos's perfect day would consist of sitting in front of his TV in his grody sweats, watching the Shockers, and munching on Ruby's chicken, followed by two or three pieces of her peach cobbler. I loved the Shockers, too, but a little popcorn was all I could handle. Whenever I got too excited, I'd yell and spit popcorn out of my mouth. It was a lot easier to clean up popcorn than pieces of greasy chicken.

When he took a breath, I saw it as an opportunity to ask the one question that had been burning in my mind ever since I got the phone call about Bitty's death. "Amos," I said, "why Bitty? She was such a good woman. She did so many wonderful things—why did she have to die?"

Amos put down his fork, allowing it to rest a moment. His hazel eyes locked on mine. "I don't know, Ivy, but my guess is that she trusted the wrong person. What's that scripture about being as wise as serpents and as harmless as doves? Your aunt trusted everyone. Unfortunately, not everyone *should* be trusted."

Although Amos's words made sense to me, I couldn't wrap my mind around why anyone would want to hurt Bitty Flanagan. What could have led someone to kill her? Was it something they wanted, or was it something she'd done?

Amos went back to his chicken. I watched him eat, glad he was enjoying his dinner, and even happier that I wasn't alone in my quest for justice.

I pushed Amos out of Ruby's around one thirty. He resisted, but I prevailed. Ruby seemed forlorn about my resistance to second helpings of everything, but I wanted to get back to the bookstore and examine Bitty's list. Besides, I'd run into Elmer, and he'd agreed to let me do some research on his computer. I had to meet him at the funeral home at five o'clock.

It was almost two by the time I made some coffee in an attempt to keep Amos awake. We sat upstairs in the kitchen so no one passing by the bookstore could see us. I didn't need Sunday visitors interrupting our research.

I handed a piece of paper to Amos. "This isn't the original list," I said. "I wrote this out so it would be easier to read."

He looked through it carefully. "Okay," he said. "Let's go through these one by one. Maybe we'll see something that will help us."

I read the first entry: *"I—PO."*

"Easy," Amos said. "Isaac—post office. We know that he did that on Wednesdays."

"Great." I put a check mark next to it.

"Pack *t.c.*"

Amos thought for a minute. "Well, the church was having a dinner that night. Could *t.c.* stand for something she was planning to take? Something that starts with a *T* and something else that starts with a *C*?"

I shook my head. "She would have written *t* and *c* if there were two things." I ran the letters through my mind a few times. "I've got it! It's *tablecloth*. I'll bet she was going to take my grandmother's tablecloth."

I got up and started rummaging through the kitchen. In one of the bottom drawers, I found what I was looking for. I held up the large Irish linen tablecloth embroidered with harps and starlings. I'd always been amazed that Bitty actually used it. I was afraid it would get stained and ruined. "Nonsense," Bitty said when I told her my feelings. "My mother worked hard on it. She created this beautiful tablecloth from her heart. When I share it with others, I'm sharing her. What's the point of having it if it's not used?"

"I recognize that," Amos said. "She brought it to every one of our church dinners."

"Well, we can mark that off our list." I slid the tablecloth back into the drawer. "Too bad it won't be used again," I said softly. "Bitty loved it so."

Amos frowned at me as I sat down next to him. "Won't be used again? What do you mean? It's yours now, Ivy. You'll use it."

I sighed with exasperation. "Why do I keep forgetting that? I know in my head that Bitty's things belong to me, but somewhere in my heart, I can't accept it."

Amos grunted. "I don't have enough time to explain *that* to you today. Maybe you should think about it yourself."

He picked up his pen and checked number two off the list. I wasn't sure what he meant by his comment, but I had the distinct feeling it wasn't a compliment. I felt a slight rush of anger. Why wasn't Amos more understanding? He knew I loved Bitty. Before I could build my resentment up a little more, he read off the next entry on our list.

"*D—coming here?*" He put the pen down. "That's easy, too. *D* is for Dewey. She was wondering if Dewey was coming to pick her up for the church supper."

I crossed my arms and sat back in my chair. "How do you know this note was about the church supper?"

Amos looked confused. "What do you mean?"

"Amos, this is the first clue we have about someone coming here on the day Bitty died."

Amos's eyebrows shot up in amusement. "You surely don't suspect Dewey Tater. That's ridiculous. Dewey wouldn't hurt anyone, especially your aunt."

"Look," I said, shaking my head, "I feel funny bringing this up, but aren't we supposed to look at the evidence logically? Without emotion?" I leaned over closer to him. "Why did Bitty postpone their wedding? What was it that changed her mind? What if she knew something about Dewey—something he couldn't risk having anyone else find out? Or what if he felt rejected and killed her in a crime of passion?"

Amos whooped with laughter. "Dewey Tater? A crime of passion? Holy cow, Ivy. Have you ever even met Dewey?"

I had to admit that it sounded silly, but I was determined to find Bitty's killer—no matter what. "Look, Amos," I said, fighting to keep my temper in check, "we can't rule out anybody. Even Dewey. Now let's move on."

We continued with the list, trying to solve the rest of Bitty's cryptic messages. I was pretty sure number seven was a note to put a casserole in the oven for the church dinner, but except for number nine, which was obviously a note to call me, we couldn't decipher anything else. I quickly wrote out another copy of the list for Amos.

"Take this with you," I said. "Maybe something will occur to you. I think we should concentrate on that particular Wednesday. We know Bitty's normal schedule, and we know there was a church dinner that night. Perhaps we'll interpret most of these entries if we focus on those two things."

Amos took the list from my hand. "You know, Ivy, there might not be anything here that will help us to find her killer."

I jabbed my finger at my list, still sitting on the table in front of me. "What about number nine?" I said. "Why was she planning to call me?"

He shook his head. "I'm not sure she was. There's a question mark next to the entry. She wasn't sure if she wanted to phone you or not."

"But that's just it, Amos. Why would she question that? She called me quite often. And I called her, too. Just because I hadn't been in town for a while didn't mean we didn't keep in touch."

He held up his hands in mock surrender. "Look, maybe she just wasn't sure she had time to call you on Wednesday. Maybe she was busy. I'm not saying you're wrong, Ivy. I just don't think we should jump to any conclusions based on this list."

"You've forgotten something very important," I said.

Amos looked at me with surprise. "And what would that be?"

"Was anything of Bitty's moved before I got here on Friday?"

Amos considered my question. "No. I don't think so. I tried to keep everything the way it was because of my initial suspicions."

"You didn't empty the trash? Anything like that?"

He shook his head slowly. "I came here and cleaned up the blood on the floor, but I threw the rags in a plastic bag and took that with me. I didn't want you to see them."

"Well then, Mister Deputy Sherriff, where is the original of this list? I've looked everywhere. It's not here."

His expression grew stormy. "Maybe Bitty threw it away somewhere else. And don't call me *Mister Deputy Sheriff*."

"Okay, okay. But where would she have disposed of the list? According to Isaac, she didn't go anywhere that morning. And anyway, this list has notes related to a dinner that was supposed to happen that night. That means she wouldn't be finished with it until after the dinner. It should be here, Amos."

Amos just stared at me. It was obvious he couldn't refute my logic.

"Someone took the list. Why? There must be something here that was too dangerous for her killer to leave behind. If we can figure it out, I think it will point right to him. We've got to keep at this until we understand each and every entry."

He stared at the list for a few moments. Finally, he looked up and scowled at me. "Ivy, it's possible you're right. It's also possible that you're putting way too much importance into this note. I hope we don't waste time on something that has nothing to do with why Bitty died."

I reached over and patted his hand. "I've got a feeling, Amos. I've just got a feeling—"

"Oh no," he responded, his worried expression deepening. "I remember when you used to tell me you 'had a feeling' when we were kids. Somehow or other, we always ended up in trouble."

I withdrew my hand. "I'm sure I have no idea what you're talking about."

"No idea what I'm talking about. Are you kidding me?" He slapped his hand on the surface of the table. "What about the time you told me you 'had a feeling' that Lymon Penwordy was stealing cows from Newton Widdle? You made me sit out in a cold, wet cow pasture in the middle of the night, I might add, for over four hours so we could catch him at it."

I smiled as sweetly as I could before I said, "And I was right, wasn't I? We saw Lymon sneak three cows out of Newton's corral."

"Oh, you were certainly right," he snorted. "'Course, it took years before Morley Watson quit telling the story of how I came running into his office the next morning hollerin', 'Deputy! I know who's been stealing all the Widdle cows!'"

It took all the fortitude I could muster not to giggle. Deputy Watson had arrested Lymon, but he'd chuckled all the way through it. I was told that after he loaded his prisoner into his car to drive him to the Stevens County Jail in Hugoton, he and Lymon were both laughing so hard you could still hear them—even after they'd left the city limits.

"And then there was the time you were convinced Sara Beasley's state fair award-winning jam was actually store-bought. 'I just have a feeling, Amos,' you said."

"And what's your point?" I asked as innocently as I could. "I was right about that, too."

"Yeah, you were right. But you weren't the one Ed Beasley threatened to stuff inside a Mason jar. I had to hide every time I saw him coming. Good thing they finally moved to Cawker City. I was finally able to walk the streets again instead of skulking around in the shadows."

"I think their daughter Mabel Mae lived in Cawker City," I said. "They probably moved there to be near her."

"They moved because they were too embarrassed to stay in Winter Break."

"Well, if they did, it isn't my fault," I replied with a sniff. "Sara's the one who cheated. Besides, Cawker City is a very nice place to live. I mean, they have that ball of twine and all."

Amos grunted. "Yes, I'm sure they moved to Cawker City because they have the world's largest ball of twine. Must be why so many people flock there."

"Cawker City is just about the same size as Winter Break," I said.

Amos raised one eyebrow. "And your point is?"

"Okay, look," I said. "I really think this list is important. If you don't, I can't do anything about that. But the truth is it's all we've got. I'm going to keep working on it."

Amos yawned, a sure sign that Ruby's chicken was finally kicking in. He stood up. "I'm going home to take a nap. I'll take the list with me and mull it over. When do we get together again?"

"I'm going to the funeral home this evening to do a little research on Elmer's computer. I've got to get some idea of how much these books are worth so I'll know whether Noel's offer is fair. I found an inventory list in Bitty's desk, but I still need to write down some information about the new books."

"Do you need help with that?" Amos asked.

I grinned at him. "You've got that dazed chicken look. I think you'd better lie down and recover. You're not much help to me in this state."

Amos stood up from the table. "I'm pretty sure you're referring to Ruby's chicken," he said wryly, "although I think you could have phrased that a little differently. What time are you going to Elmer's?"

I looked up at Aunt Bitty's red rooster clock on the wall over the oven. "I plan to get there around five," I said. "What time does church start tonight?"

"There isn't any service on Sunday nights anymore."

That surprised me. Sunday night church had been a Winter Break tradition for as long as I could remember. "What happened?" I asked.

"Most of our congregation is made up of farmers. You know they work six or seven days a week. Pastor Taylor decided that families needed some time together. Those who want to go to church Sunday nights go over to First Mennonite. The rest of them get to see their families before they head back to the fields." He shrugged. "I think it was an inspired idea."

"Well, I guess that gives me all the time I need to work on this tonight." I stood up and started toward the stairs, expecting Amos to follow me. Just as

I reached the top step, Amos reached out and grabbed me. Startled, I turned to face him.

"Listen to me, Ivy," he said, his jaw tight, his eyes narrowed, "this isn't a story from one of those Nancy Drew books you used to read. You've got to be careful. If there is a killer hiding in Winter Break, and he feels you're a threat to him. . ."

"I'll be okay, Amos," I said, not feeling as brave as I sounded. "No one even knows we're suspicious. We'll find him. We're a good team."

"I hope you're right. But if at any time you feel unsafe, you've got to promise to call me right away."

"I promise."

His eyes were fastened on mine, and his grip softened to something close to a caress. For a moment, I wondered if he was going to kiss me, but instead, he let me go. He headed down the stairs and left, Bitty's bell signaling his departure.

I stood at the top of the steps, his words still ringing in my head. He was right. This wasn't a story in a novel, nor was it Newton Widdle's cows or Sara Beasley's jam.

This was the real thing, and we had to be careful. I couldn't control the little shiver that ran like cold water down my back.

A little before five o'clock, I left the bookstore with Bitty's inventory records tucked safely under my arm, along with a list of the books from the new shipment. By matching some of the entries on the records with books on the shelves, I had deciphered Bitty's codes. *AS* meant the book was *actively stocked. SS* was *sold and shipped*, and *WS* meant *waiting to be shipped*. Thankfully, there were no outstanding books to be mailed. The entries stopped at the end of November. I was relieved to know that none of my aunt's customers were waiting for something they would never receive.

Since I'd been staying at Bitty's, I'd gotten four phone calls from book dealers. Their community proved to be a very tight-knit group, because after the last one, all the out-of-town calls abruptly ceased. I assumed the merchants had passed the word around about Bitty. All the other phone calls were from Winter Break people wanting to express their sorrow at my aunt's passing.

Alma had reminded me at church that I needed to come to the post office and pick up Bitty's mail, especially since there appeared to be so many condolence cards. I guessed that a lot of them would be from Bitty's customers. I made a mental note to go there tomorrow after the open house at Lila's. Maybe there would be something from the mysterious Olivia.

For now, though, I didn't really believe those new books were involved in Bitty's death. If someone wanted them, he could have gotten to them long ago. My only real worry was their value and how that would enter into any offer Noel might make for the inventory.

As I trudged the two blocks to Elmer's, I wondered if we were in for more precipitation. The streets were still snow packed, and the freezing temperatures weren't going to help them get cleared anytime soon. I could feel moisture in the chilly wind that whipped at my face, a sure sign of either frozen drizzle or more snow. My biggest fear was that bad weather would force some of Winter Break's rural residents to stay away from the memorial service tomorrow. I really wanted Bitty to have the kind of funeral she deserved.

I couldn't help but think about my mother, wondering if she shouldn't have made the effort to come to Winter Break. Bitty was her only aunt. My feelings wavered. I'd told her not to worry about it, but now that I was here by myself, I realized that a small seed of resentment had squirmed its way into my mind.

I was still mulling this over when Elmer opened the door for me. "Nice to see you again, Ivy," he said. Actually, he said, "Nice to tee you again, Ivy." I thought about saying *Nice to tee you, too,* but my mother had instilled good manners in me. Besides, Elmer was letting me use his computer.

He took me into his office, turned the computer on for me, and signed on to the Internet. "There's pop in the fridge, a coffeemaker in the break room next door, and the bathroom is just down the hall," he said.

I assured him I was fine and thanked him again for his help.

"I'm happy to help you in any way I can. My telephone number is right here on the desk. You know I live next door so I can be here in a flash if you need something."

I assured him that wouldn't be necessary, and with one last funeral home smile, he left me alone to tally up the worth of Bitty's timeworn empire.

I took off my coat and put it on the back of the rather lumpy padded desk chair. Then I set the inventory records next to the computer and pulled a notepad and pen from my purse. I scooted an old lamp teetering on the edge of Elmer's rickety desk next to the notepad and clicked on the light. The lamp's base was grimy and in desperate need of cleaning. The glass cover was also coated in dust. I took a tissue from my purse and cleaned away a little of the grunge. Underneath I found green, yellow, and blue leaves set against a gold-colored glass background. There was something else above it. I wasn't certain, but it looked like a bird of some kind. I couldn't help but wonder what was waiting underneath the neglect the years had deposited. I promised myself to clean it for Elmer when I had some extra time.

I started my search by looking for sites that dealt in rare books. I was happy to find that there were several search sites that covered thousands of books, old and new. When I ran up against a book that wasn't listed with a particular online location, I searched for the book by name. I usually found it listed with an auction company. Unfortunately, some of them didn't have prices, so those books took a little longer to research.

I quickly learned that condition was everything. Books were classified as *Very Fine, Fine, Near Fine, Very Good, Good,* and *Poor.* Some had dust jackets; some didn't. First editions were more valuable, but evaluating whether or not a book was a genuine first edition wasn't always easy. Pictures of the books were nice, but since I hadn't been able to drag the bookstore over to Elmer's, I had no idea of condition—or anything else.

After about two hours, I'd barely scratched the surface. What I had matched was pretty amazing. Although most of the books were in the two-hundred- to three-hundred-dollar range, several could be worth a great deal more, depending on their condition.

I leaned back in Elmer's threadbare chair, deciding that a cup of coffee was in order, but before I deserted my post for a caffeine break, I wanted to count how many pages I still had to go in the latest inventory book. If I could find most of the books on the Internet, I could at least make an educated guess about the total value of Bitty's treasured books. If not, I was going to be spending a lot of time in Elmer's funeral home. Although I wasn't really afraid, I had to admit that sitting by myself in these surroundings was a little creepy.

I flipped through the remaining pages, counting them quickly. As I reached the last one, I saw something that I hadn't noticed before. Between the final page with writing on it and the first blank page was a ragged strip of paper. I looked around the desk and found Elmer's magnifying glass. Then I pulled the lamp as close as possible and positioned the glass next to the open book. It was clear to me that a page was missing. I'd just assumed that the last entry on the back of the previous page was the end of the transactions. Had someone torn out some records in an attempt to hide something? Perhaps Bitty had made a mistake and wanted to start over. I realized right away, however, that if that were the case, the rejected page would have been before the final entry, not after. The missing page made my suspicions more real. Someone must have removed it *and* taken the list Bitty had written out and left on her desk.

I had just reached for the phone to call Amos, when I thought I heard a noise coming from somewhere inside the building. I waited a few seconds, but everything stayed quiet. I chalked it up to imagination and picked up the receiver. The tiny *bang* I'd heard before turned into a noisy crash. I definitely wasn't the only one here.

I put the receiver down and went to the door, glancing up and down the hallway, hoping to see Elmer trotting toward me. There was no one in sight.

"Elmer? Elmer, is that you?" My voice was at a higher-than-normal pitch. I sounded as frightened as I felt. I waited for an answer. Nothing. I had a couple of choices. I could either lock myself in the office and call for help or go plunging into the unknown, searching for the source of the racket just like they do in all those stupid horror movies. Not that I would know anything about that, of course. Since this definitely wasn't a movie, I slowly closed the door, turned the lock, and ran to the phone.

As I picked up the receiver, my mind flashed again to those dumb movies. I quickly repented for every single one I'd ever watched, but at that moment, some of the images were still floating around in my brain. For instance, right before the hapless victims found themselves facing certain death, they would invariably try to call for help. Of course, the phone never worked. I'd always wondered why they didn't just accept the fact that good old Ma Bell was programmed to snooze right before the insane murderer jumped out of the shadows. It would save time. Chiding myself for thinking that way, I grabbed the receiver. No dial tone. I'm not kidding. I pounded on the phone with my fist several times, figuring that somehow the silent instrument would interpret this as a very serious request and the dial tone would magically spring to life. It didn't.

Funny the stuff that goes through your mind when you imagine the worst. Probably the smartest thing for me to do would be to sit in Elmer's office until someone found me. I knew Elmer would be back sometime in the morning to take Bitty's ashes over to the church. What bothered me most was the possibility that I wouldn't have time to take a shower and dress before the service. It was probably ridiculous, but I was horrified to think I would let Aunt Bitty down in the very last thing I would ever be able to do for her. I had on jeans and a sweatshirt, and my hair was in ponytails. I couldn't possibly show up looking like this. The other thing that worried me was the realization that my staying here might be just what the killer wanted. I was isolated, easy to get to. The thought made me feel frightened and helpless. And that made me mad.

So I made a decision to make a frenzied dash out the front door and run to Elmer's house. Then I remembered the part in the movie where the heroine runs to the person she expects to help her only to find out that he is the murderer. I rolled that over in my mind a few times, but I honestly couldn't imagine poor Elmer killing anyone. The idea of the timid little funeral director pointing a gun at me and yelling, "Top or I'll toot!" didn't seem to fit my horror movie fantasy. That picture in my head was the thing that made me decide to run toward the known and away from the unknown.

I unlocked the door to the office and slowly opened it. I looked down the hall to my left and didn't see anything. Then I looked toward my right, in the direction of the front door. The coast was clear. I could either creep slowly down the hall, giving whoever was in the building plenty of time to catch up to me, or I could run as fast as I could, push open the front doors, and skedaddle to Elmer's house. I took a deep breath, prayed, and took off like Freddy Krueger was hot on my tail. As I neared the front doors, I heard something behind me. I could swear it was someone calling my name. I had no intention of turning around and letting Freddy catch up to me. Instead, I ran faster, holding my arms out to push the street-side door open so I could make my escape. But instead of ending up on the sidewalk outside, I felt something hard hit me on the head. The last thing I remembered before the darkness took over was the sense that someone stood behind me, whispering my name.

10

Having never been knocked unconscious before, I was of the opinion that people thus affected would eventually wake up without any memory of their brief visit to the state of oblivion. However, this wasn't my experience. I dreamed that someone was still chasing me. So when I opened my eyes and realized that a man whose face I couldn't clearly see was kneeling over me, touching me, I reacted in the most rational way possible. I decked him.

When he screeched, "Ow!" and put his hand to his nose, I realized I'd just smashed my fist into Amos's face.

"I see you're okay," Amos said crossly, rubbing his offended appendage. "But why did you hit me?"

I struggled to sit up. Elmer stood behind Amos, looking slightly relieved that he was out of range.

"What are you doing here?" I touched my tender forehead. A sizable bump greeted me, along with one whale of a headache.

Amos slipped his hands under my armpits and helped me to my feet. "I came by to check on you," he said. "When I looked through the front door, I saw you lying on the floor. I ran over to Elmer's so he could let me in. And once again, if I may ask, why did you hit me?"

I wasn't as concerned about his bruised ego as I was about my narrow escape from disaster. "Someone was in here, Amos. Whoever it was cut the phone lines, chased me when I tried to run out, and whacked me over the head. You must have come just in time and scared him away."

My dramatic revelation didn't produce the reaction I'd expected. Instead of throwing their arms around me in a grateful expression of overwhelming joy that I had escaped an early grave, I saw Amos and Elmer exchange a quick glance. Their expressions reminded me of the time my mother made homemade lemonade and forgot to add sugar.

"What's the deal?" I asked, feeling more than a little miffed by their seeming lack of compassion. "You believe me, don't you? Someone was after me. How do you think I got bashed on the head?"

Amos put his arm around my shoulders and guided me to one of the tired-looking overstuffed chairs in the lobby. "First of all, I want you to sit down," he said. "You still look a little shaky."

Either he was right or the room was actually spinning. I gently lowered myself into the chair, holding my head so that it wouldn't move any more than absolutely necessary.

"Elmer, will you check out the back rooms?" I asked. "See if anything looks unusual."

"Yes, I'd be glad to." Elmer patted my shoulder. "You just relax a little, Ivy," he said, trying to placate me. "Everything will be okay."

As he toddled off, I hissed at Amos. "What is wrong with you? You're the one who told me to be careful. Then when I'm actually attacked, you act like I've lost my marbles."

He knelt down next to my chair. "Listen, Ivy, I believe you thought someone was here, but the truth is. . ." He took a deep breath and brushed a strand of hair from my face. "The truth is, you ran into the front door and knocked yourself out."

"What? Are you nuts?" I was incensed. How could he think I would do something so stupid?

"Look, I'll show you." He stood up and walked over to the front door, which was made of thick glass. He patted a spiderweb-shaped crack that was right about where my forehead would be if I was standing up—or galloping full speed into an immovable object.

Even though I was still a little woozy, I pulled myself up to my feet. "But that's impossible. I hit the bar on the door with both hands. It should have opened."

"Under normal circumstances, it would have," Amos said patiently. "But there's a dead bolt on the metal doorframe." He pointed to a knob I hadn't noticed before. "Elmer locked it when he left. When you went galloping toward the door, you hit the push bar with both hands, but the dead bolt kept the door from swinging open. You crashed headfirst into the glass." He shook his head, his face creased with concern. "The truth is, you probably got off lucky. If the glass had broken. . ."

I sank back down into the chair and set my chin in my hand. "Okay, I get it. But, Amos, there *was* someone here. Maybe I caused my own headache, but I really did hear loud noises coming from down the hall. That's why I ran."

His expression made it clear that he was having a hard time believing me.

"I'm telling you the truth," I said, glaring at him. "Someone was in this building. I called out, thinking it was Elmer, but no one answered. Right before I hit my head, I heard someone call my name."

Amos started to say something but was interrupted by Elmer's return. The diminutive funeral director looked embarrassed. His eyes darted back and forth between me and Amos.

"Well, I checked out the building," he said hesitantly. "Everything seems in order."

"But I heard a loud crash," I said. "Like something metal falling to the floor."

Elmer shook his head, his face registering his pity for my mental state. "I do have some aluminum trays stacked in the embalming room," he said kindly, "but they seem to be all right, although I will have to speak to Billy Mumfree about them. I've told him a hundred times about not putting the trays directly on top of each other."

"But what about the phone?" I could hear the defensiveness in my tone, and I hated it. I recognized the voice of the old Ivy, the insecure girl who'd had no control over her own life. Angrily, I pushed her away.

Elmer stared at his shoes for a moment before answering. "I'm sorry, Ivy. I know this isn't what you want to hear, but you accidentally kicked the phone cord out of the wall jack for the phone line. It's located right next to the desk, under the jack for the computer line. The connection is loose. I do it all the time. I should have warned you about it. I'm sorry."

I wanted to defend myself, but I was tired and my head hurt like the blazes. I grabbed the arms of the chair and forced myself up again. Amos reached out to steady me, but I pushed his hand away. "I need to get my stuff out of the office," I said to no one in particular. "Then I'm going back to the bookstore to get some sleep."

"You stay here," Elmer said. "I'll get your things."

I wanted to protest, but I really wasn't sure if I could make it down the hallway without falling over.

"I've got my car out front," Amos said gently. "I'll drive you back and make sure you've got everything you need."

There wasn't anything I wanted from Amos right then, but I had no choice. There was no way I could walk all the way back to the bookstore.

Elmer came trotting down the hall with my stuff. "Let me carry these out to the car for you," he said, indicating the inventory books and my notebook.

I thanked him while Amos took my coat and helped me into it. Elmer followed behind us while Amos held on to me until we got to the car. Once I was inside and my things were in the backseat, I waved good-bye to Elmer as he stood in front of the funeral home, looking dejected. I tried to smile at him, hoping to lift his spirits a little, but it didn't seem to help much. Elmer Buskin wasn't used to being happy, so the unfortunate circumstance fit his already gloomy view of life.

"I'm going to call Dr. Barber. She needs to take a look at that bump on your head," Amos said as we pulled out into the street.

"It's nothing. It might look bad for a few days, but the swelling will go down. The only thing wrong with me is this whale of a headache. A few aspirin should take care of it." The story of how I ran into a door while being chased by an invisible intruder wasn't something I wanted dispersed throughout town.

"Ivy Towers, I'm not asking you this time. I'm telling you," Amos said harshly. "What if you have a concussion? You can't take the chance."

"I think I can decide for myself whether or not I want to see a doctor," I replied, choking back a rush of unwelcome emotion. "I am not some weak-minded little numskull who needs to be taken care of by you or anyone else."

I didn't want to cry in front of Amos, but I didn't seem to have a choice. I wasn't even certain why I was weeping. Was it a release of the fear I'd felt in the mortuary? Or was it the hurt caused by Amos's lack of trust in my version of what had happened? Probably a little of both.

Amos pulled the car over to the side of the road. "Ivy, I'm not trying to tell you what to do. I'm trying to help you." His words were clipped with irrita-tion. "Why are you so defensive? Why am I suddenly the enemy?" He turned around and stared out the windshield. His hands were clenched on the steer-ing wheel while his jaw tried to work out his frustration.

I wanted to say something, but I was too upset. I felt alone. My parents were overseas, Bitty was gone, and the one person I really trusted in Winter Break didn't believe me when I needed him most.

Finally, Amos started the car and drove me back to Bitty's. He helped me inside and got me settled on the couch in the sitting room. After running upstairs to get some aspirin and a glass of water, he covered me with a quilt and started a fire in the fireplace.

"Look, Amos," I said, trying to calm him, "I'm sorry I upset you. You're not my enemy, but back at Elmer's you certainly didn't feel like my friend. A friend believes you when you tell him something."

He sat down next to me on the stone hearth and cradled his head in his hands. When he looked up, his expression was composed. "Okay, Ivy. Even though it doesn't make sense, I believe you. I'm sorry I let you down." He ran one hand through his sandy hair. "I try hard to look at things with an eye to-ward the facts. You're asking me to take what you say on faith. I guess I need practice." He grinned at me. "I know you think being a deputy sheriff who lives in Winter Break doesn't take much effort, but you'd be surprised. This town has had its share of problems. This isn't the first time something unusual has happened here. I guess I slid into lawman mode back at the mortuary."

The look on my face made him laugh. "Believe it or not, last year a couple of big-time bank robbers holed up outside of town thinking no one would pay any attention to them here. And the year before that, I uncovered a group stealing cars and bringing them to Winter Break to strip and sell parts. There was a murder in Hugoton six months ago. Right now, the sheriff's office in

Stevens County is searching for someone who killed a spouse for the inheritance money. Law enforcement in Minnesota think the killer might be hiding out somewhere in the area." He shook his head. "It isn't all store-bought jam and stolen cows, Ivy. I've been involved in a lot of important cases."

I shot him an amused look. "Yet Hiram Ledbetter seems to slip away time after time. I guess it's because he's got such a devious criminal mind."

Amos glowered at me. "Hiram Ledbetter is a lot smarter than you give him credit for. As long as he's selling *liniment*, he's not doing anything wrong. I'll catch him someday. You can count on that."

"I think Sherlock Holmes said the same thing about Dr. Moriarty," I said innocently. "I didn't realize you were also locked into a battle of wits against an evil archenemy."

His expression made me giggle. That sent a shot of pain all the way through to the back of my head. I winced.

"I don't like this at all," Amos said. "I'm going to call Lucy and tell her what's going on. I'm not sure you should wait until tomorrow to see someone."

"For crying out loud, Amos. I told you I was okay. Don't bother the doctor." To be honest, even though I didn't want him to call Lucy Barber, I was more focused on his use of the doctor's first name. This was the second time he'd called her Lucy. I was starting to wonder if he and Dr. Barber had more than a doctor-patient relationship.

Amos ignored me, just as I knew he would, and went into the bookstore to use the phone. Even though he wasn't all that far away, I couldn't make out what he was saying. After a few minutes, he put the phone down and came back.

"Lucy seems to think you'll be okay. You haven't thrown up and you don't seem confused. . .well, at least not any more than usual."

I stuck my tongue out at him. "Very amusing. I told you I was okay. If I felt something was seriously wrong, I'd tell you. I'm not a martyr."

"She told me to ask you if you were having any problems with your vision."

"No," I said, stifling a yawn. "It's good enough to see that it's getting late, and you need to go home. I'm pretty tired."

"Okay, I can take a hint."

"Not very well," I mumbled.

"Dr. Barber will be here in the morning to check on you," he said, ignoring me. "And before you get all huffy on me, she was coming for the funeral anyway. I'll feel better knowing she's checked on you."

Miss Skiffins, who had just come into the room, jumped up on the couch and nestled down on my chest. "Well, that kind of settles that," I said. "I guess I'll spend the night on the couch."

"Maybe I should stay here, Ivy. How do you know that the person at the mortuary won't come here? I could sleep in one of these chairs."

I shook my head. "This place is locked tight. I'll be fine. If I hear any strange noises, I'll call you right away. I promise."

Although I meant what I said, I knew that Amos still had doubts about my stalker. If he'd really believed me, he would have insisted on staying without giving it a second thought. His hesitance made me want him to leave. I had some things to think about, and I couldn't do it with him here.

"Okay. I'll call you in the morning to check on you," he said. "What time?"

"No earlier than eight."

"One last thing," Amos said, crouching down next to the couch. "Please forgive me for not believing you, okay?"

"No problem."

He patted me on the arm and left, making sure to lock the door behind him. I knew I hadn't been honest with him. There was a problem. A big problem. I was now convinced that I needed to get out of Winter Break as soon as possible. I was becoming someone I didn't want to be. Someone I'd been trying not to be for a long time. It wasn't just Amos's lack of faith in me; it was more than that. It was my lack of faith in myself. I was beginning to understand that somehow, Winter Break was changing me in a way I couldn't accept.

Even though I had many conflicting thoughts rolling around inside my achy head, I made the firm decision to sell out to Noel Spivey based on my best guess as to the value of Bitty's books. That seemed to be the fastest way to get out of this one-horse town. But first, Amos and I would figure out what really happened to my great-aunt. Nothing was going to make me leave before that was accomplished.

As I lay on Bitty's couch, with the fire sputtering in the fireplace, I felt something heavy pressing down on my chest. It wasn't Miss Skiffins, who was purring with contentment. It was something else. Something I couldn't define and didn't want to.

And whatever it was frightened me a lot more than being chased in the dark through Buskin's Funeral Home.

11

I woke up around seven the next morning, feeling a little bit better. A quick check in the bathroom mirror showed the swelling had gone down. At least I was beginning to lose the look of someone who should have her own tent in the circus sideshow. However, the spot where I'd made contact with Elmer's door was now turning a lovely shade of dark purple. My only hope was to cover it with makeup. I rummaged around in Bitty's cosmetic bag and found some heavy foundation and powder. With a little luck and some creative hair styling, maybe no one would notice my colorful lump. I had no desire to answer questions that would force me to recount my late-night escapade at Buskin's.

I was already on my second cup of coffee when Amos called at eight o'clock on the dot. After assuring him I was fine and accepting a ride to the church, I headed for the shower. The hot water felt good on my shoulders. They were tight—a sure sign of tension. I stood under the nozzle for a while, thinking about the decision I'd made the night before. I was certain it was the right one. It made sense in my head. School was waiting. One more semester, and I'd have my degree. Even more important to me right now, I could go back to being the person I'd been before coming here. Samantha was beginning to feel like a long-lost relative who'd moved away, and I had every intention of finding her, and myself, again. I was starting to realize that I hadn't really lost Ivy Towers. She was alive and residing in Winter Break. If I didn't get out of here soon, I could become her again. I couldn't allow that to happen.

One obstacle I faced had to do with the money I'd make from the sale of Aunt Bitty's inventory. What would I do with it? How could I profit from her death and probable murder? Yet I knew she wanted me to have her inheritance. Perhaps I'd pay off my student loans then give a chunk of it to Faith Community. Maybe the church could even use the building that housed the bookstore. I wasn't certain what they could do with it, but if I gave it to them, all I would have to do was sign over the deed. After I took what I wanted from Bitty's possessions and fulfilled her personal bequests, the rest of her property could also be donated to the church. Her friends could each take something to remember her by, and the church could sell the rest.

With all these thoughts running through my mind, I stepped out of the shower and dried off. Then I pulled on my bathrobe and wrapped the towel around my head. I was on the way to find something to wear, when I heard a noise from downstairs. I went to the top of the stairs and looked down. Someone was at the door. I wasn't excited about the idea of greeting a visitor in my bathrobe, but there wasn't time to get dressed first. I ran downstairs and opened the door a crack, trying to peek around the side so that whoever was standing out there wouldn't see my ratty terry cloth robe.

A young woman bundled up in a parka, snow boots, and gloves stood on the porch with a black bag in her hand. "Ms. Towers?" she said. "I'm Lucy Barber. Amos Parker asked me to drop by and take a look at the bump on your head."

I hesitated a moment, feeling at a disadvantage without my clothes.

She smiled. "I see you've just gotten out of the shower. If you'll let me in, I'll be glad to wait while you get dressed."

Not seeing any way out of it, I opened the door. "Yes, please do come in. I'm sorry. It will just take me a minute to throw some clothes on."

Dr. Barber stepped inside, stomping the snow off her boots and onto the floor mat. "From what Amos said, I'm sure you're fine, but it never hurts to be absolutely certain."

I stood there clutching my threadbare robe while I watched her remove her coat and gloves. Lucy Barber was a strikingly beautiful woman with long, ebony hair and eyes the color of dark chocolate. I could see a hint of Indian heritage in her flawless features. She was tall, with a lithe body that would be the envy of any aerobics instructor.

I felt short, dumpy, and wet. "Have a seat, Dr. Barber," I said. "I'll be right back."

She smiled at me. "No problem. Take your time."

Without any hesitation, she started toward the sitting room. I was learning that this was par for the course in Winter Break. I wondered if there were any townspeople who *hadn't* spent time in Aunt Bitty's bookstore.

After pulling on some jeans and a shirt and trying to do something with my wet ringlets, I dragged my bruised noggin, along with my more severely bruised ego, into the sitting room. I felt like a soggy, slightly disfigured gnome in the presence of this natural beauty. My poor self-image shook hands with some kind of sour sludge lodged in the pit of my stomach. I knew exactly what it was—jealousy. The thing I couldn't understand was *why*. I wasn't in love with Amos Parker. What did I care if he wanted to hang out with Miss America in a doctor's uniform? It wasn't any skin off my nose.

"Why don't you sit down?" Dr. Barber said. "I want to get a good look at your injury."

I dutifully complied, allowing her to poke and prod my battered forehead. She took a small penlight from her bag and shined it in my eyes.

"How do you feel this morning?" she asked after nearly blinding me. "Any blurred vision, headache, or upset stomach?"

"No, no, and no," I said, trying to blink away the big white spots that danced before my eyes. "I had a really rotten headache right after the accident, but I took some aspirin and I feel okay now."

She jabbed my forehead once again.

"Of course, it is still a little tender," I said with tears in my eyes.

"Oh, sorry," she said. "You're fine, but you are going to have a lovely bruise for a week or so. However, I don't see any evidence of concussion." She dropped her little light back inside her bag. "If the headache comes back, or if you have any unusual symptoms, give me a call."

"Okay. Thanks."

As she turned to leave, I stopped her. "Dr. Barber, I wonder if I could ask you a few questions about my aunt's accident."

I realize that after being bonked on the head, things may seem a little fuzzy for a while, but I was perceptive enough to see a drastic change wash over Lucy Barber's face. It was as if someone had suddenly turned out the light and closed the door. Her compassionate doctor expression disappeared, and something akin to wary suspicion took its place.

"There's really nothing I can tell you," she said, still moving toward the door.

"Please. I know you saw her right after she. . .after she fell. I'm her niece. Surely you can spare a few minutes."

Her reluctance was obvious, but she came back and sat down across from me. "What is it you want to know?"

"I'd like to hear why she died. What did you see when you got here?" I had a few other questions, but I decided to ease into them. The good doctor reminded me of a cornered animal. If I moved too fast, she'd probably run away.

With a sigh of resignation, she put her bag down on the floor and leaned back into her chair. "When I arrived, your aunt was already gone. She'd fallen off the ladder, striking her head on the bottom roller cover. There was serious blunt force trauma to the right side and significant bleeding—internally and externally. The fall most likely caused an immediate lack of consciousness, followed by death." She frowned at me. "I could go into details about what happened inside her skull, but you wouldn't understand it. I don't believe she suffered."

"Did you try CPR?"

Once again, that invisible door slammed shut in my face. "She was gone, Ms. Towers. Her brain was irreparably damaged. No amount of CPR could have brought her back."

I wondered about her ability to see into my aunt's head without X-ray equipment, but I choked down my skepticism. "You ruled the death an accident and had Elmer pick up the body?"

She nodded. "That's right. I believe your aunt had already taken care of her final arrangements with Mr. Buskin. I saw no reason to interfere with those wishes."

Frankly, I was beginning to find the doctor's smugness a little irritating. I don't care how gorgeous she was, I didn't like the cavalier way she had disposed of Aunt Bitty. My attitude led to my next question, which, in retrospect, I should have phrased a little differently.

"Dr. Barber, did it ever occur to you that someone else might have caused my aunt's death? Shouldn't you have at least considered the possibility and asked for an autopsy?"

Her expression turned stormy. "Are you accusing me of something, Ms. Towers? If so, why don't you just come out with it?"

I swallowed the angry bile I felt bubble up from my chest into my throat. "I'm not accusing anyone of anything. . .yet. I just find it strange that my aunt's body was sent out and cremated before anyone had a chance to find out what actually happened. Maybe things are done that way in Winter Break, but I don't believe most health-care professionals would handle a situation like this in a similar fashion."

Dr. Barber sprang up from her chair and glared at me, her dark eyes flashing. "Now you look here. Your aunt was my friend. I cared deeply for her. If I could have saved her, I would have. You're talking about things you know nothing about. Perhaps if you'd bothered to show up once in a while, you'd know better than to sling accusations at her friends. I doubt seriously if Bitty would appreciate your actions. The only person around here who should feel guilty is you!"

She stomped her way out of the sitting room and grabbed her outer clothing from the coatrack. I followed behind her, too angry to speak. Just who did this woman think she was? She'd never had the kind of relationship I'd had with Bitty. I knew that under my ire ran a strong undercurrent of guilt. I *should* have been here. That knowledge made me more irate. "I'm not finished with this," I warned her. "I intend to find the truth about my aunt Bitty—either with you or without you."

Dr. Barber whirled around and pointed her finger at me. "You need to be careful," she said in a low voice. "Trying to blame the wrong person for Bitty's death just might land you in big trouble."

She pulled on her coat, jammed her feet into her boots, and flung the door open. Aunt Bitty's bell jangled with alarm. I watched as she tromped out to her silver SUV, shooting one last fierce look toward the bookstore. As she pulled away, I realized I was shaking. Her last words sounded like a threat. My intuition told me that Dr. Lucy Barber was hiding something, and I intended to find out what it was.

I was dressed and ready by twelve thirty when Amos pulled up outside. Rather than make him come in, I opened the door and motioned to him to wait in his car.

Although the bitter temperatures had kept the snow from melting, the sun was actually shining. It was the first time since I'd arrived in Winter Break that the sky hadn't been overcast. Maybe God had lifted the clouds out of respect for Bitty. He would have a tougher time breaking apart the dark animosity hanging over my heart.

When I had myself belted in, I looked up to find Amos staring strangely at me. "What?" I asked. "Is something wrong?" I reached up to pat my hair, making sure it wasn't out of place any more than normal. I looked down and checked the black dress I hadn't worn in years. I'd originally bought it five years ago for the funeral of a friend of my father's. But it wasn't faded, and thankfully, the hem wasn't stuck in my pantyhose.

"I. . . It's nothing," Amos said.

He looked a little flushed. Not unusual in this kind of cold, but odd for him. "Are you sure you're okay?"

He nodded. "You look nice, that's all. I'd forgotten how well you clean up."

"Oh, thanks. I must look pretty awful under normal circumstances."

He started to put the car in gear. I reached over and touched him. "Wait a minute, Amos. I need to talk to you before we get to the church."

I quickly recounted my odd meeting with Dr. Barber, finishing with her last comment. "I think she was threatening me, Amos. I'm convinced she knows something she's not telling us. I don't trust her."

"That's ridiculous, Ivy. I know Lucy very well. She cares a lot for all of her patients. She was particularly close to your aunt. You implied that she didn't do everything she could for Bitty. I don't blame her for getting upset."

"Listen," I said, "Dr. Barber was in town the day Bitty died, remember? She was at Ruby's, although we have no idea just when she got there. She could have easily gone to the bookstore before she went to the restaurant."

He shook his head and put the car into gear. "No way. You don't know Lucy."

"And you do?" I could hear the resentment dripping from my words, but I didn't care. "Seems like you and the hot doctor are pretty close. No chance that's coloring your perception some, is there?"

Amos shifted back into PARK and scowled at me. "Why would my relationship with Lucy be any of your business? You have no right to ask any questions about anyone in Winter Break. You've made it crystal clear that there's nothing here you care about. You see yourself as some strong, sophisticated person named Sam who's too good for us small-town hicks. You hate it here so much you've tried to rid yourself of the person who used to care about this place and the people who live here."

For a moment, I was struck dumb by the emotion behind his words. "Amos, I didn't mean it to sound like that," I said, finally finding my voice. "My decision to distance myself from Ivy has nothing to do with Winter Break. It's me." I could feel tears trying to make an entrance, but I forced them back. I leaned over and laid my head on his shoulder. "It's me," I said again. I stared out the front windshield, searching for the right words. "I. . .I've spent most of my life feeling like I don't belong anywhere. My parents are such self-assured people. They've always known what they were called to do. To be honest, I've just been someone in the way. A problem that had to be 'dealt with.'"

Amos started to say something, but I hushed him. "Let me finish."

He nodded and closed his mouth.

"Coming to Winter Break was, I don't know. . .different. I felt like I belonged here. But when I went home, I was still Ivy, living in my parents' shadow." I could feel a tear force its way out of the corner of my eye. I dabbed at it quickly with the side of my hand. I didn't want black streaks of mascara decorating a face that was already disfigured. "When I started college, I decided to change who I was and become the person I wanted to be." I pulled away and turned my head to look at him. "That's why I changed my name. It was a fresh start, a chance to find out what kind of person I really am. Without my parents, without feeling that I had to live up to anyone else's expectations. Winter Break was never the problem, Amos. The truth is, I love it here. But I can't go back to being Ivy. I can't pick up all that insecurity and fear again. I just can't."

Amos was silent for a moment. Then he reached over and brushed a stray curl from my face. "My beautiful Ivy," he said gently. "Have you ever considered that instead of deserting the person you used to be, you should allow God to heal her?" He shook his head. "Leaving her lost and confused doesn't sound right to me. She doesn't deserve it." He touched my cheek once again. "I know you think you can leave her behind, but I don't believe we can ever be free from our hurts without first giving them to God. Feelings buried alive never die, Ivy. No matter how deep you bury them."

He put the car into gear and pulled out into the street. We rode the rest of the way to church in silence. His words rolled over and over in my head. Was he right? Had I tried to cover up my problems instead of dealing with them? As we drove into the parking lot, I forced myself to put my questions aside for now. It was time to say good-bye to Bitty.

Amos unbuckled his seat belt and started to reach for the door handle.

"Wait a minute," I said. "Before we go in. . ." I tried to muster up a smile, although I wasn't feeling particularly cheerful. "I will think about what you said, but I want you to respond in kind."

"What do you mean?"

"I want you to honestly consider what I said about Lucy Barber. Quit coloring her with your own emotions. You told me you like to look at the facts. I think the evidence is compelling. She was in town. She was the one who pronounced Bitty dead, and she sent her to be cremated without an autopsy and without allowing anyone else to view the body. And she is definitely hiding something. Her reaction to me was way over the top."

He sighed. "What do you want me to do?"

"Nothing right now. But we need to add her to our list of suspects."

He grunted. "So far our list of suspects pretty much includes the whole town."

"I know it seems that way, but until we can find a reason to rule someone out, we can't afford to ignore anyone."

He sighed again, but at least this time he accompanied it with a small smile. "Hope my name doesn't end up scribbled in under Lucy's. You've never asked me where I was the morning of her death."

"I never suspected you," I said with a grin. "You still feel guilty about stealing strawberry pop from Dewey."

He shook his head. "You know, every time you tell that story, you leave out one very important thing."

"And that would be?" I said in my most innocent voice.

"You forget just who was waiting outside the Food-a-Rama for that second bottle."

"I have no idea what you're talking about. I think growing older has dulled your memory."

"Well," he said, looking down at his watch, "at least I can still tell time. We'd better get in there. It would be a little embarrassing for you to be late to your own aunt's funeral."

As we entered the church, I was amazed by the number of people jamming the lobby and filing into the sanctuary. It was standing room only.

When Elmer saw me, he hustled Amos and me into the pastor's office and closed the door. "We'll wait until everyone else is in place, then you'll enter and take your seat," he said. "Would you escort her, Deputy?"

Amos nodded. "I'd be happy to if it's okay with you, Ivy."

"Yes, that would be fine." I was grateful to have someone's arm to hold on to. Butterflies were beating their wings wildly inside my stomach. I wasn't sure why. I had no reason to be nervous, yet I was. I reminded myself that today was about Bitty, not me. That helped a little.

Elmer left the room, returning a few minutes later. He motioned for us to follow him. I took Amos's arm and we exited into the lobby. I could hear the strains of one of Bitty's favorite hymns being played on the organ. I could almost hear her singing: "Softly and tenderly Jesus is calling. . . ."

Elmer waved us on, and Amos and I began our long walk down the aisle to the front row. I snuck a look at some of the people waiting to bid Bitty farewell. I spotted Dewey, who gave me an encouraging smile. Lila Hatcher sobbed into her handkerchief. Lucy Barber refused to look my way, and Ruby Bird waved at me, her flaxen wig topped with a black netted pillbox hat. Although it was a style more popular in the sixties, I was touched that she had tried to tone down her audacious hairpiece. I saw Isaac sitting next to Alma Pettibone. He glanced up at me as we passed. I was startled by the grief etched into his face. I looked around for Noel. I didn't want to stare, but I thought I saw the back of his head over to the side in the fourth row.

After we sat down, the organist finished her song. Then Pastor Taylor came up to the podium. On a table in front of the stage sat Bitty's final resting place. The Bible urn was surrounded by pictures of my great-aunt. Behind the table was an easel that held a large picture of her smiling face. It was a posed shot, like something you'd see in a church directory. Bitty looked lovely. Her silver hair still had streaks of auburn. It curled softly around a face that expressed a joy that only knowing God's love could explain. The twinkle in her eyes seemed to be there just for me. I couldn't tear myself away from them. They were mirrors of the love and compassion that dwelt in the depths of Bitty's soul. Although in my mind I already knew she was dwelling in the presence of the One she loved the most, staring into those eyes confirmed it beyond a shadow of a doubt. She had always lived with her gaze focused toward heaven; taking up residence there had simply been the next natural step for her.

I opened my purse and pulled out one of the tissues I'd wisely jammed inside before leaving the bookstore. I was surprised when Amos held out his hand for one, too. I reached for another, noticing that his eyes were as teary as my own.

Pastor Taylor came up to the podium, and we all turned our attention toward him. "We are gathered together here today," he began, "to say good-bye to a friend. Although she is on a journey that will separate us for only a short while, we will still miss Bitty Flanagan. I'd venture to say that there isn't one man, woman, or child in Winter Break who isn't affected by her passing or who wasn't touched by her life."

The thought flashed through my mind that there was at least one person who wouldn't miss her. I could feel Amos glance over at me. I was pretty sure he was thinking the same thing.

"I used a word a moment ago," Pastor Taylor continued, "that epitomizes Bitty Flanagan. The word was *friend*. Bitty was a very spiritual woman, but also very human. Although I would be hard-pressed to think of any weaknesses she ever expressed, I can easily tell you one of the strengths she possessed. I can tell you the one characteristic she exhibited more perfectly than anyone I've ever known. That quality was friendship. Bitty knew how to be a friend. John 15:12–13 says, 'My command is this: Love each other as I have loved you. Greater love has no one than this, that he lay down his life for his friends.' Bitty laid her life down every day for all of us. There wasn't anything she wasn't willing to do. There wasn't anyone she wasn't willing to love." He glanced around the room. In that moment of silence, I could hear the sound of weeping. It was coming from everywhere. I realized that Amos himself was almost overcome by emotion.

An odd feeling came over me as I realized that Bitty Flanagan hadn't thrown her life away in Winter Break the way my mother had said. She'd shared it. She had impacted the lives of people in a way I could barely understand. And even though I knew today wasn't about me, I couldn't help but wonder about my own funeral someday. Would this many people come? Would they feel the kind of loss these people felt? Would they grieve this way about me?

I tried to listen to Pastor Taylor, but my mind wouldn't focus. Comparisons between my life and Bitty's kept filling my thoughts, no matter how hard I tried to push them away.

After speaking for a while, Pastor Taylor stepped away from the lectern, and a young woman walked up to the microphone. The organist began the moving strains of "What a Friend We Have in Jesus," and the girl began to sing. Perhaps we were all sitting in the small town of Winter Break, Kansas—a place most people in the world had never heard of—but I couldn't imagine that anyone, anywhere, at any time, could have sung that song more beautifully. The whole church seemed to catch its breath and hold it until the final notes faded away.

I was surprised to find tears streaming down my face. I'd forgotten all about my mascara. I started dabbing as quickly as I could, hoping it wasn't too late.

Then Pastor Taylor came back to the microphone. "We have some people who have asked to say a few words about Bitty."

He stepped back, and one by one, the citizens of Winter Break expressed their love for my aunt. Between sobs, Lila Hatcher talked about coming to Winter Break as a widow, feeling alone and abandoned. But then my aunt became her friend and gave her a reason to live, getting her involved in church and even sharing her love of books. Dewey Tater talked about the years he cared for his dying mother and the way Bitty was always there to brighten up both of their spirits. The way she spent hours reading to the elderly woman so Dewey could get some much-needed rest. He credited my aunt with teaching him about love.

One by one the people came, pouring out their hearts. It was one of the most moving things I'd ever seen or experienced.

Then Odie Rimrucker came to the front, his cheeks wet. "Bitty Flanagan saved my life," he said in a deep, rumbling voice. "Pure and simple."

He glanced around the room as if he thought he might find Bitty sitting somewhere, listening. He cleared his throat and stared down at the pulpit for a moment. I thought I saw his lips move. When he looked up again, he was a little more composed.

"I know most of you people remember when I was a drinker," he said slowly. "In fact, I was a drunk. It don't matter what it was that first drove me to drink. We all have our problems. I expect most of us have some deep sadness in our lives somewhere. For whatever reasons, I never felt like I belonged anywhere. I never felt like anyone wanted me. I thought I was just a mistake that God let slip through somehow. I was so pained on the inside that I drank, trying to make the hurt go away." He wiped his eyes with the back of his hand. "But drinkin' don't help nothin'. Drinkin' only makes it worse. 'Course, I couldn't see it back then." He smiled a little. "I thank all you people who tried to help me, especially Deputy Sheriff Watson. He never gave up on me. I sure wish he was still with us. I really do miss him." He nodded toward Mrs. Watson and her two sons, who sat a few rows from the front. "So many people tried to help me, but for some reason, none of it took. It wasn't that any of you did anything wrong. You didn't. I just couldn't listen 'cause my mind was locked up with sadness. Then one day, my beautiful wife left me and took my children. That was the end for me. I decided to drink myself away. I drank so much I thought I would go to sleep and never wake up. That's what I wanted to do, but Bitty Flanagan had another plan, and no one could stop her when she set her mind to somethin'."

A twittering of laughter swept through the room. Bitty's stubbornness was well known. I couldn't help smiling at the memory of her jutting out her jaw, pointing her finger at whomever happened to be handy and saying, "If the devil thinks he's going to make me back down, he's got another *think* coming."

I turned my attention back to Odie, who was busy battling emotions that threatened to overtake him. His mouth trembled as he spoke. "Bitty had the deputy take me to her place to sleep it off. She took care of me for several days. When I finally woke up, stinkin' of booze and vomit, she cleaned me up and poured coffee down my throat, even though I wanted nothin' of it."

Odie's rotund face flushed at the unflattering image he'd portrayed of himself. I could only imagine the strength it took for him to face the person he'd once been.

"It weren't that Bitty told me much different than anyone else had, 'bout how I needed to change my ways and let God heal me, but she did somethin' no one else had ever done."

Odie tried to choke back the tears and regain control of his unsteady voice. He quit looking at the crowd and focused on something in the back of the sanctuary—something only he could see. "Bitty Flanagan didn't just tell me what I could be. She told me who I already was. She saw somethin' good in me even then. She didn't see no dirty stinkin' bum. She saw the Odie down deep inside, the one who hurt and wanted to be loved, and she loved *him*. I didn't think no one could do that. Leastwise me. She showed me that God Almighty knew the truth about old Odie Rimrucker. And that He loved me jes' the way I was." He shook his head slowly. "I almost couldn't believe it," he said. "But I knowed Bitty Flanagan weren't no liar. And if she said God loved me, it must be the truth. She showed me what God's love really is. Love that comes to you no matter what a low-down, dirty dog you are. Love that accepts you just as you are but also believes in what you are gonna be someday. And when you know God sees you like that, well, you know you can really be somethin' different. When you finally believe you're not just a failure, a little light goes on inside that starts givin' you the strength to be somethin' else."

He looked over at me. "Miss Ivy, as you is the only living relative here at this service, I want to thank you for your aunt, Miss Bitty Flanagan. I'm here today, sober and in church, 'cause this great lady helped me to reach out and find God's love. I'm purely grateful. All I can do to honor her is to try to be the person she knew I could be. Thank you."

Odie walked away from the pulpit to the sounds of clapping. I wondered if there were very many funerals where people actually broke out in applause. But today, at the funeral of Miss Bitty Flanagan, it certainly felt right.

After a few more testimonies, we all sang two more hymns that Bitty loved. Then the service was dismissed.

Elmer came to the front of the church and directed Amos and me to the lobby. I stood there for a long while, accepting hugs and words of appreciation about Bitty. I finally saw Noel. He came up and put his arms around me, promising to call me the next day so we could talk more about the bookstore. I could barely contain the warmth that filled me at his embrace. Amos ignored him completely, turning to talk to someone else so he wouldn't have to face him.

Through a break in the crowd, I saw Isaac leaving through a side door. He stopped for a moment and looked my way. I got the feeling he wanted to say something to me, but seeing the long line of people, he gave up and walked out. It didn't matter. We were definitely going to have a conversation—and soon.

Lucy Barber also left without speaking to me, but I saw her wave at Amos. He looked her way and smiled, but he didn't wave back. Probably because he knew I was watching him.

Just when I thought everyone was about gone, Ruby Bird came flying up toward me, yelling, "My poor, poor Ivy." I couldn't help but wonder if someday, someone was going to suggest she get a hearing aid. It seemed as though she got louder every day. "Your aunt was a dear, dear friend," she hollered. "In fact, she was one of the few people I trusted in this whole world." Then crazy Ruby Bird whispered something in my ear. Well, let's say she softly shouted it. "Your aunt is the only person I ever shared my secret with," she said with a note of triumph. "She knew everything that goes into a Redbird Burger." She glanced around the almost empty room as if she really believed no one else could hear her. "And if you play your cards right, honey, I'll tell you, too, someday."

The weight of her pillbox hat was pulling her ridiculous wig over to the side of her head, making me worry that the whole thing was about to fall off, exposing what was underneath. I was pretty sure I didn't want to know. Her poor scalp hadn't seen the light of day for at least twenty years.

"Thank you, Ruby. That means so much to me. Will I see you over at Lila's?"

Also sensing the possibility of an imminent wig disaster, Amos put his hand on my back and began moving me toward the front entrance.

"Land sakes, child," Ruby bellowed, "I plumb forgot. I've got to get over to the restaurant and get the food for the open house." When she hugged me, I wanted to reach up and pull her wig back to where it was supposed to be. I forced myself to keep my hands down. "I'll see you over there," she said. Then she galloped out the front door.

Pastor Taylor watched the whole escapade. After Ruby disappeared down the steps, he broke out in giggles. I don't know if it was a release of tension or something else, but Amos and I both joined in. Finally, after we stopped laughing, Pastor Taylor wiped his eyes and shook his head. "My goodness," he said. "Ruby Bird is certain proof that God has a sense of humor." He smiled at me. "You'd better be careful, young lady. The story about Bitty knowing Ruby's secret ingredient will be all over town by the end of the day. And if she ever really tells it to you, that will be your last peaceful moment in Winter Break."

We said our good-byes, and I thanked him for the beautiful service. Amos and I went outside and got into the car.

It took only a few minutes to get to Lila's. I loved the old Biddle place. It was built in the early 1900s by a man named Silas Merryweather. Mr.

Merryweather had it in his mind to change Winter Break from a stopping point on the way west to a large, thriving city. He'd come from the East Coast, bringing lots of money and even more ambition. After building his Queen Anne–styled Victorian home, he began trying to lure other businesspeople to town. Unfortunately, after experiencing the long, harsh winters that seemed to plague Winter Break, the brave businesspeople who had ventured out west to catch the next wave of prosperity went away broken and bankrupt. Merryweather's ship never came in, and eventually he gave up and left town. Since then, many families had lived in the lovely old home with its turrets and balconies. Before the Biddles, the home had fallen into disrepair, but Cecil Biddle had worked hard to bring it back to its original splendor.

Funny how I compared all homes to this grand old structure. In my imagination, whenever I thought about having my own family someday, I saw us living in the Biddle house. Having never really lived in a place that felt like home, I found this house had become the standard, the home of my dreams.

We turned the last corner, and the Biddle homestead loomed up in front of us. Its backyard faced Lake Winter Break. The Biddles had been the guardians of the lake in the winter. Cecil would check the surface every day, and when it was finally frozen hard, he would raise a little yellow flag he'd attached to a pole in his backyard. When the flag was up, the town's children knew it was okay to venture out with their skates. Marion would make hot chocolate in a big thermos and bring it to us. I could still taste it. It was the best hot chocolate I'd ever had.

"Ivy, are you okay?" Amos asked after parking the car. "You seem a million miles away."

"I was remembering all the good times we had here. I'd forgotten about so many of them." I reached over and squeezed his arm. "Sorry. I'm ready. Let's go in."

Lila's house was packed with people. A few minutes after we arrived, Ruby poked her head in and yelled for some "big, strong men" to help her unload her truck. Lila's long banquet table was soon loaded with enough food to feed the entire town for several days. Although I wasn't hungry, I followed Amos through the line, taking small samples from the spread laid out in honor of Aunt Bitty.

Besides the food Ruby brought, there were all kinds of goodies carried in by other townspeople. The Baumgartners were out in force, so there were bowls of sauerkraut and apples, red cabbage, and potato dumplings. Someone brought a tray of bratwurst, and on the dessert table, amid Ruby's scrumptious pies, sat decorated stollen loaves, Black Forest cake, apple strudel, and my favorite, baklava.

Hannah Blevins, a longtime friend of Bitty's, donated her famous apple-and-green-tomato relish, made from a recipe that had won several prizes at the state fair. Alma Pettibone, the postmistress, brought her wonderful huckleberry jelly and homemade huckleberry muffins. Every summer, she visited her sister in Oregon, and they would put up jars and jars of preserves. Alma always brought back a huge batch of jelly, along with extra huckleberries for baking. She passed out the wonderful jelly to many of her customers in Winter Break. Of course, Aunt Bitty always got several jars. She and I would bake bread together, and when it cooled enough, we would slather huckleberry jelly on it. That jelly was a little bit of heaven in a jar.

I grabbed a couple of Alma's huckleberry muffins and a spoonful of jelly and went searching for butter. It was in the middle of the table, shaped into the image of a graceful swan. The mold used to shape the butter was very familiar. It was Bitty's, passed down from my great-grandmother and, according to Bitty, eventually destined for me.

"What's wrong?" Amos whispered. "You're holding up the line."

As I reached for some butter, someone came up behind me and gently touched my back. I turned around to see Lila standing there with tears in her red-rimmed eyes. "I suppose you recognize your aunt's butter mold?"

I nodded.

"Your aunt gave that to me because I loved it so," she said softly. "I think you should take it back, though. It should stay in your family." Lila reached into the pocket of her dress and took out a hankie. "She was too generous," she said, wiping her brimming eyes. "I'll wrap it up and give it to you to take home."

"No, Lila. If she gave it to you, you should keep it. You must have meant a great deal to her. I know how much she treasured that mold."

I finished taking everything I wanted and began looking for a place to sit down. Lila took my elbow and guided me toward a couple of empty chairs. She sat down next to me and leaned in close.

"Your aunt was the best friend I ever had," she said. "We were like two peas in a pod. We both lived similar lives, you see. Although she lost Robert when she was young, and I lost my Milton when I was in my fifties, we both understood grief. I can't tell you how much Bitty's friendship meant to me. She had a way of filling up all the empty places with hope." She dabbed at her eyes again. "I swear, I don't know what I'm going to do without her. I feel so alone."

Trying to balance my plate on my lap, I reached over and patted her hand. "There are many, many wonderful people in Winter Break," I said. "You won't be lonely. And the church has lots of activities. They'll keep you busy."

Her fingers trembled as she touched her salt-and-pepper curls. "Yes, that's true. But it's not the same as having someone in your life you can tell every-thing to." Her smile was thin and forced. "I'm sure you don't understand that. Being so young and beautiful, you must have lots of friends. But for someone my age. . .well, people like Bitty just don't come along every day."

I wanted to comfort her, but she was right. Bitty was special. She would be impossible to replace. "Lila," I said, "if Bitty hadn't considered you family, she never would have given you that mold. I'm sure she felt just as strongly about you."

The older woman broke down and sobbed into her hankie. "I don't know what to say," she whispered after she composed herself. "I hope it consoles you a little to know that Bitty had many, many friends. I know her last days were happy ones."

"Believe me," I said. "I'm beginning to realize that she was a very blessed woman."

Lila nodded. "That she was, dear. That she was." She stood up. "I hope you'll stay in Winter Break. We could be such good friends. I feel it in my bones."

My bones weren't planning to stay in Winter Break, but I smiled at her anyway and nodded. As she walked away, her words came back to me. "*Someone in your life you can tell everything to.*" It did sound wonderful. There was no one in my life now with whom I felt that comfortable. As kids, Amos and I were pretty close. We'd shared almost everything. Emily Baumgartner had also been a good friend. Correction: Emily *Taylor*. I looked through the crowd, but I didn't see her.

I was enjoying my second muffin, when Alma sidled up next to me. "I re-membered how much you always loved my jelly and my huckleberry muffins. I made that batch of muffins just for you."

"Thank you, Alma," I mumbled, my mouth full but extremely happy. "They're just as good as I remember."

"May I sit down?" she asked, motioning to the empty chair next to me.

I swallowed and wiped my mouth. "Of course, please do."

Alma Pettibone was a woman who was passionate about two things: her soaps and town gossip. She was a kindhearted woman, but her tongue had gotten her in trouble more than once. Bitty used to warn me that telling something to Alma was just like standing in the middle of Main Street with a bullhorn and announcing your business to everyone within earshot. I think she really tried to curb herself, but she was weak. It occurred to me that maybe I could take advantage of her shortcoming. The post office was right across the street from the bookstore. Alma had a clear view of everyone who came and went. It was possible she saw something that could point me in the right direction. I silently chided myself for not thinking of it sooner.

"Alma," I said quietly, looking around to make certain no one else could hear us, "the morning that Bitty died, did you happen to notice who visited her?"

She scrunched up her face and looked at the ceiling. I wasn't certain what that meant, but I surmised that she was trying to remember. "Hmm. Now that was last Wednesday, wasn't it? That was the day that Marla Mason told Dr. Naismith that his wife had been seen in the company of that nasty Brock Davis."

She stopped looking up and flashed me a triumphant smile. My blank expression must have given her a clue that I had absolutely no idea what she was talking about. She cupped her hand around her mouth and whispered conspiratorially, "I watch *As Our Lives Turn* at ten o'clock every weekday, and I sit right in front of the window. I can see everything that goes on outside."

She had obviously found a way to combine her two favorite things. I was impressed. "Did you notice anyone visiting the bookstore during the time your program was on?"

"I certainly did!" she exclaimed. "Of course, earlier that morning, Dewey went over for breakfast. He did that every morning. Then Isaac came in for work. That was before my programs started."

"I specifically want to know who went to the bookstore between ten and eleven o'clock."

Alma clucked her tongue several times. "My goodness, dear. I understand, but I'm not one of those computer machines. I can't just push out information when you press a button." Her silver topknot jiggled in frustration.

"I'm sorry, Alma," I said in an appropriately apologetic tone. "Please go on."

"Well, let me see. Oh yes. Your aunt had a couple of visitors that morning after Isaac picked up the packages from the post office." She wrinkled up her nose again. "That snooty Dr. Barber came by."

I found that information interesting. "Do you remember how long she was there?"

Alma shook her head. "No, I'm sorry. I had to make a trip to the little girl's room. I didn't see her leave."

I glanced around again, but no one was paying any attention to us. "Alma, why do you call Dr. Barber 'snooty'?"

She raised her eyebrows and pursed her mouth. "That woman had the nerve to tell me that if I'd turn off the TV and give my eyes a rest once in a while, I wouldn't get so many headaches."

I was fairly certain Dr. Barber's diagnosis was right on the money, but this wasn't the time to antagonize Alma. "You said someone else stopped by?"

The old woman nodded so vigorously, her bun looked like it was caught up in some kind of frantic dance routine. "Before the doctor stopped by, Dewey Tater went running back to the bookstore. This was a couple of hours after he'd left earlier that morning." The sparkle in her eyes showed that she was warming up to the gossip that had been thrown into her already-willing lap. "I thought that was kind of unusual. Dewey usually never leaves his store once it's opened. He looked like he was upset about something."

Her words were like ice water thrown into my face. "Can you be more specific about the time?"

"Well, if I remember right, Dr. Naismith had just started operating on Angela Marstairs." She sighed and shook her head. "That girl just never learns. I mean, she wouldn't have needed that operation to relieve the pressure on her brain if she hadn't been snooping around in things that shouldn't concern her." Alma leaned closer. I could feel her breath on my face. "You know, she is really June Anne's mother, but—"

"Alma," I said, trying to keep a note of hysteria out of my voice, "the time Dewey went to the bookstore?"

Her hand went to her chest. "Oh yes. I almost forgot." She screwed up her face again. "Why, it would have been right around ten fifteen. My show hadn't been on that long, and the operation was before the second commercial break. I'm sure of it."

"Thank you, Alma. Was there anyone else you can think of?"

She looked at me sadly. "Well, Isaac came back a little while later. Then Dr. Barber and Dewey. By then, our dear Bitty was gone." A tear crept down her face. "I know I go on and on about my soaps, dear. Bitty used to scold me about them sometimes. But she understood."

"She understood what, Alma?"

Winter Break's postmistress hung her head. When she spoke, I had to strain to hear her. "She understood that my soaps keep me from feeling alone. They keep my mind off my troubles." Her brown eyes sought mine. "Your aunt told me that I needed to get out and spend more time with people, but I'm terribly shy. I promised her I'd try someday—when I was ready. She believed me, Ivy. Even though I didn't mean a word of it."

"I'm sure she did, Alma," I said. "By any chance, did you see anyone else?"

She shook her head. "No, that's all I can remember."

"And did you leave your chair any other time except for that bathroom break?"

"No, that was it." Alma stared down at the floor for a moment. "Wait a minute. That was Wednesday. April Tooley comes in every Wednesday at ten thirty to mail a package to Marvin. He's in the army, stationed overseas. She won't set her package on the counter like everyone else does. She makes me process it right then and there." Alma's face flushed a little, and she lowered her voice to a whisper. "She says I forget things sometimes. I humor her because her brother is over there risking his life for our freedom."

"And about how long does it take to get her package ready to mail?"

"Oh, I don't know. I'd say it takes me about ten minutes. We like to gab a little. 'Course, I end up missing some of my program, but it's the least I can do for one of our men in uniform."

Her smile showed her pride in doing her part for our country. I wasn't sure that missing ten minutes of a soap opera once a week was that much of a sacrifice, but who's to say? Maybe to Alma it was a real gift from the heart. I thanked her for the information, and she wandered away, probably looking for a television somewhere.

As soon as she left, Amos edged up next to me. "We need to talk," he said in a low voice. "I've dug up some interesting dirt."

I grinned at him. "Are you trying to tell me that you're pumping people for information at my aunt's memorial service?"

He wrinkled his nose at me. "Oh, and you were in deep conversation with Alma Pettibone so you could catch up on the soaps?"

"Okay, you got me. I have something to tell you, too. I think we're going to have to wait, though, Amos. I can't leave now."

"But this is important."

His obvious frustration fueled my interest. I glanced around the room. "Let's go sit by the fireplace; no one is there."

I stood up and ambled slowly toward one of the chairs near the brick hearth on the other side of the room. Most of the guests were near the buffet table. As long as they hovered near the food, Amos and I would have some privacy.

I stopped first at the kitchen and dumped my plate into a trash container. Then I continued my slow walk toward the fireplace, hoping no one was watching me. Amos followed nonchalantly. I had a notion that we probably looked highly suspicious, but when I scanned the room, it appeared that no one had noticed us. They were too busy eating and talking.

"Okay, who goes first?" Amos asked after we were seated.

"Age before beauty," I said.

"Thanks a lot," Amos said. "But I'll take it." He glanced around us once more then scooted closer so no one could hear him. "First of all, Morris Dinwiddie told me he was coming back Sunday night from Hiram Ledbetter's farm after buying some 'medicine.'"

"So what? How does that help us?"

He sighed and shook his head. "If you'll just hush a minute and listen, you'll find out."

"Okay. Don't get snarky."

His eyebrows shot up. "*Snarky?* Is that one of those big-city words?"

I rolled my eyes. "Sorry. Don't get all het up. Is that easier for you to understand?"

"I'm not a hundred years old," he grumbled.

I was getting exasperated. "Are you going to tell me what you heard in this lifetime, or should I just plan on spending the rest of my existence in this chair waiting for you to get around to it?"

He mumbled something else that I refused to acknowledge. "Morris Dinwiddie saw Isaac skulking around in the dark near Buskin's right around the time you knocked yourself out."

I grabbed the arm of my chair. "What?"

Amos swung his head around to see if anyone had noticed my rather loud exclamation. "Shh. You heard me." He put his hand on my arm. "Ivy, I think he was coming from the mortuary."

"I told you there was someone there. He was following me."

He held up his hand like a traffic cop. "Now wait a minute. He may have been in the building, but let's remember that he didn't actually hurt you. You ran into that door all on your own."

"Maybe I beat him to it," I hissed. "You have no idea what his intention was."

"Well, you certainly were an easy target, lying on the floor all passed out. If he'd wanted to do something to you, why didn't he use the opportunity you so brilliantly provided him?"

I didn't have an answer for that.

"The point is," Amos said softly, "it was probably Isaac in the building that night. That's what you heard. We need to figure out what he was doing there."

I started to say something, but Amos hushed me. "That's not all. Here's something else interesting. Your friend Noel has been placing and receiving a lot of calls at Sarah's."

"He's a book dealer, Amos. Of course he gets a lot of calls."

Amos leaned back a little, and I could see he was definitely pleased with himself.

"Okay, give. What are you so happy about?"

"Almost all the calls are from one person."

I was growing weary of this cat-and-mouse game. "All right, I'll bite. Who were the calls from?"

"Someone named. . .Olivia."

I had to admit, I hadn't seen that one coming. "Olivia? Our Olivia?"

He shrugged. "I don't know, but I think the coincidence is intriguing at the very least."

I sat back in my chair to think for a moment. Noel was a book dealer from Denver. What could he have to do with the shipment of books sitting in the bookstore? And who was Olivia?

"I think we should try to find the Olivia who sent those books," I said. "It may be important."

"But you said the labels from the boxes were missing, and there weren't any references to any Olivia in Bitty's books."

"What about Alma? Doesn't she have to keep some kind of records?"

"I don't know," he said. "But we'll definitely ask. As far as Noel Spivey as a suspect," he said, looking skeptical, "you know I'm not crazy about the guy, but this doesn't really make much sense. He doesn't even live here; in fact, he said this was the first time he'd ever been in Winter Break."

"Even so, we have to check out every lead. Frankly, the idea of someone who didn't know Bitty killing her makes more sense than someone who did." Even as I said it, I couldn't believe it. Noel Spivey didn't seem like a killer to me.

"Now tell me what you found out," Amos said.

I informed him about Bitty's extra visitors on the day she died.

His eyebrows shot up at the mention of Lucy Barber, but he didn't say anything. However, he immediately dismissed the idea that Dewey was hiding something.

"But Alma said he looked upset," I said. "I think that's significant."

He grunted. "First of all, Alma has a flair for the dramatic. She probably confused one of her soap opera actors with Dewey. I'm telling you that Dewey had nothing to do with Bitty's death."

I started to say something about Amos believing in Dewey because he cut him slack for stealing that strawberry pop, but I was interrupted by Pastor Taylor, who suddenly came up behind us.

"This is a nice turnout, isn't it?" he said, gazing around the crowded room.

"Bitty would have been honored," I agreed.

"I hope you know how much she meant to us. I will really miss her, sitting in church and smiling at me during the service." He chuckled. "You might not believe this, but the other side of the pulpit can be rather disconcerting. Sometimes during your most rousing sermon, you're greeted with yawns and glassy-eyed stares. And that doesn't include the people who are trying to look as if they're reading their Bibles but are actually sound asleep." He sighed deeply. "But Bitty was always bright-eyed and interested. And always looked happy to be in church. Yes, I'm really going to miss that," he said again.

I started to stand, but Pastor Taylor waved me back down. "Please don't get up. I'm sure you're tired. It's been a long day. I didn't want to bother you, but I thought I might stir the fire a little. These old houses are hard to keep warm, and some of the guests are getting a little chilly."

He walked around to the hearth and grabbed some tongs hanging from a tool rack. After he turned the logs over a couple of times, the fire crackled back to life. Watching him reminded me that we still needed to buy tongs for Bitty's fireplace. I mentioned it to Amos.

"Don't know where you can get any fireplace tools in Winter Break," Pastor Taylor said. "We had to go to Hugoton for ours. I think some people order them through the mail. 'Course, you have to pay shipping that way." He put the implement back on the rack. "I see Lila has some extra tools. She'd probably give you whatever you need."

I shook my head. "That's not necessary. We're doing fine." I didn't want to say out loud that it didn't matter that much since I wouldn't be staying long enough to worry about it.

Pastor Taylor sat down on the brick hearth. "I hope you weren't offended about the cash memorials to the church. I wouldn't have brought it up if Bitty hadn't mentioned it to me."

"I'm sure it's exactly what she would have wanted. I have to say that I was touched by all the flowers that showed up anyway. People in Winter Break are very generous."

"I don't know that it was generosity. I think it was more gratefulness than anything else." His eyes misted. "Bitty touched a lot of people in her life, Ivy. More than you realize, I think." He wiped his eyes and smiled at me. "I hope you'll be around for a while. I believe Bitty left you a wonderful legacy. I'd like to see you get blessed by it."

I nodded but kept my mouth shut. I was beginning to understand that leaving Winter Break was going to be a lot tougher than I had ever imagined.

As Pastor Taylor walked away, Amos said in a low voice, "We need to get out of here. We've got a lot to talk about. I also think I figured out another entry on Bitty's list."

I started to remind him that this reception was for me and that I couldn't leave early when Dewey came up and put his hand on my shoulder. "Doing okay?" he asked.

"I'm fine, Dewey. How about you?"

He walked over and gazed into the fire. "I'm feeling the loss a little more today than I did yesterday," he said. "Don't know why. But I keep reminding myself that God's family is eternal. Even when we're apart, we're still together." He looked at me and smiled sadly. "You probably think that's silly."

"Actually, I don't. I miss Bitty, but I can't shake the feeling that somehow, she's still here."

He nodded. "Yep. I feel it, too."

"It's almost like she has some kind of unfinished business, Dewey. Like she's trying to tell us something. Have any idea what that might be?"

Amos shot me a look of warning and cleared his throat. I ignored him.

Dewey's expression darkened. "I have no idea what you're talking about,

Ivy Towers. I hope you're not spreading that ridiculous story about someone hurting Bitty. She wouldn't have stood for you doing something like that. She didn't believe in spiteful gossip."

I met his direct gaze without flinching. "I intend to do whatever I need to do to uncover the truth, Dewey. I think my aunt trusted someone she shouldn't have. I won't leave Winter Break until I find out who it is."

Dewey glared back and forth between Amos and me, his forehead knotted in frustration and his face slowly turning a nice shade of magenta. "Ivy Towers, I'm warning you. You'd better not stir things up that you can't fix, especially if you're not planning to stay around and clean up your mess." He stared at me for a moment longer then turned around and stomped off.

That was the second warning I'd received in one day. "See what I mean?" I hissed at Amos. "You keep telling me that Dewey couldn't possibly have anything to do with Bitty's death, but that isn't the way an innocent man acts."

"I don't think he's acting the least bit suspicious," Amos hissed back. "He loved your aunt and can't conceive of the idea that someone would purposely hurt her."

Amos cocked his head to the side, and my eyes followed his gesture. A group of people stood not far to our right. When they noticed us staring at them, they turned away. It was obvious they'd overhead Dewey's proclamation. I was a little embarrassed, but I was also somewhat relieved. Maybe if a few of Bitty's friends knew there was a reason to be suspicious about her death, we might uncover more information. I was certain Amos didn't share my feeling. I was right.

"I'm leaving," he said, standing up. "I think you've done enough damage here today. You can carry on without me."

"Amos, don't go. Please. I'm sorry." I tried to whisper, but my words came out louder than I intended. I didn't bother to look around. I was certain several of the guests overheard me.

He sat back down, but his mouth was tight with anger. "Ivy, I want you to ease back a little. I mean it. You don't know anything about handling an investigation. You need to trust me." His eyes snapped with emotion. "For crying out loud, this isn't rocket science. Blabbing everything we know right now could blow the entire case. We're going to shelve this discussion until we get back to the bookstore. In the meantime, I'm going to get a piece of Ruby's blackberry pie. Do you want anything?"

I shook my head. I'd kept him from abandoning me completely, but in truth, I was also a little peeved at his overbearing attitude. I cared a great deal for Dewey, but my main loyalty was to Bitty. Why was Amos so stubborn in his defense of almost everyone I suspected? At this rate, we'd never uncover the truth.

I was deep in thought when someone slipped into the chair Amos had vacated.

"Sam?"

Noel Spivey, cradling a coffee cup in his hands, looked incredibly yummy in an obviously expensive black suit. It draped his long, lean frame as if it were made specifically for him. It reminded me of a silk dress my mother had worn years ago. His eyes seemed to be an even deeper blue than before, and a lock of his wavy dark hair fell casually across his forehead.

The word *spiffy* crept into my brain. Spiffy Spivey. I bit my lip in an attempt to stop a giggle that threatened to make an inappropriate entrance. Then I remembered what Amos told me about the phone calls, and things didn't seem quite so humorous.

Perhaps it was Amos's condescending attitude, or perhaps it was just my own orneriness, but after I gave the debonair Noel my sweetest smile, I said, "Why, hello, Noel. Care to tell me who Olivia is?"

Maybe finding the truth isn't rocket science, but it doesn't take much more than a little common sense to know what it means when someone turns white as a sheet and spits a mouthful of coffee out all over you.

12

To say that Amos wasn't happy with me was an understatement. When he found me dripping with coffee and Noel trying to clean me up, he was quick enough to figure out that something noteworthy had happened. When I admitted to him that I'd brought up Noel's calls to Olivia, he ordered both of us back to the bookstore.

I made my excuses to Lila, thanking her for the lovely reception and promising to have lunch with her later in the week. Then Amos marched Noel and me out to his car and told us both to get in. No one said a word. When we arrived at the bookstore, Amos got out and pulled open the passenger door, along with the door to the backseat where Noel sat, and pointed toward the front entrance. We meekly followed his wordless instructions. My silence came from my fear that I had finally crossed the line with Amos. I couldn't ever remember him looking so angry. I had no idea why Noel was so quiet, but I suspected it was from guilt. The question was, guilt about what? Was he involved in a scam to get something valuable in Bitty's collection, or was he guilty of something much worse?

I was also beginning to worry that I had truly jumped the gun and given away something that might hurt us in our search for the truth. In my heart of hearts, I really didn't believe Noel Spivey was capable of murder. I couldn't find a motive. His only relationship with Bitty was through his long-distance business transactions with her. What possible reason would he have to come all the way to Winter Break, Kansas, to kill her? It didn't make sense. Besides, in this small town, someone would have spotted him and asked questions. New people never drift in and out of town without stirring up attention.

Amos herded us into the sitting room and pointed toward the two chairs that were immediately to meet our backsides. After we complied, he finally spoke. His first words were to Noel. He ignored me completely.

"All right, Spivey. I'm not thrilled that Ivy told you we know about your calls to Olivia, but that cow's left the barn. Now you're going to come clean. And don't try to tell me that your Olivia isn't the same one who sent two boxes of books to Bitty right before she died. There's no way that's a coincidence."

Noel didn't try to argue. Instead of responding to Amos, he addressed me. "Sam, there's one thing I want you to know before I tell you why I really came to Winter Break." Those striking eyes locked onto mine, and I found that I

113

couldn't look away. I may not be the best judge of character, but I was pretty sure I saw sincerity there.

"I didn't tell you everything, but I didn't actually lie to you, either. I meant every word I said about how special I think you are. There's something about you that I find intriguing, and I don't want the truth to ruin any chance I have to get to know you better." He hung his head, and I could barely hear his next words. "I hope you'll give me a chance to explain, and I pray you'll understand."

To be honest, I was surprised by the intensity behind his words. I was also very aware that it sounded as if we had something much more involved going on besides a dinner and a kiss on the cheek. One look at Amos made it clear that he believed the worst. Or the best, depending on which side of the fence I was on. His expression could have been placed in the dictionary next to the explanation of what *looking daggers* actually means.

"If I were you, Spivey, I'd be more concerned about what *I* think about you," Amos hissed between clenched teeth. "Ivy can't lock you up."

Noel's head jerked up. "Lock me up?" he said, his face pale. "I haven't done anything illegal, Deputy."

"Noel," I said, "how did you find out that Bitty died? The only place it was published was in the Hugoton paper. You were in town before any of the other dealers knew about her death."

"There's a book buyer who lives in Dodge City. He gets the Hugoton paper. He saw it and called me."

Amos sat down on the fireplace hearth, next to the now visibly shaken man. "Okay, let's say we believe that. Now you need to tell us who Olivia is and why you're here."

Noel ran his hands through his carefully groomed hair, mussing it only slightly. "Olivia is my sister," he said quietly. "She sent those books to Bitty."

"I don't understand," I said. "You're a book dealer. Why wouldn't your sister work with you? Why was she involved with my aunt?"

He sighed. "She did it out of anger." His fingers tightly gripped the arms of his chair. "You see, the books belong to our grandmother. She's been ill for the past several months, and Olivia has been caring for her alone. There are only the two of us to look after her. Our parents are both dead. Olivia asked me to come down and stay with Grams for a while so she could have a break." He shrugged. "I was too busy with my business, and I couldn't help her. She got upset with me and decided to cut me out of the situation. She found a nursing home for Grams and has been cleaning out her possessions."

"But if you didn't have time to help your sister, why are you here now?" Amos asked, his voice tight with hostility.

Noel shrugged. "I cleared my calendar, wrapped up all the deals I had, and went back to Cincinnati to help Olivia. I never told her I wouldn't help. I just wasn't able to come when she first asked me. By the time I got there, she'd already sent the books to Winter Break."

"But how did Olivia know about Bitty?" I asked. "She's not a book dealer, too, is she?"

He grunted. "No, Olivia doesn't know beans about rare books. She never wanted to learn anything about my business. She knew about Bitty because I'd told her about this place."

"That's very interesting," Amos said harshly. "But if she didn't care about what you did, why did you mention Bitty's bookstore to her?"

Noel smiled sadly. "Because I told her once that if I could do anything I wanted to do, I'd sell my lucrative business and open a bookstore just like this."

"But you told me that Bitty was running this place all wrong," I said.

"No, I told you that the way she ran it wasn't practical. I never said it was wrong." He gazed around the store, a faraway look in his eyes. "This is a magical place. There aren't many bookstores like this left, especially in small towns. What I wouldn't give to leave the rat race behind. . . ."

"Ivy said you made an offer for only the inventory, not the whole store," Amos said. "If you think this is such a great place, why didn't you offer to buy everything?"

Noel exhaled forcefully. "Because, old chap, I can't afford to move here and run a small bookstore. I could show Sam how to do it, but I have too many obligations to do it myself."

"Ivy," Amos said.

"Huh?" Noel stared at him in confusion.

"Ivy. Her name is Ivy. Quit calling her Sam."

I started to interrupt, but he glowered at me. I decided that in this case, discretion was the better part of valor. It seemed Noel also determined it was wise to mollify the man with the gun.

"Okay, sorry. Ivy, I mean."

"None of this explains why you came here, Noel," I said. "So your sister sold the books to my aunt. Why do you care? I've looked them over. There are some books there that are worth a few hundred dollars, but I couldn't find anything valuable enough for you to come all the way to Winter Break."

Noel straightened up in his chair. "You're absolutely right about that," he said. "But the book I'm looking for isn't in the boxes."

"What do you mean?" Amos asked.

"It's missing. There should be twenty-seven books altogether. There are only twenty-six."

"Noel, tell me about the missing book," I said. "What is it?"

"It's a first edition of Mark Twain's *The Prince and the Pauper*."

"How much is it worth?"

"Depending on the condition it's in, probably around fifteen hundred dollars," Noel said quietly. "I can't be more precise because I haven't actually seen it."

"How much did your sister sell it for?" Amos asked.

"Five hundred dollars for the lot."

"Noel," I said, "I still don't understand. Were you really that upset about the deal? Did you come all the way to Winter Break because you felt cheated out of a thousand dollars?"

He shook his head slowly. "Olivia found that book right before she sent the rest to your aunt. She was trying to get rid of all of Grams's old books, so she tossed it in one of the boxes. The fact that the book was carefully wrapped up and kept in a trunk didn't get her attention. But it should have. If she'd ever tried to learn anything about my business, she would have realized that this book was different. She would have looked more carefully and discovered that there was something very special inside."

"I'm confused," I said. "You're looking for something *inside* the book?"

"Yes," Noel responded. He clasped his hands together and shook his head. "You see, Grams has Alzheimer's. She's had symptoms for many years now, but for the most part, it expressed itself as momentary lapses of memory. For as long as I can remember, she'd tell Olivia and me about some kind of 'treasure' she had, something she was saving for us. She never told us what it was. Then suddenly her disease took over. It crept up slowly and then pounced like some kind of wild animal, pushing Grams so far away from us, we couldn't find her anymore." He wiped his eyes with the back of his hand and cleared his throat.

"She seemed to lock on to 'her treasure,' asking us to find it for her," he continued, his voice shaky with emotion. "She tried to tell us about a book with a letter in it written to my sister." He shook his head. "It didn't make any sense. We brought her every book we could find, but she'd push them away. Then, after awhile, Grams quit mentioning it altogether. To be honest, my sister and I chalked it up to her imagination—and the disease that had so viciously attacked her."

"You never found anything that your grandmother might have seen as a valuable possession? Something she would want to pass down to you?" Amos asked.

"No. Of course, she had some antiques and a few rather valuable books, but nothing that explained her frantic attempts to get us to look for this so-called treasure."

"And then something changed?" I asked.

Noel nodded and straightened up. "Yes," he said with an air of resignation. "Something definitely changed. As I said, I went home as soon as I cleared my calendar. That's when I found out that Olivia had sent all of Grams's old books to your aunt." He shrugged. "I wasn't happy about it, but I wasn't that upset, either. I knew the books Grams had. Anyway, I thought I did, and although I think I could have gotten a little more for them, it wasn't enough to worry about.

"Olivia and I made up, and I started pitching in to help her get the house cleaned out while we made arrangements to put Grams into a very nice facility that specializes in Alzheimer's patients.

"Then one day, an old friend of hers stopped by. He'd known our grandmother and grandfather for many years. He even attended their wedding. Over coffee and doughnuts, he asked me what had happened to Grams's valuable book. Of course, I had no clue what he meant, and I told him so."

"Is there an end to this story at some point?" Amos asked impatiently.

I shushed him. "Go on, Noel. Just ignore him."

Noel took a deep breath, his eyes wandering toward Amos's gun. "That's okay," he said with a weak smile.

Amos glared at the both of us.

"Grams's friend told us that my grandfather had come across a first edition of *The Prince and the Pauper* that had originally belonged to Samuel Clemens. . .Mark Twain. Inside was a letter he wrote to his wife, telling her about his idea for a new novel." Noel's expression became wistful, and his voice softened as he became consumed with his story. "It was a story about a character he introduced in *The Adventures of Tom Sawyer*. One of Tom's friends. . ."

"Huckleberry Finn?" I asked breathlessly. "Are you saying that there was an actual letter from Mark Twain outlining his ideas for Huckleberry Finn?"

Noel stared at me for a few moments as if he didn't know who I was. Finally, he nodded. "Yes. And to top it off, it was written to his wife—"

"Olivia," I said. "His wife's name was Olivia."

"That explains why your grandmother kept connecting the letter to your sister," Amos said.

"Yes. If only I'd made the connection sooner."

"How much is it worth?" I asked. "I've seen old Twain letters in antique stores. I don't remember them selling for huge amounts of money. I believe he was quite a prolific letter writer."

Noel smiled. I think he forgot about Amos for a moment. His eyes sparkled with excitement. "Yes, that's true," he said. "The worth comes from who he wrote the letter to and the subject of the letter. This letter, if it really contains Twain's outline for *Huckleberry Finn*, would be a very valuable find.

Another letter that expressed Twain's disgust with slavery recently sold for sixty thousand dollars."

"Sixty thousand dollars?" Amos said. "That's incredible."

"Yes. In fact, this letter could go as high as one hundred thousand dollars to a Twain collector."

Before I could say anything, Amos interrupted. "Sounds like enough money to encourage someone to commit murder." He stepped over and put his hand on Noel's shoulder. "I think we have our killer, Ivy."

Noel's eyes widened. "Now just a minute—"

"But Noel wasn't in town when Bitty died," I said, frowning at Amos. "Besides, why would he kill her? Why wouldn't he just break in and steal the book?"

"Because your aunt found out about the letter," Amos snapped. "She knew how much it was worth and wouldn't give it up."

I stood up and faced Amos. "First of all, if my aunt had found a valuable letter that someone had accidentally sent her, she would return it. Bitty was unbelievably honest. And second of all—"

"You're right," he said bluntly, interrupting me, "but what if our friend Noel didn't know that? Maybe he didn't stop to ask questions."

"And second of all," I continued, "he wasn't in town, Amos. There's no way he could have killed Bitty from Denver."

Amos glared at Noel, who was keeping his eyes on Amos's right hand. I was afraid that if Amos moved toward his gun, Noel would soil one of Aunt Bitty's prized chairs. "And how do you know he didn't sneak out here, kill her, and then come back like he'd never been here before?"

Before I could respond, Noel timidly raised his hand. "If you two will give me a chance," he said, "I can prove to you that I was nowhere near Winter Break the day Bitty died."

"And how do you intend to do that?" Amos growled.

"Actually, I don't think it will be at all difficult," Noel said. "You said Bitty died on Wednesday morning, correct? You see, I was being interviewed on live Denver television a little after ten thirty that day. KACL broadcasts a show called *Bookshop*, and I was the featured guest. It is physically impossible for me to be in two places at one time. It's a six-hour drive from Denver to Winter Break."

"Okay, okay," Amos said. "I get it. You couldn't have done it." He pointed a finger at Noel. "I'm going to check out your story. All I have to do is call the station."

Noel leaned back in his chair, much more relaxed than he'd been a short while ago. "Go right ahead, Deputy. You'll find I'm telling the truth."

I breathed a sigh of relief. I'd never believed that Noel was capable of murder. However, Amos looked rather disappointed. "Well," I said to my placated friend, "we know Noel couldn't have done it, and we also know something else very important."

Amos nodded. "We know why she was killed," he said. "Someone else found that book with the letter inside. Whoever it was knew how valuable it was and murdered Bitty for it."

"That's not all," I said. "We know that number eight on my aunt's list probably referred to Olivia. The murderer took the mailing labels, saw Olivia's name, and obviously suspected that Bitty was going to call *O*, the person who sent the books. Whoever did it was afraid that the missing volume would be discovered and that a search for the book would somehow lead to him. I think Bitty planned to call Olivia because there were more books in the boxes than there were supposed to be. She never saw the letter Olivia sent explaining the last-minute additions."

"That makes sense," Amos said. "Maybe that's the reason the list was taken."

I nodded. "Looks like it. Now we have to figure out who would have realized the value of a letter from Mark Twain."

He grunted. "We'd do better to figure out who *didn't* know. Anyone with half a brain would know it was worth something. I mean, we may be a little isolated in Winter Break, but we're not brain-dead."

"Yes, but not everyone in town was in the bookstore Wednesday morning. As far as we know, only three people were here," I said.

"What if someone came in the back way?" Amos asked, sighing. "Anyone could have come and gone undetected."

I went over to the door and checked the lock. The dead bolt wasn't turned, but the doorknob was locked. It would take a key to open it. Bitty used this door only during the summer when she tended her garden. In the winter, it was locked up and forgotten. There was no reason to go out that way. The trash cans were kept on the north side of the building and were easily accessible from the front entrance. Isaac's apartment was on the south side of the bookstore, and he had his own private entrance facing the street.

"Amos," I said, "did you check this door after you found Bitty?"

"As a matter of fact, I did," he said. "It was unlocked."

"And you didn't find that suspicious?" I asked. "I thought you knew everything about my aunt. Why didn't you know that she kept this door sealed tight during the winter?"

"Ivy," he said quietly, "your aunt has been buying large lots of firewood for the last couple of years. There was too much to keep in the inside log rack. She had a large outside cord rack installed next to the back door."

"I didn't know that. Sorry," I said. "I guess you really did know Bitty better than I did." I was ashamed to realize that I was a little jealous of how close Amos had been to Bitty.

"Ivy, it wasn't that I knew her *better* than you. I didn't. No one was closer to her than you were. She just happened to tell me that she was becoming more sensitive to cold and wanted to keep stocked up with firewood. It's no big deal."

I pulled the door open. Sure enough, there was a large rack that contained several cords of wood. And there was something else. Something I'd forgotten. I closed the door slowly. "Amos, there are two doors that open up into the backyard," I said. "Bitty has one and Isaac has the other. That means that Isaac could easily have come in through the back door."

He shook his head. "That doesn't make sense. Isaac was seen by almost everyone on Wednesday. He was at the post office and the store. He went to Ruby's to pick up food. Why would he sneak in the back door when everyone already knew he'd been here?"

"What about the time lapse, Amos? The twenty minutes it took him to notify you? Maybe he snuck in through the back and—"

"Excuse me," Noel interrupted. "I know you two are busy being Nancy Drew and one of the Hardy Boys, but I wonder if we shouldn't check to see if my grandmother's book is somewhere else inside the bookstore. I looked through the boxes, but I've never had time to check out the shelves."

Amos raised an eyebrow. "That sounds logical. I don't think we're going to find it, but we might as well make certain."

An hour later, we finished checking the last row of books. We'd found two copies of *The Prince and the Pauper*. One was a first edition, in pretty good shape, but there wasn't anything written inside to confirm it had belonged to Noel's grandmother. We weren't really surprised when we opened the book and found there was no letter tucked inside. The other copy wasn't a first edition. It was a hardcover reprint from the sixties, not worth much to anyone except to readers like me. I remembered sitting on the front steps of the bookstore on a mild summer day, lost in the story of Tom Canty and Prince Edward.

Looking high and low through Aunt Bitty's books had forced us to use the rolling ladder. It was difficult for me to step up onto it the first time, knowing that Bitty's last moment of life occurred there, but it was strong and secure, and after a couple of times, my nervousness evaporated.

"Well, this was a waste of time," Amos said, standing up and dusting off his pants after perusing the final row of books.

"I'm sorry," Noel said. He held up the first edition we'd found. "This could be my grandmother's book, but I can't prove it. Since I never saw it, I can't identify it. Bitty could have easily had her own copy. I was hoping for a bookplate or a signature so I could identify it as Grams's."

"Maybe there is a way to tell," I said. "I'll go through her inventory books and check to see if there's an entry that refers to this book. It might take awhile. I have no idea when it came in."

"I wonder if I might be allowed to miss out on chapter two of your escapade," Noel said in a tired voice. "This has been a very draining day, and I'd like to crawl back into my feather bed at Sarah's for a late-afternoon nap."

"Okay," Amos said. "I'll take you to your car; then I'll come back. There's something else I want to talk to you about, Ivy."

Noel pushed himself up from the floor where he sat cross-legged. "I'll return tomorrow so we can talk about the books," he said. "At least all this searching has given me a pretty good idea of what's here." He came over to where I stood and took my hand in his. "I can't stay here more than three or four more days, Sam. . .er, Ivy. Olivia still needs my help."

I smiled at him. "I understand, Noel. We'll wrap everything up tomorrow, I promise. Why don't you come over after lunch—say around one?"

I walked Noel and Amos to the front of the store. Noel pulled on his coat then paused with his gloved hand on the doorknob. "There is one thing you should both consider as far as your thief and probable murderer. There is no easy way to sell this letter. It will be considered a very important find. By that I mean you can't just post it on eBay. Your killer must have some kind of plan to dispose of it. He's certainly not going to be able to get rid of it in Winter Break. In fact, he won't even be able to sell it in Kansas. He'll have to contact someone in a big city where something like this could be handled." He shook his head. "Even then it will be almost impossible to keep it quiet. If anyone claims to have 'found' it, collectors and appraisers will still want to find out where it came from."

"What if the seller can't give them what they want?" Amos asked. "Will that make the letter any less valuable?"

"Not really," Noel said. "The only really important thing value-wise will be its authenticity. If it was really written by Twain, that's all that's needed. However, a professional dealer will want to know its history so he doesn't end up with stolen property on his hands."

"So whoever has it will either have to bide his time or get out of Kansas." I shook my head and looked at Amos. "I hope we can catch this person without waiting around for him to try to skip town. Who knows how long that might take? I have to get back to school."

"You see if you can find that book listed in the inventory," Amos said, frowning at me. "I'll be back in a little while. After I drop Noel off at his car, I've got to run over to Maybelle Flattery's farm. She thinks Bubba Campbell's dog is eating her chickens. I promised I'd go by and talk to Bubba today. It shouldn't take long."

Noel paused again before walking out the door. "So there is actually someone living here whose name is Bubba?" he asked with a smirk.

Keeping a straight face, I replied, "Well, that's Bubba Campbell. There's also Bubba Johnson, Bubba Baumgartner, and way out on the north edge of town, there's Bubba Weber, who owns a honeybee farm."

My revelation wiped the smile right off his face.

Amos grinned and winked at me. "Come on, city boy," he said to the disconcerted bookseller, "let's get you back to Sarah's."

I watched as Noel walked down the steps to Amos's patrol car, shaking his head. I closed the door behind them and locked it. After they drove away, I headed over to the desk to see if I could find any record of the Twain book.

I'd just unlocked the desk drawer and pulled out Bitty's most recent inventory book, when I heard a noise from somewhere near the sitting room. I'd barely gotten to my feet when in walked my number one suspect in Bitty's murder.

Isaac Holsapple stood at the entrance to the bookstore.

And he was holding a knife.

13

Okay, so in the right light a cake server kind of looks like a big knife. After being reassured more than once by an extremely mortified bookstore clerk that he had no intention of stabbing me—or serving me cake—I calmed down long enough to ask him why he'd snuck into the bookstore through the back door.

"I didn't sneak in, Miss Ivy," he said in his singsong, almost feminine-sounding voice. "I used that door all the time when Miss Bitty was. . .was alive." He cast his wide, dark, chocolate-colored eyes toward his feet. "I should have knocked, I'll grant you, but I just didn't think about it. Please accept my apologies."

"What do you want, Isaac?" I was wishing at that moment that Amos hadn't left. I didn't trust Isaac Holsapple, although I wasn't really afraid of him, either. He stood at only about five feet tall, so I had a good four inches on him. He was old and skinny and reminded me of an aging troll. I figured I could take him if it came to that. However, if he'd killed Bitty, he might have more going for him than met the eye.

He inched his way a little farther into the room. I had half a mind to tell him to stop where he was and drop his cake server, but I couldn't figure out how to say it without sounding like a really bad episode of some cop show. Not that I would know anything about that, of course.

"I. . .I wanted to return this," he said. "Miss Bitty lent it to me for the church dinner. I made a German chocolate cake and she gave it to me to use. It. . .it's yours now, of course."

Isaac's eyes kept darting around the room, almost as if he were afraid something was getting ready to jump out and attack him. He seemed so timid, so inconsequential, that in the light of day, the idea that he might be a murderer seemed rather ludicrous. But looks can be deceiving. He stopped a few feet from the desk and held out the silver server in his trembling hand.

"Just lay it down there on top of the shelf," I said, not wanting to get any closer to him than necessary.

He glanced at the small bookshelf next to him that held a display of children's books. He looked so hesitant at setting something where it didn't belong, it was almost funny. Bitty had been an aficionado of "a place for everything and everything in its place." He was probably hearing her voice in his head. With much effort, he finally complied with my request.

"Well. . .thank you, Miss Ivy," he squeaked. He started to turn around to leave, but then he hesitated. He swung back around and fastened his huge eyes on me. "I. . .I want you to know how sorry I am about Miss Bitty's passing."

As I watched him, I realized that one of the reasons his eyes seemed so large was the strength of the lenses he wore in his round, tortoiseshell glasses. They not only magnified his eyes; they amplified his sadness. It was obvious he'd been crying. But had he shed tears because he missed Bitty or over regret for what he'd done?

"Thank you. I understand that you are the one who found her."

"Yes," he said. "I'd just come back from the restaurant. She. . .she was lying right over there." He pointed to the spot where Amos said he'd found my aunt.

"Isaac, I have to wonder why you haven't come to see me before today. I've been here since Friday night."

He retreated a couple of steps. "I didn't want to bother you, Miss Ivy. We don't really know each other very well, and to be honest, I'm a rather shy person. I would have said something to you at the service, but there were so many people around you."

I stood up and walked in front of the desk. "I understand," I said, leaning against the edge, "but what I really don't get is why someone would want to kill my aunt Bitty. Do you?"

I'm not sure just what kind of reaction I was looking for. Guilt, perhaps— or fear. But what I saw in Isaac's face wasn't either one. It was more like relief.

"No. No, I don't know who would want Miss Bitty dead," he replied. "She was a wonderful woman. Everyone loved her."

"I must say that you don't seem surprised by my question. Do you suspect that her death was something more than just an accident?"

He clasped his hands in front of him and stared at his locked fingers while he considered my question. "Miss Ivy," he said finally, his voice soft but firm, "I am convinced of it."

"You were the one who wrote that note on the envelope I left lying on the desk, weren't you, Isaac?" Why hadn't I seen it before? Isaac had keys to the bookstore. He was one of the few people who could have come in, even if I had locked the door that day. I'd been so busy suspecting him as the killer that I hadn't realized he was the obvious choice as the note writer.

He nodded with so much gusto, his long, stringy hair bounced around like frantic little worms trying to jump off his head.

"Were you in the funeral home Sunday night?"

"Yes," he said, lowering his eyes. "I've been trying to keep an eye on you. To protect you. Sunday night I followed you to the mortuary. It wasn't hard to get in. Billy Mumfree cleans the place on the weekends, but he never remembers to lock the back door. Unfortunately, I accidentally knocked some metal trays to the floor in the back room. Instead of keeping you safe, I frightened you. It's my fault you ran into the door and knocked yourself out." He raised his head a little. "I want you to know that I checked to see if you were badly hurt. I was going to get help when Deputy Parker showed up. I only left because I knew he would give you the assistance you needed. I'm very sorry about your injury."

I wasn't certain I believed him, but at least his story explained why I'd had the uncomfortable feeling of being watched ever since I'd arrived in Winter Break. It also made it clear why the person stalking me inside Buskin's Funeral Home had left me lying on the floor instead of completing his attack.

"Okay," I said. "Now can you tell me why you believe someone killed my aunt?"

"I would be happy to," he said, "but perhaps we could sit down? My legs aren't as strong as they used to be. Sometimes they hurt me, especially when it's cold."

"All right." I followed him to the sitting room. He walked with a noticeable limp, and I wondered how old he actually was now. I'd never really thought much about Isaac as a person. He was more like a fixture in the bookstore. Like a clock or a lamp. Of course, that wasn't true. He was a human being, someone I'd never taken the time to get to know.

He gingerly lowered himself into the chair in front of the fireplace. I sat down in Bitty's rocking chair and waited for his explanation.

He cleared his throat a couple of times. "Miss Ivy," he said, "your aunt was quite adept on that ladder. If there was no other reason to think that something suspicious took place Wednesday morning, that fact alone should have caused questions."

"I agree," I said. "That was the first thing that made me wonder about her so-called accident."

"Then there were the footprints."

"Footprints? What footprints?"

"In the snow," he said slowly. "Usually, I am the only one who uses the back door, except when the weather is nice. I came in that morning after a fresh snowfall. But when I left for my apartment Wednesday, after Miss Bitty had been. . .removed, there were two sets of footprints."

"So whoever killed her left by the back way," I said, more to myself than to him. "When you say two sets of prints, Isaac, do you mean as if they had come and gone by the back door?"

"No," he said emphatically, "they used the backyard only once, when they left the bookstore. The footsteps only led away from the back door."

"Which means they came in the front door." I wasn't certain how helpful this information was, but it did show that whoever entered the bookstore that morning probably hadn't planned to kill Bitty. Something happened. Something that made this person feel the need to dispose of her. It also meant that someone might have seen the killer. The only people Alma mentioned were Dewey and Lucy Barber. I was suspicious of both of them. Alma's story about Dewey returning Wednesday morning, looking upset, concerned me. And Dr. Barber's stonewalling and defensive attitude certainly made her seem suspicious. Of course, it might not be either one. Alma had been away from her window for quite a while, helping April Tooley.

"There is something else," Isaac said, interrupting my thoughts. There was a note of triumph in his voice. "Something that no one else knows."

I raised my eyebrows as a sign to continue.

"Miss Bitty wasn't dead when I found her."

I almost jumped out of my rocking chair. "What? Dr. Barber told me she'd probably never regained consciousness."

He shook his head. "She was barely conscious when I found her. She only lived long enough to whisper two words to me."

"What did she say, Isaac?" I could hear the tremor in my voice. Aunt Bitty's last words. For some odd reason, I wanted to stop him from telling me. It made her final moments seem more real. Believing that she'd died instantly and hadn't known that someone she'd trusted had betrayed her had afforded me a measure of comfort. Now that was gone.

Isaac rubbed his hands up and down his skeletal legs. "I wonder if we could start the fire?"

"Yes, in a minute, but first I want to hear what my aunt said to you."

His owl eyes misted over. "She said. . .'I forgive.' That's all she said, Miss Ivy. And then she was gone." A tear rolled down his wrinkled face.

The reality of Bitty's state of mind in the closing seconds of her life overwhelmed me. This was the death of a true Christian woman. Her last thoughts were of forgiveness. The revelation was almost more than I could bear.

"Why didn't you tell me this before now?" I asked when I could get the words out.

He shook his head. "I wanted to, but I was afraid you'd tell the wrong person. I didn't want to see Miss Bitty's killer leave town before you had a chance to catch him."

"But you wrote me a note, Isaac. What's the difference?"

"I believed that revealing my suspicions to you in this way would give you time to think it over and come to the correct conclusion. I counted on the fact that you would consider this to be a clue, as in the Nancy Drew books you used to read so much, and not just the crazy rantings of your aunt's rather odd book clerk." His slight smile told me that he was fully aware of how I saw him.

"I'm sorry, Isaac. I wish you would have trusted me enough to come to me immediately."

His smile grew and reached his mournful eyes. Funny how he didn't look quite so peculiar to me anymore. Actually, there was quite a bit of character in his face. I'd never noticed it before.

"That's okay, Miss Ivy. Now we have a long time to get to know each other."

I got a sick feeling in the pit of my stomach as I realized that Isaac thought I was going to stay in Winter Break and run the bookstore. This place provided him with more than a job; it was his life. What would he do when I left?

"Miss Ivy, if we're going to be working together, there's something else I think you should know. It. . .it's about me. Your aunt kept it a secret, and now I'm asking you to do the same."

My already-uncomfortable insides did another cartwheel. In my experience, the words *There is something I think you should know* really meant *I'm going to tell you something you'll wish I hadn't*. What was next? *I killed my mother and buried her in the backyard? My real name is D. B. Cooper? I like to dress up in a clown's costume and chase squirrels?* Then he said the last thing on earth I ever would have expected.

"Forty-five years ago, I caused an accident. That accident took the life of Robert Simmons, your great-aunt's fiancé."

There is a popular phrase that describes a condition of surprise that causes one's mouth to drop open. I discovered that it isn't just an expression. My jaw seemed to lower and hang at the end of my face all by itself. I was literally struck speechless.

Isaac removed his glasses and took a handkerchief from his vest pocket. He wiped his eyes. "I was drunk as a skunk the night it happened. I'd had a fight with my wife, so I went to the bar. I drank until I could barely stand up. Then I got behind the wheel." His voice got softer and more somber. "Back then, driving under the influence wasn't talked about like it is now. Still, I should have known better." He wiped his face again. "I never even saw Robert's car. I ran right into him. I wasn't really hurt—just a few cuts and bruises—but Robert was thrown from his vehicle and broke his neck. He died right there on the spot." Isaac cleared his throat, wiped off his glasses, and placed them back on his face. "As I said, in those days, drunk driving wasn't the bane of the road that it is today. I got off scot-free as far as the law was concerned. Not even a ticket. It was declared an accident. But I knew what I'd done—I'd cost that young man his life." Isaac shrugged and rubbed his thin legs again. "I lost my wife, my son, and myself that night. The guilt over what I'd done drove me to drink even more, until there was almost nothing left of me. I don't believe I would have lasted much longer, but your aunt heard about my condition and she came to me." He gazed at me with a look of something close to fondness, and I wondered if he was remembering Bitty when she was younger. I'd seen pictures of her around the time she opened the bookstore. She and I could have been twins. "She forgave me, Miss Ivy. She gave me a reason to believe there was hope for me, even giving me a job in her new bookstore. Little by little, I began to find my way back to life. I served her for over forty years, and every single moment was a privilege. She taught me that God loved me, no matter what mistakes I'd made, and that He was willing to give me another chance." His mouth quivered. "I owe her everything."

I was flabbergasted by Isaac's story. Forgiveness. Aunt Bitty had excelled in it, even forgiving the person who killed her. I suddenly felt very small and shallow. Not knowing exactly what to say, I got up to put some logs in the fireplace grate. I started the fire then reached for the canister that held the fireplace tools.

And I knew.

In that instant, everything came together. I knew who had killed Aunt Bitty.

14

I sent Isaac back to his apartment and began to check out several other things to see if they would support my conclusion. By the time I was thoroughly satisfied, Amos was back from Bubba Campbell's farm.

"Well, at least that case is solved," he said, stomping the snow off his boots and onto the floor mat. "Bubba's protests about his dog being unfairly blamed fell a little flat when old Barnabas came running up with a dead chicken in his mouth."

"Leave your coat on," I said before he unzipped his parka. "We've just solved another crime, and we're going to confront the perpetrator."

"What in blue blazes are you talking about?" he snorted. "What crime have we solved?"

As I pulled on my coat, I told him about my original suspicion, along with what I found during my research afterward. The skepticism in his face melted away as I explained.

"Well I'll be a monkey's uncle," he said when I finished. "It was there all the time. I should have picked up on it myself."

I grinned at him and opened the door. "It was elementary, my dear Watson."

"Okay, first of all, I'm not going to be Watson to your Sherlock," he grumbled, "and secondly, I thought you were an English major. You should know that Sherlock Holmes never even said that."

"Yes, I know that," I said, "but I'm surprised you do."

Amos tapped the top of my stocking-capped head with his finger. "We're not all a bunch of dumb yokels here, you know."

"I guess I do now, Deputy."

The joy of finally figuring out who had killed Bitty dissipated as we neared our destination. This wasn't just the end of a puzzle; we were getting ready to confront a killer, the person who had taken Bitty away from the people who loved her. I could feel anger bubbling inside me, but Bitty's last words kept playing over and over again in my mind, like the time the old McDonald's jingle got stuck there. *"You deserve a break today"* was replaced by *"I forgive, I forgive, I forgive. . . ."* Unfortunately, I wasn't sure I was capable of being as loving as Bitty had been in her final moments.

About fifteen minutes later, Amos and I were sitting next to a crackling fire, being served tea and cookies. I put my cup down and stared at my aunt's murderer, who smiled at me as sweetly as she could. "So, Lila," I said, "how did it feel to kill your best friend?"

The blood drained from the woman's face, and her teacup slipped from her fingers, hitting the side of the coffee table and smashing to pieces. "Wha–what? What are you talking about?" she stuttered. She turned to Amos. "Deputy Parker, is this some kind of a sick joke?"

"No, Lila," he said gruffly, "this is definitely not a joke. I certainly don't feel like laughing."

Lila tried to pick up the pieces of her ruined china, but her hands shook so hard, she kept dropping them. Finally, she gave up. "I have no idea what you're talking about," she said, her pale blue eyes wide with fright. "You must be insane."

"I don't think so, Lila. You almost got away with it, didn't you? You know what finally tripped you up?"

I didn't actually expect an answer, and I didn't get one. "It was Aunt Bitty herself. Her penchant for perfection: 'a place for everything and everything in its place.'"

"I'm sure I don't know what you mean," Lila said, her eyes shifting away from me and toward the door.

"I don't think I'd try it if I were you, Lila," I said. "I can guarantee you that Amos and I are faster than you. You'd never make it, and in the mood the deputy is in, I'm not sure what kind of force he would use to stop you."

That seemed to remove any thought of escape, but she wasn't admitting defeat yet. "There is no way in this world you can tie me to Bitty's death," she said. "Bitty fell. It was an accident."

"Actually, it wasn't that at all, and you know it. Would you like me to tell you exactly how it happened?"

Lila didn't answer. She still looked unconvinced, but I didn't expect her denial to last long. "Wednesday morning, you went to the bookstore to borrow my aunt's butter mold. You wanted to use it for the church dinner that night."

"Your aunt gave me that butter mold," Lila sputtered, "because we were such close friends."

"No, Lila. I should have known that story wasn't true. Bitty had already told me that she wanted me to have that mold. She never would have changed her mind without talking to me about it. That would have been going back on her word, and that was something she never did.

"You came over to borrow the butter mold," I continued. "My aunt probably went upstairs to get it. While she was up there, she put on some water for tea and put the tea bags in the cups. While she was gone, you noticed a shipment of new books, and being curious, you looked through them. You found a first edition of *The Prince and the Pauper*. You opened it and looked inside, making an incredible discovery. There was a letter written by Mark Twain to his wife, Olivia. You knew it was valuable, and you were convinced that my aunt didn't know anything about it since she had just opened the box and hadn't had time to go through it. You probably slipped the book and the letter into your purse thinking that you would be able to claim the book as your own, without anyone being suspicious. In the meantime, you might have glanced around for a packing slip—anything that might give a clue to the fact that the book with the letter was inside the box.

"Although you couldn't find anything like that, you did find a list on my aunt's desk. Number eight on the list mentioned *O* and that there was a question about something *extra*. You knew from reading the mailing label on the outside of the box that the books had come from someone named Olivia. Obviously, my aunt intended to contact her about the shipment. You were afraid that if my aunt made that call, she would find out about the book. Even if the seller knew nothing about the letter, Bitty would know that someone had removed the book from the boxes. You'd never be able to explain how the book or the letter came into your possession without it pointing back to Bitty."

I paused for a moment. "That might have been the moment you decided to kill her. You needed to create a story that would be believed—a legitimate reason for you to have the book. I don't know when you put the book on the shelf, whether it was before or after you killed Bitty, but my guess is afterward. Just so you know, you put the book in the wrong place. My aunt never put books that were for sale with the books that were available for reading, yet I found two copies of *The Prince and the Pauper* on a shelf with regular books. The first edition didn't belong there."

Lila hadn't moved since I'd started talking, but she looked like a blow-up doll with a leak. With every new revelation, the wind went out of her a little more.

"After Bitty came downstairs, she either went up the ladder herself, or you sent her up for some reason. When she started down, you hit her on the side of the head with the fireplace tongs you'd removed from the canister."

Amos interrupted. "That's what Ivy meant about Bitty being the one who gave us the first clue," he said. "I'd complained about her lack of proper fireplace tongs. In fact, we were planning to buy some. Then, today, it hit Ivy. Bitty Flanagan would *never* be without the correct tool. Especially since she'd taken to using her fireplace so much. 'A place for everything and everything in its place.' Isaac confirmed for us today that he'd stirred the fire Wednesday morning and seen the tongs in the canister with the other tools." Amos stood up and walked over to Lila's tool rack. He reached behind the rack and held up a second set of tongs. They were brass, just like Bitty's set.

Lila ignored him and looked away with an air of resignation.

"You might have only knocked her out," I said, "but when she fell off the ladder and hit her head on the wheel cover, you were set. The original injury you caused was covered up by the massive wound that occurred because of her fall. You tried to position her in a way that made it look as if she'd gotten tangled up on one of the ladder rungs. Then you went looking for things that could point directly to you or to the missing book. You had to cover your tracks *and* end up with that letter in your possession."

"By then you'd realized you had no way of selling that letter," Amos said. "How would you say you found it? Would the letter tie you back to Bitty?"

"So you had an idea," I continued. "You removed the list from Bitty's pad so no one would know that you had been there or that Bitty had planned to contact Olivia. Then you took her keys and unlocked her desk drawer. You removed the page in the account book that mentioned the purchase from Olivia. You also knew about the list she'd made of things she wanted to leave her friends. You crossed off your name and added it again at the bottom. This time, you wrote in the first edition of *The Prince and the Pauper*. You put the book back on the shelf, knowing that someone would make sure you got it. That way, you could pretend to find the letter. You were fairly certain that even if I looked inside the book, I wouldn't check every page, so your claim of finding the letter wouldn't be challenged. Since you knew Bitty so well, you knew I would be the person in charge of her estate and that I probably wouldn't try to take that letter back. You were fairly confident you would be home free. The book was legally yours since my aunt had left it to you, and you could explain just how the book and the letter came into your possession. Since the original owner had sent Bitty the book, you assumed they didn't know anything about the letter. You hoped that any chance of connecting the book with that person was now gone."

Amos took the next part of the story. "You were lucky in some respects, Lila. You entered the bookstore while Alma was away from her window. Of course, after you killed Bitty, you couldn't take the chance that someone might see you, so you left by the back door. But you made some big mistakes. Isaac Holsapple saw your footprints in the snow. He knew someone had left the bookstore that morning by the back door. And you forgot that Bitty was making tea upstairs for the both of you."

"We were able to recreate a copy of the list Bitty made, Lila," I continued. "You were on it. Number four on the list was *BM for L—Don't forget!* Amos and I made a mistake when we read it. We thought the *L* was an *I*. Tracing over indentations from a missing piece of paper isn't an exact science. It loses something in the translation. Once I suspected you, I looked over the list again and realized that number four was a reminder that you would be picking up the butter mold to use for the church supper Wednesday night. That list was written Wednesday morning, Lila. That proves my aunt was expecting you. It also confirms that you *were* there because you have the butter mold. The only way you could have gotten it was to see my aunt on that very morning, sometime before she died."

Lila was staring at the floor. Finally, she said, "It all sounds very interesting, but can you prove a word of it?"

Amos gingerly carried the fireplace tongs in his gloved hand, being careful to stay away from the curved end. "If you're not convicted by all of the circumstantial evidence, Lila, I'm pretty sure this will be the final nail in your coffin. You may think you've removed all the evidence from it, but it's much harder to remove blood than you think. And there's no reason for you to have Bitty's tongs—unless you took them after you killed her."

"And of course, the letter is here somewhere, Lila," I said. "It will be found eventually."

"Yes, I suppose it will," Lila said. "I'll save you the trouble. It's in a box in my closet."

I was relieved to hear her confess, but at the same time, listening to her admit she'd killed Bitty filled me with intense anger.

"Lila, I have to ask you why you left the tongs lying out where they could be seen," Amos said. "Why didn't you dispose of them?"

Lila shook her head forlornly. "My goodness, Deputy, this is Winter Break. We have one trash hauler. That moron Maynard Sims thinks it's his business to check through everything I throw out. I can't tell you how many times he's come to my front door showing me something in my trash, asking if I really meant to throw it away." She sighed with exasperation. "I was afraid to throw out the tongs. Eventually, I decided to leave them near the fireplace since no one would think it odd." She stared at Amos with a look of disdain. "I'd been so clever at the bookstore, I thought I was safe. I hope this doesn't offend you, but you didn't seem sharp enough to figure out what I'd done." She swung her gaze at me. "But leave it to a relative of Bitty Flanagan's to refuse to let it go. If you'd just taken care of your aunt's business and left town, everything would have been all right."

It took every ounce of strength in my body not to jump off the couch and strangle her. Amos shot me a warning look.

"So what happens now?" Lila asked, smoothing her skirt. "I suppose you will arrest me, Deputy Parker."

"Yes, that's right," Amos said. "I'll take you to Hugoton and turn you over to them. There's a jail there. They'll take charge of you."

"I understand," she replied. "Ivy, I know this won't make any difference to you, but I want you to know that I didn't have any other choice. Bitty really was a good friend to me, but I'd run out of all the money I received from my husband's estate. I had no way to survive. Your aunt had plenty of money, you know. In fact, she had everything." She sighed and shook her head. "It really wasn't fair. I was tired of being the poor companion." She picked up a napkin from the tea tray and dabbed at her eyes. "You see, some people are simply not as fortunate as others. When I saw that letter, I knew I'd found my salvation. In my attempt to keep it, I panicked. I never took the time to think it out until it was over. The only thing on my mind was that if I wanted to make the letter mine, I had to get Bitty out of the picture. My decision was made in seconds. Bitty climbed up the ladder, and I grabbed a tool from her fireplace set. As she came down, I hit her, although as you suspected, it wasn't hard enough to kill her. If she hadn't fallen off and struck her head, she might have survived." She touched the napkin to her eyes again. "I'm sorry she had to die. I wish it could have been different."

Amos took a step toward her, his face crimson with anger. "You must be insane," he growled. "Other people aren't on this earth just to fulfill your selfish desires. Bitty Flanagan was a person. She had the right to live. It wasn't your choice to take that from her."

"Amos, stay where you are," I said. "Losing your temper now will only help Lila."

He stopped his advance, but he didn't look happy about it.

"Did you know Bitty was still alive when you left her there, Lila?" I asked.

She looked up, obviously startled. "No. I was certain she was dead."

"No. She was just unconscious. She spoke to Isaac when he found her. Would you like to know what she said?"

Lila's narrowed blue eyes sought mine. I looked away. "She said she forgave you."

"Yes, she would, wouldn't she?" There was no more life left in her voice, just resignation. She stood up slowly. "I guess we need to get going, Deputy. May I pack a few things first?"

Amos followed her into her bedroom while Lila got a suitcase and packed the items she thought she might need for a few days. I wasn't certain the jail in Hugoton would allow her to have them, but I didn't feel like saying anything about it and neither did Amos. Lila handed me the box with the letter in it as we were leaving.

Amos drove to the bookstore, pulling up in front and parking so I could get out. He came around to help me navigate over the eternally frozen street. But before I stepped out and accepted his arm, I turned around to face the woman who had killed my aunt. "Lila, it will take me awhile to get rid of the anger I have toward you. I know God will help me with that. But I have to say something to you, even though I don't want to. Even though it goes against everything I'm feeling right now."

Lila stared back at me without emotion.

"I forgive you, Lila," I whispered. "I forgive you because Bitty forgave you. I hope that someday you will be able to forgive yourself."

I got out of the car and took Amos's hand. He helped me up the steps and waited while I unlocked the door.

"Wait a minute," he said, grabbing my shoulders and turning me around to look at him. "That was a brave thing you did," he said. "You've given me the courage to tell you something I should have told you a long time ago."

His eyes misted, and he touched my face with his gloved hand. "When I left Winter Break to live with my father, it wasn't just because I wanted to be with him. It was also because I couldn't be around you anymore. You see, I loved you so much, but you were determined to get out of this town and start a life somewhere else. You didn't care for me the way I wanted you to, so I thought that going away would help me to forget you. It didn't." He smiled and shook his head. "I still love you, Ivy Towers. You're a part of me, and I believe you always will be. Now you're getting ready to make a choice. If you have any feelings for me at all, I hope you'll stay in Winter Break and see if something important develops. If you decide to leave, I'll try to understand. I truly want you to be happy, however it affects me." He let go of me and stepped back. "I wanted you to know how I felt before you made your final decision."

He walked away and got into his car without looking back. I stayed where I was and watched him drive away. Then I sat down on the steps of my aunt's bookstore while the sun began to set upon another frigid day in Winter Break. I stared down the road where he'd disappeared until I was so cold I could no longer feel my feet.

15

A mos didn't return until Tuesday evening. When he finally arrived, I was waiting for him.

"Hey there," he said as he came in the door. Although the sun was peeking through the clouds, another cold front had moved in, bringing wind gusts strong enough to rattle the windows. So instead of being in the single digits, we had plunged a few degrees below zero.

I waited while he struggled out of his heavy winter coat, gloves, hat, and scarf. "So is Lila safely tucked away?" I asked when he had finally unencumbered himself.

"Now there's an interesting question," he said, grinning. He came over to the desk and perched on the edge. "*Lila* is not safely tucked away. However, Rosemary Maxwell is locked up and will most probably stay that way for the rest of her sorry life."

"Rosemary Maxwell? What are you talking about?"

His lopsided smirk reminded me of Alice's Cheshire Cat.

"Remember I told you that someone who killed their spouse was supposed to be hiding out somewhere in Stevens County? Well, it seems that *Lila Hatcher* was a phony name cooked up to cover her tracks. She picked Winter Break because she didn't think anyone would ever find her here. Her real name is Rosemary Maxwell, and she's wanted in Minnesota for killing her husband and taking off with the inheritance. Police didn't suspect her until she disappeared; then they did some investigating and found out that her husband, Edwin, didn't die of a heart attack after all. They've been looking for her ever since she came here. They are quite willing to welcome her back. She's being extradited to Minnesota this week."

"That's amazing," I said. "But how did you find out who she really was?"

Amos shrugged. "The sheriff in Hugoton thought she looked familiar and found her picture on a bulletin from Minnesota. Although she looked a little different, she admitted she was Rosemary Maxwell." He grinned broadly. "And besides putting Rosemary in prison where she belongs, something else good came out of all this. Since I was 'instrumental' in apprehending their suspect, they're going to equip the office in Winter Break with all the newfangled devices they have available to them in Hugoton."

"And what newfangled devices are we talking about?"

His grin broke into a chuckle. "A computer and a fax machine. It seems that the sheriff realized that if I'd had a chance to see the bulletin for myself, I might have recognized Rosemary much earlier. So now the office in Winter Break is becoming high tech."

He spotted Bitty's list on the desk. "We never did get around to talking about this. I told you I'd figured out something else on this list."

"Oh, you did? And what is that?"

"Number six is. . ."

"Wind clock," I said quickly.

Amos chuckled. "So you got that one, too, huh?"

"That's not all," I said, smiling. "I solved the rest of the entries on the list, *and* I uncovered some new information you might find interesting."

A gust of winter wind shook the windows. "Let's go where it's warm," I said through chattering teeth.

"Okay, but first I have a gift for you."

He grabbed something wrapped in newspaper, lying next to the coatrack. When we were in the sitting room, he unwrapped the package and pulled out a pair of fireplace tongs. They matched the rest of the set perfectly.

"These weren't easy to find," he said as he slid them into the holder with the rest of the implements. "I had to look through three antique stores. Bitty had this set for a long while."

"Thank you, Amos," I said gratefully. "Now it won't be so obvious something is missing. It reminds me. . ."

"I know," he said gently. "I figured as much." He plopped down in the chair across from me. "Now tell me your news."

"Okay, but I have to warn you that I've been quite busy since you left. First of all, I know why Bitty canceled her wedding to Dewey. I also know why he was so upset that Wednesday morning."

"Wow, I'm impressed. Tell me."

"Shortly before Bitty and Dewey planned to set a wedding date, Dewey found out he was diabetic. Even though Lucy told him it was serious, he refused to make the changes she suggested. Aunt Bitty was upset with him and worried about his health. She canceled their plans until he promised to follow all of Lucy's instructions. Wednesday morning, he came flying over to the bookstore to tell her that he'd set an appointment with Lucy so he could get copies of his new diet and start taking his medication. He wasn't really upset. He was just determined to get a date set. Number ten on Bitty's list, the last thing she wrote, was *PT—Ap W?* Remember? I'm convinced it meant *Pastor Taylor—April Wedding?*"

"And how did you find this out?" Amos asked, his eyes wide with surprise.

"Easy. I asked." I grinned at him. "I decided it was time for honesty. Bitty's murder is solved. I was tired of suspecting everyone of something nefarious, so I made a few visits."

"Uh-oh. And who else did you interrogate?"

"I did not interrogate anyone. I *visited* them."

"Sorry, my mistake," Amos said with a laugh. "Okay, who else did you *visit*?"

"Lucy Barber for one," I answered. "We've buried the hatchet. I was right. She was keeping a secret about my aunt."

"A secret? What kind of a secret?" he asked, frowning.

I couldn't help but be a little tickled. His ego was probably a little bruised because he'd been kept out of the loop. I'd come to the conclusion that Amos was just about as nosy as I was.

"There are a lot of people in Winter Break who either don't have health insurance or don't have enough," I said. "Bitty was paying their bills, Amos. She made Lucy promise not to ever tell anyone what she was doing. That's why Lucy was over here so much, and that's why Bitty wrote *DRL—chk* on the list. She planned to give Dr. Lucy a check to cover medicine for several of the town's residents. Lucy wouldn't allow her to pay her fees when someone couldn't afford to, but she did let Bitty pay for medicines and treatments that she couldn't provide by herself." I shook my head. "Lucy wasn't upset with me at all. She was just worried about her patients. She did come to the bookstore Wednesday morning to pick up the check. When she didn't see my aunt, she left. I suspect that Bitty was lying on the floor where Lucy couldn't see her."

"I'm not surprised about Lucy's anxiety about her patients. I told you that she's a dedicated doctor."

"I know. I'm going to continue the work my aunt started. I've already written her one check, and I intend to give her more when she needs it."

Actually, I didn't tell him everything Lucy confessed to me. She had feelings for Amos, and even though they'd dated a few times, it hadn't taken her long to discover that he was in love with someone else. When I came to town, she figured out that I was the person he couldn't seem to forget. At first she was jealous of me, but eventually she faced the realization that she and Amos had no future. She apologized for her reaction to me, and we mended our broken fences.

"Is that everything, Sherlock?" Amos asked.

I shook my head. "No, not quite. The other day when we were searching the shelves for *The Prince and the Pauper*, I came across an old book about a company that used to make decorative lamps. They've been out of business for a long time. Something about the lamp on the cover made me remember something I'd seen."

"What are you talking about?"

"Elmer Buskin has an old lamp on his desk. I cleaned a little of the dust off of it the night I was there, and I'd planned to go back and finish the job."

"You're not making any sense, Ivy. What does this have to do with anything?"

"Keep your shirt on, smarty-pants," I said, grinning triumphantly. "I found the same lamp in the book. I borrowed Elmer's computer again and did an Internet search." I paused for dramatic effect. Amos took the bait.

"And. . ."

"And I found that the very same model was recently sold at an auction for forty-five thousand dollars."

Amos was speechless.

"So now Elmer will be able to fix up the funeral home and get on his feet."

"You're an amazing woman, Ivy Towers," Amos said finally. "I swear, I never know what you're going to come up with next."

I shook my head. "It was Great-Aunt Bitty who was amazing, Amos. In fact, I intend to try my best to be more like her. I believe people like Bitty can keep teaching us, even when they're gone, if we listen carefully to the legacy they left behind."

He nodded. "That sounds like an excellent idea. You aunt would be honored to know the impact she's still having in the lives of the people who love her." He leaned back in his chair and stared at the fireplace. "And did you meet with Noel about the store?" He was so quiet I had to strain to hear him. Any feeling of joviality blew out of the room just like the wind that had whipped up such a frenzy outside a few minutes before.

"Yes, I did," I said softly. "And he made me a very good offer."

"How much?" Amos was calm and controlled, but I could see his jaw working furiously.

"He offered me sixty thousand dollars for everything."

"And what did you say?"

"I told him that I couldn't accept. You see, Noel showed me something I hadn't seen before. He told us that running this bookstore was his dream job, but he couldn't afford to do it. I may be a little slow, but I finally figured out he was right. I have a chance to live out my dream job and to be near the man I love. How could I turn that down?"

Amos jumped to his feet and grabbed my hands, pulling me up next to him. The tears in his eyes matched my own.

"I've been praying that God would show me the place He had for me," I said. "I'd started thinking that I didn't belong anywhere. But all the time it was—"

"Standing right in front of you," he finished. His arms surrounded me, and I fell into his embrace.

"That was what Aunt Bitty meant in her letter," I whispered. "She knew all along where I was supposed to be."

I gazed over his shoulder at the bookstore that was now mine. "There's just one thing," I said.

"What's that?" Amos asked softly.

"How in the world am I going to explain this to my mother?"

Amos laughed. "I have no idea, but we'll figure it out together. We have the rest of our lives."

Right before I kissed him, I said, "Good. That's probably about how long it's going to take."

Alma Pettibone's Huckleberry Muffins

¾ cup butter
1 cup white sugar
1 egg
¾ cup milk
1 teaspoon vanilla extract
1¾ cups sifted all-purpose flour
2½ teaspoons baking powder
½ teaspoon salt
1 cup huckleberries
1 tablespoon all-purpose flour

Directions:

Preheat the oven to 400°F (200°C). Grease 15 muffin cups or line with muffin papers.

In a large bowl, cream together the butter and sugar until smooth. Mix in the egg, milk, and vanilla until well blended. Combine 1¾ cups flour, baking powder, and salt; stir into the batter until just moistened. Toss huckleberries with remaining flour to coat. Then fold them into the batter. Spoon batter into muffin cups, filling at least ⅔ full.

Bake for 15 minutes in the preheated oven, or until the tops spring back when lightly pressed.

Serve warm with butter or huckleberry jelly!

BYE BYE BERTIE

Dedication

To Juanita Dunlap, who introduced me to the Third Person of the Trinity—and changed my life forever. God bless you.

Acknowledgments

My thanks to Deputy Sheriff Robert P. (Pat) Taylor from Kingman County, Kansas. You brought Amos to life! Rick Brazill, Deputy Chief of Operations for Sedgwick County, Kansas. Thank you for responding to an odd e-mail from someone claiming to be an author. David Diamantes, a true "fire expert." Your help was invaluable. Ken Chau. I appreciate the help with Mandarin. I also want to thank you for the way you entertain my husband when you're both supposed to be working. But I won't tell. Susan Downs, the world's best editor and most patient human being. I'm blessed to know you. My agent, Janet Benrey. Thanks for hanging in there. Once again, I thank my family for their constant support and prayers. I love you!

1

I stepped outside the front door of Miss Bitty's Bygone Bookstore, a cup of steaming hot coffee in my hands. I could almost breathe in the approaching sunshine and joie de vivre of a fresh new season.

Spring comes slowly to Winter Break, Kansas. But when it finally arrives, the whole town blossoms. Doors closed tightly against frozen temperatures burst open much like the first fresh green blades of grass seeking warmth and sunshine. The townspeople put away their snow shovels in exchange for trowels and gardening forks. Flowering bulbs that spent the winter sleeping beneath the frozen earth are gently urged to life. Flora and fauna are welcomed with open arms, and life in the small town is colored with vibrant flowers and the sound of children's laughter.

"Hope you've got another cup of joe waiting for an old man who desperately needs his caffeine."

Dewey Tater, owner of Laban's Food-a-Rama, and the mayor of Winter Break, shuffled across the street toward me. He and my great-aunt Bitty had shared breakfast together every weekday morning for many years. Now that she was gone, Dewey and I continued the tradition. I looked forward to our time together. Dewey filled a spot in my life left vacant by my father and mother, who were serving as missionaries in China.

"There's plenty of coffee and some warm huckleberry muffins, fresh from the oven," I replied. I'd been working on a low-sugar/low-fat version of Dewey's much-loved muffins. Substituting applesauce and a little of Bubba Weber's honey for the sugar had proved tricky, but in the end, I'd finally found what I hoped was the right balance.

We followed exactly the same routine almost every morning. Dewey enjoyed hearing what was on the menu almost as much as I looked forward to telling him. For someone who'd never been a breakfast person, I was putting a lot of time and effort into creating special morning meals while making certain Dewey's food fit his new lifestyle. Diagnosed with diabetes, he had been forced to make a few changes in his food choices. In the scheme of things, however, this sacrifice seemed small compared to the loss of the woman he'd loved.

Dewey and my great-aunt Bitty had been what is commonly referred to as an *item*. If she hadn't been murdered inside her bookstore by someone she thought was her friend, Bitty and Dewey would have already been married.

"Huckleberry muffins, huh?" Dewey said with a grin. "You're getting mighty fancy for a girl who said she couldn't cook breakfast worth spit."

I held the door open, and the elderly man stepped inside. "Well, I can't allow you to start your day all cranky and out of sorts. Bitty wouldn't like it."

We headed to the sitting room located toward the back of the first floor, passing through the heart of the bookstore. Old books lined the walls from the floor to the ceiling. The smell of lemon oil, aged leather, and musty pages masked the aroma of my fresh-baked muffins until we reached the sitting room where I'd laid out breakfast on the big oak table used for town meetings and book club get-togethers. We could have eaten upstairs in my tiny apartment, but the kitchen was small and uncomfortable for two adults, although it was just right for one human being and a small calico cat. Miss Skiffins had come downstairs with me and was curled up on one of the overstuffed chairs scattered around the sitting room. Although the room contained a large fireplace that was used to warm the space throughout the winter, I'd left it alone the past few days. The mornings were still a bit chilly, but by midmorning the temperature was almost perfect. I'd started opening the windows so the mild springtime air and gentle breezes could sweep through the store, anointing it with the scent of wild honeysuckle. It grew in abundance in Winter Break, covering fences, lining sidewalks, and sometimes invading gardens where it wasn't wanted. But I loved it. To me, it was Winter Break's spring perfume.

My eyes gravitated to the decorative urn that graced the mantel above the fireplace. Designed to look like a book with a cross on the side, it contained my late great-aunt's ashes. Of course, I knew that Bitty wasn't really here. She was waiting for us in a place even better than our beloved bookstore. A place where no one would ever be able to separate us again. But for now, having the urn comforted me a little. It was a reminder of the wonderful woman who had made such a difference in my life.

I poured Dewey's coffee from the carafe I'd carried downstairs; then I added a little cream and sweetener, just the way he liked it. "I still say seven o'clock is too early to be eating breakfast. Maybe you and Bitty liked to get up with the chickens, but I'd like to stay under the covers just a little longer."

Dewey chuckled. "Why, Ivy Samantha Towers, we both have businesses to run. You know that as well as I do. Breakfast at seven. Open at nine. That's just the way it is."

"Maybe for you, but why am I opening the bookstore at nine every day? Hardly anyone actually comes here. Almost all my business is done through the mail."

Dewey set his cup down and stared at it thoughtfully. "School will be out soon and you'll have kids wandering in. You know, Bitty couldn't stand to turn anyone away. Especially a child who wanted to read a book. Maybe the best reason you have for opening the store every morning is because Bitty did it that way. That's good enough for me."

I grinned at him and took a sip of coffee. "It's good enough for me, too, Dewey, but someday you're going to have to realize that I'm not Bitty. What happens when I actually do something a little differently than she did?"

He sniffed and raised one eyebrow. "You're already doing that. Bitty didn't take much stock in the Internet. Thanks to that nosy Noel Spivey, you're getting ready to put Bitty's business out there for the entire world to see."

I set my cup down and frowned at him. "Dewey Tater. First of all, Noel Spivey isn't nosy. His expertise with rare books has been an invaluable help to me. He's taken time from his own business in Denver to answer all of my dumb questions. To be honest, I don't know what I would do without him. And secondly, much as I hate to say it, this is *my* business now. Just because Bitty didn't know anything about the Internet doesn't mean I can't use it. I'll be able to sell more books and stay in touch with other dealers. It will be a big boost for the store."

Dewey took a bite of his muffin and chewed quietly, ignoring me. Finally, through muffin crumbs, he mumbled, "I'm just pointing out that Bitty didn't need the Internet to sell books."

I sighed and poured a little more coffee into his cup. "I don't intend to change the bookstore. I love it the way it is. I only want to make it as successful as possible so it can continue." I touched his hand. "Bitty trusted me enough to leave me this place. Can't you trust me, too?"

Before he had a chance to answer, I heard the bell over the front door jingle. I could have leaned back in my chair to see who'd come in, but it wasn't necessary. I knew who it was since he came by every morning about the same time.

"Any leftovers for a starving deputy sheriff?"

"Got a couple of homemade huckleberry muffins," I called out. "But if you don't hurry, I can't promise anything."

Amos Parker strolled into the sitting room, a big grin on his face. "Huckleberry muffins, huh? Sounds good."

Dewey smiled at Amos. "This gal of yours is getting quite proficient in the kitchen. A positive sign, I'd say."

Amos kissed me on the top of the head and pulled up a chair. "I knew if I waited around long enough, her domestic side would finally surface."

"Ha-ha. Very funny." I put a cup in front of him and poured some coffee into it. "Thanks to Bitty, I'm a very good cook, I'll have you know. But in my parents' house, breakfast was just something we stuffed into our mouths before we left for work and school. Dry cereal, hard-boiled eggs, toast, breakfast bars. . .that's about it. I've certainly been adding to my repertoire, what with Dewey's insistence on a 'decent breakfast.'"

Dewey snorted. "Those first few meals weren't decent. And they assuredly weren't breakfast. They weren't even fit for Miss Skiffins. Lumpy oatmeal and dry toast." He shook his head sorrowfully. "Bubba Johnson feeds his pigs better slop than that."

"Thank you for the encouragement," I replied sarcastically. "You really know how to inspire people."

Dewey grinned and shoved another piece of muffin into his mouth. "It's a tough job, but someone's got to do it."

I put a muffin on the small plate I'd set aside for Amos and handed it to him. "What's on today's schedule?"

"So far not much," he answered. "I have to drive to Hugoton and check in with the sheriff. Seems someone is picking up cows grazing near the highway and taking off with them. Also got some civil papers to serve for bad checks. Hopefully it won't take all day to find our phony-check writers." Amos took a bite of his muffin and followed it with a swig of coffee. "How 'bout you?"

"Actually, Noel is taking our Mark Twain letter to the museum in Hannibal today. It's pretty exciting."

"Hope you know what you're doing," Amos said. "You two could have gotten a lot of money out of that letter."

"I'm not sure I should have gotten anything at all," I said. "It was Noel and Olivia's letter. Not mine."

"But Bitty bought it from Noel's sister," Dewey said, reaching for a second muffin. "By rights, it was yours."

"Bitty bought a book. She had no idea the letter was inside. She would have returned it to Olivia, and that's what I decided to do."

"I'll give Noel and his sister credit for one thing," Dewey said. "Giving the letter to the museum took a lot of class."

"Yes. Yes, it did. When he offered to split whatever he got at auction with me, and I told him I couldn't possibly take money made from Bitty's murder, he understood immediately."

"I think his grandmother's death sealed the deal," Amos said, taking a break from chewing. "What a wonderful tribute to her and to Bitty, donating the letter to the museum in their names."

"Bitty and I visited that museum when I was ten," I said. "It's a wonderful place. I'm so happy to be able to entrust Mr. Twain's letter to a place where it will be viewed and enjoyed by so many people."

"Why don't we plan to drive down there sometime this summer and see the display?" Amos asked.

"That's a wonderful idea," I said. "I would love to see the letter showcased next to a plaque with Bitty's name on it."

"I'm sure you two young people wouldn't want to take an old geezer with you," Dewey grumbled. "Maybe you could bring me back some pictures so I could pretend I got to see it in person."

I chuckled. "Like Amos and I thought we could get out of town without you. Of course you can go." I caught Amos's eye and winked at him so Dewey couldn't see me. "Maybe we could invite Alma to go with us, too. She would probably enjoy spending a few days with a certain 'old geezer.'"

Dewey banged his coffee cup against the tabletop, his faced locked in a scowl. "I have no intention whatsoever of spending time with Alma Pettibone. I'm not interested in soap operas, and I certainly am not looking for a replacement for Bitty, even if she thinks I am."

I felt a little sorry for Winter Break's postmistress. She was a lonely woman whose family consisted of actors and actresses on her daily television serials. Although several people had tried to get her to spend more time with actual human beings and less time obsessing about the fantasy world she surrounded herself with every day, she continued to pass the time handing out mail in the Winter Break Post Office with one eye glued to the small TV she kept nearby. Recently, however, she had begun to show some interest in Dewey, much to his chagrin. Every time I picked up my mail, she would ask me how he was getting along.

"Oh, don't get so upset," I said teasingly. "You've got to realize that handsome, debonair men are going to attract single ladies."

Amos sighed and picked up his coffee cup. "She's right, Dewey. It's a curse men like us have to bear."

Dewey smiled, even though I suspected he was still a little upset. I decided it was an excellent time to change the subject.

"Isn't it about time to open that store of yours, Mr. Tater?" I asked teasingly. "I wouldn't want you to be a minute late unlocking your door."

"You just take care of yourself, Miss Towers," he said, smiling. He looked at his watch. "Got some beautiful watermelons in from Marvin Hostettler. You should come over and pick one out."

"Maybe I'll do that after I get Isaac lined up. Of course, I may have to push through the throngs of excited customers, but I'll try to find a few minutes this afternoon."

Dewey pushed his chair away from the table and stood up, shaking his head. "Since you think you're so funny, maybe you should try out for *Hee Haw* or something."

Amos snickered. "*Hee Haw*? How long has it been since you watched television, Dewey?"

Dewey grinned and shrugged his broad shoulders. "It's probably been ten years since I watched anything on TV except for basketball and football. It got so silly and full of garbage, I gave it up. I read instead. I've been through almost every book in this place—except those on the top shelves. They're next on my list."

"Good for you," I said. I didn't mention the small color TV sitting upstairs on my dresser. I'd brought it back with me from Wichita when I'd gone there to get the rest of my meager possessions. The truth was, I was anxious for Dewey and Amos to get busy with their daily activities so I could plug in the TV and adjust the rabbit ears I'd had to buy. Even though we could only get four channels in Winter Break, I was excited about it.

"I haven't gotten to those top shelves yet," I said to Dewey. "I'll start pulling some of the books down in the next few days so we can both go through them. I'll let you know when I get that far. Inventory is taking a long time because I have to research each one. I know the books on the shelves that face east are all valuable and for sale, and the books that face south are for reading, but I can't be sure that some of them didn't get mixed up since Bitty died. That means that each and every book has to be investigated."

"Surely Isaac is helping you with that," Amos said.

I shrugged. "Isaac knows a little, but he admits that his interest is more in what's between the covers of a book than in its monetary value. I think Bitty tried to teach him as much as she could, but eventually she gave up. Unfortunately, his lack of knowledge about what makes one book more valuable than another isn't helping me much right now."

"Well, I'm going to respect *our* differences and go open my store *on time*," Dewey said.

I waved my hand at him. "I didn't say I wouldn't open at nine. I'll unlock my door the same second you do."

"See that you do," Dewey said with a smile, "unless you want to be haunted by your aunt. I expect opening the doors at nine fifteen would cause an uproar in heaven itself."

"I'll remember. I wouldn't want to be responsible for anything that catastrophic."

Dewey chuckled as he ambled through the store and out the front door.

"I'd better get on my way, too," Amos said. "I'll check in later this afternoon. I have no idea what time I'll get back. How about dinner at Ruby's tonight?"

Ruby's Redbird Café. The only restaurant in town, run by a woman who had turned raising her customers' cholesterol numbers into an art form.

I shook my head. "I can't tonight. I've got to set up a special e-mail account and start letting Bitty's book dealers know how to reach me."

"Okay, then how about tomorrow night?"

"I don't know. What's the special on Tuesday nights?"

Amos grinned. "Tuesday's blue plate special is chicken-fried steak and mashed potatoes."

"Oh no. I have no intention of attacking one of those plate-sized fried wonders. Besides its being double-fried in who-knows-what, Ruby covers everything on the plate in mounds of gravy. Too many meals there, and you'll have to start rolling me around town. If I want to keep my girlish figure, I really shouldn't go anywhere near Ruby's ever again."

Amos crossed his arms and stared at me as if I'd lost my mind. Ruby's was revered by the people in Winter Break. I was surprised they'd elected Dewey as their mayor instead of Ruby. It probably had to do with the infamous Redbird Burger controversy. A pound of fried beef with extra sharp New York cheddar cheese, onions, and jalapeños mixed in and more cheddar cheese on the top, it sported a secret ingredient that Ruby wouldn't share with anyone. There had been many attempts to wrestle it from her, but so far, all plans had failed.

"Ruby added grilled chicken to her menu just for you, Ivy," Amos said with a scowl. "She's bending over backward to make you happy."

"Are you kidding me? She grills chicken, all right. But after she cooks it on that greasy grill, she slaps melted cheese, green onions, and bacon on top. I hardly think that qualifies it as a healthy addition to her menu."

"Well, order a salad or some fruit, then. She's canned some wonderful peaches. You love peaches."

I sighed. "Yes, but the only way Ruby serves them is in a pie or on top of ice cream."

"Come on, Ivy. You're a wonderful cook, but I want to go out this week. I'm sure you can find something healthy at Ruby's."

"It would be easier to find the Lost Gambler's Gold than anything at Ruby's that still contains an ounce of nutrition."

"Well, people have been looking for that gold for many, many years. I guess that means you still have plenty of time to instruct Ruby on the finer points of wholesome eating."

I stood up and started stacking our dishes so I could carry them upstairs. "Do you remember the summer we dug up the peach grove looking for the Gambler's Gold?"

Amos chortled. "Yes, I do. The only thing I got out of it was blisters and a scolding from Harvey Bruenwalder. Filling up the holes was a lot of fun, too. Thanks for all the help."

I smiled innocently. "Harvey felt that young ladies shouldn't be forced to do manual labor. I think that was very sweet of him."

"Sure. Especially since the whole thing was your idea."

"I have no clue what you're talking about. I distinctly remember that you were the one who was excited about finding George Slocum's treasure."

Amos shook his head. "You have a very selective memory. The whole thing started off with. . .'I just have a feeling, Amos.'"

I still believed the story about Slocum burying his gold right before an Indian raid. Amos and I spent an entire summer looking for it, but we'd never uncovered the secret treasure. The tale of the Lost Gambler's Gold was mentioned in several memoirs written by Winter Break citizens in the late 1800s. Rumors put it somewhere near the peach orchards outside of town, but it had never been found.

"Speaking of peaches," Amos said, "are we on for Ruby's tomorrow?"

"You have a one-track mind, don't you?" I replied, sounding more irritated than I felt.

Amos pushed his chair away from the table. "I'll take that as a yes. I've got to get to Hugoton, but I'll stop by tonight when I get back." He kissed me and then strolled out the front door, looking a little too pleased with himself.

I didn't really mind going to Ruby's. I enjoyed the camaraderie in the restaurant. Besides church, Ruby's Redbird Café was the place everyone liked to gather to check up on each other. I was getting a little tired of my own cooking, so going out would be a welcome treat. My problem with Ruby's centered on Dewey's struggle with diabetes. I felt responsible for him. I was committed to giving him, and the other citizens of Winter Break, a few options that didn't include melted cheese, gravy, bacon, slabs of butter, and fried coverings to everything—including vegetables. Ruby fried okra, mushrooms, cauliflower, broccoli, peppers, and even corn. She'd never met a fruit or vegetable she couldn't throw into her deep-fat fryer.

I took the dishes upstairs, loaded the dishwasher, started it, and then went back downstairs to get ready for Isaac. He worked Mondays, Tuesdays, and Wednesdays from nine in the morning until two in the afternoon. Unfortunately, there wasn't much for him to do yet. When Bitty was alive, one of his duties was to catalog newly purchased books. I wasn't ready to buy much, so for now, Isaac was helping me to inventory and research all the books on the shelves. I compared our list with Bitty's, making certain everything matched up. Although many of the books had an estimated value written next to their entries in her inventory lists, quite a few didn't. This meant I had to research their values on the Internet. Since the only service available in Winter Break was dial-up, it was a time-consuming and exasperating task.

I gazed up at the books on the top shelves, wondering just what I would discover there. I was curious about them, but I was more committed to hooking up my TV. I had only a few minutes to get it done and then get back downstairs to unlock my front door. A few intrepid souls might actually wander in to borrow a book. Many times, visitors ended up in the sitting room, reading the afternoon away. Or, in some cases, catching a catnap with a book balanced precariously on their laps. But that was one of the reasons Great-Aunt Bitty opened her bookstore so many years ago. She loved literature and she wanted to share it with everyone in Winter Break.

I hurried upstairs and into my bedroom. It wasn't hard to get inside since my room didn't have a door. It was more like an alcove, really. The only real bedroom in the small apartment was Bitty's, and I had no intention of sleeping there. It was Bitty's room, and I wasn't ready to turn it into anything else. Anyway, I liked my room. It was where I'd always slept as a child whenever I visited Aunt Bitty during holidays and summers.

The TV was sitting on the dresser, and the rabbit ears were on the floor next to it. I pushed on the dresser so I could move it away from the wall and plug in the TV. When I did, I heard a crash. The gold jewelry box with the big, fake rubies had fallen off the dresser and landed on the floor. It was cheap and rather garish, but it was mine. Bitty had given it to me when I was little. Back then, I thought it was the most beautiful thing I'd ever seen. It had once graced my great-aunt's bedroom, but when she realized how much I loved it, she'd given it to me. Now, thanks to my negligence, it lay in pieces on the floor. I knelt down to pick it up. A folded piece of paper was sticking out from underneath the shattered jewelry tray that had been attached to the inside of the box. Because it was rather brittle and yellowed, I slowly unfolded it. A quick perusal revealed words, written in faded ink, that made a tickle of excitement run through my body.

It was a map. And in old cursive writing at the top were the words *My Treasure*. My conversation with Amos earlier that morning flashed through my mind. Was it possible? Could the story of the Lost Gambler's Gold be true?

Taking special care, I refolded the map and stuck it in my pocket. Then I cleaned up the pieces of the ruined jewelry box, tossed them in the trash, and finished hooking up the TV. When I was done, I ran downstairs and locked the map in the top drawer of my desk. I'd been enthralled by the story of the Lost Gambler ever since I was a little girl. In fact, the whole town of Winter Break was fascinated by it.

Could it be that the answer to the mystery had finally been uncovered? Was it possible that I would be the one to break the secret and find the treasure?

2

At nine o'clock on the dot, the back door of the store opened and Isaac Holsapple stepped inside. Since he lived in an apartment attached to the bookstore, it was easier for him to exit through his back door and come in through the sitting room.

Isaac was an odd little man, and I'd spent my childhood being distrustful of him. However, after Bitty died, I found out more about him. Many years ago, Isaac had caused an accident that killed Bitty's fiancé, Robert. Isaac's guilt had almost ruined his life. But Bitty had reached out to him with forgiveness and the offer of a job. Now Isaac worked for me, and we'd become good friends.

"Good morning, Miss Ivy!" Isaac sang out in his high-pitched voice. As usual, he was dressed to the nines, although his clothes reminded me more of something worn in the previous century. He always sported a long-sleeved white shirt with a wool vest. His ever-present pocket watch was in his vest pocket, the chain attached to one of his buttons. He looked like an English valet and acted a lot like the way I imagined one would act. Isaac was very prim and proper. Everything in his life seemed in perfect order except for his rather long, graying hair, which was always disheveled. I was curious as to why he paid so much attention to his clothing but didn't seem interested in taking care of his hair. However, it was one mystery I intended to leave unsolved. I wouldn't hurt his feelings for the world.

I returned his greeting, and soon we were knee-deep in books. Isaac would read the titles, check the inventory list for an entry, and then read the information to me so that I could set up computer records and research values and condition issues online. I tried as hard as I could to concentrate on our task and put my excitement about the map out of my mind, but it was almost impossible. I was certain Isaac noticed my distraction, but thankfully, he didn't mention it. Until I could find out more about it, I wanted to keep my discovery secret from everyone but Amos.

We plugged away all morning. By twelve o'clock, I was hungry and wondering what to make for lunch.

"Miss Ivy," Isaac said, interrupting my thoughts. "If you haven't already prepared something for our noon repast, I wonder if you would allow me to provide our meal." His smile told me he had something special in mind.

"That would be wonderful, Isaac," I said. "I'm afraid I don't have much on hand. I was thinking about going to Dewey's for some watermelon, but we could have that tomorrow if you'd rather."

He clapped his hands together and then scurried out the back door to his apartment. A few minutes later, he returned with a large covered bowl, two smaller bowls, and a couple of forks.

"I know how hard you're trying to bring some healthy foods into your diet," he said. "Although my own garden isn't quite ready to harvest, I have a friend who has a farm near Dodge City. His crops are weeks ahead of mine. I visited him Saturday and he sent me home with some wonderful things. I thought maybe you'd like to share a vegetable salad today."

I could feel my body leap for joy at the idea of fresh, farm-grown vegetables. "Oh, that sounds so good, Isaac. Thank you."

I went upstairs and fixed us each a glass of iced tea. I'd set a gallon-sized glass container of water with tea bags outside yesterday, letting it slowly brew in the warm afternoon sunshine. I preferred sun tea to the quickly prepared version made with boiling water. It took me awhile to get Isaac to try it, since he shunned all drinks with caffeine, but after I convinced him that I used only caffeine-free tea, he decided to give it a chance. Now he looked forward to a daily glass.

By the time I brought our drinks downstairs, Isaac had prepared our salads. Soon we were happily munching away on fresh lettuce, spinach, grape tomatoes, red onions, radishes, and crunchy cucumbers. Isaac's homemade balsamic dressing added just the right touch.

"Isaac," I said when I finally put my fork down, "what do you know about the Lost Gambler's Gold?"

He finished chewing and wiped his mouth with his napkin. "Honestly, Miss Ivy, I believe the story. I know it sounds fantastic, like something someone made up, but after studying various accounts, I'm convinced it's true."

"I'd love to hear what you've learned. Except for reading a few old memoirs, my only knowledge comes from the tall tales we kids used to tell each other during slumber parties or late-night excursions into the peach orchard. We weren't really going for historical accuracy."

Isaac leaned forward a little, seemingly prodded by my encouragement. "According to stories written by the early settlers of Winter Break, George Slocum was a gambler on his way back east where he was born and raised. Supposedly he'd won a fortune in gold from a miner who'd struck it rich during the great gold rush of the 1860s."

"Was that in Colorado?" I asked.

"Well, the first gold rush occurred in California, but in 1859, gold was found in what is now known as Colorado. Of course, then it was actually a part of the Kansas Territory. Colorado Territory was established in 1861."

I shook my head. "My goodness, Isaac. You're a walking history book."

He smiled. "Now, Miss Ivy, I've been working in this bookstore for over forty years. What do you think I do in my spare time? I've read almost everything that's ever passed through this wonderful place. Books can teach you so many things." He sighed. "I truly feel sorry for people who don't read."

"Back to George Slocum...," I gently reminded him.

"Oh yes, now where was I?"

"He was on his way back east."

"Yes. It was 1861. Fort Sumter had been attacked by Confederate troops and the Civil War had begun. Slocum wanted to get back to Kentucky before the fighting escalated. He stopped in Winter Break to rest his horse for a couple of days before continuing home. Unfortunately, news of an imminent attack from a tribe of Indians forced him to change his plans. Fearing that his gold would be stolen, he buried it and then joined with Winter Break residents to stand against the Indians. Although the town was saved, Slocum was lost." Isaac took a sip of iced tea and smiled at me. Then he lowered his voice to a conspiratorial whisper. "The rumor was that he wasn't actually killed by an Indian arrow, but instead by a Winter Break citizen who knew about the gold." He shrugged and waved a hand in the air. "But who knows?" he said with a final flourish. "Whether the person who killed George Slocum found the gold is impossible to know. Town gossip says it was never discovered. Thus began the legend of the Lost Gambler's Gold."

"And the stories we kids used to tell each other."

Isaac chuckled. "Oh, you mean about the Gambler's ghostly hand reaching up from under the ground to drag you down to his grave?"

"Yes. I had a few nightmares because of it, let me tell you." I shuddered at the memory.

Isaac stacked our empty salad bowls and stood up. "I'll take these back to my apartment; then we'll get started again." He headed toward the back door but stopped before reaching it. "I hope I answered your question."

I grinned at him. "Goodness, Isaac. I learned more from you in a few minutes than I have from years of listening to childish rumors and reading old memoirs."

He nodded with satisfaction. "Good. Of course, you know there isn't likely to be any treasure still buried here, don't you?"

"Why do you say that?"

He looked at me with amusement. "Why, Miss Ivy, I doubt that Mr. Slocum had much time to bury his treasure. That would mean it wasn't too far from the surface. This is primarily a farming community. After all this time, someone plowing a field would surely have found it. Most probably, however, someone saw Slocum with his gold and killed him for it. It's probably long gone by now."

As the door closed behind him, I began to ponder the logic of his conclusion. I truly hoped he was wrong. I could hardly wait to show the map to Amos and get his opinion. Even more exciting was the idea of following the map and digging at the spot marked with a big red X.

Isaac and I worked diligently the rest of the afternoon. At two o'clock, he went home, leaving me some time to look a little more closely at the mysterious map. Before I had a chance to take it out of my desk, the bell over the front door tinkled, and Alma Pettibone stepped in. She glanced nervously around the store until her gaze rested on me. I was surprised to see her for two reasons. First of all because she never left the post office during the day due to what she called her "important postal duties" and second because her soaps weren't over until three o'clock.

"Ivy!" she said rather breathlessly. She reached up with one hand and tried to tug her silver hair back into its original topknot. It must have come undone in her hurry to get across the street. "I just had to bring this to you right away. The postmark says *China!*"

I got up from the desk and took the letter from her. Sure enough, it had come all the way from Hong Kong. But why would my parents write to me instead of calling? The handwriting on the envelope was definitely my mother's. "Thanks, Alma," I said. "It's from my mother and father. I think I told you they're missionaries overseas."

"Yes, dear. I do remember. But why would they mail you a letter? I mean, even at Christmas they didn't send anything."

"My parents won't send packages from China," I said. "It's very expensive, and many times, items are lost along the way."

Alma looked at me sympathetically. "I'm sure that's it, dear," she said.

I thought about defending myself by assuring her that my parents didn't ignore me at Christmas because they didn't love me but realized I was getting sidetracked. I wanted to read my letter. In private.

"Thanks for bringing it over, Alma," I said, scooting behind her so I could hold the door open. "I really appreciate it."

She paused for a moment and stared at the envelope in my hand. I knew she wanted me to read it in her presence, but I had no intention of doing so. Finally, she threw me a forced smile and hurried back to her precious afternoon serials. I waited until I saw her enter the post office; then I took the letter back to my desk and opened it. It wasn't until I reached the third paragraph that I discovered the real reason my mother had sent me a letter instead of calling.

We are taking a brief sabbatical so we can spend some time with you in Winter Break. Recent decisions you've made have caused us quite a bit of concern, Ivy. We want to make absolutely certain you haven't embarked upon a path that will bring you great heartache.

We will arrive in Wichita on the sixteenth and then rent a car and drive to Winter Break. We will arrive in town on the seventeenth. Don't worry about accommodations; we've already made arrangements.

I hope you will be glad to see us. We certainly are looking forward to being with you.

Love,
Mother

The seventeenth? Things move a little slowly in Winter Break, and for the life of me, I couldn't remember today's date. I flipped open my day planner and scanned the calendar. Today was the fifteenth! They would be here in two days. My mother hadn't warned me earlier about their visit because she knew I would have tried to talk her out of it. Now it was too late. They'd already left China.

Miss Skiffins ambled up next to me and rubbed my leg. I picked her up and buried my face in her soft fur. "We'd better get all our ducks in a row, sweetie. In a couple of days we're going to war." I didn't mean literal combat, but there would certainly be an emotional battle for my future. My mother had not accepted my decision to move to Winter Break with grace. She saw my choice to stay here and continue Aunt Bitty's bookstore as an act of rebellion. My mother wanted me to join her and my father in China. Although I respected their commitment to evangelism, I didn't feel it was the place God called me to be. My efforts to convince them of that obviously hadn't been successful.

I wondered where they planned to stay. Since there weren't any motels in Winter Break, the closest they could get would be Hugoton. It wasn't much, but at least there would be a little distance between us. A gentle swat with her fluffy paw told me Miss Skiffins had been squeezed enough for a while. I put her down and turned my attention to the treasure map. There was nothing I could do at that moment about my parents, so I tried to push worry from my mind by focusing on the possibility of finding long-hidden gold.

I took the map from its hiding place and carefully smoothed it out. Winter Break was drawn as a series of small squares. The road out of town wound past the graveyard and toward the peach orchards. In the middle of the orchards, there was an object sketched in. It was round with tiny lines inside its borders. There were words written next to it, but they were so smudged I couldn't make them out. From that point, tiny footprints had been drawn, each one heading north, until they stopped at an object marked with a large red *X*.

"*X* marks the spot," I said softly to myself. As I felt a rush of excitement about the map, seeds of worry also crept into my mind. The Lost Gambler's Gold had held on to its resting place for a long time. Would I be as tenacious when my mother tried to uproot me from Winter Break? I steeled myself for what lay ahead, asking God for the courage to stand strong and to hold on to the life I believed He'd called me to live.

3

By early evening, dark clouds began to gather over Winter Break. I'd spent the afternoon going over the account books on the big table in the sitting room. I closed the last one and checked my watch. I had plans to pop some popcorn and watch a little TV before bed. It sounded like a perfect plan for a rainy night. Although I had a few favorite shows, I tried to watch television sparingly. Bitty had never owned a "mind trap," as she called all television sets, and I'd never really noticed its absence during our summers and holidays together. She'd told me more than once that a good book was much more beneficial to the brain than TV. "Books activate thought and imagination, Ivy," she'd say. "TV on—imagination off." Although I hadn't adapted my life to her choice of no TV at all, I certainly wasn't planning to emulate Alma Pettibone by getting stuck on certain programs and allowing them to run my life. I intended to exercise one of the most difficult but necessary fruits of the Spirit: self-control.

I was stacking the account books in a neat pile when I heard the front door open. Stretching, I got up to see who it was and found Amos standing on the landing. I expected to see his usual smile. Instead I discovered a decidedly somber expression.

"What's wrong?" I asked.

When he didn't answer, I hurried over to my desk and sat down, motioning to the chair next to me. I could hardly wait to show him the map. He sat down with a grunt, his forehead creased with worry. "You remember those cows I told you about?" he said finally. "The ones being stolen?"

I nodded.

"It's become an epidemic. Cows are disappearing all over the place."

"Maybe it's aliens," I said, trying not to smile. "I saw something on TV once—"

"It's not funny, Ivy," Amos said in a low voice. "I think we may know one of the people involved."

I pulled the map out of my drawer and put it on top of the desk, waiting for the cow conversation to end so I could show it to him. "Who do you think it is?"

Amos sighed. "The description I got matches Odie Rimrucker."

I couldn't keep the indignation out of my voice. "Amos! It couldn't be Odie.

He'd never do anything like that."

He nodded, but his expression didn't change. "I know what you're saying, but it sounds just like him. Even down to a description of his truck."

I couldn't believe it. At one time, Odie had been the town drunk. He'd lost his family, his job, and most of his friends to drinking. But several years ago my aunt Bitty helped to straighten him out. He was a deacon in the church now and a model citizen. "I refuse to accept that. It can't be true."

He smiled weakly. "If I ever get in any big trouble, remind me to call you right away, will you? You're a very loyal friend."

"Well, thank you. That's a very nice thing to say, but I'm not defending Odie because I'm loyal. I'm defending him because I truly believe he would never be involved in something like this. Even when he was drinking, he wasn't the type to steal from others. Especially from people in Winter Break. He loves it here."

"I know that. I don't want to believe it either, but what am I supposed to do? I can't ignore this."

I could feel my chest tighten with concern. "What will happen to Odie if you accuse him of stealing from his neighbors? What if he starts drinking again?"

Amos jumped up from his chair, pulling off his hat and smoothing his ash blond hair with his free hand. "You think I haven't thought of that?" He scowled at me. "You act as if you're the only one who's concerned about Odie."

"I never said you didn't care about him. I know you do."

Amos put his hat back on and shook his head. "I'm sorry. I didn't mean to take this out on you."

"That's okay. I understand." I really did. It was easy for me to have an opinion, but I wasn't the one who would have to speak to Odie about it. Amos was under a lot of pressure. "What are you going to do?"

He sat down again. "I'm going to wait as long as I can before I confront Odie. I've got dates and approximate times that cattle were stolen. Before talking to him, I'll nose around a bit and see if I can't find an alibi for him. If I can prove he was in town, doing something else at the time of the thefts, I'll know he wasn't involved. I won't even bring up his name to the sheriff." Amos stared at me and shrugged. "That's all I can do, Ivy. But if I can't find an alibi. . ." His voice trailed off. He didn't need to finish his sentence. We both knew what would happen. Without warning, Amos clapped his hands together, making me jump. "Now let's change the subject," he said. "Anything interesting happen while I was gone?"

It took a moment for me to respond. I'd been so caught up by Odie's predicament, I'd almost forgotten about the map. "Yes. Which do you want first? The good news or the bad news?"

"There's bad news?" Amos shook his head. "I can't imagine anything worse than what I just told you. . .unless someone died. Did someone die?"

"No. Well, yes, I suppose somewhere in the world someone died, but everyone *I* know is still breathing."

Amos raised one eyebrow and fixed his incredible hazel eyes on me. "You may have noticed that I'm not really in the mood for your twisted humor right now. Why don't you tell me your bad news and get it out of the way."

I took a deep breath. "My parents are on their way to Winter Break. They'll be here Wednesday."

I expected him to commiserate with me, but instead he smiled. "That's not bad news. I'm sure you'll be glad to see them."

"Glad to see them!" I said. "They're coming here for the express purpose of ruining my life. They want me to leave Winter Break."

Amos chuckled. "That's ludicrous. Your parents love you. They'll listen to what you have to say. I think you're letting your imagination run wild."

I held my hand up like a cop stopping traffic. "Wait a minute. You don't really know my parents. You may have met them a few times when we were kids, but you've never spent any *quality* time with them. You have no idea—"

He reached over and grabbed my hand. "I may not know them, but I do know this: God brought us together. *He* says you belong here, with me. Your parents are godly people. They'll recognize His hand in this."

I couldn't think of a response. Amos was going on pure, unadulterated faith, and in my book, and in God's book, nothing on earth was more powerful than that. I felt a sense of relief. Even if I had to cling to Amos's faith alone, at least I could see a life preserver floating in my sea of doubt. It was enough to hold on to for now.

Amos squeezed my hand. "Now what's the good news?"

I felt anticipation build inside me as I pushed the map toward him. "Look what I found hidden inside that old jewelry box Bitty gave me. I think it might be a map to the Lost Gambler's Gold!"

Amos laughed and unfolded the yellowed, brittle paper. "You think George Slocum hid his map in Bitty's jewelry box? That's ridiculous, Ivy. My mom had a jewelry box just like yours. She got it at a carnival. It certainly isn't old enough to belong to Slocum."

I got up and came around the desk so we could look at it together. "Of course I don't think George Slocum put it there. But someone else might have. Someone who was trying to hide it. I mean, what else could it be? As far as I know, there isn't any other treasure around here."

As Amos looked carefully at the details, he shook his head. "This map isn't old enough to belong to George Slocum."

"What are you talking about?" I asked, feeling a rush of indignation. "Of course it is."

"This clearly shows the orchard. Those trees were planted by Harvey Bruenwalder's father in the late forties or early fifties. The orchard didn't exist when George Slocum was alive."

I couldn't argue with him; he was right. My enthusiasm had clouded my judgment. But the flush of disappointment I felt was slowly replaced with a ray of hope as I contemplated the markings on the old piece of paper. "Okay, so it's not a map to Slocum's gold," I said. "But it's a map to something. Something important enough to bury. Maybe this is even bigger than the Gambler's Gold. Maybe—"

Amos's sudden burst of laughter made me jump. "That imagination of yours is something else." He leaned over and kissed me. "It's one of the reasons I love you so much. You're extremely unique."

I smiled at him as sweetly as I could. "Thank you, Amos. I think you're special, too. I also think we should find out what's buried on the far edge of the orchard. I just have a feeling—"

Amos jerked as if he'd been burned. "Oh no. Not again. This never ends well. Somehow I always land knee-deep in trouble when you 'have a feeling.'"

"Well, fine." I sniffed. "I intend to find out what's buried there. With or without you. This map came to me for a reason. It's my destiny to dig it up."

"Your destiny?" Amos shook his head vigorously. "What if this turns out to be something we shouldn't uncover? Has that possibility crossed your mind at all?"

"Nope," I said happily. "I have a feeling this is going to be a good thing. It's too late tonight to go out there, but I'm headed to the orchard tomorrow with a shovel. You can come if you wish. It's totally up to you."

"Do you intend to ask Harvey if it's okay for you to go digging around in his orchard? If I remember right, the last time we did that, he threatened to call the authorities."

I plopped myself on Amos's lap and wrapped my arms around his neck. "But you *are* the authorities, Amos. So if he calls anyone, he'd have to call you. I'd say we're in good shape, wouldn't you?"

"Oh, man. Now I'm the one who has a feeling. And my feeling says that—"

I kissed him before he could finish his sentence.

"Okay, I'll call Harvey and see if he'll let us check this out," he said after I pulled back. He gently pushed me off his lap and stood up. "But I wouldn't count on anything. We're certainly not his favorite people."

Amos headed toward the front door, but before he opened it, he turned around and pointed his finger at me. "Do you promise to stay away from there until I come for you tomorrow afternoon?"

I nodded my head with enthusiasm. "I promise. As long as you get here before it gets late."

"I'll be here by three o'clock. *If* Harvey says it's okay, we'll go to the orchard; then we'll go to Ruby's for dinner, okay?"

I almost jumped with excitement. "Sounds great."

He pulled the door open but turned back once more and frowned at me. "Now, Ivy, I'm willing to dig in one spot and one spot only. If we don't find anything within, say, an hour, we're out of there. Understood?"

"Sure. I've got it."

"I mean it."

"Okay, okay. An hour," I said impatiently. "Now get going. I'll see you tomorrow."

The bell jangled violently as the door slammed behind him. Maybe I hadn't discovered the Lost Gambler's Gold, but something was buried out in the orchard, and we were going to find it. I picked up the map and looked at it again. By tomorrow evening, its secret would be revealed.

Although I'd dismissed his concerns at the time, Amos's words of warning about things that shouldn't be uncovered floated back to me. In fact, they haunted me the rest of evening. Even the TV couldn't distract me completely from an odd sense of foreboding. Around midnight, I turned off the television and fell into a troubled sleep. I dreamed I was walking through the orchard when suddenly a bony hand shot up from underneath the ground and grabbed my ankle. I woke up in a sweat, certain I'd cried out. Miss Skiffins was crouching, staring at me. A peal of thunder added to the frightened cat's panic. I picked her up and comforted her until she began to purr. After she settled down and went back to sleep, I snuggled under the covers and listened to the sound of rain hitting the roof while I contemplated my nightmare. It was similar to the one I'd had as a kid after being told the story of the Gambler's ghost, but there was an obvious difference that made this dream even more frightening.

This time, the person in the orchard wasn't George Slocum. Someone else was buried there.

And he was waiting for me.

4

Tuesday morning dragged by. When Isaac left at two o'clock, I was about ready to jump out of my skin. I could hardly wait to find out what was buried beneath the earth at the edge of the peach grove. The trepidation I'd felt the night before had evaporated like early morning mist in the glow of my unbridled enthusiasm.

By two thirty, I was ready to go, sitting at my desk, gazing out the window. By three o'clock, I was antsy and intently focused on my desk clock's second hand.

By three thirty, I was holding a small shovel and on my way out the door. Amos had promised to meet me by three. He was probably just tied up somewhere, looking for more missing cows. I reassured myself that if Harvey had said we couldn't dig in the orchard, Amos would have called me right away. It sounded okay in my head, and I was so determined to see just what kind of treasure the map would reveal, I didn't allow any other thoughts to interfere with what I wanted to think.

I drove away as quickly as I could without drawing attention to myself, the map lying beside me on the car seat. As I neared the edge of town, I found myself looking around for signs of a familiar patrol car. I'd tried to convince myself that I had nothing to feel guilty about, but the fact that I kept checking for Amos was most likely a good indication that my conscience wasn't completely clear.

"Amos knows where I'm going," I said aloud to no one. "He probably intends to meet me at the grove." When several minutes passed without a lightning strike, I decided to ignore the uncomfortable feeling in the pit of my stomach.

I drove slowly past Harvey's place. His old, battered truck wasn't there, and I didn't see anyone stirring. I pulled onto the dirt road that led to the orchard and parked as far away from Harvey's house as I could. Then with the map in one hand and my shovel in the other, I made my way to the center of the orchard.

I quickly discovered that the odd drawing in the middle of the map was an old campfire pit. Years ago, Harvey and his wife had hosted jamborees for Scout troops from the small towns that surrounded Winter Break. I was too young to have seen this myself, but I'd heard about it. When Harvey's wife took off, he'd shut down the campfires, but I could still see the depression where the pit had been. There were still a few old, rotted logs that lay scattered haphazardly around its edges.

With a few glances around to ensure I was alone, I counted off the steps drawn on the map. There were thirty-one. Since I had no idea who had drawn the map, or how big their steps were, I was at a disadvantage. Thirty-one steps for my short legs might be twenty for someone with a larger stride. However, the tracks seemed to stop at the edge of the orchard. If the tree line was the same, I should be able to approximate it fairly closely.

After one more furtive look around, I stepped forward and started counting. "One, two, three, four, five..." When I finally said, "Thirty-one," I stopped and looked down. I was at the edge of the orchard, but was I really in the right spot? Then I noticed something odd sticking out of the ground, near the base of the tree in front of me. I knelt down to look at it for a moment before trying to pull it out. It took several hard tugs to break it free. Although most people would have no idea what it was, I did. It was an old barrel tapper, used to cut holes in barrels of whiskey. Amos and I had found one once when we were kids. Deputy Sheriff Watson noticed us with it and was extremely interested in where we'd discovered it. The only person in Winter Break who would have need of something to tap barrels of booze was Hiram Ledbetter. Always on the lookout for Hiram's still, Morley Watson took off toward the spot by Winter Break Lake where we'd found the barrel tapper lying under the dock. It hadn't done any good; Hiram wasn't anywhere near the lake. The deputy sheriff had hit another dead end.

I gazed down at the tapper, wondering why anyone would stick something like this in the dirt. Then it dawned on me. They were marking the spot. The tapper looked old enough to have been there for a long, long time.

I put it on the ground next to me. I was so excited I felt as though my insides were doing cartwheels. This was the place. After one more look around, I picked up my shovel and started digging. It was much harder work than I thought it would be. Thank goodness, the ground was soft due to the rain overnight, but the wet dirt was heavy. I carved out a circle about five feet across since I had no idea how close to the old tool the treasure might be.

After about forty minutes, my arms were stiff and sore. At one point, I almost gave up, but my natural nosiness wouldn't allow me to walk away. It took another twenty minutes before the tip of my shovel hit something solid. With growing excitement, I dug around the area a little more and then jumped down into the shallow hole. I brushed some remaining dirt off the top of a rectangular object until I could get my fingers around it and pull it out. It was an old metal box. I felt the hair on the back of my neck stand up. Maybe this really was the Lost Gambler's Gold! Could Amos be wrong about the map?

I brushed the grime off the front of the box the best I could. The metal was crusted with dirt and rust, and I could feel it flaking apart in my hands. I decided to wait and open it under more controlled conditions, but as I stepped out of the hole, I lost my grip and the box tumbled from my hands. The ancient clasp holding it shut broke off on impact, and the box's contents spilled out, tumbling back into the hole.

"Shoot and bother," I grumbled. I knelt down and picked up each item, placing them gently back into the box. Unfortunately, there wasn't any gold. There were some metal objects, a couple of pictures, and a few other things I didn't bother to look at too closely. I wanted to get my discovery out of the hole, cover up the mess I'd made in Harvey's peach grove, and go someplace where I could have a more leisurely look at the box and its contents.

I'd placed everything I could find back in the decaying container, when I realized there was still something lying at the bottom of the hole. I'd almost missed it. It was so corroded I'd mistaken it for a part of the dirt that surrounded it. I got on my knees, reached down, and grabbed it, but it seemed to be caught on something. I pulled a little harder, and it finally came loose, breaking a chain that had been attached. I held it up. It looked like a medal of some kind, but it was hard to tell. It needed to be cleaned. Before I got up, I noticed long, light-colored sticks snaking under the earth, running parallel to each other. They were probably tree roots, although one of them had broken apart when I yanked the medal out of the ground. Roots that dry didn't bode well for the tree they belonged to, but the tree looked perfectly healthy. I stood up and grabbed my shovel. It was heavy with impacted dirt. I hit it several times against the tree to loosen the mud before I realized I'd made several cuts into the trunk. "Oh, phooey," I said out loud. Harvey wasn't going to take kindly to this injury. I touched the grooves with my fingers. They were deep but probably not bad enough to cause any real damage. I noticed that the ruts made an almost perfect *H*. Maybe Harvey would be forgiving since I'd carved his initial into the tree.

Fat chance.

I carried my find carefully to the car. Thankfully, there was an empty paper bag in my trunk that I could put the fragile container in. The clasp was gone, and I didn't want another accident.

It took me awhile to cover up the hole and put the barrel tapper back where I'd found it. By the time I got back to my car, it was almost time to meet Amos at Ruby's. I stopped for a moment at Harvey's, since his truck was still gone, and availed myself of his outdoor water pump. After washing my hands and face and brushing off my clothes the best I could, I'd done everything possible to look presentable. Under normal circumstances, I would never enter a restaurant in my current condition, but in Winter Break, many of the farmers who came in to get a bite of lunch or dinner at Ruby's were still grimy from the fields. I'd probably fit right in.

Besides my obvious unkempt appearance, I was beginning to deal with my similarly soiled conscience. I'd come up with several seemingly valid excuses for my jaunt to Harvey's, but I knew down deep inside that I should have waited for Amos. My overwhelming enthusiasm had drowned out the still, small voice inside me—again. Getting what I wanted sometimes seemed more important than doing what I knew was right. It was one of my greatest weaknesses.

As I neared Ruby's, I kept trying to come up with ways to explain my actions to Amos, but it wasn't working. "I'm sorry, Lord," I said quietly before I got out of the car. "I did it again, didn't I? Please forgive me."

As I pushed open the front door of Ruby's, I was determined to tell Amos the truth, admit my duplicity, and take whatever I deserved. I could only hope that Harvey had said yes to our request. Then Amos wouldn't be quite so upset with me. I looked through the sea of people crowded into wooden booths with red-padded seats and red-checked tablecloths. Finally, I saw him seated at a table in the middle of the room. Great. I'd hoped we'd get one of the booths against the wall. Now I was going to have to confess my sins surrounded by half the population of Winter Break.

Amos looked my way, and I waved at him while giving him one of my most innocent smiles. However, one look at me and the bag in my hands, and Amos's expression changed. He knew what I'd done.

"Ivy Towers," he hissed as I slid into the chair across from him, "I told you to wait for me. What did you do?"

Forgetting my previous good intentions, I automatically went on the defensive. "You promised to pick me up at three," I shot back. "Where were you?"

"Questioning Odie Rimrucker about those stolen cows," Amos said, frowning. "It took a lot longer than I planned."

"What? I thought you weren't going to bother him about it."

Amos's right eyebrow shot up. "You have a very selective memory, you know that? I told you I would try to check out his alibi. If I could confirm that he was somewhere else during the thefts, I'd leave him alone." He sighed, pulled off his hat, and ran his hand across his face. "I asked around. No one could tell me if he was in town during the times the cows went missing."

"I still say Odie wouldn't steal. You know him better than that."

He grunted. "I think I know you, too, Ivy, but then you do something that makes me wonder."

"Look, you told me to wait until three o'clock—"

"Just stop it," he retorted angrily. "You knew I didn't want you going to the orchard by yourself. I made it very clear that—"

"You can stop hollering at me," I said, interrupting what promised to be a long diatribe. "I know I messed up. I should have waited." I reached over and took his hand. "I'm sorry. I really am."

Amos looked like a cat whose canary had just flown away. "Well, I. . .I mean. . ." He frowned at me. "It's no fun when you admit you're wrong, you know," he said. "I have nowhere to go. And I wasn't hollering. I was speaking distinctly."

I risked a small smile. "I don't like it when you 'speak distinctly.' It makes me feel like you're mad at me."

Amos shook his head. "I wasn't able to get in touch with Harvey."

"You mean we didn't have permission to dig in the orchard?"

"No. If you'd waited on me, you'd have learned that."

Now I really felt guilty. "I guess I'll have to go to him and admit what I did, won't I?" I asked the question hoping Amos would come up with some reason I should keep the incident to myself. He didn't.

"Yes, you're going to tell him. And right away. In fact, I want you to go over to Harvey's either tonight or first thing in the morning."

I knew there was no point in arguing. Amos was as stubborn as I was. When he made up his mind, it was useless to try to change it.

"Amos," I said, hoping my transgressions hadn't completely ruined the excitement of my discovery, "I found a box buried right where the map said it would be."

Before he had a chance to respond, Bonnie Peavey, Ruby's longtime waitress, stepped up to our booth. "Whatcha havin'?" she asked in a quiet voice.

Bonnie had lived in Winter Break her entire life. Her parents, along with her two brothers and twin sister, still lived on the original family homestead. One of her brothers, Earl, lived in the same house as her parents, while Connie and Billy Ray, her younger brother, had their own houses built on Peavey land. Bonnie, the renegade of the bunch, rented a room at Sarah Johnson's. She always seemed rather lonely, and I felt sorry for her.

After Amos and I had ordered and Bonnie had strolled away, I set the sack on the table.

"I don't know if we should be looking at this, Ivy," Amos said. "This is actually Harvey's property. Maybe it's too late to put it back, but I don't think I'm comfortable with going through it unless Harvey knows about it."

"I've already seen what's inside," I said, "so that horse has left the barn. After I explain everything to Harvey, if he wants the box back, we'll give it to him. I just want one close look at the contents; then I'll be satisfied."

Amos seemed to consider this for a moment. I could tell he was just as curious as I was. "Okay," he said finally. "One good look—then we turn the box and the contents over to Harvey. Agreed?"

I nodded so vigorously, I almost gave myself a headache. I slowly pulled the box out of the bag and set it on top of the sack so it wouldn't mess up Ruby's clean table.

Amos picked up his napkin and started wiping off the top of the container. Although the paint was faded and sections were eaten away by rust, a picture began to emerge. He peered closely at the place he'd cleared and frowned. He wiped a little more then set his napkin down and started to chuckle.

"What's so funny?" I asked, feeling a little offended.

He shook his head. "Oh dear. I almost hate to tell you this."

"What? What is it?"

Amos started to laugh again, and I reached out for the container, determined to see for myself just what it was that was so humorous.

Amos pushed it toward me. "You have certainly uncovered a very valuable treasure," he sputtered, his face red with exertion. "Ivy Towers, you have unearthed an actual Bonanza lunch box!"

"A what?" Sure enough, peering back from the top of the box were Hoss and Ben Cartright. I was pretty sure the green-shirted arm to their right was Little Joe. Well, unless the Lost Gambler was a lot more contemporary than the stories suggested, this hadn't belonged to him at all. Amos snorted as he launched into another round of giggles.

I glared at him in an attempt to shut him up. People were beginning to stare. I decided to ignore him and carefully removed the cover and set it down next to the box. I unrolled the napkin that held my silverware and laid it out on the table. One by one, I began taking items from the box. Although they were obviously old, most of them were in pretty good shape. There was also a piece of aluminum foil that must have been wrapped around the objects until I'd dropped them into the hole.

Amos finally settled down, and although our previous level of enthusiasm had leveled off quite a bit, looking at items that had meant so much to someone so long ago was still extremely interesting. He leaned over to watch me as I carefully removed each object and gently put them on my napkin.

"These look like some kind of medals," I said.

Amos took them from me and turned them over in his hand. "They're track medals," he said. "Whoever they belonged to was pretty good, I'd say."

He put them on the napkin as I lifted out an old knife. Amos grabbed that from me also.

"It's an old Boy Scout knife," he said. "Odie has one just like it. I guess he used to belong to a Scout troop here in Winter Break when he was a kid. Dewey was the scoutmaster."

"Dewey?" I was surprised. I thought I knew everything about Dewey Tater, but I didn't remember ever hearing this before.

"What else is in there?" Amos asked, his interest obviously piqued.

"There are some pictures," I said. "Maybe they'll give us a clue as to who owns this lunch box."

One of the photographs was of a man standing next to a tractor. The other picture showed a beautiful young girl. She was holding something, but the picture was too faded for me to see what it was. The background made me think of a country fair. All the photographs were in remarkably good shape except for a little fading and something that looked like mold around the edges. But no one in the pictures looked the least bit familiar.

"Is that everything?" Amos asked.

"No, there's a small Bible here." As I lifted the Bible out of the box, the cover began flaking apart in my hands. A small, dried flower that had been pressed between the pages fell out onto the table.

Amos carefully picked up the flower and put it on the napkin. "Look at the front pages and see if anyone's name is written inside."

Before I had a chance to open the cover, I heard a gasp from behind me. I turned to see Ruby Bird looking over my shoulder, her face drained of color, her eyes wide. Thankfully, Amos jumped up just in time to catch her before she fainted.

5

Any chance of keeping our discovery quiet disappeared with Ruby's strange reaction to seeing the lunch box and the things inside it sprawled out across our table. We had quite a crowd gathered around, and everyone wanted to know where the box had come from and to whom it belonged. My search for secret treasure had turned into a group event. Making things even worse, Harvey Bruenwalder walked in the door right after Ruby's fainting spell. My hope of confessing my sins in private disappeared like smoke in the wind.

"Everybody move back and give Ruby some room," Amos barked to the throng of people leaning over to see what was going on. Reluctantly, several Winter Break folks took a step backward, but everyone seemed determined to stay within hearing distance.

I looked around me. It seemed as if half the town was in Ruby's. I saw Elmer Buskin, the funeral director, and Isaac was standing next to Alma Pettibone. Standing off a bit from the crowd was Odie Rimrucker. His gaze was locked on Amos, and his expression was anything but happy. I felt someone touch my shoulder.

"Ivy, what's going on? Is there anything I can do to help?"

I turned to see Pastor Taylor and his wife at the table behind us. My old childhood friend Emily Taylor and her husband, Buddy, the pastor's son, were sitting with them. Emily smiled at me, and I smiled back. "Maybe so, Pastor," I said. "Could you check to see if Ruby is okay? I think she fainted, and I—"

"Ivy Towers!"

Ruby's loud voice cut through the air, stopping any further conversation. "Where in the world did you get this?"

The restaurant owner was obviously feeling better. Her hearing problems raised her voice several decibels above normal human tones. I began to wonder if I shouldn't just stand up on the table and shout out the whole situation.

Ruby straightened her Marilyn Monroe–styled wig, which was now slightly askew, and gazed down at the contents of the box. Amos had helped her into the chair next to him right before she hit the ground. Since he was surrounded by curious onlookers, he was now a prisoner. And he wasn't happy about it. I glanced over at him, hoping he would field Ruby's question. He gave me a look that could freeze molten lava. I was definitely on my own.

"It was buried in the peach grove, Ruby," I said, trying not to look at Harvey. "I went there because I found this." I pulled the map out of my purse and handed it to her. Ruby unfolded it and started to cry. All around us, I could hear people whispering to one another.

"She found it where?"

"What is it?"

"What'd she say, Bertha? What'd she say?"

I recognized Marybelle Widdle's voice. Great. She was here with Bertha Pennypacker. They went everywhere together. Bertha had it in for me. I had no idea why, but the woman detested me. No matter what I said to her, or how I tried to befriend her, she would always defeat my attempts with an icy stare or a snide comment. This was going to give her a lot of fuel for her "I hate Ivy" fire.

I noticed Harvey Bruenwalder standing behind Elmer. His fierce expression made it clear that I was going to have a lot of explaining to do. He didn't say anything, and this wasn't the time for me to talk to him about my transgression. But I was aware that I would certainly have to mend my fences with him as soon as possible.

Trying to ignore the sick feeling in my stomach, I turned my attention away from our audience and tried to concentrate on Ruby. Reaching across the table, I let my fingers lightly touch her arm. "Ruby, what is it? Who does this belong to?"

Without answering me, she put the map down on the table and lifted the moldy cover of the little Bible. Still visible, although it was faded and had traces of mildew, was a scrawled signature: *Bert Bird.*

Bert Bird? Ruby's son? I'd heard stories about him when I was a kid. About how he'd left town when he was a teenager and never came back.

"This was my boy's lunch pail," Ruby said loudly enough for everyone to hear. "And these are his track medals. This is his Bible." She picked up one of the pictures. As she gazed at the man next to the tractor, she began to cry harder. "My husband, Elbert," she croaked through her sobs. "This was taken a couple of months before he died. That's me standing next to him."

I took the picture from her trembling fingers. I hadn't noticed the wisp of a woman standing beside the tractor. If I had, I doubt I would have recognized her. Ruby's dark, expressive eyes were wide and innocent, and her face was framed by thick ebony hair plaited into a long braid that fell over her shoulder. Her shy smile and delicate features reminded me of a gentle fawn. This woman was a far cry from the tough, leather-skinned Ruby of today. As I looked a little closer, I could finally see the similarities in her features. The hair was what really threw me, since I'd never actually seen Ruby's hair.

Amos handed her his handkerchief, which she gratefully accepted. After she wiped her eyes and took a few deep breaths, she picked up the second picture.

"Oh my goodness," she said.

"What is it, Ruby?" I asked as softly as I dared. Ruby's hearing problems didn't allow for a lot of subtlety.

"Bonnie! Bonnie Peavey!" Ruby suddenly screeched.

Poor Bonnie jumped as if someone had plugged her into an electric outlet. One look at the picture made her turn as white as Ruby had moments earlier. I wasn't worried about Bonnie falling to the floor, since there were so many people gathered around her. If she passed out, the worst that could happen was that she would end up leaning a little to the left.

"Bonnie Peavey!" Ruby squealed again. "What is your picture doing in my son's lunch box?"

Now all eyes were focused on the hapless waitress. Her usually somber features were alive with emotion. "I. . .I. . .I don't know. That was thirty years ago, Ruby," she said softly. Too softly for the crowd trying to figure out what was going on.

"What did she say?" Bertha Pennypacker said in her eternally whiny voice. "I can't hear her."

"Something about the picture bein' dirty," a raspy male voice said. "Move over, Elmer. I can't see it."

"She said *thirty*, not *dirty*," Elmer Buskin squeaked. Of course, with his speech impediment, it actually came out, "*tirty*, not *dirty*."

"Huh?" someone else said. "What was that?"

I'd had enough. I managed to wiggle out of my chair. Then I pushed a few people back so I could get some breathing room. "Would all of you please go back to your seats and let us talk to Ruby? If anything important comes up, we'll make sure you all know about it."

"And just how do you propose to do that?" Bertha Pennypacker asked icily.

"Why don't you just tell it to Alma Pettibone?" someone asked with a snicker.

I looked over at Alma. She flushed beet red and began to fight her way through the crowd, most probably heading toward the front door. Isaac turned to watch her leave and then followed after her. Good. His compassionate nature would help to soothe her hurt feelings.

"I mean it, everyone," I said with a little more force. "Go sit down. Give Ruby a little space."

Of course, no one moved. I was trying to come up with something a little more threatening, when Amos stood up and addressed the crowd.

"Now listen here, folks," he said in his down-home, unthreatening style,

"I know you all care very much about Ruby and just want to help her. For right now, the best thing you can do is to give her a little space so she can look over her son's possessions. Let's give her some respect and peace. In a few days, I'm sure Ruby will be more than happy to share her feelings with you. But not right now, okay?"

Some people began moving, but several just glared at Amos and stood their ground. Just then, Dewey Tater made his way through the crowd. "You heard Amos," he said loudly. "You people start minding your own business. This is Ruby's business. Let's leave her to it."

As if Dewey were the Pied Piper himself, the rest of the rats turned and scattered back to their respective holes. Their reaction made it clear why Dewey was the mayor. The fact that I compared the good citizens of Winter Break to rats made it obvious I wasn't cut out for political office.

Once the crowd had dispersed, the only people near Ruby were Dewey, Amos, and me. Dewey started to walk away, but Ruby grabbed his arm and asked him to stay.

At first Ruby was silent, turning each item over in her fingers, gazing at it longingly. She picked up the medal that was the most dirt encrusted and stared at it for a moment. "I don't recognize this," she said finally. "Maybe if it was cleaned up some."

"I'll scrub it for you, Ruby," I said. "In fact, I'll clean everything up as much as I can." Aunt Bitty had used saddle soap to clean the covers of some of the old leather-bound books in her collection. Bert's Bible might be beyond that stage, but I could contact some other rare book dealers for advice. Amos could help with the rusty medals. I wanted to give Ruby back her newfound treasures in better shape than they were in now.

"Thank you, Ivy," the old woman said. "Why don't you take the box and bring it back when you're done? I don't think I can look at this stuff anymore right now."

Her thin fingers slowly closed the lid on the fragile lunch box. I was pretty sure it wasn't going to make it through any kind of cleanup. It was in pretty bad shape, but I didn't want to bring that up now.

Ruby reached over and patted the chair next to her, motioning Dewey to sit down, which he did.

Pastor Taylor stood up and came over to us. "Ruby, we're going to take our food to another table. We don't want to intrude on a private conversation—"

"No, no, Pastor," Ruby said. "I wish you would stay. It would comfort me."

Pastor Taylor nodded and sat back down. He turned his chair slightly so Ruby could see him; then he smiled at her. "So these things belonged to your son, Bert? I don't know much about him, Ruby, since we weren't in Winter Break yet when he left. Would you like to tell us a little about him?"

I smiled appreciatively at him. His soft-spoken, caring style was just what Ruby needed. She looked up, tears streaming down her weather-beaten face as if they had a life of their own. "Bert was a wonderful boy," she said. "He always helped out on the farm, glad to do anything he could to help his daddy. He was the joy of my life, always tryin' to make me laugh. And he loved my cookin'. In fact, he was the one who used to tell me I could open a restaurant. When I sold the farm, I opened the diner because of him." She stopped. Amos offered her his handkerchief, and she wiped her face with it.

"I never knew that, Ruby," Dewey said.

She shook her head slowly. "I don't think I ever told anyone." She stared at him for a moment, her eyes shiny with tears. "You remember Bert, don't you, Dewey? You were his scoutmaster. In fact, I think you gave him this Boy Scout knife."

"Yes, I did. And of course I remember him," Dewey said gently. "He was a fine boy. One of the best boys I ever worked with."

Ruby nodded. "Yes, he really was a wonderful young man. But after his daddy died so unexpectedly, he began to change. He was angry, I think. Angry at God. Angry at me. I don't know." She paused and blew her nose.

I doubted Amos was going to want that handkerchief back.

"It was too much for him," she continued. "Tryin' to be a boy and a man at the same time. It was too much to ask. I shouldn't have put him in that position."

"Nonsense," Dewey said. "It wasn't your fault. You were trying to keep the farm afloat."

"Is that why he left, Ruby?" I asked.

Ruby stiffened as if someone had thrown cold water into her face.

"I sent him to stay with relatives," she said icily. "He just never came back." She shoved the box toward me. "I'd appreciate it if you would clean this up. I'd like to have Bert's stuff as mementos. I guess he buried it sometime before he left and forgot about it." She turned and hollered at poor Bonnie, who was taking orders at a nearby table. "Maybe when we close up tonight, Bonnie, you can explain to me why your picture is in my son's lunch box."

Bonnie's eyes widened, and she scampered off toward the kitchen. I was pretty interested in the answer to that question. Had Bert and Bonnie dated? They would have been rather young.

Ruby stood up and faced us. "I want to thank you all for listenin' to me. I know you care, and that means a lot. This discovery shook me up some, I admit that. But Bert is gone, and I don't think he's ever comin' back. I will treasure these things you found, Ivy. Thank you. But it's time to go on with life. I can't live in the past. There's just no purpose in it."

With that, she turned on her heel and headed toward the kitchen. The quiet atmosphere in the diner, the result of people trying to listen in on our conversation, exploded with voices, everyone talking about the strange situation we'd just encountered. Bonnie scurried away behind Ruby.

"I'm sorry," I said to Amos and Dewey. "I should have kept my mouth shut. I had no idea she would close up like that."

"It's not you, Ivy," Dewey said. "She's been like that ever since Bert left. A lot of people have tried to talk to her about it, but she just clams up."

"Why would she do that?" someone said behind me. I'd forgotten about Pastor Taylor and jumped at the sound of his voice.

"It doesn't make sense," I said. "If Bert went to stay with relatives while Ruby straightened out her problems with the farm, why didn't he come back? There's obviously something Ruby doesn't want to tell anyone."

"I imagine it's just too painful for her to discuss," Dewey said. "I'm sure it's very difficult to admit that your own flesh and blood decided to live with someone else. Ruby's never gotten over it."

Though I didn't respond to Dewey's remark, I wasn't sure I agreed with him. Ruby's abrupt change of attitude smacked of some kind of secret. What happened next only deepened my conviction that there was a mystery of some kind lurking beneath the disappearance of Bert Bird.

"Where's the map?" I asked, noticing that it was gone. We looked under the napkins and on the floor, but it was nowhere to be found. Had Ruby taken it? The only thing I'd seen clutched in her hands when she left was Amos's handkerchief. And if she didn't have the map, who did? And why?

6

But that doesn't make any sense," I told Amos as we sat together on the front porch of the bookstore. I'd purchased a pair of white rocking chairs in Hugoton so that Amos and I could sit outside and watch the town come alive with spring colors and smells. The cicadas supplied our background music. Their throbbing cadence at dusk was irritating to some, but I found it incredibly soothing. The throaty contralto voices sang backup to the many birds that made Winter Break their home. In my mind, cicadas were the harbingers of spring and the oft-maligned troubadours of summer.

"You're reading too much into this, Ivy," he said gruffly. "You think there's a mystery behind everything unusual that happens. The map probably fell on the floor, and someone picked it up and threw it away, thinking it was trash."

I took a deep breath and mentally counted to five. "So the treasure map that led us to finding Bert's possessions, clearly marked with the words *My Treasure*, the same map that created so much interest in the diner, suddenly got confused with garbage?"

I could hear a note of hysteria in my voice, but I was frustrated. Amos was a sheriff's deputy. It seemed to me that he should be able to see that the theft of the map was extremely suspicious.

He sighed and rocked a little harder, a sure sign I was getting on his nerves. "Yes, I think it's possible, Ivy. There's no earthly reason anyone would want that map. Bert's box has already been dug up—thanks to you. The map is worthless now. Meaningless. The only person who might want it would be Ruby. Maybe she took it. After all, her son drew it."

"But why wouldn't she say something about it? Why would she hide it under your handkerchief?"

"Maybe she wasn't trying to hide it at all. Maybe the handkerchief just covered it up. I think you need to leave it alone. You sure can't ask her for it. It isn't yours."

I didn't have an answer for that. He was right. I changed the subject. "What do you know about Bert Bird's disappearance?"

Amos's rocking slowed a little, and in the fading light, I could see his forehead wrinkle. "I've heard a lot of different things. Most of it seems to line up with Ruby's story. Trying to be the man of the house was too much for a sixteen-year-old boy. He went to stay with relatives and just never came back."

"You said 'most' of it lined up with Ruby's story. What do you mean? Do you know something you're not telling me?"

Amos stopped rocking and sighed. "I hesitate to tell you this because of your overactive imagination, but now that I've thought about it, I do remember a conversation I overheard when I was a kid. Morley Watson and Dewey were talking about Bert's leaving, and Morley said something really odd."

I waited while Amos resumed rocking and staring at the sunset. After what seemed like an eternity, I said, "Would you like to share it with me, or do you want me to try to read your mind?"

"Oh, sorry. I was just thinking about Odie."

I couldn't keep the exasperation out of my voice. "Will you please tell me what Morley said about Bert? We'll have to worry about Odie later. I can only handle one problem at a time."

Amos looked surprised by the impatience in my voice. He was used to living in a small town where everything moved like molasses in the Arctic. I still had big-city blood flowing in my veins. Patience was not so much a virtue as it was an inconvenience.

Amos stopped rocking again. "Well, Ruby kept saying that Bert would be back, but after a while, when he never showed up, I guess they got a little suspicious."

"What do you mean by 'suspicious'?"

"I mean Morley and Dewey wondered if something had happened to Bert. If maybe someone had done something to him."

"What do you mean, 'done something to him'?"

Amos turned and looked at me. "Are you going to keep asking me what I mean?"

I ignored him. "You mean they wondered if Bert was dead?"

He nodded. "Dewey asked Morley if he'd ever suspected that someone had killed Bert."

I couldn't believe what I was hearing. "What did Deputy Watson say?"

Amos shrugged. "He said he didn't have any evidence of it, but he thought the whole thing was pretty strange. Then he asked Dewey if he'd ever suspected Ruby of being the kind of person who might do away with her son. Dewey said he didn't know her well enough to hazard a guess."

"Amos Parker, why didn't you ever tell me about this? You used to tell me everything when we were kids."

Amos zipped up his jacket and gazed off into the horizon. "At the time, I think it was because it scared me a little. This happened right before my mother married Truman McAlister and took off for California. We weren't getting along, and I felt like I was in her way. I hadn't thought about this for years. Not until today."

I scooted my rocking chair closer to him and grabbed his arm. "Your mother loved you, Amos. She just got caught up with Truman and thought she'd find some kind of happiness with him."

He nodded. "I know. I've made peace with it. We talked several times before she died. I flew out to see her just a month before she passed away. I think we put the past to rest."

"Someday you'll have to do the same with your father," I said softly.

"Let's get back to Bert, okay?" Amos's tone was harsh. His father was still a forbidden subject between us. I wasn't sure why, but I was willing to wait until he was ready to open up. I could sense that pushing him would only make him more defensive.

"Okay. I'm sorry."

We rocked silently for a while. I was turning over the idea of Ruby's being involved in Bert's disappearance, but I just couldn't see it. I didn't pretend to know Ruby that well, but I'd always had a sense about people. My gut told me that Ruby truly loved her son and missed him. But I still couldn't understand why Bert had never come back after all these years. Even if he'd chosen to grow up somewhere else, why hadn't he visited his mother when he was older? And why was Ruby so defensive about it? It just didn't add up.

"I wonder if Ruby even knows where Bert is," I said. "It's obvious she's heartbroken that he's never come back."

"Let it go, Ivy," Amos said. "Once you clean Bert's stuff up and give everything to Ruby, you'll have to walk away and leave her with her memories. That's all she has now. Besides, you need to be thinking about Harvey."

I put my head on Amos's shoulder. "Couldn't you talk to him? He'd accept it better coming from—"

"No," he said, interrupting my heartfelt plea. "You need to do this yourself. You caused this mess. Now you clean it up."

"But, Amos—"

"Don't 'but, Amos' me. You knew I didn't want you going there without me. Your curiosity got out of control again."

"I know, I know." I snuggled up as close as I could to him with the arms of the rocking chairs between us. "I take full responsibility. I'll see Harvey first thing in the morning."

"What time are your parents supposed to get here?" he asked, his tone a little gentler.

"Your guess is as good as mine. I'll drive over to Harvey's first thing in the morning and plan to be back here no later than eleven. They're traveling all the way from Wichita. That's about a six-hour trip. Even if they left at six in the morning, they couldn't be here until noon."

"Do you really think they'd leave that early?"

I laughed. "You really don't know my mother at all, do you? She'd leave even earlier if my dad would let her. And because she's on her way here to 'save me,' she won't waste a minute of her time. She's a very determined woman."

"Well, so are you, Ivy," Amos said. "And together, we're unbeatable."

"Yes, we are," I said as I reached over to accept his kiss.

"I'll pick you up at nine thirty in the morning. We'll visit Harvey together."

I kissed him again and then went inside before he could change his mind. I felt better knowing he would be by my side when I confessed my lack of judgment to Harvey Bruenwalder. Harvey struck me as an eternally grumpy man. I had no idea how he'd take my apology. Unfortunately, Amos and I had been a thorn in his side ever since we were kids. Everyone had their limits.

From the doorway, I watched as Amos's taillights disappeared around the corner. After I shut the door, I went over to my desk where the rusting box sat on a towel. I slowly pulled back the top while the hinges creaked with resistance.

I held the pictures in the desk lamp's light and looked closely at the faces that stared back at me. Elbert Bird had a kind face, with deep-set, dark eyes that suggested a sense of humor. He had the kind of smile that could come only from a man who was truly happy, who had almost everything he wanted in life. Ruby's expression was full of hope, with no doubt of the future before them. I remembered Ruby saying that shortly after this picture was taken, Elbert was killed. I was sad for him, for Ruby, and for Bert.

I put that picture back and picked up the photograph of Bonnie Peavey. If someone hadn't told me who it was, I never would have known. The Bonnie I knew was a shadow of the vibrant young girl with the dazzling smile. Bonnie had been a waitress at Ruby's for as long as I could remember. She was the kind of person who seemed to melt into her surroundings, like a chair or a table. She was there, yet she wasn't. Had Bert's departure robbed her of her vivacity? The girl staring back at me was happy. Her expression went beyond having her picture taken, as if her smile was intended for the person behind the camera. Was it Bert? I couldn't know for sure, but in my heart, I believed it was. Maybe Bonnie had lost the love of her life thirty years ago. Of course, Amos would probably tell me that my imagination was running away with me again, but I wasn't so sure.

I grabbed a sewing box I'd found in Aunt Bitty's room and began putting the items from the lunch box inside it. Bert's friends from the Ponderosa weren't long for this world. His treasures needed a new home.

I set the photographs aside while I carefully fingered each of the medals. The only one that would be hard to clean was the oddly shaped one that had been snagged on tree roots. I couldn't understand why it was so dirty when the other medals were corroded but clean. It was almost as if it had been placed in the box already crusted with dirt and grime. But why would Bert do that?

I was beginning to feel sleepy, and tomorrow was going to be a big day. My parents' arrival would most probably turn my semi-orderly world into chaos. There was a part of me that looked forward to seeing them again—especially my dad. It had been almost two years since I'd had one of his wonderful hugs. My mother was the real problem. Why couldn't I ever seem to please her? My prayer was that she would see how happy I was then go back to China at peace with my choices.

Of course, I also had hopes of someday waking up and finding that I had supernaturally been given a voice like Céline Dion's and a face like Julia Roberts's. So far, that hadn't happened either.

I closed the box and rounded up Miss Skiffins. We hit the mattress around midnight. It was a little after 3:00 a.m. when I woke up with a start. The tiny cat was digging her claws into my arm with a death grip. As I grabbed her and shook her loose, I realized I could smell smoke. I reached over and clicked on the lamp next to my bed. Miss Skiffins stared at me, her eyes wide with terror. I tucked her under my arm and ran into the hallway. I could see smoke downstairs. I was really thankful that my room had no door, or I might have assumed the cat was having a bad dream and gone back to sleep. For a moment, I hesitated, wondering if I should try to climb out an upstairs window. I looked down at my sweat suit. It was heavy enough, but my feet were bare. While trying to control the struggling feline under my arm, I quickly shoved my feet into my sneakers. Just then, Isaac called my name.

"Ivy! Are you up there?"

"I'm here, Isaac. Is it safe to come downstairs?"

"Yes!" he yelled. "But hurry!"

I ran down the stairs. He was waiting at the bottom. "How bad is it?"

"It's just in the corner by your desk," he said, coughing.

I could see the fire now. It was moving up the wall near the front windows. "We've got to call Milton!"

Isaac was guiding me to the back of the store. "I already called him, Miss Ivy," he said. "He'll be here any minute. You go around front. I'm going to get the fire extinguisher and see if I can't stop this from getting any worse."

"Be careful, Isaac," I yelled as he ran back inside. I tromped around the side of the bookstore. Miss Skiffins was fighting me for all she was worth. Thankfully, my car was unlocked, so I put her inside. I didn't want to drop her and have her run away.

I watched the street in front of the bookstore for the fire department truck. Milton Baumgartner ran the volunteer fire department in Winter Break. We had only one old engine, but the volunteers had protected many a building from destruction in the tiny town.

Within a couple of minutes, I saw the out-of-date, dusty red engine pulling up. Milton was driving. His wife, Mavis, sat next to him in the front seat while their two sons hung on to the sides of the vehicle for dear life. As the Baumgartners piled out, Dewey came running out of his store, still buttoning his shirt. I was glad he lived close by. His presence gave me some reassurance. I knew he would do everything he could to save the bookstore.

Almost immediately, Mavis began barking out orders to her family. She was a large woman with bright lemon yellow hair piled precariously on top of her head. Mavis Baumgartner was a force to be reckoned with, and she ran her family like a drill sergeant cursed with an unruly command. Although all our volunteers had been given firefighters' outfits by the Stevens County Fire Department, only the men had them on. Mavis was so massive she couldn't fit into hers. Instead, she wore a big, bright yellow rain poncho over her long flannel nightgown. As she clomped around in enormous black rubber boots, with her poncho flapping in the breeze and her overly bleached bun beginning to come loose from the hairpins that were trying valiantly to keep it secure, she looked like Big Bird with an attitude and a bad dye job.

Before long, other people started showing up. It was the nature of a small town. When one person was in trouble, everyone joined in to help. I felt someone grab my arm. It was Amos.

"Ivy! What happened?"

I fell back into his arms. "I. . .I don't know. I was sleeping. Isaac got us out."

Isaac. I turned to find him, but he was helping the Baumgartners get the hose from the truck. Our fire truck was a tanker truck, which meant it had water inside. Of course, this made the engine heavy and rather slow, but since the fire station was only six blocks away, it hadn't cost us much time. However, if they couldn't put out the fire with the water they had, there would be a big problem. Although Winter Break had a few fire hydrants, the bookstore was almost two blocks away from one. I prayed that the water they had would be enough.

Amos ran over to help with the hose. When the water gushed out, it took only a few minutes for the fire to fizzle and die out. By the time it was over, thankfully, I could see that only one corner of the store was affected. With Miss Skiffins finally calmed down some in the backseat of my car, Amos and I went inside to survey the damage. It seemed to be confined to the area near my desk. Aunt Bitty's antique desk was ruined, as was her chair and the portion of the room that surrounded it.

Isaac walked up behind me. "Thank God the books are all right," he said. "But are the records gone? All our work. . ."

I turned around and hugged him. Isaac had never been very touchy-feely before, but he hugged me back, not seeming to have a problem with our sudden bout of intimacy.

"Thankfully, I've been working on the books in the sitting room and didn't put them back in the desk. They're fine. But even more important than that," I said earnestly, "thank you for getting Miss Skiffins and me out of there."

He smiled in the dusky room, illuminated only by the fire engine's headlights. "I had no choice. You pay my salary."

I ignored his attempt to lighten the situation. "I mean it, Isaac."

"It could have been much worse," he said. "The fire was still small enough so that I could get most of it under control with the extinguisher. Thankfully, I smelled the smoke when I got up to get some milk because I couldn't sleep. It's a good thing my apartment is right next door."

"And it's a good thing you picked tonight to have insomnia."

Amos slapped Isaac on the back. "It doesn't matter how large the fire was, Isaac. You handled it like a pro. Good job."

Even in the semidarkness, I could see Isaac blush. "Well, be that as it may, Deputy, I am still concerned about our books. I wonder if the smoke will affect them."

Mavis came clomping up to us. "The fire was contained to this one area, and most of the smoke drifted toward the door and windows. You're going to have to do some cleanup, but my guess is that you'll find most of your books in fine shape. You really caught it early. All in all, things turned out as well as could be expected." She shone her flashlight at the wall behind us. "Looks like it started right here." The beam of light focused on a charred outlet in the wall.

"Must have been an electrical problem," I said.

Mavis stomped over to the switch and then knelt down and put her nose next to it. She shook her head and stood up slowly. "You smell something?" she asked Amos.

Amos leaned down and sniffed. "Gasoline?"

Mavis nodded vigorously, her hair flying frantically around her head.

"What are you saying?" I asked. "Someone. . .someone set this fire on purpose?"

"We can't be sure of that, Ivy," Amos said. "But it certainly looks suspicious."

"But why?"

Mavis and Amos just looked at me. Isaac shook his head sadly. I was flabbergasted. Who in the world would want to burn the bookstore—with me in it?

"Whoever did this had to know I was here," I said slowly. "Could they have been trying to hurt me?"

"If someone had wanted to hurt you, Ivy," Mavis said kindly, "I think they would have tried starting the fire somewhere else. Seems to me like their goal was the building." She studied the burned fixture for a moment. "I think someone wanted us to think a short circuit started the blaze." She smiled at me. "Sorry I can't tell you more. This isn't *CSI*. It's just Winter Break. Our job is to put out fires. I don't know much about arson. Only remember one arson fire. Ben Willard thought he could get some insurance money for burning down his barn. Silly fool used so much gasoline he lost his house and his tractor to boot." She shook her head. "At least all you've got is minor damage. I guess we can be thankful for that."

Mavis might know how to put out a fire, but she sure didn't understand what "minor damage" was. Aunt Bitty's beautiful desk and antique chair were gone. That wasn't minor to me. However, I was grateful the whole store hadn't gone up in flames.

Just then, one of Mavis's boys came around the corner. "Think everything's under control, Ma. We wet down the outside real good. This fire shouldn't be startin' up again."

"Thanks, Pervis," she said.

"You need to find another place to stay," Mavis said. "We smashed your door in, and it's gonna stink in here for a while. It'd be best if you could go somewhere for a few days while things get repaired."

Amos put his arm around me. "She's right, Ivy. Why don't you go upstairs and grab a few things? I'll take you somewhere else for tonight at least."

I pulled away from him. "I don't want to go, Amos. This is my home. Besides, I'll be upstairs. I'll be okay."

Mavis shook her head. "That's the worst place you could be. Even though we've drenched this area, we can't guarantee it won't flare up again. You can't be here until we're absolutely sure it's safe."

"How could someone get in, Mavis? I'm sure the door was locked."

Using her grime-encrusted hand, she reached up to stabilize her quickly disintegrating bun. "Can't really tell, honey. Maybe someone jimmied the lock. Could be they just kicked it in. It's also possible you just thought the door was locked. That was a pretty door, but it sure wasn't very durable." She put her hand on my shoulder. "It won't take us long to clean this up. We'll have things as good as new before you know it. I'll make sure you get a door that's pretty *and* strong, okay?"

"She's right, Ivy," Milton said from behind me. I turned around to see his sons nodding their agreement.

"But. . .but it isn't your job to fix this," I said, waving my hand toward the blackened furniture and the wall behind it.

"You know better than that," Dewey said as he came toward us. "Folks in Winter Break see themselves as family. What hurts you hurts all of us. You get your stuff and stay away for a few days. I'll keep an eye on things. We'll start the cleanup tomorrow. First thing you know, you'll be back in business."

"Thank you," I sputtered, feeling overwhelmed by the generosity being shown to me. "Thank you, everyone. But, Amos, where will I stay? Sarah Johnson is full up. I can't think of any other place."

I knew Dewey would have asked me to stay with him, but his apartment above the store was as tiny as mine. There wasn't room.

"I have an idea," Amos said. "You just go and pack. Everything will be okay."

I started toward the stairs when I remembered something. "Oh no! Amos, I had Bert's lunch box on the desk!"

I hurried over to the charred remains of the desk. Mavis shone her flashlight over the surface. Everything was there, including my ruined laptop, the charred desk lamp, the blackened pencil holder, the melted stapler, and my overly cooked phone.

But Bert Bird's lunch box and personal treasures were gone.

7

You can't ignore this, Amos," I said after he shuffled me into his patrol car. "Whoever tried to burn down the bookstore was after Bert's lunch box. There is something nefarious going on here, and we have to figure out what it is!"

"Nefarious?" Amos said. "Why do you have to talk like that? Who uses words like *nefarious*?"

"I do, that's who," I snapped. I wanted immediate action. It seemed to me that Amos was so wrapped up in small-town reticence, it was going to take forever to get things moving. "What's your plan? Wait until someone is dead and then take this whole thing seriously?"

Amos pulled the car over. "Ivy," he said, twisting in his seat so he could properly glare at me. "I'm not an idiot, although you act like I am. I dragged you away because you can't keep your mouth shut. Your curiosity about Bert was one thing. I could even overlook the map's disappearance, but the fire and the theft of Bert's things? There is obviously something going on here. I'd like a chance to find out what it is, but it's going to be tough if you're busy telling everybody and their neighbor that we're suspicious."

"Oh." I patted his arm. "I'm sorry. I should have known better. At least the only people who could have overheard me were people we can trust." I blinked back an attack of pesky tears. "I guess I'm just emotional about the bookstore. Aunt Bitty expected me to take care of it. I didn't do a very good job."

Amos reached over and took my chin in his hand. His hazel eyes locked onto mine. "You listen here. This wasn't your fault at all. We're going to figure out what's going on, and we're going to get the bookstore back up on its feet. Don't worry about it, okay?"

I nodded. Then I reached over and kissed him. "Okay. I won't. But this is really going to give my mother something to rant about. How am I going to explain it?"

Amos let go of my face and leaned back in his seat. "You won't. Let her assume it was an accident, and don't tell anyone else that the box and its contents are missing."

"What about Ruby?" I asked. "I'll have to tell her something."

He thought for a moment. "You tell her the truth. There was a small fire. I doubt she'll assume that Bert's stuff was burned up."

187

"But what if she asks me specifically about it? Then what?"

Amos sighed. "Then we'll deal with it, but I'd sure like to keep this as quiet as possible."

"You're hoping we can catch the thief before he disposes of everything."

"Actually, I was hoping that *I* could catch the thief before he disposes of everything, but I suppose there isn't any earthly way to keep you out of this." He flashed me a hopeful smile. "Is there?"

I returned his smile with one of my own. "Not in this lifetime, bucko. Not after the scumbag set my bookstore on fire and almost scared the life out of Miss Skiffins."

"I figured that. And don't call me bucko ever again."

"Okay. Now what's our first move?"

Amos started the car and pulled back out into the street. "First we get you settled in. Then, without much sleep, we go see Harvey. After that, you entertain your parents while I sniff around a little bit."

I started to protest.

"Don't get snarky," Amos interrupted. "I'll keep you updated on anything I find out."

"You bet you will," I said emphatically. "And you shouldn't say 'snarky.' It doesn't sound right coming from you."

"I'm trying to update my vocabulary. I have you to thank for it."

"Glad I could help," I said. "Now, out of curiosity, just where are you taking me? I'm certain we're not going to your place. You know I can't stay with you."

He nodded. "And not just because it would cause a scandal; I don't have a spare bedroom. In fact, I don't even have a bedroom. I sleep on the couch."

"But you still live in your mom's old house. I thought there were two bedrooms."

"There were. But I let RoseAnn Flattery store some of the things she inherited from her mother in one room, and Bubba Weber needed a place to keep extra jars of honey."

"It takes a whole room to collect a few jars of honey?"

Amos grinned. "If you're storing over a thousand jars, it does."

My mouth dropped open. "A thousand jars? My goodness! I know he sells a lot of honey, but surely you can't stockpile it too long without it going bad."

"He sells some; then he brings more jars. Besides, raw honey keeps almost forever, according to Bubba. Something about low moisture content. I wasn't really listening."

"Amos, you're a saint, and I appreciate your desire to help people, but do you really think you should have given up both of your bedrooms?"

He shrugged. "Maybe not, but I was spending most of my nights on the couch anyway. It made sense at the time."

I was pretty sure Amos wasn't happy living in the same house he'd shared with his mother and father. It had been a sad little house with peeling paint and a broken-down porch when his parents lived there. I'd visited a few times when we were young, but he hardly ever invited me over. Now we never mentioned it. Even though Amos had fixed the house up, we still never went there. It was as if it was a part of a past we weren't allowed to share. I didn't push it, although I felt that someday we would have to talk more about his childhood.

"So back to my original question. Where are we going?" I valued my privacy and wasn't interested in giving it up to stay with someone else, no matter how well intentioned they were.

Amos didn't answer me, but when he turned onto Oak Road, I knew the answer. "The Biddle house? Are you serious?"

The beautiful, cornflower blue Victorian structure that sat next to Lake Winter Break was my favorite house in the entire world. It was my dream home. Cecil and Marion Biddle had left it behind several years ago when they moved to Florida because of Cecil's arthritis. The icy Winter Break weather had been too much for him. They had rented out the house for a while, but thankfully, the woman living there was gone from Winter Break.

"But how—" I started to ask.

"Cecil called me yesterday to tell me that someone was going to be staying in the house for a week or so," Amos said. "He left me a set of keys and asked if I would unlock the house. I planned to tell you at dinner, but as you know, things got a little crazy and I forgot. I'm sorry."

"I don't understand," I said. "Someone else will be staying there, too? Who—" Then it hit me. "Wait a minute. Oh no. . . ."

Amos pulled up in front of the Biddle house. "Now, Ivy. It's a big house, and they are your parents. You'll be fine. Besides, we'll get the bookstore fixed before you know it."

The sense of dread I'd felt since I found out my parents were coming to Winter Break grew little legs and started dancing the cha-cha in my intestines. "How in the world did my parents get hold of the Biddles?"

"I have no idea. Maybe they kept in touch. Your mom and dad have been to Winter Break more than once. If I remember right, they really connected with Marion and Cecil."

I'd forgotten about that. "But I don't see how they knew to reach them in Florida."

"Maybe you should ask Dewey. My guess is that he hooked them up. Your mom used to call him when Bitty broke her leg several years ago. He knew the Biddles had rented out the house before."

That was most likely the answer. Dewey probably thought he was doing me a favor. "I don't think this is a good idea, Amos. I'll be an easy target here.

At least at home, I can get away if I need to."

"Ivy," Amos said forcefully, "your parents aren't your enemies, for goodness' sake! You should be thankful you have parents who love you." He glared at me in frustration. "Some of us would give anything for that."

Amos's chastisement hit home. My attitude *was* negative. It wasn't going to help me get along with my parents, and I was certain it wasn't pleasing to God. I sent up a silent prayer, asking the Lord to help me change before my folks arrived.

Amos carried my luggage inside the house. Everything looked just as it had when I was a child. The Biddles had left almost all their furniture and appliances behind, choosing to buy new things in Florida rather than try to transport all their belongings. The beautiful decor was perfect for the house. Comfortable, with a Victorian influence, the lovely maroon, gold, and cerulean colors were a theme carried into each room.

My favorite room was the huge dining room. One entire wall was made up of windows, with French doors that opened out to the patio. It offered a beautiful view of Lake Winter Break. Marion had hosted many dinner parties around the gorgeous mahogany dining room set that was positioned just in front of the windows. In the summer, the adults would eat inside with the doors open, and the kids would eat on the patio. I could almost smell Cecil's famous barbequed ribs as they crackled on the grill.

The thing I loved most in the room was a tapestry that hung on the wall, over the buffet. It was huge—at least seven feet long and six feet across. Marion had painted it herself. There was the lake, with children skating and snow falling. Cecil's flagpole was visible, with his little yellow flag waving in the wind. It was our sign that the water had frozen hard enough for skating. Once the yellow flag went up, children raced to the lake, where we spent hours and hours skating and drinking Marion's hot chocolate.

I could pick out each person in the painting. Amos and I skated together, holding hands. My best friend, Emily Baumgartner, sat on a bench near the lake while accepting a cup of hot chocolate from Buddy Taylor. I'd forgotten about that. How touching that Marion had painted them together since they were now married. I'd had no idea that they had been anything more than friends. Had Marion seen something the rest of us hadn't? I decided to ask her about it someday.

I lightly touched the image of Aunt Bitty, sitting next to Emily, waving to me with one hand while holding a book with the other one. That was Aunt Bitty all right. Her great-niece and her books. Her two favorite things.

"That painting is very special, isn't it?"

I jumped involuntarily. I'd forgotten for a moment that Amos had followed me inside.

"Yes," I said softly. "It's very, very special. I'm still surprised that Marion left it here."

Amos set my bags down. "She said it belonged to Winter Break."

I was so entranced by the tapestry, I didn't respond. He seemed to understand and came up next to me, pulling me close to him. We stood there for quite a while, locked in an embrace, staring at Marion's labor of love.

When Amos finally spoke, his voice cracked with emotion. "The first time I ever saw you, you were only seven years old. You were standing next to the lake with your skates in your hands. Big white flakes of snow swirled around you, and the glow from the Biddles' backyard light made you look like an angel. You were the most beautiful thing I'd ever seen. You took my breath away. I was only nine, but I knew I would love you forever. I've never wanted anyone else since that moment."

"And I was thinking you were the handsomest boy I'd ever seen," I said. "Until that moment, I thought boys were nothing more than a necessary nuisance. What I felt that night was something brand-new. Something wonderful."

He leaned over and brushed my lips with his. "I'd better go," he whispered. "I'll be back at nine."

I let him go and watched him walk out the front door. I'd been brokenhearted when I first came back to Winter Break. Losing Aunt Bitty was devastating. Funny how a little bit of time could change everything. I'd not only found a new life for myself in this small town, but I'd rediscovered love, as well. I knew beyond a shadow of a doubt that there was absolutely nothing in this world that could make me leave Winter Break. Not my parents and not the person who had tried to burn down my store.

I felt a kind of resolve inside that I'd never experienced before. Anyone who thought I could be run out of town was in for the fight of a lifetime.

I grabbed my bags, put Miss Skiffins's pet carrier under my arm, and went upstairs. There were four bedrooms at the top of the stairs, along with two bathrooms, but I climbed one more set of stairs until I reached the door to the attic. I hadn't seen this room for many years, but I was hopeful things hadn't changed. Sure enough, when I switched on the light, I found another bedroom. It used to belong to Marion and Cecil's daughter, Mary. We'd spent many rainy days playing in her bedroom when we were children. Mary was now a doctor in Wichita. We'd had lunch a few times when I was going to school, and she'd told me about her bid to have a room away from her three brothers. Cecil had designed this attic room for her. It had a sloping ceiling, with a large window next to a bed covered with a beautiful handmade quilt. The window looked out on the lake. Around the window and across the ceiling were small stars painted with silver fluorescent paint. Mary had asked her father if he could "bring the stars inside," and he had given them to her. I put my bags in the large armoire that sat against the wall, let Miss Skiffins out of her carrier, and then plopped down on the bed without changing my clothes. The little cat curled up next to me; I was so tired, I was asleep within minutes.

I dreamed I was frantically searching for something hidden beneath a dark velvet sky of twinkling stars.

8

Thankfully, I woke up at seven and had time to shower and change before Amos arrived. I'd found some instant coffee in the cupboard and made a cup, but there wasn't much else on the shelves or in the refrigerator. I would have liked to shop for my mother and father so they would have food available when they arrived, but Mother was so picky I knew it wouldn't do any good. It was better if she went to Dewey's herself and selected whatever she wanted.

After a quick cup of coffee, Amos and I got in the patrol car and drove out to Harvey's.

"Let me tell him about it," Amos said as we neared the house. "You keep quiet and look remorseful."

"That won't be difficult," I said morosely. "I feel really bad about what I did. Funny how something can sound so right in your head and turn out so wrong when you actually do it."

Amos sighed. "Here's a revolutionary idea. You could listen to the person who tried to warn you not to listen to that voice in your head."

"I wish it were that easy. I don't like to be told what to do. It's one of my greatest weaknesses."

Amos reached over and patted my shoulder. "And one of your greatest strengths is your ability to face the truth about yourself, Ivy. Some people never do that."

"Some people don't get as much practice as I do," I said wryly.

As he laughed, I thought about asking why he'd done such an about-face over my problem with Harvey. Originally, he'd declared that I would have to face the music alone. Now he was telling me to be quiet and let him handle it. I was beginning to learn that if I let him have enough rope, I might not have to hang for my trespasses. While I was debating whether I could ethically use this personality trait to my advantage, he stopped the car and got out. He had just opened my door when Harvey came strolling around the side of the house. He stopped as soon as he saw us and shot me a look that could have frozen even Hiram Ledbetter's Life-Preserving Liniment. I was obviously in deep trouble. Suddenly, Amos's offer to speak for me seemed extremely appealing.

"Hey, Harvey," Amos called out. "Can we talk to you for a minute?"

Harvey looked at us as if we were foxes who had come to inspect his henhouse. "What do you want, Deputy?" he called out.

"Ivy is here to apologize to you," Amos said. "She knows she shouldn't have gone into the orchard without your permission. I hope you'll be understanding about it."

Harvey sidled up close to us, his thin, sallow face locked in a perpetual scowl. "Understanding? You two don't seem to be able to mind your own business. You already desecrated my orchard once, and here you go again. I ought to file a complaint with your superiors."

Amos removed his hat and ran a hand through his hair. "Now, Harvey," he said in a soothing tone, "you know Ivy and I were only kids when we dug those holes. And nothing was desecrated. We didn't hurt the trees at all."

"Well, you aren't kids now, are you?" Harvey hissed. "So what's your excuse this time?"

"Harvey," I interjected, "this was all my fault. I found that map and wanted to see what was buried in the orchard. Amos planned to ask your permission before we stepped one foot on your property. I was the one who jumped the gun. Amos didn't know anything about it."

Harvey spit a stream of tobacco juice onto the ground. "That doesn't surprise me one little bit," he said, brown liquid dribbling down his stubbly chin. He reached up to wipe it off, but his dirt-encrusted hand made an even bigger mess. "You were always trouble, Ivy Towers. You were a mess when you were a kid, and you're a mess now."

"Now just a minute," Amos said, taking a step forward. "There's no call to talk to Ivy like that. Either you can accept her apology and be done with it, or we can certainly take this to the next level."

I had no idea what "the next level" meant, but Harvey took a step backward. After another spittle projectile, he locked his bloodshot eyes on me. His expression was as sour as his attitude.

"I guess we'll let it go this time, but I'd better not ever find you on my property again, do you understand?" he said, pointing his finger at me.

"I promise, Harvey," I said in a contrite voice. "Unless you invite me, I have no intention of coming anywhere near your place."

"You don't have to worry about any invitations, Ivy Towers," he replied in a low voice. "None will be forthcoming."

"I saw you at Ruby's yesterday," I said. "You know that we found a lunch box buried in your orchard? One that belonged to Bert Bird?"

"Just goes to show you two weren't the only brats fooling around on my property," he said harshly. "If you're asking me if I want it back, the answer is no. You let Ruby keep it."

Amos touched my back with his hand. "Okay, Harvey. I hope we can let bygones be bygones. Is there anything else you have to say about the matter?"

Another stream of brown liquid hit the dirt. A few drops splattered against Amos's boot, but he acted as though he didn't notice.

"No, there's nothing else to say, Deputy, except good day to you."

"Thank you, Harvey," I said in my humblest tone. "You'll have no more problems from me."

I could hear Harvey mumble something under his breath, but Amos was steering me so quickly toward the car, I didn't catch it. I was pretty sure he wasn't complimenting me on my hairstyle or wardrobe.

Once we were in the car, Amos blew out his breath between clenched teeth. "That old so-and-so can be meaner than a rattlesnake on a diet. I can hardly believe he used to host jamborees here for the Scouts. Doesn't sound like something he'd do."

"People change. I guess when his wife left him, it made him bitter. We should feel sorry for Harvey. I'm sure he's a lonely, sad man."

"Acting that way certainly won't change anything."

"That's true, Amos. Maybe Harvey needs a friend."

Amos swung around and stared at me. "For crying out loud. Now you want me to be best pals with Harvey Bruenwalder?"

"Well, maybe not best pals, but it wouldn't hurt for you to reach out to him a little." Harvey was the kind of person it would be easy to walk away from, but I could hear Aunt Bitty's voice in my head. *"God doesn't give us credit for loving the people who are easy to love, Ivy,"* she'd say. *"It's loving the unlovely that really shows Christ's love."*

"You beat all, you know that?" Amos said, shaking his head. "You want to help Harvey, a man who wouldn't care if he never laid eyes on you again, but you don't trust your own parents, who love you to pieces. Sometimes I can't figure you out at all."

I smiled sweetly at him. "Good. That will keep a little mystery in our relationship."

Amos grunted. "I don't think that will be a problem. You certainly keep me on my toes."

I decided it was time to change the subject. "At least Harvey didn't insist we return Bert's box."

Amos shook his head. "I'm not sure whether it's because of his compassion for Ruby or because he just couldn't care less about it. I guarantee you that if you'd actually uncovered the Lost Gambler's Gold, he'd be putting a claim on it."

We drove the rest of the way in silence. I was turning the situation with the store over in my mind, trying to figure out who would want to set fire to Winter Break's only bookstore and what Bert's paltry trinkets had to do with it. I had no idea what Amos was thinking, but my guess was that he was still worrying over Odie and those missing cows. I was concerned, too, but the bookstore fire had taken top priority in my mind.

As we pulled up to the Biddle house, I was surprised to see Dr. Lucy Barber's SUV parked in the circular driveway. Lucy and I had started out on the wrong foot after Aunt Bitty died, but now we got along just fine. I counted her among my friends. In fact, I quietly carried on the work my great-aunt had started by helping with bills and medicines for some of the townspeople who couldn't afford what they needed. Lucy donated everything she could, and I made up the difference. I was going to have to start making some money with the bookstore soon, however. Bitty's inheritance was getting smaller and smaller.

The only real tension between us now came from the fact that Amos and Lucy had dated a little before I came to town. Amos hadn't been serious about her, and she had always known that he was in love with someone else, but she still wasn't thrilled when I showed up after Bitty died. And I wasn't sure that there weren't still some leftover feelings of resentment on her part. It wasn't obvious, just an undercurrent I thought I felt sometimes. Of course, my imagination could be running away with me again.

"I wonder why Lucy is here," I said. "How did she know I would be staying at the Biddles'?"

"I told her," Amos said. "I know you feel okay, but you breathed in a lot of smoke last night. I want her to take a look at you."

"Amos," I grumbled as he parked the car, "why don't you just ask me if I need to see a doctor? I'm not a child!"

He plastered a big, goofy grin on his face. "You'd better smile and act like everything's okay. If Lucy sees us fighting, she may think I'm available again."

I reached over and slapped his arm. "If you keep trying to run my life, you *will* be back on the market." Since there was no way to make an escape, I climbed out of the car, determined to make the best of it.

Lucy saw us and jumped down from her vehicle. "Hey, you two! It's been awhile."

"It took a fire at the bookstore to bring you around," I said. "I'm not sure I can come up with an encore to that. Maybe you could just stop by to say hi once in a while without all the drama."

Lucy chuckled. "I think I can do that. Let's get you inside so I can see if you're going to live one more day." She was carrying a paper bag and handed it to me.

"What's this?" I asked.

"Just some things I thought you might need. Amos told me you'd be staying here for a while. I was pretty sure there weren't many supplies, since the house has been vacant for so long."

I peered into the sack and saw coffee, sugar, milk, bread, butter, eggs, and bacon. My stomach rumbled in appreciation. "This means you have to stay for breakfast."

"I don't have much time, Ivy," she said. "I have several people to see this morning. But I would love a cup of coffee. I was out pretty late last night at Cyrus Penwiddie's place. He's got a bad case of shingles, and it took me a long time to get him comfortable."

"Did you catch any of the excitement surrounding our mysterious fire?" I asked as we entered the house.

Lucy shook her head. "No. Cyrus's place is almost two miles outside of town. I never actually came into Winter Break. I was shocked when Amos told me about it."

I got busy fixing a fresh pot of coffee. I definitely needed another caffeine kick in the pants. And I was pretty sure Amos was as tired as I was. A glance at the clock in the kitchen told me my parents could swoop down on me at any minute.

With the coffeemaker chortling in the background, Lucy inspected my throat with her trusty tongue depressor. "Any hoarseness? Difficulty breathing? Coughing spells? Mental confusion?"

I answered, "Nuh-uh," to each question. It's hard to say anything more coherent with a large wooden stick holding your tongue down.

"Can I take that last question?" Amos asked.

"I don't think so," Lucy said. "I assume any woman who gets herself mixed up with you is suffering some kind of dementia."

"Oh, very nice," Amos said, shaking his head. "I can't believe the trials I am forced to endure for love."

His hangdog expression made Lucy and me laugh. My laughter almost ended tragically, however. Guffawing with a tongue depressor down your throat is a recipe for disaster. Lucy pulled it out. "Sorry," she said.

"Well, now I *am* coughing," I sputtered.

"You look fine. I don't see anything to be concerned about. If you have any symptoms, let me know, okay?"

"Symptoms of what?" a loud feminine voice interjected.

I turned around to see my mother and father standing in the doorway. "Mom! Dad!" I said, trying to redirect the attention somewhere else. My next step was to state the obvious. "You're here!"

My father's face erupted into a broad grin, and his arms opened wide. I flew into them. I hadn't realized until that moment how much I needed one of my father's bear hugs.

"Hello, punkin. I've missed you so much."

"I've missed you, too, Daddy," I mumbled from the folds of his coat.

"Nice to see you, Amos," my dad said with his arms still wrapped around me.

"Good to see you, too, sir. It's been a long time."

"Symptoms of what, Ivy?" My mother's forceful voice cut through my brief but joyous reunion with my father.

"Why, hello, Mother," I said, stepping back. "I'm happy to see you."

She reached over and gave me a quick, perfunctory hug. "Quit trying to avoid the subject, Ivy," she retorted. "What symptoms?"

"Are you okay, honey?" my father asked. His face showed his concern. My mother's expression was the same one I'd seen all my life. She was waiting for my next major foul-up. I rarely disappointed her.

"There was a small fire in the bookstore last night, Mother," I said. "Amos was afraid I'd breathed in some smoke." I pointed toward Lucy. "Mom and Dad, I'd like you to meet Lucy Barber. She's Winter Break's doctor."

My mother extended her hand to Lucy. "I'm relieved to know that Winter Break *has* a doctor. It's nice to know you, Dr. Barber. Do you live nearby?"

Shoot and bother. My mother had some kind of advanced radar that always seemed to zoom in on anything I didn't want her to know. I'd never seen anything like it.

"No, Mrs. Towers, I live in Hugoton, but I come here frequently."

Mom looked as if she'd bitten into something sour. "What happens if there's a real emergency? How long does it take you to get here?"

Lucy, to her credit, responded with a relaxed smile. "I can get here in a little over thirty minutes. And I have a trained nursing assistant who can take care of things until I arrive." She turned to me. "I planned to tell you that Sarah Johnson is now stocked with emergency supplies in case of an accident or a sudden medical emergency. We've been working together for a couple of weeks. I hope this will help folks in Winter Break feel a little safer."

"That's a great idea, Lucy. Between you and Sarah, I'm sure we're covered." I smiled at my mother, hoping to convince her that I would survive should I accidentally set myself on fire or explode from eating one of Ruby's Redbird Burgers. "Lucy's very committed to us. In fact, she drove to Winter Break late last night because someone called her."

"Unfortunately, it was a case that Sarah couldn't handle," Lucy explained helpfully.

I threw a quick, stern look her way. I was pretty sure she was only making things worse. "But you drove here right away, right? As soon as you received the phone call?"

"Of. . .of course, I was happy to come," she said cheerfully, getting the hint. "Anything I can do to help. . . ."

"I know everyone in Winter Break appreciates you." My saccharine attempt to build up Winter Break's doctor was starting to make me feel a little nauseated.

Lucy smiled broadly at all of us. "And to that end, I'd better skedaddle. Bubba Weber got stung by one of his bees and thinks the wound is infected. If I don't get there soon, he'll start trying to treat himself. The last time he did that, he almost lost his hand."

"Thanks again," I said gratefully. "And don't forget what I said about stopping by sometime just to visit."

"I definitely will do that, Ivy," she said, eyeing my mother. "Maybe sometime in the next week or two?" Her question was code for *Will your mother be gone by then?*

"That sounds about right," I said as innocently as I could.

"It was very nice to meet you, Mr. and Mrs. Towers," she said as she made her getaway. "I hope you enjoy your stay in Winter Break."

"Nice to meet you, too, Dr. Barber," my dad said. "Maybe we'll see you again before we leave."

A look of panic crossed Lucy's face. She nodded and then quickly executed her escape.

"She's very attractive," Mother said. "Is she Indian?"

"She's part Cherokee," Amos said. "On her mother's side. Would you two like to sit down while Ivy and I get us some coffee?"

"Thanks, Amos," my dad said jovially. "We've been driving for quite a while. I'm a little tired. A cup of coffee sounds perfect."

My parents sat at the breakfast bar while I poured coffee and Amos put away the groceries, leaving the sugar and milk out in case anyone wanted some. My dad took his coffee with two spoons of sugar and a dollop of milk. My mom was a no-nonsense coffee drinker. Black. And the thicker the better. I drank my coffee black but couldn't stand thick, bitter coffee. My mother called my coffee "hot, dirty water." I handed her a cup. She took a sip and shook her head. I ignored her.

"I'm going to have to get out of here, too," Amos said. "But why don't I take your bags upstairs before I go?"

"Why, thank you," my dad said with a grin. "My back isn't what it used to be. I'd be grateful for the help." He reached into his pocket and pulled out a single car key with a rental tag attached to it. "If you'll just put everything at the top of the stairs, I'll move it into whatever room Margie picks."

I wanted to ask why my father couldn't pick their room, but we all knew the answer, so I kept quiet.

"So how long has Dr. Barber been serving Winter Break?" my mother asked as soon as Amos left the room.

"A couple of years, I think," I said. I had a bad feeling that we were going someplace I didn't want to go.

"Hmm," Mom said, tapping her nails against her coffee cup. "Amos certainly seems to know a lot about her."

Bingo. There it was. "Yes, Mother," I said with a smile plastered on my face. "And before you go there, they dated for a while before I came back to town. It was never serious. It's been over for a long time, and Lucy and I get along fine. So you can quit looking for something that isn't there."

My mother's raised eyebrow was the sign that I'd overreacted again. According to my mother, I was always overreacting.

"You said there was a small fire at the bookstore?" my dad asked, deftly changing the subject.

"Yes. It looks like it started at a receptacle." That wasn't a lie. It did start at the receptacle. I wasn't going to offer any information about *how* it started unless I was asked specifically.

"That old bookstore is a fire hazard," Mother huffed. "It should have been torn down a long time ago."

I could feel the blood rush to my head. My mother was an expert at pushing my buttons. I'd made a promise to myself that I wouldn't respond to any of her cutting remarks as long as she was in Winter Break. With great effort, I pushed back the words I really wanted to say. "The people who live here love that bookstore, Mother. And I love it. No one's going to tear it down."

"It's been years since I've seen the bookstore, Ivy," my dad said. "I'm looking forward to it. Let's get unpacked and settled; then we'll drive over there. We'll also need to buy some groceries while we're out."

"I do want to check on the bookstore," I said, "but we may have to wait a couple of days for any kind of a tour. There will have to be some repairs, and I'm sure it doesn't smell very good right now."

"So where are you staying?" Mother asked. "Surely you're not still living in that tiny room above the store."

"No, Mother. Not right now. Not until things are cleaned up."

"So where *are* you staying, Ivy?" Dad asked.

"Well, for a few days, I guess I'm staying here with you. If that's okay."

My father's round, cherubic face lit up. "How wonderful! We'll be a family again—at least for a little while."

I knew what he meant, but I wasn't sure we'd been a real family in a long time. My mother seemed pleased by this turn of events, although I was afraid it might be because she realized I was now a captive audience. *Will you walk into my parlor?" said the spider to the fly.*

"That's wonderful," she said, smiling for the first time since she'd arrived. "This will give us plenty of time to talk."

Of course, her upbeat mood didn't last long. Miss Skiffins picked that moment to rub up against her leg.

"Ooh!" my mother yelped. "Where did this mangy thing come from?"

The startled cat ran around the other side of the breakfast bar, obviously frightened by my mother's screeching. I hurried over to pick her up. "Mother! This is Miss Skiffins, Aunt Bitty's cat." I held the trembling animal, trying to calm her. "She's my cat now. Please don't holler at her. She's had it rough. First she loses Bitty, then she wakes up in the middle of a fire, and now she's away from her home."

"Oh, for pity's sake," my mother said. "It's just a cat, Ivy. I remember how you used to assign human traits to animals. It isn't healthy."

"Now, Marjorie Christine," my father said in a stern voice. "We're only going to be here for a short while. You can be nice to this precious little kitty during our visit. Let's not have any more yelling at the poor thing."

My father rarely stood up to my mother, but whenever he said "Marjorie Christine," which was my mother's real name, she backed down without a fight. It was one of the reasons my dad was my hero. In my whole life, he was the only person who had ever managed to control my mother.

She didn't say anything, but I knew, at least for now, this battle was on hold.

"I think that's everything," Amos said as he strode into the room. He handed the car key back to my father and then leaned over and kissed my cheek. "I'll call you later."

I wanted to grab his arm and beg him not to leave, but I couldn't. I flashed him my bravest smile and watched him walk out the front door.

"So let's plan our day," my dad said with a sparkle in his eyes. "I particularly want to eat at that wonderful restaurant in town. What was it called?"

"Ruby's Redbird Café."

"Oh my goodness," my mother said disgustedly. "Are you telling me that place is still open? They might as well pile their plates with lard and hand people a shovel."

My mother is a beautiful woman. Copper hair, creamy skin, and large emerald-colored eyes. While my looks are rather untamed and pedestrian, hers are refined and elegant. I'd always wanted to look like my mother, but for the first time in my life, I actually saw myself in her. And I didn't like it. Was that what I sounded like when I complained about Ruby's food?

"Ruby Bird is a wonderful cook, Mother. She goes out of her way to make things she thinks people will enjoy. I'm sure you can find something to your liking if you try." I felt a surge of emotion that I couldn't understand at first. But then it became clear. This was my home, and Ruby Bird was part of my family. If someone from Winter Break criticized my mother or father, I would feel the same way. Defensive.

My mother sniffed her disapproval. "Well, hopefully Dewey Tater will have some decent things in his store. I'll try to prepare some healthy meals for all of us."

I didn't say anything, but I had made a quick, silent pact with myself. No more holier-than-thou attitude toward Ruby and her restaurant.

I glanced at my watch. "Why don't you guys freshen up and unpack? Then we'll head over to Ruby's for lunch. After that, we can check on the bookstore and go to Dewey's."

Not going to work in Miss Bitty's Bygone Bookstore felt strange. I'd grown used to it. I loved living among old books and new friends. I was happy with my life, and this change in my routine left me feeling unsettled.

While my parents chose one of the upstairs rooms and unpacked, I went out through the dining room and onto the large patio deck that Cecil had built onto the back of the house. It was hard to add a feature as modern as a deck to a Victorian house and retain its style, but Cecil Biddle had done a marvelous job. The white, weathered boards reached out toward steps that led past blooming flower beds to a dock that stretched almost twenty feet into the lake. I'd spent many hours sitting on that dock, wiggling my toes in the water while I thought about all the things young girls think about.

I sat down in one of the wooden deck chairs and breathed in the warming air, fragrant with the scent of honeysuckle and lilac bushes. I spent a few minutes thanking God for the day ahead and praying that He would help me to walk in love. "*This is the day the Lord has made; let us rejoice and be glad in it.*" I felt God's peace settle over me. Everything would be okay. *Love never fails.*

As I meditated on the unfailing goodness of God, I wondered what He had planned for my life. I knew He had a design, and that it was good, but I was the kind of person who always wanted to know what was coming. I was learning that God doesn't always lay things out ahead of time. Learning to trust Him was more important than knowing everything before it happened. "I trust You, Lord," I whispered. "Help me to walk in Your will and stay on the path You have laid out for me. Please help me to forgive the person who set fire to the bookstore, but help us to find out why whoever it was took Bert's things." Then another thought crossed my mind. "And, Lord, if he's alive, please bring Bert Bird home. Ruby needs to see her son again."

I felt a sense of peace come over me. That, coupled with the lack of sleep from the night before, caused me to doze off. Right before my mother woke me up, I thought I heard Aunt Bitty whisper, "*God does have a plan, Ivy. Someday soon, you will bring Bert Bird home.*"

9

Since my mother wanted to go to the grocery store first, we decided to have lunch afterward then visit the bookstore. From across the street I could see Milton and his sons clearing out burned boards and working on a new door. I wanted to go over and help them, but I knew I'd just be in the way. I waved at them, and then I followed my parents into the Food-a-Rama. I'd found out that it *was* Dewey who'd suggested my parents stay at the Biddle house. I intended to thank him for his suggestion later, in private. It didn't take long, however, before I realized it wasn't necessary. Dewey was already suffering for his interference in my life. Although it wasn't any surprise to me, our trip to Laban's Food-a-Rama wasn't a great success.

"You don't have rice flour?" Mother asked when Dewey handed her a bag of regular white flour.

Dewey scratched his head and looked puzzled. "Sorry, Margie, but I only sell white and wheat. I didn't even know they made flour from rice."

"It's fine, Dewey," my dad said. "Flour is flour."

"Flour is not flour," my mother huffed. "I can't make *changfen* with white rice. And there's no sesame seed oil. Thank goodness you can buy rice in Winter Break. At least we can still have *congee* for breakfast."

"I said it's fine, Margie. Why don't you just cook some of the good old American dishes you used to make? We'll have lots of time to eat Chinese food when we get back." My dad frowned at my mother, who immediately stomped off to look at something on one of the shelves in the back of the store.

Dewey didn't seem offended by my mother's less-than-gracious attitude. His face held its usual good-natured expression, and his smile was still in place. While my father explained to him that changfen is rice noodles and congee is a kind of Chinese porridge, I grabbed a basket and did a little shopping of my own. If I had to stay with my parents for a while, I wanted some food I liked in the house. I grabbed some microwave popcorn, one of my favorite things, and added some natural peanut butter along with a jar of Bubba Weber's honey. Then I sorted through the fresh fruits and vegetables brought in by Winter Break residents. Some lettuce, radishes, carrots, and a few not-quite-ripe peaches also found their way into my basket. I was looking over the extra-virgin olive oil when my mother's voice behind me made me jump.

"Ivy, why in the world are you buying groceries? I asked you what you wanted. I intended to get enough for all of us."

"I don't expect you to provide for me completely, Mother," I said in as calm a voice as I could muster. "I've been taking care of myself for quite some time."

"What do you mean by that?"

My mother's sharp retort so surprised me, at first I couldn't think of anything to say. "I—I didn't mean anything by it," I finally sputtered. "I just meant that I can cook for myself. I don't expect you to buy my food and prepare my meals."

"Buy whatever you want. You can choose to eat with your parents or by yourself. It's your prerogative."

As she whirled around and headed down another aisle, I stood there and wondered why it seemed that almost everything I said made my mother mad. It hadn't always been that way. At one time, we were very close. We'd started having problems a couple of years before they left for China. Most of it had been my fault. I'd seen their plans as some kind of personal rejection. I regretted the sniping that went on between us back then, wishing we'd used the time we had together more constructively. Of course, we were together now and things were just as bad.

I grabbed a few more items before I checked out with Dewey. Mother and Dad were already in the car by the time I got out. Since Mom had purchased some perishable items, we ran the groceries home before we went to Ruby's for lunch. The café was already packed by the time we arrived, but Ruby hollered at a couple of farmers to sit at the counter and get out of their booth so that "Ivy Tower's parents can have a good sit-down meal." I thought it was a sweet gesture, but my mother looked embarrassed.

"Mickey and Margie Towers!" Ruby yelled at them after they slid into their side of the booth. "It's been nigh on forever since you been to town. Where you been keepin' yourselves?"

While my dad explained their mission in China, my mother eyed the big chalkboard mounted on the wall, which served as the only available menu at Ruby's. We were on the other side of the room, so it was difficult to make out her rather shaky handwriting. My mother took her glasses out of her purse, put them on, and glared at the Winter Break residents crowded next to the cash register to pay their bills, since they were blocking her field of vision.

"Margie, put those glasses away," my father said sternly. "Redbird Burgers all around, Ruby," he said with a grin. "Next to seeing my only child, your burgers are the best thing in Winter Break."

Ruby put her hands on her narrow hips and smiled with approval. "For you, Mickey, I'll make 'em extra special."

She looked over at me as if she wanted to say something else, but I glanced away, unwilling to meet her eyes. I didn't want her to bring up the lunch box now. Not in front of my parents. The less they knew, the better. Besides, I still hadn't figured out how to tell Ruby that the box and its contents had disappeared. My ruse worked. She sailed down the aisle on her way to make her famous one-pound hamburgers with all the fixin's. Except for ketchup. Ruby didn't allow anyone to put ketchup on her burgers. In fact, the mere mention of this particular condiment had led to more than one banishment from Ruby's establishment. As far as Ruby was concerned, ketchup was made for fries and meatloaf—and that was it. Period.

I'd successfully steered clear of Redbird Burgers for a month and a half. I felt as if I'd lost most of the five pounds they had added to my hips. I guessed since I'd lost the weight once, I could do it again.

"Mickey Towers," my mother hissed. "Why in the world would you order me one of those horrible hamburgers? I don't want it! And heaven knows you don't need it."

I wasn't surprised. My mother was always nagging my dad about his weight. He wasn't really fat, just rotund. With a beard and a red costume, he would make the perfect Santa Claus. His soft, silver hair, sparkling eyes, and rosy cheeks made him a perfect match for the jolly old elf.

My father turned to her with a twinkle in his eye. "Then why did you tell me that Ruby's Redbird Burger was the best thing you ever tasted?"

"I—I never said any such thing," she sputtered, looking at me. "Why would you say that?"

"Yes, you did, Margie," my dad said, smiling. "You said it the very last time we were in Winter Break."

"I—I—I couldn't have." My mother's face was as red as the checkered tablecloth on the table.

"Marjorie Christine," my father said in a low voice, "you not only said it, but hamburger grease was dribbling down your chin at the time. I remember thinking how cute you looked." He gazed at her fondly; then he shook his finger at her. "Now loosen up a little bit. Let's try to enjoy our time here." A large smile spread across his face. "I intend to have some fun with my daughter and eat myself silly. We don't get this kind of food in China."

I was certain my mother had blocked out everything she had once liked about Winter Break—including Redbird Burgers. She'd always felt that Bitty had wasted her life here, and she was determined that I wouldn't do the same thing.

"Ivy, I need to put some gas in the rental car. Where's the nearest gas station?"

"You'll have to get back to the highway, Dad. There's a station about ten miles from here. No one in Winter Break sells gas."

"Well, my goodness. What if someone runs out?" my mother asked. "You're just out of luck?"

"No. Several people keep extra gas stockpiled on their farms in case they need it. Some people, like Dr. Barber, carry around a can of gas in the back of their vehicles, although it sure doesn't seem safe to me."

Before my mother had the chance to respond, an unpleasant, nasal voice interrupted our conversation.

"Well, who do we have here?" Bertha Pennypacker sidled up to our booth. Her dyed jet black hair was tightly knotted in a frizzy ponytail, making her face look almost Oriental. Before I had a chance to say anything, Bertha stuck her large hand out toward my father. "I'm Bertha Pennypacker, a friend of Ivy's." Her mouth opened in an expression that was supposed to be a smile but looked more like the effects of gas pains. I was trying figure out just when we became friends while my father shook her hand and introduced himself and my mother. Bertha extended her hand to my mother, which meant that she had to reach across my face. I realized that she was desperately trying to show me the large diamond ring that sparkled on one of her fat fingers.

"Goodness, Bertha," I said helpfully, "what a beautiful ring. Is it new?"

"Why yes, Ivy," she simpered. "My husband, Delbert, gave it to me as a birthday present." She giggled girlishly. All of her chins wiggled like out-of-control Jell-O. "Along with a brand-new car and a fur coat."

I wanted to ask her what she was going to do with a fur coat in May, but I didn't want to encourage her to share any more of her time with me. "Why, that's wonderful. I'm glad Delbert is doing so well for himself." It was common knowledge that the Pennypacker boys kept the farm going while Delbert spent most of his time partaking of Hiram Ledbetter's Life-Preserving Liniment.

"My parents are visiting from China," I said, changing the subject before we were subjected to any further details of the Pennypackers' sudden good fortune. But Bertha quickly revealed that she had another reason for stopping by my table.

"Why, Ivy," she said with a smirk, "I heard someone set fire to your little store and stole that box you dug up in Harvey's orchard. How odd. Why would anyone want that silly little box?"

I was flabbergasted. How did Bertha know about that? Then I remembered Amos's reprimand about mentioning the theft in public. The only place it had happened was in the bookstore, right after the fire. Who had spilled the beans to Bertha? "Where did you hear a story like that, Bertha?"

That weird smile again. "Now I can't tell you that. Let's just say that a little birdie told me. You're not the only one in Winter Break with secrets, you know." With that comment, she slinked away. Well, okay, she waddled away, but it was as good as slinking.

"What in the world is that woman talking about?" my mother said as soon as Bertha was out of earshot. "Who set fire to the bookstore? And why are you digging in someone's orchard?"

Since I had no choice, I told my parents the story about Bert Bird's box, leaving out as many details as possible. I tried to give them enough to explain Bertha's comments, but not enough to alarm them. I deftly left out the part about Harvey and his tirade. I had just finished when Bonnie brought our hamburgers. Thankfully, their attention turned from me and onto Ruby's Redbird Burgers. That was fine with me. I wasn't certain, but I could have sworn that I saw a tear in my father's eye. My mother just shook her head and clucked her tongue at the monstrosity in front of her. Ruby's Redbird Burger was so big nothing else would fit on the plate. Bonnie's next trip produced a large basket lined with napkins to soak up the grease from Ruby's homemade, fresh-cut french fries.

We bowed our heads as my father prayed what could easily be the fastest prayer ever recorded. Before I had a chance to say amen, he had chomped down on his burger. Melting cheddar cheese dripped from between the buns and plopped down on his plate.

He mumbled something that sounded like "Mmm, dis a bey burber eva maba," which I translated into "Mmm, this is the best burger ever made." My mother rolled her eyes again, but she did slice off a piece of her hamburger with her knife and delicately put it in her mouth. She didn't comment, but she started chiseling away at a very determined pace, and her eyes seemed to glaze over a bit.

When my dad reached a resting point, he wiped his mouth and looked at me with concern. "So you think someone purposely took that box and set the fire? Why would anyone care about an old box buried by a boy who moved away so long ago?"

Shoot and bother. Ruby's burger had just taken second place. I was obviously up to bat again. "That's the million-dollar question, Dad," I said. "It doesn't make any sense. And actually, there are two boxes. Bert's old lunchbox and another box I used to protect his stuff. Trust me, there wasn't anything there of value, except perhaps to Bert and his mother."

"You need to stay out of it, Ivy," my mother said. "This isn't your concern."

"It's my concern when someone tries to destroy my bookstore, Mother. Besides, they ruined Aunt Bitty's desk. That desk meant a lot to me."

"You really do love that old bookstore, don't you, sweetheart?" my dad said gently. "I didn't realize—"

"Oh, Mickey, don't encourage her. What kind of a life will she have in Winter Break, Kansas? My goodness, Ivy, someone as talented and intelligent as you shouldn't allow herself to get trapped in a small town on its way to nowhere." My mother hit the side of the table with her slender hand. "Why can't you see that?"

"And why can't you understand that I'm not you, Mother?" I said a little more harshly than I meant to. "I have to live the life I feel God gave me. It may not be what you're called to do, but I love it here. I feel at home, and I haven't felt that for a long, long time. Not since the last time I was in Winter Break."

My mother's face turned crimson. Without another word, she scooted out of the booth and headed for the door. I started to get up, but my father grabbed my arm and pulled me back.

"Let her go," he said. "She has some things to work out. You can't do them for her."

I sighed in frustration. "Why does everything I say set her off? Why is she so mad at me?"

"She isn't mad at you, you know; she's unhappy with herself."

I plopped back down into my side of the booth. "What are you talking about, Dad? I'm pretty sure I'm the person she thinks is throwing her life away. Why should she be upset with herself?"

My father smiled at me. "Because she's afraid she's the one who made the wrong choices, honey." He cast one longing glance at the rest of his burger, but unselfishly he ignored the temptation and grabbed my hand. "You know your mother and I have always felt called to be missionaries. We've had China in our hearts for a long, long time. But I wanted to wait until you were settled down, maybe married. In my mind, being your father has always been the most important job God ever gave me."

"Mother certainly didn't feel that way," I said, trying to keep the bitterness out of my voice. "I've always felt like I was in the way of her real goals."

"And that's just it. She has come to the realization that she may have failed you some. It's tearing her up."

I couldn't believe what I was hearing. "Is that the real reason you guys took this trip?"

He patted my hand before letting go of it. "Well, for me it was a chance to see you. For your mother, however, it was. . ."

"A chance to redeem herself," I said.

"Yes. I'm afraid that's the truth." My father shook his head slowly. "I think she's decided that if she stops you from 'throwing your life away in Winter Break,' she will prove to herself that she really is a good mother."

"But, Dad, I really am happy here. I believe with all my heart that this is where I'm supposed to be."

"I see that, Ivy, and I'm happy for you. The tough part will be making your mother believe it."

I wanted to say that I shouldn't have to do that. At twenty-one, I was an adult and responsible for my own life.

A vision of Aunt Bitty and me sitting on the Biddles' dock one summer floated into my mind. I had just aired my latest complaint about my parents. "Ivy," she'd said with a smile as she dipped her bare toes into the lake, "I never had children, but I know what it's like to love a child." She scooted closer and put her arm around me. "I'm pretty sure the hardest part of being a parent must be letting go. Frankly, just thinking about it scares me. When you're here with me, I know where you are. I know you're safe. But when you're away from me, I worry about things that could hurt you. One of these days, your parents will have to watch you start your own life, without being near enough to catch you if you fall. It will be incredibly difficult for them. I have no idea how people without God in their lives survive it. It takes great faith, Ivy. It will be hardest for your mother when that day comes."

Once again, my wise aunt had foreseen my future. For the first time in a long time, I admitted to myself that I'd never really doubted my mother's love for me. My abandonment issues weren't all her fault. Some of them came from my own unwillingness to see my mother's point of view.

"We'll get through this, Dad," I said. "Thanks for telling me the truth. Hopefully it will help me to understand Mom a little more."

My father smiled and attacked the drippy remains of his burger with gusto. I chomped on my own Redbird Burger until all that was left were some of the messy innards. And speaking of innards, I felt as if mine were going to burst. I encouraged my dad to go for a walk with me to burn off some calories before I exploded. We paid Bonnie and scooted out the front door. I was glad Ruby was too busy to notice. Even though the lunch box was no longer a secret from my parents, I still didn't want to tell Ruby that her missing son's property was also missing. Of course, Bertha and her big mouth might end up solving the problem for me, but that wasn't the way I wanted to handle it. Ruby had a right to know, and it was my job to tell her. I wondered briefly if this might be something I could foist off on Amos, but I pushed the thought out of my mind. Using him to get me out of the mess with Harvey was enough. I needed to take responsibility for this one.

I figured Mom would be sitting in the car, but it was empty. "Maybe we should look for her," I said.

"I think we should let her be, Ivy. Sometimes your mom needs time to herself to work things out." He grabbed my hand as we strolled down the street. "One of the things I love so much about your mother is that when she's wrong, she'll eventually face it and apologize. Trust me; she's harder on herself than she is on anyone else—even you."

I stopped walking and grabbed my father's arm. "Dad, Amos said the same thing about me. Am I. . . I mean, am I. . ."

My father laughed. "Are you like your mother?" He stopped in the middle of the street and put his hands on my shoulders. "Why do you think you and your mother fight so much, Ivy? It's because you're so similar."

"I don't think I'd ever leave my daughter behind so I could go to some other country, Dad. That doesn't sound like me at all."

My father smiled one of those wise-father smiles that meant I was about to find myself on the losing end of an argument. "But you would drop out of school and move to a town so small most people in Kansas have never even heard of it because you're convinced it's what God wants you to do?"

"But that's not the same. . . ."

"Maybe it's not exactly the same situation, but can't you see that both of you are passionate about what you believe? You and your mother are both looking for God's will in your lives." He sighed. "Maybe your mother and I moved too quickly. Maybe our timing was a little off, I don't know. But your mother's passion for souls and her willingness to give up everything for the people she believes she is called to help makes me respect her more than I can say." My dad's eyes were moist. "And I feel the same way about you. You've taken a big step of faith because you believe you've found the place you belong. You're making a brand-new life, teaching yourself how to run a bookstore, and reaching out for love. That takes courage, sweetheart. The kind of courage I see in your mother." His voice caught as he looked into my eyes. "I am so proud of both of you."

I wanted to argue, but I couldn't. My mother and I *were* alike. Passionate, committed, and above all, just plain stubborn.

My father let go of my shoulders, and we continued our walk down Main Street. In Winter Break, that means you must stop and say hello to half the town before you get more than two blocks from your starting point. While Dad extended warm greetings to residents who remembered him and introduced himself to those who didn't, I considered his admonition. By the time we turned around and headed back to the car, I'd concluded that my father was a much wiser man than I'd ever realized. Maybe it was time to let my mother off the hook. Perhaps we could bury the hatchet and start all over. I hoped so. Even more important, I decided to spend some time on my knees about the situation. Although I could see that change was needed, God was the only One who could actually clean up my heart.

We were rounding the corner on our way back to the car when Elmer Buskin stepped out of Buskin's Funeral Home. His thick gray eyebrows arched in surprise when he saw us. "Why hello, Ivy," he said. "Isn't this your father?" The only way I'd ever been able to describe Elmer's odd voice was to say it sounded somewhat like a cross between Darth Vader and Tweety Pie. Elmer's attempts to present himself the way he thought a solemn and proper funeral director should were ruined by his high-pitched voice and pronounced speech impediment. "I'm so happy to see you again, Mr. Towers," he said. Of course it came out "I'm toe happy to tee you again, Mittah Towahs."

My dad didn't miss a beat. "I'm happy to see you, too, Mr. Buskin. How long *has* it been? Five or six years?"

"At least that," Elmer said, smiling. "Please, I'd love for you to come inside and see what a blessing your daughter has been to me."

My father shot me a questioning look, but I shook my head and followed Elmer inside the funeral home. Just a few months before, Buskin's Funeral Home had been a tattered and used-up secondhand Rose. Now the floors shone and the carpets were thick and plush. The lobby held beautiful high-backed chairs covered in velvet. The old, rickety furniture was gone. Style and elegance were the watchword at Buskin's. Even Elmer's bald head seemed shinier.

Billy Mumfree, who used to clean the building on the weekends, was sitting at a highly polished table over in one part of the large outer room. A couple sat with him, looking at an oversized album filled with pictures. Billy, whose biggest goal in life used to be doing a wheelie on his ever-present skateboard, was dressed in a dark suit, his once-scraggly hair trimmed and neatly combed. I'd heard that Elmer had hired Billy as an assistant.

"Why, Elmer, the place is beautiful," my dad said in a low voice so as not to disturb the couple talking to Billy. "I'm impressed."

Elmer steered us down the hall to his office. When he opened the door, I couldn't believe it. The walls had been repapered, the carpet replaced, and new furniture filled the room. Elmer pointed at two handsome leather chairs positioned in front of his English-style, cherrywood desk.

"Everything you see is because of your daughter," Elmer said. He looked at me. "You haven't told him?"

I shook my head. It wasn't a big thing—not as big as Elmer made it out to be. I felt my cheeks start to tingle. I'm sure I was beginning to resemble an overcooked beet, but Elmer ignored my obvious discomfort.

"Your daughter discovered that an old desk lamp I'd been using for years was actually a valuable antique. I was able to sell it for a little over sixty thousand dollars." Elmer's voice broke, and his round, owl-like eyes moistened. "That money saved my business. Now, not only do the people in Winter Break come here, but people from other towns entrust their loved ones to me because Buskin's Funeral Home is a place they can be proud of."

"Why, Ivy," my dad said, "I didn't know you knew anything about antiques."

"I didn't—I *don't*. We can thank Aunt Bitty for that." I explained about finding an old book in the store that had a picture of the lamp in Elmer's office.

That book had given me my first clue that the lamp was valuable. It showcased lamps made by the Handel Company. Once I found the lamp, a quick Internet check told me that Elmer had a gold mine sitting under years of dust and grime. I smiled at Elmer. "I like to think that somehow Aunt Bitty arranged the whole thing so she could thank Elmer for all his kindness to her."

"Well, I don't know about that," my father said, "but if she did have anything to do with it, I'm sure she needed her kindhearted great-niece to carry out her plan."

The attention from my dad felt great, but I was ready to change the subject. With hair the color of a red stoplight, I had no hope of blushing attractively. Before I had the chance to turn our conversation in a different direction, Elmer did it for me.

"I hear you found an old box that belonged to Bert Bird."

I sighed. "My goodness, does the whole town know about this?"

Elmer chuckled. "You've been in Winter Break long enough to know that news travels faster than the speed of light."

"Yeah," I said dryly. "As fast as the speed of Bertha Pennypacker's mouth."

Elmer nodded. "You got that right."

"Elmer, did you know Bert Bird?" I asked.

"Yes, in fact, he used to help me sometimes. After his father died, I would pay him to sweep out the place. I couldn't give him much, but I hoped that whatever he managed to earn here would help out his family a little."

"Were you surprised when he left?" I asked.

Elmer frowned. "Well, no. Ruby told everyone he was going to stay with relatives from out of town. Things were really tough for her then. What surprised me was that he never came back."

"Other people tell me he was so frustrated with trying to keep the farm going that he stayed away because it was too much for him."

Elmer leaned forward as if there might be someone else in the room besides my dad and me. "Ivy," he said in a low voice, "I never believed that. After his father's death, Bert's number one concern was his mother." He shook his head slowly. "That boy was dedicated to her. Yes, it might have been hard on him for a while there, but I still don't understand why he's stayed away all these years. It just doesn't make sense."

"Then what do you think happened, Elmer?"

"I think he's dead," he said softly. "If that boy could have come home, he would have." He shrugged his small, rounded shoulders.

Amos's story about overhearing Morley Watson and Dewey talk about Bert flooded my mind. "Surely someone would have been notified if he'd passed away, Elmer."

Elmer sighed. "Depends on how he died. Maybe there was foul play. We just handled a funeral for a man who disappeared from Dodge City a couple of years ago. Someone found his body buried in a field about ten miles out of town. The farmer that dug him up didn't even know it was a skeleton at first. Thought he'd uncovered some old tree roots."

I felt the blood drain from my head and run straight down to my toes. I stood up in an attempt to force the blood back up to my brain where I seriously needed it now. "And a city girl might think they're tree roots, too," I mumbled. "Elmer, I think you'd better find a shovel and follow me out to the peach orchard. I'm pretty sure I know just where we'll find Bert Bird."

After speaking to Amos, I hung up the phone harder than I meant to. I was more than a little miffed. He'd wanted to know why I hadn't realized that the "roots" Bert's medal had been stuck on were actually human bones. I admit that my answer could have been more gracious. "I have no idea why I didn't immediately jump to the conclusion that someone had buried a young boy in a peach grove, Amos," I'd responded sarcastically. "I mean, that's what any normal person would have realized right off the bat, right?"

After advising me to calm down, Amos told me he'd meet me at the grove. As I ran toward the car, followed closely by my father and Elmer, I saw my mother sitting in the passenger seat. Shoot and bother; now I'd have to tell her about the body. Another nail in the "Why would anyone want to live in Winter Break?" coffin.

We all jumped into the car while my dad tried to explain to my mother just where we were going. I slumped down in the backseat next to Elmer, hoping it would make me a smaller target. It occurred to me that since I hadn't buried Bert in the peach orchard, I shouldn't be feeling guilty. Somehow, though, I knew my mother would see this as a result of my choosing to live in Winter Break. Surely there was some kind of connection.

My mother listened to my father's rushed account of my morbid discovery without saying anything. It was a bad sign. Whenever my mother grew silent, things were spiraling into the danger zone.

On the way to the grove, I tried to quit thinking about Mom's reaction to this strange turn of events. Instead, I attempted to connect the pieces of an increasingly odd puzzle into a clearer picture. Was the person who buried Bert in the peach orchard the same person who stole his belongings? Was it Ruby? Was she trying to cover her tracks? Try as I might, I just couldn't make sense out of it. Ruby didn't seem like someone who would kill her own son. She was truly touched when she saw Bert's box and the things inside. Was something else going on here? What was I missing?

My dad stopped the car, forcing me to abandon my rather confused ponderings.

"You're going to have to tell me where to go from here, honey," he said.

I looked out the car window. We were at the edge of the peach orchard.

We had already passed Harvey's house. I was considering whether we should go back and tell him what we were doing when Amos's patrol card pulled up next to us. Harvey was in the passenger seat, glaring at me.

Amos got out of the car and walked up to my window. "Harvey's fit to be tied, Ivy," he said with a sigh. "He says you probably dug up some old animal bones. There are a few of them buried around here. Are you sure these bones are human?"

"About as certain as I can be, Amos. I haven't seen a lot of human remains, so I'm going on instinct here, but something tells me that no one's rib cage should be resting under Bert Bird's most prized possessions."

The tone of my voice made his mouth tighten. "All right, all right. You're going to have to lead the way, because none of us have seen this spot. With the map gone, I hope you can still find it."

"Odd how everything connected to Bert Bird keeps disappearing just like Bert did," I said. "Do you see a pattern here, Deputy Sheriff Man?"

He crossed his arms and glowered at me. "Yes, I do. And don't ever call me Deputy Sheriff Man again. Got it?"

I nodded and batted my eyelashes at him. "Just follow me, O Great Detective."

My dad started pulling away before Amos could tell me not to call him O Great Detective. "Where are we going, Ivy?" he asked.

I directed him around the edge of the grove. A dirt road encircled the entire orchard. When we were close to the place where I'd found the box, I told him to stop. Amos and Harvey pulled up behind us, and we all piled out of our respective cars. Amos grabbed a shovel out of his trunk. Elmer took the shovel he'd thrown into our trunk before we left, and he stood next to Amos.

My dad held out his hand for Elmer's shovel. "You shouldn't get that nice suit dirty," he said to Elmer with a smile. "Why don't you let me do this?"

Reluctantly, the funeral director handed it to him. I was somewhat relieved. Elmer was a small man, not used to physical labor. It would have certainly taken longer if he'd insisted on digging.

"Okay, Ivy," Amos said. "Lead the way."

Even though I didn't have the map to guide me, I was pretty sure I could find the spot. I noticed a big tree I thought looked familiar. Then I remembered something. "The spot is marked with a barrel tapper," I said.

"What's a barrel tapper?" my father asked.

While Amos explained the intricacies of a barrel tapper, I glanced back at my mother. She followed silently behind the rest of us, her eyes focused on the ground, which was rough and uneven. I had no idea what she was thinking, but I was pretty sure I wasn't going to enjoy the aftereffects of today's adventure.

The tree I thought I'd recognized suddenly loomed up in front of us. "I . . . I'm sure this is the place," I said, staring at the ground in front of the tree. The dirt had been recently turned over, but the barrel tapper was nowhere to be seen. I got down on my knees, thinking it might have simply fallen over.

"Forget it, Ivy," Amos said. "Anything could have happened to it. If you're sure this is the place you found the box, that's all we need."

I stood up and looked around me, trying to remember what I'd seen the day before. "Yes, I'm certain," I said finally. "This is definitely the place."

Amos turned to the indignant property owner, who stood with his arms crossed and his foot tapping out an angry refrain. "Harvey, is there any other reason for the dirt to be turned over here?"

"Of course," Harvey said. "If you'd bother looking around a little bit, you'd notice all kinds of holes around here. I'm replacing my irrigation system."

Amos didn't respond, but his eyes narrowed. I wasn't worried. When the bones were uncovered, I would be exonerated. In fact, I would be a hero, finally closing a thirty-year-old case. I kept these positive thoughts foremost in my mind when Amos and my dad dug down a foot. I even held on to them at the three-foot level. At about four feet down, they disappeared.

"Ivy," my father said as Amos helped him out of the empty hole, "there doesn't seem to be anything here. Are you sure this is where you found the box?"

Was I sure? Could this be the wrong spot? I was asking myself these questions when I remembered something. I walked over to the tree and felt along the side. Sure enough, there on the side of the trunk were the marks I'd made when I was trying to clean my shovel.

"This is it," I said, looking into the faces of four people whose expressions were anything but reassuring. "Someone has moved the body."

"See what I told you, Sheriff?" Harvey said in an explosion of emotion. "I tried to tell you this woman is crazy—off her rocker! It's about time you listened to me and did something about her. I don't want her ever to set foot on my property again. She's a menace—a real nutcase."

"Harvey," I said, trying to stop the torrent of anger flowing from him, "there really was something here. I swear I didn't make it up. I—I don't know what to say."

Harvey took a step toward me, his face twisted with rage. I saw Amos move his way, but before either one of them reached me, someone else stepped between us.

"Now you listen to me, Mr. Bruenwalder," my mother said in a tone that caused all of us to stop in our tracks. "You're not going to talk to my daughter that way. If Ivy says there was something buried here, then there was something buried here. It has obviously been moved. May I suggest that your energy would be better spent trying to find out who did it? And may I also point out that this person, whoever he is, also came onto your property without your permission? I guarantee you he wasn't here trying to do the right thing—like my daughter is." My mother pulled herself up to her complete height of five feet, three inches and declared loudly, "And one more thing, sir. Don't you ever call my daughter crazy again. I hope I am making myself abundantly clear." My mother's emerald eyes flashed with anger, and her body trembled.

Harvey took two steps back. He looked as though he wanted to say something, but after seeing the expression on my mother's face, he clamped his lips tightly shut. It was probably a defensive move. I guess there's nothing more dangerous than an angry mother.

"I'm going to post someone out here for a while, Harvey," Amos said. "I don't want anyone else fooling around until we get a handle on this thing."

Harvey started to sputter something, but Amos stopped him. "This isn't up for debate, so let it be. And one other question: Just where were *you* last night?"

Harvey clucked his tongue several times. "Sorry, Sheriff, but trying to place the blame on me won't work. I was in Hugoton last night. Headed there right after your little show at Ruby's. I went to help my sister get ready for her garage sale. Didn't get back until about thirty minutes before you came by this morning. You can't pin anything on me."

"I'm sure your sister will confirm this, Harvey?"

He flashed Amos a self-satisfied smile. "Yes, she will. And so will the members of her church who were there, too."

"I hope they will. Right now, I'm taking you home. I want you to stay in town for the next few days. Do you understand?"

Harvey nodded, but he didn't look happy about it. Amos ordered him to get into the patrol car. As soon as Harvey was out of earshot, he sighed and shook his head.

"I can't pull anyone from the department in on this right now," he said to us in a low voice. "Even though we all believe Ivy, I have no proof there was a body here."

"Then how will you watch the orchard?" my dad asked.

"There are a couple of guys in town who will help me unofficially," he said. "That's all I can do. I doubt we'll catch anyone who shouldn't be here. I think they already got what they wanted."

"Amos," my dad said, "if you need me, I'd be willing to take a shift."

"Dad! I don't want you out here. What if something happened to you?"

"Now, Ivy," he said with a smile, "nothing is going to happen to me, and this will give me something to do. You know I'm not the kind of person who can just sit around and do nothing." He put his arm around me. "Besides, someone is trying to mess with my little girl. You couldn't keep me from getting involved if you tried. So don't."

They say that a daughter compares every man to her father. I guess it must be true. As I stared into my dad's clear, sky blue eyes, set into a kind face, I saw something in him that I recognized in Amos. Not only were their smiles the same, but so was their unwavering support for me. Even though we hadn't found a body, Amos was proceeding as if he had no doubt in my story.

As I gave my father a big hug, I breathed in his trademark Old Spice. "Thanks, Daddy," I whispered. When I pulled away from him, I turned toward my mother. "And thanks, Mom," I said. "What you said meant a lot to me."

I don't know exactly what I was expecting, but if I thought my relationship with my mother had turned some kind of corner, I was mistaken. "I don't want you to think I've changed my mind about this place, Ivy," she said with determination. "I still think you need to get out of Winter Break. Not only is this place a dead end, but now it's become dangerous, as well."

"So you think I should just cut and run, Mother?" I said, not able to keep a note of exasperation out of my voice. "I should leave Ruby behind to wonder what happened to her son? And I should let the person who tried to burn the bookstore walk away? Let the place that Bitty loved just cease to exist?" I shook my head in frustration. "It's not going to happen, Mother." I took a deep breath and tried to pull on any reserve of courage I had inside me. "Besides, I have no intention of leaving behind the man I love with all my heart."

To say that I knocked the wind out of my mother's sails was an understatement. I'm sure she'd been wondering about my relationship with Amos, but there it was. I'd just tossed my inner feelings out for everyone to see. I hoped they weren't going to get trampled on and thrown back to me. I wanted to look at Amos, but I couldn't.

My mother's eyes narrowed, and her lips became a thin line. She spun around and headed for the car. My father grinned at me and grabbed Amos's hand. After shaking it vigorously, he followed my mother and slid into the driver's seat next to her. I could hear him saying something, his tone hushed but firm. After discreetly waiting a bit until there was a lull in the conversation, Elmer flashed Amos and me a broad smile before getting in the car.

I turned to find Amos standing only a few inches away from me. He put his hands on my shoulders. "Did you mean what you said?" he asked, his voice husky.

"Well, I didn't say it because I thought that declaring your love next to someone's grave site was particularly romantic." I stared up into his eyes and felt a little tickle run all the way through me and settle somewhere inside my toes. In fact, I think I actually felt them curl up a little.

Amos shook his head. "For once in your life, couldn't you just answer a question yes or no? You always have to give the long version of—"

I put my fingers on his lips. "Yes," I said softly. "The answer is yes."

Amos moved his right hand up to my face and held my chin. Then he leaned over and kissed me lightly on the lips. When he drew back, his expression was serious. "Why don't you keep practicing that? I have another question to ask you when things settle down a little."

I was grateful there was time for practice. At that particular moment, I couldn't seem to remember any words at all. He kissed me on the nose, got in his patrol car, and drove off, with Harvey still staring daggers at me.

11

After leaving the orchard and dropping Elmer off, we drove to the bookstore. I'd noticed Milton and his sons working around the place earlier when we were at the grocery store, but I wasn't prepared for what I discovered once we walked past my newly installed front door. At least ten other people were inside the bookstore cleaning, hammering, painting, and fixing things up. Pastor Ephraim Taylor and his son, Buddy, were replacing burned wallboard. Bev Taylor, the pastor's wife, was cleaning soot and grime from the floor. Emily was down on her knees, scrubbing one of the blackened carpets that lay on the wooden floor. Someone else was helping her, but I couldn't tell who it was since her back was turned to me. My eyes filled with tears of gratitude to see these dear friends working so hard to help me in a time of crisis. In the corner, several men were on their knees, tearing out charred flooring.

One of them turned and waved at me. "Hello there, Miss Ivy," Isaac said with a big grin. "Can you believe how fast this is going? In two or three days, we should have everything back to normal."

"That's wonderful, Isaac." I motioned toward my parents. "Do you remember my mom and dad?"

"Oh yes." He stood up and wiped his dirty hands on a denim apron he wore over his clothes. He stuck his hand out toward my father, who shook it heartily.

"How are you, Isaac?" my father asked. "I'm so glad you stayed on to help Ivy. I know you and Bitty were very close friends. I'm sure her death was devastating to you."

Isaac paused for a moment before answering. "Yes, yes, it was," he said quietly, "but God sent Ivy to take her place. If He hadn't, I might feel that Bitty was really gone. As it is, part of her lives on, not only in the bookstore, but in my life. I'm very grateful for your daughter."

My dad put his hand on Isaac's shoulder. "I'm very grateful for you, Isaac. I hear you were instrumental in getting Ivy out of here before the fire spread."

Isaac shook his head. "As you can see, the fire wasn't that bad. She would have easily made it out without my help."

"But you were there for her. That means a lot to her mother and me. We know that someone is looking out for her in our absence. Thank you."

Isaac looked embarrassed, but I could tell my father's sincere appreciation for his intervention meant a lot to him. After a quick, shy smile, he turned around and went back to work. Isaac felt like a part of my family. But I guess that's the way it's supposed to be with Christians. We really are family. Unfortunately, while some people take the concept to heart, others, like Bertha Pennypacker, don't ever seem to understand it.

I stepped carefully over the holes in the floor caused by burned boards being ripped out and touched Pastor Taylor on the back.

"Ivy!" he said when he'd turned around. "How good to see you." He leaned over and hugged me. Spackling dust left a mark on my dark blue sweatshirt. "Oh, I'm so sorry," he said. "Look what I've done."

"Don't be silly," I said, smiling at him. "You could pour that whole pail of spackle on my head, and it wouldn't matter one bit. I don't know how to thank you for what you're doing."

"Helping someone you love is a joy. We're having a wonderful time."

"Pastor, I need to reimburse everyone for all these supplies. I hope you intend to give me the receipts."

"Ivy, Ivy, Ivy," he responded with a grin, "do you want us to lose our blessing? You know the Lord repays a lot better than you can. I think I'll take those blessings that are 'shaken together and running over' if you don't mind. I can't speak for anyone else here. You might get a bill or two, but I wouldn't count on it."

I couldn't think of anything to say. I truly believed Luke 6:38. I'd seen it work time and time again. Finally, I said, "I know we have some kind of insurance. I paid the bill not long after Bitty died. It's possible that it will cover some of this restoration. I'll check it out. In the meantime, will you please tell everyone that if they need reimbursement, all they have to do is let me know? Whether the insurance covers it or I do, I don't want anyone to feel stuck."

He nodded. "I'll be happy to, but I wouldn't be pulling out your checkbook anytime soon."

Fortunately, my parents picked that moment to find me, interrupting our conversation before I began to blubber with gratitude. "Pastor Taylor, do you remember my father, Mickey Towers, and my mother, Marjorie Towers?"

Pastor Taylor took off his gloves and shook hands with my parents. "Of course, I remember you both. It's been a long time. I understand you're ministering in China now? Bitty was so proud of both of you. She used to talk about you all the time." He paused for a moment. "Say, I wonder if you might talk about your ministry tonight at church. Just tell us what you're doing and how things are going over there. If this isn't enough notice, I'll completely understand. Maybe we can schedule it for another day." The hopeful look on his face made me smile. Pastor Taylor was so interested in missions, I almost wondered if he wasn't going to hop a plane to some overseas country one day.

My father gave one of his big Santa Claus laughs. And yes, it actually sounded like "*Ho, ho, ho.*" "Pastor," he said, "as you get to know us better, you'll discover we have no problem talking about our ministry. We'd be delighted to speak in the service tonight. You just point at us when you're ready, and we'll be more than happy to spend a few minutes sharing our adventures in China."

"Great!" When he slapped my dad on the back, a small plume of white dust rose from his glove.

"Ephraim Taylor!" a voice rang out. "Quit messing up those people's clothes." His wife, Bev, came up and greeted my parents. Soon she and my mother were jabbering away like two jaybirds on a telephone line. My mother could be quite cordial to other people. It just didn't seem to extend to me.

My dad took off his jacket and was soon working away with Pastor Taylor. I decided to see if I could help Emily. She seemed focused on the rug, and when I patted her on the arm, she jumped. "Ivy!" she exclaimed. "I didn't realize you were here."

The girl working with her turned around. I was shocked to see a pale face with eyes outlined in dark eyeliner and lips smeared with dark red, almost black lipstick. Although she wore an apron over her clothes, she was dressed all in black. Her eyebrow was pierced. Seeing someone dressed in Goth regalia in Winter Break was a definite shock. I'm sure my face showed it.

"Ivy, this is Faith," Emily said. "She's my second cousin. Her mother and father passed away in an automobile accident last month. Faith has come here to live with us."

I was certain there was more to that story, but this wasn't the time to ask questions. "I'm happy to meet you, Faith," I said gently. "I'm so sorry for your loss. I can't thank you enough for helping out."

The girl glared at me. "She made me come here," was all she said.

"Well. . .well, still, I appreciate it."

"Whatever," the girl said, turning her back to me and directing her concentration back to the job at hand.

"You keep at it; I'll be right back," Emily said as she stood up. She grabbed my hand and pulled me a few feet away from all the action. "I just have to tell you something," she said with a big grin on her face. "We just found out. I'm pregnant!"

I started to squeal, but Emily clamped her hand on my mouth. "Shh," she said. "Pervis might hear you."

I was more than a little confused. Pervis, Milton and Mavis's son, was a Baumgartner like Emily. I figured the Baumgartners shared everything.

"Pervis is dating May Pennypacker," she whispered. "If he hears you and tells May, she'll tell her mother and it will be all over town by nightfall. Buddy

and I want a little time to tell people in our own way. I know you understand."
She gently removed her hand from my mouth.

"Of course I understand," I whispered back. "I'm so excited for you!"

Emily's deep cocoa-colored eyes glowed. "You know, Ivy, I may have a large family—okay, an insanely large family—but when we were kids, you were more like a sister to me than any of my real sisters. I'm so glad you came back to Winter Break."

Simultaneously, our eyes filled with tears—which made us laugh. "What a pair," I said, attempting to choke back something that tried to combine a laugh and a sob. It reminded me of the story Emily had told me when we were young, about some man who supposedly coughed, hiccupped, sneezed, and laughed all at the same time. With eyes as big as saucers, Emily had said the man dropped dead. Until I was almost sixteen, whenever I got a cold, I worried that I might be attacked by that deadly combination. I reminded my friend about her odd story, and we launched into a spasm of laughter. I glanced behind us to see several people watching us with concern. Unfortunately, it just made everything funnier. I was certain my Winter Break friends had decided that the fire had dislodged the last loose screw holding my sanity together. After a couple of minutes, we were able to find a measure of control. With a promise to call me later, Emily went back to work.

I was going through a few books on the shelves, sniffing them to see if they smelled like smoke, when someone called my name. It was Isaac.

"I heard you mention something about insurance to Pastor Taylor," he said. "Miss Bitty had insurance on the bookstore through the Farm and Field Insurance Company in Dodge City. Some man named Shackleford was the agent. Unfortunately, the deductible was so high, I'm sure it won't help you." He sighed. "Bitty didn't want to spend money on insurance. She got the cheapest policy she could."

I patted his shoulder. "I'm not really surprised. I think she knew that if something happened, she was covered. Either by angels or the people of this town." I struggled to contain the overwhelming gratitude that threatened to surface and turn me into a sobbing mass of jelly. "Right now, it's hard for me to see much of a difference between the two."

Isaac nodded. "I've felt that way myself many times."

After he walked away, I went back to checking the books. To my relief, they seemed fine. Mavis must have been right. The smoke had drifted toward the front door and the windows. There's something to be said for drafty old bookstores that aren't completely airtight.

At one point, Milton and his sons took me over to the new door to show me their workmanship. They had installed the door along with a beautiful carved frame that surrounded the outside entrance. It was perfect. My concerns about losing the original door evaporated.

"It looks like wood, don't it?" Milton said with a lopsided grin.

I agreed that it certainly did.

"Nope," he said with an air of pride. "Solid steel. Ain't nobody gonna be able to knock this thing down." He reached into his pocket and pulled out a set of keys. "These are yours. This one is to the doorknob, and this one is for the dead bolt."

I thanked him and took the keys. I was about to ask him how much the door cost when I noticed Pervis picking up supplies from the front porch. I excused myself and ran down the steps in an attempt to stop him before he got into his truck.

"Pervis," I called out. "Can you wait just a minute?"

He paused at the back of the truck and stared at me. Pervis was a good-looking kid. Tall and lanky, he'd inherited his mother's height and coloring, but thankfully for him, his other features were more directly connected to his father.

"Pervis," I said, "first of all I want to thank you for everything you're doing for me. There's no way I could ever repay your kindness."

A slow smile spread across his freckled face. "It's no problem." His voice was surprisingly deep. "I'm happy to do it."

"I hope you won't be offended by my next question." Even before I asked it, Pervis cast his eyes toward the ground, looking distinctly uncomfortable.

"The night of the fire, I noticed that two boxes that were sitting on my desk were missing. I only mentioned it to Amos, but somehow the story got out. I wonder if you know how that happened."

At my words, his face fell. "I'm real sorry, Ivy," he said. "I overheard what you said and mentioned it in passing to May Pennypacker. I think she told her mama. I wouldn't have said a word if I'd realized what would happen. May and I had a long talk about it. I told her that spreading tales was a sin and that I didn't cotton to it." The look of remorse on his face was real. "May feels real bad about it, too. It's caused some real trouble between her and her mama."

"I'm sorry to hear that, Pervis. I hope you learned a lesson here, though. Spreading stories can cause a lot of problems. I really didn't want anyone to know that the boxes were missing."

With that, Pervis looked so upset, I had to put him out of his misery. "Let's not worry about it anymore, okay? What happened, happened. But I would appreciate it if you would keep anything else you hear about me to yourself. Do you think you can do that?"

Shamefaced, he hung his head. "Yes. You have my word."

I reached over and touched his arm. "Thanks, Pervis. Now let's forget about it, okay?"

"Okay," he mumbled. He got into his truck, and I started back up the stairs. I felt sorry for him, and I really didn't blame him for what Bertha did with the information he'd inadvertently given her. That was on her. Of course, now that she'd spread the story all over town, it was going to make finding out who took the box a lot more difficult.

Before I got to the door, I noticed Alma Pettibone coming toward me, carrying a large plastic box. I raised my hand in greeting. "Hi, Alma. What have you got there?"

She almost flew up the stairs. "I just thought with everyone working so hard, maybe they'd like some cookies and lemonade. If you'll take these inside, I'll go back and get my thermos and some cups."

"Alma, that's such a nice thing to do. Thank you." It was then that I noticed that Alma's habitual topknot was gone. In its place was a lovely, soft hairstyle that framed her face with a silver glow. And she was wearing makeup. Not much, just enough to bring out her eyes. Funny that I'd never noticed she had such beautiful eyes. My question as to why Alma had changed her looks was answered only seconds after I held my hands out for the box. She hesitated for a moment after handing me the cookies. The container was heavier than I'd expected. There had to be seven or eight dozen cookies packed inside.

"I wonder. . . ," she said lightly, a blush spreading from her neck into her checks, "if Isaac is inside. I mean, is he one of the men working. . . I mean, do you know where he might. . . I mean. . ."

I could tell that if I didn't stop her, we would be standing on the steps all afternoon, waiting through hundreds of "I means."

"Alma," I said as kindly as I could, "Isaac is inside working. I know he'll really appreciate the cookies and lemonade. Why don't you go get your thermos and together we'll set this up in the store. Maybe you can stay and serve everyone." By everyone, I meant Isaac.

"That would be. . . I mean. . .that would be wonderful, Ivy," she said. As she scurried down the steps, I was left with the distinct impression that Dewey wasn't going to have to worry about unwanted attention from Alma Pettibone anymore. Isaac and Alma. Interesting. Under normal circumstances, it was a relationship I wouldn't place any bets on. But when the bell over the church rang three times, I realized that Alma Pettibone was missing one of her favorite soap operas, *The Gallant and the Gorgeous*. Before today, I wouldn't have believed she'd miss that sordid tale for anything. "Wow," I whispered to myself, "there's a lot more than flowers in bloom in Winter Break, Kansas."

As I started back up the steps, I noticed something sticking out from underneath a pile of lumber. I put the cookie box down, walked to the bottom of the steps, and moved the boards aside. I reached down and pulled out a gas can. Somebody had piled building supplies on top of it, probably not realizing that it might belong to the person who started the fire. Although it appeared to be just like every other gas can I'd seen in Winter Break, I looked it over carefully for any signs of ownership. When I turned it over, there, written in marker on the bottom of the can, were the initials *LB.*

Lucy Barber.

A mos was late getting to church that night. I deposited my parents in the sanctuary and waited in the lobby as long as I could, but I finally gave up and went inside. I'd have to wait until after the service to tell him what I'd found. I couldn't help but wonder how he would react. Would he defend Lucy? Would he believe she'd started the fire? I certainly had my doubts. The only reason I could come up with for her wanting to burn down the bookstore would be to get me out of town. I had to admit to myself that I'd been wondering if she still had feelings for Amos, but I just couldn't see her doing something like this. Since coming to Winter Break, I'd discovered that she was a compassionate doctor who cared deeply about people. So what were the alternatives? Could the initials belong to someone else? Was it possible the gas can had been stolen and left by the steps to throw suspicion on Lucy? I had no idea what the truth was, but the one thing I was sure of was that the can was placed there for a reason. It hadn't been there before the fire; I would have noticed it. The gas can was one more piece of a puzzle that didn't seem to fit together into any final image that made sense.

I was turning all these things over in my mind when Pastor Taylor stepped up to the podium, and Amos slid into the pew next to me. He squeezed my arm and focused his attention on what the pastor was saying. I tried to listen, but my mind kept wandering. I caught Amos looking at me a couple of times. He could tell I was restless. I fumbled around in my purse until I found a scrap of paper. I scribbled, "I need to talk to you after church," on it then passed it to him when my mother was looking the other way. Here I was, twenty-one years old and worried that my mother might catch me passing a note in church. Amos took the slip of paper, read it, and then slid it into his pocket after nodding his agreement.

I forced myself to put my concerns about Lucy Barber on hold and pay attention to the sermon. Pastor Taylor was reading the story of the prodigal son in the fifteenth chapter of Luke. When he got to the part about the father welcoming his son home, I couldn't help but look across the room at Ruby. Was she thinking about her missing son? Where was Bert Bird? Was he really dead? And if so, who had killed him? I still couldn't believe it was Ruby, no matter what Dewey and Morley Watson might have said years ago. And whose bones had I found in the orchard? Harvey's claim that they were animal bones popped into my head. But time spent in biology classes told me they were human. Besides, why would someone go to all the trouble of moving old animal bones? That really didn't make any sense. My mind was churning over so many questions, I was giving myself a headache. Then I heard Aunt Bitty's voice whispering in my ear, *"Real faith means letting go, Ivy. If you ask God for something, you must believe He's working on the answer. If you're still chewing on it, that problem's still sitting on your plate."* She was right, of course. I had a tendency to try to work everything out myself. I needed Him to show me the truth. A verse in Matthew popped into my mind. *"There is nothing concealed that will not be disclosed, or hidden that will not be made known."* I whispered a quiet prayer, asking God to reveal what was hidden and to help Ruby find peace. I also asked Him to bring Bert home if he was still alive. I suddenly realized that I was still staring at Ruby. But now she was looking right back at me, and the look on her face startled me. Was it anger that twisted her features? She turned her head away, but the expression on her face haunted me throughout the rest of the service.

About fifteen minutes before the time we normally dismissed on Wednesday nights, Pastor Taylor called my parents up front. As they talked about China, I heard something in my mother's voice I'd rarely heard before. Passion. My mother was passionate about China—about the people who lived there.

My dad began telling a story about a tour guide who was hired to show them around Hong Kong. While they were inside one of the many temples in and around the city, the small woman who was their guide pulled my father over to the side and said, "I understand you are a Christian minister?"

My father, a little concerned that she was going to object to his presence inside one of their holy sites, hesitantly admitted that he was.

"Oh, sir," the woman said with tears in her eyes, "I have been praying for twenty years for God to send someone to tell me about Jesus. Will you please tell me the story of the Savior?"

As my father shared that the woman was marvelously converted and now serves with them in China, I noticed that my mother was crying. How many times had she heard that story? Yet it still touched her. I began to understand that my mother only wanted me to feel the kind of fervor she did. She wasn't trying to ruin my life; she was trying to help me find it. I reached over and took Amos's hand. It was going to be my job to make her see that although my calling wasn't the same as hers, it was just as real and just as strong.

When Pastor Taylor closed the service, many of the parishioners rushed toward my parents. I could see I wasn't the only person touched by their story. With the welcome distraction, I grabbed Amos's arm and pulled him out of the sanctuary. The door to the library was unlocked, so we slipped inside. Although the main lights were off, a small lamp that sat on a table near two stuffed chairs gave out enough illumination for us to see.

I immediately launched into the story about finding the gas can with Lucy's initials. When I finished, Amos frowned.

"Ivy, I don't believe for one minute that Lucy set that fire. She just isn't that kind of person."

"I have to agree with you, Amos. For a while I wondered if Lucy was still madly in love with you. Maybe she tried to burn down the bookstore so I would leave town and she'd have you all to herself."

Amos shook his head. "First of all, Lucy Barber is not madly in love with me. I think I'd know. And second, how do you explain the theft of the boxes? Why would Lucy want them?"

I sighed. "She wouldn't. That's what's so confusing. Everything looks suspicious; the theft of the boxes, the fire—but nothing seems to connect." I grinned at him. "And as far Lucy goes, if she were crazy about you, you'd never know it. Men are absolutely clueless about love."

Amos grabbed me and pulled me close to him. "You're wrong there, you know. I know you're wildly, madly, and completely in love with me."

"You have quite an ego there, don't you, champ?"

"No," he said softly. "And don't call me champ."

My retort was curtailed by his kiss. Finally, I pushed him away. "Making out in the church library. You have no shame, do you?"

"No," he answered simply. "Come back here."

"Amos, stop it! We have to talk. I don't know when I'll get another chance. My parents follow me everywhere I go."

"Okay, okay," he said, plopping down in one of the chairs near the lamp. "But you owe me lots of lip time when they leave."

"Just keep a running total of my debt, will you?" His grumpy expression made me laugh.

I sat down in the chair on the other side of the table. "Why don't you ask Lucy about the gas can, Amos? Show it to her. Maybe she can shed some light on it. I'd like to know if it was stolen, and if so, when."

"I guess I can do that," he said, "but I'll do it in a way that won't make it seem like I'm accusing her of anything."

"Fine. I have it in my trunk. I'll give it to you when we leave."

"Is there anything else?"

"Yes." In the glow of the lamp, he looked so handsome I was having a hard time concentrating. I forced myself to gather my thoughts. "I've been thinking. The bones I saw could have belonged to Bert Bird. I mean, as far as we know, he's the only person who is missing from Winter Break. But the problem is, just how did Bert manage to die and then bury his treasure box on top of himself? It doesn't make sense."

Amos folded his arms across his chest and looked at the floor as he thought about what I'd said. I could almost hear gears turning in his head. Finally, he looked up. "You know, that *doesn't* make any sense. Unless he was killed while he was burying the box. Someone found him, killed him, and then buried him and the box."

"Okay, that's possible. But there's something else here I can't figure out."

"What?"

"Why did Bert want to bury his most treasured possessions in the first place? Why not just take them with him? Why draw a map so he could find them again? And how in the world did the map get inside Bitty's jewelry box? And the big question, why would anyone want to kill Bert Bird? What possible threat could he have been to anyone?" I turned to stare at Amos. He looked as puzzled as I felt.

"Those are good questions. I'm afraid I don't have answers for them," Amos said.

"One other thing I've been thinking about. I know Harvey said he wasn't in town during the time someone dug up the bones and moved them, but he could have done it. I mean, it is his property. He seems to be the most likely suspect."

"Why would he do that?" Amos asked. "Unless he put them there in the first place."

"Well, maybe he did."

Amos laughed. "So you think Harvey caught Bert digging in the orchard, got mad, whacked him, and threw in his lunch box for good measure? I think that's a little harsh even for Harvey. And besides, if he was that upset about Bert trespassing on his property, you and I should have been six feet under a long time ago."

"Okay. Point taken. Obviously someone else moved the bones." I reached over and grabbed his hand. "Look, this may be a waste of time, but I'd like to find out who else left town around the same time Bert did. He was just a boy. He probably wasn't traveling alone. Maybe he left with someone else—someone who dropped him off with these elusive relatives Ruby keeps mentioning."

"But what if Ruby's relatives came here to get him?"

"I think someone would have seen them, Amos. Winter Break is a pretty small town. I'm not saying it isn't possible, but so far, no one has mentioned anything like that."

"I don't know. That was a long time ago. I doubt we can find much."

"I know," I said. "But let's try. I'm going to talk to Dewey. He's been here forever, and people open up to him. Maybe he'll have some helpful information. And I'm also going to pay Bonnie a visit. If she was Bert's girlfriend, she might be able to shed some light on what happened when he left."

"You'd better do it when Ruby's not around. I don't think she'd appreciate your questioning her only employee." He shook his head. "You know, Ruby's the person we should be asking. She's the only one who really knows the truth."

"No," I said emphatically. "It's obvious she's not going to tell us anything. I think we need to keep her in the dark until we figure out what's going on. All we have right now are several strange occurrences that aren't leading us to anything solid. I don't want to stir her up with a bunch of meaningless suspicions."

"There's still the possibility she might be involved, Ivy. She's definitely keeping some kind of secret. I hope it doesn't turn out to be the worst-case scenario here, but you need to prepare yourself."

"Maybe. But do you really believe that Ruby set my bookstore on fire and moved Bert's body? I just don't see it."

Amos stood up, stretched, and yawned. "Right now I'm not thinking about much of anything except getting some sleep. I'm heading home, Ivy. It's been a long day."

"I forgot to ask you, how are things going with Odie? I saw him in the sanctuary. He didn't look too happy."

Amos ran his hand through his hair and sighed. "No, he's not happy at all. But the truth is, there isn't enough evidence to charge him with anything. And there isn't enough proof to let him off the hook, either. All I've managed to do is to make him feel defensive. It's not a good place for two Christian brothers to find themselves in. I don't know what to do."

I grabbed his arm and pulled myself up, leaning into his strong shoulder. "The thirteenth chapter of First Corinthians tell us that 'love always hopes, always perseveres.' I guess all you can do is persevere in believing the best about Odie."

Amos stroked my hair. "I wish I could do that," he said softly. "But as a law enforcement officer, my first reaction is usually suspicion."

"Maybe Odie senses that, Amos."

He kissed the top of my head. "You're probably right. Maybe I should sit down with him and talk to him like a brother. He needs to understand that just because I have to do my job, it doesn't mean I don't believe in his innocence."

"Do you believe he's innocent?"

Amos sighed so deeply, I felt my hair move. "You know, Ivy, I really do. I train myself not to make judgments on guilt or innocence. But I truly don't believe that Odie Rimrucker would steal cattle. I just don't."

I looked up and kissed him lightly on the lips. "Then tell him that."

"I will." After one more long, lingering kiss, he left the library. I wanted a few minutes to sort out my thoughts, and I knew I wouldn't get the chance for a while with my parents around. I'd just sat back down, when I heard a noise behind one of the bookshelves. Wondering if there were mice in the library, I got up to check it out. Instead of a mouse, I found someone sitting on the floor in the corner. Hidden in the shadows, the lurker wasn't immediately identifiable, but a closer look revealed Faith, Emily's young Goth cousin.

"Faith, what are you doing here?"

"I wasn't trying to listen to you, if that's what you think," she said in a surly tone.

"I didn't say you were. I just wondered why you were in here instead of in the sanctuary."

She jumped to her feet and stepped into the light where I could see her. The black streaks under her eyes revealed that she'd been crying. "I don't like churches, and I don't believe in God."

"And why is that?"

Her upper lip curled in a sneer. "I suppose if you believe in a God that would kill your parents, that's up to you. I sure don't." She pushed past me and headed toward the door.

"I don't believe in a God who would do that," I said toward her fleeing back. "I believe in a God who gives life, not death."

She whirled around and glared at me. "My cousin Emily says the same thing. So how do you explain what happened to my parents?"

I smiled at her in the dim light. "I don't. I didn't know your parents and wouldn't even begin to hazard a reason for their tragedy. But I will tell you that God doesn't go around killing people. We don't live in a perfect world, Faith. There's evil, pain, and tragedy. But God's not the author of it."

Her face crumbled with grief. "Then why didn't He save them?"

I walked up to her and put my hand on her arm. "I can't answer that either."

She pulled away from me and took two steps back. "You sure don't know much, do you, lady?"

"Maybe not," I said gently, "but I know that God is good, and I know He loves you very much. If you give Him a chance, someday He'll answer your questions. For now, though, I think you need to let Him help you through this."

She shook her head. "No thanks. I'm doing just fine without Him."

She turned and started for the door but then stopped with her hand on the doorknob and looked back at me. "This kid, Bert. The one you were talking about?"

Feeling that this wasn't the time to chide the girl for eavesdropping, I just nodded.

"He planned to come back."

"What do you mean?"

The light from the lamp illuminated her face—and the sadness I saw etched there. "He wouldn't have left things behind that meant so much to him. He would have taken them with him unless he planned to come back to them someday. It was like a promise, you know? A vow to return."

I started to ask her how she knew this but realized it wasn't necessary. I could see it in her eyes. She'd left something of her own behind, hoping that someday she'd go home. But in Faith's case, there didn't seem to be anyone to go home to. Without another word, she opened the door and left the library.

I pondered her words while I rounded up my parents and said good-bye to Pastor Taylor and his wife. Emily came up and hugged me, promising to get together with me later in the week. I noticed Faith standing behind her, but she wouldn't look at me or acknowledge my presence.

When we got to the parking lot, I saw that Amos's patrol car was gone. He'd left without getting the gas can. I made a mental note to remind myself to give it to him the next time I saw him. I also wanted to tell him what Faith had said about Bert. It made a lot of sense, but it also raised a lot of new questions. I chewed on everything while driving back to the Biddle house. My father was talking most of the way home, but I was so distracted I caught only part of what he said.

When we unlocked the front door and stepped inside, I heard my dad say, "Well, what do you suppose this is?"

He leaned down and picked up an envelope that had been slipped under the door. He handed it to me, since my name was scrawled on the front. I opened it while my parents stared at me. Inside, on a piece of paper, someone had written, *Don't look for Bert Bird unless you want to see someone get hurt.*

13

After being grilled by my parents into the wee hours of the morning, I found it hard to roll out of bed with only a few hours' sleep. I'd called Amos after we found the letter, and he'd promised to come over in the morning to discuss it. I hurried around and tried to make myself look presentable. The circles under my eyes were still there after I touched them up with concealer, but at least they were less obvious.

I listened at the top of the stairs, hoping my parents had changed years of routine and slept late, but my hopes were dashed when I heard their voices in the kitchen. As I came down the stairs, my father was just going out the front door.

"Good morning, sunshine!" he called out. "I'm taking the rental car into Hugoton for some gas. We're sucking fumes. Is there anything you need from the big city?"

I laughed. "Hugoton really isn't very big. You might be disappointed."

He grinned. "If you could see some of the villages we've been to in China, I bet you'd think Hugoton was a progressive metropolis."

I shook my head at him, and he reached over and hugged me before going out the door. My mother sat at the kitchen counter with a look that told me our conversation from the night before wasn't finished.

"Before you say anything, Mother, Amos is supposed to be here any minute. Let's let him take a look at the letter before we jump to any further conclusions."

"Ivy Samantha Towers," she said, irritation spewing through each syllable of my name. "Why in the world would you value the advice of some deputy sheriff who lives in a place like Winter Break over the concerns of your own parents?"

I poured a big cup of coffee then plopped down on the stool next to her. "What do you mean when you say, 'a place like Winter Break'? I love this town and the people who live here. There's nothing wrong with Winter Break, Kansas. Frankly, your comment sounds absolutely snobbish. What if I asked you and Daddy why you'd live in 'a place like China'? Would that offend you?"

My mother rolled her eyes and sighed. "China and Winter Break are not the least bit comparable, Ivy. Quit trying to change the subject. It's clear to me that you're not safe here. First Bitty is murdered, and now someone is threatening you."

I fought to contain the growing resentment that nibbled viciously at me. I wanted to remind my mother that I was now an adult and capable of making my own decisions. I also wanted to tell her that it would take a visitation from God for me to believe I wasn't supposed to be in Winter Break, and that I didn't believe the Holy Spirit had vacated His job and given my mother the position. However, I knew that it was my responsibility to honor my parents, and those comments would most probably fall outside the "honor" guidelines. I took a deep breath and let my words come out in measured slowness. "Mother, you and Dad taught me to listen to God's voice. You told me that I should strive to be led by Him. I try to do that every day. I truly believe I am supposed to be here. I don't know exactly why, but I'm convinced that one of the reasons has to do with 'some deputy sheriff,' as you called him."

Mom started to say something, but I hushed her. "Listen, Mother. Let's give this a rest, okay? We went over this same ground last night so many times, I think I've memorized the entire debate. I'm not leaving. I'm sorry it upsets you; I really am. I'd like to think you were happy about the life I've found in Winter Break. It would be wonderful if you could share in my happiness, but if that's not possible, so be it. I'd like today to be a peaceful day if at all possible. I didn't get much sleep, and I'm probably a little cranky."

My mother took a long sip of her coffee but then stared into her cup for what seemed like an eternity. I steeled myself for whatever new assault was being prepared for launch. I wasn't prepared for her to look up at me and smile.

"What?" I asked, worrying that this was some kind of new tactic designed to throw me off track.

"Oh, Ivy," she said in a soft voice. "I was just remembering the argument I had with your grandmother when I told her my heart's desire was to go to China as a missionary. She spouted some of the same things to me that I've been saying to you. And my reply to her was almost word for word what you just said to me." She shook her head slowly. "Why did I forget about that until just this minute?"

She reached over and took my hand. "I really do want you to be in God's perfect will, honey, but I am worried about you. Your father and I pray over you every day, and we believe in God's protection. But you know that even the most cautious of us can open a door to trouble without meaning to. Your Aunt Bitty did that by trusting someone she shouldn't have. I need to be certain that's not what's happening here."

"I understand that, Mother, I really do. But I *do* belong in Winter Break. And as far as the letter last night and the things that have been happening, I believe I've been given an opportunity to solve a mystery that might restore a son to his mother. Whether Bert Bird is alive or dead, I'd like Ruby to finally be able to lay his disappearance to rest. It's obvious that someone thinks I can do it, and believed it enough to have sent me this warning."

"And tried to burn down the bookstore," my mother added.

I nodded. "There's something strange going on, and I think I'm close to the answer."

"You said you want to help Ruby find closure, but how do you know she doesn't already know where Bert is?"

"I don't know that, but my gut reaction tells me that her cover story about relatives isn't true. If you'd seen her reaction to the sight of Bert's lunch box and the things inside it, you wouldn't believe it either. Ruby misses her son. I'm sure of it. Something else is going on. And even if Ruby does know where he is, and I doubt it, I want to know what happened to Bert Bird. Someone's gone to a lot of trouble to keep his whereabouts secret. I want to know why."

My mother got up and refilled our coffee cups. "Okay, Ivy," she said, sitting down next to me and handing me my cup, "why don't you start from the beginning? Tell me everything. Maybe I can help."

By the time Amos knocked on the front door, I'd recounted the entire story, from finding the map up to the discovery of the letter the night before. This time, I didn't leave out anything. Although my mother didn't say a word throughout my long-winded discourse, I could tell she was chewing things over in her mind. It was great to feel as if we were actually working together on something, but I still had to wonder if our sudden bonding experience wasn't going to end up causing me some kind of grief.

Amos was looking at the letter when my father burst through the front door. "Amos?" he yelled out. "Amos, where are you?"

"I'm in here, Mickey," Amos said loudly enough for him to hear.

When my father entered the kitchen, it was obvious to all of us that he was upset.

"Mickey," my mother said, "what in the world is wrong?"

My father's usually serene features were tight with anger. He directed his attention to Amos, ignoring my mother and me. "Some crazy fools ran me off the road," he said, his voice quivering with rage. "This nut was tailgating me even though I was going the speed limit. Then he decides to pass me in a no-passing lane. He takes off to go around me with some yahoo driving a truck full of cattle following him. They couldn't possibly have seen what was coming up over the hill. Sure enough, as they sped past me, a big semi was coming toward them in the other lane. I was sure they were going to hit, so I put my car in the ditch to get out of the way."

"Oh, Mickey," my mother said, jumping up and grabbing my father. "Are you okay?"

"I'm fine," my father grumbled. "Just a bit shaken up. I checked the car over, and it looks okay, too, but I certainly put some angels to the test out there."

I ran over and hugged him. "Oh my goodness, Dad. You could have been seriously hurt!"

"I'm okay, honey. Not any worse for wear."

"So what happened?" Amos asked. "Was there an accident?"

"No, it was a miracle someone didn't get hurt. The first guy sped up and made it into the other lane before the semi reached him, and the cattle truck pulled back into my lane. It was a good thing I drove off the road, though, or he would have hit me."

"This just happened?" Amos asked, pulling his notebook out of his pocket.

He was now in deputy sheriff mode. I liked it when he acted all official. Not just because I was proud of him, but more important, because he was really just too cute for words.

"Yes," my dad said. "I turned around and came back. There can't be a drop of gas left in that car."

"Can you describe both of the trucks?" Amos asked, scribbling in his notepad.

"Well, the cattle truck was pretty rickety. It was painted a dark green, but there were gray patches on the hood and the doors. You know, like the primer that goes on before a paint job. The other truck was a regular pickup truck. Newer. Red. I think it was a Ford, but I'm not certain. To be honest, I had my eye on the semi, not the truck."

Amos lowered his notebook and stared at me with an odd expression. Then he turned his attention back to my father. "A red Ford truck?" he asked slowly. "Mickey, this is very important. Did this truck have an extended cab?"

"Sorry," my father said. "I'm not a truck person. You'll have to explain what you mean."

"Did it look like there was more than just a front seat?" Amos asked patiently. "Were there small windows behind the driver's side window?"

My father thought for a few moments. "Now that you mention it," he said slowly, "there were two windows behind the main side window. I hadn't thought about it until now, but I saw the windows as the guy passed me."

Amos's excitement was beginning to show. "Did you happen to notice if there was a metal running board along the side?"

Again my father contemplated Amos's question. Finally, he shook his head. "Sorry, Amos. I just don't remember. It seems to me that there was, but everything happened so quickly, I can't say for sure."

"Dad," I interjected, "did you see the driver of the red pickup?"

He shook his head. "No, his windows were tinted. To be honest, I was more focused on where the truck was than I was on the driver."

"Then we can't be sure it wasn't Odie," I said to Amos.

To my surprise, he grinned at me. "Actually, we can," he said. "I took your advice, Ivy. I went to see Odie. I told him that I believed he was innocent."

"But how does that prove. . . ?"

"It proves it because I just left him at Ruby's," he said excitedly. "We had breakfast together. Odie couldn't have been the one on the highway because he was with me."

"Oh, Amos," I said. "It really isn't Odie! I'm so relieved!"

He held out his arms, and I almost flew into them. "Sounds like you were having some trouble believing the best about Odie, too."

I laughed and pulled back. "Who, me? Nah. I believed in him the whole time."

"Mickey," Amos said, "will you come with me to look for these guys? I think they're the ones who've been stealing cattle all over the county. I'd like to catch them if we could."

"Sure, I'd love to throw a rope around those yahoos. Let's go!"

Amos planted a kiss on my cheek. "I'll talk to you about the note when I get back," he said. "For now, you stay here with your mother. Don't leave the house." He looked toward Mom, who nodded her agreement. Then he and my father hurried out the front door.

"You mentioned someone named Odie," my mother said. "Did you mean Odie Rimrucker?"

I turned and went back into the kitchen. "Yes. I didn't know you knew him."

My mother motioned toward the French doors in the dining room. "Let's finish our coffee outside, okay?"

We stepped out onto the patio, the brisk morning air enveloping us with scented arms of honeysuckle. The rising sun sparkled on the lake while a flock of Canada geese lazily bobbed on the water near the shore. We made ourselves comfortable in the soft wicker patio chairs with their beautiful tropical-colored cushions.

My mother suddenly seemed a million miles away. There was obviously something on her mind. Finally, she cleared her throat and smiled at me. "Since we're being so honest with each other this morning, I'm going to tell you something you don't know. Something that may surprise you. Years and years ago, before I met your father, I was in love with Odie Rimrucker."

She could have told me that she and my father found me in a crater caused by a crashed spaceship from the planet Krypton, and it wouldn't have shocked me as much as this revelation. I couldn't seem to frame any kind of response. Chubby old Odie Rimrucker? Odorous Odie, the town drunk? My mother and this uneducated. . .although I didn't like the connotation the word provided, the only word that came to mind was. . .*hick*.

Sensing my total confusion, Mom laughed lightly. "You young people seem to think the rest of us were born old, but that isn't true. You see, you're not the only person who used to come to Winter Break during holidays. I spent several summers here as a girl." Her expression became dreamy. "Aunt Bitty and I used to be very close. Why do you think I sent you here so often? I wanted you to enjoy Bitty's companionship the same way I had."

"I—I don't remember you telling me that you'd spent any time here except when you brought me to Winter Break or picked me up." I tried to remember if Bitty had mentioned it. I could remember her talking about my mother with a note of sadness in her voice. At the time, I hadn't paid much attention. Or perhaps I just didn't care. I wouldn't admit this to my mother, but coming to Winter Break had meant trying to forget about her for a while.

"I didn't bring it up much," she said softly, gazing out at the lake. "Probably because I didn't want to think about Odie—and this place." She took a long sip of coffee and then put her cup on the glass table in front of us. "The truth is, I left Odie and Winter Break behind after the summer we broke up. A few years later, I met your dad, and my whole life changed. I put the past in the past and moved on." She shook her head slowly. "Or at least I thought I had. Now I'm beginning to wonder."

"But, Mother, Odie? I—I can't imagine...."

She smiled at me, the sides of her mouth quivering in amusement. "If you ever get the chance to look at a picture of Odie Rimrucker when he was a teenager, take it. You'll see a strong, handsome young man with a smile that could melt your heart. It's true that he wasn't as well educated as I was. His grammar left a lot to be desired, but he was romantic, intelligent, and very, very sweet."

I was listening intently, but a vision of my life as the daughter of Odie Rimrucker was tap-dancing through my brain. And it wasn't pretty. I pushed the unflattering picture out of my consciousness and into a dark closet in my mind where, hopefully, it would never escape. "So what happened, Mother?" I asked.

"Unfortunately, Odie's problems with alcohol began early," my mother said sadly. "His father was a raging drunk who beat him and his mother, and although Odie swore he would never become like his father, he was drawn to the bottle. In the end, he gave in. His choice tortured him, and he drank even more. It was an endless cycle."

"A stronghold," I said, remembering a sermon in which Pastor Taylor had addressed the subject.

My mother nodded. "That's right, Ivy. There was a spiritual stronghold of alcohol in that family. Even though Odie resisted it, the power of it was too strong for him, and he lost his battle." My mother sighed and crossed her arms across her chest as if trying to warm herself. "Of course, I didn't realize it then. I blamed him for being weak. And I left." She looked up at me, and I was surprised to see tears in her eyes. "I left him to deal with it alone."

"It got really bad, Mom," I said. "Eventually Odie lost his family because of it."

"I know." She wiped her eyes with the back of her hand. "Bitty kept me up-to-date. She knew how much I cared for him."

Something suddenly became clear to me. The story I'd heard about Aunt Bitty nursing Odie through his last and almost fatal bender made sense. "Is that why Bitty took him in when he almost died? Because of you?"

My mother's smile was sad and wistful. "I think Bitty would probably have helped him anyway; that's the kind of person she was. But the answer to your question is yes. When I heard about his situation, I asked her to help him if she could."

"But you and Daddy were married by then."

My mother put her hand up to shield her eyes from the sun, which was beginning to peek over the patio roof. "I never stopped caring about him, Ivy. Not having a romantic relationship with someone doesn't mean you automatically stop being concerned about him. Your father knew all about it. We prayed for Odie together."

The idea of my father praying for my mother's old boyfriend was another shock to my already-battered system. I decided right there and then that I didn't really know my parents all that well after all. And I still had a lot of growing up to do.

"So right now, Daddy is out trying to catch the real cattle thieves. If he does, he will have helped to exonerate Odie."

"God answers prayers, Ivy," my mother said with a chuckle. "Maybe He's using us to help Odie because we truly care about him."

"And He sent Amos to talk to Odie while Daddy was dealing with the real thieves so Amos would know Odie was innocent."

My mother reached over and touched my hand. "And He used you to put the idea of talking to Odie in Amos's head. Without that, none of this would have worked out the way it did." She squeezed my fingers.

I nodded dumbly. Sometimes God's love and mercy overwhelm me. I felt that way now.

"Remember, faith only works through love," my mother said. "Our prayers for Odie were activated by our love for him." She let go of my hand and leaned back in her chair.

I sat silently, watching the geese chase something around in the water. Finally, I said, "Then God can use my love for Ruby to help her find her son."

"Wrong," my mother said, her voice so soft I could barely hear her. "God can use *our* love to find Ruby's son."

I turned to stare at my mother, the woman I'd thought I had all figured out. "You're going to help me?"

She grinned at me. "Where do you think you got those Nancy Drew skills, missy? I read all those books in Bitty's collection long before you cracked them open."

I was speechless. The geese waddled out of the lake and begin to nibble on the fresh blades of grass sprouting up around the edge of the water. Although geese could glide beautifully on the water, on land their gait was ungainly and awkward. I was pretty sure I knew how they felt. At that moment, I was a goose out of water. This was new territory for me—and for my mother.

"So our next step is to talk to someone who can tell us who else left town around the time Bert disappeared?" my mom asked.

"Yes, that was my plan. Of course, Dewey was here then. I'm hoping he'll be able to remember something helpful."

"Let's go talk to him now. We have no idea when Amos and your father will be back."

"Amos told us to stay put," I said.

My mother leaned forward in her chair. "Okay. Then why don't we get Dewey to come here?"

"He's running a store, Mother," I said. "We can't ask him to shut it down because we want to have a chat with him."

She thought for a moment. "Well, he eats lunch, doesn't he? Why not invite him over for lunch?" My mother glanced at her wristwatch. "It's ten thirty now. I could put together some tuna sandwiches and a nice salad."

"I think that would work. He closes from noon to one anyway. I'll call him right now."

By the time Dewey knocked on the front door, my mother had set out a nice meal, even taking time to brew and chill a pitcher of tea, seasoned with a little fresh mint from Marion's yard.

After a few pleasantries, we sat down to lunch on the patio. It was a perfect afternoon. A slight breeze wafted up from the lake, bringing with it a hint of the spring flowers beginning to bloom near the water. I almost hated to say anything that might disrupt nature's gentle ambiance, but those missing bones just wouldn't be still. They called to me.

"Dewey," I said, interrupting a benign conversation about some of the fresh vegetables he would be getting into his store next week. "I need to ask you some questions about Bert Bird. Do you mind?"

He wiped his mouth with his napkin and shook his head. "I was wondering about the real reason you two lovely women asked me to lunch. I'd hoped it was because you couldn't do without my sparkling personality and scintillating conversation."

I grinned at him. "Of course that was the main reason, but I must admit to a small ulterior motive."

Although Dewey and I had no secrets from each other, our morning breakfast meetings had been disrupted, and things had happened that I hadn't had time to tell him. I brought him up to speed about the fire, the lunch box, the bones, and even the warning note. My mother frowned at me when I mentioned the mysterious letter shoved under my front door, but as I said, I had no secrets from Dewey.

When I finished, Dewey sat back in his chair and folded his arms. His forehead was knotted with concern. "I've been wondering about Bert Bird for a long time. I never could figure out why he didn't come back. After a few years, I quit believing he was really living with relatives. He loved it here. And he loved his mother. It was such a mystery." He shook his head slowly. "To be honest with you, at one time I even suspected Ruby of doing away with him." He chuckled. "Of course, after I got to know her better, I knew that wasn't true."

"Was there anyone else you suspected?" I asked.

He took a drink and put his glass down. "Nope. There wasn't anyone in town that had anything against that boy. He was a great kid. I led the Boy Scout troop he was in." He got a faraway look in his eyes. "After his dad died, Bert became almost like a son to me. I mean, he had no father and I didn't have children. I guess we kind of bonded."

"If Bert wasn't planning on coming back," my mother said, "wouldn't he have told you?"

He smiled at her. "You just hit the nail on the head, Margie. That's one thing that still bothers me." His eyes narrowed. "Either we weren't as close as I thought, or something bad happened to that boy."

"And there's the lunch box, Dewey. Someone told me that if he buried it, it was because he knew he *was* coming back. He wouldn't have left something he referred to as his *treasure* if he knew he'd never see it again."

"That sounds right. Of course, we didn't know anything about the lunch box back then."

"I'm curious about something else. Do you remember any of Ruby's relatives coming to pick Bert up? I know it was a long time ago."

"Nope. That's another strange thing. One day he was just gone. If I'd have actually seen someone come for him, I probably wouldn't have been so suspicious of Ruby's story down through the years."

"Dewey," my mother said, "can you remember anyone else who left town around the same time Bert did? Ivy and I wonder if he might have traveled out of town with someone who was leaving Winter Break. At his age, he surely wasn't traveling alone."

He sat back in his chair with a sigh. "It's been a long, long time, but let me see. Well, there was Edith Bruenwalder, but that had nothing to do with Bert. Edith just had enough of Harvey and took off to live with her sister in Topeka." Dewey's bushy silver eyebrows worked together as he tried to pull up memories from the past. "There were the Carvers. Ben and Tillie were the parents. They had two girls. . .Margaret and. . .what was that other one? Something like RaeAnne. . .can't quite remember. Ben got a job in Nebraska somewhere. I remember when they left because they had an account in the store that needed to be settled first. Ruby owed some, too, although I had no intention of collecting it. This was after Albert died and Ruby was really struggling. Ben asked about her account and offered to pay it. 'Course, almost all the townspeople were pitching in to help her. It's too bad it wasn't enough to keep Bert here. Oh, and there were a couple of Baumgartner kids that took off." He shrugged. "That happens from time to time. Being a Baumgartner is a hard life. I wish I could remember their names, but I just can't at the moment."

The Baumgartner family now numbered well over one hundred due to new marriages and brand-new children and grandchildren. Almost all of them lived and worked south of town and attended the First Mennonite Church. It was originally founded by Baumgartners, and elder Baumgartners were dedicated to keeping it going. However, down through the years, a rebellious Baumgartner escaped once in a while. The wayward lambs either disappeared forever or repented and came back to the fold. There were a few exceptions. My friend Emily was allowed to attend Faith Community Church since she was married to a member. But in her family's eyes, she was now and always would be a Baumgartner. The family certainly wasn't mean-spirited or tyrannical. They were some of the nicest people you'd ever want to meet. But they were dedicated to their church—and their family. Kind of in that order.

"You can't remember either one of them, Dewey?" I asked.

"Wait a minute. Emily's mother was one of them. But of course, she came back." He drew his eyebrows together once again. "Right now I just can't remember who the other one was. But I don't think he ever returned. It was a boy as I recall. Darrel? Darrin?" He shook his head. "Inez would recollect it, since he left about the same time. I'm just not sure."

Inez was Emily's mother. That would be easy enough to check out. Inez had always liked me. She was almost like a second mother to me when I was young. I remembered that Emily had already mentioned getting together sometime this week. Maybe we could meet for coffee. I made a mental note to call her later today and set up a time to get together.

"Was there anyone else, Dewey?" my mother asked.

He sighed. "Sorry. That's all I can remember. There haven't been that many people in and out of Winter Break over the years, so that's liable to be about it. Of course, I can't be completely sure any of these people left exactly when Bert did. I could be off some. Trying to recall something that happened thirty years ago isn't that easy." He shook his head. "You really think this will help you figure out what happened to Bert?"

I shrugged. "I have no idea, Dewey, but say a prayer for me. I'm running out of ideas."

"You know, there is someone you should talk to," he said. "Bonnie Peavey."

"I intend to. I'm just waiting for a chance to get her alone. She's always with Ruby."

Dewey nodded. "I've never told anyone this before, but I'm going to tell you, Ivy. Bert and Bonnie were about as crazy about each other as any two people have ever been. I saw them together quite a bit because they'd come in the store to buy candy after school. But Bonnie's family wouldn't have put up with her having a boyfriend, and Ruby would have blown her stack if she'd known Bert was making goo-goo eyes at Bonnie. Ruby and Bonnie's mothers didn't get along. In my opinion, Bonnie Peavey knows as much as anyone about what happened to Bert Bird."

I thanked Dewey for his help before he headed back to the store. My next move would be to talk to Bonnie Peavey.

14

It was almost nine o'clock that night before we heard from Amos and my father. When they finally ambled through the front door, there was a look of satisfaction on their faces.

"You got them?" I asked with anticipation.

Amos grinned slowly and slapped my father on the back. "Thanks to your dad, the cattle thieves are behind bars this evening. We even recovered some of the cattle. A couple of lowlifes out of Richfield were working together to steal cows and sell them to a guy in Dodge City who didn't care if they were branded or not."

"That's great. Does Odie know?"

"Not yet," Amos said. "But he's about to." He strolled into the library, where there was a phone and a little privacy.

I was thrilled that he'd told Odie he believed in him before the real thieves were caught. Now Odie would never think that Amos's words came as a result of the capture. At least that situation was behind us.

"Well, I guess your old boyfriend is in the clear, Margie," Dad said. "God answers prayers."

"Yes, He does," my mother said, giving my father a big hug. "And you're living proof of that."

Although I hadn't expected to feel this way when I found out my parents were coming to Winter Break, I was suddenly really glad they were here. I'd almost forgotten how great they could be.

My dad mentioned that he and Amos hadn't gotten a chance to eat all evening, so my mother and I fixed them sandwiches and fruit. I'd just cut Amos's sandwich in half when he came around the corner after talking to Odie. The smile on his face told me everything I needed to know.

"Thanks again for your advice, Ivy," he said. "I'm glad this is over as far as Odie is concerned." Even though he seemed relieved, the look on his face still held an uneasiness.

"Is something else bothering you?" I asked.

Amos studied the pattern in the rug as if something was written there. Finally, he looked up. "These guys we picked up don't seem like they have enough sense to put together something like this. I have to wonder if someone else is pulling the strings. Someone who set this up and used them to carry out his plan."

"Why don't you eat something and think about it later," I said. "You and Dad need to relax for a while and celebrate your victory. I'm just grateful you're both all right."

"Except for the ten years those cattle thieves took off my life," my dad grumbled.

"Now, Mickey," my mother said, "don't say things like that. I plan for you to be around a long, long time." She handed him his plate, and he sat down at the bar to eat. Then she put her arms around his neck and kissed the top of his head. "I have to have someone to boss around, you know."

My dad sighed. "I know. It's my cross to bear."

Amos and I laughed. The thought entered my mind that I hoped I would be as happily married someday as my parents were. Without thinking, I glanced over at Amos. I was surprised to find him looking at me with an odd expression. We both turned our eyes away quickly, but I could feel a warm flush spread across my face. I looked down at my feet, hoping my face would tone itself down a few shades before anyone noticed. I wondered what Amos was thinking. Surely we hadn't been turning over the same idea in our heads. I couldn't help but remember that he'd said he had a question to ask me. I didn't want to get my hopes up.

The truth was, I had no idea if Amos was even interested in getting married. I could still remember the pain he suffered when his folks got divorced. "I'm never getting married," he'd said tearfully. "It just doesn't work." Of course, that happened a long time ago, when he was just a kid. I hoped he didn't still feel the same way.

My dad's booming voice broke my reverie. "Let's all get some sleep. This has been an exciting day. I'm taking everyone out for breakfast in the morning. Ruby's hotcakes and sausage for me!" I glanced over at my mother, but to her credit, she just smiled at me and nodded.

I grabbed Amos's arm. "I'll walk you out," I said.

After Amos said his good-byes to my parents, we strolled out into a cool, star-filled night. The cicadas sang to us, and the full moon shone down, highlighting the budding trees that surrounded the house and lined the road back to town.

"I love this house," I said softly. "I've always wanted to live here. It's been wonderful, even if it's almost time to leave."

Amos smacked his forehead. "Oh, shoot. With everything going on, I totally forgot. I ran into Milton today. He said you should be able to open up the bookstore on Saturday. Almost everything is done. They're just waiting for the spackling to dry so they can paint the walls. They'll finish that tomorrow. After a day of letting the place air out, you're good to go."

I breathed a sigh of relief. "I'm so glad and so thankful for everyone who pitched in to help." I grabbed his hand. "Let's throw a party to thank every-one, okay? We could have it here—just like one of the parties Marion used to throw. We'll pull out Cecil's old grill and fix hot dogs and hamburgers. The kids could swim in the lake. What do you think?"

"Well, I think it would be best to call Cecil and Marion to see if they'd mind, but I think it's a wonderful idea," he said. "I'll be glad to help."

I laughed. "As if Cecil and Marion would say no. They loved throwing parties here. I bet they'll be thrilled."

He turned to leave but hesitated on the last step. "Ivy," he said in a tone so low I had to strain to hear him. "I...I'm...I mean, I..." He swung around and stared at me. I was shocked to see tears shining in his eyes. "Never mind," he whispered. "We'll talk about it some other time."

"What is it, Amos? Is something wrong?"

"No. No, everything's fine. We need to talk about something, but this isn't the time." He pulled on his hat and strode toward the patrol car without looking back at me. As he drove away, I couldn't help but wonder what was bothering him. Things were going so well, surely there wasn't a problem with our relationship. Just a few minutes ago I was thinking about what it would be like to marry Amos, and now I was feeling insecure. I pushed away the worry that wanted to burrow down and get comfortable in my psyche before it took root. It was ridiculous. Amos and I were fine. We'd deal with whatever was on his mind when he was ready to discuss it. When I went back inside the house, I almost missed seeing my mother, who sat silently at the breakfast bar, staring at me.

"Is everything all right?" she asked, looking concerned.

I guess my expression hadn't caught up to my resolve. "Yes. Sure," I said, trying to sound as upbeat as possible. I had no intention of airing out my love life right now. No matter how well my mother and I were getting along.

"We need to talk to Bonnie," she said. The abrupt change in conversation threw me.

"What?"

She frowned and shot me one of those looks mothers perfect so well. It always made me feel that she was wondering if I was really her child—or whether she might have picked up the wrong package at the hospital.

"Bonnie Peavey," she said slowly so I could grasp the complicated concept.

"Oh, right." The stress and excitement of the day were beginning to take their toll on me. I was mentally wiped out. "It will be impossible to talk to her during the morning rush. We'll have to find a way to get her alone."

"She smokes," my mother said. "I saw her hiding behind the restaurant the other day with a cigarette. We'll just wait until she goes outside; then we'll go out there and talk to her."

I wasn't crazy about the idea of standing anywhere near cigarette smoke, but if I could find a place upwind, it would be a good time to trap Bonnie without everyone in town listening to our conversation.

"Sounds good, Mother," I said. "But I'm exhausted. I'm going upstairs to bed. Let's take this up in the morning."

"Is everything all right, Ivy? You look worried. Are things okay with you and Amos?"

My mother's radar was activated and tracking nicely. "As far as I know, everything's fine," I said. "I'm just beat. I've got to get some sleep."

"Okay, dear," she replied with a smile. "I'll see you in the morning, bright and early."

It might be early, but right at that moment, I wasn't sure how bright I'd be.

I climbed the stairs to the attic room. After changing my clothes and crawling into bed, I stared up at the pretend stars that glowed on the ceiling. I wanted to lie in bed and think about all the things that were going on, but I remembered Aunt Bitty's advice about piling things on my plate. I decided to hand it over to the One who could actually clean it up, make it sparkle, and hand it back to me full of blessings. Then I drifted off into a peaceful sleep.

15

The next morning, I awoke to my mother's gentle prodding. "Wake up, Sleeping Beauty," she whispered into my ear. She'd awakened me the same way every morning when I was little. Now that I was an adult, it seemed childish—but it still made me feel good.

By the time I got downstairs, my parents were ready to go. I'd barely swallowed two gulps of coffee before we were out the door. As I started down the drive, my dad went over the events of the previous evening for about the third time. The excitement in his voice made me smile, but I was hoping this would be the last go-round. His eyes shone as he described the feeling of racing after the bad guys. Although I was pretty sure my mother wanted to chew him out for getting himself in the middle of a dangerous situation, she kept quiet. She was allowing him to have his moment in the sun. I knew her well enough to know that he was scheduled for a serious talking-to in the near future.

We turned off the long path from the house onto the road that led into town. On the way, we passed several farmhouses. However, I saw something at Homer Wilson's house that made me stop and pull up to the driveway. Lucy Barber's SUV was parked at the end of the drive, and its back door was wide open.

"I'll be right back," I said to my surprised parents. I crept up slowly to the SUV, keeping my eye on Homer's front door. There was no gas can anywhere to be found in the back of the vehicle. I tiptoed around to the side. Near the backseat, lying on the floor, was something that took my breath away. I felt dizzy for a moment, but when I realized that at any second Lucy could come out and find me inspecting her car, I turned and ran back to where my parents waited with inquisitive expressions.

"What are you doing?" my mother asked as soon as I slid back behind the wheel. I pulled away as slowly as I could. Driving on gravel roads is a noisy business, and I didn't want to draw attention to myself.

When we were well away from Homer's house, I pulled the car over. Before I could get a word out, she said, "Ivy, you look like you've seen a ghost. What in the world is going on?"

"It was in her car, Mother. But it doesn't make sense—"

"What was in her car, Ivy? What are you talking about?" My mother's stern tone shook me out of my stupor.

"The barrel tapper," I said slowly. "Lucy Barber has a barrel tapper in her SUV."

My father, who had been listening patiently to our conversation, interrupted. "What are you two talking about? What's a barrel tapper?"

I reminded him that it was the same device that Amos had already described in Harvey's orchard when we were looking for a nonexistent body.

"So what's so funny about the lady doctor having one of her own?" he asked in a grumpy voice. "You can't tell me that there's only one of those silly things in the whole world. Out in this neck of the woods, there must be lots of them."

"I don't think so, Dad. They're not that common. Besides, it looked like the exact one I found marking the body in the orchard."

"But, Ivy," my mother chimed in, "your dad has a point. There's no way to tell if it's the same one. Are you certain you saw it clearly? Maybe it was something else—something that reminded you of the instrument you saw."

I was certain about what I'd seen—until my mother managed to put doubts in my mind. I would have to look again—but more closely this time. I needed to remove the tapper from Lucy's SUV. Instead of gazing at it through smoky, dark glass, I wanted to hold it in my hands and make certain it was the tapper that had been used to indicate Bert's grave.

Of course, thinking that Lucy was somehow involved in Bert's death was ludicrous. She wasn't even alive when he disappeared. But why did she have the tapper? Did she know who killed him—and who moved the body? Was she involved somehow?

These questions bumped around in my head until I couldn't think straight. And I still didn't have any answers.

We pulled up to Ruby's a few minutes later. Amos's patrol car was already parked outside. When we got inside, I spotted him in a booth next to the wall. When he saw us, he waved us over. As we made our way to where he waited, I spotted Emily and Buddy having breakfast.

"Go ahead," I told my parents. "I'll be with you in a minute."

"Hello there, Ivy!" Buddy bellowed as I approached their table. "Looks like you've got the whole crew out for breakfast."

"I wanted to give you a kiss on the cheek, Buddy," I said. I bent over next to him and whispered, "Emily told me the wonderful news. I'm so happy for you."

Buddy's grin nearly split his face in two. "Thanks, Ivy," he said softly. "And thanks for keeping it to yourself until we can make the official announcement. Emily couldn't stand to keep it from you. I'm glad she has someone she trusts so much."

"I am, too," I said, patting his broad shoulder.

I turned my attention to the beaming mother-to-be. "Emily, I want to ask you a favor. I'm trying to find out who left town around the time Bert Bird disappeared. I heard your mother may have gone away for a while right around the same time. She might remember someone else who left either in the weeks before or after Bert went missing. Could you ask her for me?"

"Sure, Ivy," she said. "I'd be happy to." A frown colored her perfect features. "I didn't know Mother ever left Winter Break. This is the first I've heard of it." She reached over and touched my arm. "I'll dig up some information for you, Sherlock, if you'll meet me here for coffee this afternoon." She smiled at me. "I won't keep you long—not so long that your parents would be offended. But long enough for you to get what I imagine is a much-needed break."

I grinned back at her. "You know me too well, you know that? I was going to suggest the very same thing." I glanced over at my parents, who smiled broadly. "What time?"

"How about three o'clock?" Emily said.

I leaned down and kissed her cheek. "I'll be here."

My parents sat together on one side of the booth. I slid in next to Amos, who didn't bother to greet me. He was focused on the menu written on the dry-erase board at the front of the restaurant.

My mother kicked me under the table when Bonnie appeared next to us with her order pad. I shook my head at her. Ruby was flying around the room. There wasn't any way to talk to Bonnie now. I ended up ordering only coffee and toast, and I wasn't certain I could even get that down. I had butterflies in my stomach from the discovery in Lucy's SUV. There wasn't a lot of room left for food.

After Bonnie walked away, I leaned closer to Amos. "I thought you'd like to know that I might have found the barrel tapper this morning," I said quietly.

"What?" Amos said.

"The barrel tapper. I think I know where it is."

His confused look told me he'd forgotten about it. "The barrel tapper that marked the place where Bert's box was buried—along with a slightly missing body?"

"Oh, yeah. Sorry," he said sheepishly. "I was thinking about something else."

"Sorry to disturb you," I said sarcastically. "I just thought you might like to know who has an item that was taken when the body was removed from its burial site."

"She found it in Lucy Barber's car," my mother blurted out, stealing my thunder.

His mouth dropped open. "I don't believe it. Why would she have it?"

"Well, that's the sixty-four-thousand-dollar question, isn't it?" I said. "It doesn't make any sense unless she was in the orchard. But why would Lucy Barber move Bert's body? Lucy only started working in Winter Break a couple of years ago. She couldn't possibly have known Bert Bird. Even if she'd lived near Winter Break all her life, she wasn't even born when he left." I sighed. "You know, the more clues we get, the more confusing this whole thing is."

"Ivy, you keep saying that the body in the orchard is Bert Bird," my dad interjected. "But you have no way of knowing that, do you?"

"No," I said, "but he's the only one missing."

"Not necessarily," Amos said. "Maybe it was someone else."

"Maybe," I said. "The only thing we know for sure is that *someone* was buried there, and it wasn't an animal. No one would have gone to so much trouble to move a dead cow."

"I think you're right," my mother said, "but Amos has a point. What if it's someone completely different? Someone who disappeared years later—or earlier—than the time you're concerned with?"

I shook my head. "Unless someone else buried Bert's lunch box after he left, the body had to be placed there first. Either Bert buried his box on top of the body, or someone buried Bert Bird and his box at the same time. Bert is the key to this mystery. If we can find out what happened to him, we'll figure out the rest of the story." I sighed and put my head in my hands. "Hopefully we'll get the answers we're looking for sometime in my lifetime."

Bonnie came back with Amos's orange juice and a carafe of coffee for the rest of us. As she poured coffee into my cup, I looked around for Ruby. She was at the cash register, ringing up customers. I made a quick decision. "Bonnie," I said, keeping my voice low, "I need to talk to you. In private. It's about Bert Bird. I need to ask you some questions about what happened when he left Winter Break."

It's a good thing I have fast reflexes. Bonnie almost lost her grip on the carafe, and coffee spilled right where I'd been resting my arm.

"I–I'm sorry," she sputtered. "Are you all right?"

"Yes, I'm okay. Please don't worry about it." I used my napkin to wipe up the mess before it dripped down on my jeans.

Bonnie's eyes darted quickly toward the front of the room—to where Ruby stood talking to a customer. "Come by tonight," she said in a low voice. "After we close. I always stay late and lock up. Come around ten." She glanced once again toward Ruby. "But if *she's* here, keep going. She can't know that I'm talking to you."

"All right, Bonnie. I'll be here."

She turned on her heel and swept past us.

"I'm coming with you," my mother whispered.

I shook my head. "Bonnie doesn't know you, Mom," I said. "It would be better if I came by myself."

"I'll drive you," Amos said. "With the way things have been going, I want to be nearby in case something else happens." I started to argue with him, but he shook his head. "It's not negotiable, Ivy. I'll park around the side of the building. Bonnie will never know I'm here."

"Thanks, Amos," my dad said. "That will make me feel better."

My mother wasn't saying anything, but I knew she was upset. I reached over and patted her hand. "I promise, I'll rush home after I talk to Bonnie and tell you every single thing we talked about, okay?"

She smiled. "Okay, as long as you don't leave anything out."

"I won't. I promise."

Our conversation was suddenly interrupted by someone speaking loudly. I immediately recognized the voice. Three tables away from us, Bertha and Delbert Pennypacker were giving Bonnie their breakfast order.

"I'll have the steak and eggs, please," Bertha said in a shrill voice. "And make certain that steak is medium, will you, please? The last time we were here, my steak was terribly overcooked." She batted her eyes and glanced around the room to see if anyone was paying any attention to her. I turned my head so she wouldn't think I was listening. I noticed that most of the other people in the restaurant were also ignoring her.

Delbert seemed to be looking at his place mat intently. When he finally ordered, he barely acknowledged Bonnie—or his wife. Although Delbert Pennypacker had a reputation for being lazy, drinking too much, and chasing other women, I almost felt sorry for him. I couldn't imagine what life with Bertha had to be like. The thought made me shiver.

While my dad made small talk with Amos, I tried to piece together all the confusing facts that surrounded the missing Bert Bird. It reminded me of a hot, lazy summer afternoon years ago, when Emily and I tried to put together one of her mother's huge puzzles. We worked on that thing for hours, but we couldn't get more than a few of the pieces to fit. When Inez came home and found us, she burst out laughing.

"Oh no, girls," she'd said. "I dumped three different puzzles that were missing pieces into that box. I was going to throw them away!"

I felt the same way now, as if I were trying to piece together one picture, but there were too many pieces that didn't match. Maybe my meeting with Bonnie would help me to see the final image a little more clearly.

While my father recounted some story about the difficulty of finding good American food in China, I chewed on my dry toast and tried to ignore Amos as he shoveled mounds of Ruby's stuffed French toast into his mouth. The incredible aroma made my stomach rumble. Watching him consume forkfuls of hot berries and cream cheese tucked into Ruby's homemade bread, which had been baked in butter and covered in real maple syrup, made me feel as if I were trying to ingest cardboard.

Maybe it was my decision to look away from the gastric performance playing itself out next to me or maybe it was just God nudging my head in the right direction, but my eye caught something that made me choke on my toast.

Amos's slapping me on the back and my mother's trying to get me to take a drink of water made it more than a little difficult to talk, but I finally was able to sputter, "I'm okay. I'm okay! Quit hitting me!"

"Are you sure you're all right, punkin?" my dad asked in a worried tone.

I coughed a few more times, gave Amos a dirty look for his overenthusiastic beating, and croaked out, "The note. I know who wrote the note warning me to stop looking for Bert Bird."

16

"I wish you'd just left things alone. It won't do no good to dig up the past this way. Bert is gone, and it's for the best."

Amos, my parents, and I sat in the empty restaurant alone with Ruby. After I'd confronted her, telling her I realized the handwriting on the note matched the scrawled menu items on her large dry-erase board, she'd promised to talk to us after the morning rush. We waited for people to eat their fill and then head back home or out to the fields. Finally, around ten thirty, Ruby shooed the last of the "lollygaggers," as she called them, out the front door. She locked it and turned the CLOSED sign around to prevent further interruptions. Then she reluctantly joined us at our table.

"Ruby," Amos said, "there's still a missing body out there. I can't look the other way because you tell me to. You know that. You've got to tell me the truth. What happened to Bert?"

Ruby pulled a chair up next to our booth. Her wrinkled face sagged with weariness, and her eyes were full of long-held pain. "I don't know nothin''bout a body, Deputy," she said in a tired voice. "You see, my Bert ain't dead as far as I know."

"You. . .you know Bert's alive?" I said. "Where is he?"

She shook her head, her platinum wig jiggling like it had a mind of its own and was in complete agreement with its ancient owner. "I have no idea where my boy is. I haven't known for a long, long time."

"Why don't you start at the beginning," my mother said soothingly. "We'll just hush and let you tell the story your way."

Ruby flashed her a grateful look. "Thank you, Margie. I believe that would be the best way to go." She took a deep breath and blew it out. "First of all, let me say that I'm plumb sorry I wrote you that note, Ivy." She looked at me with tearful eyes. "At the time I wrote it, it sounded okay to me. But the more I thought about it, the more I realized you might have thought I was threatenin' you in some way." A tear spilled from one of her red-rimmed eyes and splashed down on her careworn cheek. "Nothing could be further from the truth. I appreciate you findin' Bert's stuff, and I appreciate the way you care about him—and me. But I can't have you lookin' for him. He was the one I was talkin' about in that note. The one I was afraid would wind up hurt."

Ruby took the edge of her apron and wiped her eyes. Then she breathed a sigh that seemed to come from somewhere deep inside her soul. "Before I tell you what happened to my Bert, I have to ask you to keep what I'm about to tell you to yourselves. It wouldn't do no good for folks to know."

While the rest of us mumbled our agreement, Amos kept quiet. Ruby stared at him with one eyebrow raised. "I didn't hear nothin' from you, Amos Parker."

"I can't make that promise, Ruby," he said. "You know that. If there's foul play..."

"Ain't no foul play, Deputy," she answered. "Not the legal kind, anyway."

"If that's true, you have my word, as well," Amos said. "I'll keep your secret if I possibly can."

That appeared to satisfy her. She took another deep, shaky breath. "When Elbert and I came to Winter Break, we had such high hopes. We'd been tryin' to scrape out a livin' in Oklahoma, but it was hard. Elbert was workin' for a man who owned a feed store. He wasn't gettin' paid much in the first place, but then the man started cheatin' him. He blamed Elbert for weighin' the feed wrong. Said it was costin' the store money. His boss would short Elbert's pay, sayin' he was just collectin' what he owed." Even after all these years, Ruby's eyes sparkled with righteous indignation. "Elbert Bird wouldn't take a dime that didn't belong to him. He wouldn't even pick up money dropped in the street. 'Why, Ruby,' he'd say, 'someone might be lookin' for that. Might be all they have to pay for their dinner. We better let it sit right there so the owner can retrace his steps and find it.' Man like that ain't stealin' anything from anybody. Well, anyways, baby Bert come right around that time. Elbert was tryin' his best to take care of us, but things got harder and harder. Then we got a telegraph from Elbert's uncle Leonard, tellin' us he was sick and askin' us would we please come to Kansas and help run his farm." Ruby smiled. "It was the answer to a prayer. We packed up and came to Winter Break."

She seemed to drift away a little, probably seeing happier times in her mind's eye. Then she shook herself and refocused on her story. "It was tough takin' care of Uncle Leonard, don't get me wrong, but he was a kind man. I truly loved him. It was hard when he passed, but then we found out that he'd left everything to us. We finally had a chance to have somethin' of our own— to turn our lives around in a positive direction. And we did just that." Ruby's smile held a note of pride. "Elbert and me made that place into a right fine dairy farm. The best around. For the first time in our lives, we had everything we needed, and life was good."

The light left Ruby's eyes, and she stared down toward the floor. "Then it happened. Elbert went out one day to tend the cows, and he never came home. I told him not to go out in that lightnin' storm. Somethin' told me he wasn't supposed to be out there, but he wouldn't listen." She wiped her face with her apron again. "I wish like everything I'd insisted he stay inside. I shoulda run out there after him and dragged him back into the house. But I didn't, and he died."

Ruby raised her hand to pat down her wig. Her fingers trembled visibly. "So. . .I was left alone to raise Bert. I tried to keep the farm going, I really did. Bert did everything he could to help me, but I made him go to school. School came first. The farm second." Ruby shook her head. "I truly believe that boy woulda worked himself into the ground if I'd let him. But I wanted him to be something more than a farmer, depending on the weather and such. I wanted him to have a good job—a better life than Elbert and me."

Ruby grew silent, staring at something across the room. We waited for what seemed like an eternity but was really only a few seconds. Finally, my mother touched Ruby's arm.

"Go on, Ruby," she said gently. "Tell us what happened next."

The old woman's body shuddered. "It's hard to tell this next part. No matter how I say it, it makes me sound like a rotten mother. At the time, though, I thought it was the best thing for Bert." Her pleading gaze seemed to lock on each one of us, searching for some kind of understanding.

"Go on," my mother said again.

"Our neighbors," Ruby said in a voice so low we all leaned forward to hear her, "Ben and Tillie Carver, were leaving for Nebraska. Ben got a job at a farm implement company as a salesman. It was a good job with good pay. They had two daughters, Margaret and DeAnn. Bert was friends with the girls. They seemed like such a nice family."

Again Ruby paused in her narrative, seemingly reluctant to continue. Finally, she began again. Her voice shook, making it hard to understand her. "Ben Carver offered to take Bert with them to Nebraska for a couple of months. He knew I was having problems and couldn't take care of him properly." She put her head in her hands. "I. . .I thought Bert would be better off gettin' away from here for a while. I didn't want him to worry no more. It was summer and school was out, so it seemed like the perfect solution while I decided what to do." She paused again before raising her head to look at us. Her expression was one of bewilderment. "It was just for a while," she said again. "Until I could sell the farm and make things better for us. Maybe I was wrong, but I didn't know what else to do. It was gettin' so I couldn't keep the boy fed proper."

"Why did you tell everyone Bert was going to stay with family?" my father asked. "You didn't do anything wrong. Why make up a story?"

She shook her head. "Pride," she said slowly. "Nothin' more than stinkin' pride. Everyone in town had been trying to help me out so much, I was too embarrassed to tell them I couldn't care for my own son, even with their help. I figured if I said Bert was stayin' with relatives out of town, no one would ask any questions, and I could concentrate on finding a way out of my problems without havin' to take any more charity."

"What happened, Ruby?" I asked. "Why didn't Bert come back?"

"I promised him, Ivy," she said, tears beginning to make shiny trails down her cheeks. "I promised him I would come for him as soon as I could. I sold the farm, and with the money I made, I opened this restaurant." A small smile shone through her tears. "I got the idea from Bert. He'd tell me, 'Mama, you are the best cook in the whole world. If you had a restaurant, everyone in town would eat there.'" She wiped her face with her apron. "I remembered him sayin' that, so I bought this building and started cookin'. Sure enough, people started comin' and I began to get ahead a little. Right away, I called the Carvers and told 'em I was coming for Bert. Ben Carver told me that Bert didn't want to come home. That he was happier livin' with them."

"I don't get it," Amos said. "Bert was with them only a few months, right? Why would he say something like that?"

Ruby nodded, her wig jumping up and down. "That's exactly what I wondered," she said. "I knew my boy loved me. Why wouldn't he want to come home? I told them I was comin' to get him anyway. But then I got his letter."

"He sent a letter?" my mother asked. "You didn't actually talk to him?"

Ruby shook her head. "No, Ben said he didn't want to talk to me. He said he wrote down everything he wanted to say."

"What was in the letter, Ruby?" I asked.

She covered her face with her apron for a moment. When she lowered it, I wanted to cry. In all my life, I don't think I'd ever seen so much sorrow in any person's face.

"He said he was happy livin' with the Carvers. That he didn't need me, and he didn't want to live in Winter Break. That there was lots of things in Nebraska that Winter Break didn't have. He said it would be best if we just left each other alone." Ruby's last words were wrapped around her sobs. She pulled her apron up over her face again, this time crying bitterly into it.

My mother scooted next to her and wrapped her arms around the grieving woman. I reached across the table and put my hand on her arm. There wasn't anything to say. All we could do was try to comfort her.

Finally, her crying lessened and she pulled the apron down. "I couldn't believe it at first," she sputtered. "My Bert wouldn't say those kinds of things to me. After awhile, I decided to go to Beatrice—that's where they was livin'—and just make him come home. He was still a boy, and I was his mama. He'd have to come if I made him. But the Carvers were gone. I looked for them for a long time, callin' their relatives and friends, tryin' to find out where they were. I even went to the police in town and asked for their help. They checked around a little, but they couldn't find no sign of them either. After awhile

I quit lookin'. I decided that if Bert wanted to come home, he knew where I was. He'd been with the Carvers awhile by then. He must have been happier with them than he'd been with me, and I wanted him to be happy more than anything. I been waitin' in Winter Break all these years just in case he changed his mind and came home. But that was thirty-some years ago. He probably has a wife and kids by now. He doesn't want anything to do with me; that's obvious." She reached over and grabbed my hand. "That's why I pushed that note under your door, Ivy. You're a smart girl. I was afraid you'd uncover the truth and go lookin' for Bert. I know it's easier to find people now, what with the Internet and all, but I don't want to interfere in his life. I don't want to mess him up any more. I'm really sorry about the note," she said. "I truly didn't mean to scare you."

My mother patted Ruby's shoulder. "She understands, Ruby," she said. "Don't worry about it."

Ruby locked her pain-filled eyes on mine. "Will you promise to keep my secret?" she asked in a strained voice. "Will you please just leave this alone now?"

Before I could answer, my mother spoke up again. "Ivy won't look for Bert anymore, Ruby," she said. "I promise."

I was beginning to feel like a puppet with my mother pulling the strings. "Amos?" Ruby said. "What about you?"

"I'm sorry you've gone through so much, Ruby. Whatever you want to do is fine with me."

"Good. Good," she said with a deep, slow sigh. She slapped her hand on the top of the table. "Now I've got to get things going for the lunch rush. You folks need to head on out of here."

It was as if a strong wind had suddenly swept the past few minutes away. Ruby was her old self. She stood up and headed for her kitchen, ready to go on with life as if nothing had happened, her pain shut behind a door she'd kept closed for many years. Before she reached the door to the kitchen, she stopped and whirled back around.

"I'd still like my boy's lunch box and keepsakes," she said. "It would give me somethin' to remember him by." With that, she was gone. Within seconds, the sounds of chopping came from the kitchen, along with the aroma of jalapeños. Ruby's Redbird Burgers were getting ready to make another appearance. My breakfast of dry toast lay cold and flat in my stomach. I could swear I heard it whispering, "Redbird Burger. Redbird Burger."

"Let's get going," my mother said.

I started to say something, but she shushed me. "Outside," she whispered. Her face was set and angry. I couldn't begin to imagine why. I knew why *I* was hopping mad. My mother had given Ruby a promise I hadn't made. And I still had lots of questions.

When we got outside, my mother turned to me. "Sorry about speaking for you, Ivy," she said. "But I had to get us out of there."

"Something's wrong with Ruby's story," my dad said. "Your mother picked it up, too."

"What do you mean?" Amos asked. "Don't you believe her?"

"Well, first of all," my mother said, "it bothers me that Ruby never got to talk to Bert himself. Who knows why he wrote that letter—or if he even did?"

My dad put his arm around me. "Parents and children have a bond, Amos. It can't be broken that easily. Even if Bert did want to stay with the Carvers, he should have wanted to visit his mother at least once in the last thirty years. Even kids with lousy parents usually try to mend fences at some point. Something about this whole thing stinks like dead fish left lying in the sun."

Amos had an odd look on his face. He'd tried to reach out to his own father, although his attempt hadn't been successful. Maybe my parents were right.

"Well," I said, "if I'm finally allowed to talk, may I say that you put me in an awful position when you promised Ruby that I was going to leave this alone? I don't think I can do that. I want to find Bert. With the Internet, I'll bet—"

"Ivy," my mother said, "I only said that so that Ruby wouldn't put the rest of us on the spot. *I* didn't promise anything. I intend to do exactly what you said. Look for Bert Bird online. If he's listed in any phone book in the nation, we'll find him."

"Why, Mother," I said. "How delightfully devious of you. And you being a missionary and all. . ."

"There are many facets to your old mother, my dear," she said. "The detective side of me has been awakened."

"May I suggest to you and Dr. Watson," my dad said, "that we continue this conversation somewhere else. Ruby might get suspicious if she sees us out here jabbering."

My parents and I climbed into my car. Amos came around to my side and leaned in. "We learned something else this morning," he said, frowning. "Ruby didn't set that fire. She doesn't know that Bert's box is gone."

"And I'm surprised about that," I said. "With Bertha running off at the mouth, how could Ruby have missed out on that information?"

"Easy," he replied. "In a room full of customers, she can't hear hardly anything. There are too many sounds for her to sort out. That's why Bonnie takes almost all the orders. Bertha could have explained the situation in depth to her, and Ruby would have just smiled and nodded—and not picked up one single word."

"And here's another thing," I interjected. "Whoever was buried in the orchard isn't Bert Bird. So we have a body floating around somewhere. Odds are that whoever moved it set the fire. Somehow the box, the body, and Bert Bird are all connected. We have to find out how."

Amos shook his head. "I swear this thing gets goofier every day. Every time we turn over a rock, another snake crawls out."

"Amos," I said as I started the engine, "I hate to completely change the subject, but I need to bring up something else. I have a feeling—"

"Oh no," he said, standing straight and holding his hands up in surrender. "I stayed a few seconds longer than I should have."

"Let me finish. You said that there had to be someone else connected to those cattle thieves. Someone who was planning everything?"

Amos leaned down again. "You have an idea?"

I smiled and nodded. "I have a feeling that you should check out Delbert Pennypacker. Either Bertha won the lottery, or Delbert got a job. Since neither one of those possibilities seems likely, I got to thinking. . ."

"That Delbert's been doing something *nefarious* on the side?"

I slapped him on the arm. "I knew I could improve your vocabulary with a little effort."

Amos stood up. "I'll make a little trip over to see the Pennypackers. Where are you going now?"

"We're going over to the bookstore. I want to see how things are coming along."

Amos said good-bye to my folks, gave me a quick kiss, got in his car, and drove away. I had a distinct feeling that his visit to the Pennypackers wasn't going to help my relationship with Bertha. I was trying not to worry about it as I turned the car around and drove to the bookstore. My mother interrupted my thoughts with a question about a computer.

"Mine melted in the fire, Mom," I said. "I know Elmer Buskin would let us use his."

"We brought our laptop, Ivy," my dad interjected. "Maybe we could just plug it in at your place."

"Well, let's see if we'll have any privacy first," I said. "I'm not sure if everyone's finished working."

Everything looked quiet when we pulled up in front of the bookstore. My parents followed me up the steps and waited as I slid the key Milton had given me into the lock and opened the brand-new door. We were greeted with complete silence. No one was inside. I flipped on the light and looked around. The main room was beautiful—just as it had been before. As I looked over at the spot where Bitty's desk used to be, I got a surprise that almost made me drop my keys. Sitting a few feet away from where the old desk had been was what looked like the exact same desk! How could it be? I blinked my eyes a couple of times to make sure I wasn't seeing things. Maybe the stress of the fire and everything. . . Nope. It was still there.

"What. . .how. . ." was all I could manage to get out.

Hearty laughter came from behind me. I turned to find Dewey standing there, enjoying my complete bewilderment.

"Something you didn't know, Ivy," he said, grinning, "was that I was with your aunt when she bought her desk. It was not long after she opened the bookstore. A farmer out near Sublette passed away, and Bitty and I went to his estate sale. We bought several pieces of furniture, including a *pair* of matching desks. I've had this one upstairs in my apartment for all these years. It's beautiful, but I have a big old oak desk I use for everything. This one was always a little too girlie for me. It would make me very happy if you would take it."

I had a lump in my throat so big I couldn't get an answer out. Instead, I rushed over and threw my arms around my old friend.

"I think that means yes, Dewey," my dad said, laughing.

I nodded vigorously. "Yes. Yes, it does," I finally croaked out. "Thank you, Dewey."

He squeezed me hard before he gently pushed me away. "You're gonna get me bawlin' if I don't get out of here," he said in a husky voice. "I've got to get back to work." He walked toward the door but then stopped. "I almost forgot. I'm supposed to tell you that everything is done but that you need to stay away from the new section of flooring for a few days. Milton and his boys refinished the surrounding area so the new boards would blend in. You can put the carpet down and move the desk back when the finish dries completely."

"No problem," I said with a smile. "And, Dewey, thanks again. You don't know what this means to me."

The old man stared at me for a moment. "Yes, I think I do, Ivy. I think I do." With that, he ambled out the door, and I was left feeling blessed by God to know someone like Dewey Tater.

"Everything looks great," Dad said. "Your friends did a wonderful job."

"Yes, they did," I said. "I guess I can move back home."

My mother touched my shoulder. "Before anyone moves anywhere, let's get our laptop set up. I want to do some Googling."

I looked over at my dad and grinned. Mom had always been rather technically challenged. I wasn't sure she was up to doing a thorough search.

"Don't worry, Ivy," my dad said. "Your mother has become a Net junkie. She can surf with the best of them."

"Oh, for goodness' sake," my mother said in an irritated voice. "I am *not* an Internet junkie. I've had to learn how to use the blasted thing so we can get the supplies and things we need in China." She sighed and shook her finger at my father. "You make me sound like some kind of computer addict."

"Not an addict, dear, just a very competent researcher. If anyone can find Bert Bird in cyberspace, it's you." He looked at both of us with a serious expression. "If we locate him, what are we going to do? Have you thought about that?"

"I just want him to know how much his mother loves him," I said. "I also want to find out why he's never come home. If he really doesn't want to be here, so be it. We leave it alone and walk away. Ruby never needs to know. But if the Carvers lied to him, which I think is a possibility, it's time he heard the truth."

"I agree," my mother said, "but you're going to have to keep your word and let your father and me handle this."

"Well, I suggest we go get your laptop," I said. "I'll pack up my stuff; then we'll all come back here. I'm meeting Emily around three for coffee. I'll leave you two on your own to investigate the whereabouts of the missing Bert Bird."

"Let's go," my father said. "I feel like a part of some famous detective team." He thought for a moment. "I can't seem to think of any teams with three detectives, though."

My mother walked to the front door and pulled it open. "I can," she said. "How about Nick and Nora Charles?"

He frowned. "That's only two."

She turned and smiled at him. "You're forgetting Asta, their dog. Let's go, boy."

My dad and I laughed and followed her out to the car. As we drove back to the Biddle house, I had the strangest feeling that the search for Bert Bird would soon be coming to an end.

17

With my parents safely ensconced at the bookstore, I headed over to Ruby's to meet Emily for coffee. Although Ruby only served full meals during certain hours, she usually left her doors open so townsfolk could come inside for coffee and something already made. Bonnie served pie and cake and occasionally made a sandwich. Ruby kept the coffee going all day, though, because she felt anytime was a good time for a cup of coffee and a friendly conversation.

I pulled into a parking space right by the front door. Winter Break had been experiencing gorgeous spring weather, but we were definitely in that spring-showers-bringing-May-flowers stage. Clouds had begun to gather overhead, and as I stepped from my car, I felt a couple of raindrops on my arm. I had my hand on the door to the restaurant when I noticed Lucy Barber's SUV pull up across the street at Sally's Sew 'n' Such. Sally Redfield was diabetic, and Lucy almost always stopped by to see her whenever she was in town.

I knew Amos planned to talk to Lucy about the barrel tapper, but I wasn't sure how long that was going to take. I felt an urge to get answers now. I'd been pretty patient, but enough was enough.

"Lucy! Lucy, wait a minute," I hollered at her. She turned around and waved at me. I ran across the street, pelted by raindrops that were getting bigger by the second.

"Hi there," she said with a smile when I stepped under the welcome protection of the overhang in front of Sally's. "How are things going with your parents?"

"Believe it or not, they're going pretty well," I said. "My mother and I are actually talking about something besides how messed up I am."

"That's wonderful, Ivy," Lucy said. "I'm happy for you."

I couldn't help but think about how my relationship with Lucy had also improved over the last several months. She really was becoming a good friend.

"Did you need something?" she asked.

"Yes, I do," I said. "I need your help. Some weird things have been going on lately. I have a couple of questions that may seem odd. Do you mind if I ask them?"

She set her black leather bag down and frowned at me. "I. . .I suppose not," she said slowly.

"Lucy, what happened to the gas can you used to carry in your car?"

"Why, did you find it?" she asked.

"Are your initials on the bottom?"

She nodded.

"Then yes, I believe I did. When did you lose it?"

"It was Tuesday night while I was at Cyrus Penwiddie's house. I left the back of my truck open, and when I came out, I noticed right away that it was gone."

"That was the same night as the fire at the bookstore," I said more to myself than to anyone else.

"What are you talking about?" she asked. "You're not saying that someone used *my* gas can to start that fire." Lucy's face had gone pale.

I nodded. "That's exactly what I'm saying. They used your can and then left it near the building so someone would find it."

"Why?" she asked.

"I think they were trying to make me suspect you set the fire."

"And do you, Ivy?"

"No. No, I don't." I smiled at her. "I guess whoever started the fire thought that since you and Amos used to date, I'd jump to the conclusion that you were capable of burning down the bookstore."

She nodded. "I'm glad it didn't work. You know, I was jealous of you when you first came to Winter Break. I never officially apologized to you for that, and I'm truly sorry."

I reached out and patted her shoulder. "I've had my own bouts of jealousy, Lucy. Let's just forget it, okay?"

"You've got a deal," she said and sealed it with a hug.

"I said I had two questions. Can I ask you the second one?"

She let go of my shoulders. "Sure. Go ahead."

"I noticed something in your car the other day. A barrel tapper. Can I ask you where you got it?"

"You were looking in my car? I assume it was to see if my gas can was there?"

I grinned. "Yeah, sorry."

She laughed. "I'm happy to answer your question, but next time you need to inspect my car, just ask, okay?"

I nodded. "You have my promise."

"I got the barrel tapper at a yard sale."

"A yard sale? Where?"

She hesitated, wrinkling her forehead as she thought. "Ivy, I really don't know. This past week, I've been to all kinds of sales. With the weather getting nicer, everyone and his brother is having a yard sale. If you'd looked further, you'd have seen lots of other things in my car. I buy lots of stuff in an attempt to satisfy my hobby."

"What's your hobby?" I asked.

"Tools. Old farm tools, old medical tools. Even some kitchen equipment. I think they're fascinating." She stepped out into the rain, which was falling pretty heavily by now, and opened her back car door. Then she bent over to grab something from the floorboards. She slammed the door shut and ran back to our temporary shelter. "Is this what you're talking about? Do you need it for some reason?"

I took it from her hand and looked at it closely. I was certain it was the same tapper. "Lucy, I've got to go. Someone's waiting for me at Ruby's. But would you please try to remember where you bought this? It's very, very important." I handed the tapper back to her.

"Sure, and please let me know when you find out who set your store on fire. I'll have a few words to say to the creep."

I reached over and gave her a quick hug. "I'll do that. Thanks. Your gas can is in my car—do you want me to get it now?"

She looked up at the sky. "Looks like we're in for a real downpour. I'll get it later, if that's okay."

I thanked her again and ran across the street to the restaurant. Big raindrops chased me. I was certain I resembled a drowned rat by the time I sat down with Emily, who looked as perfect as she always did. Never a hair out of place or a wrinkle in her clothes. Emily was the kind of person I knew I could never be. I was messy and rambunctious. Emily was soft, sweet, and spiritual. And I loved her to pieces.

"I'm so glad we finally got some time together," she said while I shook the water out of my hair and all over the table.

"Sorry. I feel like a wet dog."

Her laugh was light and lilting. "Well, you certainly don't look like a wet dog. You look beautiful."

"I guess pregnant women are subject to delusions."

"Oh, Ivy, you're too self-deprecating. I've always envied your spectacular looks."

My stunned silence was interrupted by Bonnie Peavey. "Whatcha havin'?" she asked, pouring us two cups of coffee without asking. Bonnie pretty much knew what everyone wanted before they opened their mouths.

I was starving. "I hate to even ask this, Bonnie," I said, "but is there any stuffed French toast left?"

She looked over her shoulder. "There's some made up in the fridge. All I have to do is bake it. It will take about thirty minutes. Can you wait that long?"

"I'll wait as long as I have to," I said. "Are you sure Ruby won't mind?"

She shook her head. "She's not here. She had to go to Hugoton for supplies. She should be back around four thirty."

I glanced over at the dry-erase board. In big letters at the top Ruby had written: DINNER STARTS AT 6:00 P.M. FRIDAY NIGHT SPECIAL: ROAST BEEF AND RED POTATOES. Ruby served food pretty much when she felt like it. Pushing things back an hour or two was par for the course, especially when she had to do some shopping. She bought everything she could from Dewey, but he couldn't stock enough food for the kind of crowds she cooked for. Once a week at least, she would go to Hugoton for additional provisions. Usually she went in the morning. I suspected that our intense conversation after breakfast explained the late-afternoon trip.

"I'd love some French toast, too, Bonnie," Emily said. "But I think I'll have a glass of milk instead of coffee today."

"Oh, really?" Bonnie said with a smile. "Is there anything you want to tell me?"

"Not yet," Emily said with a wink.

"I'll get you that milk, honey. And maybe a little extra French toast." With that, she took off for the kitchen.

Although it wasn't as important to talk to Emily now, since Ruby had explained the reasons behind Bert's departure, I was still curious about his relationship with Bonnie. With Ruby gone, it seemed like a perfect time to ask her a few questions. "Emily, please forgive me. I want to talk to Bonnie for a moment. I'll be right back."

Emily was used to my mercurial personality, so she just smiled and waved me on.

I swung the kitchen door open and found Bonnie pouring a glass of milk for Emily. She seemed startled by my invasion of Ruby's inner sanctum. "Did I forget something?" she asked.

"No. Listen, Bonnie, I know you told me to come by tonight to talk to you, but with the bad weather, I thought maybe you could give me a couple of minutes now. Some really strange things have been happening, and they seem to be tied to Bert Bird. Is there anything you can tell me about him?"

Bonnie stared down at her feet for several seconds before finally looking up at me and nodding. "I don't know if I can help you, but I'm willing to do what I can. Let me take this milk to Emily. I'll be right back."

I used my time alone to poke around a little in Ruby's kitchen. Everything was clean and organized. It was obvious that Ruby ran a tight ship. I could smell her tender roast beef, the aroma coming from two very large ovens. I peeked under three huge metal trays that were covered with tinfoil. Buttery boiled red potatoes sat waiting to make their appearance tonight. I'd just put the foil back when Bonnie swung the door open.

"When's Emily's baby due?" she asked.

I laughed. "You knew that because she ordered milk?"

"Sure. Emily loves her coffee. A baby is the only thing that would make her order milk."

"Well, keep it a secret. She and Buddy haven't told all their family yet."

"No problem," Bonnie said quietly. "I don't really have anyone to tell anyway."

She opened the refrigerator and took out a large tin tray of Ruby's stuffed French toast. She cut two slices, grabbed a pan, and shoved it into one of the ovens, next to a big roaster.

"Now tell me about you and Bert," I said gently after she'd closed the oven door.

Bonnie worked at tucking strands of loose, straw-colored hair under her brown hairnet. "We were only fourteen when we fell in love," she said. Each word was pronounced carefully, as if the story had been rehearsed many times. I stood close to her so the sound of rain hitting the metal roof over our heads wouldn't drown out her voice. "And yes, it really was love. To say that teenagers can't fall in love is ridiculous. My parents got married when they were fourteen. They've been together over fifty years now. Bert and I loved each other so much, it hurt. But he kept it from his mother because she was so devastated by his father's death. Bert didn't want to do or say anything to upset her. Then one day, he came to see me. I could tell he'd been crying. When I asked him what was wrong, he told me that Ruby was sending him away to stay with the Carvers. I couldn't believe it. He was so upset, Ivy. I didn't know what to do—what to say. Bert was trying to understand, but he felt abandoned. First he loses his father, and now his mother sends him away."

"But Ruby was only thinking about him, Bonnie," I said. "She was trying to protect him."

"I tried to tell him that," she said, nodding, "but he wouldn't listen. He wanted to stay here and help his mother through her troubles. He wanted to be the man of the family. Instead, she treated him like some child that needed protection." She looked at me. "Can you understand that?"

"As a matter of fact, I can," I answered slowly. "I guess I'd feel the same way."

"Sure you would. Anyway, before he left, Bert told me he loved me and that he would come home as soon as he could. He gave me a lunch box with all his most prized possessions. But I couldn't keep it. My mother didn't like Bert because she had something against Ruby. I have no idea what it was. To be honest, my mother is mad at most of the people she knows. Somehow Ruby just ended up on her list. You can imagine how happy she is that I work here." Bonnie smiled briefly. I had the feeling that upsetting her mother didn't bother her too much. "Anyway, I was certain if she found the lunch box, she'd make me get rid of it. So we decided to bury it in the peach orchard." Tears formed in Bonnie's eyes.

"Bonnie, were you with him when he buried it?"

The waitress nodded her head. "We buried it together. It wasn't easy. There hadn't been any rain for several weeks, and the ground was hard. Thankfully, we found a spot where the dirt had been recently turned over. We buried the box there."

"Did you ever think about retrieving it?"

"No."

"Because if you dug up the box. . ."

"It would mean he wasn't coming back," she said sadly.

"And the map?"

Bonnie smiled. "Did you see the picture of me in Bert's box?"

I nodded.

"It was taken at a traveling carnival that was in Hugoton. If the picture hadn't been faded, you would have seen me holding the jewelry box that Bert won for me. He put the map in there. He wanted to make sure we could find the place where we buried the lunch box."

"But how did my aunt Bitty end up with it?"

"When I moved out of my folks' place, my mother put it in the church bazaar. In fact, she donated all my things out of spite." She looked up at me. "You see, they wanted everyone in the family to stay on the homestead. But I wanted my own life, so I took a room at Sarah Johnson's. I went to retrieve the jewelry box, but I was too late. I tried to find it at the bazaar, but it was already gone. I guess it was your aunt who bought it."

"Bonnie, why do you think Bert never returned to Winter Break?"

She sighed and looked at her red, dry hands. "I don't know. I've asked myself that so many times, I can't think about it anymore. As crazy as it sounds, Ivy, I still believe he'll come back to me someday."

"Have you and Ruby ever talked about Bert?"

She shook her head. "No. She knew we liked each other, but when she told Bert she wanted him to concentrate on saving the farm instead of fooling around with me, he decided to keep our relationship a secret. His mother had been so hurt already by the loss of his dad, he couldn't stand to add anything else to her worries."

I was pretty sure Bonnie didn't know about Bert's letter asking to stay with the Carvers. She really had no idea why he hadn't kept his promise to return to her.

"Thank you, Bonnie. This information helps me. But I have one other question."

"Let me guess," she said with a wry smile. "Why am I still in Winter Break and why have I worked for Ruby all these years?"

"You're trying to take care of Bert's mother—for his sake?"

Once again, Bonnie pushed her straying strands of hair back into her hairnet. "It's all I have left of him," she said softly. Then she turned around and began stirring something on the stove.

I took that as my signal to leave and went back to the table, where Emily sat staring at my cup of coffee. "This milk thing is going to be a real challenge for me," she said.

I sat down and picked up my cup. The coffee was lukewarm, but I didn't care. Bonnie's story had really touched me. That kind of love. . .love that had bloomed when they were children; it was a lot like my relationship with Amos.

Emily and I spent awhile talking about our families. She told me about their search for baby names, and I told her about the plans I had for the store. Then she mentioned Faith and her concern for the young girl.

"Why don't you send her to help me in the store after things get up and running?" I said. "I could use some assistance, and it sounds like Faith needs something to do."

"I don't know, Ivy. She's quite a handful. Are you sure you want to tackle someone like her?"

"Aunt Bitty would have said yes, Emily. And so will I. There's nothing too difficult for God. If He can use me to help her, I'd consider it a privilege."

The rain spattering on the roof and the heavenly smells coming from the kitchen blended together to create a cozy atmosphere. Even though Emily and I had been apart for several years before I came back to Winter Break, it seemed as if I'd left only yesterday. For the first time in days, I felt really relaxed. Finally, Bonnie brought out two plates of Ruby's stuffed French toast. My determination to eat healthily grew little wings and flew away. I consoled myself in the belief that nothing was really off limits as long as most of the time I made good choices. An occasional treat was good for the soul. And my soul was singing, "Hallelujah!"

Emily and I ate as if we hadn't seen food in a week. Of course, Emily was eating for two. I didn't have that excuse. About halfway through I remembered why it was best to eat Ruby's food with caution. The French toast wasn't the only thing that was stuffed.

"Oh, Ivy, I almost forgot," Emily said while I was letting my fork cool down, "you wanted me to ask my mother about people who left town around the same time she did."

I really didn't need the information now, but I wasn't certain I could tell Emily that without revealing why it was no longer necessary. I'd promised Ruby that I wouldn't tell anyone about Bert, so I just nodded.

"I'm glad you asked about it, because it forced my mother to admit that she took off for a while after she graduated from high school. She wasn't sure she wanted to live in Winter Break, surrounded by Baumgartners." Emily laughed. "Somehow it made her seem a little more human to me."

"Wow. So your mom was one of the renegade Baumgartners, huh? I've heard about them, but I think she's the first one I've known."

Emily snorted. "Yeah, my mom the rebel."

I had to giggle at the idea of Inez Baumgartner as a rebel. She was about as down-to-earth and mild mannered as anyone I'd ever known.

Emily took another bite of French toast and rolled her eyes. "I've got to quit eating this," she mumbled. After a few more chews and a swallow, she took a drink of milk. "Mom said that she and her second cousin Darrel took off for Wichita. After a couple of weeks, Mom came back. She didn't like life outside of Winter Break. But Darrel stayed. He's an attorney in Topeka now."

"Wow. Someone who made it out."

She shrugged. "Yeah. At least he stays in touch. My mom's aunt Edith left Winter Break right around the same time and no one ever heard from her again."

"Edith. Are you talking about Edith Bruenwalder?"

Emily nodded. "Yes. Harvey's wife." Although the restaurant was almost empty, Emily leaned closer to me. "According to my mother, poor Edith was a very nice woman. She loved kids even though she and Harvey never had any. It was her idea to host the Scout jamborees in the orchard. Eventually Harvey shut them down out of spite. Mom suspected that Harvey abused her. She noticed bruises sometimes, although Edith did her best to hide them. When she left, no one was surprised. I'm sure she took off for her own protection. I guess she never contacted anyone again because she couldn't risk letting Harvey know where she was." Emily reached down and picked up her bag. "My mom gave me a picture of Edith for my family album. I've got it here if you want to see it."

I wasn't really surprised to find out about Harvey, but it made me sad. I guess his mean streak wasn't anything new. He'd been working on it for most of his life. I was glad his wife got away.

Emily pulled out a large envelope then slid a picture out and put it on the table in front of me. It was a photograph of Harvey and Edith. They must have been in their thirties. Harvey was smiling, but it didn't seem to reach his eyes. Edith's smile was thin and her expression stoic. This wasn't a happy couple.

I started to hand the picture back to Emily, when I noticed something that made my blood feel like ice water. "Emily," I said breathlessly. "Can I borrow this picture? I'll get it back to you."

"Why, Ivy," she said. "Of course you can, but what in the world? You're as white as a sheet."

I grabbed my purse and threw some money on the table. "I have to go. I can't explain now. I'll call you later."

With my heart thumping as if it wanted to jump out of my chest, I tucked the old photo under the protection of my shirt and ran out the front door of Ruby's. Lucy Barber was just coming out of Sally's. I put the picture in the front seat of my car and ran across the street. A bolt of lightning cracked somewhere off in the distance. By the time I got to Lucy, I was soaked to the skin. The rain had dropped the temperature several degrees. I felt as if I'd been shoved into a freezer. Through chattering teeth I asked her a question I was certain I already knew the answer to. Lucy thought for a moment but then confirmed my suspicions. I thanked her and ran to the car. It took me only a couple of minutes to get to the bookstore. I ran inside, startling my mom and dad, who were crouched over their laptop.

"Ivy!" my mother said. "You're absolutely waterlogged. What—"

"Not—not now, M–Mom," I said. "You've got to dis–disconnect. I—I n–need to use the phone."

"But, Ivy," my father said, "we found—"

"Dad, p–p–please. I–I've got to c–call Amos right now. P–please—"

"You've got to call who?" a voice said behind me. Amos was standing on the rug by the front door, wiping his wet feet.

"Amos! I—I know what hap–happened! We–we've got to g–go."

"Go?" he said with a bewildered look on his face. "Go where? I just got here."

I ran over to him and pulled a jacket off the coatrack. I was shaking so hard I couldn't get it on. He took it from me and then held it out so I could get my arms in the sleeves.

I grabbed him and started pushing him toward the front door. "We're going. . . We're going. . ." I stopped, took a deep breath, and forced myself to calm down enough to say, "Amos, we're going to arrest a murderer."

18

"S o let me see if I have this right," my dad said as we sat around the Biddles' kitchen, drinking coffee and trying to forget how much of Ruby's fried chicken we'd consumed after Sunday morning service. "Harvey Bruenwalder killed his wife, Edith, because he found out she was going to leave him."

It was a lovely spring day. Through the large windows and the French doors that opened onto the patio, I could see the sun sparkling off Lake Winter Break. The ducks and geese that lived there were splashing happily around in the water, celebrating the end of winter's hibernation. I waved at Amos, who was out on the patio. He smiled and waved back at me. Then he returned his attention to what looked like an intense conversation.

"Right," I said, pulling my concentration back to my dad. "Several people knew he abused her, so when she vanished, everyone assumed she'd simply had enough and taken off for greener pastures."

"You'd think someone would have questioned it, though." My father stared into his coffee cup. "If either one of you disappeared, I'd like to think people would search for you."

"Most people just assumed Edith was hiding out from Harvey," I said. "Some of her family saw her leaving as merely another Baumgartner desertion. They just waited for her to come to her senses and come back to Winter Break. Unfortunately, no one ever followed up. It's really sad."

"So Harvey killed her and buried her in the peach orchard," he continued. "Then Bert Bird comes along to bury his box of treasures and finds a place where the ground is soft enough to dig up."

"Yep. He plants his box right on top of Edith, never knowing he was that close to a corpse."

"Who put the barrel tapper in the ground by the body?" my mother asked.

"Harvey," I said. "He couldn't take a chance of forgetting where she was. Of course, now we know why he got so bent out of shape when Amos and I dug up his orchard when we were kids. Fortunately for Harvey, we didn't get near that spot. After I found Bert's box, he removed the barrel tapper, hoping I wouldn't be able to find my way back."

"Then he took it to his sister's yard sale." My dad laughed and shook his head. "Even that went wrong for old Harvey. That barrel tapper made its way back to Winter Break when Dr. Barber bought it and put it in her car."

"But what really led you to the truth was the photo Emily showed you," my mother said. "When you saw that picture of Edith Bruenwalder, you noticed her pendant and realized it was one of the items in Bert's box."

I nodded. "That was the clue that pulled all the pieces of the puzzle together. After I spilled Bert's belongings on the ground in the orchard, I spotted the pendant in the dirt. I thought it had tumbled out of the box, but it hadn't. I'd uncovered it, and Edith, when I was digging. I'd always wondered why that medal was so dirty while the others were only slightly rusted. Now, of course, it makes sense."

"When you put Bert's things out on the table at Ruby's, Harvey saw the pendant. He knew right away what had happened," my dad said. "Boy, I would have loved to see his face."

I chuckled. "I thought he was looking that way because I'd trespassed on his property." I got up and poured another cup of coffee. The caffeine was beginning to make me jittery, but I hadn't slept much the night before. Too much excitement. I knew Amos was just as tired as I was. After dropping Harvey off at the sheriff's office in Hugoton, he'd gone all the way to Wichita. It was almost midnight by the time he'd returned last night.

"I'm glad Amos and the other deputies found Edith's remains behind Harvey's house. Now she can have a decent burial," my mother said. There was a hint of sadness in her voice.

My father shook his head. "Harvey must have moved her right after he discovered you'd been out in his orchard. I'll bet he almost had a heart attack when he realized how close you'd come to uncovering his secret."

I smiled. "I'm sure he did."

"I think he took Dr. Barber's gas can to divert suspicion in case someone figured out that the fire was purposely set," Mom interjected.

"He certainly tried to cover all his bases," my dad said. "But things didn't go the way he planned. The store didn't burn as quickly as he thought it would. The fire didn't even hide the fact that the whole thing was set just to hide the theft of those boxes. He couldn't allow anyone to get a good look at that pendant. If someone who'd known Edith saw it, it might have raised questions he didn't want asked."

"He probably took Dr. Barber's gas can because it was available. I doubt that he knew anything about your history with her," Mom said.

I sighed. "Thank goodness I didn't go too far down that road. If I'd really suspected Lucy, things might not have turned out the way they did."

"Well, it's a good thing Harvey tried to make it look like an electrical fire and kept everything near that one outlet," my father said. "If he'd poured gasoline everywhere, the whole store might have gone up like a dead Christmas tree—with you in it."

Dad's words made me shiver. That particular outcome was something I didn't want to think about.

"Bert's stuff is probably hidden somewhere at Harvey's," I said, changing the subject, "including the map he took, hoping I wouldn't be able to find my way back to Edith's grave. I hope we find everything. I'm sure Ruby will want all of it."

My mother smiled. "Yes, she probably will, Ivy, but I don't think it will be as important as it once was."

"I'm sure you're right," I said, glancing back toward Amos.

My father grunted. "This whole experience makes me want to go back to China. Believe it or not, things seemed a lot clearer there."

Mom laughed. "You mean like the time you tried to tell someone in Mandarin that you needed to buy a new pair of shoes and instead informed them that you were in the market for young children?"

"Oh, hush, Margie. It was an understandable mistake." Although he tried to sound gruff, he couldn't hide a smile.

"Wow, Dad," I said teasingly. "Not a good thing for a minister to request from the local yokels. How did you get out of that one?"

"It took a lot of explaining, believe me," my mother said, still grinning. "Lucky for us, our obvious ignorance of the language smoothed things over."

I glanced at my watch again. It was almost three o'clock. Ruby had promised to come by after the last of her fried-chicken-engorged customers waddled out of her restaurant. Good thing Ruby's was closed Sunday evenings. It was the only time she really had to herself. She was going to need every second of it today.

Suddenly the doorbell rang, making me almost jump off my stool. I glanced at my parents, who looked as nervous as I felt. Since no one else moved, I got up and opened the front door.

"What in heaven's name is so important I had to come here as soon as I closed up?" Ruby grumbled when I swung the door open. "I'm missing my Sunday afternoon nap. I hope this is important."

"I think this is pretty important, Ruby," I said. "Please come in."

She clomped her way into the kitchen. "My, my," she said, looking around. "This place looks just the same as it did when Cecil and Marion lived here. Always was the prettiest house in Winter Break."

We walked through the living room to the kitchen, where my mother stood waiting. My father had gone out to the patio to alert Amos.

"Hello there, Margie," Ruby said. My mother opened her mouth, but nothing came out. Instead, she started to cry.

"Well, I must say that's a strange way to greet someone," Ruby said. "Just what in blue blazes is going on here?"

"Ruby," I said, "sit down. Please." I pulled one of the kitchen stools over to her.

"Now you're startin' to scare me, Ivy Towers," she said. With a little bit of a struggle and some help from me, she managed to wriggle up on top of the stool. It was a little high for someone of her stature.

"Ruby," I began, "there is something I must tell you. I...I..." I reminded myself to speak up so she could hear me. I had no intention of having to repeat what I was about to say. I could feel my insides starting to churn. Unless I did this quickly, I was going to end up blubbering like my mother. As it was, I couldn't look at her even though I could hear her hiccupping and sniffling behind me.

"Ruby," I began again, talking as quickly and loudly as I could without sounding like a gibbering idiot, "Ben Carver lied to Bert. He told him that you didn't want him. He told him that you had deserted him. That's why Bert wrote you that angry letter. He was striking back at you, trying to make you think he didn't need you either. Bert never knew you looked for him, and he never knew you wanted him back."

Ruby's face was ashen. "What? How could he have thought... How do you know this, Ivy Towers?" Her voice shook as she wriggled down off the stool. "How could you possibly know anything about this?"

I hadn't heard the French doors to the patio open, so I was startled when a deep voice came from behind me.

"She knows that because I told her, Mama."

Ruby stepped away from me, her eyes locking on the nice-looking man with salt-and-pepper hair who stood next to Amos.

I reached over to grab her in case she fainted, but it wasn't necessary. Her body was ramrod straight, and every fiber of her being was focused on her son, Bert Bird. My mother, who was overcome with emotion, snorted. In any other circumstance, I would have found it funny. But at that moment, it only caused the tears I'd been holding in to start rolling down my cheeks.

"Is that really you, son?" Ruby asked, her voice trembling. "Have you really come home?"

Bert left Amos's side and went to his mother. "It's really me, Mama. Have I changed that much?"

Ruby reached up with a trembling hand and touched his face. "No. No, I see you, son. I see you."

With that, Bert wrapped his arms around his tiny mother and held her. They were both crying now, and I was close to snorting louder than my mother. I motioned for everyone to leave the room and let the two have their long-awaited reunion in peace. We all quietly exited through the French doors and stepped out onto the patio.

"So Bert really believed his mother had abandoned him all those years ago?" my father asked Amos after he'd pulled the doors shut behind us.

"Yes," Amos said with a sigh. "I guess the Carvers were pretty persuasive. With the loss of his dad, and his mother struggling so hard to take care of him, Bert was vulnerable."

"I have a question," I said as soon as I could get the words out. "I didn't ask Bert this last night because it seemed, well, too personal, but how did the Carvers treat him?"

Amos stood next to the wood railing that surrounded the deck. We'd stepped down toward the end of the patio so we couldn't see Ruby and Bert. "As surprising as this sounds, Bert told me they were good parents. They were strict but treated him kindly."

"I don't call lying to a child and taking him away from his mother kind," Mom said, wiping her eyes with my dad's handkerchief. "I call it cruel."

"Not much to be done about that," Dad said. "They're both dead. No one to blame. No one to prosecute."

"Bert wouldn't have allowed that anyway," Amos said. "He thinks they were just trying to protect him—keep him safe from a bad situation. Of course, it's clear that they had no right to make that decision for him and Ruby. That's something he'll have to come to terms with someday."

"It took you quite a bit of persuading to get him to return here, didn't it?" I asked.

Amos nodded. "Your mother located a few possibilities on the Internet, and I finally found him in Texas. After I got him on the phone, it took the good part of an hour to explain who I was and why I was sticking my nose in his business. But once he believed I knew his mother and that she really hadn't abandoned him all those years ago, he couldn't get a flight out fast enough. When I picked him up at the airport in Wichita, he was anxious to get to Winter Break and see her."

"And now what?" I wondered out loud. "Will he try to build a relationship with Ruby, or will he go back to Texas and get on with his life?"

Amos shrugged. "It's only a guess, but when we first drove into Winter Break, he seemed pretty happy. He's divorced, no children, and he recently got laid off from his job. Maybe he'll decide to move back here. Try to make up for some of the time he and Ruby lost."

"Wouldn't that be something?" I said, grinning. "Bert and Ruby together again. You know, it was Bert's idea for Ruby to open a restaurant. Maybe he could help her—"

"Whoa," Amos said with a smile. "You're beginning to get ahead of yourself there, little lady. Let's give them time to get to know each other again." He put his arms around me. "You just solved two crimes, you know. When

I started questioning Delbert Pennypecker about his newfound wealth, he folded like a cheap card table."

"You mean he really was behind those cattle thefts?"

"You nailed him. He's going to be spending some time away from Bertha." He grinned widely. "I'm not sure if he'll see that as punishment, though."

I felt sorry for Bertha. I also hoped she'd never find out that I had anything to do with bringing Delbert to justice.

"I wonder if Bonnie and Bert will end up getting reacquainted," I asked, changing the subject.

Amos chuckled. "He asked on the way up here if Bonnie still lived in Winter Break. I saw the look in his eye. He'll definitely drop by to see her."

"And how would you know what that look in his eye meant?" I asked teasingly.

He didn't answer me. Instead, he glanced over at my parents, who were beginning to experience the aftereffects of Ruby's fried chicken. I knew they would be dozing soon.

"Let's take a walk by the lake," Amos said.

I told Mom and Dad where we'd be, but they were already drifting away on clouds of fried chicken and mashed potatoes. I wasn't sure they heard me.

Amos grabbed my hand and guided me down the wooden steps that led to the the edge of Lake Winter Break. The ducks and geese came up to see if we had any food. When they were satisfied that we were useless to them, they swam away to pursue other possibilities.

Amos led me over to the same bench that was depicted in Marion's painting. It was the spot where Bitty sat, waving at me. I could almost feel her with me, as if she were sitting right next to us.

"I have something to say to you, Ivy," he said. I was surprised to see tears in his eyes.

"Amos, what is it?"

He hung his head slowly and stared down at the ground. "My background... my mother and father. During all this time we were wondering what happened to Bert Bird, I realized that in a way, I'd disappeared, too. When I went to live with my father, I was so disappointed in him. He was a drunk, Ivy. And he hit me."

"Oh, Amos."

"Instead of dealing with the hurt I'd felt because of my family, I hid it. Not only from you, but from me, too. I didn't want to talk about it. I didn't want to think about it. I disappeared on the inside, Ivy." Amos wiped his eyes with the back of his hand, and then he turned toward me. "But that's not the way to live. I don't want to lose any more time because of the past. Ruby and Bert have given up so much. I'm not willing to do the same." He reached into his pocket and took out a small velvet box. Then he let go of my hand and got down on one knee in front of me. "Ivy Towers," he said, his voice breaking, "I can't imagine living another day of my life without you in it. Will you marry me?"

I don't know who jumped up first, but I found myself in his arms, his lips on mine. It's hard to talk when you're kissing someone, but somehow I got out, "Yes! Yes! Yes!" before I was completely lip-locked and unable to speak.

Finally, we both sank back down onto the bench. Now Amos was laughing and I was crying. What a team.

"I had to step away from the past," he said. "I couldn't live inside other people's mistakes anymore. I'm not saying I'm perfect and that you won't have to slap me down once in a while, but I want you to know that I intend to do everything in my power to make you happy. You're a part of me. You always were, ever since the day I first set eyes on you."

"I feel the same way, Amos. We're not even married yet, but I understand what it means to be one person. I couldn't imagine living without you either."

Amos slipped the beautiful diamond engagement ring on my finger. It fit perfectly—as though it was always meant to be there.

Then, with a mischievous smile, he reached into his other pocket and took out another velvet box. He held it out to me, and I took it.

"What in the world, Amos?"

"Just open it. I'll explain everything."

I opened the box to find a key inside. "What's this?" I asked with a smile. "The key to your heart?"

Amos shook his head. "No. It's my step of faith. It's something I did because I believed with all my being that you and I were going to spend the rest of our lives together." His beautiful hazel eyes sought mine. "It's the key to your new home. God is giving you the desire of your heart."

I shook my head in confusion. "My new home? I don't understand. . . ."

"It's this house, Ivy. I bought the Biddle house. We're going to live here after we're married. You're going to live here now."

"But how. . .how could. . ."

He grabbed my hands. "I called Cecil and Marion. They said they'd never sold the house because they were waiting for the right people. The people God sent to them. When I told them why I wanted to buy it, they offered it to us at a ridiculous price. Way below what it's worth." Amos choked up. "Marion said that the house was meant for us, Ivy. Just like you and I were meant for each other."

I gazed into the eyes of the man with whom I would spend the rest of my life and realized that home was more than a town. It was even more than a house. Home was a place God created within our hearts.

And I was truly home.

Ruby Bird's Stuffed Berry French Toast

Ingredients:

1 loaf white bread
1 bag frozen mixed berries
8 ounces cream cheese
½ cup melted butter
10 eggs
⅓ cup maple syrup
1½ cups half-and-half

Instructions:

Spray a 9x13-inch baking pan with nonstick spray. Cut the bread into 1-inch cubes and line pan with half of the bread. (Use mushy white bread so it doesn't get too crunchy when baking.) Defrost the mixed berries and scatter over bread. Dot cream cheese over bread. Cover the berries and cream cheese with the other half of the bread. Combine melted butter, eggs, maple syrup, and half-and-half in a bowl. Mix well. Pour over the bread evenly. Chill, covered, overnight. Preheat oven to 350°F. Bake uncovered for 40 to 50 minutes.

FOR WHOM THE WEDDING BELL TOLLS

Dedication:

Grandmothers are one of God's special blessings. My friend, Shauna Sparlin, remembers her grandmother, Bula Tuell, as someone who helped to instill character in those around her. She lived her faith every day. My own grandmother, Kathleen Holderby, was the same way. She loved God and taught me to do the same. This book is dedicated to Bula and Kathleen. They were instrumental in creating the fictional character of Bitty Flanagan, as well as shaping the real-life lives of those who loved them. Through Bitty, Shauna and I share our wonderful grandmothers with all of you.

Acknowledgments:

As always, my thanks to Deputy Sheriff Robert P. (Pat) Taylor from Kingman County, Kansas. Your help has been crucial! Thank you to my "Mandarin specialists," Ken Chau and Kevin Hill. And to my husband, Norman, and my son, Danny: Thank you for all your love and support.

1

Planning a wedding is a lot like planning a funeral. There's a church and a minister. People dress up and food is served. If you are the star of the event, what you wear is very important. Your makeup is crucial and shouldn't be overdone; otherwise guests will look at you and say, "She just doesn't look natural." The biggest *difference* between the two ceremonies is that you get more rest during the funeral. However, you may actually wish for death by the time the wedding is over.

I expressed these feelings to my best friend, Emily Taylor, over lunch at a coffee shop in Hugoton. We'd just left the bridal shop where I'd tried on every dress they had and found absolutely nothing. Don't get me wrong, their dresses were beautiful. They just weren't *me*.

"We can drive to Dodge City," Emily said helpfully. "Maybe you'll find your dress there."

I shook my head. "I doubt it. For some reason, nothing I've seen *feels* right. Maybe I'm just not the wedding dress type."

Emily reached over to touch my arm, her long chestnut hair falling over her slim shoulder. "Ivy, you're getting married. That *makes* you the 'wedding dress type.'" She smiled sweetly, which was easy for her since she is the epitome of sweetness. I felt like the poster child for petulance. "You can't walk down the aisle in your underwear. We have to find something. We've been at this for over two months. There's not much time left."

I sipped my coffee and stared at her. Emily Taylor née Baumgartner was the picture of perfection. Her hair was shiny and manageable, her skin flawless. Her face could easily adorn the cover of *Cosmopolitan*—not that she would be caught dead being associated with a magazine that hyped the *modern woman*. Emily was as old-fashioned as anyone could be. She was also extremely responsible. I'm sure her wedding had been planned out months in advance. I was in a major time crunch now because I'd kept putting things off. I really wanted to be married; I just didn't seem to be able to find the time to get anything accomplished. And now I was in trouble.

A few days ago, Emily'd shown me her wedding pictures. Staring back at me from the white, lace-covered album was the consummate bride. Her dress looked as if it had been tailored especially for her. Emily Baumgartner was born to be a bride.

I, on the other hand, seemed totally unsuited for the role. In every wedding gown I'd tried on, my wild, curly, dark red hair, in contrast to the pale color of the dress, made me look like my head was on fire. Veering away from a white dress didn't seem to be the answer. What if people thought it signified something? I could just see Bertha Pennypacker turn to Marybelle Widdle with a smug smile as I walked down the aisle and whisper, "I knew it all along."

"Maybe I'll just elope," I said glumly. "That way I can wear my green corduroy jumper. Amos likes it."

Emily's light, lilting laugh took a little of the edge off my bad humor. She really was a wonderful friend. I was grateful for her companionship, especially during the times I acted like a spoiled brat. Not many friends can see you at your worst and still find you amusing.

"There's no way you can elope, Ivy," she said. "People in Winter Break love you and Amos. We're not so much like a small town as we are a very large family." She gave me a sympathetic smile. "You know that."

I nodded and forced myself to smile back at her. "You're right. I guess no matter how horrid I look, the most important thing will be that Amos and I are finally married."

She shook her finger at me. "Now, you stop that. You could never look horrid, no matter what you wear. I've never known anyone who had so little sense of her own beauty. I'd love to have red hair and emerald green eyes. I'm so colorless; brown hair and brown eyes. You're. . .you're. . .*vibrant*, Ivy. That's what you are. Vibrant!"

I couldn't help but laugh at her description. "Okay, now you're just getting silly. If you promise to stop, I'll keep looking for the right gown."

She held up her delicate hand. "I swear. No more adjectives."

I took a bite of my tuna salad sandwich and thumbed through some of the bridal magazines Emily had brought with her. The dresses were beautiful, but most of them were strapless. Winter Break, Kansas, in February wasn't a good time to leave even an inch of skin uncovered unless the lovely shade of *frostbite* goes with your ensemble. I finished the last magazine and pushed it across the table toward her. "I don't see anything here I like."

Emily sighed. "Okay, tell me what kind of dress you envision. Maybe we need to start there and work toward finding *that* gown."

I chewed for a moment, thinking. What *did* I see when I pictured myself walking down the aisle? The answer startled me. "I have no idea, Emily. I've never thought about it."

Emily put her fork down and looked at me like I really had set my head on fire. "Why, Ivy Towers. Every little girl thinks about her wedding day. Are you trying to tell me that you've never dreamed of the perfect wedding?"

"Yes, I've thought about it. I just forgot about the part that had to do with me walking down the aisle, sporting big, pouffy hair while jammed inside a white satin straitjacket. Obviously, that was a mistake."

Emily was quiet for a moment. Then she slowly shook her head. "Most girls only envision themselves on their wedding day. You think about everything else *except* you. You're truly one of a kind." She stared at me quizzically. "I take that back. You do remind me of someone else. Bitty. You two are like peas out of the same pod. Almost every time I'm around you, I see her. It's stronger now than it was when she was alive."

My eyes flushed with tears, and I had to look away. It was a little over a year since my great-aunt Bitty had been murdered inside her bookstore, yet I still felt her presence with me every day. When it came to human beings, there was no greater compliment anyone could pay me than to compare me to her. She was a genuine Christian who loved everyone and had never turned her back on anyone in need. I had no doubt that God would easily be able to say to her, "Well done, good and faithful servant." Now that she was gone, I found myself struggling to carry on her legacy.

Emily scooted her chair next to mine and put her arm around me. "I'm sorry. I didn't mean to upset you."

I patted her hand. "You didn't. I still miss her, you know?"

"I know. I miss her, too."

After a few seconds of silence, I picked up the top magazine on the stack Emily had carted to lunch, and Emily went back to nibbling on her salad. "Okay, let me give this another go. It's only four weeks until the wedding. Unfortunately, that underwear comment you made could become reality."

Emily chuckled. "Well, remember what I said. If you find something but we can't get it here in time, Mama said all we'd have to do is show her a picture and buy some material. She can sew anything."

"That's very sweet, but I wouldn't dream of asking her to make my gown. It's way too much work."

Emily shook her head, and her expression turned serious. "The truth is, I think you'd be doing her a favor. Ever since Daddy passed away, she seems almost lost. Making your wedding dress might actually help her to feel useful again."

"Really?" I chewed on her comment along with my sandwich. "You know what? If you're sure she'd really want to do it, I'd be thrilled to have her help. I love your mom to pieces, Emily. A dress she made would mean so much more to me than anything I could buy."

"Oh, Ivy. Are you sure?"

I nodded happily. "I'm absolutely certain. I already feel better. Now my dress will be really special."

Emily clapped her hands together. "That was it all along. You wanted a dress that meant something to you. I should have realized that in the first place."

"Don't get too happy. I still have to pick a pattern. We're just preparing to walk into another minefield."

"I have an idea," she said. "Let's find a very basic pattern. Then Mama can customize it for you. That way, you two can work together to make it just the right dress."

"That's a good idea. Now, can we talk about something else? This wedding stuff is starting to get on my nerves."

Emily frowned. "Goodness, you've barely begun. There are a lot of details to planning a wedding. There are the decorations, the flowers, the food, the bridesmaids dresses, the theme, the—"

"Stop!" I spoke louder than I meant to. People sitting around us turned to stare. I lowered my voice. "How in the world am I supposed to plan this entire thing and run the bookstore? I just started buying and selling on the Internet. Orders are coming in steadily now. I can't lose momentum if I want to make the bookstore the kind of success I know it can be."

"I told you I'd help you, Ivy," Emily said quietly. "Don't worry about it. Together we'll—"

"Nonsense," I said, interrupting her again. "You have a new baby to take care of. I appreciate the offer, but you can't give me the kind of help I need."

Emily sighed. "You're probably right. Taking care of Charlie and fixing up the house takes up most of my time."

"Besides, you've already given me the best gift possible."

"What do you mean?"

I smiled at her. "Agreeing to be my matron of honor, silly. There's nothing else you could do that would mean more to me."

"Why, Ivy," she said, her beautiful eyes shining with emotion, "it's an honor."

"Thanks. Now let's change the subject before we both start bawling."

She laughed. "Okay, what would you like to talk about?"

"Tell me what it's like to own a peach orchard."

Emily smiled dreamily. "The orchard is beautiful, and it's wonderful to own all that land. Come spring, we'll see if we can grow peaches. Mama has plans to put up lots of preserves. And now that Buddy and his dad have redone most of the house, I'm really starting to feel at home there."

The Bruenwalder property had some shady history, but after Harvey went to prison, Emily's mother inherited it since she was directly related to Harvey's late wife. She promptly passed the house and land along to Buddy and Emily. The tradition of helping newlyweds was a long-held practice among the

Baumgartner clan. The Baumgartners were a force to be reckoned with in Winter Break. Over one hundred strong now, they had their own church, First Mennonite, and their family stuck together like glue.

I took another sip of coffee. It was lukewarm. I signaled to the waitress and pointed at my cup. She smiled and went to get the pot. "I'm glad, Emily. It's really a pretty place."

She nodded her agreement. "Thanks. We'd love to have you and Amos over for dinner soon. Sure haven't seen much of him lately."

"These bank robberies are keeping him really busy. The sheriff has him hopping all over the county."

"It's so weird," Emily said. "Why is this guy only robbing banks in Stevens County? It's almost like he's targeting *us*. It feels personal somehow."

"It's not personal. He's hit a couple of banks in Seward County, too. But you're right. Most of them are certainly close by. He must live somewhere in the area. He's in his comfort zone. Most criminals like to do their dirty deeds in an area they're familiar with."

Emily raised one of her perfectly shaped eyebrows. "There you go again. Are you a bookstore owner or a private detective at heart? Sometimes I can't tell."

I waited until the waitress had warmed up my coffee before I said, "Maybe a little of both. That Nancy Drew gene is hard to ignore."

Emily laughed and looked at her watch. "I think it's time to head back to Winter Break. I need to defrost something for dinner, and you need to work on your wedding list."

I would have objected to the list comment, but it was useless to argue. Making daily lists was another thing I had in common with Aunt Bitty. Then there were the project lists—like the one I'd created for my wedding. Unfortunately, very little had been crossed off.

We paid our ticket and headed back to town. As if crossing an invisible line about a mile before the city limits, the clear roads gave way to blowing and drifting snow. No one knew why Winter Break had snow all winter long while the rest of the state welcomed winter weather only sporadically. It's just the way it was. People in Winter Break accepted it. Funny thing was, you never heard anyone complain. Winter Break seemed to be filled with people who loved winter. A few had moved away to warmer climates, but for the most part, people who were born in Winter Break stayed in Winter Break. Personally, I loved snow. Give me a snowy day over a sunny one anytime. I'd been extremely frustrated while living in Wichita. Snowstorms seemed to drift around the city as if they were afraid to enter. I had nicknamed Wichita "the donut hole of winter."

I may have never had a vision of myself at my wedding, but I'd always known it would be a winter ceremony with twinkling silver lights and fat snowflakes drifting down on me like sparkling confetti. Living in Winter Break gave me a good chance of seeing that dream come true.

I loved life in this special town. A little over six hundred people resided within its borders. A lot of them were farmers. Most of them were wonderful, God-fearing people who shunned life in the big city and were content to live out their days in a place where values still meant something and being a good neighbor was taken for granted. Although Main Street wasn't very long, we actually did have one. Dewey Tater ran the town's only grocery store, Laban's Food-a-Rama. We also had a funeral home, two churches, a restaurant, a post office, a sewing emporium, and a small sheriff's office. In the past year, we'd added a real estate office and an insurance agency. And then, of course, there was the bookstore.

Emily dropped me off in front of Miss Bitty's Bygone Bookstore. I waved good-bye, promising to call her the next day. When I opened the door, the bell above it rang out, welcoming me home. Isaac Holsapple, my assistant, smiled up at me. He was sitting on the floor next to a large stack of books.

"Anything important happen while I was gone?" I hung up my coat and scarf on the coatrack next to the door.

"Not really," he replied. "Miss Hartwell from the library dropped by to see if you had any further donations."

Winter Break was getting ready to welcome its first library. Noel Spivey, a book collector and friend from Denver, had answered my plea for some start-up money that would allow us to open a small, private collection owned and run by the town. After the donation of a building from Dewey, we were working hard to get the library open by early spring. Even though I had a small selection of books that could be borrowed from the bookstore, Winter Break citizens really needed a full range of literary genres to choose from. Hope Hartwell, a young woman who moved to town from Ensign, Kansas, a tiny town outside of Dodge City, had been hired as our librarian. She'd stayed with me for almost a month when she first arrived. Although the city council wasn't able to scrape up as much money as I would have liked, Sarah Johnson, a widow with a large boardinghouse and an even bigger heart, had offered the young librarian a permanent place to live. She had also invited Hope to share supper with her every evening. Ruby Bird, who ran Ruby's Redbird Café, told Hope she was welcome to eat in the restaurant anytime for free. Winter Break had rallied around the young librarian, making her feel welcome. In some ways, Hope reminded me of Bitty, who came to Winter Break looking for a place to start over after the death of her fiancé. Hope had cared for her beloved grandmother until she passed away. She had no other living relatives.

"I do have some new books for her," I said to Isaac. "Between the residents of Winter Break and the bookstore owners I've contacted through the

Internet, we'll have quite a selection by the time we open the doors."

Isaac smiled up at me. "It's an outstanding thing you've done, Miss Ivy. You're making Miss Bitty's dream of making fine literature accessible to everyone in this town come true. She would be very proud of you. I know I am."

The elderly man, who had also been Bitty's assistant before he became mine, had grown to be a very close friend. Although we shared our lives on many levels, I knew that Isaac had been lonely for the kind of intimacy Amos and I couldn't give him. For many years, ever since he'd come to Winter Break, the bookstore had been his whole life. Recently, however, he had expanded his interests a little. Isaac had begun dating Alma Pettibone, Winter Break's postmistress. Alma, a timid woman who hid behind her soap operas, and Isaac, who spent his life with books, had somehow found each other. In my wildest dreams, I would never have paired the two. Isaac was fussy and terminally neat, while Alma was disorganized and forgetful. But somehow they seemed to fulfill a need in each other for companionship.

"I didn't start the library by myself, you know," I said. "The whole town pitched in. Noel and Dewey gave us the foundation we needed."

"You did much more than you give yourself credit for. You lit the fire that got everyone excited about the project. I'm especially happy for the town's children. They will certainly benefit."

I glanced through the stacks of books that Isaac was putting on our bookshelves. A recent purchase from an estate sale had brought us several fine, rare books for our collection, including an early edition of John Bunyan's *Pilgrim's Progress*. I watched as Isaac carefully placed it on the shelf. "Did you hear from Faith today?" I asked.

"No. I'm certain she's over at the library helping Miss Hartwell. She is turning out to be quite a blessing to her."

"Yes, she is. I have to admit that I miss her, though." Faith was a teenager who had attached herself to me during a time of crisis in her life. I'd grown to love her like a daughter, but since Hope had come to town, Faith had thrown herself into helping at the library. It had become a joke around town that our new library was being built on Hope and Faith.

Isaac took off his large, round, tortoiseshell glasses and pulled a handkerchief from his pocket. "Now, Miss Ivy," he said in a low voice, "you aren't jealous, are you? You're the one who brought the two of them together."

I thought about his question for a moment. "Maybe a little bit," I said slowly. "I know that's terribly immature."

After thoroughly polishing his spectacles, Isaac slipped them back on and stared at me through lenses so thick he reminded me of an owl. "It isn't immature. It's human. Might I suggest that you, as they say, cut yourself a little slack?" He grinned and then went back to inspecting the next book in the stack. "Besides, if you criticize yourself for your actions, it takes all the enjoyment out of it for the rest of us."

I laughed at his last comment. Isaac had recently started to develop a sense of humor. I found this change in his personality very amusing, mostly because it seemed so out of character, but also because he was really quite funny. "I'm so glad that straightening me out is such an important part of life for everyone. I guess I should be happy that I've brought such meaning into your lives."

"It's a dirty job," he sighed. "But someone's got to do it." He smiled at me and then bent over to peruse a list of books that had been cataloged for inclusion into our group of rare books that were for sale. He marked off the last book placed on the shelf then picked up the next book in the stack. "How did your trip to Hugoton go?" he asked. "Did you finally select a dress?"

I had just started to tell him about my lack of success, when the front door was pushed open with so much force, I thought the bell was going to fall off. I turned to see Delaphine Shackleford, another new resident of Winter Break, waving her fur-covered arms around like some giant bird trying to take flight. Delaphine was the wife of Barney Shackleford, a salesman for Farm and Field Insurance, a company specializing in rural accounts. Barney had been relocated from Dodge City so he could oversee the company's policyholders in western Kansas. Delaphine, who fancied herself some kind of society queen unfairly banished from her subjects, had made it clear that life in Winter Break was a trial worthy of a true martyr. Pastor Ephraim Taylor, the pastor at Faith Community Church—and Emily's father-in-law—had tried valiantly to involve her in some kind of ministry so she could get her mind off herself and on to something more constructive, but so far, all attempts had failed.

"Ivy Towers!" she called out in her high-pitched voice. "I am here on a mission. I have come to save you!"

Delaphine had a slight Southern accent that deepened when she was being dramatic—which was most of the time. No one could figure out just where it came from since she'd grown up in Spearville, a Kansas town about the size of Winter Break. At the present moment, it was as thick as peanut butter.

"Well, actually I've already been saved, Delaphine."

After removing her black fur coat, matching hat, and muff, and carefully inspecting my coatrack for cooties, she hung up her garments and pranced toward the spot where Isaac and I waited.

"Silly, I'm not talking about religious stuff," she declared grandly. "This is something *really* important."

Isaac and I exchanged glances. He looked like he'd just put a lemon in his mouth and was surprised to find out it was sour.

"Delaphine, why don't you have a seat?" I pointed toward the sitting room in the back of the store where an eclectic collection of comfy couches and chairs were arranged for the benefit of those who wanted to snuggle up with a good book and spend the day carried away on the wings of the written word. This special room had also provided the setting for quite a few afternoon naps enjoyed by a variety of Winter Break residents. I had experienced more than one myself. "Can I get you a cup of coffee or a glass of iced tea?"

"No, thank you, dear," she said, clapping her hands together. "I have an idea that has given me all the stimulation I need!"

I followed her to the back of the store after rolling my eyes and folding my hands together as a sign to Isaac that prayer would be appreciated. He just grinned and shrugged his shoulders.

I motioned to a nice burgundy chair. After judging it to be worthy of her royal behind, Delaphine sat down gingerly. I had barely taken the seat next to her when she exploded with enthusiasm. "I am so excited, and you will be, too, when you hear my idea. It's the answer to everything!"

I was fairly certain there were some things in the world that would still not be addressed after her revelation, but I nodded at her, trying to exude some kind of confidence in what I was about to hear. "You've certainly piqued my interest, Delaphine. What is your idea?"

She wiggled her bejeweled fingers at me. "Now, dear, you must call me Dela. All my real friends do."

I smiled. "Okay, Dela. Thank you."

She nodded at me graciously, as if I had just been awarded knighthood. "I heard from Alma Pettibone that you are worried about getting everything done for your wedding. I am here to save the day, Ivy. You don't have to worry about another thing. I am now your *wedding planner!*" She sat back in her chair, a look of triumph on her face. "Now what do you think of that?"

I was dumbstruck. What did I think of that? A wedding planner? Delaphine Shackleford?

"Before you say anything," she said earnestly, "I've done this before—many times. I have a real knack for weddings. I've planned quite a few for my friends. In fact," she lowered her voice to a conspiratorial whisper, "I made all the arrangements for the nuptials of an ex-governor of Kansas. He told me it was the best wedding he'd ever had. Out of all four of them!"

I wasn't sure this was actually a glowing recommendation. Seemed to me that our ex-governor needed to quit worrying about the ceremony and try to figure out what the actual marriage was all about, but still, I could see the excitement in Dela's face—and I *did* need help. . . .

"What would you do, Dela?" I asked. "And what would you charge me?"

"Oh, Ivy," she replied, her tone almost pleading, "I wouldn't charge you anything. I just want to help. I have absolutely nothing to do, and this would make me feel like I'm contributing something." She blinked back tears as she pulled an embroidered handkerchief from her designer handbag and dabbed at her mascara-laden eyes. "Everything here is so different. Sometimes I don't feel like I belong at all. This would help me to feel like a part of Winter Break." She patted her bleached, coiffed hair. "I could bring a little class to this town if you would just give me a chance."

I thought Winter Break's residents were pretty classy already, but I could see her point. I was hoping for a ceremony a little different than the one Amos and I had attended last November. I'm as down-home as the next person, but using your pet pig to carry the ring down the aisle was a little much even for me. Maybe it was the vision of Lulu-belle the pig with a pink pillow tied to her back, or perhaps it was the list I'd started that had almost nothing crossed off, but I found myself nodding at Dela. This really *could* be the answer to my problems. Someone else could worry about all the wedding details while I concentrated on the bookstore. And, Dela could make some new friends in the bargain. It sounded like the perfect solution.

What could possibly go wrong?

2

"You did *what*? Are you out of your mind?"

Amos's reaction wasn't really what I'd been hoping for. I'd been congratulating myself all day for being very clever. Dela Shackleford was ecstatic and already hard at work. She'd called me just before I left for dinner, claiming to have already come up with several "enchanting" ideas for the wedding. We had an appointment in the morning to go over them.

"I don't think you need to be so negative," I said crossly, taking a bite of my fruit salad while Amos stuck a forkful of Ruby's Monday night special in his mouth. Monday was chicken-fried steak and mashed potatoes, both smothered in thick chicken gravy. After much cajoling, Ruby had finally added some healthy dishes to the choices at Ruby's Redbird Café, the only restaurant in Winter Break. Her long-lost son, Bert, had returned to town last summer and was helping her run things. His influence had certainly added some support to my campaign for less saturated fat on the menu. Together, Bert and I convinced Ruby that fruit didn't have to be served in a pie and vegetables didn't exist just so they could be breaded and fried in lard. My concern for Dewey Tater's diabetes and my waistline had instigated my crusade, but now, many of Winter Break's citizens were ordering salads, steamed vegetables, whole grains, and fresh fruits. These pioneers would most likely never be in the majority, but it did my heart good to know that at least some of our residents might actually enjoy the feeling of unclogged arteries for once. However, as in most fierce battles, I had been forced to concede one thing: Ruby's Redbird Burgers. They were less like food and more like a drug happily ingested by the entire population of Winter Break. Her burgers were heaven on a bun. That is if heaven had fried meat, cheddar cheese, and a secret ingredient that most Winter Break residents would give their firstborn for. I'd accepted the healthy menu additions as a victory and hadn't even attempted to attack the Holy Grail of Ruby's Redbird Café. They say that wisdom is knowing how to pick your battles.

After stuffing a couple of large bites of mashed potatoes in his mouth, Amos swallowed, put his fork down, and gaped at me. "I'm not being negative, Ivy. But Delaphine Shackleford is nuts. She's called me out to her place at least a dozen times since she and Barney moved here. She's always *hearing* something or *seeing* something outside her house. Once I found Newton Widdle's cow wandering around on their property and another time she swore someone was calling her name. It was a barn owl in the tree next to their bedroom window. She just needs to understand that living in the country isn't the same thing as living in the city. She actually asked me once if I would spend the night in my car and keep a watch over her place. I tried to explain that I work for the sheriff in Hugoton and that just because I live here doesn't mean I'm available to her day and night."

I jabbed a juicy, sweet piece of melon with my fork. Ruby had canned and frozen lots of fruit for the winter. Even though I knew she used some sugar in the process, the result was still yummy and better for me than the rest of the cholesterol-laden menu.

"It's hard for people to understand, Amos," I said. "You have an office here. People think they can call you whenever they need help."

"In most situations, they can. I just have to clear it through the sheriff. I'm certain he wouldn't want me staking out Dela's house on a whim." He frowned and stared down at his food. "Anyway, that office isn't mine. It was put here for any deputy who needed a place to park themselves if they couldn't get to Hugoton for some reason. It's not my fault that none of the other deputies ever come to Winter Break."

He sounded sincere, but I knew he viewed the small space as his own. God help any deputy sheriff who came to town and expected to be welcomed into that office with open arms.

"Look, I really need help with the wedding. You're out chasing bank robbers, and I'm trying to run the bookstore. I need Dela and she needs me. You know how hard it's been for her to adjust to life here."

Amos snorted. "Delaphine Shackleford would have a hard time adjusting wherever she went. She's a self-centered woman who is only interested in things that benefit *her*. She's getting something she wants out of helping you. I'm afraid you'll discover that our wedding is not her top priority."

I set my fork down. "Amos Parker. Whatever happened to not judging people? Did you conveniently forget what the Bible says?" I gave him my most angelic look. "'Do not judge, or you too will be judged...and with the measure you use, it will be measured to you.'"

"Okay, Miss Holier-Than-Thou. You can take a break." He waved his knife at me. "I seem to remember a few comments you made about Bertha Pennypacker last week. Let's see, what was it? You called her a nosy—"

"That's enough," I interrupted. "Two wrongs don't make a right. Besides, I don't think you should be bringing up things from the past. It's not very Christian."

Amos laughed and stabbed another piece of steak. "Marriage to you is certainly going to be interesting. You're something else, you know that?"

"Well, anyway," I said, "I'm willing to try this. From what I've heard, Barney's company intends for him to be here awhile. He and Dela need to make some friends."

Amos quit chewing and stared at me, his boyish face twisted with concern. "You don't want anyone to be unhappy, do you? The thing that worries me is that the one person you don't think about is yourself. I'm just trying to look after you." He reached over, took my chin in his hand, and stared into my eyes. "I intend to spend the rest of my life doing that."

I kissed him—even with the smell of chicken-fried steak on his breath. "Thank you. I look forward to it. But right now I need you to give Dela a chance. Will you do that, please? For me?"

He leaned back in his seat and let out a sigh of resignation. "Okay, Ivy. Let Delaphine Shackleford plan the wedding. But if this doesn't work. . ."

"It will, Amos. I'm sure it will." The words sounded good when I said them, but there was a little niggling twinge of worry inside my gut. I sent a silent prayer heavenward. If this turned out badly, I was going to be eating something besides wedding cake. A heaping dish of crow wasn't going to go down as easily.

"Have you seen that dog again?" Amos asked, thankfully changing the subject. A stray dog had started showing up around my house. Although he was dirty and his hair was matted, I was pretty sure he was a Border collie. Black and white, with an intelligent face, he would prowl around the lake, coming close to the house. But when I called him or got within a few feet of him, he would run away. "He was sitting near the lake when I left this morning."

"Don't feed him, Ivy. He could be dangerous. There's no way to know how long he's been running loose."

It was a sad fact of life that people who wanted to get rid of their pets would sometimes dump them in rural areas. Winter Break had certainly seen its share of stray dogs. Unfortunately, after awhile many of them would start acting wild and running in packs. Once that started, it was almost impossible to tame them again.

"He's always by himself, Amos. There aren't any dogs with him. Maybe he'll learn to trust me."

He shook his head. "I really don't want you putting yourself in danger. He might be vicious. He could even have rabies. Please stay away from him."

I smiled, but I didn't say anything. I'd been putting food and water out for him every day for a week. I couldn't turn my back on him now. He had the saddest eyes I'd ever seen. He'd probably watched his family drive away without him, abandoning him to a life of loneliness and desperation. Rejection hurt, especially when you couldn't understand what was happening.

I tried to push my concerns about the dog away for a while so I could concentrate on finishing my meal. Amos launched into a story about chasing down some guy who'd been writing bad checks in Hugoton. I tried to listen, but my thoughts kept bouncing back and forth between the abandoned dog and Dela. I wasn't sure which one worried me most.

On the way home, Amos warned me once again about the dog. I wondered if my silence gave me away, but I couldn't just walk away from the pitiful animal—even if I wanted to. And I didn't. After a good-night kiss and a reminder about an important meeting the next day, I said good-bye and went inside my house. After Amos left, I checked outside, but I didn't see the dog anywhere.

Tuesday morning I had breakfast with Dewey Tater, just like every weekday morning. As much as I enjoyed our breakfasts, I found myself rushing through it. Dela was bringing over her wedding ideas, and I was finally starting to get excited. I felt a little guilty about Dewey. He was a good friend. He had been engaged to marry Bitty before she died. They'd shared breakfast together every day before they each opened the doors to their respective businesses. Although I'd hoped he'd develop another special relationship, at almost eighty years old, Dewey wasn't interested. "Bitty was the love of my life," he'd declared more than once. "Guess I'll just stop now while I'm ahead." And that was it. He believed he would be with Bitty again someday, and he didn't want any other female "mucking up" his reunion. "How would I explain that to Bitty?" he'd grumble when I tried to encourage him to find a new lady friend. I'd finally given up. Someday Dewey would breathe his last. It would be a sad day for me, but I knew in my heart that as soon as Dewey closed his eyes on this earth, he'd open them in heaven, and Bitty would be waiting there to welcome him home.

About eight thirty, Dewey ambled out of the bookstore so he could open Laban's Food-a-Rama to the public. I cleaned up our breakfast dishes and made another pot of coffee in the small kitchen upstairs where I'd lived when I first came to Winter Break. It had been Bitty's apartment then mine. Now that I lived in my dream house by the lake, I'd turned the apartment into a storage area for books and other things. However, I kept the kitchen stocked so I could make something to eat without going all the way home or being forced to eat at Ruby's every day. I put some bagels and cream cheese on a plate and carried everything downstairs to the sitting room. I'd just reset the table, when Dela came flying through the front door.

"Ivy?" she sang out in her Southern-tinged falsetto. "Ivy Towers! Your wedding guru has arrived!"

I waved at her. "I'm back here, Dela."

She bounced back to where I stood waiting. She looked like a skinny version of Mrs. Claus. She wore a red velvet dress with white fur around the wrists and neck. Perched on her ash blond head was a white fur hat, and on her feet were knee-high black leather boots. I glanced down at my jeans and sweater. I was suddenly glad that I'd already formulated a plan for my wedding dress. I wasn't certain Dela and I had the same taste in clothes.

I motioned toward the table. "Let's sit here, Dela, so we'll have plenty of room. Would you like some coffee?"

She pulled out a chair and sat down, pushing the food tray out of her way. Then she took a large folder from her attaché case. She raised her eyebrows and looked at the coffeepot in my hand. "I'm only drinking Peruvian Organic now. I don't suppose. . ."

I set the pot down. "No. It's just plain American coffee."

She raised her nose in the air just a smidgen. Not so much so that I could say she was actually rude, but just enough so that I knew she wouldn't be caught dead drinking good old Folgers.

"What about a bagel?" Silly me, not willing to quit while I was behind.

Dela looked at the tray I'd prepared as if I were serving roadkill. "No, nothing for me, thank you," she said in an overly polite tone.

Well, things were certainly starting off well. The inside of my stomach was beginning to feel like the cast of Riverdance had taken up residence. What was I getting into? I poured myself a cup of coffee and moved the food tray out of the way. Dela, seemingly relieved to be distanced from my low-class hillbilly brunch, spread her papers out in front of us.

"Now, dear," she said in an excited voice, "I have some of the most wonderful ideas for your wedding. Wait until you hear them! First of all, we need to establish a theme. It should be something new and innovative. You know—something avant-garde!"

Her fake Southern accent, combined with an attempt at a French phrase, was incredibly comical. I kept my mouth shut tight so as not to giggle and offend her.

"Oh, I'm sorry," she said. "Avant-garde means—"

"I know what it means, Dela," I interrupted, feeling my face flush. "Let's just look at your ideas, okay?" My momentary attack of humor had turned quickly into irritation. My clipped response sounded harsh, even though I hadn't planned it.

Dela's smile disappeared. She reached over and patted my knee with her perfectly trimmed fingers. "I'm sorry, honey," she said softly. "I get a little carried away sometimes. I don't mean anything by it." Her brightly polished nails looked like drops of blood against my jeans. They matched the large gold and ruby red ring she wore on her right hand. On her left, she supported a sparkling wedding ring set that must have cost a pretty penny. A large rhinestone bracelet slid down her wrist and onto her hand. It seemed too big for her, but almost everything about Dela was larger than life. Her clothes, her jewelry, her accent, and her attitude. I couldn't begin to guess how many pieces of jewelry she owned. A few of the women at church had remarked that she changed her jewelry more than her clothes, sometimes sporting as many as three different sets a day.

And I hadn't meant to hurt her feelings. My goal was to encourage her. "I'm sorry, Dela. Really. I guess I'm just a little nervous about getting everything done in time for the wedding."

She immediately brightened up. "I understand. I'm here to make everything better. Now let's take a look at my ideas."

She pulled out several pictures and laid them in front of me. The first one showed a woman in a short white wedding dress with an open bodice in the shape of a heart. I could almost see her navel. The bridesmaids were in pink velvet mini-dresses with puffy sleeves. They looked decidedly grim. I certainly couldn't blame them.

"Isn't this lovely?" Dela gushed. "It's all built around a Valentine's Day theme." She picked up her notebook and began to read. "The chapel will be decorated with red roses and calla lilies. Red hearts will be everywhere; hanging from the ceiling, on the walls, even red hearts set down like footsteps up to the altar. Two children will walk down the aisle, throwing red rose petals. They will be dressed like cherubs." She sighed and put her hand to her chest as if trying to rein in her utter excitement. "Amos will wear a classic black tuxedo with a red tie and cummerbund. Your bridal bouquet will be red roses in the shape of a heart. Of course, you will walk down the aisle to Mendelssohn's 'Wedding March,' but there will be other music, as well. I suggest 'Sheep May Safely Graze' by Bach or 'Dance of the Blessed Spirits' by Glück." She waved her hand dismissively. "Of course, some people want 'Canon in D' by Pachelbel. It's become rather pedestrian, but it's your wedding. We can include it if you wish. And the food. . ." At this she broke out in a girlish giggle. "In keeping with our romantic theme, we'll have an oyster bar, asparagus, chicken with mole sauce, and a chocolate fountain with strawberries and bananas for dipping."

I should have said something right after seeing the hideous bridesmaid dresses and the peek-a-boo wedding gown, but somehow I seemed to have lost the ability to speak. As it was, I had to try several times to get anything coherent out of my mouth. "But. . .I can't. . . Are you serious. . .I mean. . ." Finally, I stopped and took another run at it. "I don't know where to start, Dela," I said. I didn't want to cause her any further emotional distress, but I was somewhat manic by then. "This just isn't me. And I don't want any red hearts at my wedding, even if it is Valentine's Day."

Those red hearts hanging everywhere reminded me of second grade when we all made big red hearts out of construction paper and decorated them.

Some of them were to take home to our parents, and some of them were for classmates. Miss Curtis, our teacher, put bags with our names on them on the large corkboard on the wall. We had just moved to the district and I didn't know any of the kids very well. I was the only child in class who didn't get a valentine.

"Well, maybe if we cut down the number—"

"No, Dela. No red hearts. None. I'm sorry."

She tried to interrupt me, but I raised my hand up and put it near her face.

"No red hearts. Anywhere. At all. Ever. Never."

She clamped her mouth shut so tightly, it was just a thin line surrounded by white. Her eyes narrowed with annoyance, but to her credit, she stayed quiet.

"And I'm not showing my stomach—or anything else. Besides, Inez Baumgartner is making my dress. That's already taken care of. And Amos already has his tux picked out."

"Well, it would have been nice if you'd told me about the wedding clothes before I spent all this time looking through gowns and tuxedos," she said, her words quick and clipped.

"I'm sorry," I said, trying my best to smooth things over now that the blood was once again flowing to my brain. "You're right."

"Is there anything else I should know?" She raised one eyebrow and stared at me coldly.

"I don't know. I really don't have anything specific in mind, but there are a few things that are important to me." This was turning out badly, and I really wanted it to work. For me and for Dela. I thought for a moment while she glared at me. I decided to swallow my pride. It was either that or confess to Amos that I'd made a mistake. I took the easier route. "I haven't been fair to you, Dela. I should have told you about my dress and Amos's tuxedo before you put so much time into this. I'm so sorry. I just didn't think about it."

Dela didn't respond, but her expression softened a little.

"I want things to be tasteful and simple. And I'd like a winter theme. I want to be married in the church, but I want the reception at my house." I shook my head. "I think that's about it."

"First of all," Dela said, her words like small, sharp blasts of machine gun fire, "anything *I* do will be tasteful."

I glanced at the poor pink bridesmaids, their humiliation captured forever in a glossy eight-by-ten. Dela and I definitely had different ideas of what "tasteful" meant.

"Secondly," she continued, "you absolutely cannot have the reception at your house."

If the hearts and flowers wedding theme hadn't convinced me that I'd made a terrible error in judgment, Dela's declaration cemented it. "What do you mean?" I said slowly enough so she could understand me. "I'm having the reception at my house."

She sat back in her chair with her mouth open in horror. "I have already planned for it in the community room at the church, and I simply can't re-work it." She crossed her arms and gazed at me defiantly. "Besides, I've already booked it."

I held my breath and silently counted to ten—something my father had taught me to do when dealing with my mother. When I reached nine, I took a deep breath. "Dela, I really appreciate your help with my wedding, but the re-ception is going to be at my house. Ruby and Bert are going to do the cooking. I am quite open to your suggestions about the wedding and even the recep-tion, but please check with me before booking anything else, okay?"

Dela started grabbing things from the table, pushing papers together in a huff. "I can't work like this," she declared.

My first reaction was sheer joy. She was quitting. I was free! But then she started to cry. I have to admit that a brief battle ensued inside me. If I let her walk out now, my life would be much easier, and I could prevent loom-ing disaster. Instead, I found myself saying, "I'm sorry, Dela. Please let me see your other ideas. Just because I didn't like that one, it doesn't mean I won't like some-thing else."

There were three reasons I said what I did. Number one: Dela was lonely and needed to feel connected to her new community. Number two: I was too stubborn to tell Amos he was right all along. And number three: I knew what my aunt Bitty would have done in the same circumstances. She would have considered Dela's feelings more important than her wedding plans. There may have been a fourth reason that had to do with a slight case of insanity, but I didn't have time to come up with any other explanations for my behavior.

Dela quit maniacally shuffling papers around and grabbed her designer handbag. She took out a hankie and wiped her eyes. "I don't know," she said be-tween high-pitched hiccups. "I've never been treated like this before. Everyone else loves my ideas. The ex-governor told me that I'd created the wedding to end all weddings." She sniffed a few times then blew her nose. "And they're still together, I might add."

I wasn't really surprised. The poor man probably couldn't face another Dela Shackleford wedding. "I'm sure it's just me, Dela. Let's look over your other proposals. I'll bet there's something here that will be absolutely perfect."

She put her handkerchief back in her purse. "I do have a couple of other ideas. . . ."

"I'd love to see them." I was praying as hard as I could without looking like I was storming heaven. It wasn't easy. There was a little, invisible version of myself on the inside, jumping up and down and yelling as loudly as possible, asking God if He could drop everything for just a few seconds and save me from this imminent wedding nightmare.

Dela searched through her stack and pulled out another folder. "Now, these pictures are of *my* wedding."

She paused and looked up toward the ceiling. I almost followed her gaze to see what was so interesting but stopped myself just in time.

"It was the most beautiful wedding I've ever seen," she said dreamily. "Why, people in Dodge City didn't know what to think." She kept staring heavenward for several seconds. Finally, she lowered her head and smiled at me. "Do you know that every single person who attended said the same thing?"

"And what was that, Dela?"

"That they'd never seen anything like it." She shook her head slowly. "And now I am going to do the same thing for you."

That little invisible person jumping up and down inside of me sat down with a *thunk*. Obviously this was one of God's busier days.

In my worst imagination, I wasn't prepared for what awaited me. The first thing I saw was a picture of Dela decked out in a red silk gown with a large yellow dragon splayed across the front. On her head she wore some kind of gold crown with a red veil. Short, stocky Barney was stuffed into a red tux with a matching yellow dragon on the jacket front. He looked like one of those chubby, plastic boy dolls you find in gift stores that has been draped in a cheap Chinese costume. The next picture was a shot of the bridesmaids and the groomsmen. It wasn't any better. They were all dressed in yellow satin. The bridesmaids had red sashes around their middles that made them look decidedly frumpy and overweight, and they clutched sandalwood fans in their hands. One of the women held hers up to her face. Although she was trying hard to make the gesture look playful, I suspect she was hoping it might keep her from having to leave town and create a whole new identity. The men all wore shiny yellow tuxedos with red accents. That's all that needs to be said about that.

The next several pictures showed the inside of the church. Lanterns hung from every available space. Red banners with gold Chinese figures were draped around the room. And hanging behind the stage was a large papier-mâché dragon. Dela tried to push another picture in front of me, but I couldn't take my eyes off that dragon for some reason. I wanted to look away—but I couldn't.

When I finally gazed down at the last picture, I saw the aisles in the church decorated with Chinese fans and orchids. It was the only part of the monstrosity I could say something positive about. "I...I like what you did here. The orchids are lovely."

Dela clapped her hands together with delight. "I knew you'd love this. With your parents being missionaries in China and all. . ."

I was fairly certain my parents would not only hate this, they would most probably disown me if they ever saw this make-believe Chinese monstrosity. I thought fast. "You know, Dela, it's very thoughtful of you to think of my parents, but the truth is, I think they'd rather not see a Chinese wedding. I mean, they've been in China a long time now. I think they are expecting something more. . .American. Do you understand?" I wasn't sure how she could possibly understand since it didn't even make sense to me, but I smiled like what I'd said was perfectly logical.

Dela stared at me with narrowed eyes. "Well, I don't know. . . ." She grabbed the attaché case from under the table. "I brought some favors with me for you to look at." She dumped several things out in front of me. "These are napkin rings for the reception. They're in the shape of fortune cookies. And here are some paper parasols." She reached farther inside the bag. "Now these are really special." She pulled out a box and set it in front of me. "Every guest will get a set of chopsticks with the bride and groom's names on them. Of course, those will be wooden. But this set is for you and Amos." She opened the box to reveal a set of long, bronze chopsticks with pointed ends. Engraved on one side were the names *Delaphine and Barney Shackleford—May 6th, 1986*. She took them out of the box and handed them to me.

I was startled to hear someone behind me clear his throat. Fearful that it was Amos, I turned around and was relieved to find Isaac standing just to the left of my chair.

"Sorry to disturb you," he said. "I'm getting ready to start work. Any special instructions?"

I shook my head, numb with embarrassment. I could tell by the look on his face that he found my predicament extremely entertaining. I was just as aware that he knew exactly what needed to be done. He'd just wanted to get a gander at those awful pictures. He was looking for ammunition—something he could tease me about. This would certainly keep him equipped for quite some time.

After he left, Dela leaned in close to me. "Why don't you give this some thought, Ivy? If you really think your parents wouldn't like it, that's okay." She sighed. "To be honest, I doubt that the magic of this event could ever be duplicated. I struggled with even showing this to you. I don't want you and Amos to feel that you have to try to live up to a standard that's. . . well, out of your reach." She shot me a look of pity that made me want to tell her what I really thought of her wonderful wedding—but I didn't.

"You're absolutely right. We would probably come off as poor imitations. I hate to do anything that might cast a bad light on your unique event."

I seemed to hit the right nerve. Dela nodded and began gathering up the mementos of her nightmarish Chinese ceremony. I handed her the chopsticks and sent a quick prayer of thanks to God along with my apologies for ever doubting Him. I hoped that Dela interpreted my sigh of relief as a sign of my great disappointment.

After fiddling with what seemed to be a defective clasp on the box that held the chopsticks, she finally put it into her purse. "I've got to have Barney fix that fastener before I lose something that can't possibly be replaced."

My guess was that whoever came up with the engraved chopsticks idea was probably no longer in business. Therefore, Dela's observation had some real merit.

"I do have one more idea that might be more your style," she purred.

I seriously doubted that Dela and I would ever have the same kind of style, but to my surprise, when she opened the final notebook in her case, the results were surprising. "This is a fairytale wedding," Dela said. "It lacks the color and verve of my wedding, but I think there's something quite magical about it."

The bride's gown was ivory satin with a beaded bodice. Small rhinestones were scattered throughout the white beads, giving the dress a lovely shimmer. The sleeves were long, made out of lace, and the bride held a white winter muff. Instead of a long veil, a small, sparkly band threaded through her hair.

The bridesmaids wore simple dresses, touched with a hint of dusky grey. Although they were sleeveless, each girl had a matching shawl draped around her shoulders.

The church was decorated with small, twinkling lights and crystal snow-flakes that hung from the ceiling. White orchids graced the platform with silver candlesticks.

"Why, Dela," I said. "This is beautiful. I think you've captured the winter look I want."

The smile on Dela's face told me she was pleased. However, she couldn't resist one last dig. "I guess the other weddings were just a little too imaginative for you," she said, patting my hand. Although her tone was obviously patronizing, I was just happy that this whole thing hadn't blown up in my face. Telling Amos that accepting Dela's help hadn't been the disaster he'd anticipated almost made viewing Barney Shackleford in a red satin tux worth it. Almost.

"Can I have this picture of the wedding dress?" I asked. "I'd like to show it to Inez. It can be our guide."

"Absolutely," she said. "Why don't you keep this folder? You can go over everything and make a list of any changes. I will need to meet with you again in a couple of days so we can start ordering our supplies." She handed me the folder. "What kind of budget are we talking about, dear?"

I mentioned a figure Amos and I had agreed on. At first, we'd decided that we didn't want my parents to help with the cost of the wedding. As missionaries, we felt their finances should be protected. My dad had sent us a check anyway, insisting that helping us was a joy and reminding me that they actually did have money of their own, thank you. We applied his check along with what we believed we could afford, and came up with a sum we felt was completely sufficient for our needs. Dela's reaction made it evident that our budget would seriously constrain her creativity.

"Oh, my," she said, a frown darkening her face. "We'll have to do better than that. I can't even begin to pull this wedding off for that much. You'll have to at least double your budget."

"Dela, I appreciate everything you're doing, but that's the amount we have to spend. Period. If we can't do it, we can't do it. I appreciate your help anyway." I smiled at her and stood up, sticking out my hand. My bluff worked, just as I knew it would.

"Well, I'll just have to find some way to pull it off," she said, shaking her head and ignoring my extended digits. "I am the kind of person who likes challenges. This certainly will test my mettle." She stared up at me, determination on her face. I was now Delaphine Shackleford's pet project. She stood up. "I will need to see your house now," she said matter-of-factly. "If I am to plan the reception there, I must see what I'm working with." The look of resignation on her face conveyed her fears that I most probably lived in a van by the river. I wondered what she would think when she saw my Queen Anne-style Victorian house next to Lake Winter Break. It was a gorgeous house, the prettiest in Winter Break.

"I'm sorry, but as you can see, I'm working right now. I just can't spare the time. Why don't we make an appointment for another day?"

Dela's smile froze on her face. "Pardon me, honey," she said icily, her pseudo-Southern accent as thick as sorghum, "but my time is important, too. I've taken the morning off so I can help you. I think the least you can do is to treat my offer of free services with respect, don't you?"

"Excuse me." Isaac appeared behind us, supposedly looking for something on a shelf near the sitting room. "I've got everything under control, Miss Ivy. Why don't you go ahead and take Mrs. Shackleford to your house? I'll watch the store."

His smile looked sincere, but I could see the twinkle in his eye. "Well, thank you so much, Isaac," I said. "I will certainly return the favor to you at an appropriate moment in the future."

He swept his arm in front of him with a slight bow. "I appreciate that," he said with a grin. "I will be watching for it most carefully."

I glared at him as I tagged along behind Dela to the front door. She followed me over to my house. Once we got there, it took her over an hour to inspect my living room, dining room, and kitchen. Although she made clucking noises every couple of minutes, in the end, she grudgingly admitted that she could probably pull off an acceptable reception there. The dining room had large windows and French doors that faced Lake Winter Break. Dela decided that this feature could be used to our advantage.

"I have all kinds of ideas," she told me. "But I want some time to sketch them out, and I have an errand in town I must take care of. Why don't I stop by tomorrow and we can discuss them?"

I agreed to meet her the next day at the bookstore, and after an odd kiss near my cheek that never actually touched my face, she left. Since it was almost noon, I decided to have lunch before I went back to work. I fixed a sandwich, sat at the dining room table, and gazed out at Lake Winter Break. Since it was thoroughly frozen over, I'd raised the yellow flag on a pole near the lake. Cecil Biddle, who had once owned my house, had installed the pole when I was a kid as a way to let folks in Winter Break know that the lake was safe for skating. On the weekends it was full of children. I loved to watch them from my window. This was probably my favorite place in the house to sit and read my Bible, pray, or just daydream. It gave me a sense of peace.

I'd just finished my sandwich when I saw the dog. He was skulking around the backyard deck. The pan of food I'd set out for him was still a little over half full, so he wasn't hungry. I got the feeling he was curious. I didn't want to spook him again, so I stayed where I was. After a few minutes he looked my way, but this time he stood still and stared at me. His expression was still melancholy, but for the first time, he also looked inquisitive—as if he were trying to figure me out. Finally, he turned and ran back through the trees that surrounded one side of the lake.

The past few weeks had been pretty cold, and we were set for another snowstorm. I couldn't help but worry about him. But along with concern for the dog, I felt something else stirring inside me. Something on a deeper level. I remembered what Aunt Bitty told me once about what she used to call "God's fire alarm." "When God rings that fire alarm inside you," she'd say, "it means you better pay attention. Something somewhere needs a dose of prayer."

I happened to glance up at the clock on the wall. It was later than I'd thought. I prayed quietly while I cleaned up the kitchen and put the food away, but I could swear that alarm got even louder.

3

I finished up my work at the bookstore and rushed home. After a quick dinner and a change of clothes, I headed to the church. The Winter Break City Council, led by Mayor Dewey Tater, had called a special meeting for seven o'clock. He planned to announce his selection of citizens to serve as the new library's advisory board. I knew my name was on the list, but for the most part, Dewey had kept his final selections to himself. He'd asked my opinion about what qualities I thought were important for a library board member, but he didn't mention any names. I knew he took his role as Winter Break's mayor seriously, even though there wasn't much for him to do. City council meetings were usually boring affairs, where the placement of street signs and trash Dumpsters topped the agenda. However, the whole town was excited about the library, and quite a few people had expressed a desire to be on the board. Tonight promised to hold some actual excitement.

When I arrived, the meeting had just started. I wasn't the least bit surprised to see Dela sitting on the front row, still dressed in her red velvet and fur outfit. She was determined to be the cream of society wherever she was—even if it was in Winter Break, Kansas.

Alma Pettibone, who served not only as our postmistress but also as the city clerk, called the meeting to order. Elmer Buskin, owner of Buskin's Funeral Home, had just moved to have the minutes from the last meeting approved, when Amos came in the door and scooted into the chair next to me. He slid off his parka and hung it on the back of the chair. Then he kissed me on the cheek. I grabbed his hand and held it while Mort Benniker seconded the motion. I noticed that one of the council seats at the table was empty. J.D. Feldhammer was missing. J.D. and his wife, Ina Mae, had only lived in Winter Break for about six months. He was a real estate agent who had moved here from Liberal, Kansas. He handled a lot of farm properties and had put together the deal for my home. He'd been recommended to Cecil and Marion Biddle, who'd sold the house to Amos as a surprise for me. When Ina Mae needed to be close to her sickly mother who lived in Hugoton, J.D. had purchased Lester Simmons's property. Lester's house had been vacant for quite a while, and rumor had it that J.D. got it for a really good price. He seemed very happy here and was well liked by everyone who had gotten to know him. I liked Ina Mae, too, although she was painfully shy. It had taken awhile for me to get past her reserved persona, but now she was in the habit of dropping by the bookstore every few days to visit and have a cup of coffee. I looked through the crowd and spotted her sitting by herself near the back of the room. Because of J.D.'s business, Ina Mae often needed a ride to church or to events like this evening's meeting. I made a mental note to check with her before we left to see if she had a way home.

I focused my attention back to Dewey, who announced the reason for tonight's meeting. "We're here to set up a board for the library," he said, trying to speak loudly enough for everyone to hear. "As you all probably know, we asked for a letter from anyone interested in being a part of the board, with an explanation as to why you think you are qualified for this position. I was asked to read those letters then recommend some folks for the board, subject to the council's approval." He pulled his glasses out of his pocket and perched them on his nose. "After a careful review, I am recommending the following people for the board." He picked up a piece of paper from the table and began to read. "Ivy Towers, Isaac Holsapple, Bev Taylor, Bertha Pennypacker, Evan Baumgartner, and Delaphine Shackleford."

I was horrified. Dewey had nominated Bertha Pennypacker and Dela? He knew how difficult they were to get along with. What was he thinking? I was happy to know that I would be serving with Isaac, and Bev Taylor, Pastor Taylor's wife. And Evan Baumgartner, one of the teachers from the grade school in Hugoton, was a good choice. But Bertha and Dela?

"I didn't see that coming," Amos whispered to me.

I'm sure the lack of blood in my face indicated my agreement, but I didn't say anything. I was afraid to.

Bubba Weber seconded Dewey's nominations, and Dewey called for a vote. His list was passed unanimously. I wanted to cry. My dreams of a library board working together for the good of the community seemed lost, as well as my election as board president. Bertha, the town's gossip, had taken a dislike to me right after I came to Winter Break. Dewey told me that she had always been jealous of Bitty and had transferred her attitude onto me. Of course, the fact that I'd helped Amos break up her husband's cow-stealing ring hadn't helped anything. Good old Delbert was now cooling his heels in the Hutchinson Correctional Facility, and Bertha hated me even more.

After encouraging the board to meet and start writing out its goals and then present them to the city council at their next regular assembly, the meeting was dismissed. Ruby had set up a table with desserts and coffee. People made a beeline for it, leaving Amos and me standing in the back of the room.

"Let's go," I hissed. "I'm so mad I could spit nails."

Amos looked surprised. "Why are you upset? I thought you wanted to be on the board."

I stared at him in amazement. "You think I'm happy that Dewey picked Bertha and Dela? What in the world makes them suitable to serve on a library board?" I shook my head. "Dewey must have lost his mind. We'll never get anything accomplished if we have to kowtow to those two prima donnas."

"Ivy Towers," someone said from behind me, "maybe we should just let the entire council go and put you in charge of everything."

I turned around to find Dewey standing there. To say I was mortified was an understatement. "I—I—I. . ." was all that would come out of my mouth.

"You might be surprised to find out that Bertha Pennypacker's mother was a librarian, and that she was practically raised in a library. And you might also be surprised to learn that Delaphine Shackleford was on the Dodge City Library Board. She has just the kind of experience we need."

I wanted to say that she probably only served because it nicely filled out her social calendar, but I'd already said too much. I decided to cut my losses and shut up.

Dewey looked at me with an expression I'd never seen on his face before: disappointment. Then he said the one thing that had the power to make me feel worse than I already did. "Your aunt Bitty would be ashamed of you right now. I don't remember her ever saying an unkind word about anyone."

With that, he turned and walked away, leaving me to stand there with my bad attitude hanging out for all the world to see. People were beginning to drift around the room—their plates stacked high with Ruby's scrumptious desserts. I wasn't certain who'd heard Dewey scold me, but I was mortified. Almost everyone I knew was at the meeting.

"Let's go," I said to Amos. I could feel tears sting my eyelids, and I had no intention of blubbering in front of the city council and my new library board pals.

Before he had a chance to respond, a shrill voice cut through the sound of regular conversation in the room. "Hello there, Ivy! Who would have thought you and I would be serving on the same board!" Dela's Southern screech shot through the room like an errant bullet. "I'm so excited to know that we will be working together on *two* important projects." She linked her arm through mine like we were best friends. "And I want you to know that I will be happy to serve as board president since I have so much experience."

Her smile had a touch of triumph in it. I wondered if she'd already been campaigning for the position. As if on cue, Bertha Pennypacker sidled up next to her. "Oh, Dela," she said in syrupy tones, "you would make the perfect president. Don't you think so, Ivy?"

I just nodded since I didn't trust myself enough to open my mouth. Bertha took this as a vote of confidence. "Then I'm sure you'll convince the other members of the board to vote for our dear Dela, won't you?"

Bertha, in her cheap dress and home perm, was preening for attention from someone who probably saw her only as a means to an end. Curiously, I found myself feeling rather sorry for her. Having a husband in prison certainly couldn't be a boost to her self-esteem.

"We'll see, Bertha," I said. "Why don't we wait and discuss it at our first meeting? Can we set a time for it now?"

"Why, Ivy," Dela simpered. "I think that's a wonderful idea. When should we meet? What about tomorrow night?"

"That's a church night," I said, wondering if she already knew that. "What about Thursday night? We could meet at the bookstore."

"Hmm," Dela said. "I suppose we could get together there, but why don't you let me bring the hors d'oeuvres? I have some recipes that would be, uh, appropriate."

I was thinking about telling her just what she could do with her "appropriate" hors d'oeuvres, but I already had Dewey mad at me. Creating more strife would only make things worse.

I returned her saccharine smile with one of my own. Amos's lopsided grin told me I probably looked more constipated than amused. "Thank you, Dela. That's very nice of you. Thursday night it is. We'll need to let the others know."

"Bertha," Dela said, "why don't you take care of telling Mrs. Taylor? I'll be glad to talk to Evan. And, Ivy, you can inform your assistant about the meeting."

She was handing out orders like she was already the board president. I could feel my blood beginning to boil. Since I tend to turn beet red when I get upset, Amos knew I needed help. He linked his arm with mine and gave me a look meant to warn me to back down. Between Dewey's admonishment and the expression on Amos's face, I realized I was taking this situation too seriously. I was thinking about myself instead of what was best for the library. Sending a quick apology heavenward, I decided it was time to take the high road. Quite a few people had gathered around us, probably wanting to congratulate us on our appointments. This certainly wasn't the time or place for an emotional meltdown.

"I'll be happy to do that, Dela," came out of my mouth instead of the angry words I wanted to throw at her. I looked up at Amos. "Why don't we get to the dessert table before all of that wonderful lemon meringue pie is gone?"

He knew I was looking for a way of escape and quickly agreed, but before we could make our getaway, Dela grabbed my arm.

"Honey," she said loudly enough for everyone to hear, "I brought my measuring tape with me tonight so I could get some measurements at your house." She glanced around at all the people who stood nearby. "I'm Ivy's wedding planner, you know."

COZY IN KANSAS

From the mumbled responses, nodding heads, and smiles sent my way, it seemed that most people were impressed. However, I thought I detected a few looks of abject pity.

I had to think fast. I had no intention of spending any more time that night with her. "I'm a little tired tonight, Dela," I said. "Why don't we do it tomorrow?"

She shook her head sorrowfully. "Oh, I can't do that, dear," she said. "I have plans tomorrow." She turned her head sideways and peered up at me with a look of amazement. "Now, Ivy," she said so everyone could hear her, "as I've already told you, I don't mind helping you with your wedding, but the least I expect is for you to work around *my* schedule. I don't think that's asking too much, do you?"

Before I could answer, Amos interrupted. "Dela, Ivy and I are going over to the bookstore after we leave here. Why don't you take Ivy's keys and go on to the house. If you finish before we get there, put the keys on the dining room table. That way we won't be there to interrupt you. I'm sure you don't need us interfering with your. . .your measurements."

I wanted to kiss Amos on the lips. Right there in front of everyone.

"That would be fine," she said. "It would be much better if I could work undisturbed." She held out her hand while I fished out a spare set of keys from my purse.

"What are you going to be measuring, Dela?" I asked.

"Oh, honey," she declared in her overly mushy, Southern tones, "I have to find a way to get as many people as possible into your limited space. Of course, we'll have to move out some of the furniture. And then there are the decorations. I will need some wall space, so some of your little pictures will have to come down. Especially that huge, horrible tapestry in the dining room. It takes up too much space and the colors are just awful."

Amos tightened his grip on my arm. That "horrible tapestry" Dela referred to was my very favorite object in the house. It had been painted by Marion Biddle. It was a lovely picture of the back of the house and the lake during winter. Several children stood near the lake with their skates in their hands, while others skated on its frozen surface. I was one of those children. Marion had left it hanging in the house when they moved to Florida. "It needs to stay there, Ivy," she told me when I'd asked her about it. "That tapestry belongs to Winter Break." She knew how much I loved it, so I was thrilled when she told me it was mine.

"I'm sure we can remove it for the reception," Amos said quickly. "That won't be a problem." He shot me another look meant to keep me quiet. "Let's go, Ivy. We really need to get to the bookstore."

Before Amos pushed me out the door, I remembered Ina Mae. I looked quickly through the crowd that was focused on Dela and her halftime show. Near the coffeepot, I saw J.D. standing next to his wife. Since she wouldn't need a ride after all, I made my exit, grabbing my jacket from the small coat-room by the door.

I'd hoped I was free of Dela, but unfortunately she followed us out the door. "Don't worry about anything, honey," she called.

Since she was parked right next to Amos's patrol car, there was no way I could get away without responding. "Thanks, Dela," I said with a smile. It took almost everything I had to answer her in a civil way. Dewey's face and his comment about Bitty were the only things keeping me from throwing a real fit.

"That woman has some nerve," I said forcefully when we got inside the car. "If I want that tapestry up during our reception, it will stay up! How in the world does she think she can tell me what—"

"I told you this was a bad idea," Amos snapped, interrupting me. "But you wouldn't listen. Whatever happens now is on *your* head."

This was exactly what I'd been dreading, an "I told you so" from Amos. I sat in sullen silence while he drove us to the bookstore. Unfortunately, I had to face the truth. Maybe I had every *right* to be upset, but that didn't make my reaction acceptable. Aunt Bitty's voice resonated in my heart. *"Anyone can love people who are easy to get along with, Ivy. It's loving difficult people in spite of their faults that gives us the chance to walk in God's love."* I'd really had the best intentions for allowing Dela to be involved in my wedding, but I realized that unless I could adjust my attitude, this situation was going to turn into a big mess.

Once inside the store, with a fire going in the fireplace and Amos and me together on the couch in the sitting room, I felt the need to confess. "I let my emotions get away with me, Amos," I said. "I'm sorry. You're mad at me, Dewey's mad at me." The tears I'd managed to push away at the church made a return entrance. "I told Dela she could plan our wedding, so now I have to try to work with her and not be so touchy. And I'm sure she and Bertha will have some good ideas about the library."

Amos opened his arms, and I cuddled up against him.

"I'm proud of you," he said softly. "You know, Ivy, I love a lot of things about you, but one thing I really respect is your ability to face your faults. It's a wonderful quality."

I wiped my face with the back of my sleeve. I needed a tissue, but I didn't want to leave Amos's embrace. "I know. You've told me that more than once." I ended my comment with a hiccup.

Amos chuckled. Then he pulled a handkerchief out of his pocket and handed it to me. "Maybe you need to hear it again. It might remind you that

311

you're not a complete failure as a human being." He squeezed me and kissed the top of my head. "I love that you're so honest with yourself—and with me. It's one of the reasons I trust you."

I could have pointed out that I wouldn't have to use my so-called wonderful quality as often if I just quit goofing up so much, but I decided to stop while I was ahead. I wiped my face and spent the next couple of hours cuddled up with the man I loved. Finally, since it was getting late, we reluctantly untangled ourselves, and Amos drove me home.

As we pulled into my long, curving driveway, I noticed that Dela's car was parked in front of the garage. I'd almost missed it in the dark. At least she wasn't blocking the drive. "For crying out loud," I said. "She's still here? What in the world could take this long?" I grabbed Amos's arm. "Let's drive around a little longer, okay?"

Amos laughed. "No way. I have to get up early in the morning and so do you. This is a test of that new attitude of yours. Go in there and make nice, okay?"

I sighed. Great, another test. I was getting a little tired of them. "Okay, okay." I turned my face toward his for a good-night kiss and then got out of the car. I steeled myself for what lay ahead.

I waved at Amos as his patrol car pulled away. Then I climbed up the steps to my front door. I was surprised to find it locked. When I stepped inside the house, I called out, "Dela?" When I didn't get a response, I called for her again. My house was strangely silent. I walked through the living room and checked out the kitchen. No Dela. A quick walk down the hall only revealed Miss Skiffins, my small, calico cat, napping in the spare room. I even checked the patio even though no one in their right mind would be out there as cold as it was outside. I yelled upstairs. Nothing. Would she have gone up there? Surely not. I climbed the stairs, calling her name, but all the rooms were empty. Confused, I went downstairs and stepped back outside. Her car was still parked in the driveway. I flipped on the yard light and thought I saw someone in the front seat. Why would Dela just sit there and ignore me? I felt a flash of frustration. This was Delaphine Shackleford. Common sense wasn't one of her virtues. I stomped down the stairs and marched over to her car. No reaction. Trying to push back my growing irritation, I tapped lightly on the driver's side window. She still refused to look at me. Finally, I opened the car door.

Dela's limp body fell sideways, hanging out the door. Her eyes were wide open and staring at me. And one of those stupid chopsticks was stuck beneath her ribcage.

I heard someone screaming, but it took several seconds before I realized it was me.

4

And what time did you say you left the church?"

"For the fifth or sixth time, Sheriff, it was around eight o'clock. I didn't check my watch."

Sheriff Milt Hitchens was a large man with a florid face and fingers the size of plump sausages. However, most of his bulk seemed to be muscle. I knew Amos took him seriously, and I would imagine that any criminal would think twice about crossing him.

"I'm sorry to keep goin' over this, Miss Towers," he said in a low, gravelly voice, "but it's very important we get all the details straight."

I wished Amos was here. He'd gone with another deputy to tell Barney Shackleford that his wife had been murdered. The pictures Dela had shown me of her dumb Chinese wedding kept flashing through my mind. I couldn't keep my eyes from tearing up. Strange how they seemed so ridiculous when I'd first seen them, and now. . . Okay, they were still ridiculous, but there was something endearing about a man who would dress up like that for the woman he loved. Barney didn't deserve the news he would receive tonight.

The sheriff and I were sitting in my living room while various law enforcement personnel availed themselves of my phone and, it seemed, the contents of my refrigerator. I didn't really care. Amos had told them to help themselves.

"Excuse me, Sheriff, may I talk to you a minute?"

A rather nondescript man in a dark suit interrupted us. I was getting used to it. It had been happening all evening. According to Amos, when there is a murder in a small, rural town like Winter Break, the sheriff's department and the Kansas Bureau of Investigation work the case together. This guy was most likely KBI. They all looked the same. Suits and serious expressions.

After speaking quietly for several minutes, Sheriff Hitchens came back and sat down next to me again. "Sorry for the interruption, Miss Towers. You said that the only thing you touched was the car door?"

"Yes, the car door." I blew my breath out through clenched teeth. I could feel the pressure building inside me. Dela was dead. In my driveway. My home had been invaded by law enforcement officers, and my fiancé's boss was treating me like a suspect. What more could go wrong?

"Miss Towers, I want you to think about that question very carefully. We will be fingerprintin' you so that we can eliminate your prints from any others on Mrs. Shackleford's car." He shook his head, his jowls bouncing like a nervous basset hound. "Sometimes people will try to pull out a knife or move a gun without thinkin'. You're certain you didn't do anything like that?"

I glared at him. "I've told you over and over the only thing I touched was the car door. I didn't touch Dela because it was obvious she was dead. And I'm not brain dead. I would never have. . ." A sudden, sickening memory popped into my mind. To say that my whole body felt numb was an understatement. I looked at the sheriff in horror. "I—I—I, uh. . ."

He raised one eyebrow at me. "I take it you have somethin' to say to me, Miss Towers?"

I nodded dumbly.

"Would you like to actually tell me what it is, or would you like me to guess?"

I shook my head. "I—I—I mean, I think I may have touched the chopstick."

The sheriff's already ruddy face darkened several shades. "What do you mean, you *think* you may have touched the murder weapon?"

I wanted to protest that "chopstick" sounded better than "murder weapon," but it didn't seem to be appropriate. "Dela, that is, Mrs. Shackleford, was showing the chopsticks to me this afternoon in my bookstore. I. . .I picked them up. My. . .my fingerprints might still be. . ." I couldn't finish my sentence. The sheriff was looking at me the same way I imagine a hawk might stare at a mouse. I felt like dinner. "Sheriff, I assure you I did not kill Dela Shackleford. I wasn't anywhere near my house. I was with Amos Parker all evening. He can vouch for me." I wished I could get the squeaky tone out of my voice.

"I'll need you to come to my office tomorrow morning, Miss Towers. You can have Deputy Parker drive you if you'd feel safer. The roads are still pretty bad."

All I could do was nod. In my mind, I was trying to see things from the sheriff's point of view. Dela was dead in my driveway. My fingerprints were on her car door *and* on the murder weapon. Nope. This didn't look good. As I watched the activity around me, I remembered that I had no motive. Sheriff Hitchens would see that. Besides, Amos was my alibi, and he worked for the sheriff. The convulsing butterflies in my stomach began to settle down a little. Perhaps murder might be a temptation *after* a Delaphine Shackleford wedding, but before? It didn't make sense.

As Hitchens walked away, I thought about pointing out my obvious innocence to him, but before I had a chance, Amos walked in the front door. I was so glad to see him I could barely contain myself, and I promptly forgot all about building a case for my exoneration.

I jumped up and hurried over to him. His expression was grim. I was certain telling Barney the bad news had been tough. "Are you okay?" I asked.

"Not really," he said, his eyes narrow and his jaw tight. "This whole thing is unbelievable."

"How's Barney?"

Amos shook his head slowly. "He didn't take it well, Ivy. Not well at all."

Before he could tell me more, one of the other deputies called his name. He walked away and joined a group of several deputies and a couple of KBI agents. They began talking to each other in low voices. Finally, Amos came back.

"Where is Miss Skiffins?" he asked. "With the front door opening and closing so many times. . ."

"Don't worry. I put her in the upstairs bedroom." I moved closer to him. "Someone followed me upstairs when I locked her up, Amos," I whispered. "It was like they thought I was up to something. What's going on?"

He sighed. "That's just the way it is. The KBI is tough on crime scenes. They keep us on our toes. Everything is important. Everyone is a suspect. When they first got here they were upset because we came in the house."

"What? But it's obvious she was killed in her car. Why would they want to check inside the house?"

"They're just being careful, Ivy. They need to make certain Dela wasn't attacked in here first." He shook his head. "I'm the one who told the guys they could come in and get something to eat."

"I'm sorry. Are you in any trouble?"

"No. The crime scene investigators concluded that Delaphine was definitely killed in her car. They think she'd been dead a couple of hours when you found her. Doesn't look like she ever made it into the house. She was stabbed once. The chopstick was pushed up under her ribs and hit her heart. She never had a chance."

I turned around and went back to the couch. I was starting to feel lightheaded. The night's events, the realization that my fingerprints were on the chopstick that killed Dela, and the fact that it was after two o'clock in the morning and I was ready to drop combined to make me feel slightly woozy.

Then as suddenly as they had come, sheriff's deputies, KBI agents, and some other people I'd never been able to identify began moving toward my front door like rats leaving a sinking ship.

"What's going on?"

"Wait here," he said firmly. "I'll be right back."

He joined behind the strange exodus. In a matter of seconds, my house was quiet again. Except for some empty pop cans and plates with the remains of cold cuts and chips littering my kitchen, everything was back to normal. It was as if a bad dream had come to an end. Unfortunately, I was pretty sure it would be waiting for me in the morning.

After a few minutes, Amos came back, closing the door behind him. "The coroner has taken Dela away, and her car has been towed to the sheriff's impound lot." He went into the kitchen and started cleaning up. I wanted to tell him to forget it, but I was too tired and too heartsick to say anything. When my kitchen finally had some semblance of order, he came over and sat down next to me. Without saying a word, he opened his arms and I melted into him. Now, the tears I'd been holding on to came without inhibition. Amos let me bawl for a while. When my sobs finally turned to sniffles, he handed me a paper towel he'd wisely carried with him from the kitchen. I wiped off my face and straightened up.

"Amos, the sheriff thinks I killed Dela."

"The sheriff does *not* think you killed Dela, but he has no choice but to follow up on every piece of evidence. Your fingerprints are on the car door and she was killed in your driveway. He can't ignore that. It doesn't mean he thinks you're a suspect."

"But what about that stupid chopstick? Aren't you worried about that?"

The calm expression Amos had been exhibiting for my benefit crumpled. "What about the chopstick?" he said slowly.

He hadn't heard. "My fingerprints are probably on it. Dela handed them to me today at the bookstore and I—I held them."

"You touched the murder weapon?" The size of his pupils and the lack of color in his face told me I was in trouble.

"Yes, Amos," I said sharply. "Although now I wonder why it didn't occur to me that just a few hours later, someone would drive one of those chopsticks into Dela's chest. What in the world was I thinking?"

Amos leaned over and put his head in his hands. After a few seconds he straightened up. "Everything will be okay. You were with me. He'll believe that."

I jumped to my feet. "He'll *believe that*? It sounds like you're trying to concoct an alibi! I *was* with you." I went to the refrigerator and grabbed a cold can of root beer. My throat was as dry as parchment. "You and I went straight from the church to the bookstore. Of course, I could have run out when you went upstairs to the bathroom. Let's see, you were gone what? Three or four minutes? Plenty of time for me to hurry outside, jump in my car, drive to my house, confront Dela in her car, and kill her with a chopstick from her wedding!" I waved my root beer can around like a conductor's wand. "That's it, ladies and gentlemen! Ivy Towers murdered the victim so she wouldn't have to walk down the aisle in a go-go dress!"

Amos raised his eyebrows and stared at me. "You're really overreacting, you know. And why would you get married in a go-go dress?"

I sat down on one of the stools at the kitchen breakfast bar and sighed. "Never mind. I'm being ridiculous. Here I'm worrying about myself, and I should be thinking about poor Barney."

Amos stood up and stretched. It had been a long night. I glanced at the clock. Correction. Long night and even longer morning.

"He was devastated," Amos said. "We asked him if he had any idea who might have attacked her. He didn't have a clue. As far as he knew, everyone loved her."

I shook my head. "I guess love really is blind. Dela ruffled a lot of feathers with her highbrow ideas and snotty attitude, but I can't think of a single person who would actually want her dead. In her own way, I think she really wanted to make our wedding special."

Amos came over and grabbed my hands. "We could get married in the grocery store with you holding a stalk of celery for your bouquet, and it would be special. I don't care about all the trappings. I just want to be your husband." My husband-to-be leaned over and kissed me. For the first time since I'd found Dela slumped in her car, I felt better.

"If you're planning to drive me to the sheriff's office in the morning, you need to go home." I looked at the clock on the kitchen wall. "We're not going to get much sleep."

"You go on upstairs," Amos said. "I'm going to stay down here."

I shook my head. "I can't let you do that. It doesn't look right."

His eyes narrowed and he put his hands on his hips. I knew what that meant. This wasn't going to be easy. "Ivy, someone was killed right outside your door. Most likely, the target was Dela, but I can't be sure. You cannot stay in this house by yourself until I'm sure it's safe. Right now I'm not the least bit concerned about 'how it looks.' I'll stretch out on the couch. Tomorrow we'll find someone else to come and stay with you."

I started to protest, but he pressed his fingers against my lips. "This is not open for debate. You get to bed, set your alarm, and wake me up at seven. We'll get some breakfast at Ruby's and then we'll drive to Hugoton."

I was too tired to argue, so I headed upstairs, released Miss Skiffins from her temporary prison, and fell into bed with her tucked under my arm.

I dreamed I was being chased by a large, ugly, papier-mâché dragon.

5

Ruby's Redbird Café was bustling. Pictures of Winter Break families, past and present, hung on the whitewashed walls, and the aroma of coffee and bacon permeated the air. Even though it was only a little after seven, almost every seat was taken. Most of Ruby's customers were farmers. Snow-covered fields didn't bring a halt to their heavy responsibilities. Farm animals had to be fed and tended to. Wood needed to be chopped to keep the fireplace going, and important repairs to equipment and buildings that hadn't been done during a busy crop season had to be addressed before spring.

Along with the farmers, other Winter Break residents gathered together because they liked to start the day with their neighbors. Quite a bit of gossip flowed through Ruby's every morning. Today was no exception. Diners leaned across the plastic red-checked tablecloths, deep in conversation. The topic, of course, was Dela Shackleford. As soon as I walked through the door, I was surrounded by people asking for details. Ruby had rescued me by pushing through the crowd and hollering at everyone to "mind your own business or hit the road." Although a few nosy souls might have been willing to tempt her, in the end, no one was willing to miss out on one of Ruby's famous breakfasts. They were revered in Winter Break. No one could turn out a spread quite like Ruby—except Bert. He had already acquired his mother's talent for a perfectly formed omelet, and his blueberry pancakes were a crowd favorite. Together, Bert and Ruby ran the café with the skill of a highly trained drill team. Bert had added something new to Ruby's experience. His years as a fry cook in Texas had birthed a new language between him and his mother. It was something to behold. "A cuppa joe" was easy enough. But I had to ask Bert what "a pair of drawers" meant. Turned out to be two cups of coffee. For those who chose to pick up their food and take it home, Ruby would holler out the order followed by "and it's going for a walk!"

Although Ruby was still loud, thankfully she'd toned down some. Hard of hearing, she'd resisted a hearing aid for years. When Bert came home, he insisted she see a doctor. Now she sported a hearing device that lowered her screeching several decibels. Having Ruby sneak up behind you and yell so loudly your dinner ended up in your lap had been an everyday occurrence at the Redbird Café. Now at least her customers had a fighting chance.

"What'cha havin'?" Bonnie Peavey, the only waitress at the Redbird Café, leaned over the booth and smiled at Amos and me. Her dark eyes matched her ebony hair, which had been twisted into a braided bun. A little makeup brought out her flawless complexion. The change in Bonnie in a few months' time was remarkable. A year ago Bonnie had been a washed-out wisp of a woman, someone who seemed to blend into the background. Along with Ruby, she had been transformed by Bert's return.

We gave her our orders and told her that Dewey would also be joining us.

"I'll watch for him," she said, "but he always gets the same thing when he comes in for breakfast on Saturdays. Plain English muffin, poached eggs, a bowl of melon, and a cup of coffee."

I grinned at her. "Good for him. He's staying on track."

"We keep a close eye on him." She raised one eyebrow and looked around the room. "Boy, the place is sure buzzing. Someone said you found poor Mrs. Shackleford's body. You okay?"

I noticed that Newton and Marybelle Widdle, who were sitting at a table near our booth, leaned toward us, obviously hoping to hear something new about the dreadful murder. Since Marybelle was Bertha's best friend, I knew that whatever I said would be carried faster than the speed of light to my seeming archenemy.

I scooted closer to Bonnie and lowered my voice. "Yes, she was in my driveway. It was just awful."

"I'm sorry, honey," Bonnie said. She also noticed Marybelle and Newton's interest. "You need something, folks?" she asked loudly.

Marybelle and Newton flashed their most innocent expressions and went back to their breakfasts.

"Do they have any idea who did it?" Bonnie asked. "The whole town is on edge. People who never lock their doors are installing dead bolts."

"It's never a bad idea to be safe," Amos told her, "but the killer is probably someone who knew Dela and was only targeting her. I don't think you have anything to worry about."

Bonnie nodded, but she didn't look convinced. Someone stepped up behind her, carrying a couple of plates.

"Well, now I know why my food is piling up in the back." Bert grinned at us and then handed steaming plates of eggs, bacon, and pancakes to the booth in back of ours. After checking to make sure his customers had everything they needed, he turned his attention back to us.

"It's probably because nobody wants your cruddy old food," Bonnie said, her dark eyes flashing with humor.

Bert sighed loudly. "See what I put up with? A true artist is never appreciated in his own time."

Amos laughed. "I feel exactly the same way," he said, looking at me.

"You poor things," I said, winking at Bonnie. "You're definitely legends in your own minds."

Bert chuckled, put his arm around Bonnie, and kissed her on the cheek. His salt-and-pepper hair framed an intelligent face with gray blue eyes. He and Bonnie made an attractive couple. I wondered if we'd be getting some news one of these days. Maybe there would be more than one wedding in Winter Break before spring came.

After a couple of minutes of small talk, Bert grabbed our order from Bonnie, waved a quick good-bye, and headed toward the kitchen. I heard him yell at Ruby, "Fry two, let the sun shine with two little piggies in the alley!" That was Amos's order of two eggs sunny-side up and a side order of sausage. I was getting pretty good at interpreting "diner speak."

Ruby's Redbird Café had always had a family feel to it, but now that Bert was here, there was a new energy. I saw Ruby walk out of the kitchen and step up to the cash register by the door. Maybe Bert had persuaded her to get a hearing aid, but he hadn't changed Ruby's outward appearance. She still sported a big Marilyn Monroe-styled wig. It was white blond, and it looked ludicrous on her ancient, wrinkled face. Ruby, like so many other women who'd spent time working outside on farms when they were young, had leatherlike skin with deep cracks that ran down her cheeks. She usually wore no makeup except a slash of bright red lipstick that always caked up into the corners of her mouth by the lunch rush. Although her outward appearance was rather odd, folks were drawn immediately to her bright blue eyes, which sparkled with personality. To be honest, I was a little relieved that Bert hadn't been able to update his mother's look. I liked Ruby just the way she was. Brash, caustic, eccentric, and uniquely Ruby.

Amos was saying something about wishing he'd ordered pancakes instead of toast, when I saw Dewey walk in the front door. I waved to him and he began to thread his way through the crowded restaurant to our table.

"Boy, things sure are quieter when we have breakfast at the bookstore," he said as he slid into the other side of the booth across from Amos and me. "Even Saturday mornings aren't usually this bad." He nodded at Amos. "Good morning, son."

"Sorry, Dewey," I said, "but Amos and I have to drive to Hugoton this morning. I thought it would be better to grab a bite here so we could get away early. I'm beginning to wonder if that was a good idea."

Dewey reached over and took hold of my hand. "I could hardly believe it when you called and told me about Delaphine. How are you doing?"

It was the second time this morning someone had asked me if I was all right. I patted Dewey's hand. "I'm fine. Thanks for asking. This situation sure makes my temper tantrum from last night seem ridiculous."

Dewey peered at me from under his thick silver eyebrows. "I shouldn't have gotten on to you like that, Ivy. I'm sorry. To be honest, I was getting so much pressure from people wanting to be on the board, I was just happy to be done with it."

I waved my hand at him. "No. You were right. Aunt Bitty would have accepted everyone selected as being picked by God Himself. She used to always say. . ."

" 'God has a plan, and He doesn't always check with me before He formulates it,' " Dewey quoted.

I grinned at him. "I see Bitty's still talking in your head the way she does in mine."

Amos chuckled. "I'll find myself about to do something, and I swear I can hear her asking me, 'Have you spent any knee time on that decision, Amos?' " He shook his head. "I've had to back up and take another look at quite a few of my bright ideas."

Bonnie sidled up next to our booth. "Good morning there, Dewey," she said, patting him on the back. "The usual?"

Dewey crossed his arms across his chest and gazed up at the ceiling. "No, ma'am," he said in a deep voice. "I believe I'll start out with a sausage and cheese omelet. And use cheddar cheese on that. Four links of Ruby's homemade spicy sausage. And a side of blueberry pancakes. Lots of butter and syrup. Oh, and don't forget to bring an extra order of those wonderful hash browns. I like mine extra-crispy around the edges." He sighed with contentment and gazed at Bonnie with a twinkle in his eye.

"You bet. Right away. Poached eggs, melon, and a dry English muffin coming right up."

Dewey's pleased expression turned into a scowl. "My goodness, woman," he grumbled. "You sure know how to take the fun out of a meal."

Bonnie leaned over and kissed him on the head while Amos and I snickered. "We're just trying to take care of you, you crotchety old geezer."

"Bonnie," I said, interrupting Dewey's mumbling about too many people telling him what to do, "can we pay you ahead of time for our ticket? Amos and I have to get to the sheriff's office in Hugoton, and I want to get out of here as soon as we eat."

Bonnie came over to our side of the booth and leaned closer to me. "Sure. That's no problem. Let me total it and I'll bring it back. You can just pay me at the table."

I thanked her, but she stayed where she was. Obviously there was something else she wanted to say.

"I hope this doesn't offend you, Ivy," she said quietly. "I overheard someone say that the sheriff suspected you of killing Dela. Some folks said you had words with her last night at the city council meeting. Are you really under suspicion?"

I was startled to hear someone actually verbalize it. The idea had been floating around in my mind, but while it was locked inside my head, it seemed much more harmless.

"She's not actually a suspect, Bonnie," Amos said, coming to my defense. "The sheriff has to start ruling out people. Since Dela was killed in Ivy's drive-way, she's got to be eliminated."

I was glad he hadn't mentioned that my fingerprints were also on the murder weapon. That was a story I didn't want circulating around town.

Bonnie looked around and leaned in even closer. "Listen, I don't like to repeat things I hear, but this place is a hotbed of gossip." She glanced at the Widdles, but they were deep in conversation. "I've heard more than one person say that Delaphine Shackleford was fooling around. You know, with someone besides her husband. I've been wondering if it might be important."

"It just might," Amos interjected. "Do you have any idea who it was?"

She shook her head. "Not a clue, Amos. If I'd wanted to find out, I probably could have, but as I said, I don't cotton to gossip."

"If you do hear anything more," Amos said, "will you let me know?"

Bonnie straightened up. "You bet. I have a feeling the stories are going to be flying like bees in heat. Poor Dela will be skewered six ways to Sunday before this thing is all said and done." With that, she turned and hurried off to put in Dewey's order.

"I can't believe the sheriff suspects you," Dewey blustered. His face was red with indignation. "While he's wasting taxpayer money bothering you, the real murderer could be halfway to Timbuktu by now."

"It's like Amos said, Dewey. He has to question everyone who's connected in any way, no matter how slight. He'll clear me soon. Please calm down. It's not good for you to get so upset."

"Well, I just never heard of anything so ridiculous."

At that moment it wasn't Dewey's diabetes that concerned me. It was his blood pressure. I reached over and stroked his arm. "Don't worry. Everything will be fine. I promise." My reassurances seemed to do the trick. Dewey's color began to return to normal. Feeling that he would be all right, I turned my attention to Amos. "What do you think about that? If Dela really was having an affair, the sheriff should know, shouldn't he?"

"Of course," Amos said solemnly. "If there's proof. Then we'd have to figure out what it means."

"It means that her boyfriend is a suspect," I said. "And so is Barney. Look, Amos, we need to be very careful about spreading rumors. Maybe I can poke around a little and find out something."

"I think you need to keep out of this," Dewey said gruffly. "If you don't stop sticking your nose in other people's business, you might get it chopped off one of these days."

"Dewey Tater," I said louder than I meant to, "I do not stick my nose in other people's business. Somehow I just seem to tumble into it. Besides, when someone is killed in my driveway, and I'm suspected, it becomes *my* business!"

"About that pretty nose of yours," Amos said. "You still need to find someone to stay with you for a few days, at least until we have a better idea as to why Dela was killed. How about calling your mom and asking her to come a little early? She and your dad plan to be here in a couple of weeks anyway."

I sighed. "It's not like they can take vacation whenever they want to, you know. They're running a mission. I don't know if she can just up and leave because her grown-up daughter has gotten herself into another mess."

"I understand, but maybe she can come now and your dad can run things by himself for a little while. Someone needs to stay with you, and I can't think of anyone else. Emily's taking care of a baby, and according to you, I can't spend another night in our house without a chaperone."

"Why can't I move in for a while?" Dewey said. "At least until Margie gets here. Living in that small apartment over the store can get downright boring. A change of scenery would be nice."

Amos slapped the top of our table. "I think that would be a great idea. You could ride in to work together each morning. What do you think, Ivy?"

I smiled at the both of them. "I can't think of anyone I'd rather have as a roommate. Let's do it. And I'll call my mom tonight. I guess it doesn't hurt to ask." Of course, I actually could think of someone else I would rather have living in my house, but I'd have to wait a few more weeks for that.

Bonnie showed up with our food, so further conversation was suspended for a while. I tried to concentrate on my breakfast, but the idea of Dela having an affair made my stomach feel queasy. All I could see was Barney's funny, happy face, standing at the altar in that ludicrous tuxedo. His wife was gone—his marriage ended. Was he getting ready to receive another terrible shock? A betrayal that Dela would never have a chance to repair? Or could it be that Barney wasn't the person he seemed to be? Could he have killed his wife with a chopstick from their wedding? I began to wish I'd never seen those goofy pictures, but for some reason, they made me feel very protective toward Dela and her memory. While Dewey and Amos chatted about something else, I sent a prayer heavenward, asking for help to uncover the truth about the murder of Dela Shackleford.

6

"I thought you said you knew this was standard procedure, Ivy."

Amos's attempts to make me feel more relaxed weren't working. Even though I'd done my best to calm Dewey's concerns about the sheriff's interest in me, there simply wasn't any way I could reconcile the concept of being fingerprinted with anything other than criminal behavior. "Will there be a mug shot?" I asked Amos, using what he referred to as my "whiney voice." Newspaper reports with matching pictures paraded through my head. Celebrities who held little resemblance to their Hollywood glamour shots, staring at the camera with that stunned deer-in-the-headlights expression on their faces. Would I look just as ridiculous?

"Of course not. You're not being charged with a crime. For crying out loud, Ivy. Quit letting your imagination run away with you."

"I'm trying not to, but we're driving to the sheriff's office in a patrol car, and I'm going to be fingerprinted like a common criminal. It's hard not to feel like I'm on the wrong side of the law."

Amos drew a deep breath and blew it out slowly. "Okay, you believe whatever you want to. When you get this way, there's nothing I can do about it."

He directed his attention to the highway. Conditions were beginning to get treacherous. A snowstorm had moved into the area. Most of western Kansas was getting a nice winter blanket of white, but since Winter Break already had about six inches on the ground, we were now up to about nine inches. Our windshield wipers beat a steady rhythm, trying to push away big, fat snowflakes that blew against our field of vision. It reminded me of the day I first came back to Winter Break to bury Aunt Bitty and decide what was going to happen to her beloved bookstore. I drove into town at night, snow almost blinding me, my own windshield wipers barely able to keep up. My intention was to get things squared away and get back to my life in Wichita. Yet here I was, a little over a year later, running the bookstore, engaged to the man of my dreams, and feeling as if I'd finally found the path God had prepared for me. It occurred to me that even in these strange circumstances, God's plan hadn't changed. This turn of events wasn't a surprise to Him, nor was it too much for Him to handle. "God doesn't ask us to walk by what we see and think, Ivy," Bitty used to say. "He tells us to walk by faith. What does faith tell you?" What I could see and feel was telling me that things didn't look good, but my faith told me that God had everything under control. It was my job to lean on His promises and trust Him to carry me through whatever came my way. I made the decision to go with the voice of faith, and as I did, a sense of peace settled over me and pushed away the self-pity that had seemed so strong only moments before. I scooted closer to Amos and hooked my arm around his. "I'm sorry. You're right. The most important thing is that we find out who killed Dela. I've only been thinking about myself."

The tightness in Amos's jaw relaxed, and he smiled at me. "I guess I'm a little tense, too. I'm sorry. You're the last person in the world who would ever hurt anyone. My deputy sheriff side seems to be in conflict with my fiancé side."

I squeezed his arm. "As someone who loves both your sides, I suggest you call a truce. Everything will be okay." I meant what I said, but as we pulled into a parking space in front of the sheriff's office, I felt a twinge of alarm. I made a conscious effort to reject it.

"Hello, Parker. Miss Towers." The sheriff's deep voice greeted us as we stepped inside the small office. Sheriff Hitchens stood next to a desk belonging to Marge McCarty. Nicknamed Big Marge because of her size, she didn't help to foster an atmosphere of friendliness to visitors who happened to wander into the sheriff's office. Of course, most guests didn't cross the doorway of their own volition. Unfortunately, I was one of those.

"Good morning, Sheriff. Hello, Marge." I flashed them both a smile I hoped was the very expression of total and complete innocence.

Sheriff Hitchens didn't seem moved, and Big Marge glowered at me. But that was par for the course with Marge. I reassured myself with the knowledge that she looked the same way at everyone.

"Someone from the KBI was supposed to be here this morning and interview you, but I guess a little snow was too much for him. Probably didn't want to mess up his cute little suit. So I guess it's just me. Lucky you. This way, please." We followed the sheriff to a room in the back where he quickly rolled some ink from a pad over a glass plate. He placed each of my fingers on the plate and moved them back and forth, getting the best possible coverage. After that, he placed them against several cards and handed me a damp towel when he was finished. It only took a few minutes, and it wasn't as bad as I had imagined. Then he put on plastic gloves, grabbed a long cotton swab, and motioned for me to open my mouth. He ran the swab over the inside of my cheek rather vigorously then dropped it into a plastic bag which he labeled and put in a metal container.

"That's all there is to it, Miss Towers," he said when he was finished. "Not as bad as you thought, was it?"

I shook my head. "No. Thank you, Sheriff."

He walked over and pulled the door closed, cutting us off from Big Marge and the outside world. "Sit down, please." He pointed to an old upholstered chair that had seen better days. I took a seat, trying to avoid the big rip in the fake leather. Amos came up next to me and put his arm on the back of the chair, resting it on my shoulders.

"When you saw Mrs. Shackleford Tuesday night at the town meeting, was she wearin' the same clothes she had on that morning?"

"Yes, she was."

He reached for an envelope lying on a desk behind him. He pulled out some papers and handed one to me. "This is a list of everything we found on her. I'd like you to look it over. Tell me if anything is missin'—or if there's somethin' on the list that you *didn't* notice that morning." He looked back and forth between Amos and me. "Coffee?"

Although it was a nice gesture, it sounded more like an order the way he said it. We both nodded, even though I really didn't want any.

When he left the room I whispered to Amos, "What is he looking for on this list?"

"Anything different," Amos replied in a low voice. "Something that changed. It could point to motive. Especially if there's an item missing."

I looked the list over and was shocked to see that it even listed Dela's underwear. Her clothing, her purse and its contents, along with her jewelry, were also cataloged. "Her attaché case isn't here, but she probably took it home before going to the meeting." I started to put the sheet of paper back on the desk, but Amos grabbed my arm.

"Look it over again, Ivy," he said sternly. "I know it seems like a waste of time, but if you see anything, anything at all, it could really help."

I sighed and glanced over the record again. First I read through the contents of her purse: *Makeup case, pocketbook with credit cards, driver's license, twenty-seven dollars in cash, two lipsticks, set of keys, aspirin, three writing pens, small notebook, breath mints.* Then I started on the other list of belongings: *red velvet skirt, red velvet matching jacket, black boots, gold and green ring with matching earrings and necklace, diamond and white gold wedding set.* . . The sound of the door opening behind me drew my attention away from the macabre list.

"How's it comin', Miss Towers?" The sheriff's booming tone made me jump, even though I knew he'd come back. He had the kind of voice that demanded attention.

"The only thing I don't see is her attaché case, Sheriff. But I imagine she took it home before the meeting that night."

Hitchens handed Amos and me each a cup of coffee in a Styrofoam cup. "What was inside the case?"

I briefly explained my discussion that morning with Dela, including the pictures of different wedding scenarios.

"Could there have been anything else inside that case?"

"I—I don't think so," I said, trying to remember. "I believe it only held pictures and ideas for weddings. Of course, I can't be completely sure."

"And she kept the chopsticks in her purse?"

"No. Originally they were also in the case. She put them in her purse after she had a hard time closing the clasp of the box they were in."

The sheriff leaned against the side of the desk and stared at me. "Is there anything else you can tell me?"

I glanced over the list once more. When I got to Dela's jewelry, I suddenly remembered something. "Her bracelet." I looked up at the sheriff. "Her bracelet's not here. The only reason I even recall it was because it seemed too big for her. At one point, it almost slid off her hand."

Hitchens took a small notepad out of his pocket and started writing in it. "Describe the bracelet, please."

"It was quite beautiful. Silver with clear rhinestones and..." I tried to bring a picture of the bracelet back to my mind. "Blue stones on the sides. I don't know, Sheriff, I didn't stare at it. I just noticed that it didn't seem to fit her."

Hitchens wrote a few more things in his notebook. Then he put it down and reached out for the list I still held in my lap. I handed it to him.

"Thank you, Miss Towers. That's quite helpful. Since she probably went home before the evenin' meetin', we'll check with her husband to see if she actually did drop off her case and her bracelet. Of course, if we can't find them, it would indicate that they were stolen."

I choked back a laugh. Sheriff Hitchens didn't look like someone who would find anything about a murder case particularly funny. "I really can't see that, Sheriff. The wedding pictures wouldn't be a good motive for murder, and the bracelet was obviously costume jewelry." I wanted to add that perhaps it would be prudent to track down all the humiliated bridesmaids from the go-go wedding and Dela's nuptials, but again, I doubted Hitchens would see the humor in my suggestion.

The sheriff slid the list of Dela's belongings back into the folder. "Are you a jewelry expert, Miss Towers?"

"No, but if Dela's bracelet was the real thing, it would have been worth a great deal of money. I doubt that she would be wearing it during the day. I also think she would have had it shortened to fit her. She wouldn't want to lose something that valuable."

Sheriff Hitchens raised his eyebrows and gave me a slow grin. "Quite an interesting observation. I've heard about you, Miss Towers. How you fancy yourself to be some kind of amateur detective." His smile disappeared and was replaced with something close to a snarl. "Let me make this perfectly clear. This isn't one of those silly novels where somebody who thinks they're Sherlock Holmes, Junior, outsmarts actual law enforcement personnel. I advise you to stay on your side of the fence and let me do my job. If you get in my way, even one time, I'll fix up a cell for you, and you'll sit out the whole investigation as a guest of the county. Do I make myself clear?"

I felt blood race to my face. I wanted to defend myself. Finding my aunt's killer and uncovering a murder that had happened many years ago in Winter Break hadn't happened because I was trying to be an "amateur detective." The suggestion was not only untrue, but it made it seem as if each situation was nothing more than some kind of trivial fishing expedition. And they were anything but that. I started to say something, when Amos squeezed my shoulder.

"Is there anything else, Sheriff?" His words were carefully measured. I knew he was close to losing his temper, and I couldn't let it happen. Amos loved his job almost as much as he loved me.

Hitchens cleared his throat. "As a matter of fact, there is. First of all, I want you both to keep the missin' case and bracelet to yourselves. Until I find out if they were taken from the car, I don't want this information punted around by the bumpkins that hang around Ruby's Café. Secondly, I think you need to know, Miss Towers, that we received a call around eight thirty this morning from someone claiming that you killed Delaphine Shackleford."

I know my mouth dropped open, and I felt Amos's grip tighten on my shoulder. This wasn't good. I gently pried his fingers off before he caused me permanent damage.

"Before you get all hot and bothered, it wasn't anything I'd begin to take seriously." Sheriff Hitchens stood up and walked over to the door. "The woman believes you killed Mrs. Shackleford because you didn't want her on some library board." He seemed amused by our reactions. "I don't honestly think you killed her over some silly, small-town appointment. But I think you need to know that you may have an enemy out there. Deputy Parker will tell you that we always get a few nutcases who call in tips when there's a murder. We learn to spot the phonies from the real thing." He swung the door open and waved at us to leave. As Amos walked past him, the sheriff grabbed his arm. "I want you to keep an eye on things in Winter Break, Deputy. It will be a few days before we start getting much information from the coroner's office or the KBI boys. I want you to poke around and see if you can find someone who had a real reason for wantin' Mrs. Shackleford dead." He fastened his narrowed eyes on me. "And I expect you to use *your* training skills. I don't want to hear that your girlfriend here is stickin' her nose in where it doesn't belong."

This was the second time in one day my nose was the topic of conversation. I was getting tired of it. "Thank you, Sheriff," I said as sweetly as I could. "I'm sure Amos won't need my help. He's quite capable of doing his job."

Hitchens opened his mouth to reply but was cut off by Big Marge, who was holding the phone next to her ear. "Sheriff, there's another one," she said loudly. "This time it's in Morgan City."

Hitchens swore under his breath and grabbed his coat. "You come with me," he barked at Amos.

"You better call Dewey and ask him to come and get you." Amos hugged me and ran out the door, right on the heels of the sheriff. It was like some kind of instant evacuation. I didn't even have time to say good-bye. I could hear the tires of the sheriff's patrol car squeal as he pulled out of his parking space.

I turned around to find Big Marge staring at me. Well, this was going to be fun. I opened my mouth to ask if I could use the phone, but she pointed at a desk in the corner where another phone sat. While she began contacting other deputies and ordering them to Morgan City, I called Dewey. I glanced at my watch. It was only a little after ten o'clock in the morning, but I felt like I'd been at the sheriff's office all day.

As I sat near the front window, waiting for Dewey under the watchful eye of Big Marge, I kept wondering who in the world would suspect me of killing Dela. Was it someone who knew me? Someone who really believed I was capable of such a heinous crime because I wanted to be president of the library board? The idea was ridiculous. Still, it was disconcerting to be accused of murder.

I forced my thoughts back to Dela. Then I remembered Bonnie's comment about Dela having a boyfriend. I'd meant to bring it up to the sheriff. Now, I was glad I hadn't. I'd let Amos do it. I needed to heed the two warnings I'd already received and leave the investigation to him. Besides, I had a wedding to plan. I tried to mentally picture my wedding to-do list, but my thoughts kept wandering to that phone call. Did someone in Winter Break actually believe I was a murderer? Who could have made that phone call? And why?

7

Due to the snowstorm, Dewey and I didn't get back to Winter Break until after one o'clock. He dropped me off at the bookstore and went across the street to the Food-a-Rama. Because of the weather, we decided to have dinner at Ruby's then head to church without going home first. The road that led to my house could be tricky in the snow. I knew Amos would be glad to drive us back after the service. His patrol car was equipped with special tires that kept him out of ditches when the roads were icy or snow packed. My car, on the other hand, didn't seem to have any capacity for traction. Amos had pulled me out of so many snowbanks we'd pretty much abandoned using my car in the winter.

I sat down at my desk, looked up the number of the mission in China, and phoned my mother even though I knew it was very early in Hong Kong. I figured that if I'd ever had a good reason for waking up my parents, being suspected of murder was probably it.

After a few false starts, she finally figured out who I was. I tried to make the situation sound better than it was, but it didn't work.

"Another murder?" My mother's tone generally got higher the more upset she was. At that moment, I was pretty sure there were some operatic sopranos out there who would be jealous of her amazing reach. "What is going on out there? What is Winter Break, the murder capital of the world?"

As I assured her that we were still a long way from that distinction, I could hear my father speaking in the background. He's the calming influence in our family. Gradually, my mother's voice drifted down into normal ranges.

"I'll try to book a flight out this afternoon. But I probably won't get into Wichita until late tomorrow evening. Can Amos come to Wichita to pick me up?" Wichita was the closest large airport. It was possible to get a commuter plane to one of the smaller cities nearer to us, but they were horribly expensive.

"We'll figure something out, Mom. Just call me back at the house and let me know your flight information and exactly when you'll get in."

"Now, Ivy. That's *if* I can get a flight out today. I'll do my best."

"I hope this isn't going to cause you too much trouble." I had to wonder if dragging my mother away from her missions work was the right thing to do. Was I being selfish?

"Nonsense," she said. "We were coming in a few weeks anyway for the wedding. I've even talked to your father about arriving early so I could help. I'll be thrilled to see you and Amos." A male voice drifted through the receiver. "Just a minute, Ivy. Your father wants to say hello."

"Hi, *gong zhu*! I just wanted to say *wo ai ni*!" My father's deep Santa Claus laugh burst through the receiver.

Although in Mandarin *princess* didn't sound quite so delicate, gong zhu was my dad's new nickname for me. My previous moniker had been *bao bei*, which meant "precious." When he'd graduated to *wo de xin gan bao bei*, I'd been forced to ask him to find something else since it actually translated into "my precious." I was pretty sure even nasty hobbitses would find the phrase rather spine-tingling. Of course, my parents hadn't seen a movie for years, so when I tried to explain the reasoning behind my request, I ended up sounding slightly insane.

"Hello, *Ba ba*. I love you, too."

"I understand your mother is coming a little early. Wish I could join her, but I have a few things to wrap up here."

"That's okay. I'll just be happy to see you."

I said good-bye to my father and then my mother got back on the phone to reassure me that she would let me know her flight arrangements as soon as she could. After we hung up, I realized how much I missed them. My relationship with my mother had certainly improved since I'd moved to Winter Break. She had been horrified when I made the decision to make my home here and run my aunt's bookstore. Life in a small town wasn't my mother's cup of tea. But we'd finally come to an understanding and now, next to Amos, she was my best friend.

"Everything okay?" Isaac stood next to my desk, a look of concern on his face.

"Yes. My mother's coming to stay with me. She should get into Wichita sometime tomorrow night." I sighed. "I'm a little concerned about how we're going to get her here. With Amos spending so much time on these bank robberies, I'm not sure he'll be able to get the time off to pick her up. My car is useless in this kind of weather, and she won't want to rent a car. She doesn't like to drive in the snow."

His wizened face crinkled into a frown. "I wish I could help. I'm so useless in situations like these."

Isaac didn't drive. It really wasn't necessary in Winter Break, but that wasn't why he didn't own a car. He'd given up driving years ago, after being involved in a fatal accident.

"Don't worry," I said. "We'll figure out something."

He pulled a chair up next to my desk. "This rash of bank robberies seems so strange, doesn't it? I would think someone who wanted to acquire a large sum of money would target one of the larger financial institutions."

I sighed and leaned back in my chair. A look out the window told me it was snowing even harder. "Amos said the same thing. I think it's one of the reasons they're having such a hard time finding this guy. In a way, hitting smaller banks is pretty smart. They're easier to rob, but you're right, I don't imagine they keep much money readily available."

The front door of the bookstore flew open, helped along by a hefty gust of wind. Amos stepped inside. He stomped his boots on the entry mat and pulled off his gloves. "Boy, it sure feels nice and warm in here. It's awful out there."

After hanging up his coat and removing his boots, he came over and parked himself on the edge of my desk.

"So what happened?" I asked. "Isaac and I were just talking about the bank robberies."

He rubbed his hands together to warm them. "It's the strangest thing I've ever seen. It appears to be one man. Somehow, he knows just when to hit the banks."

"What do you mean?" Isaac asked. "Is one time better than another?"

"Yep. Usually in small towns, there's not much cash in the till. Except on certain occasions. Like the bank in Mollyville. The only real money that comes in is after a big weekend at the Mollyville Hotel Restaurant. You know, that big tourist attraction on Highway 54?"

We both nodded. Converted from a hotel built in the 1800s, the Mollyville Hotel drew people from all over Kansas—and other states. They only served one thing: family-styled fried chicken dinners with all the fixings. It was always busy, and those who didn't make reservations generally didn't have much luck getting in.

"So this guy strikes after someone brings in a large deposit?" I asked.

Amos took off his hat and smoothed his honey blond hair. "That's what's happened every time. In Chevron he struck the Savings and Loan right after the county fair."

"But that would mean he knows the local routines," Isaac said. "So it would appear that he is someone known by the residents."

Amos nodded. "That's exactly what it means." The frustration in his voice was evident. "But how could one guy know so much about so many different towns? We've checked with all kinds of people. No one has any idea who it could be."

"What about people who don't belong?" I asked. "Someone new in the area?"

"We've tried that, too. No one has reported anyone suspicious." He chuckled. "Except in Brinkman. There was a story about a strange man hanging around the bank the day before the robbery. Turned out to be a sign painter from Liberal. The bank was updating the lettering on the front door. He wasn't too happy about being suspected of bank robbery."

"Surely the banks in Stevens County are taking better precautions now," Isaac said.

"We've been doing everything possible to get them to implement necessary safety measures. So far only one of them even had a security camera. And it wasn't working. I'm not sure what's going on in other counties where this guy's been, but my guess is they're doing the same things we are to try to prevent another robbery."

"I haven't heard any reports of violence," Isaac said. "I guess that's a blessing."

"Unfortunately, that's not true," Amos said. "He shot a customer in Chevron who tried to stop him."

"Why, Amos," I said, "this is the first time I've heard that. It wasn't in the newspaper."

Amos shrugged. "The wound wasn't serious. The robber shot the guy in the leg, but he's fine. We're keeping that particular detail under wraps along with a few other things. In any investigation, it's important to have a few secrets. Helps us to make sure we've got the right person."

"But shouldn't people know he's armed?" I asked. "For their own protection?"

"The banks in Kansas know about it. But to be honest, I don't think he's dangerous. He's never tried to hurt anyone else. The man who was shot made a foolish move. Our robber friend fired in an attempt to stop him, not kill him."

"What about his getaway car?" I asked. "Has it been seen?"

Amos crossed his arms across his chest and stared at us. "Are you two thinking about joining the investigation?"

"Don't be silly," I snapped. "We're just interested. It's better than thinking about Dela's murder."

Amos sighed. "Well, you're right about that. And yes, his cars have been spotted almost every time."

"You said 'cars,'" Isaac said. "He drives more than one?"

"He steals someone's car, drives it to the bank, and robs it. Then he drops the car off somewhere and takes his own vehicle to make his getaway. Actually, it's pretty smart. Pinching a car in a small town is too easy. People leave their keys in the ignition. They think they're immune because they're not in the big city." He shook his finger at us. "And before you ask, there are no fingerprints, so he's obviously wearing gloves. Not too unusual in the winter. And we haven't found any usable tire tracks. Either the stolen car is found in a parking lot, or it's abandoned in a place where there's so many vehicles going in and out, we can't tell what he's driving. This morning we found the truck he used parked at a large twenty-four-hour bingo parlor outside of Morgan City. So many people had come and gone, we couldn't get any information on him or his car."

"Well, Deputy," Isaac said, "I don't envy you with this one."

"I have a hunch you won't be chasing this guy much longer," I said.

Amos frowned at me. "What do you mean?"

"He can't keep this up. He's attracting too much attention. My guess is he's trying to grab as much money as he can from these little banks because they're easier to hit. That's going to change, and he knows it. I'll bet you a jar of huckleberry jelly that his reign of terror will come to an end any day now."

"You might be right," Amos said thoughtfully. "Which means if we don't catch him soon, we may never bring him in. And that reminds me. Alma gave us four more jars of jelly. And I've got about ten more jars of Bubba Weber's honey."

"Bubba's going to have to find a place to store his honey," I said crossly. "First he fills up your house, now he's loading up my basement. Cecil built those shelves downstairs to house Marion's preserves, not Bubba Weber's honey."

Amos grinned. "Are you thinking about putting up your own preserves?"

"Even if I wanted to, I don't have the room. I'm too busy hoarding honey."

Amos shrugged. "You're right, but it won't be much longer. Dewey's cleared out one of his back storage rooms in the store. He's going to start keeping the honey there."

"Good. I like Bubba, but this has gone on too long."

"After we're married, we're going to have to do something with that basement. It needs to be updated, and we need to do something different with the laundry. Carrying clothes up and down the stairs is too much trouble."

I smiled at him. "I like my basement. It has character. And I don't mind carrying the laundry. It's good exercise."

"A lot of the older houses around here were equipped with dumbwaiters," Isaac interjected. "Besides the washing, basements were used to store fruits and vegetables. It was cooler down there and produce kept longer. It was a simple matter to send food or clothes up and down with the dumbwaiter."

"Unfortunately, my house doesn't seem to have one," I said. "But maybe my handsome, soon-to-be husband can design something himself."

Amos chuckled. "Or your handsome soon-to-be husband can find a place upstairs to move the washer and dryer. I don't like those stairs. They're too rickety. Besides, you've got to be tired of chasing Miss Skiffins out of the basement every time you open the door."

My small calico cat had developed an obsession for huckleberry jelly. I'd caught her on the kitchen counter more than once, licking the jelly off my toast or English muffin. She'd figured out there was jelly in the basement, but thankfully she hadn't figured out how to open the jars yet.

Isaac stood up and offered Amos his chair. "Well, this was a most stimulating discussion, but I need to go home and prepare for church." He smiled and looked a little embarrassed. "Alma and I will also be dining at Ruby's before this evening's service."

I wanted to tease him about Alma, but I'd found out the hard way that there were certain things Isaac took very seriously. And his relationship with Alma was one of them.

He excused himself and left through the sitting room. He lived right next door. In fact, his home was actually part of the bookstore. Aunt Bitty had turned part of the building into an apartment for her faithful employee and close friend.

Amos slumped down into the chair vacated by Isaac. "Let's quit talking about the bank robberies for a while, okay? I need a break. This whole thing is giving me a headache." He scooted the chair closer to me and reached for my hand. "Sorry about this morning. I respect Sheriff Hitchens, but sometimes he can be a real jerk."

"I'm okay. Don't worry about me. Are you going to check with Barney about Dela's attaché case and bracelet?"

He nodded. "Yeah, Hitchens asked me to follow up and let him know. I can't imagine the killing had anything to do with either one of them. Dela probably left the case at home because she didn't need it for the meeting, and if the bracelet was as loose as you say, maybe she took it off because she didn't want to lose it."

I stared at him for a moment. "Yeah, maybe."

"What's wrong? Is there something bothering you?"

"This sounds silly, Amos, but the more I think about it, the more I realize that the bracelet didn't belong."

Amos cocked his head to the side and looked at me quizzically. "What do you mean, it 'didn't belong'?"

"Dela was always so *coordinated*. Everything went together, you know. Fashionwise, colorwise. But the bracelet didn't go with her outfit. It was too dressy and had blue stones set in silver. Her earrings, necklace, and ring all had red stones set in gold. Dela was always super coordinated. Her jewelry always matched her outfits and all the pieces matched each other."

Amos pursed his lips. "That's interesting." He stood up. "Why don't I pick you up around five for dinner? I think I'll run over to Barney's now. If the bracelet's not there. . ."

"It could mean something," I finished for him.

Amos learned over and kissed me on the nose. "Just for the record, I love your nose. You can stick it into my business whenever you want to."

I reached up and hugged him as hard as I could. "Thank you. Maybe I'll only stick it where it's wanted from now on."

"That might be a good idea, for a while at least."

I suddenly remembered my mother and asked him about picking her up tomorrow night.

"I don't think that will be a problem. Our robber keeps banker's hours. Let me know as soon as you have all the flight information."

After he left, I realized I had only a little over an hour before we left for Ruby's. I cleaned my desk and checked my e-mail. I had several inquiries about books. Noel had sent me a message about some new editions he'd acquired for the library, including an entire set of Charles Dickens. I wanted to let Hope and Faith know, and I also wanted to see how the library was coming along, so I decided to have Amos pick me up there. It would also give me a chance to see Faith. We'd become really close over the summer. She'd been despondent over the death of her parents in an automobile accident, and I was someone who was willing to listen. Someone outside of her family. She was living with her aunt, Inez Baumgartner, Emily's mother. She had definitely made strides toward healing, and working in the library had given her something constructive to do.

I wrote a note on a sheet of paper telling Amos that I would be at the library and taped it to the front door. Thankfully, the glass storm door would keep it from getting soaked by blowing snow. It was a primitive way to communicate, but there wasn't any cell phone service in Winter Break. Unless another larger city sprang up near us, no cellular company was going to put up a tower for a town our size. At first, it was a major inconvenience. But now, it didn't bother me much at all. Except for times like this. I could call Amos's dispatcher, but unfortunately, that was Big Marge. I could have also called Barney, but I didn't want to disturb him quite yet.

Trekking two blocks in a blizzard isn't easy. One step forward is usually accompanied by two steps back, but I finally made it. I had to bang my fist on the library door since it was locked. Finally, Hope pulled up the shade on the window and peered out to see who was making so much racket.

"Ivy!" she said after pulling the door open. "Get in here before you freeze solid."

I gratefully stumbled inside. It took awhile to get my blood circulating again, but after stomping my feet a few times and rubbing my hands together, I felt confident enough to venture forward. I gazed around the room and was thrilled to see the progress that had been made.

"It looks great," I said as I took off my coat. "You two have really been working hard."

Hope grinned. Her short ash blond hair and turned-up nose always made me think of a pixie I saw once in an illustrated book. Her small stature added to the picture in my head.

"I think we'll be ready to open right after Valentine's Day. You've brought us so many books it's taking us a long time to catalog everything." She laughed. "Isn't that wonderful?"

I was delighted by Hope's enthusiasm. When she first came to Winter Break, the grief of losing her grandmother was still very fresh. She was so quiet and introverted, I wondered sometimes if she would ever come out of her shell. But here she was, excited about the library and making new friends.

"Hi, Ivy!" Faith came around the corner of a long row of bookshelves. She was another person who had changed after coming to Winter Break. Strange how so many people had found redemption in this small town.

"Hello! I was just telling Hope how impressed I am by how far along the library has come. It sure looks better than it did the first time Dewey showed us this old building."

Hope held out her hand for my coat. I slid it off and handed it to her. She carefully laid it across the back of a nearby chair.

Faith laughed. "I was really excited about the library until we stepped inside the front door. Boy, I wasn't certain whether this place was a blessing or a curse!"

I shook my head. "After the feed store closed down, Dewey just locked the door and forgot about it. Too bad the mice didn't forget."

"And the birds who found their way in through the hole in the roof," Hope said. "But then so many people pitched in to clean it up and make repairs, it came back to life." She smiled and looked around. "I think it's just perfect now."

The building was still pretty old, and it certainly wasn't what I'd call "perfect," but it definitely had charm. The exposed pipes that ran across the ceiling had been painted white, and some of the men from church had painted the walls a deep green, repaired the wooden floor, and built shelves that ran along the walls and down through the middle of the main room. Up near the front was a large desk for checkouts and a seating area set aside for library clients. We still needed some nice, comfy chairs for future bookworms. So far, we'd only collected a few beat-up folding chairs from the church basement.

The library reminded me only a little of the bookstore. It would never have quite the same relaxed ambience of Miss Bitty's, but it would still be a terrific resource for the residents of Winter Break. Although my interest was heading more and more toward collectible and rare volumes, I would always keep some special volumes to be read by residents who wanted to enjoy a cold winter afternoon next to a crackling fire or hide out from the rain and dream between the pages of a book. Bitty would have wanted it that way.

I handed Hope a list of the new books Noel was donating to us.

"Oh, my," she said softly. "A complete set of Dickens? And the Father Brown mysteries? How wonderful."

G. K. Chesterton was a favorite of mine. His character, Father Brown, had entertained me on many occasions. "And I'm working on completing our Agatha Christie selections." I smiled. "With all the Nancy Drew editions we already have, we're going to end up with a wonderful selection of mysteries." Hope and Faith both grinned at my comment. We were all mystery buffs.

"How about some coffee, Ivy?" Faith asked. "Inez gave us her extra coffee-maker so we could have something hot to drink while we're working. It does get a little cold in here when the wind blows hard."

Although I'd felt warm when I'd first come inside, now I could feel a definite draft around the windows. "I'd love some coffee. I'll also speak to Dewey about making this place a little more airtight. No one will want to stay very long if we can't keep the winter wind out."

I took my coat from the back of the chair where Hope had placed it and put it around my shoulders. Then I sat down in the chair. "If I'm in the way, just kick me out. Amos will be picking me up for dinner in a while."

"Don't be silly," Hope said. "We can visit while I finish cataloging this stack of books."

We spent some time talking about literature. Then the discussion turned to Dela's murder and my upcoming nuptials. I was beginning to see that both events were going to get tied together in people's minds since almost everyone knew that Dela had been my wedding planner. For the first time, I started to wonder if Amos and I shouldn't postpone our marriage for a couple of months. The danger was that we could find ourselves waiting until spring. Although Winter Break usually got more measurable snow than anyplace else in the state, waiting until April was taking a chance. I really wanted to be married in the snow—on Valentine's Day.

I'd just started telling Hope and Faith about my trouble finding a gown, when someone pounded on the front door. I was closest to the door so I opened it to find Amos standing outside. As he stepped through the door, a blast of cold air pushed snow in after him.

"Sorry," he said, looking down at the clump of snow quickly melting on the small carpet in front of the door. "It's snowing like blue blazes out there—even for Winter Break."

"No problem," Hope said, jumping up from where she'd been sitting on the floor with a pile of books. "We've been cleaning it up all day." She grabbed a towel from the desk and tossed it down toward Amos's wet boots. "Just stomp on it some so it will soak up the water."

"How about a quick cup of coffee?" I asked him. "We still have plenty of time."

He grinned. "Sounds great. The heater in the patrol car is having a tough time against the wind. I'm frozen to the bone."

Faith poked her head around the corner of one of the bookshelves where she'd been working. "I'll get it. How do you take it, Amos?"

"Black is fine," he said. "Right now the only thing I care about is how hot it is."

"Excuse me for a few minutes, will you?" Hope said. "I'm missing a book. It's probably at the bottom of one of those boxes in the back room."

"If you need any help let me know," Amos said, scooping up the wet towel from the floor and handing it to me.

She thanked him and disappeared, leaving Amos and me alone. I laid the wet towel on top of some plastic sheeting in the corner.

"Did you talk to Barney?" I asked in a low voice.

Amos's gaze moved toward the spot where Hope had been standing. "Yes. Dela's satchel is there."

"What about the bracelet?"

Amos looked around once again. "He didn't know what I was talking about. He even showed me Dela's jewelry collection. It's huge, but I went through it carefully. There wasn't anything like what you described: a silver bracelet with clear rhinestones and blue stones on the sides."

"So it wasn't there?"

He shook his head. "That bracelet's gone, Ivy. Whoever killed Dela took it. All we have to do is find it and we've got our murderer."

The sound of shattering glass startled us. We turned around to find Faith staring at us, the coffee cup lying in pieces on the floor, and her face as white as the snow swirling around outside the window.

8

We checked to see if Faith had been burned by the coffee that splashed up against her jeans, but she was fine. It was obvious to Amos and me that her reaction was connected to our discussion, but Faith wouldn't admit it. She kept repeating that she'd simply lost her grip on the coffee cup. Her expression was grim and she was obviously distracted. Hope kept shooting me worried looks behind Faith's back, but all I could do was shrug at her. There was no way I could tell her what we'd been talking about since Sheriff Hitchens had warned us to keep our mouths shut about the bracelet.

Amos made some excuse about wanting to get to Ruby's before it got any later. I hugged Hope and Faith before I left. I could feel how tense Faith was under her sweatshirt. We'd spent so many long afternoons talking about her life and the death of her parents that knowing she was shutting me out hurt my feelings a little. I whispered in her ear, "If you need to talk to me about anything, all you have to do is call." The only response I got was an almost imperceptible nod.

Amos and I fought our way to the car. When we got inside, he started the engine and turned the heater up full blast. We were greeted with a burst of icy air.

"Well, what in the world was that?" I asked through chattering teeth.

"I don't know," Amos said in a grim voice. "But we were supposed to keep that little fact about the missing bracelet to ourselves. Good job."

"What do you mean, 'good job'? Seems to me you were the one shooting your mouth off in there. Besides, we didn't actually tell anyone. Faith overheard us." I turned toward him, pulling my coat around me as tightly as I could. "Amos, she knows something about that bracelet. It was obvious."

He stared out the car window at the library. "I'd like to think she just got rattled hearing us talk about the murder, but here's something I didn't get a chance to 'shoot my mouth off' about. I got a call from Hitchens as I was leaving Barney's. You know that call that came into the office claiming you'd killed Dela?"

"Yes, of course I remember. I can't get it out of my mind."

Amos turned toward me and lowered his voice as if someone might be hiding in the backseat, listening to our conversation. "It seems it was only the first of several so-called tips."

I felt my heart leap inside my chest. "You mean someone else has accused me of murder?"

"No. Not you."

"Not me? Then who?"

He removed one of his gloves and put his hand in front of the heater. "Let's see. One person called to confirm what Bonnie told us. That Dela was having an affair and Barney killed her. Someone else said that Barney killed her because she was going to uncover some kind of insurance fraud he was involved in. And another advised the sheriff to look for a missing bracelet. That robbery was the motive."

"They knew about the bracelet? Amos, where are these calls coming from?"

"Unfortunately, from different places. Two of them were from the kind of cell phone you can buy at any discount store. We can't trace them. And the other one was from a pay phone in Hugoton."

I turned this new information over in my mind. "The tip about Dela having a boyfriend could be made up by anyone. And Barney being involved in some kind of fraud could be conjured up by someone who knows he works in insurance, but how many people would know about the bracelet?"

"I have no idea, but right now most of the tips point to Barney." Amos put his glove back on. "Look, we'll talk more about this later. Let's get to Ruby's before we freeze to death out here. I don't think I want to add to the wild speculation spinning around town. Some anonymous caller is liable to decide we committed suicide to hide our guilt over killing Dela."

I hit him on the arm. "Amos! Don't make a joke out of this. It isn't funny."

He rubbed his arm. "I didn't say it was funny. Quit beating me up." He put the car in gear and we slowly turned around in the snow-packed street and headed toward the restaurant.

"You can see why I'm concerned about Faith's reaction," he said through chattering teeth. "I need to know what's going on. Do you think you could talk to her? You guys are good friends."

I scooted up as close as I could to him, pointing the still-cold air from the heater toward us. "I'll try, but ever since she's been helping at the library, we haven't spent much time together. All I can do is give it my best shot. I'm sure she had nothing to do with Dela's death."

"I don't think she did either, but we need to find out what she knows about the bracelet before she slips up and says something that could get her into trouble."

"Oh, Amos. Do you think she could be in danger?"

"Who knows? This whole situation is really confusing. I don't suppose you're ready to come up with one of your Sherlock Holmes moments and tell me who the murderer is?" His eyes crinkled with humor, but his expression certainly wasn't jovial.

"Don't let Sheriff Hitchens ever hear you say that. The truth is I can't even come up with a Watson moment." I saw Ruby's up ahead. It was already filling up and it was only around five thirty. Something I'd been trying to remember took that moment to pop into my head. "You know what this reminds me of?"

"I don't have a clue." He successfully steered us into a parking space. I thanked God once again for the great all-weather tires the county put on its patrol cars.

"A mystery I read once. I can't remember who wrote it."

"Great," Amos fumed. "The heater's finally starting to work." He put the car in PARK but kept the motor running. "What about it?"

"There was a murder. Then all kinds of people in the town started getting letters that accused them of different things. Adultery. Murder. Larceny. All kinds of disreputable happenings."

Amos looked amused. "Disreputable happenings, huh? How did it turn out?"

"The murderer was sending the letters. He did it to throw suspicion off himself. But the interesting thing was, he realized that he had to include himself among those who received a letter, because if he didn't, it could point to him as the author—and the murderer."

Amos turned off the engine and stared at me. "That's interesting, but how does that apply to our situation?"

"Who knows? What's normal in a situation like this? In a small town like Winter Break, everyone knows your business. Are there really that many people who think they have pertinent information about Dela's murder, or could all the calls be coming from one person?"

Amos stared at the snow piling up on the windshield. "We've gotten lots of tips before over all kinds of things, but I'd have to say that this is different. All of these calls are anonymous. That's not normal. I mean, why wouldn't people leave their names? Or just come into the office and talk to the sheriff if they thought they knew something important? Or even come to me? I don't relish telling Barney that someone accused him of killing his wife. Even mentioning that she may have been fooling around isn't something I look forward to. Especially now. Unless we find Dela's killer quickly, we'll have to follow up on these tips. We won't have any choice."

The tiny amount of warmth we'd been able to generate was rapidly disappearing. "Look, you haven't been around much lately," I said. "Maybe these people who are calling will come to you if they know you're available. Let's get inside Ruby's so the word will spread that you're in town. Besides, I'd like to lose this nice shade of blue I'm developing."

I put my hand on the door handle, but Amos reached over to stop me. "One more thing," he said. "I also tracked down the phone used by your anonymous caller." He pointed toward the pay phone near the front door of Ruby's Café.

"That phone?" I asked incredulously. "It's clearly visible from inside Ruby's. Maybe someone saw who called."

"My thinking exactly. Let's talk to Ruby and Bonnie. See if they can remember seeing anyone using the phone this morning."

"What time did the sheriff say that call came in? We were having breakfast between seven and eight o'clock."

"The sheriff said the call came in around eight thirty."

"So whoever called waited until we left Ruby's. I wonder if they knew we were going to see the sheriff."

"Look," Amos said, "it won't do any good to guess who called. Let's see if anyone noticed someone on the phone around eight thirty." He released my arm and we got out of the car. The steps up to the restaurant hadn't been cleared so Amos held on to me so I wouldn't slip. Once we opened the front door to Ruby's, welcome heat washed over us. We threaded our way through the full tables and found a booth in the back. The table was still dirty, and Bonnie's tip was sitting there, but we didn't care. We were cold and hungry, and Ruby's was the place to be under those conditions.

We'd just sat down, when Emily came up to the booth and slid in next to me. "Hey! I've been trying to call you all day. Where've you been?"

I shook my head. "If I told you, you wouldn't believe me." The last thing I wanted to do was to recount my time being fingerprinted at the sheriff's office. "Let's save that story for our next girls' gabfest, okay? What's going on?"

"I talked to Mama. Ivy, she's so thrilled about the dress. She can hardly wait to get started. She would like to meet with you and do a few measurements."

"Oh, great. My very favorite thing. Can't she just measure you and double it?"

Emily laughed. "No, because it would be too big, you silly woman." She stood up. "Just give me a call, and we'll set something up soon. I better get back to Buddy. We're having a 'night out' together. I didn't want to take Charlie out in this weather, so Mama's watching him."

I saw Buddy sitting across the room with a big, sloppy grin on his face. I waved at him. "Looks like your hubby's pretty happy to have some time alone with his wife."

Emily smiled and gazed around the crowded restaurant. "If you call this having some time alone. But I guess we'll have to take what we can get."

I grabbed her arm before she could get away. "You and Buddy plan a real grown-up evening soon, okay? Go to Hugoton for dinner. Amos and I will watch Charlie."

Amos's eyebrows shot up so high they almost disappeared into his hair. "Whoa. What are you volunteering me for?"

I batted my eyes at him. "You need to get some practice, Amos. Someday we might hear the patter of little feet."

"Well, at least for a while, they better belong to Miss Skiffins," he said, shaking his head.

Emily and I both laughed, and she leaned over and hugged me. As she waded through the crowd toward Buddy, I couldn't help but notice how happy they looked. I could hardly wait until Amos and I were married. I was even more excited now since I wasn't too worried about all the planning that still needed to be done. My mother was a human tornado. I was confident she would whip everything together when she got here.

"Hey, you two." Ruby pulled the dirty dishes off our table and dumped them into a large plastic basket. Holding the basket under one arm, she wiped down our table with a wet rag. "How's it goin'?"

I could have said a variety of things, but instead I smiled and said, "Fine. How about you?"

Ruby gave us a look at her false teeth. "Couldn't be better. Seems like you and Amos ain't the only people gettin' hitched."

"Oh, Ruby! Bonnie and Bert?"

She nodded so hard I was afraid her wig was going to bounce off. "He asked, she said yes." She slapped her rag back inside the basket. "If you'd told me a year ago that I'd be announcin' Bert's weddin', I woulda called you a two-faced lyin' weasel." Her eyes got shiny. "But look at me now. And it's thanks to you two." She wiped her hand across her eyes. "Dinner's on me tonight, folks. And dessert, too. You better eat up, 'cause you know how stingy I usually am."

Amos chuckled. "Ruby, you're about the least stingy person I know. Thanks for the dinner. We'll gladly accept."

She started to leave but then turned around again and leaned over next to me. "I promise, honey, you're gonna have a weddin' feast like you never imagined. I'm pullin' out all the stops. And I'm givin' you somethin' for a weddin' gift that most of the people in this town would give their right arm for." She grinned widely and left, yelling at people in her way to "move it or lose it!"

Amos stared at me with his mouth open. "Wow, Ivy. Maybe she's going to give you the recipe."

That was really all he needed to say. "The recipe" could only be one thing. The secret formula for Ruby's Redbird Burgers. Down through the years, many people had tried to wheedle it out of Ruby through bribery, threats, and coercion. In fact, there had once been a town meeting called to figure out how to get Ruby to fork over her burger secrets before she kicked the bucket. So far, all avenues had led to defeat. The only person she'd ever told was my aunt Bitty. And Bitty wouldn't even tell me. "A promise is a promise, Ivy," she'd said. "If people can't trust our word, how can they believe us when we tell them they can take God at His?" She'd died with the secret of the Redbird Burger. Now, it seemed that I was to be given the greatest honor Ruby Bird could bestow. Maybe to some people it might seem silly, but to me it was one of the most touching gifts anyone had ever given me.

"Maybe you better not count your burgers before they're hatched," I told Amos. "She might mean she's passing along one of her wigs. How do you think I would look?"

He chuckled. "Not so good. Let's hope that never happens."

"What'cha havin?" Bonnie stood poised with her order pad, a big smile on her face.

"I hear congratulations are in order," I said. "I'm so thrilled, Bonnie."

She blushed. "Well, don't go telling a bunch of people about it. We're trying to keep it kinda quiet. We're thinking about a small ceremony."

"I think you should have whatever you want, Bonnie. But I imagine the whole town would turn out to see you two get married. It's a real love story." I choked up over the last few words. Two people loving each other for over thirty years, finally getting a chance to be together. It didn't get more romantic.

"Oh, for crying out loud," Amos said with a smirk. "You women and *romance*. Good thing we men are more practical."

Bonnie grinned. "Bert took me to the peach orchard where we buried that box of his trinkets so long ago before he left town. He gave me a new jewelry box full of all those old things. And right in the middle was a small velvet case with my ring in it. Then he got down on one knee and asked me to marry him." She sighed. "He might be a man, but he's as romantic as they come." She wrinkled her nose at Amos. "Besides, you're a big talker, but my guess is you're pretty romantic yourself."

Amos held his hands up. "I plead the fifth."

Bonnie laughed and lowered her voice to a whisper. "By the way, I tried to find out who poor Dela was fooling around with, but the only thing I could figure out was that it didn't happen here. It was back in Dodge City where she came from. Some relative of Marybelle Widdle's who lives there told her that they'd seen Dela out several times with some good-lookin' man. But no one I talked to has any idea who it was." She clucked her tongue. "If you want my opinion, it's just a nasty piece of gossip without anything to back it up. I'd forget about it."

"Thanks, Bonnie," Amos said. "I appreciate your help."

She scribbled something on her order pad. "Ruby said dinner's on the house tonight. Bert's got a new dish. This is the first time we've served it. I think you ought to give it a try."

"What is it?" Amos sounded a little suspicious. Change at Ruby's didn't come easily.

Bonnie looked a little embarrassed. "Veal Marsala with risotto and steamed asparagus."

Amos and I just stared at each other. Veal Marsala in Ruby's Redbird Café? It just didn't sound right.

"No one's ordering it," Bonnie said. "They're all afraid to try it."

I knew Amos had been looking forward to Ruby's famous Wednesday night meatloaf, but some things are more important than meatloaf. "Bring us two orders of Veal Marsala, Bonnie," I said as loudly as I could without looking totally deranged. "It sounds wonderful."

Amos looked like he wanted to say something, but he just offered Bonnie a weak smile and a nod.

"Thanks, folks," she said quietly.

When she walked away, Amos scowled at me. "Thanks for ordering for me. What if I hate Veal Marsala?"

"Have you ever had it?"

"No, but that's not the point. I—"

"Oh, hush up," I whispered. "You were going to order it anyway. We both know it."

We were getting stares from several of the tables around us. I noticed J.D. and Ina Mae Feldhammer sitting in a booth across the room. I waved at Ina Mae. She smiled and held up her hand. She hadn't been to the bookstore for about a week. I pretended to pick up a cup and drink from it and she nodded. J.D. didn't seem to notice. In fact, he was going over some paperwork and didn't appear to realize his wife was even there. I wondered if her marriage was the source of her sadness. She never talked about anything personal when she came to visit. We just shared recipes and talked about books we liked.

I noticed Bertha Pennypacker sitting with the Widdles. Bertha and Marybelle had their heads together, and they were looking at Amos and me. As usual, I seemed to be the topic of conversation. Newton just stared off into space, lost in his own thoughts.

When Bonnie came back with our coffee, I remembered to ask her about the phone call.

"This morning?" she said, wrinkling her nose. "Boy, we were so busy, I can't remember if I even looked out the window. I'll ask Ruby and Bert if they noticed anything and get back to you. Is it important?"

"It really is, Bonnie," Amos said in a low voice. "But please keep it to yourself, okay?"

"Sure thing," she said, leaning in close so no one around us could hear her. "I'll let you know what I find out. Maybe you better deputize me, Amos. I'm sure doing a lot of nosing around for you."

"I would if I could, Bonnie," he said with a grin. "You're better than some of the deputies I work with."

She laughed and walked back to the kitchen.

After she left, I started to ask Amos a little bit more about the phone calls that had come into the sheriff's office, but he hushed me. "I can't take the chance that someone will overhear us. We've already spilled the beans once today. Let's talk about it later when we're alone."

We spent the next few minutes talking about picking up my mom and what would happen if the snow got much deeper. I wasn't sure if I wanted to come back into town tomorrow to open the bookstore. I was pretty sure no one was going to want to wade through all the white stuff to read a book, and Isaac had finished his work for the week. I had just mentioned my concerns to Amos when Isaac and Alma came in. They looked so cute together, Isaac in his black topcoat that appeared to have been styled in the '50s and Alma dressed in a deep blue wool cloak with a matching knit hat. The table next to our booth was empty, so Isaac steered Alma our way.

"Hello," Alma said in her soft, demure voice. "How nice to see you both."

Isaac, ever the gentleman, came over and shook Amos's hand. "Good evening, Deputy." He turned and gave me a little bow. "And you, too, Miss Ivy."

"Hi there, Isaac. Getting a little dinner before church?" Amos asked.

Isaac helped Alma off with her coat and held out her chair. "Yes. It seemed the thing to do. Alma was going to cook for us, but I decided she needed a night out." He smiled and took off his own coat. "But I must tell you that she is a culinary master. I have thoroughly enjoyed all her meals." He patted his small stomach. "I might actually be putting on weight."

Isaac was a wisp of a man. Even a pound would help. As strong as the wind was sometimes in Winter Break, I was afraid he was going to be carried away one day.

Suddenly, the doors of the kitchen swung open. Bert Bird was bringing out two plates of steaming food. Bonnie followed behind with a bread basket. Either we were being treated to a very small parade or Amos and I were getting ready to be presented with our dinners. With all the flair he could manage, Bert deposited our plates in front of us.

"Veal Marsala," he said loudly. "I'm glad someone in Winter Break is willing to take a risk. Bon appétit! " Then he whirled away, leaving Amos and me the center of attention at Ruby's.

Bonnie set the bread basket down and turned to Isaac and Alma. "What'cha havin'?" she asked.

COZY IN KANSAS

Isaac looked at me and smiled. Then he raised his eyebrows at Alma. "I believe we will have the Veal Marsala, too. It looks wonderful."

Bonnie winked at him and yelled to Bert, who was standing in front of the doors to the kitchen, watching us. "Two more Italian moo moos!" Bert flashed us a big grin and disappeared into the kitchen.

While Amos said a prayer over our food, I silently told God that I had no intention of being deceitful, but I was determined to say the Marsala was good, no matter what it tasted like. Amos and I speared a forkful of veal, mushrooms, and sauce and stuck it in our mouths at the same time. The explosion of garlic and butter sauce, along with the tender medallion of veal, was incredible. "Delicious!" I said. I had half a mind to stand up and give a review so everyone could get back to their own lives.

Amos nodded, smiled big, and took another bite. I think he was just trying to get out of saying anything, but the gusto he displayed seemed to work. Everyone went back to their conversations. In the next few minutes, I heard several people call Bonnie over and ask if it was too late to change their orders. The Veal Marsala was a hit, and Ruby's had a new favorite. I couldn't help wonder if Bert would still be here someday when Ruby was gone, cooking the old standbys but bringing some new taste treats to the town of Winter Break.

We ate quickly since it was getting late and we wanted to avoid the stampede to the church. I'd just finished my last bite when Bonnie came back to our booth. "I asked around about the people using the phone this morning," she said quietly. "Bubba Weber told me he used the phone after he dropped off our jars of honey. But he had to wait for Bertha Pennypacker to get off the phone. She seemed real secretive about whoever she was talking to. She told Bubba to wait inside until she was finished."

"Did you ask Bubba what time that was, Bonnie?" Amos asked.

She nodded. "He said it was right around eight thirty. He remembers because he needed to deliver some honey over to Marvin Baumgartner's place. He lives quite a way outside of town and Bubba wanted to make sure he and Edith were back from visiting her sister in Cawker City."

"Thanks, Bonnie," I said. "That's exactly what I needed to know."

She handed me a bag she was holding. "I heard about the dog. Thought you'd like to have some bones." She smiled and patted my shoulder. "You come by any time, and we'll give you some scraps. Poor thing needs to get inside where it's warm. Good luck."

I thanked her before she scurried back to the kitchen. Then I flashed Amos my most superior expression. "Who do you suppose could have told Bonnie about the dog? It sure wasn't me."

Amos frowned at me. "You caught me, Nancy Drew. I think he's a lost cause, but I know you well enough to realize you're not going to give up. I'm afraid you may have to learn that some creatures never heal from abuse."

"But I truly believe that with God all things are possible, Amos. For that reason alone, I have to try. I've never found anything so broken that God couldn't mend it." For some reason my eyes wandered toward Bertha Pennypacker, who was glaring at me. I wondered what was really causing her to hate me so much. Was her anger coming from some past pain?

I looked at Amos. "I can hardly believe that Bertha despises me so much she would actually try to implicate me in a murder investigation."

"I'm sorry, Ivy," he said gently, "but you have to remember that Bertha's problems aren't your fault. For some reason, she's decided to focus her unhappiness on you. My guess is that she's jealous of you for some reason. You represent something she wants and doesn't think she has."

"I know that, but to actually accuse me of killing Dela. . ."

"Thankfully, it wasn't successful. I know what she did was wrong, but I think we need to put Bertha on the shelf for a while. We have other things to think about that are a little more important right now."

I agreed with him, but there was still a wound in my soul. I'd never been disliked so fiercely before. And it hurt.

We joined the mass exodus of Ruby's patrons on their way to church. Amos stood in the street and directed some of the cars trying to back up and head for the church so we wouldn't end up with a huge pileup. By the time we drove into the church parking lot, there weren't many spaces left. He let me off near the entrance while he parked the car. When I stepped into the foyer, I almost ran into Ina Mae Feldhammer. She seemed to be waiting for someone.

"Hi, Ina Mae," I said, smiling. "How's your mother?"

The corners of her mouth turned up quickly then dropped as if they weren't used to going in that direction. "She's hanging in there," she said, her voice so faint I could barely hear her. "I think she's looking a little better."

"I'm so glad. Are you waiting for J.D.?"

"No. I was waiting for you." She looked up at me, her large, chocolate brown eyes and her sad expression reminding me of the lost dog that was hanging around my house. "I was wondering if you were going to open the bookstore tomorrow. I mean with all the snow and everything. . ."

"I really hadn't made up my mind yet." I got the feeling that her question was more of a request than an inquiry. "Can I call you tomorrow and let you know?"

She nodded quickly and walked away.

"Where's J.D.?" I asked, not wanting her to leave yet.

"He has to see someone about a property."

"It's pretty bad weather for that, isn't it?" I asked.

She stared down at her shoes. "J.D. says the real estate business is a twenty-four-hour-a-day job." She shrugged. "He goes wherever he has to. Business comes first."

I wasn't so sure she accepted his priorities as easily as she said. The front door opened and Amos came in. I put my arm around Ina Mae. "Are you sitting by yourself tonight?"

She looked away from me and nodded.

"Why don't you sit with Amos and me?"

Again, a small smile twitched the corners of her lips. "That would be nice."

We entered into the sanctuary as the music began. While we sang, I prayed that God would show me how to help the small, timid woman. She certainly needed a friend.

After praise and worship, Pastor Taylor stepped up to the podium. I respected him as much as anyone I'd ever known. Not only was he a wonderful source of spiritual strength when it was needed, he truly lived what he preached. Winter Break residents knew if they needed anything, he would be there. When a fire destroyed part of the bookstore last year, Pastor Taylor and Bev were among the first people on the scene, helping to repair the damage and put Miss Bitty's Bygone Bookstore back together. Although God had used him to touch my heart on many occasions, one thing he'd said when I was a kid had always stuck with me. *"The goodness of God gives me strength."* I trusted in that goodness—in every circumstance. I'd met people who believed God was a fiery judge, just waiting to punish them for their mistakes. But I'd learned that God loved me, accepted me warts and all, and *always* wanted the best for me. And Pastor Taylor was right. It gave me strength.

He looked out at the congregation, his expression solemn. "Before tonight's lesson, I want to pray for Barney Shackleford and his family. And I want to remind everyone that although we might not be related to Barney in a physical sense, we are related in the Spirit. Please reach out to our brother during this tragic time. Barney has expressed his wish to have Dela's service here in Winter Break, and he asked me to extend his personal invitation to all of you. There is no date set at this time. When I have more information, I will pass it along to you. Barney does have several relatives staying with him, so if you can deliver some food to them, I know they would appreciate it. Please contact my wife. She has a sign-up sheet for meals."

I was surprised that the funeral would be held here. I'd assumed it would be in Dodge City, and I couldn't help but wonder about the arrangements. Pastor Taylor led us in a beautiful prayer, thanking God for welcoming Dela into His kingdom and asking for peace and comfort for Barney and the families. Then he asked us to turn to the eighteenth chapter of John, where he read about Peter's denial of Christ at His crucifixion. After that, we turned to Matthew 10:33, where he read, " 'But whoever disowns me before men, I will disown him before my Father in heaven.' " Pastor put down his Bible and looked out at us. "So by his own words, Peter deserved to be disowned. Rejected by Jesus in front of the Father. But what did Jesus do?" Then he read the story of the women who went to the tomb and found it empty. "They found an angel inside the tomb. Jesus was gone. What did the angel say?" Pastor Taylor smiled. "Remember that Christ had every right to turn His back on Peter. In the hour of His greatest need, the disciple who claimed to love Him denied he even knew Him. But notice that the angel says this: 'You are looking for Jesus the Nazarene, who was crucified. He has risen! He is not here. See the place where they laid him. But go, tell his disciples and Peter, "He is going ahead of you into Galilee. There you will see him, just as he told you." ' " Pastor Taylor closed his Bible. "Notice that Jesus singled out Peter. He wanted to make certain Peter knew He was coming to see him and that He still loved him and still considered him to be His friend. You see, God's love is eternal. There isn't anything you've ever done that will cause God to turn His back on you. We give up on ourselves sometimes, but God is always there, calling to us. He wants you to know that no failure is too much for Him. There is nothing you've ever done that could break your relationship with Him so badly that it can't be mended."

I remembered what I'd told Amos about the dog. It was similar to what Pastor Taylor had just said about our own bond with God. I heard an odd choking sound next to me. When I turned to look at Ina Mae, I saw that tears were streaming down her face. Not knowing quite what to do, I reached over and took her hand in mine. When she looked up at me, there was so much pain in her face, I wasn't sure what to say or do. But she squeezed my hand and hung on. We stayed like that throughout the rest of the service.

Pastor Taylor brought up many more examples from the Bible of God's unchanging love. When he was finished he asked if there was anyone in the congregation who'd felt estranged from God and needed to restore fellowship with Him. I felt Ina Mae's grip strengthen, but she stayed seated as several others went forward. Finally, I whispered in her ear, "If you want to go up front, I'll go with you." It was all she needed. Still holding my hand, she stood to her feet and we walked up together. When Pastor Taylor prayed for her, she cried harder, but when he was done, I saw the first real smile I'd ever seen on her face. By the time she let go of my hand, it was almost numb. I had to open and close it several times to get all the feeling back. After everyone had been prayed for, we went back to our seats and waited to be dismissed. When Pastor Taylor gave the final blessing, I asked Ina Mae if J.D. was going to pick her up. She shook her head.

"I don't think so. He said he might be really late."

"Why don't you let me drive you home?" Amos said, overhearing our conversation.

"Thank you. That would be wonderful." Again, a smile lit up her face. As we stood to leave, I saw Faith standing next to Emily. She saw me, too, and turned her head.

"Amos, why don't you get the car?" He nodded and took off for the foyer. "Ina Mae, I need to talk to someone for just a minute. Can I meet you by the front door?"

She nodded. "I'd like to stop by the bathroom for a minute anyway. I must look a mess."

I grinned. "I've had raccoon eyes so many times in church, people think it's the way I wear my makeup."

She laughed. "I won't be long. I'll wait for you in the front."

We went our separate ways and I began searching for Faith. I found her standing next to the coatrack. I had the feeling she was hiding—from me. I grabbed her arm. "I want to talk to you. Let's go to the library."

I led her to the church library, which was unlocked. After pulling her inside, I locked the door to discourage anyone else from entering, and then I pointed to a pair of chairs with a table and a lamp between them. Faith plopped down into one of them, but she didn't look very happy about it.

"Faith," I said as gently as I could, "I'm concerned about you. Today at the library—"

"I told you," she said, interrupting me, "I just lost my grip on the coffee cup. Why don't you believe me?"

I could almost see the petulant child I'd first met months ago when she first came to Winter Break. The change in her had started right here—in this library. Now here we were again. I shook my head. "Honey, we've shared almost everything there is to share. I thought you trusted me. What happened?"

Her eyes filled with tears. "Oh, Ivy. I don't know what to do. I know you care about me, but I don't want to get anyone in trouble."

"Faith," I said as gently as I could, "Dela Shackleford is dead. She had the right to finish her life. Someone took that away from her. When it comes to murder, there can't be any secrets. Don't you see that? If you know something that could lead to uncovering her murderer, it's your responsibility to tell someone. If you don't want to tell me, you can talk to Amos."

She hung her head. Her dark, straight hair hung down, covering her face. When she raised her head, tears were running down her cheeks. "What if I say something that makes someone look guilty who isn't? That's not right."

"That's not up to you to decide. We have laws and people whose job it is to uphold them. If this person isn't guilty, he or she won't be charged with anything. But you can't decide what's right and wrong. It's not your job."

I could see the torture in her face, and it disturbed me. "Honey, please trust me. Tell me why you reacted so strongly when Amos and I were talking about Dela's murder."

She didn't say anything for several seconds. Then she sat up straight and looked into my eyes. "That bracelet? The one Amos was describing?"

I nodded, encouraging her to continue.

She took a deep breath. "I saw it, Ivy. Hope has it."

9

With Ina Mae and Dewey secured in the backseat, Amos maneuvered his car carefully through the snow-covered streets to Ina Mae's house. As soon as the heavy snow was through falling, several Winter Break farmers would attach snow plows to their tractors and clear the roads. It was one of the side benefits of living in a farming community. Our downtown streets would probably be cleared by tomorrow afternoon. The only down side was that after being plowed, there was usually a sheet of ice left behind. Businesses would put down Ice Melt or salt to clear their own walks, but it was too expensive for the town to salt all the streets. Besides, salting might make a difference for a day or two, but then snow would surely move in again. In Winter Break, a superior sense of balance, along with a good pair of snow boots, weren't luxuries. They were necessities.

It was still snowing, but thankfully the wind had died down. Harsh, blowing flurries had changed to big, fluffy flakes drifting down from the sky, creating a beautiful winter dance that was highlighted by the glow of streetlamps. I would have enjoyed it more if Faith's words hadn't kept resonating in my mind. Why would Hope have the bracelet? I'd mulled over the problem pretty well by the time we reached the Feldhammer house.

Amos got out of the car and opened the door to the backseat, helping Ina Mae to step out.

"Thank you, Ivy," she said before she closed the car door. "You don't know how much tonight helped me. I'm so glad you were with me."

Although I didn't know what her battle was, I knew the feeling of reaching out to God and having Him reach back. I'd never forgotten the story of a young man who'd been brought up in another religion. He'd spent his life trying to get attention from the god he'd been taught to follow. Yet there was never any response, no matter what he did or how much he prayed. Then someone told him about Jesus. The first time the young man cried out to Him, God answered, showering him with His love and forgiveness. He was amazed to find a God who really listened; who really cared for him and was actually able to change his heart. The young man became a Christian and spent his life as a missionary in his own country. Seeing the expression on Ina Mae's face brought that wonderful story to my mind.

"Please come by for coffee when you can," I said. "I may not open the bookstore tomorrow, but I plan to be there Friday. I'll call you tomorrow and let you know for sure."

She nodded. "Thanks, Ivy. Goodnight, Dewey."

She smiled and shut the door. I watched her make her way up to the front door, Amos holding her arm so she wouldn't slip. *Nothing so broken that God can't mend it.* I'd seen this truth played out time and time again. *With God nothing is impossible.*

"Quite a night," Dewey said from the backseat. "I'm glad you were there for Ina Mae."

"Me, too," I said, twisting around to look at him. "I was just wondering why we try so hard to solve our own problems before we turn them over to God."

Dewey shook his head. "I guess it's because most of us haven't figured out how helpless we are without Him. We might be able to do all things through Him, but by ourselves we're pretty puny."

I chuckled. "Isn't that the truth?"

The driver's side door swung open and Amos climbed inside. I wanted to tell him about the bracelet, but Sheriff Hitchens's admonition kept me from saying anything in front of Dewey. I waited until Amos pulled up in my driveway and got the car as close to the front door as possible.

"Dewey, do you mind going on in?" I asked, handing him the keys. "I'd like to talk to Amos for a minute."

Dewey grinned. "You two aren't gonna sit out here and neck, are you?"

"Now that you mention it, I think that sounds like a pretty good idea," Amos said innocently.

I slugged him on the arm. "Oh, hush up. It's too cold to 'neck.' Our lips would freeze together."

Dewey opened the car door in the back. "I don't know, Amos. That doesn't sound too bad. Maybe you should give it a try."

"Shut the door and get in the house, old man," I said, laughing. "I'll deal with you later." We watched Dewey walk up the steps. He had a small satchel with him. I assumed his pajamas were inside. "I just realized," I said with a sigh, "Dewey's my babysitter."

"Don't be silly," Amos said. "Now, what's up?"

I told him about Faith and the bracelet.

Amos sat back in his seat and let out a low whistle when I finished. "Hope Hartwell has the bracelet?" He thought for a moment and then shook his head. "Why in the world would she kill Dela for some cheap bracelet?" He turned to stare at me. "You know, you said you got a pretty good look at that thing. Are you sure it was rhinestones? Could it have been diamonds?"

I held up my hands in mock surrender. "How would I know, Amos? The only diamond I've ever had is the one in my engagement ring. I assumed it was costume jewelry because no one in their right mind would wear something that expensive unless they were at some kind of formal dinner. And trust me, the meeting I had with Dela yesterday morning wasn't that fancy."

"Okay, settle down. I'm just trying to figure this out. The truth is we can't be sure the bracelet Faith saw is actually Dela's. Maybe she saw a bracelet that was similar."

"You've got a point, but it would certainly be an odd coincidence. Two identical bracelets showing up at the same time?"

"Did Faith say it had blue stones like the other one?"

"Yes, she described exactly what I saw, Amos. I really think it's Dela's."

Amos grunted. I could almost hear the gears turning in his head. "The point is, whoever took the bracelet removed it from Dela's body for one of two reasons. Either it was valuable, or somehow it would tie them to the murder."

"That makes sense," I said, "but I have a hard time seeing Hope as a cold-blooded killer. Usually I get a pretty good sense about people."

Amos snorted. "You're great with piecing clues together, but you've spent time around two different murderers and your 'Spidey sense' never kicked in one time. I think we better stick to the facts."

I stuck my tongue out at him. "Okay, maybe you're right. But I still can't imagine Hope driving a chopstick through Dela Shackleford's heart because of a bracelet. She seems like such a nice person."

"The truth is we don't really know Hope. She hasn't been in Winter Break very long. We certainly can't rule her out because she 'seems like such a nice person.'"

With the car idling, I could feel the cold creeping in again. I tried wrapping my arms around my body to generate some warmth. It wasn't working.

"So now what? Do we talk to Hope? Or just turn this information over to the sheriff?"

"*We* don't do anything," Amos said. "Sheriff Hitchens asked *me* to investigate this murder. I should tell him about Hope, but I haven't actually seen the bracelet. I don't know if I can just take Faith's word for it." He put his arm up on the back of the seat and rubbed my shoulder. "I don't suppose you told Faith not to mention to Hope that she talked to you?"

"Yes, I did, smarty-pants. I'm not completely brain dead."

"Good job. And don't call me smarty-pants." He leaned over and kissed me. And our lips didn't stick together. "You get inside. Make sure all the doors are locked. When you hear something from your mother, let me know."

"I will." I kissed him again. "Call me in the morning, okay?"

"You got it. If anything unusual happens tonight, you call me right away. Promise me."

I reached over and touched his cheek. "I promise, but the only unusual thing I'm likely to hear is Dewey's snoring. No one is after me, Amos. Please stop worrying."

He shook his head. "I'm not worrying. I'm just trying to be wise. You're the most important person in my life. I want to make sure you stay safe."

"I understand," I said with a smile. "I feel the same way about you." I kissed him once more, then I turned to open the car door.

"Hey, wait a minute," Amos said. "I've got Bubba's honey and those jars of huckleberry jelly in the trunk. We need to get them inside before they freeze."

I waited while he retrieved a large box from the trunk. When we got to the front door, I started to open it and then I stopped. "Amos, where are my keys?"

He frowned. "I think your brain's frozen. You gave them to Dewey. Now open the door. This box is heavy."

"No, I gave Dewey my regular set of keys. I'm talking about the spare keys I gave to Dela at the church. I just realized that I never got them back. And the list of Dela's belongings at the sheriff's office only listed one set of keys. She had to have her own set. She was driving her car. Where are mine?"

"I looked at that list, too. You're right. There was only one set of keys." He stared at me with a worried expression. "I don't like not knowing where those keys are. I'll check with the sheriff. Maybe they just forgot to document both sets." He shifted the weight of the box in his arms. "Right now, though, I'd appreciate it if you'd just open the door. Unless you want a front porch littered with broken jars of honey and huckleberry jelly."

"Sorry." I pushed on the door and found it unlocked. After directing Amos to put the box on the kitchen counter, I hugged him while Dewey watched us.

"I'll let you know what I find out," he said when he let me go. He looked at Dewey. "Keep an eye on our girl, Dewey. I'm counting on you."

When he left, I stood at the front door and watched him pull out of the driveway, his brake lights disappearing behind a curtain of snow. I glanced around once before closing the door, but I didn't see the dog. I said a silent prayer, asking God to keep him safe. I also asked for help finding my keys. I didn't want to panic. There was probably a good explanation for their disappearance, but knowing that the last person who had them was a victim of murder made me nervous.

Once inside, I finally started thawing out. Dewey and I drank hot chocolate and sat in front of the fireplace in the living room while Miss Skiffins curled up next to me and slept. We talked for a while about the bookstore. I was just telling him about my attempts to acquire a first edition of *Little*

Women by Louisa May Alcott, when there was a knock on the front door.

Dewey got to his feet. "You expecting anyone?" he asked.

I shook my head and checked my watch. It was a little after ten o'clock. "Nope."

He went to the front door and looked through the peephole. "Well, I'll be," he said. "It's J.D." Dewey swung the door open. Sure enough, J.D. Feldhammer stood on the porch.

"Goodness gracious, J.D.," I said when he stepped inside. "What are you doing out in this kind of weather?"

"I'm really sorry to bother you folks," he said. "But my car slid off the road. I'm stuck in the ditch just a little ways down from the entrance to your driveway."

Dewey closed the door behind J.D., and I jumped up and went over to where he stood, shivering. "Here, give me your coat. Let's get you warmed up."

J.D. smiled and handed me his all-weather coat. Then he took off his black rubber snow boots and set them on the mat. "Sure glad you're living out here, Ivy. The nearest farm is Bubba Weber's, and that's about another mile up the road."

J.D. took off his gloves and his knit cap. I took those, too. "Let's lay these out near the fire," I said. "See if we can dry them out some."

He followed Dewey and me into the living room. "Maybe I can get Odie to come and pull me out. He's got that big truck."

"I'm sure he'd be more than happy to help," I said, "but let's call Amos first. He's always pulling people out of the snow. He's got chains in his trunk. I'll bet he can have you back on the road in a jiffy."

J.D. looked relieved. "Well, if you don't think it would be too much trouble. . ."

"Not at all. You sit down in front of the fire and warm up. I'll call Amos and get you a cup of hot chocolate."

"Thanks, Ivy. I really appreciate it." J.D. followed Dewey over to the couch. I went into the kitchen to phone Amos. I could tell by his voice that I woke him, but Amos was first and foremost a protector and defender of the people. If someone needed help, he figured it was his job to respond. Promising to be there as soon as he could, he hung up. I mixed up some more chocolate syrup and milk and then shoved the cup into the microwave.

It felt odd to have J.D. in my house after the evening I'd spent with his wife. I had no intention of mentioning Ina Mae's experience in church. It was her responsibility to tell him about it if she chose to do so. I had to wonder if her marriage had contributed to her problems. J.D. was a nice enough man, always friendly and personable, but sometimes I wondered if his job had become too time-consuming. He seemed rather driven, not only by his profession, but in other ways as well. Once he moved to town, he jumped quickly into what passed for Winter Break's social circle. With a little arm-twisting, he'd wrangled a spot on the city council. I wasn't sure how prestigious the position was since he shared his council spot with Mort Benniker, a local pig farmer whose only claim to fame was that he could burp the alphabet after taking only one breath. But J.D. seemed happy to have a place where he could contribute to the town's future. I certainly couldn't fault him for that.

I'd just removed the cup from the microwave when the phone rang. It was my mother.

"Ivy, my plane leaves at four o'clock this afternoon, my time. I won't get into the Wichita airport until one in the morning on Friday. Are you sure Amos can still pick me up?"

"You know Amos, Mom. He gets by on very little sleep. He says he can do it, but if he gets tired, stop at a motel and rest awhile. There's no rush. I want you both to be safe."

"Is everything all right there? Has anything else happened?"

"No, Mom. No more dead bodies. Dewey's staying with me until you get here, but I don't think I'm in any danger." The missing keys popped into my mind. "But better safe than sorry, I guess."

"Okay, sweetie. See you Friday."

"Bye, Mom." I put the phone down, wishing my parents lived closer. I really missed them. They'd felt the call to China for years. Now they were there, laying their lives down for the gospel. I knew wanting them here was selfish, but I couldn't help it.

I plopped some mini marshmallows into J.D.'s cup and carried it into the living room. He and Dewey were deep in a conversation about the library.

"Why not use the facility in the evenings for book clubs? If we charged a small rental fee, we could use the money toward upkeep and new books," J.D. was saying.

"It's a good idea," Dewey answered. He looked at me when I walked into the room. "Ivy, aren't there a couple of clubs that meet at the bookstore?"

"Yes, the romance club meets once a month, and the Zane Grey club meets every other month. Oh, and Hope and I were talking about a mystery book club. To be honest, though, I have to either drive back into town or stay late to let them in. If you want to move the clubs to the library, it would be fine with me."

"Hope is living at Sarah Johnson's, isn't she?" J.D. said. "She's much closer to the library than you are to the bookstore."

I nodded and handed him his cup. "It *would* be easier for her to open the library."

He put his hot chocolate down on the coffee table. "Ivy, I'd love to see what you've done with the house. I haven't been here since I closed the deal with Amos."

I started to tell him that things hadn't changed much. Cecil and Marion had left almost all their furniture when they moved to Florida. But I had brought quite a few of Bitty's things in. Her oak antique sideboard sat against one wall of the dining room. Her mother's Blue Willow china was displayed on it. And her oak rocking chair was near a window with her old brass floor lamp next to it. I'd also framed some pictures of Bitty and dedicated a wall to chronicle her life. The guest room held her bedroom furniture. "Sure. I'd be happy to give you a quick tour." I looked at Dewey. "You want to come?"

He shook his head. "I've already seen every room in this house. Right now the only one I care about is the one I'm going to be sleeping in."

"Go on to bed then, Dewey. I'll be fine. J.D. is here, and Amos is on his way. You don't need to stay up with me."

He cocked his head to one side and raised his eyebrows. "You sure?"

I grinned. "I'm certain. I'm suspending your babysitter responsibilities for tonight."

It didn't take much encouragement. He headed toward the stairs. "You'd better show J.D. the upstairs first. I'm going to be sawing logs in the guest-room in a few minutes."

"I think we better take that threat seriously, J.D."

He laughed and we followed Dewey upstairs. I showed J.D. through the upstairs bedrooms, then we went back downstairs. When we reached the dining room, J.D. stopped.

"Ivy, I hope I'm not out of line, but what did you mean by Dewey being your 'babysitter'?"

"You're not out of line. Amos feels that since Dela Shackleford was killed in my driveway, I might be in danger, too. I think he's wrong, but Amos is Amos. When he gets something in his mind, that's it."

J.D. smiled. "Sounds like a man in love."

I'd never really paid much attention to J.D., but I realized that he really was a nice-looking man. His dark brown hair framed an intelligent face, and his eyes were so blue, they almost looked fake. I wondered if he wore colored contacts.

"Yes, he does, doesn't he?"

J.D.'s gaze moved to Marion's tapestry. "It's really something."

"Yes, it is. I love it."

"That's you and Amos, isn't it?" he asked, pointing to the spot where Amos and I held hands and skated on the frozen lake.

"Yes. You know, Marion painted us as a couple. She also painted Buddy and Emily together. Odd, huh?"

He smiled. "Maybe Marion was prophetic. I think it's very special. I hear you're having your wedding reception here. Will you leave the tapestry up?"

"Absolutely. You know, Dela thought it should come down. We would have had a battle over that one." I laughed. "She was about as stubborn as I am. I wonder who would have won."

J.D. walked over to the French doors that led to the deck. Snow was still falling, but it was lighter now. He stared out the window for a few seconds and then shook his head. "I still can't believe she's dead." His voice was soft and there was a hint of pain. The anonymous tip about Dela having an affair popped into my mind, along with the sadness I'd seen in Ina Mae's face. Could it be. . . ?

"I didn't realize you knew Dela and Barney that well."

J.D. turned around. I saw the hurt in his eyes. "I sold their house in Dodge City and helped them find the new one in Winter Break. Ina Mae and I moved here a couple of months before Dela and Barney. A mutual friend referred me to them. During the process, Barney was gone a lot, on the road, you know. I spent most of my time with Dela." He pointed to the dining room table. "Do you mind if we sit down?"

I shook my head. "Of course not. I'll get our hot chocolate." I retrieved our cups and joined him at the table.

"I want you to understand something, Ivy," he said in slow, measured syllables. "I have never cheated on Ina Mae, but I was attracted to Dela." His eyes went back toward the window. I got the feeling he could say what he had to say more easily if he wasn't looking at me. "We started out talking about the house, but before long, we began sharing other things from our lives." He smiled, but it was empty and melancholy. "Dela was so different from Ina Mae. Vivacious. Interesting. Flamboyant. I found her compelling and. . .challenging." He turned to look at me. "I know how selfish that sounds. I'm really sorry it happened. Especially because Ina Mae got it in her head that Dela and I were actually having an affair." He shook his head. "She started going through my billfold, checking my pockets, even looking through my office for signs that I was cheating on her. It wasn't true, but I couldn't convince her of it. And then one day, she found some jewelry I'd picked up for Dela at an estate sale." His eyes locked on mine. "Dela was always buying jewelry. She liked to find expensive things at estate sales, yard sales, thrift stores. . .you know, places where she could pay a fraction of what they were worth. When Barney was out of town, I'd go with her sometimes. She hid a lot of her purchases from Barney. He's not a selfish guy, but he did ask Dela to show some restraint." He chuckled. "She tried, but it just wasn't in her nature. This one time, she sent me back to pick up a pearl necklace and matching earrings. The guy who was selling them had called her. He wanted to get rid of them and had cut the price in half. She couldn't get them without Barney finding out, so she asked me to keep them for her until she could retrieve them. I had them in my dresser drawer." He stared down at his hands. "I tried to explain it to Ina Mae, but she never would believe me."

"She thought you bought them as a gift for Dela?"

He nodded. "To this day, she thinks I betrayed her. She still doesn't trust me. We don't talk much anymore. To be honest, I've kind of thrown myself into my work. I guess it's so I won't have to deal with the way things are between us."

"Maybe you need to try again. It might be different this time."

"I don't know. She was so angry, Ivy." He looked up at me. "And then when I found out Dela had been murdered. . ."

I didn't know what to say. Did he really think Ina Mae had killed Dela? *Could* she have done it? I thought about her actions at church. Was it absolution she'd been seeking? I had a hard knot in my stomach. "J.D., after you picked Ina Mae up at the church the night of the city council meeting, did you go right home?"

"Yes. I was really tired. I'd been out of town showing two properties. When we got home, I went straight to bed." He stared at me, worry lines creasing his mouth and eyes. "And no, I don't know if Ina Mae left after I went to bed. I just can't believe she could have. . ." He stopped and shook his head. "I've been with Ina Mae for twenty years. She doesn't have a violent bone in her whole body. There's just no way. Really."

I got the distinct feeling J.D. was trying hard to convince both of us that Ina Mae couldn't have killed Dela. But scorned women, whether their rejection was real or imagined, had committed violent acts before. The possibility was obvious, but there was something else working in my mind. The bracelet Dela wore. The reason it was too big. "J.D.," I said, "during your jewelry buying trips with Dela, did you ever see her buy a rhinestone bracelet with blue stones?"

He looked startled. "Can I ask why you're interested in that bracelet?"

I sighed. "You can, but unfortunately for now, I can't answer your question. I can tell you that it's really important. You said 'that bracelet.' Do you know the one I'm talking about?"

He nodded. "I remember it because the family of the woman who sold it to Dela got really upset about it. They said it had been sold for a fraction of its worth."

"What did Dela do about it?"

He shrugged. "She wasn't concerned. She said a deal was a deal. I don't think she was trying to be harsh, but people like Dela are looking for a 'steal' when they go to estate sales. When they find one, they take it. There's just as much risk the other way. You know, buying something you think is valuable and finding out later it's not what you thought it was."

"Did you talk to the people who sold the bracelet yourself?"

"No. Dela told me all about it. She'd gotten several calls from someone related to the original owner. After awhile, the calls began to get scary. Threatening. I insisted she contact the police, but she wouldn't do it. Then she and Barney moved to Winter Break." He smiled. "Not a place most people would think of looking, I guess. Dela never heard from them again." He cupped his hands around his cup as if trying to warm them. "I don't know. At the time Dela's reasoning made sense. Now that I think about it, maybe she should have tried to make it right." He looked at me quizzically. "Does that help you?"

"I'm not sure," I said honestly. "But I appreciate the information. J.D., could Ina Mae have known anything about the bracelet?"

He thought for a moment. "Maybe. She listens in on a lot of my phone calls, although she'd never admit it. I can't really be certain." He took a sip from his cup then he set it down. "You make a great cup of cocoa, and you're a wonderful listener. Sorry I dumped all that on you. Guess I've been stuffing my concerns for so long they were waiting to come out to the first kind person who cared enough to let me talk. I hope I haven't made you uncomfortable."

"Not at all," I said. "My great-aunt Bitty used to say that the difference between a friend and a stranger was a cup of hot chocolate and a good conversation. I'm glad you felt comfortable enough to share your feelings."

He chuckled. "I guess that makes us friends."

"I guess it does," I said with a smile. "Could I make a suggestion, J.D.?"

He nodded. "Of course."

"Why don't you and Ina Mae meet with Pastor Taylor? I'm afraid I'm not an expert on marriage, but Pastor Taylor is a pretty smart man. I think if you two could get honest about your feelings, he could probably help you."

J.D. stared out the window at the snow. "You might be right. I should have suggested it a long time ago. I guess I was just so ashamed of having feelings for Dela. But if admitting my sin in front of my pastor will save my marriage, I'll do it." His gaze shifted to me, and he reached over and squeezed my hand. "Thanks, Ivy."

"I really believe you two will be okay," I said. "How about another shot of cocoa?"

He handed me his cup. "I'd love it."

I was on my way to the kitchen, when I heard a strange thumping sound. A glance toward the front door revealed the origin. Miss Skiffins was wrapped around one of J.D.'s snow boots.

"Miss Skiffins!" I hollered. "Get away from there!" She rewarded my command by totally ignoring me. I put our cups on the kitchen counter and looked at J.D., who seemed to find the whole thing funny. "I'm really sorry. She has this thing about certain shoes." Up until that moment, she'd been focused on my slippers and a pair of my sneakers. I'd discovered her more than once with her head inside one of them.

Thankfully, she wasn't actually inside one of J.D.'s boots, but she was certainly enamored by them. She had pushed it over and was licking the bottom as if it were her kitten. Luckily, she was enjoying herself so much she didn't run from me when I approached her. It took a little effort to separate her from her new rubber friend, but after a few pulls and some severe scolding, she let go. I carried the small calico kitten into the kitchen.

"I have no idea what got into her," I said to a very amused J.D. "There's something about your boots she really likes."

"Don't worry about it," he said with a grin. "If I didn't need them tonight, I'd leave them here for her. She certainly enjoys them more than I do."

I set the cat down next to her food bowl in the kitchen. Then I reached into the cabinet for a can of cat food. Usually, that was all it took to get her attention. But as soon as I released her, she made a beeline back to the boots. I ran after her, but she reached her goal before I could scoop her up. Again, she fastened her claws around one of the boots and I had to pry her off. It was really rather embarrassing. J.D.'s hoots of laughter didn't help. Once again, I relieved my obsessed feline from the object of her affection. "You're on a time-out, missy," I scolded. "I'm sorry, J.D. I'll be right back." I ran up the stairs and deposited the cat in one of the bedrooms. "You sit in here and think about your manners," I hissed at her. Unfortunately, she didn't look the least bit repentant. I closed the door and hurried back down the stairs. When I rounded the corner, J.D. was still laughing.

"I'm glad you think it's funny," I said with a smile. "If she's poked a hole in your boot, you might not find it so humorous the next time you step in a puddle."

He waved his hand toward me. "Don't worry about it. I'm actually glad I got stuck in the snow tonight. I've had a wonderful time. Miss Skiffins was simply the entertainment section of our evening."

I noticed that J.D.'s overall appearance had changed since he'd come in the front door. His guarded persona had been replaced with an easy affability. I shook my head and snickered. "I guess it *was* pretty funny. Cats are really unusual animals. They have minds of their own. Seems like dogs work hard to obey you. Cats work twice as hard to ignore you."

J.D. grinned. "I had a cat when I was a kid, and you're right. He was quite a character. Ina Mae and I have two springer spaniels. They're our babies, I guess. Maybe we should add a cat to the mix. I have to admit my dogs aren't nearly as entertaining as your Miss Skiffins."

I'd just made two more cups of hot chocolate, when there was a knock on the door. "That should be Amos." I handed him his cup. "You drink that first, then we'll take care of your car."

I set my cup down on the table and hurried to the door. When I opened it, I found Amos standing there with an odd look on his face. I could immediately see that something was wrong. He stepped inside and stomped his boots on the carpet without saying a word to me.

"What's the matter, Amos?" I asked. "Has something happened?"

He grabbed my hand and led me into the dining room where J.D. sat sipping from his cup. "J.D.," he said in a somber voice, "I received a call from my dispatcher on my way over here. Your neighbors heard your dogs barking for over an hour, so they went over to your place to see what was wrong. They found Ina Mae at the bottom of your back steps. I'm so sorry, J. D., but she's dead."

10

Amos and J.D. left to go to his house. Emergency medical personnel were still there with Ina Mae's body. Dr. Lucy Barber had also responded. Her practice was in Hugoton, but she came to Winter Break frequently to take care of its citizens. She was also a friend of mine. Amos told me that Lucy determined Ina Mae's death was an unfortunate accident. She had gone outside to check on the dogs and slipped on the icy back stairs and broken her neck. Lucy had already released the body to Elmer Buskin at Buskin's Funeral Home, but they were waiting for J.D. to arrive and tell them if he wanted her sent somewhere else. Since the Feldhammers weren't originally from Winter Break, it was possible he would want another mortuary to handle things.

I was tired, but I couldn't sleep. I heated up my cold cup of chocolate and sat at the dining room table where J.D. and I had laughed at Miss Skiffins a little over an hour earlier. I couldn't believe that Ina Mae was dead. It seemed so strange, talking with her at church, and then suddenly, she was gone. All I could do was pray for J.D. Our time together had definitely brought us closer. Odd how a stranger can become a friend in such a short amount of time. Now, his pain was mine. I doubted that I would ever forget the look on his face when Amos told him about his wife. It was as if the bottom had dropped out of his world. And it probably had. I couldn't help but wonder if he was regretting the rift in his marriage and wishing he'd had a chance to repair it.

A movement out near the lake caught my eye. There he was. The collie was trotting around the shore. He stopped and looked my way. I got up and checked the refrigerator. There was some roast beef left from Sunday. I took it out and set it on the cabinet. Then I got my coat and opened the French doors. The dishes I'd left outside for the dog were on the ground next to the deck stairs. As I stepped down the slick stairs to get them, I realized that this was exactly what Ina Mae had done. The thought sent a shiver of alarm through my body. I held on tightly to the stair rail going down and coming back up. On my way back toward the house, I got an idea. There was a small storage shed on the deck where the lawn tools were kept. I unlatched the door, pulled the string for the overhead light, and looked inside. It wasn't big, but there was enough room for a small Border collie. I went inside the house and checked out the linen closet. I found an old comforter that I hardly ever used. I put the roast in the food pan and carried it and the comforter out to the shed. Then I took the frozen water bowl to the kitchen and cleaned it out. I put the fresh water in the shed and put a small gardening trowel under the door so that it would remain open a crack. I also left the light on. If the dog could find enough courage and trust to go inside the shed, he'd be safe from the cold.

I watched from inside until I was finally exhausted enough to go upstairs and try to sleep. Maybe it was thinking about Ina Mae and the look in her eyes before she went up for prayer at the church, but I was determined to help that dog. Ina Mae was certainly more important than an animal, but the Border collie had become a symbol for me—that the impossible *was* possible. That there was no one so broken, God couldn't mend them. No creature so hurt that they couldn't be redeemed. Since I'd put the food into the shed, I hadn't seen the dog. It was up to him now. Help was extended. He'd have to decide whether or not to accept it.

I went upstairs and collapsed on my bed. As I lay there, staring up at the ceiling, I realized that a lot of people were in the same condition as the abandoned collie. They felt lost and alone, deserted by the people they'd trusted the most. Yet there was Someone still waiting for them, Someone who had been calling them their whole lives. He was holding out a life full of love, acceptance, and peace, yet because of fear, many of them turned a deaf ear to that call. And just like the small, lost dog, their very lives depended on taking a step of faith out of the cold and into warmth and safety. As I fell asleep, I prayed for the collie and for all the people in the world who had never felt the kind of love that God has for anyone who will simply accept it.

I woke up in the morning to the smell of bacon and coffee. For a moment, I was confused. Then I remembered that Dewey was staying with me. However, bacon wasn't on Dewey's list of approved foods. I got out of bed, pulled on a pair of jeans and a sweatshirt, ran my hands through my hair, and stumbled down the stairs to the kitchen. Dewey was sitting at the kitchen counter, eating oatmeal. Amos was at the stove, cooking bacon and scrambled eggs.

"What are you doing here?" I asked. "And...what are you doing?"

"I'm making your breakfast, Sherlock," Amos said with a mocking smile. "Boy, you don't wake up too sharp, do you?"

Dewey didn't say anything, but he chuckled.

"Okay, I guess I deserved that, but *why* are you making my breakfast?"

He put his fork down on the spoon rest next to the stove. Then he came over and put his arms around me. "Because last night I realized how really blessed I am." His voice cracked a little. He stepped back and looked into my eyes. "Watching J.D. come to grips with losing his wife brought me to the conclusion that no matter what happens in life, I can do anything with you by my side." Without any warning, he kissed me.

When he finished, I put my hand up to my mouth. "Shoot and bother, Amos! I haven't even brushed my teeth yet!"

He laughed and kissed me again. "I don't care. After we're married, I intend to kiss you every morning of your life!"

I stepped away before he could grab me again. "You keep cooking. I'll be back." I ran upstairs to the bathroom, brushed my teeth and my hair, and put on some mascara. By the time I got back, Amos was putting my food on a plate. Before I sat down, I checked outside. I could hardly believe what I saw. Sticking out of the tool shed was the tip of a black tail. I resisted the urge to go out there. I kept my mouth shut and went back to the kitchen. It wasn't that I was trying to keep my progress with the dog from Amos. Okay, yes, I was. For now, I thought it would be best to keep it to myself.

"Amos told me about Ina Mae," Dewey said when I sat down on the stool at the counter. "I can't believe it. We just saw her last night. It doesn't seem real."

I prayed over my food and then stuck a forkful of eggs in my mouth. "I know," I said after I swallowed. I was hungrier than I'd expected, and the eggs were delicious. "I can't imagine what J.D. is going through today. First Barney and now J.D. It's terrible."

"I thought maybe we'd go by and see him," Amos said. He'd fixed himself a plate but ate it standing up, leaning against the counter in the kitchen. "Milton Baumgartner and his sons were already out this morning, clearing Main Street. You can go to the bookstore for a while if you want to, and we can stop by J.D.'s on the way home."

Milton Baumgartner ran Winter Break's volunteer fire department. He also owned a farm outside of town. Milton and his sons were always the first ones out after a snowfall, cleaning the snow from our downtown streets.

"Sounds like a good idea," I said. "Are you going with us, Dewey?"

The old man nodded. "I'd really like to open the store. When it snows like this, folks like to stock up." He stood up and pushed the kitchen stool to the side. "If it won't cause any trouble, I'd like to get a quick shower first. Besides," he said, "I'd rather not watch you two shovel down bacon and scrambled eggs."

I grinned at him. "I understand. Go ahead. I'll get a shower when you're done. Don't use up all the hot water."

He shot me a dirty look. "Thanks for giving me ideas. Perhaps the cold water will stir up your sense of compassion. Next time you can eat oatmeal with me."

"Oatmeal?" Amos said with a smirk. "Only old people eat oatmeal."

Dewey wadded up his napkin and threw it, bouncing it perfectly off Amos's forehead, making us all laugh. As soon as Dewey went up the stairs,

I said, "I've got so much to tell you!"

"Me, too," Amos said. "You go first."

I told him about J.D.'s interest in Dela and how suspicious Ina Mae had been of her husband's activities.

He set his plate down next to the sink and folded his arms across his chest. "Are you saying he thinks Ina Mae killed Dela?"

"He didn't say that, Amos. In fact, he defended her. But I could tell the thought had crossed his mind."

"I wonder if she could have taken Dela's bracelet. Maybe she hid it somewhere in her house." He reached over and poured himself a cup of coffee. He held out the pot to me but I shook my head. I'd barely started on my first cup.

"Not if the bracelet Hope has is the one we're looking for."

Amos rubbed his temples. "Here we go again. You know, we've faced a few confusing situations, but we've never tackled anything with so many rabbit trails. I start down one, and another one pops up. I can't seem to find a clear path."

I took a big sip of coffee. The jolt of caffeine helped to wake me up a little. "Well, what do we have so far? I mean, we know I didn't do it."

Amos grinned. "You know, if you'd just confess, we could wrap this up. I'm really tired of thinking about it."

"You're very funny. Will you please try to concentrate?"

He threw his hands up in a gesture of surrender.

"We think Hope has the bracelet," I said slowly, "but there's nothing to tie her to Dela. And as far as this 'affair' tip you got, the only affair seems to be one that was in J.D.'s mind, and according to him, it never went anywhere. The only real motive we've come up with so far belongs to Ina Mae. She thought her husband was having an affair with Dela. But if she did it, what about the bracelet? You know, this bracelet doesn't seem to fit anywhere. It's confusing." I took another sip then put my cup down. "Anything from the KBI yet?"

Amos shook his head. "They're going over the car, but so far the only fingerprints they've found are yours, Dela's, and Barney's. It's a new car, so any other prints could belong to the killer. And the only fingerprints on the chopstick are yours and Dela's. Of course, we already expected that." He sighed. "The recurring theme here seems to be you."

"Obviously the killer wore gloves," I murmured.

"I'd like to suggest that you start wearing gloves," Amos grumbled. "It would certainly solve a lot of problems."

I chose to ignore him. "Do you think the sheriff still suspects me?"

"I don't know. If he really thought you'd done it, you'd be behind bars. But it's not over yet, Ivy. He still has to follow the clues, and right now they point toward you. And here's the newest information—and this only adds to the puzzle. Remember the tip that mentioned Barney and insurance fraud?"

"Yes?"

Amos sighed again and absentmindedly ran his hand through his hair. "There may be some truth to it."

I almost dropped my fork. "What are you talking about?"

"Barney's company didn't send him to western Kansas just because he needed to be closer to his clients. There were some suspicions about a couple of properties that burned down. The owners increased their coverage through Barney, and then suddenly, the buildings went up in smoke. One was a restaurant in Dodge City that wasn't doing very well. Another was a farm belonging to a guy who lived a few miles outside the city. Seems he was getting ready to lose everything. He increases his coverage, and his house and outbuildings burn down." He shrugged. "There wasn't any clear evidence of wrongdoing, so the company paid, but the suspicion was so strong, the top dogs wanted to distance themselves from Barney. They couldn't fire him without proof, so moving him out here was the only answer they could come up with."

"But what does that have to do with Dela's death?"

"If Dela knew Barney was getting payoffs from his clients, he could have killed her to shut her up. Maybe she was planning to turn him in."

"So he stabbed her with a bronze chopstick from their wedding? Really good plan." Actually, for the first time, I realized how using the chopstick had a twisted justice to it. Barney in the dragon suit flashed in my mind. Could he have endured a ceremony like that and then killed the woman he was willing to humiliate himself for?

"Unfortunately, that's not all. Barney recently took out a large life insurance policy on Dela. He stands to rake in a million dollars."

"A million dollars?" I could hardly believe it. Things were certainly piling up against Barney.

"Of course, if he killed Dela, he'll never see the money."

I drank some more coffee, trying to clear the cobwebs out of my head. "But what would the bracelet have to do with anything? Barney didn't need to steal it. He could have gotten it anytime he wanted to. And why kill her in a car in my driveway? It would have been easier somewhere else." I thought for a moment. "You know something, Amos? Those chopsticks bother me."

"What do you mean?"

"How could anyone know she had them in her purse? Originally, they were in her attaché case. And who would even know she had them in the first place, or had moved them to her purse, except me? If you plan to kill someone, you're not going to hope they have a pair of chopsticks in their purse. You're going to bring a weapon with you. It doesn't make any sense."

"From what you've just told me, I have even more reason to think you did it."

I shot him a dirty look.

"I'm starting to wonder if this bracelet is getting us off track," he said. "If we take it out of the equation, things look a lot clearer."

"But we can't forget about it. Dela had it on when she was alive. When she was dead, it was gone. Now Hope may have it. We've got to follow that rabbit trail. Even if it leads us the wrong way."

"I guess we just add it to everything else." Amos finished his eggs and rinsed off his dish. Then he picked up the frying pan and dumped a large amount of scrambled eggs into a bowl which he set in front of me.

"Thanks, but I'm full. Are you trying to fatten me up so I can't possibly fit into my wedding dress, should I ever have one?"

He came around the counter and kissed me on the head. "No. I thought maybe your toolshed guest might like them."

My mouth dropped open. "You know about that?"

"When I got here, I looked out the back windows to see if the snow had stopped. I saw him looking out the door."

"Did he see you?"

"No. I stepped back before he noticed me." Amos's face crinkled in a frown. "I understand what you're trying to do, Ivy. But I mean it about being careful. Don't approach him. You let him come to you—if he ever does. This might be as close as he'll ever get. You understand that, right?"

I smiled and nodded. Of course I didn't understand it. *Nothing so broken that God can't mend it.*

He shook his head like he knew what I was thinking. "I'm going to talk to Hope about that bracelet. Then I've got to ask Barney about the fraud allegations. I'll come back as soon as I can to get you and Dewey."

"Amos, my mom called. She's getting into Wichita about one in the morning."

His expression didn't change, but his eyes widened for a second. "No problem."

"I don't think you should do it. You have too much going on. I'll get her."

"Hey, now that's a good idea. Or, we could just go out and push your car into a snowdrift and get it over with." He wrapped his arms around me. "Don't worry about it. We're a team. I'll get your mother. Everything will be fine." He leaned down to kiss me. "You get your shower. I'll be back as soon as I can." He started to walk away, then he stopped and turned around. "And say a prayer for me, will you? There's no way I can ask Barney these questions without making it obvious he's a suspect. That's not something I really want to do."

"I will. Amos, maybe you should take me with you to talk to Hope. You know, because I'm a woman. It might make things easier."

He took his coat off the rack. "Yes, I've noticed you're a woman." He slid on his coat and paused with his hand on the door. "You know what? Maybe I'll take you with me on both visits. You haven't had a chance to offer Barney your condolences, and I could use your insight. Maybe you could make him your famous tuna casserole. But, Ivy," he said, frowning at me, "let me ask the questions, okay? I don't want it to get back to Hitchens that you're interrogating witnesses."

I nodded at him and smiled. I knew Amos wanted my help, but his "official side" had boundaries. It was my job to try not to step over them. I was going to have to keep my nosiness in check.

"Why don't you get ready, and I'll pick you and Dewey up around noon. I want to see how the snow removal's going, and I need to stop by Dorian Harker's place. Seems he loaned his camper to Pete Bennett so his brother could stay in it until he got a job and found a place to live. He moved out a couple of months ago and no one told Dorian." A slow smile spread across his face. "I guess the door was left open and a family of raccoons moved in. He's got a camper full of raccoon droppings and he's fit to be tied." He shook his head and chortled. "Who ever said the life of a deputy sheriff isn't glamorous?"

I didn't envy Amos his raccoon detail, but I was thrilled to go with him. I wanted to hear what Barney and Hope had to say. Maybe we'd uncover our murderer today. Although, I had to admit that neither one of them seemed like good suspects to me. "Thanks, Amos. I'll be ready."

He blew me a kiss and went out the door. I really was concerned about the long trip to Wichita. Amos wasn't getting much sleep. I wondered if there was another way to get my mother here. I decided to look up bus schedules when I got to the bookstore. I doubted that she would care. She and my dad frequently used public transportation in Hong Kong. They were constantly utilizing buses, trams, or mass transit. Although I knew there weren't any buses to Winter Break, maybe we could at least get her close.

Dewey was still upstairs taking a shower so I had a little extra time. I carried the eggs outside, but the shed was empty. All the roast beef was gone and most of the water. The water that remained was frozen. The comforter had obviously been slept on. I emptied the eggs into the food bowl and carried the water bowl into the house. After filling it with fresh water, I put it back in the shed. I looked around for the dog but didn't see him. As I closed the French door, I thought I saw something black moving in the yard, on the side of the deck where I couldn't get a clear view. I walked away from the doors so he wouldn't see me and get spooked.

I was rinsing our dishes and putting them in the dishwasher when I noticed the box of honey and jelly Amos had carried in the night before. Since I had a little time, I decided to take it downstairs. First I took one of the jars of jelly out and set it on the counter. I had some in the refrigerator, but it was almost gone. I was addicted to huckleberry jelly. Hopefully, Alma would keep it coming. Every year she visited her sister in Oregon and together they put up jelly and preserves. She even brought back whole huckleberries for baking. I tried to pace myself so I wouldn't run out before the next trip, but it wasn't easy.

The box wasn't too heavy, but after I switched on the basement light, I held on tightly to the stair rail with one hand and the box with the other. The stairs were pretty unstable and needed to be replaced. I made it down to the bottom and carried the box over to the shelves that lined the wall. They reached almost to the ceiling. The shelves were wide and deep and anchored to thick wood backs. Cecil had built them for Marion's peach preserves and homemade applesauce, and he hadn't taken any chances that the shelves would ever break and lose their precious cargo. Marion's peach preserves were fantastic, and she made the best applesauce I'd ever tasted. In the final steps she added red-hot candies. It gave the sauce a wonderful flavor. I'd promised myself that someday I'd learn how to make it just the way she had. For now, though, the shelves were lined with jars of Bubba Weber's honey. I was really happy that Dewey was clearing out one of his storerooms so the honey would finally have a permanent home.

I put the box on top of my washer, then I took the jars of honey from the box and lined them up next to the fifty or sixty other jars we already had. When I finished, I took out the remaining three jars of jelly. When I put them next to the other jars, I got a surprise. And it wasn't a good one. I was certain I'd had five jars left from the last batch Alma gave me. But there were only four. I stood there for a moment trying to remember if I'd counted wrong, but I was sure I hadn't. Could Amos have taken a jar upstairs? I'd checked the fridge yesterday. I was sure there was only a partial jar there. I looked around the room and checked the rest of the shelves to see if a jar had been inadvertently moved, but there was no missing jelly to be found.

"Well, shoot and bother," I said out loud. It wasn't going to do any good to stand here and stare at the remaining jars. I was pretty sure another jar of huckleberry jelly wasn't going to magically appear.

Finally, I picked up the empty box and took it over to the big trash can in the corner. I tossed it in and started to leave, when something caught my eye. I got down on my knees and looked under the shelf that held the jelly. A piece of broken glass was lodged under the bottom shelf. I carefully pulled it out. It was part of a jelly jar. Amos must have broken one and not told me. I tossed the glass in the trash can. Although I thought it a little odd he hadn't mentioned it, he was probably just afraid to get between me and my huckleberry jelly. It was actually kind of funny. I made a vow to lighten up on my huckleberry jelly obsession. It was obviously frightening my future husband.

By the time I got upstairs, Dewey was helping himself to a cup of coffee, and behind his back Miss Skiffins was helping herself to the jar of jelly I'd left on the counter. She was licking the jar with all her might, hoping, I guess, that she would eventually wear the glass down and make her way to the prize inside.

"Miss Skiffins!" I yelled. Dewey almost jumped out of his shoes. "Sorry," I said while I chased the chastised cat off my counter. "There was an act of larceny being perpetrated on my huckleberry jelly jar while you weren't watching."

"Next time maybe you could warn an old man who lives alone before you scream at your cat—or anything else," he said, shaking his head. "No one ever yells at my house. I'm not used to it."

I came around the counter and hugged him. "Again, sorry. Maybe you should get a cat. That way you could spend half your time shouting at it to stay out of things. It seems to be an integral part of sharing your life with someone of the feline persuasion."

"I think I'll pass," he said. "My heart doesn't need all the excitement."

I told him about Amos picking us up around noon. Then I put a tuna casserole together and popped it in the oven. By the time I'd showered and changed, Amos was back. I made some sandwiches, took the casserole out of the oven, and we all piled into Amos's car. First we dropped Dewey off at his store, and then we went to the library. Barney's house was a little way out of town, just like mine, except in the opposite direction. Amos wanted to go to Barney's after the library and stop by J.D.'s on the way home. I was wondering how much time I would actually spend in Miss Bitty's Bygone Bookstore today.

The light was on in the library. I was rather certain Hope would be there since Sarah Johnson's house was only a couple of blocks away, but I doubted that Faith had come in. Inez Baumgartner's place was not too far from mine, and the roads were still snow packed. Amos knocked on the door and Hope peeked out. Sure enough, when we stepped inside, there wasn't any sign of Faith.

"I figured you wouldn't venture out today, Ivy," Hope said. "If the sidewalks hadn't been cleared, I'd probably still be at Sarah's." She wrinkled her turned-up nose. "It's too cold out there. How about a cup of coffee?"

"No thanks," Amos said, speaking for both of us.

"Actually, I'd love a cup," I said, sitting down in the chair by the door. "Thanks, Hope." When she left to get the coffee, I poked Amos in the side. "The more relaxed you make this, the more information you'll get, Deputy," I whispered. "Don't give her the third degree, just talk to her."

He bent over and put his mouth near my ear. "You're not actually a law enforcement officer, Ivy," he whispered. "I know my job."

I squeezed his arm. "I know you do, cutie pie, but cleaning out raccoon excrement doesn't really qualify you for interrogation, does it?"

"First of all, I didn't clean out raccoon excrement. I just told Pete Bennett to do it. And secondly, don't call me cutie pie." He sounded mad, but I saw him trying to hide a smile.

Hope came back into the room carrying my coffee. After handing it to me, she leaned against the nearby desk. "Now what can I do for you two?" she asked.

Amos pulled out his notepad. "Hope, I need to ask you something. It's about a bracelet..."

Hope's eyes widened. "A bracelet? How would you know about that?"

I jumped in before Amos could answer. If there was any way to keep Faith out of this, I wanted to do it. "Someone saw it, Hope. It doesn't matter who it was. They just happened to mention it."

She looked confused. "I don't understand why it would be important to you."

Amos cleared his throat. "It's important because Dela Shackleford was wearing a rhinestone bracelet in the morning, but when we found her body that night, it was gone. We need to know what happened to it. If you have it, I need you to explain to me how it came into your possession."

The color drained from Hope's face. "Are you saying you suspect me of killing Dela Shackleford?" She slumped against the desk. For a moment, I was afraid she was going to faint.

I shot a look of warning to Amos. "No, of course not. No one thinks you had anything to do with her murder. Amos just needs to tie up all the loose ends. It's part of his job."

Hope glanced from me to Amos. "The bracelet isn't rhinestones, Amos. It's made out of diamonds and sapphires. It's worth almost seven thousand dollars."

Now I was the one who felt faint. This information certainly didn't make Hope look innocent. She'd just given herself a motive for murder. "Is it the same bracelet I saw Dela wearing Wednesday morning?" I asked.

Hope nodded. "Yes, it is."

"Can you tell me how you gained possession of it?" Amos asked.

Since he was ignoring my advice and talking in his official "deputy sheriff" voice, I jumped in. "You're not in any trouble," I said with a smile. "I'm sure there's a simple explanation."

She pulled herself up onto the desk, her legs dangling over the side. "I'm afraid the explanation isn't that simple, Ivy. Dela came by here Wednesday afternoon and gave it to me."

Even I had a hard time accepting that. Amos's expression was one of pure skepticism. "Why would she give you a bracelet worth seven thousand dollars?" I asked.

She shrugged. "That's simple. Because it's mine." She folded her arms in front of her. "Look, it belonged to my grandmother. After she first became ill, I moved in to help her. But eventually, she got so bad I couldn't give her proper care. We put an ad in the local paper so we could sell some of her things and hopefully get enough money for her move to a nursing home. The only item she had that was really valuable was the bracelet. At first, she didn't want to sell it. But once she realized how dire things really were, she agreed to let it go. I told her that I would take it to someone who could get us a good price for it. Like a professional jeweler or collector. But one afternoon while I was out, a woman came by inquiring about the jewelry. My grandmother, who had Alzheimer's, sold her the bracelet for two hundred dollars. When I returned home and found out, I was frantic. Thank goodness the woman had left her name and number in case there were any more pieces my grandmother wanted to sell."

"It was Dela?" I asked.

She nodded. "Yes. I called her several times, asking her to return the bracelet, but she kept putting me off."

"Why didn't you call the police?" I asked.

"It wouldn't have done any good," Amos said. "The bracelet wasn't stolen. The only thing she could have done would have been to take Dela to court."

"That's right," Hope said. "Unless the court decided that my grandmother wasn't competent to make the deal she had, we had no case. Alzheimer's is kind of like a roller coaster. Some days were good, some were bad. If they questioned her on a good day, she would have sounded completely rational." She sighed. "I didn't know what to do. I guess I should have pursued it, but then my grandmother died, and I gave up."

"Until you found out Dela was living in Winter Break?" Amos asked.

"Yes. I didn't know her by sight, but I certainly knew her name. When she was introduced to me as someone interested in the library, I was shocked, to say the least. She obviously didn't remember my name. A couple of days after that, I went to see her. I told her who I was and explained how much I needed that bracelet. You see, there wasn't enough money to pay for all the funeral expenses, and I had to take out a loan. Making the payments has been very difficult. My grandmother had a few other debts that passed to me. I have to find a way to pay them off. My only choice is to sell the bracelet."

"Look, Hope," I said slowly, "I don't want to cast aspersions on Dela when she can't defend herself, but why would she suddenly decide to give you back the bracelet? It doesn't sound like her."

"You may find this hard to believe, but she told me that once I'd put a face to the situation, she couldn't keep the bracelet. She even apologized for not making things right sooner. And she wouldn't even let me pay her back the two hundred dollars. Dela turned out to be a much nicer person than I'd imagined her to be."

"Where's the bracelet now?" Amos asked.

"It's in my room at Sarah's. I planned to get a safety deposit box in Hugoton, but then the weather got so bad." A look of panic swept across her face. "You aren't going to take it, are you?"

"Well, not yet," Amos said solemnly, "but I can't guarantee that the sheriff won't order me to confiscate it at some point. It may be evidence. If we do take it, it will be safe, and if it's determined that it has nothing to do with Dela's murder, it will be returned to you."

Hope slid off the desk and stood in front of him. "You don't believe me, do you? You really think I'm involved in this somehow." Her voice has harsh with resentment.

"I'm not forming an opinion one way or the other. It's not my job. I'm only trying to find out what happened to Delaphine Shackleford. I think her killer should be brought to justice, don't you?" The glint in his narrowed eyes went toe-to-toe with Hope's determined expression. I wasn't sure who was winning, but I felt it was time to call a truce.

"Amos, we need to get going. That casserole I made for Barney is going to be frozen solid if we don't get it to him soon." I stood up and stepped between them, giving Hope a hug. "I'm sure everything will be okay. Please don't worry. We'll find the truth, I'm sure of it."

Hope didn't really hug me back, she just stood there. But at least she didn't pull away. I said good-bye, then steered Amos out the front door. When we stepped out on the sidewalk, he broke my grip on his arm.

"Why did you do that, Ivy? There were a few other things I wanted to ask her."

"Let's get in the car. She was getting angry, Amos. And frightened. Do you want her to skip town? If she really is involved, you'd have to find her. I don't think you want to do that."

"You can't interfere when I'm questioning a suspect. I asked for your insight, not your interference."

I knew I'd crossed over the line. "I'm sorry. I really was only trying to calm her down. I'll watch it."

He shook his head and helped me down the steps to the car. We climbed inside and he started the engine. After staring out the window for several seconds he turned toward me. "I accept your apology, Ivy. I know this is hard on you. I really want your help, but I have to be careful. You're not a law enforcement official. You can't do my job for me. From now on, let me take the lead, okay?"

"I will, I promise."

The tightness around his jaw relaxed a little. "Do you really believe that story about Dela giving her back the bracelet?" he asked. "Doesn't sound right to me."

"No, it doesn't. But to be honest, neither one of us really knew Dela. I mean, we can't actually *know* someone unless we've really spent some quality time with them, can we?"

"That sounds good. Now tell me what your gut instinct says."

I sighed deeply. "It is extremely suspicious of Hope's story."

He put the car in gear. "Let's go see Barney. And could you please let me do my job without interrupting?"

I batted my eyelashes at him. "If you'd do your job correctly, I wouldn't have to interrupt."

Amos mumbled something under his breath that I didn't catch. For the sake of our relationship, I decided to let it go.

About fifteen minutes later, we pulled up in front of Barney's house. There were a couple of other cars parked there. I got the casserole out of the backseat and followed Amos to the front door. A woman I'd never seen before opened it to let us in.

Amos introduced himself and asked if Barney was available. The woman took my casserole and led us into the back of the house. Barney was seated in the family room, and there were several other people with him.

"Amos and Ivy," he said when we walked in. "How nice of you to come by." He introduced us to each of his relatives. His brother and sister-in-law from Dodge City, his cousin from Missouri, and Dela's sister and brother. Dela's sister looked a lot like her, but she was younger and not as flashy. I felt bad for her. I'd never had a sister, but I could imagine that losing one must be terrible.

"Barney, I hate to bother you at a time like this, but could I talk to you for a few minutes?" Amos asked politely.

"Of course you can," Barney said, rising to his feet. "Let's go into the living room."

I told everyone how nice it had been to meet them and followed Amos and Barney into the other room. The living room was toward the front of the house. Dela's touch was apparent. The decor was modern and rather unconventional for Winter Break, Kansas. But all in all, it was attractive and well put together. I couldn't help comparing Dela's style to mine. Everything in Dela's house was *coordinated*. *Eclectic* was the only way to describe my home, but I liked the way everything went together. It was comfortable and homey.

Amos and I sat down on a white sofa with zebra-striped throw pillows.

Barney sat next to us on a sleek black leather chair. A large, square glass coffee table was in front of us. The walls were painted a warm raspberry, and they were lined with black-framed black-and-white pictures of Barney and Dela. A shiny black piano was against one wall. I wondered if Dela had played. There was so much about her I didn't know.

"Now, what can I do for you, Amos? Have you found out who killed my wife?"

I caught myself comparing Barney's chubby face with that of a Shih Tzu. I was going to have to stop the dog versus people comparisons. My similes were in bad need of revamping.

"I'm sorry, Barney. We haven't arrested anyone yet, but we're trying hard to get at the truth. Unfortunately, I have to ask you some questions now that won't be comfortable, but I assure you that the only reason I'm asking is so we can eliminate everything that isn't important." Amos took his notepad and pencil out of his pocket and handed them to me. I was surprised but more than happy to help. Maybe Amos was trying to seem a little less official this time around.

"I think I understand," Barney said, looking back and forth between us. "What can I possibly tell you that will help?"

Amos cleared his throat. I knew this was difficult for him. He was connecting to Barney in a way he hadn't with Hope. I felt strongly that I should be quiet and let him find his own way.

"We've received some tips at the office," Amos said carefully. "I want you to know that although we have to follow up on all of them, we don't take anonymous tips too seriously. People call and leave information for a lot of reasons. Some calls are from people who have nothing better to do than to waste our time. Then there are others who have their own axes to grind."

"What are you trying to say, Amos?" Barney said with a frown. "Has someone called in with a tip about my wife's murder?"

"More than one, I'm afraid." Amos leaned forward and clasped his hands together. "Look, Barney, here it is. Just remember, I'm not asking you about these things because I believe them. I'm asking you because it may lead us to Dela's killer."

Barney's face relaxed a bit. "Okay. I understand. Please tell me what these people had to say."

Amos leaned back, clearly relieved that Barney was receptive. "Well, one person said Ivy killed Dela because she wanted to be president of the library board."

Barney's eyes widened and he laughed. "That's ridiculous. Are they all like that?"

Amos nodded. "Pretty much. Someone else claimed that Dela was having an affair and her lover killed her. Another claimed that she was killed over the missing bracelet I told you about. And someone else claimed that you killed her because you were trying to hide some kind of insurance fraud."

I noticed that Amos had left out the accusation about Barney being the killer because of jealousy over an affair. I guess one allegation of murder was enough. I also noticed that his face turned an even pastier white than usual. Because Amos had lumped all of the accusations together, I wasn't certain which one had hit its mark, but unless I missed my guess, at least one of them had caused a definite reaction.

"What can you tell me about these charges, Barney?" Amos asked gently.

"I—I'm flabbergasted," he answered haltingly. "How could anyone think that Dela was cheating on me? It—it's just cruel. And completely untrue." He began to cry. And I don't mean a little bit. He boo-hooed so loudly, the woman who'd opened the front door for us came running into the room.

"Barney! What's the matter? Do you need—"

"I'm all right, Irma," he blubbered. "Leave us alone. Please."

Irma shot Amos and me a dirty look. I immediately felt defensive. As if I'd personally attacked Barney during his most vulnerable moment. All I could do was offer her a sickly smile and shrug my shoulders. When she left, I got up and sat next to him.

"It's okay," I said as soothingly as I could. "It's probably just someone who didn't know you and Dela. Please don't be so upset." I patted his arm and waited for him to get control of himself. I really *did* feel bad for him.

"I'm sorry," he said when his sobs lessened enough for us to understand him. "I guess I never could understand why someone as wonderful as Dela would love someone like me." He shook his head and gave me a small, sad smile. "Believe me, I know I'm not a catch. Dela was so. . .so. . .wonderful. She was the toast of the town in Dodge City, you know. Everyone knew her. I was just the man who followed her around, living in her glory." He reached into his pocket and took out a handkerchief. He wiped his eyes. "But you know what? She truly loved me. The Dela the public saw wasn't the Dela I knew. She was kind and thoughtful. And as silly as it sounds, she was crazy about me. I know that sounds almost impossible, but it's true."

"What about the other charges?" Amos asked cautiously. "Can you tell me anything helpful about them? Is there anyone you think might have made them?"

Barney shook his head. "There were a couple of instances in Dodge City that looked suspicious. People who insured through me and had fires not long after that. But if they were scams to get insurance money, I had nothing to do with it. I know someone at our agency cast aspersions on me, but it wasn't true. There was never any evidence. If there had been, I would have been fired." He thought for a few moments. "And as I told you just the other day, I don't remember the bracelet you described. It doesn't mean that Dela didn't have it at one time. She may have. I showed you Dela's jewelry collection the other day. It's very large. I couldn't keep track of all the pieces. I'm afraid I'd scolded her more than once about buying so much. I'm pretty sure she didn't tell me about everything she purchased."

"We found the bracelet," I said. "Hope Hartwell at the library has it. Can you think of any reason Dela would give her jewelry?"

"No, but it doesn't mean she didn't do it. Dela loved to give jewelry as presents." He suddenly straightened up. "Oh, my goodness. I'm so glad you reminded me." He stood up. "Please, wait here. I'll be right back."

After he left the room, Amos wagged his finger at me. "I'm not sure we should have told Barney about Hope. We're going to have to follow up with her, and I'd rather not have everyone knowing we suspect her."

"I know," I said in a low voice, keeping an eye out for Irma. "But if he had given us a connection between Hope and Dela, it might have made Hope's story more believable."

"What about Dela having an affair? He sure reacted to that."

"Yes, he did," I said. "If he was so secure in his relationship, would he have gotten so emotional? I'm not sure. But I have to say, Dela certainly seemed devoted to him."

He raised his eyebrows. "I hate to say it, but people cheat sometimes even though they claim to love their spouses. I don't think we can rule Barney out."

I started to bring up J. D. Feldhammer again. If Dela was going to cheat with anyone, why not him? He was certainly good looking enough. I'd just opened my mouth to share my thoughts when I heard a door close. Barney was on his way back.

"I found it right away," he said as he walked back into the room. "Dela had put it on top of the dresser with this note."

He handed me a long black case. I opened it to find a beautiful emerald green necklace with a matching bracelet and earrings. The deep green baguettes on the necklace and bracelet were edged with sparkling rhinestones set in silver. The earrings were slightly curved with three large green stones in the middle and small rhinestones on each side. The set was breathtaking.

"I'm sorry, Barney," I said. "I don't understand."

"Read the card," he said, his eyes tearing up again. "It will explain everything."

I opened up the envelope he'd handed me. Dela's perfume drifted up from inside. I pulled out the ivory card and read:

COZY IN KANSAS

Dearest Ivy,

    I've noticed how lovely you look in green. I thought perhaps this set would bring out your gorgeous red hair and green eyes. Please accept it from me as your "something old." These pieces actually belonged to my mother. I can't think of anyone else I'd rather see wear them. Thank you for letting me be a part of your wedding. Your friendship has been a tremendous blessing.

Your friend, Dela

Now my own eyes were tearing up. "Oh, Barney, she wanted to loan these to me for my wedding?"

He shook his head vigorously. "No, no, Ivy. She wanted you to have them. They're yours. But please, if you don't like them, don't feel under obligation to wear them. Dela's taste could be somewhat extravagant. This might not be something you'd wear. . . ."

"Nonsense," I sputtered, tears running down my face. "They're absolutely beautiful. I'd be honored to wear them. But I don't think I should keep them. Maybe someone in the family. . ."

Barney wiped his eyes and smiled. "To be honest," he said, his voice lowered so only Amos and I could hear him, "Dela couldn't stand my family much, and she despised hers even more. But she thought the world of you. If you don't take this gift, she will probably come back to haunt both of us." He reached over and took my hand in his. "Please, Ivy. I know it would mean so much to Dela, and it would mean a lot to me, too."

I was so overcome with emotion, I could only nod. I hugged Barney and noticed Irma peeking from around the corner to see what was going on. "Okay," I whispered in Barney's ear. "I'll wear these at my wedding as long as you're there to see me in them."

He released me. "I would love to be there. Thank you, Ivy. And I believe this is for you also." He picked up the folder he'd carried in with the jewelry box. "I believe these are sketches Dela was working on for you."

"Thank you. I'm going to make certain Dela's ideas are incorporated. It will make our special day even more memorable." I slid the file into my purse.

Amos cleared his throat, and I turned around to see him frowning at me. I suppose I wasn't being very *professional*, but I didn't really care.

"We need to get going, Barney," he said. "Thank you for giving us your time. If I hear anything helpful, I'll contact you."

"Do you have any idea when they will release Dela?" Barney asked. "It's hard to plan her funeral without knowing. . ."

"I'm sorry," Amos said. "The coroner should release the bod—I mean, Dela, any day now. As soon as I hear something, I'll let you know immediately.

Where are you having the funeral?"

"Right here in Winter Break," Barney said. "You know, even though Dela was well known in Dodge City, she never really felt at home there. Everyone was so kind to her here, she was beginning to feel as if she finally belonged somewhere. Helping you with your wedding was the icing on the cake, Ivy. And being chosen to serve on the library board meant the world to her. One consolation I have is that the night Dela died, she was very happy. I love it here, too. I intend to stay, and I want her nearby."

Amos shook his hand and I hugged him again. As we left, weasel-faced Irma watched us all the way to the front door. I was certain she was staring at the jewelry box in my hands, but I didn't feel bad. For some reason, I was happy she wouldn't be getting her hands on it.

"Well, what do you think?" Amos said as soon as we got in the car.

I sighed and stared out the window at the house where Dela had once lived. "I have to tell you, Amos, we've questioned every possible suspect, and I have absolutely no idea who killed Dela Shackleford. After talking to Barney, I realize that I didn't know Dela at all. I thought she hated Winter Break, and I didn't think she was too crazy about me either." I stared at the jewelry box in my hands. "I guess I was wrong."

Amos started the car and turned toward me. "We have too many leads. I can't separate one from the other." He rubbed his gloves together. "I'm going to drop you off at the bookstore for a while. Then we'll visit J.D. on the way home. I've got to go to the office and see if anything new has popped up with this case or with our bank robber. Hopefully, someone else has had more luck than we've had."

He put the car in gear and drove slowly toward town. I couldn't shake a feeling that we were missing something. That the answer was in front of us, but we weren't seeing it. I prayed that God would give us wisdom and that Dela's killer would be brought to justice. For now, I was going on pure faith. A scripture in Proverbs three jumped into my mind: *"Trust in the Lord with all your heart and lean not on your own understanding; in all your ways acknowledge him, and he will make your paths straight."*

"Lord," I whispered, "if we ever needed You to make the path straight, this is it. Please help us to put all the pieces together. We can't do it by ourselves. I'm putting my trust in You." A sense of peace washed over me, and by the time we got to the bookstore, I felt like a big burden had been lifted.

11

As soon as Amos dropped me off at the bookstore, I got on my computer and began looking up bus schedules. I hadn't taken my laptop home yesterday or I could have looked up the information I needed last night. I was going to have to break down and put a computer in the house. I'd been putting it off, but it was no longer a luxury. It was becoming a necessity. I waited for what seemed forever for dial-up service, the only option right now for Winter Break. It took awhile for me to discover that there was no bus that would get my mother close enough to make a difference, but I found a train that could get my mom from Newton, which wasn't too far from Wichita, to Dodge City. It would take Amos only two hours to get to Dodge City. A much better prospect. The problem was that I had no way to call my mother. She was already on her way. I phoned an old friend of the family in Wichita. A deacon at our former church, he was happy to hear from me and perfectly willing to pick up my mother at the airport and drive her to Newton, even though her train wouldn't leave until three thirty in the morning. After speaking to him, I ordered her ticket. It would be waiting for her when she arrived at the train station.

With that problem solved, I packed up some books for mailing, but I could look across the street and see that the post office wasn't open. Alma lived even farther out of town than I did. I was pretty sure she wouldn't venture in to work until tomorrow. Maybe. Oh, the joys of small-town living.

It was after five o'clock before Amos finally made it back. I called J.D. to see if it was okay to stop by. He seemed pleased to have company. He was even happier when I offered to stop by Ruby's and pick up dinner. On the way over to Ruby's, I told Amos about putting my mother on a train. Although he had been a trouper about picking her up in Wichita, the difference between a twelve-hour and a four-hour round-trip was obviously a huge relief to him. It also meant he could get some sleep tonight before he hit the road. I'd entertained the idea of going with him, but in the end, I decided that coming to get me at three o'clock in the morning would just make things more difficult for him. Besides, I was exhausted, and a good night's sleep was something I craved more than an early morning car ride to Dodge City.

We left the café a little after five thirty with four roast beef dinners and Dewey in tow. When we pulled into J.D.'s driveway, we ran into Inez

Baumgartner backing out of the driveway. I jumped out of Amos's car and ran up to her window. She smiled at me and rolled it down.

"Why, Ivy," she said, "how nice of you to bring J.D. dinner. I left him some sliced ham and cheese for sandwiches. He should have enough to get by for a while."

Although Inez was at least twenty years older than her beautiful daughter, Emily, she could have been mistaken for her sister. During the vacations I'd spent in Winter Break with Aunt Bitty, I'd loved hanging around Emily's house so I could spend time around her mother. She was so different than mine. Inez could sew anything, was a fantastic cook, and her family absolutely adored her. Her late husband, Jake, used to light up whenever she came in the room. Inez had the unique ability to make a house a home. I'd watch her as she bustled around, always humming hymns. I learned to love several of the old hymns because of Aunt Bitty and Inez. They both loved the same songs. My favorites were "Softly and Tenderly," "The Old Rugged Cross," and "Blessed Assurance." Whenever I heard these songs, I was reminded of one rainy afternoon when Bitty and I visited at Emily's house. Inez played the piano while she and Bitty sang hymns. Emily and I sat on the floor and listened, scarfing down Inez's chocolate pecan cookies, fresh from the oven. It had been a perfect afternoon.

"I'm so glad to see you," I said, reaching through the car window to hug her while Amos juggled three Styrofoam containers of food. Dewey was holding on to his for all he was worth. "Thank you so much for offering to make my wedding dress. I really appreciate it."

Her large doe brown eyes sparkled. "I was so excited to be asked. I've already found a basic pattern I think you will like."

I remembered the photo in Dela's folder. "Dela Shackelford gave me a picture of a wonderful dress. I'll make a copy and get it to you." I sighed. "With Dela's death and Ina Mae's accident, wedding plans have been put on the back burner."

She shook her head. "It hasn't been a good week in Winter Break, has it? A few people in town keep saying that disasters come in threes. They're waiting for something else terrible to happen. I think that's foolish, but it does make you wonder a bit."

"Hopefully, the next catastrophe will belong to Dela's killer," Amos said. "I think his time of reckoning is coming."

"My goodness, I hope so," Inez said. "You all better get inside before that food gets cold." She waved at Dewey, who was more focused on dinner than being neighborly. "Good to see you, Dewey. I've got some shopping to do. I'll see you tomorrow." She smiled at me. "Let me know when I can get a picture of that dress, Ivy. I'm so excited to see it."

I gave her my assurances and she pulled out. Amos, Dewey, and I tramped through the snow to J.D.'s front door. As we came up the driveway, I could see the steps in the backyard. I tried not to stare at them, but just a quick glimpse made me shiver with something besides the cold. J.D. answered the door after our first knock. I was grateful because my hands were freezing, even in gloves.

"Come on in," he said with a smile. "How nice of you to bring dinner." He held the door open for us. The mat on the inside already held J.D.'s rubber boots. They were soon joined by three more sets. Boots were a part of everyone's wardrobe in Winter Break. With 90 percent of the winter spent wading through snow, they were almost a part of our bodies. Without them, cold feet and ruined shoes were the only possible result.

Although the house was small, it was neat and clean. A brown recliner sat near the fireplace. An old oak rocker was positioned near a forest green couch. A gorgeous patchwork quilt lay over its back. Against the wall was a curio cabinet. Its shelves were lined with framed pictures and statues of angels.

"Did Ina Mae collect angels?" I asked.

"Yes, she did," J.D. said. "She loved them."

"And did she make this quilt?" I couldn't take my eyes off of it. It had a cream-colored backing, and each corner had five interlocking rings with flowers. The center of the quilt also had five colorful rings with a center of bright flowers. I'd never seen anything like it.

"Yes," J.D. said softly. "Ina Mae was really talented, but she never wanted to sell her work. She always gave away the things she made." His voice broke.

"I. . .I'm sorry, J.D.," I said. "Maybe I shouldn't have said anything."

"No, I like hearing about her. It's like she's still here." He pointed toward the back of the house. "Let's take this food into the kitchen before it gets cold."

Ina Mae's kitchen was also a reflection of her creativity. Homemade oven mitts hung from kitchen drawer knobs, and patchwork curtains framed the windows. It was a homey, cozy kitchen, obviously owned by someone who liked to spend time there. J. D. moved a suitcase off the table and put in on the floor near the back door.

"I'm going to Liberal tomorrow," he said, pointing at the suitcase. "Elmer is taking Ina Mae there for the funeral. I hope you can all come. I hate to make it inconvenient for our friends in Winter Break, but except for her mother, all of Ina Mae's family lives in Liberal."

"Will her mother be able to attend the funeral?" Dewey asked.

"Unfortunately, no. She's very ill. To be honest, no one has told her about Ina Mae. They don't think she'll last much longer, and we don't have the heart to cause her that kind of pain. Of course, she's been in and out of reality for so long I doubt she'll even realize Ina Mae hasn't come to see her."

"That's a shame." I could understand the decision not to tell her about her daughter's death, but somehow it seemed worse for the old woman to think she'd been deserted. I hoped J.D. was right and she wouldn't be aware of Ina Mae's absence.

We sat down at the table and opened our containers. The aroma of Ruby's incredible roast beef wafted through the room. J.D. got us silverware and napkins. Then he took a pitcher of iced tea out of the refrigerator and filled glasses he set on the table.

"Anything else?" he asked, looking back and forth at each of us.

"Can't think of a thing," Dewey said, "except grace. Do you mind if I pray?"

J.D. smiled. "I'd be honored."

Dewey blessed the food and prayed that God would comfort J.D. and help him through the next few days. He also asked the Lord to console Barney and bring Dela's killer to justice. We all added our "amens" and started shoveling food into our mouths like we hadn't eaten in days. That just kind of happened with Ruby and Bert's food. Dewey grumbled a little because his roast beef was sans gravy, and instead of a potato, he had fresh green beans and a piece of whole grain bread, but all in all, he was satisfied.

We talked some about Ina Mae's service. J.D. wasn't sure when the funeral would be held. "My guess is Monday or Tuesday," he said. "Taking her to the mortuary on Saturday means we'll have to wait a bit before she's ready. I'll call you and let you know as soon as I know something definite."

"Will you come right back?" Amos asked.

J.D. shook his head, his eyes full of sorrow. "I'll probably stay there awhile. I think it will help to have Ina Mae's family around, and of course, we have old, dear friends there." He smiled at us. "Not that you're not good friends."

I reached over and grabbed his hand. "We all understand. You need to do whatever helps you. But we're here for you if you need us."

His eyes filled up with tears which he wiped away on his sleeve. "Thank you. You have no idea what that means to me."

We chatted for a while longer about some of the goings on in Winter Break. I checked my watch and saw that it was getting late. "I hate to break this up, but Amos has to drive to Dodge City around three o'clock in the morning to pick my mother up at the train station. He needs his beauty sleep."

"Before you go," J.D. said, looking at me, "I want to give you something for your wedding. Something from Ina Mae." He pointed toward the living room. "Would you like to have that quilt? I know Ina Mae would be blessed to know it went to you. It's the way she was."

I started to protest but realized that if I refused, it might hurt his feelings.

"I'd love it, J.D.," I said. "It's the most beautiful quilt I've ever seen."

"I'll get a plastic bag for it before you leave. I'm so happy you like it. Maybe you'll remember her when you see it."

"Goodness," Amos said. "Barney gave you some of Dela's jewelry, now J.D.'s giving you Ina Mae's quilt."

J.D. picked up our food containers and carried them to the trash can. "Barney gave you some of Dela's jewelry? That's was really nice of him. I'm sure Dela would be pleased."

"Actually, she'd already picked it out for me. She wanted me to wear it at my wedding." I pulled the jewelry box out of my purse. Dewey hadn't had a chance to see it either.

"Why, Ivy, those are absolutely beautiful," Dewey said when I opened the box. "Dela was right. You definitely should wear them at your wedding."

"That's exactly what I intend to do. Dela thought they would go with my hair."

Amos smiled. "She was right."

I popped the lid shut. "I think she was wearing an emerald necklace with matching earrings the night she. . ." I couldn't finish.

J.D. came up behind me and patted my shoulder. "Ivy, I'm not a jewelry expert, but that set was designed a lot differently than this one and it was set in gold, not silver. Please don't let the fact that the stones are the same color ruin Dela's gift to you. They're not connected."

I fought back tears. "You're right. Thanks, J.D. Guess I'm feeling a little emotional tonight." I put the box back in my purse. "The important thing is that Dela's gift was from the heart. They could all be made out of plastic and it wouldn't make any difference."

Amos grunted. "So I could have given you an engagement ring from a Cracker Jack box and it would have meant as much to you as what you're wearing? I wish you'd told me that *before* I spent all that money."

"Oh hush," I said brusquely. "Spending money on someone you love is good for the soul. I was only helping you."

"Uh-oh," Dewey said with a grin. "That womanly reasoning only gets worse as time goes on. You might as well hand over your wallet and be done with it."

"You watch out, old man," I said, laughing. "You're sleeping in my house tonight, you know. You better keep one eye open."

J.D. put Ina Mae's quilt in a bag and handed it to me as we left. I hugged him. "Thank you so much, and let us know about the service. I'm sure we'll be there."

J.D. stood in the doorway, waving as we left. He looked so forlorn and alone, I almost made Amos drive back, but I couldn't think of anything else we could do for him but pray. We got home around seven o'clock. I made Amos a pot of coffee while Dewey watched TV in the living room.

"Thanks for picking my mother up," I said. "Sorry I'm punking out on you. I've got to get some sleep. I'm exhausted, and my mother's going to take all the energy I have. At least I won't have to worry about the wedding. She'll have things whipped into shape in no time."

Amos chuckled. "I don't doubt that."

I set a cup of hot coffee in front of him and made myself a cup of caffeine-free raspberry tea. I didn't want anything keeping me awake tonight. "Anything new on your bank robber?"

Amos sighed deeply. "Absolutely nothing. I'm beginning to wonder if we'll ever catch him. But I don't want to talk about him now. Let's discuss our visits today. I've been going over several different scenarios in my mind." He scooted his stool up closer to the counter and stared into his cup. "Most of the time when a spouse is murdered, the husband or the wife is guilty. Therefore, I can't rule out Barney. Statistically, he's the number-one suspect. I know it seems as if he really loved Dela, but playing the bereaved partner has certainly been done before. I'd like to find out if she really was having an affair. That would make things a lot clearer."

"I'm not convinced she was," I said doubtfully. "It's entirely possible that the man she was seen with in Dodge City was J.D. But we can't be sure about that. There may be someone else involved who isn't even on our radar screen."

"That's true. And then I have to look at Ina Mae. She sure was carrying some heavy burden—something she felt she needed prayer for. Maybe she followed Dela that night to your house and attacked her. Whoever killed her didn't plan it ahead of time. A fight over J. D. fits the bill exactly."

"And J.D. can't give her an alibi. She could have left the house that night."

"And Hope isn't out of the picture. So far, she has the clearest motive." He rubbed his hands across his face. "You know what bothers me? Why didn't Dela tell Barney about that bracelet? Was it really because he told her not to buy so much jewelry? This whole bracelet business. I think it might be important."

"Yes, it could be, but I still don't think Hope is a killer."

Amos reached over and stroked my hair. "My beautiful Ivy, you don't think anyone is capable of murder."

"I'm afraid that's not true anymore," I said, taking his hand in mine. "I've learned people are capable of great evil, but it's hard to spot them because they never see themselves as villains. In some twisted way, they believe they're victims trying to right some terrible wrong done to them."

"You're right. It doesn't matter what crime someone's committed, they always seem to have an excuse. I guess the first step toward murder is convincing yourself you have a valid reason to eradicate a human being who has interfered in your life. It's the worst kind of selfishness."

I sighed. "This is getting too deep for me and my tired brain."

Amos stood up. "I'm going home to get some sleep before driving to Dodge City." He leaned over and kissed me. "And God bless you for coming up with this new plan. If I had to drive to Wichita tonight, I don't know what I'd do." He walked over to the French doors in the dining room. "What's going on with your visitor?"

"I don't know. I gave him your eggs this morning. Is he out there?"

"I can't tell, but I don't see him." He pushed the door open and stepped outside. He came back a moment later. "Sorry, honey," he said. "The eggs are still there and so is the water. Either he didn't come back today or he doesn't like eggs."

I felt my emotions well up, but I didn't want to cry in front of Amos because he'd already warned me about getting attached to the dog. Truth was, I was in desperate need of a happy ending.

"Oh, well," I said as casually as possible. "I'll put out something else before I go to bed. It's probably a critique of your cooking."

"Oh, thanks." He wrapped his arms around me. "I'll see you in the morning. I'm looking forward to spending some time with your mother. She's a super lady."

"Yes, she is. I'm glad she's coming, too. Dewey can finally go home tomorrow."

Amos glanced toward Dewey, who was watching one of the cable news channels. "I'm not so sure he'll be happy to leave," he whispered. "I think he likes it here."

"I love having him here. Maybe we can adopt him and he can live with us after we're married."

He wrinkled his nose like he was considering it. "Hmm. Well, I was thinking more toward someone younger, but maybe we could make do with Dewey."

I bopped him on the head, and he kissed me again. "I love you, you know," he said softly into my ear.

"I know. I'm fond of you, too."

He laughed and let me go. "I better quit while I'm behind." He headed for the front door. "See you tomorrow, Dewey," he said as he walked past the couch.

" 'Night, Amos."

Before Amos closed the door, he blew me a kiss. I went back to the kitchen and finished my tea. Then I went outside to check on the dog. Just as Amos had said, the eggs were still there. I brought both the bowls inside and cleaned them out. I went through my refrigerator, but I couldn't find anything I thought a dog would like. I checked the pantry and found some cans of corned beef hash. I dumped the contents of two of them into the food bowl, filled the other one with water, and carried them outside. After I put the bowls in the toolshed, I stared out into the dark, hoping to see the dog. The temperature was really dropping. I would have loved to set up a small heater in the shed, but it was too dangerous. Since the shed backed up next to the house, I hoped it would help to provide a little warmth.

By the time I got back inside the house, Dewey had turned off the TV. "Think I'll head upstairs to bed," he said. "I'm not real tired, but I have some reading I want to do. Burrowing under the covers with a book sounds like the perfect evening."

"It does sound nice, but I don't think I'd make it past the first page. I'm heading up in a few minutes." I went over to my old friend and gave him a big hug. He hugged me back.

"Good night, sweetheart," he said. "You know, Ivy, I couldn't love you more if you were my own child."

"I know that," I answered, blinking back tears. "You're as much family as anyone in my life."

He let his arms drop and turned to go upstairs. "Sometimes I miss your aunt Bitty so much I can hardly stand it," he said in a quiet voice. "And then sometimes, like right now, I could swear she was still here." He smiled at me, but I knew he was seeing Bitty. And it was okay with me. With that, he walked carefully up the stairs, holding tightly to the handrail. For the first time, I realized how much slower he was moving these days. Dewey was getting older, and I couldn't imagine my life without him. Someday he would be gone. I just hoped that day was a long time coming.

I went back to the kitchen and made another cup of tea, toasted an English muffin, and slathered it with butter and huckleberry jelly. All I wanted to do was fall into bed, but for some reason I was reluctant to go upstairs. I felt like there was something I'd forgotten or something I was supposed to do. I sat down at the dining room table and stared out into the night. The only illumination came from the lights near the lake. Cecil had strung them years ago for night skating. Amos frequently had to replace bulbs. He wanted the city to install some decorative light poles around the lake. So far, it hadn't been approved.

My foot hit something and I looked down. My purse was lying on the floor where I'd dropped it when we came in. I picked it up and set it on the table. Remembering the jewelry box, I reached into my purse and took it out. When I opened it, I was captivated again by how beautiful the pieces were. Green really was my best color.

COZY IN KANSAS

Once again, the feeling that there was something I was missing flitted through my brain. "What is it?" I whispered. "What am I not seeing?" I suddenly remembered something Aunt Bitty said once about worrying. Truth was, she had several admonitions when it came to worry. She believed faith and worry were absolute opposites. *"Worrying never solved a single problem, Ivy. Casting your care on the Lord gives Him a chance to work things out."* I took a deep breath and tried to relax a little.

When I took a bite of my muffin, a thought jumped into my mind. Something that had been said that didn't make sense—until I began to put it with all the other strange pieces of the deadly riddle Amos and I had been working on.

That "Sherlock Holmes moment" Amos hoped for had finally arrived, but there were still a few odd puzzle pieces that didn't seem to fit. Unless I could match them into all the remaining blank spaces and create a comprehensible final picture, a murderer was going to go free.

12

Sitting in the dark waiting to confront a killer is an interesting experience. On one hand, you feel triumphant because you're getting ready to
catch someone who's committed a truly evil deed. On the other hand,
you wonder just how many brain cells you could possibly have if you're willing
to put yourself within range of the person who's committed a truly evil deed.
These thoughts had been running through my mind for a little over an hour.
Of course it could have been fifteen minutes. . .or two hours. I had no idea.
It's hard to see your watch in the dark. I was getting extremely uncomfortable
seated on an old step stool Cecil and Marion had left in the basement when
they moved. It definitely had been made for feet—not bottoms.

Even though I'd been expecting it for quite some time, when I heard the
door to the basement open and steps coming near me, my heart felt as if it
would jump right out of my chest. From my vantage point, I could see the dark
shape of the killer pass by me. A flashlight came on and swept over the shelves
that held Bubba Weber's honey and my precious huckleberry jelly. I waited
until gloved hands began to take the jars from the shelves and set them on top
of my washer and dryer. Then I flipped on the light switch next to me.

"You're not going to get away with it, you know," I said, trying to keep my
voice from shaking. "I know what you did."

My intruder quickly swung around, eyes wide with shock. "What? What
are you doing down here?"

"Well, I live here. I'm pretty sure you're the person who doesn't belong."

"I. . .I was worried about you. With Amos gone and. . ."

I would have laughed if I wasn't so nervous. "You thought you'd break into
my house, check out how much huckleberry jelly I had, and somehow that
would keep me safe?"

The realization that there was no way to explain the situation seemed to
finally dawn on him. "No. I guess I don't expect you to believe that." He sighed
and leaned against my washing machine, his eyes never leaving my face. His
original look of surprise had been replaced with amusement. "Okay, I'll bite.
Tell me what you think I did, Ivy."

I cleared my throat. Nerves were making it hard for me to catch my breath.
My obvious discomfort seemed to add to his pleasure. "If you don't mind, I'd
rather start with what tipped me off. What it was that finally helped me to see

that you were the only person who could have killed Dela."

"I thought I covered myself pretty well. I'd be interested to hear what gave me away."

I tried to wiggle into a more comfortable position on the step stool. Instead of stabilizing myself, I was afraid I detected a slight shift in the old, rather rotten wood. I purposely leaned against the wall. Having my stool collapse beneath me would certainly reduce the drama of the moment. This was what mystery writers call the *denouement*—the moment when all the clues are revealed. And I didn't want to spend it in a heap on the floor. Still feeling rather vulnerable, I gave him my best Sherlock Holmes look. "It was the jewelry that Dela gave me. You compared it to the jewelry she was wearing when she died. Both sets had green stones."

"So?" J.D. said, looking puzzled. "I was right about that."

"Yes, you were. But how would you know what color her jewelry was? You came in late to the city council meeting, and you and Ina Mae were almost thirty feet away from us. Dela left when we did. You never got close enough to see the color of her accessories."

J.D. laughed. "That's it? That's what revealed me as the killer?" He shook his head. "I ran into her earlier in the day, before I left town. That's when I saw what she was wearing."

"Just my point. You see, Dela was wearing *red* and gold jewelry until right before the meeting when she changed to *green* and gold. You know as well as I do that Dela would sometimes switch her accessories several times a day. Yet not only did you know she was wearing green jewelry, you even knew they were set in gold, not silver like mine. You corrected me when I compared my jewelry to what she was wearing when she died. The only way you could have known that was if you saw her sometime after the city council meeting. Since she went straight to my house, you had to see her there—when you killed her."

He raised one eyebrow and considered this. "Okay. I'll give you that point. Go on."

"After realizing it was you, all kinds of other things fell into place. For one thing, you are the only person who could have called in all those tips. Except the one that Bertha Pennypacker phoned in."

"Bertha Pennypacker? What kind of tip would she have?"

"Never mind, it's not important. What *is* important is that you were the only one who knew about the bracelet. It wasn't hard to figure out that Dela also told you about the trouble with Barney. You told me that you and Dela spent a lot of time together while you were selling their house. It stands to reason that Dela told you *why* they had to move."

"Wait a minute." J.D. scratched his chin for a moment. "Barney could have phoned in those tips. He had all the same information."

"No. He didn't know anything about the bracelet. He never even knew Dela had it."

J.D. shifted his weight and crossed his arms. "How do you know that?"

"Easy. He told us. The bracelet must have been one of the pieces she kept secret. And it was pretty easy to figure out why you placed those phone calls. You were trying to misdirect the authorities. To keep them busy looking somewhere else. If they were investigating Barney or Hope, or even Ina Mae, it would give you time. You were trying to create as many red herrings as possible in an attempt to keep yourself off the radar screen."

"What about Hope? She could have done it."

I shook my head. "No. She was just an innocent bystander. Her story was absolutely true. Dela did feel badly about buying the bracelet for so little. She returned it. Dela must have told you she was going to do it."

A slow smile spread across his face, but his eyes were dead and cold. They reminded me of the pictures I'd seen of sharks. There was no remorse, no fear, only icy, clear calculation. I wondered if he was weighing his options about me. "She told me Sunday afternoon. Then on my way out of town on Tuesday, I saw her entering the library. It wasn't hard to figure out what she was up to."

"You lied when you said the person who wanted the bracelet was threatening Dela. You wanted me to think that Hope might have killed her for the bracelet."

He straightened up but made no move toward me. I was watching him, waiting for him to make a threatening gesture. But to him, this was a game, and he was too engrossed in it to stop it now. And too curious to know how I had tracked his moves.

"So far I'm impressed," he said, still smiling. "But there's more, isn't there? I mean—"

"You mean why are we here?"

"Exactly."

"Two reasons." There was definite movement from beneath me. "I've got to stand up. I've been sitting here too long. Do you mind?"

He gave me a quick bow. "Be my guest."

I slowly lowered myself from the stool, being careful to stay as far away from him as possible. I took a couple of steps to the left of my creaky, wooden nemesis and leaned against the wall. The circulation was returning to my extremities, but I was still well out of his reach. Of course if he moved quickly. . .

"That's close enough," he snapped. "Get to it, please. I have someplace I have to be. I can't give you much more of my time."

Maybe he wasn't as absorbed in our game as I thought. I felt a chill run through me. But since it was cold in the basement, it was hard to tell if my reaction was from fear or temperature. "Before we talk about why we're both shivering in my basement, I want to know something."

Again, he bowed with a flourish. "Ask away. It seems we have no secrets anymore."

"Did you intend to kill Dela when you met her at my house?"

For the first time, I saw a hint of remorse on his face. He hung his head slightly and lost some of the swagger he'd been exhibiting. "No. I followed her after the meeting. When she pulled into your driveway, I parked behind her and got out. I told her I wanted to talk to her and she let me get into her car. I asked her to. . .well, you seem to know what I asked her. Instead of trusting me, she got suspicious. I ended up telling her the truth. I pleaded with her to come away with me—to share everything I had. But she wouldn't listen. She told me she loved that Pillsbury Doughboy of a husband of hers, and she threatened to turn me in. We struggled and her purse hit the floor. Those stupid chopsticks fell out. Before I knew it, I'd grabbed one and I—I stabbed her." His eyes sought mine. "I didn't mean to hurt her. I loved her." Then his expression hardened again. "But she gave me no choice. It was her own fault. There wasn't anything else I could do."

"Nothing else you could do?" I said incredulously. "You could have let her live. You could have walked away." He took a step closer to me. It was casual but definite. I forced myself not to react. I needed more time.

"I couldn't walk away. If you truly know everything—you must understand why. Let's hear what you've figured out. I want to know if you're as smart as you think you are."

Actually, right at that moment I wasn't feeling too intelligent, but our game hadn't been played out yet. I had a few more moves to make. "Okay. I have no idea when you decided to start robbing banks. My guess is that as you handled properties in lots of rural communities, you began to see how unprotected some of the small banks were. It was easy for you to learn when big deposits were being made. If you couldn't get the information from your client, a few lunches in the local cafés gave you everything you needed."

He laughed. "Good job. You *are* sharp. Go on."

I cleared my throat again. I wasn't sure whether it was the dust in the basement or nerves, but my throat felt scratchy. "I suspect you told me the truth about Ina Mae. She really was suspicious of you. I'm pretty sure she had good reason to be, even though you weren't having an affair with Dela. She probably *was* going through your things, looking for evidence that you were cheating. Because of that, I doubt that you had any decent hiding places for your booty. But then you had an idea. A safe place that no one else knew about."

"Now, wait a minute," J.D. said in a rather irritated tone. "I can see how you made all your other assumptions, but there is no way you could have known about the hiding place. I've checked regularly to make sure no one but me has moved things. You're going to have to explain this one."

Even though I was somewhat fearful for my safety, I couldn't suppress a slight smile. "It was really Miss Skiffins who gave it away."

He frowned. "Your cat? I don't get it."

"Well, Miss Skiffins and huckleberry jelly." J.D.'s puzzled expression told me he still hadn't put it together. "First of all, I found a piece of the jar you broke while you were down here hiding the money. At the time, I didn't think anything about it. I figured Amos broke the jar and didn't tell me. But then, Miss Skiffins acted so strangely around your boots. Earlier this evening, when I was trying to piece all of this together, I was eating an English muffin with huckleberry jelly. And I realized that she was attracted to your boots because you had them on when you broke the jar of jelly. Even though you thought you'd cleaned up the mess, you missed one piece of the jar, and you really didn't clean your boots off very well. You see, Miss Skiffins is crazy about huckleberry jelly. She was trying to lick it off your boots."

Now he really did look confused. "But I walked through the snow. There shouldn't have been any jelly left on my boots."

"You don't know much about jelly, do you? It's sticky and hard to clean off. Maybe if it had been warmer in Winter Break and you'd been walking in wet, sloppy snow, you'd have had a chance. But since our temperatures haven't risen above freezing since your visit to my basement, your boots retained enough jelly to attract my cat."

He shook his head and took one more step toward me. "Anything else?"

"Yes. You started hiding the money in my basement when the house was still empty. Of course you had a key. You were the real estate agent handling the property. You still have a key to my front door. When Amos bought the house, you probably weren't too worried. The house can't be seen from the road. You could come here anytime I wasn't here, let yourself in, and hide more money."

"Since we don't have much time left," he interjected, "why don't you let me finish tying up all the loose ends?"

"Be my guest."

"Thank you." His gaze swept around the room, then rested on the shelves against the wall. "I'd already been working on a plan to rob several banks, hide the money, then leave town and start a new life. You see, I was tired of Ina Mae, tired of being married, and yes, there were other women. One in particular. She doesn't live in Winter Break and she has no idea I'm married. We have plans to move to somewhere warm. Somewhere safe where no one will ever find me. But I was having problems figuring out where to hide what you call my 'booty.' Then one day I was on the phone with Cecil Biddle, and he was telling me about how he had redone the old kitchen in this house. How it used to actually be part of what's now your dining room. He just happened to mention the old dumbwaiter behind the shelves in the basement. It was the perfect place. Since all the parts were finally in place, I put my plan in action. But two things happened I didn't count on."

"Me and Dela."

"Kind of. You and your wedding. That was what changed everything."

I stared at him and shook my head. "You know now that I wouldn't have had that tapestry taken down, don't you? You killed Dela for no reason whatsoever."

He shrugged and stared at the floor. "I gave her a chance. I knew if you found the other door to the dumbwaiter behind the tapestry, you would have discovered my money. I told Dela all she had to do was to tell you to leave the tapestry up and wait for me to get the money from the last bank. Then we could leave this one-horse town together. We could have been happy."

"What about your girlfriend?"

"I really would have taken Dela instead. She was the most intriguing woman I ever met."

"Unfortunately for you, she was not only in love with her husband, she was too ethical to live on stolen money."

J.D. sighed. "This has been very interesting, but I really have to get going."

"Just two more things I want to clear up." I'd been keeping my eyes on his body language. He was getting restless. I had one final card to play, but I wanted to hold it until the very last moment. I could see that it was coming quickly. "Why are you still here? Why haven't you left town? Hanging around so you could get caught doesn't make much sense."

He eyes narrowed and he glared at me. "I couldn't possibly have taken off right after Dela was killed. It would have looked too suspicious. Besides, I had one more bank to hit to bring me to my goal of half a million dollars."

"But if you'd just taken what you already had and left Winter Break, Dela would still be alive. You could have gotten the money out before anyone took down the tapestry. No one would have ever suspected you."

He frowned at me like I'd lost my mind. "I couldn't take the chance that Dela wasn't going to start fooling around with the tapestry Tuesday night. Even if she hadn't, leaving early wasn't in my plan. I'd worked too hard to set everything up. I had one more bank, and I had no intention of letting anything keep me from getting everything I was entitled to. This really wasn't my fault, you know," he said, glowering at me. "If you'd been capable of planning your own wedding, everything would have turned out fine."

It was obvious to me that J.D. was so locked up in chains of evil that the idea of not fulfilling his selfish goals had never occurred to him. "That brings me to one last question." For the first time since we'd begun our strange exchange, my emotions got the better of me, and I couldn't stop the tears that formed in my eyes. "Why did you have to kill Ina Mae?"

He grinned. "I had everything I needed except a way out of town. Ina Mae gave me the perfect excuse." He stuck out his bottom lip and tried to look sad. "I have to bury my wife, and because of my incredible grief, I'm going away for a while." His forced melancholy expression disappeared and his lips parted in a big grin. "No one would ever think to follow me. You know, Ina Mae really was taking food to the dogs. A small push from me was all it took on those slippery stairs. Thank goodness the fall killed her. Of course, I would have been more than willing to finish the job if it had been necessary, but it wasn't. Her 'accident' solved everything. Then I drove over here, put my car in a ditch, and used you for my alibi. It seemed like the perfect solution. It also gave me a chance to make sure the tapestry was still where it should be."

"And now you're back to pick up your money."

He grinned. "I needed to get it before I left town, and you let me know when your boyfriend would be gone. With just you and Dewey in the house and Amos too far away to do anything to stop me..."

"You figured you had the perfect setup."

"That's it." He reached into his pocket and pulled out a gun. "Too bad you decided to play Miss Detective. I'm afraid your snooping is going to end very badly. I'll shoot you if I have to, but I don't think it will be necessary. Unfortunately, I'm afraid you're about to have an accident yourself. Those stairs don't look very safe, do they? I think you came down here to get something and you slipped and fell."

"Another murder, J.D.?" I asked.

For just a moment, the look in his eyes changed and I saw a trace of vulnerability. "I didn't start out with the intention of hurting anyone. I wouldn't have shot the guy in Chevron, but he forced my hand. And I didn't want to kill Dela." He took a deep, ragged breath. "The weird thing is that each time it gets easier. I don't really understand why. But it does." The hardness came back into his face.

"The more you give to the devil, the more he owns you," I said softly. "He's got a stronghold on you now. I pray someday you'll kick him out and give yourself to God. Even with everything you've done, He'll still forgive you and love you."

This time he threw his head back and laughed heartily. But he who had the last laugh. . .well, you know. It was time for the last play of this game. I raised my voice. "Take nothing on its looks; take everything on evidence. There's no better rule."

Before J.D. had the chance to wipe the puzzled look from his face, a voice came from behind him. "Put the gun down, J.D. There's nowhere to go and no way out of here." J.D. swung around to see Amos, who had stepped around the corner and had his gun pointed right at his chest. As he lifted his gun around toward the man I loved, I finally moved from my spot. A jar of huckleberry jelly is good for many things. Conking a killer on the head wouldn't have normally been on my list, but it did the job. He didn't lose consciousness, but he dropped his gun. That was good enough for Amos.

"I thought I told you to stay put, little lady," Sheriff Hitchens said harshly. "I had it covered." He stepped up behind Amos, his gun also drawn.

"Sorry, Sheriff," I said, "but I couldn't take a chance."

While Amos put cuffs on J.D., the sheriff yelled up the stairs for the other deputies who were waiting. "Bag that gun," he barked at one of them. "I'm pretty sure it will match the bullet we have from the robbery in Chevron." He got up in J.D.'s face, which had gone completely ashen. "We gotcha good, son," he droned in his deep, bullfrog voice. "You not only confessed to all those bank robberies, we got you on assault and two counts of murder. You're goin' away for a long, long time."

With that, the sheriff turned and smiled at me. I was shaking so hard, I wasn't certain I was capable of staying upright. Had I really just attacked a cold-blooded killer with a jelly jar?

"You can thank this young woman for puttin' you away," he continued. "After she figured out you were the guy we were lookin' for, she called us. And just so you know, we took that bank money out of here before you ever arrived."

J.D. was speechless. He looked sicker than any human being I'd ever seen in my life. The sheriff handed him to one of the deputies who stood near us. "Put him in the car and stay with him. We're not lettin' this yahoo get away." He put his face near J.D.'s and glowered at him. "And Deputy Biggins, if Mr. Feldhammer here so much as moves an eyebrow, shoot him, will you?"

J.D.'s eyes widened and he went limp. As the deputy pushed him up the stairs, he looked completely defeated. And I guess he was.

Sheriff Hitchens stuck his hand out and I took it. "Little lady, I guess you really are Sherlock Holmes, Junior. Sorry I ever doubted you. Our friend here could have been layin' on a beach in Acapulco before we ever figured this one out. You did a good job. If you're ever interested in working for the sheriff's department. . ."

I grinned at him. "After tonight, Sheriff, I'm ready to exchange my cape and magnifying glass for a wedding dress and a quiet life in Winter Break. I'm afraid there will only be one deputy sheriff in this family."

"I understand." He smiled and squeezed my hand. Then he left, following his deputies upstairs and, thankfully, out of my house.

Amos grabbed me and squeezed me so hard I yelped. After a long hug and an even longer kiss, he pulled back and gazed into my eyes. "That was a harebrained idea, Ivy. Luring J.D. down here and getting him to confess to everything."

"It was the only way we could be sure to put him away for good, Amos," I said. "You know that. All we had was circumstantial evidence. Except for the bullet in his gun. But we needed to get him for the murders, not just the bank robberies. We all discussed it before we made the decision. Even Sheriff Hitchens agreed it was a good idea."

"But when he took out that gun. . .what if he'd shot you before we had a chance to get to you?" Amos's eyes were wet. I reached up and wiped a tear from the corner of one of his beautiful eyes.

"But he didn't. And now we know that Dela and Ina Mae's killer will pay for what he did. It was all worth it."

"Let's not argue about it anymore," he said. "I'm freezing. We need to go upstairs and warm up a little." He looked at his watch. "Deputy Winslow should be back with your mother around seven thirty or eight. You can still get a little sleep before she arrives."

"A little sleep? That's where you're wrong, bucko. I'm going to sleep until I can't sleep anymore. You tell my mother to make herself comfortable. I'll see her when I see her."

His face turned pale. "You're going to make me explain to her that you put yourself in danger to solve another murder? That should go over well. And don't call me bucko."

I kissed him. "And good luck to you. Hope the fireworks have died down by the time I wake up."

I started to leave but he grabbed me once again. "And will I also have to explain the cue you made us use so we'd know when to arrest J.D.?"

"You mean, 'Take nothing on its looks; take everything on evidence. There's no better rule'?"

He nodded. "We didn't have much time to set things up, but don't you think we could have come up with something better than that?"

"Like what?" I asked, laughing. "Like 'Hey, Amos, please get in here before he kills me'? I think that might have taken away the element of surprise."

Amos smiled and shook his head. "I was standing back there repeating that stupid phrase over and over so I'd recognize it when you said it."

"Why, Amos, I thought you told me you'd read all the classics. I'm surprised you didn't recognize a quote from *Great Expectations*."

"Charles Dickens. For crying out loud."

"Well, I think it was a perfect choice. In honor of Miss Skiffins. She's the real hero of this story, you know."

"Speaking of Miss Skiffins, let's buy her a whole fish of her own. She deserves it."

I took his hand. "That's a wonderful idea." I reached over and put my other hand on the light switch. But first I took a long look around at the room. "You know, we really should do something with this old basement. It deserves to be updated."

"I agree. But let's get married first and leave the redecorating for later, okay?"

"You've got a deal." I switched off the light and we went upstairs. As I closed the door to the basement, I noticed that it was terribly cold as we walked into the kitchen. A look toward the dining room told the story. One of the officers had left the French door to the deck open.

"Please tell me you put Miss Skiffins up before the sheriff got here," Amos said.

The whole evening had been so confusing, for a moment I couldn't remember. "Yes. . .yes, I did. I put her in the bathroom down the hall."

Amos hurried down toward the bathroom door. "It's open," he said.

We both began calling the tiny calico cat. Of course, even under the best circumstances cats will treat anyone who beckons them with utter and complete disregard, but cat owners never give up. I finally pulled a can of cat food out of the pantry and put it under the electric can opener. This always produced an immediate reaction. But no cat came running around the corner.

Amos had gone upstairs to check for her, but when he reached the bottom of the stairs, I knew he hadn't found her. "Oh, Amos," I said. "She's gotten out. We've got to go look for her. It's way below freezing out there."

Without another word, we bundled up and stepped out into the cold, dark morning. It was snowing again, making it even harder to see. We turned on all the back lights and the lights around the lake. Amos and I both had flashlights. We began calling Miss Skiffins. The idea of her outside in these conditions terrified me. She was so little. . . "*Trust God, child.*" Aunt Bitty's admonition welled up from inside of me. How many times had she encouraged me to walk in faith? "*Perfect love casts out fear, Ivy. Don't be full of fear, be full of faith.*" "Easy for you to say, Bitty," I said under my breath. "You're dead." But I knew she was right. I grabbed Amos's hand and prayed, "God, please help us find Miss Skiffins. You know how much we love her. She needs You now and so do we."

"Amen," Amos said. We searched the deck and were just getting ready to go out into the yard, when Amos took hold of my arm and stopped me.

"What's that?" he asked.

There was something moving through the yard, coming toward us. But it was too big to be Miss Skiffins. Amos swung his flashlight toward it and it stopped.

"Oh no!" I cried. It was the dog, and he had something in his mouth. As he started to come closer, I started to say something, but Amos shushed me.

"Ivy, just be quiet," he whispered. "Don't say a word. I mean it."

It wasn't hard to follow his advice. I was heartbroken. Tears were running down my face. I'd befriended this dog and he'd killed Miss Skiffins. It was all my fault. The dog kept advancing, slowly, carefully. Keeping his eyes focused on us.

"Don't move, Ivy," Amos said softly. "Stay perfectly still."

I looked up at him. Amos didn't look very upset. In fact, there was a small smile on his face. Was it possible? Could she still be alive? I turned to watch the collie walk deliberately up the stairs to the deck. Gradually, one paw in front of the other, he advanced until he was only a few feet away from us. He lowered his mouth and gingerly released a rather offended calico cat that ran straight to us, completely unharmed. She delivered one hiss of complaint to the dog before allowing me to scoop her up into my arms.

"Ivy," Amos said softly, "take Miss Skiffins inside, and for crying out loud, close all the doors. I'm staying out here for a while."

I started to say something, but he shushed me. I was getting a little tired of being told to be quiet, but I was so grateful to have Miss Skiffins back and unharmed, I didn't care. I carefully backed up toward the house and went inside. After feeding Miss Skiffins, hugging her until she swatted at me, and finally letting her curl up on the sofa next to the fire, I sat down at the table next to the French doors and watched Amos. He was sitting on the deck, only a few feet away from the dog. He had to be almost frozen, but he didn't move. And surprisingly enough, neither did the dog. I could see Amos's lips moving, so I knew he was talking to the small collie. And the dog was watching him—with interest. Finally, after about thirty minutes of encouragement, the dog moved closer to Amos. And within another few minutes, Amos was petting him and the dog was doing something I'd never seen him do before. He was wagging his tail. And then the most incredible thing happened. Amos got up and walked to the door. He opened it and turned to look at the dog who stood there, staring back and forth between Amos and me. And then he trotted inside my house. Amos went into the kitchen and took two bowls from the shelves. He put water in one and opened a can of beef stew from the pantry and plopped it into the other bowl. "We're going to have to get some actual dog food," he said to me with a smile. "We can't keep feeding Pal people food."

"Pal?"

Amos came up next to me. "I think his name is Pal. It fits him."

I had to agree. It did fit. *Nothing so broken that God can't mend it.* Those words kept going through my mind. They were true. With God, nothing at all was impossible.

While we waited for Pal to finish eating, we stood next to the windows and watched the snow fall. Amos wrapped his arms around my waist and nuzzled my neck. After a few minutes of watching the fat, white flakes drift down from the sky, I checked the lock on the door and turned around to walk Amos to the front door. I happened to glance toward the tapestry. Then I stopped cold and leaned in closer, looking at it carefully. How could there be something in this painting I'd never noticed before?

"Amos," I said slowly. "What is this? Do you see what I see?"

My great-aunt Bitty still sat on the bench by the lake, Emily Baumgartner next to her, and she was still waving to me, but for the first time I noticed the dog lying by her feet. A black and white Border collie.

"I don't get it," Amos said. "I've looked at this thing a hundred times. Why didn't I ever see. . ."

I leaned over and kissed him before he could say anything else. "Sometimes you just accept miracles, Amos," I whispered. "You don't question them."

13

"H ard to believe it's all over."

Amos and I were watching snowflakes drift lazily to the ground. The lights on Lake Winter Break were twinkling and the house was still decorated for the reception. All our guests had left, and we were finally alone.

"It was a perfect wedding," Amos said, scooting his chair next to mine and putting his arm around me. He'd changed out of his tux and had on jeans and a sweater. I'd taken off my wedding dress and put on my green jumper. "You looked like an angel coming down the aisle. I don't believe I've ever seen anything so beautiful in all my life." He leaned over and kissed me. It was long, lingering, and delicious.

When he finally pulled away, I smiled at him. "Even with our choice of ring bearer?"

Amos chuckled and looked down at Pal sleeping peacefully at our feet. Miss Skiffins was snuggled up next to him like some kind of oddly shaped puppy. "*Especially* with our choice of ring bearer. He did a wonderful job."

He really had been cute in his little doggy tux, prancing proudly down the aisle with our rings strapped to his back. He'd brought them straight to us, then sat absolutely still while Amos removed the pillow from his back. When my dad snapped his fingers, Pal had taken his place of honor on the front row, next to my proud parents. He'd done a much better job than Lulu-belle the pig, the ring bearer for the other recent Winter Break wedding we'd attended. She had let out a squeal and run the wrong way. She'd finally been sacked by the groom, but all in all, any attempt at decorum had been destroyed. It was pretty funny, though.

I sighed and stared out the window. The same big, gorgeous white flakes had fallen all during our ceremony. Pastor Taylor had removed the drapes that covered the windows on both sides of the sanctuary. Then he and Odie Rimrucker placed small lights around the outside of the building so that the fat flakes were highlighted as I walked down the aisle. The church was decorated with tiny, sparkling lights and luminous glass snowflakes. And Inez had made the gown of my dreams, just like the one Dela had shown me. And I wore the jewelry she left me. The beautiful green stones helped to draw some of the attention away from my bright red hair. Thanks to Dela, Emily said it definitely didn't look like my head was on fire. I couldn't have asked for more. But the most wonderful part of my wedding was that my father proudly walked me down the aisle, my mother cried, and I married the most handsome, incredible man in the world.

The church had been packed to the rafters. It was as if everyone in Winter Break had turned out. And they just might have. Including Bertha Pennypacker. Of course, it would have been difficult for her to have not been there, seeing that she was one of my bridesmaids. Yes, a bridesmaid. After I nominated her to be the president of the library board, things began to change for us. *Nothing so broken that God can't mend it.* Emily, my matron of honor, and all my other bridesmaids had welcomed her with open arms, helping her to feel as if she fit right in. I couldn't help but glance at her as I approached the front of the church. I'd never seen her look so happy. I was determined she was going to stay that way if I had anything to say about it.

Dewey was Amos's best man. I was thrilled to have my old friend involved in my wedding. I was even happier to finally shake hands with Amos's father. After my insistence, Amos had contacted him. After years of estrangement because of his dad's drinking, I won't say that things weren't a little tense, but it was a work in progress. I was confident that one of these days, they would be able to put the past behind them and develop a real father and son relationship. *Nothing so broken that God can't mend it.*

It had taken a few days to calm my mother down when she found out about Ina Mae's murder and the trap we set for J.D. "You're just like that Jessica Fletcher in *Murder She Wrote*," she'd snapped. "Everyone around her dropped dead. I'm surprised there was anyone left alive. Winter Break is your Cabot Cove." As much as I'd loved *Murder She Wrote*, I'd always had suspicions about Jessica. I mean, how many people have to die before you look at the one person who was always nearby? And she makes her living writing mystery novels? Please. However, I had no intention of debating the point with my mother, especially since I'd been a murder suspect for a little while myself. At least now Mom was enjoying being a mother-in-law. Jessica Fletcher, Cabot Cove, and Winter Break's murder rate were all on a back burner while she began to meddle not only in my life but also in her son-in-law's. Funny thing was, Amos loved it. Since his own mother had passed away a few years earlier, having someone clucking over him and getting into his business made him feel like he had a mom again. I was very grateful for my mother, not only for making my husband happy, but for joining forces with Inez Baumgartner. Together they had created the wedding of my dreams. Of course, I didn't credit them for sending the snow. In my heart, I believed it was a wedding gift from God.

"Sheriff Hitchens gave me your keys after the ceremony," Amos said. "I'm glad the KBI found them in Dela's car where she dropped them, but it would have been nice if they'd told us earlier."

"The important thing is that we got them back. And by the way, they're *our* keys now. In fact, everything is ours. It feels good to share everything with someone you love, doesn't it?" He didn't answer me, but another long kiss told me he felt the same way.

A few weeks earlier, I'd compared a wedding to a funeral, but I'd discovered I was wrong about that. After attending two funerals, one for Dela and another for Ina Mae, I realized that funerals were a way to say good-bye to a life that was over while weddings were a way to say hello to a life that was beginning. A big difference.

"We're going to have to send thank-you cards for all the gifts," I said, looking over the stack of presents piled up on a table against the wall. Amos and I would never need a toaster again as long as we lived, and we had enough crystal goblets to supply Ruby's café should she ever decide to get really fancy. I got up from my chair and got a large envelope from the top of the stack. "I think you'll be interested in this one. I haven't had time to open it."

"What is it?"

I plopped back down in the chair next to him. "What do you think it is?"

He sat up straight and his eyes got big. "Is it—is it. . ."

I put my fingers on his lips. "Stop before you hurt yourself. Yes, Ruby gave it to me."

"Open it. Open it."

Men and meat. Sheesh. I slowly opened the envelope, just because I knew it would drive him crazy. I pulled out a card congratulating us on our wedding. Tucked inside the card was a folded piece of paper. I unfolded it and started to read.

Dear Ivy and Amos,

I've only given this recipe to one other person outside my family. That was Bitty Flanagan, your aunt. But now I want to give it to you. I ask you not to pass it along to anyone else until I'm gone and then only to people you can trust. It isn't that it's such a big secret, but as long as everyone thinks it is, it makes it special. Hope you understand.

I could never thank you both enough for bringing my Bert back to me. This isn't even close, but here's the other part of my gift. Free Redbird Burgers for as long as I live—and Bert lives. After that, I can't guarantee anything. Ha ha.

All my love,
Ruby Bird

What followed was the recipe for Redbird Burgers. There weren't really any surprises. I'd already guessed at most of the ingredients.

"Well, what's this secret component everyone's been trying to get their hands on?" Amos asked. "I don't see anything that unusual."

"Wait a minute. There's more." Down at the bottom of the page Ruby's scrawled handwriting began again.

People in Winter Break have been trying to find out my secret ingredient for years. Now I'm going to tell it to you. (over) I flipped the paper over and there it was. *My secret ingredient is prayer. I pray over every single burger. That's my way of knowing that I've lifted almost every person in Winter Break up to God. I ask God's blessings over everyone who eats one of my burgers. I pray that their family would walk in health, peace, and prosperity. And I pray that they all find God's will for their lives. I hope you're not disappointed, but I think taking time to pray for someone else is the greatest "ingredient" there is in this life. Don't you?*

"Well, I'll be switched," Amos said with amazement. "All this time we thought she was putting some top-secret ingredient in her burgers, and she was. Just not the kind we had in mind."

"Oh, Amos," I said, laying my head on his shoulder. "Winter Break is really a special place, isn't it?"

He nodded. "I've always thought so."

I kissed him again. "And you don't mind going on our honeymoon in the spring?"

"No. I'm glad we decided to stay here for the winter." He kissed my earlobe. "The funny thing is, there isn't anywhere else in the world I want to be more than here, in this house, with you. To me, this is the perfect honeymoon."

Mom and Dad were staying in Hugoton for a couple of days so Amos and I could have some time alone. Then they would stay with us for another week before heading back to China. I would miss them, but now I had my own family. I wasn't alone anymore. Pal made a growling noise in his sleep, and Miss Skiffins patted his nose to tell him to settle down.

"I've got an idea. . . ," I started to say.

"Oh no. Not again," Amos said, smiling.

"No, not that kind of idea." I watched the snow dance in front of us like it was celebrating our wedding. "I've got an idea about Winter Break."

Amos kissed my cheek. "And what is it?"

"Winter Break is not so much a town as it is a place inside the heart. Everyone has a spot where they belong, right in the center of God's will. It's a special place where you find your heart's desires and where miracles happen all the time. But to find it, you have to lay down all your own ideas and plans. You must give God everything you thought you owned. That's when you will find your own Winter Break. It's out there for all of God's children. He's already prepared it." I hugged Amos. "What do you think about that?"

He laughed. "I think you're delirious. Let's go upstairs."

I stood up and checked the lock on the back door. Pal woke up and watched me. He and Miss Skiffins liked to sleep in my bedroom, but I was thinking that tonight they might have to get comfortable in the guest room. I stopped in front of the tapestry and stared at it. Amos came up behind me and put his arms around me.

"It's really special, isn't it?" he said.

"Yes, it is." Aunt Bitty waved to me from the bench by the lake. She watched Amos and me skating together on the frozen lake with a knowing smile on her face. Even though she wasn't with me physically at my wedding, I'd felt her presence the entire time. It was my aunt Bitty who introduced me to Winter Break when I was a child, and Aunt Bitty who led me back as an adult. Her legacy was one of love, faith, and destiny. I was determined that someday I would give to someone else what she'd given to me. I kissed my fingertips and reached up to press them to her painted face.

And with that, my new husband and I marched upstairs, ready to begin our new life together. Behind us, a small calico cat and a very contented Border collie brought up the rear.

Ruby's Redbird Burger

(This recipe makes 4 one-pound burgers or 8 half-pound burgers. Ruby's are actually one-pound monsters, but yours can be smaller!)

Cook 8 slices of peppered bacon in large skillet. Cook until crisp. Remove from skillet and set aside.

Remove all bacon grease from the pan except for approximately 2 tablespoons. (Set aside the remaining grease.) In grease, sauté half a large, chopped white onion, along with 2 tablespoons finely chopped jalapeños. (Canned or from a jar are fine.) Cook until soft.

Season 4 pounds hamburger (80/20) with:
Sautéed onions and jalapeños
4 tablespoons Ruby's Burger Mix (See recipe below.)

Knead seasonings into hamburger, but do not overwork the meat. Make 8 (or 16) patties. You can use a hamburger mold or a large mayonnaise lid to shape the burgers into a consistent size.

Place approximately 1 ounce shredded extra sharp or sharp cheddar cheese in the middle of each patty. Do not go all the way to the edges. Sprinkle approximately 1 tablespoon crumbled peppered bacon on top of the cheese. Then place another patty on top, and crimp the edges to totally seal the burger.

Cook over moderate heat in skillet seasoned with bacon grease. Once both sides are browned, cover skillet to keep burgers juicy. Cook to desired doneness. Do not turn burgers more than twice. Add 2 slices sharp cheddar cheese on top right before you remove the burgers.

Slice remaining half of onion and cook in remaining grease until rings are soft and fairly translucent. Add onions to top of burgers. Place on large deli buns (toast the buns in the oven with real butter). Follow with lettuce, slice of tomato, small spoonful of pickle relish, and mustard. You can make a special mustard using Dijon with a little horseradish or simply use regular yellow mustard. (This is Ruby's choice. She doesn't cotton to that fancy schmancy mustard!) *Do not ever use ketchup on a Ruby's Redbird Burger. If Ruby finds out, you will never be allowed to eat another Redbird Burger again!*

REDBIRD BURGER MIX

(This makes more than enough for the recipe)

3 tablespoons kosher salt
4 tablespoons coarse black pepper
2 tablespoons dry minced garlic
½ to 1 tablespoon dry crushed red pepper, to taste
½ tablespoon paprika

Mix all dry ingredients together and store in an airtight container. Does not need to be refrigerated. This mix also works as a steak rub!

Don't forget the most important ingredient for a Ruby's Redbird Burger—prayer! Ruby prays for everyone who orders a burger. She prays that God will bless them with health, prosperity, a heart to hear from God, and the willingness to follow Him wherever He leads. For anyone eating a Redbird Burger, the victim. . .I mean, customer's health could probably use a double dose of prayer!

NANCY MEHL'S novels are all set in her home state of Kansas. "Although some people think of Kansas as nothing more than flat land and cattle, we really are quite interesting!" she says.

Nancy is a mystery buff who loves the genre and is excited to see more inspirational mysteries becoming available to readers who share her passion. Her "Ivy Towers Mystery Series" combines two of her favorite things—mystery and snow.

"Unfortunately, our past several winters have been pretty dry. I enjoy writing fiction because I can make it snow as much as I want!"

Nancy works for the City of Wichita, assisting low-income seniors and the disabled. Her volunteer group, Wichita Homebound Outreach, seeks to demonstrate the love of God to special people who need to know that someone cares.

She lives in Wichita, Kansas, with her husband of thirty-five years, Norman. Her son, Danny, is a graphic designer who has designed several of her book covers. They attend Believer's Tabernacle Church.

Her Web site is www.nancymehl.com.

You may correspond with this author by writing:
Nancy Mehl
Author Relations
PO Box 721
Uhrichsville, OH 44683

ALIBIS IN ARKANSAS

Three Romance Mysteries

by Christine Lynxwiler, Jan Reynolds, and Sandy Gaskin

$7.97

ISBN 978-1-60260-229-8

Two sisters find mystery and love in small-town Arkansas.

No matter where southern sisters Jenna and Carly go, murder turns up like a bad penny. When the local newspaper editor is killed and Carly's son is a suspect, Jenna decides to go undercover to get the scoop on the murder. A vacation in Branson, Missouri, sounds like fun, but Jenna and Carly are surprised to find that the glittering lights and twanging tunes make a perfect backdrop for...murder! Back home in Lakeview, Carly's new diner is really cooking. But last time she looked, murder was *not* on the menu. So why is there a body outside her backdoor?

Arkansas sisters **Christine Lynxwiler**, **Jan Reynolds**, and **Sandy Gaskin** are usually on the same page...most often a page from their favorite mystery.

Available Wherever Books Are Sold.